The Butterfly Hunter

Max Malk

PaperBooks

Paperbooks Publishing
2 London Wall Buildings,
London EC2M 5UU
info@newgenerationpublishing.info
www.newgenerationpublishing.info

Contents © Max Malik 2011

The right of the above author to be identified as the author of this work has been asserted in accordance with the Copyright, Designs and Patent Act 1988.

British Library Cataloguing in Publication Data available.

ISBN 978-1-9082486-0-2

1

All characters, other than those clearly in the public domain, and place names, other than those well-established such as towns and cities, are fictitious and any resemblance is purely coincidental.

Set in Times
Printed by CPI Books, United Kingdom

Cover design by T. Norwolf

All rights reserved. No part of this publication may be reproduced, stored in or introduced into a retrieval system, or transmitted, in any form, or by any means electronic, mechanical, photocopying, recording or otherwise, without the prior permission of the publisher. Any person who commits any unauthorised act in relation to this publication may be liable to criminal prosecution and civil claims for damages.

For my Butterfly…

It is only through the lies of fiction we can tell the truths of life.
Max Malik

Acknowledgments

This book simply would not have been possible without Imran Akram of Brit Writers.

Imran has given unending inspiration, shown indomitable courage and provided the vision to see a new horizon in publishing.

Tom Chalmers, CEO of Legend Press, for having the belief to see the potential.

This novel would never have been written had it not been for my sister-in-law, Saiqa, who encouraged me to enter the first Muslim Writers' Awards. At that time the novel was simply a frightened little idea, too ashamed to come out and be seen; she did not even have a name.

After I won the MWA Creative Writer 2007 Award, for a different collection of my writing, I then had the conviction to help turn my shy creature into a debutant. Embarrassed and self-conscious, maybe, and in a dress too flowery, it seemed an idea too large to clothe. *The Butterfly Hunter* grew but hid under shadows, whilst other novels danced in bright light.

After many dress changes and repairs and make-up sessions, the novel felt grown up enough to socialise. This emergence would have been impossible without the continuing support and advice of numerous people. I must mention the Canon Hill Writers' Group who stopped *The Butterfly Hunter* from tripping over the hems of her ball gown.

Solihull Writers' Group have been invaluable and rarely have I had the privilege to be advised by so many talented storytellers. A special thank you amongst those must go to Dennis Zaslona, who has provided years' of insightful critique.

My true friends for teaching me what counts in life. Siraj: for showing me what a real man can be.

Thank you is never enough for family. Kausar, my mother: my first inspiration in storytelling. Saima, my sister: my first inspiration in literature. Nadeem, my brother: my first inspiration in humanity.

My son shows me everyday why I must live – Salman: my ultimate joy.

Prologue

Birmingham

The bomb exploded on Platform Four of New Street train station, just as the 7:43 started to move.

Carriages blew apart like paper bags. Windows shattered and splintered so small that the glass shards were invisible. The proof of the morning rush hour was now strewn across eight platforms: briefcases, laptops, and early morning coffee cups. The evidence of anatomy, the parts that had not been fragmented, was spread over a wide area of the railway station. A cap and rucksack lay in the middle of the track, with no other sign of the schoolboy. Mobile phones rang on, eerily, in the silence following the rupturing explosion. The ringtones became lost amongst the shouts for help, the yelps that implored for relief.

The screaming started with wide-eyed shrieks of terror; seminal sounds in the original language of Adam. Before that, a moment of absolute silence ruled, where no birds flew, no mouths sounded, and no machines moved. A primordial, pristine quiescence, dragged screeching into the modern world. Something that belonged to a phase in history before Time began, when matter did not exist and a pure silence reigned. Silence that could not face the prospect of a world so cacophonic and discordant, and so it disappeared, melted by the screams into the ether.

Arms, legs, limbs unrecognisable, spectacles, pieces of skull with scalp and hair attached – all spread across the station.

The mobile phone of the suicide bomber played Chris Daughtry's *Home*. The bomber had dropped the phone in the station, lost, before exploding the bomb:

*I'm staring out into the night, trying to hide the pain.
I'm going home, to the place where I belong.*

The ringtone rang and rang, providing evidence of a world somewhere else still normal; but for the people on the platform and on the train, the universe had changed forever.

Blood-splattered survivors came out, running and wailing. Some were trapped in the wreckage and others under part of the station roof that had collapsed. Within a few minutes the sirens of the emergency services drowned all other noise as they took over, and an air ambulance helicopter descended on the dual carriageway of Smallbrook Queensway, bludgeoning the air. Birmingham New Street train station turned into moonscape rubble. The explosion had destroyed six platforms, and most of the building.

The suicide bomber had worn the explosives in a black belt across his chest, close to his heart, next to the tiny copy of the Qur'an he always kept in his breast pocket. He ensured he could not be recognised, his face could not be identified. He did not leave behind enough flesh.

CHAPTER 1

Birmingham – Central

The fragrance from the coriander filled the kitchen as Jessica chopped and sighed; the green from the *dhaniya* an alien stain on her fingertips. Hamid, her fiancé, had said that for any English girl to be accepted as part of a traditional Asian family she must have the stamina of a statue and a tongue of marble.

Jessica's thoughts turned to the multitude of questions Hamid's mother would inevitably ask. His mother had agreed at last, and today she and Jessica's parents were due to come for dinner. Hamid had forced his mother, despite all her objections and initial rejection, to formally accept the fact that they were engaged and to bless their upcoming marriage.

Jessica glanced at the clock radio; every minute seemed to contain only six seconds today. She wondered if the yogurt would be sufficient for the Hyderabadi *Biryani*, if the mixture was right, the combination of spices too bland or too piquant. She had started the preparations the night before, marinating the chicken, and preparing the meatballs for the koftas. Food – eating, drinking, and then more eating – was all-important in Asian culture, especially to her future mother-in-law.

Jessica remembered how Hamid had barely been able to lift his feet and his chin seemed stuck to his chest when he had returned after his encounter with his mother last Monday. Initially when Jessica had tried asking him about it he had not answered, but she had ways of drawing information out of him, like a spice blender hand-squeezing, mixing and draining the last drops of hidden fragrance from a secret recipe.

*

'Hey, are you ok?' Jessica asked, as he dragged himself through the door of their flat. She smiled and helped him out of his wet coat, but he did not glance at her. Jessica knew without having to ask, even without the grimace Hamid made as he kicked off his shoes, how things had gone with his mother. He had made a special visit to invite her to dinner.

A few weeks ago, he had told her he had been seeing Jessica secretly for nearly three years. Hamid had finally told his mother, officially revealed their hidden world, although his sisters had suspected for two years. Since the confessional, every time he had tried to discuss Jessica with his mother she rejected the remotest possibility of marriage. Hamid slumped on the sofa, hair lank and sweat sheening his brow.

Jessica persisted with her smile. She pushed his hair back, towelled his forehead, and massaged his shoulders.

'So?'

Hamid still did not open his eyes. 'Hammie, come on! I've waited three years for this.'

Hamid groaned, and covered his face with the towel.

'Oh no you don't!' She snatched the cloth from his face. 'It might be bad news, but tell me, now.'

The phone rang and Jessica grabbed it off its cradle, her fingers turning white as she recognised the voice on the other end.

'Yes, it's me, Penny. I already told you! I don't want the Baghdad assignment. I can't go to Bradford, let alone Baghdad. I'm going to get married, and it's not in my plans.' She slammed the phone down.

Hamid groaned again and covered his eyes with his hands. 'You talk to your boss like that?'

'Maybe we'll have an extended honeymoon if she sacks me, eh?'

'Maybe we'll have no honeymoon at all.'

'Oh my sweet baby, Hammie,' she said, her tone changing. Jessica noticed how he half-smiled, but his eyes seemed to writhe in agony.

'My sweet *Gul-e-Shabnam*,' said Hamid. As always his translation of her surname, of Flowerdew, into a romanticised Urdu version made her crack and giggle.

'I still can't say it.' Then she gave him her imploring doll-eyes-look and stroked his ear, her breathing warm, faster. She brushed his ears with her lips, with her pierced tongue, which made Hamid chuckle. In reply he stroked her neck, exposed the tattoo behind her ear, which she hid under her long hair. He kissed the small white butterfly that she had had done in an impetuous moment as a teenager. His kiss left its own brand, a mark that seemed to tingle and burn with hope and the promise of permanence. She shivered.

Hamid pulled away and said, 'She called you a *Gandee Goree*.' Jessica wondered if it was her pierced tongue or her tattoo. She knew she was making excuses for their racism.

Jessica guffawed. 'I've heard that one before. *Dirty White Woman*. I thought everyone at the mosque used it? I kinda like the title *Gandee Goree*. Almost like Lord or Lady, but better.'

Hamid told her that his mother had responded in the expected way, with shock and horror and rejection. Hamid did not look at her as he relayed his mother's words: '*How can you marry one of them? A Goree? White Woman? What race and religion would your children be? A Gandee Goree! A Dirty White Woman!*'

She stayed silent but noticed the colour in his cheeks like reddening chillies, as he spoke through gritted teeth. 'I don't know what I can say. I've tried. Every time I mention it, she looks like a stony weatherworn gargoyle. Unforgiving. Ancient and brown with tradition.' He shouted and ranted at his mother's comments. Jessica just listened as he relayed the stories. The font of Hamid's anger, Jessica assumed, was his embarrassment. 'She also called you a witch.'

Jessica sprang up. 'A witch?'

'A cursed witch that stole her son.'

'Well, I can be a white witch.' She straddled Hamid, changing her mood deliberately; she felt nothing would be gained by letting her future mother-in-law's words control her life. She wanted her approval because it would make life so much easier, but Jessica knew she would marry Hamid anyway, without his family's involvement if she had to; if only she could get Hamid to agree to that. She put her arms around him, and nuzzled his neck. 'I can be a dirty white witch.'

'Jessy!' He pushed her away gently. 'This is serious.' He held her eyes for the first time since he had entered. '*Ami* accused you of being a cursed witch.'

Jessica stood up with her lower lip hanging, her arms outstretched, palms up, imploring. Hamid smiled at her and said, 'But she'll come to dinner.'

Jessica shrieked, jumped up and threw her fists into the air. 'Yes!' She paused, becoming serious. 'Does that mean yes? It does mean yes, doesn't it? In Asian code? It's still no but it's really a yes?'

'If she likes your food.'

'What?'

'That's what *Ami* said. She'll think about you, if you can make a traditional feast,' he said.

Jessica's eyebrows knotted. She raised her hands up to her forehead and pushed her hair away. Hamid continued, 'Good job I taught you all the Asian spices.'

'So we can do it? Finally? Get your mum to accept me? Get married?'

'Hmm...maybe.'

'Maybe's better than *no way, white bitch*, which it's been –'

'I know, I know.'

She leaned forward and snuggled into his neck again. 'Oh, well done, Hammie!'

'I wish you wouldn't. If *Ami* ever hears you calling me Hammie...'

Jessica had called him that since she had made him make her a bacon sandwich in the early days. Then she had told him she was a vegetarian anyway. More than the joke, his retching afterwards had made her laugh harder.

'Wanna be my wild boar?' She moved to sit on his lap, straddling him again with ease, like a habit.

'Don't think I've got the strength tonight after –'

Jessica covered his mouth, smothered him in smooches, her lips tingling with every caress as if each kiss was the first one. When he was breathless, she pulled away.

'Are we getting married?' She shook him by his shoulders. 'Sod everything. It's been three years. I'll cook your mother every bloody dish under the Indian sun. And even puddings never imagined by the monsoon. But are we getting married or not?'

He groaned and covered his eyes again.

'No. Not now. Not this time. It's *yes* or screw you Hammie, wild boar or not.'

'Yes. Next month.'

'Are you sure?'

'No matter what anyone says.' He sat up straight and she looked into his unflickering brown eyes.

'No matter what your –'

'*Ami* says.' He paused but did not move his eyes from hers. 'I'll handle the *Biradari*, the community – but even worse, I'll take on mum.'

She squealed, pulled him up off the sofa and hugged him.

'We're getting married, Hammie!' She threw her arms around him, and put a hand on each of his buttocks and squeezed. 'Come on, Wild Boar.'

'Maybe we should go through a few dishes...recipes and spices, I mean. She's coming to dinner this Friday.'

She pulled him towards their room. 'Fuck the recipes. Let's go to bed. I'm spicy enough.'

*

Jessica stopped her chopping for a moment, as she heard a dull thud. She looked up through the window and saw birds flying from the trees, like souls leaving the branches. She wondered if it could be thunder, but the sky was blue. She considered ringing Hamid to remind him not to be late tonight, but put the phone down.

Dread, like a dark miasma, rose within Jessica from some unfathomable depth when she thought about what Hamid's mother might say that night. She chopped harder, faster with an increasing strength. *How clever of Hamid to arrange the dinner on the third anniversary since we first met*, she thought. It seemed as if she had never had a life before him.

Although she used fresh coriander regularly, it still smelt exotic; her pale fingertips retained a foreign memory of green even after Jessica wiped them on the dishcloth. She brushed her honey-gold hair away from her eyes. Hamid's mother had never seen Jessica; she wondered what her future mother-in-law would make of her blue eyes, her full lips and tapering jaw, her thin nose slightly upturned at the end, blonde hair to her shoulders that kept falling over the left side of her face.

This was her final labour: she had to produce an overflowing cornucopia of dishes until there was no room on the dining table, and to force feed the guests until they were gravity-bound, or at least ill with oversatiety, especially Hamid's mother. Jessica had to impress her if she was ever going to succeed in being a fully-fledged member of his family. Their relationship would no longer be a dirty secret: no more sneaking around and hiding and lying to his family.

A flutter ran through her stomach as she thought *will I be accepted?* Despite the traditional clothes, the wedding *lengha*, she would look so entirely different on her wedding day from the typical Asian bride. She smiled as she remembered how, when she had tried the dress in the shop, her lithe limbs had been too long for the standard sizes; she had already chosen a maroon-coloured outfit covered in gold embroidery with Hamid last weekend. The henna patterns she imagined on her hands would make a brighter contrast on her clear, pale skin.

Jessica chewed her lower lip, and blinked hard a few times. The pain would be worth it once they were married. So she wore her patience like armour. She knew she would lance through their comments at the right time, and so cut open the pustular boil of racist objections. Somehow Hamid's mother would end up accepting her, even liking her, once they met. Somehow.

Jessica heard the clamour of more sirens, getting closer, hungrier. She swirled hot water in the china teapot for one. With the special teaspoon, she measured just the right amount of white tea. She took out the catalogue of wedding dresses from the back of a drawer. She thought about ringing Hamid, needing to hear his voice, but decided to let him relax with his coffee at the station that he had every morning on his way to work.

Jessica had invited both families to her place in Solihull, which would be more formal than telling them about this secret flat in Birmingham city centre, although this had been her sanctuary with Hamid for the past two years. Here they had spent last night talking and planning, and today she had made an early start on dinner so she could take the food over to her house later. She found it hard to think of anything except his mother's approval at the feast. She hoped his mother had realised that Hamid would not give her up, no matter what anyone said. Hamid had often told her over the last few days that he would fight his whole parochial Pakistani village and his tribe, if he had to, for her.

Jessica walked into her bedroom, and took off her top and pyjamas ready for the morning shower. She jumped as the phone rang: a Bollywood love song that Hamid had set as her ringtone, although she still could not quite understand what it meant, even after Hamid had translated the lyrics for her. She knew it would be Holly; no one else would ring her this early in the morning.

'Hi, Jessy. I hope you're not still in your bed, inventing new animal shapes with your man, even if it *is* your anniversary?'

Jessica laughed. 'Wish I was. Hamid's left for work, couldn't get a day off even today.'

'Are you sure about his mother?'

'Oh Holly, not again. I know you're suspicious –'

'I know, I know, but I'm worried about his mother, because they're just so different and you still haven't met his family. Your mother-in-law might be a Gorgon.' Holly laughed. Jessica knew Holly could never be fully serious, regardless of the situation. 'Looked that one up for you on Wikidpedia.' Holly always called it that, since she had told Jessica how *wickedly cool* it was.

Jessica chuckled. 'Maybe she's related to Medusa, although I don't think this one has snakes for hair.'

'That's the point. You just don't know, do you? Well, you can always say no. Just like drugs. It's better to say it now if you're not sure, than at the altar, or whatever these lot call it, when you're fully addicted.'

'Too late for that. I'm mainlining, and I'm high on Hamid.'

'I'm not going to say anything about Hamid. You know what I think - I've said enough before. I know you love him. I'm just trying to help you get through this ordeal by food, before you cook yourself into one of the dishes.'

He's the only man who's loved me for me, Jessica thought, *and who never wanted to change me*. She knew Holly found it hard, after becoming a single parent and leaving an abusive partner, to accept that some men might be different. Hamid never minded what others said, and those small memories and habits were more important than the florid gestures of love. Strange things had made them grow closer together; things that might have made others doubt their compatibility.

'Do you really love him, no matter what the differences?'

'Of course I love him. You know the things I adore about him. The way Hamid stands up for me against his family... he's even threatened to disown them if they don't accept us getting married!' Jessica loved the way he always asked her how her day was, and then listened patiently. The way he made her a martini just the way she liked it. When she told him how shit the world was and moaned he did not shut her up, or try to solve her problems like most men. Instead, he listened. He knew when she needed holding, but mostly he just listened to her talking about her mum and dad, and shopping, and work at the BBC, and the new head of section...

'Anyway, I just want you to be happy and safe; you never know. I've heard some of these Muzlins can be violent.'

Jessica laughed at the way Holly always mispronounced the word. 'He's the only Muslim you know. Was Sally's dad a Muslim?' Jessica had never mentioned the abuse Holly and her daughter had suffered. 'I'm sorry. I love Sally. But he battered you into a new shape, didn't he? You've known Hamid for long enough and he hardly ever talks about religion. He keeps it private.'

'Well, if you're sure you wanna fight Medusa then I can always come and give you a hand, like I said.'

'You've got Sally. Oh – one thing. Do you think I should use *garam masala*, sprinkled on top of the *biryani*, at the end?' Jessica turned her head slightly towards the window as she heard police sirens blurring past.

'Haven't got a clue, even though I've seen you make it enough times...always tastes good, though.'

'Thanks Holly, I'll manage. Better get on with it. I was just about to step into the shower.' Jessica had started working in the kitchen about an hour ago, a little while before Hamid had left for New Street station. She had cooked the lamb curry the evening before, but the sauce still needed thickening.

'You're gassing away to me with nothing on?'

'Bye, Holly – wish me luck for tonight. I hope Hamid can become my very own Perseus.'

'What?'

'Look it up on Wikidpedia.' Jessica put the phone down, shivered and skipped into the shower. She heard the television just before she got in: *There's been a bombing…*

London – Southall

Ahmad Regus lay dying. His deathbed did not seem grand. No throne or high priest's altar, no acclaim from the mosque's pulpit. This was not how he had imagined he would die. Ahmad had not thought his bedroom would become his death chamber.

He had lived in the same place since his arrival from Pakistan, a small house in a narrow back street of Southall. Glancing at the over-familiar Wilton carpet brought back memories of his children growing up, which mixed in his mind like the crimson swirls on the sulphurous brown background of the thinning carpet. Beige curtains hung limp and let in differing amounts of light depending on the time of the day, but never the sun. He lay on an ageing pine bed in one corner of the room that changed shades of agate yellow, depending on the light, like an ancient chameleon that cannot quite manage to maintain one colour anymore. Washing-powder-advert bed sheets lay crisp and unruffled over his gaunt body, highlighting thin elbows folded over his chest.

Ahmad's breathing was barely visible as the immaculate white sheets rose and fell, but the *shloop* caused by the intake of every breath merged with the sibilance of the crisp sheets, as they moved over his body. Sofia, his wife, straightened the sheets and crept away; he attempted a smile as she turned to check on him again, and then lay still, feigning comfort.

Ahmad heard Jimmy, his youngest son, turn the door handle almost imperceptibly as he walked in without knocking. He knew Jimmy probably hoped he was asleep so that he could avoid talking to him. Things existed between them like an opaque plastic wall, issues that for years Ahmad had avoided looking too deeply into, like a cling-film barrier stuck over his mouth that would suffocate any other kinship. Ahmad's love and concern for his son made him continue to try and guide him. He half-turned to Jimmy, and slightly lifted his head off the pillow.

'Jimmy, my *Betah*, how are you?' he said, and looked at his son through half-closed eyes. The effort of lifting his head covered his brow in sweat.

Jimmy's real name was Yusuf, but no one ever called him that. Ahmad had nicknamed him after the cricketer, Jim Laker of England. Ahmad had been a fan of the elegant off-spin bowler and had grown up with stories of Australia's defeat, told to him by his father. Tales of the historic test match that had taken place in 1956, the year Ahmad was born, had been instilled in him. In his youth he had become an impetuous batsman and even more passionate leg spin bowler. Cricket was a passion that ran through the family, so he began calling his eldest son 'Tony' after another of his favourite bowlers. Ahmad wanted a link to remain between his children and the grandfather they had never seen; he had died in Pakistan a decade after Ahmad's arrival in England. Ahmad had insisted that his boys stayed 'Tony' and 'Jimmy' with the support of the *Imam*, Younis: his childhood friend, who had played cricket with Ahmad and loved it as much. They had succeeded in this, despite the opposition of his family and the mosque community.

Some of the conversation between his wife, Sofia, and Zoya, his daughter, drifted up to him like a summer breeze as they prepared the evening meal. Their voices and fragrance from the kitchen gave him comfort; he knew he would not die alone and neglected. He watched intently as his son perched his large frame onto the edge of the bed, trying to take up as little space as possible.

'How are you? *Abbo*, listen. I've been talking to Dr Patel – he's spoken to the surgeon,' said Jimmy, speaking Urdu.

Ahmad knew he would try to take control. Jimmy had used '*Abbo*' since childhood as an informal way of saying 'father', it really just meant 'dad', but Ahmad felt some Urdu words seemed more respectful and more intimate. 'Dr Patel came to see me yesterday, *Betah*.'

'I know, I know. He's going to get a second opinion from another surgeon, a friend of his.'

Jimmy scratched his scar on the right side of his face, which would become more livid when he became agitated. 'It doesn't matter...'

Ahmad sank back into the pillow. He felt tired, but he knew Jimmy was stubborn, more lead-headed than Ahmad had been in his youth. He closed his eyes, and lay back on his sweat-soaked sheets.

'There's nothing he can do. The first surgeon already said that.' He sensed movement outside his room and realised that Sofia had come to check on them, to ensure that they had not deteriorated into one of their downward-spiralling arguments, like a whirlpool, from which there had often seemed no escape in the past.

'They can do the operation, they'll cut the fuckin' thing out, and it'll be gone.' Jimmy said the second part of the sentence in English.

Ahmad did not pretend to like Jimmy's expletives, but had long since learnt to live with them. It was either that, or lose his son. 'My son, it has – it has – spread – the surgeon said it has spread.'

He saw the shock and pain clearly on his son's face, which screwed up, and the scar became angry and swollen. Jimmy's large nose, like Ahmad's, was a Regus family trait, except Ahmad knew his own face had changed and looked as if it had been pinched in a vice, so his nose seemed even larger than usual. He looked into Jimmy's small, deep-set eyes below thick eyebrows and broad forehead, noticed as always the scar that stopped on the right side of his face by the angle of his square jaw. The scar started below his right eye and ran down the side of the nose past his thick full lips, narrowly missing a vital artery, down almost to his neck.

Ahmad remembered the doctor had told him how lucky the boy had been. Ahmad had not let the emergency crew touch Jimmy; he had nearly bled to death when he had carried him out of the ambulance into Ealing Hospital Accident and Emergency department. The body lay pale; not a child but not yet a man, cold and almost lifeless as most of his blood poured over Ahmad's hands. He knew it had been Jimmy's first serious fight at thirteen in the drug world, but he had never questioned him about it.

Now he hated his son's continuing optimism, and wanted to crush the naivety that went with it. Ahmad's physical pain alone was more than he could bear. 'I've had an ultrasound, and my liver has cancer.'

'But Dr Patel said that he personally knows Mr Willow, he's a brilliant surgeon. He's done loads of these operations, innit? People get better all the time…'

Ahmad did not hear the rest of Jimmy's sentence, as exhaustion overtook him; he closed his eyes and drifted off momentarily.

As usual, in these recent days of his illness, his thoughts turned to Younis. The *Imam*, Younis, his childhood best friend, who had not visited him since he had become bedbound. They had come to England together as young men, sharing their hopes and aspirations. Ahmad still remembered their excitement rising as the New World unfolded before them, tall buildings and a congested city, as the jumbo jet descended and made a final turn, before landing at Heathrow.

Everything was so different from their village in Pakistan. They had jabbered in Punjabi and pointed repeatedly out of the window. '*Landan! Landan! Hai oh haie Landaan!*' was all either of them could shout. They would have felt ridiculous had they been able to see themselves, but their chattering made them oblivious to their fellow travellers. They did not know anyone in England. Ahmad remembered how at that time they had had a sense of adventure, long-lost ever since the new land had transformed itself into home, a place that had forced them into the crucible of foreignness. They had grown up with the myth of England, which had always seemed like alchemy, the riches of the 'White Country' that had seemed just out of reach during their childhoods. Despite both Ahmad and Younis promising their parents they would never fall for the charms of white women or change in any way; it was England itself that had inevitably metamorphosed them, turned them into different versions of themselves and then transformed them into their current avatars. *How far we have both come, Younis? But how far, really?* thought Ahmad. *Aren't we – underneath my Southall Skin and your Imam's Impermeable Jacket – aren't we both the same boys that left Ramnagar all those years ago?*

Ahmad allowed the full memory of their arrival to come to him for the first time since he had become a respectable member of the community. The guilty pleasure of that embarrassing moment flooded over him. He forgot the cancer and pain for a while, and held a smile fleetingly. Younis became the *Imam* on their arrival and so the leader of the local mosque, and therefore the community. Ahmad knew that his friend had mentioned him in last week's *Jummah Khutbah*, the Friday sermon. Now everyone knew he was dying.

The mosque regulars had told Ahmad how the *Imam* had droned a routine and much-practised liturgy. In his mind he could clearly see Younis speaking:

'All those people in the back rows are kindly requested to move forward...' A short pause as the men shuffled forwards. '...Pray for the Mohammed Qasim GCSE results; £1,000 his father paid for mosque work... pray for our dear brother Ahmad Regus who is *suffering terrible cann-cerr...*' He pictured his voice becoming singsong, and trailing off for emphasis.

Ahmad could imagine Younis stating the money as he did every *Jummah*. 'And the mosque income was £1,342.67 last week, and the expenses were £3,678...' A pause and a barely perceptible sigh to let the figures sink in. 'The building works you see outside – it is for the Allah, and it is only your generous supports with money...' Ahmad imagined he paused, and then continued in Urdu, because Younis did not know the words in English for *exegesis* and *rote learning*. '...that allows the new wing for Qur'an exegesis lessons on Saturday for girls between eleven and sixteen to continue... The new green dome will cost £76,000...'

And there it was: *cancer*. That word again, thrown in casually, between the weekly announcements and balance sheet.

Only Allah cures, and all illness comes when Allah wills, wondered Ahmad's febrile mind. *It comes to test us. To see what mettle we are made of, and how we will respond.* His thoughts should have consoled him; this was a trial. Instead, he screwed up his face. He felt as if icy metallic claws had gripped his rectum, and torn it out through his throat. He vomited for the sixth time that day, leaning over to the sick-bucket. He ignored Jimmy's attempts to help, and wiped his mouth with a tissue. He realised Jimmy had not moved when he had drifted off, in case he disturbed Ahmad.

I am no worse than any of the others: why not Abdul Wahid or Mohammed Qayum? he thought. He made it to the front row, on bad days also, for most of his prayers. Even for *Fajr*, the first prayer of the day, he was in the third row, at worst. And did not the *Imam* say, only two Fridays ago, those who make it for the Morning Prayer are blessed and special? Why couldn't it have been someone from the fifth row? Or the seventh, or the tenth? *Ya mereh Allah!* he thought. There were people who didn't make it to the mosque at all. Could it have been only two *Jummahs* ago? He had sat in the front row looking up at his childhood friend, who had become fiery as ever during his speech. That time, it had been the opposing *Imam*, Abdullah, from the mosque on the 'other' side who received the full treatment; his mosque was literally across the street. Younis had saved his full *mirch* and *masala*, his chilli and spice, for his personal adversary that week.

Ahmad regretted not being in the first row since then. There was a special feeling about sitting in the front, right in the centre, at the feet of the *Imam*. Ahmad had made every *Jummah*, for the last thirteen years since they had moved to the new mosque. The PA system went past those near Younis, and it felt to Ahmad as if the *Imam*'s words addressed him personally. Those in the front could feel the passion in the voice of Maulana Mohammed Younis Khan *Imam* Sahib; they could clearly see his cheeks reddening as the drops of globular spittle spray landed on those in the front rows at moments of especial fury in the Friday speech, as he condemned the excesses of the opposing *Imam*.

Through his restlessness, Ahmad heard Zoya and Sofia cooking in the kitchen. The smells and noise of their chatter permeated the small house, and felt like a warm blanket. Then Sofia entered the room again. She seemed to be forever flitting in and out. He looked at her without blinking, almost in surprise that she should be back again so soon.

Ahmad grimaced and turned off the radio, which was reporting a bomb attack at a railway station somewhere. He removed the single earphone; his lifelong habit of listening to the radio news irritated him now.

'Thank you. Sorry…' he said to Sofia, as she straightened his new sheets and took the bucket away. His wife carried his soiled covers and vomit, and smiled at him in her usual way before she left the room. Ahmad turned away from his son slightly. Jimmy fidgeted with the rings on his fingers, and said nothing.

*

It was at times like this that Jimmy wished that they would speak in English. It did not feel abnormal to speak Urdu with his father because that had always been the family language. His father had not allowed him to speak English at home since he was a child. *You will learn English soon enough my son, at school and with your brother and sister and friends – but with me you will always speak Urdu, or I will not answer you.* Jimmy could hear him telling him off, his voice clear and strong, rich like dark honey and treacle, loud without shouting. His father had commanded the room without effort when he spoke.

His father would always ask him what he had learnt in school that day. Today his father's voice was weak and thin; an ancient cotton thread brittle and about to break, so fragile. He did not allow himself to think of Ahmad's insides bleeding, the blood slowly wasting into his bowels, draining his life force almost as he lay there.

Ahmad sat up, grunting with effort. Jimmy leaned forward as Ahmad took his weight onto his elbows Jimmy helped his father, and then plumped up the pillows, before Ahmad's his head fell back.

'Do you remember that trip we took to Pakistan when you were fifteen? I have never seen you happy since that time.'

Jimmy smiled at the unexpected recollection. It had been the most extraordinary trip of his life and he had gained, in small part, an insight into his father's free and unfettered childhood. When he got to Pakistan he found that, although he was older than most of the other children of the village, he still ran with them unashamedly; ran through the green wheat fields and splashed in the *nulla*. He stole mounds of oranges and feasted on innumerable *loquats*, scaring the small green parakeets off the branches in his uncle's orchards, and broke the golden-ripened heads of corn and cooked them on hot coals right there in the field. He then snapped off sugar canes for dessert, washed them in the fast flowing, cool stream. The sugar cane was so sweet and refreshing. He chewed them and sucked every last drop of juice from them, before spitting out the husks into the river. Freedom. A small glimpse of his father's childhood that he tried to copy passionately during his two-month-long stay in Pakistan, and that had tied him to the land of his ancestors', that had given him more association than just genetics. Then the memory of the most frightening event overcame Jimmy; an experience he had barely allowed himself to remember.

He had visited the graves of his ancestors. He had seen rows upon rows of them, generations of clay headstones. Some of the newer ones were marble, but most of the graves were mud bricks lined up in the dusty red-brown earth, stretching back into history. Ahmad had shown him the place. An almost secret grove, on the first Friday of their visit after *Jummah* prayers. They had held up their hands and said a prayer together for the departed souls.

A few days after that, Jimmy left home in the middle of the afternoon. As everyone else slept in the village, he had taken it on himself to visit the remote location of his family graveyard on the far side of Ramnagar; he especially wanted to see his grandfather, Dadda Jan's grave again. The graveyard was hard to find, beyond the fields, past the *nulla*, and hidden in between the orchards. Jimmy eventually managed to rediscover the isolated cemetery. He had missed Dadda Jan all his life, just from the stories that Ahmad had told him. That grave seemed to draw him into the burial area more than any of the others. Jimmy wished he could have seen and spent time with his grandfather, to whom he had written regular childish letters, as if he had known him intimately. He stood in the afternoon heat of a Pakistani summer that blistered his feet in the Afghan sandals, staring at his ancestors' graves, and at Dadda Jan's in particular.

The heat haze started affecting Jimmy's eyes. He twisted away from the graves for a moment, and when he turned back his heart lurched as he saw the earth open. He felt it move under his feet as two more fresh rectangular holes were created in front of his eyes, adding to the long row of graves. He almost pitched forward into the abyss. The chasms gaped at him, empty, with no headstones. Then, abruptly, two headstones pushed themselves up, fast, out of the ground. One had his father's name on it and the other had his name on it. *Mohammed Yusuf Regus*. It did not say Jimmy; he had almost forgotten his real name from disuse. He read the rest of the golden inscription on the jet-black marble of the headstone.

Mohammed Yusuf Regus. Underneath his name was a quote from the Qur'an:

*Think not of those who are killed in the way of Allah as dead.
Nay, they are alive, with their Lord, and they have provision.* Surah
3, Verse 169
*Martyr of Islam
Rest in Paradise with the Martyrs
May you be in Firdous – the Highest of Gardens. Be happy
in* Jannat Al Firdous

> *May you be enshrouded with Allah's Love, covered by His Mercy*
> *Live close to His face forever. Live forever.*

Jimmy wondered how he could read Urdu. The graves challenged him as they whispered to him. At first he thought he had imagined the whispers, but they kept repeating something – words he could not make out, a weird humming sound.

Then he saw the spirits and souls rising out of the graves in front of his eyes in the midday heat, like vapour mist that rises from a tarmacadam road. He could not count them as they surrounded him. They started swaying from side to side, but he stood steady, without moving.

Jimmy could hear the ghostly apparitions talking to him, questioning him: he could not make out the words or understand the language, but they persisted and came closer and closer, pressing into him, onto him. They floated above him, seemed to merge with him, and squeezed him tight from the inside so that he felt constricted, without breath. His scar throbbed and slithered as if it was a python wrapped around his face, constricting his skin tighter and tighter. When he felt the blood rush from his brain, just as he thought he would black out and collapse, he understood them.

'What are you? Who are you? What are you? Who are you?' The voices clamoured and clawed at him and then the strange language of the apparitions became clearer. They seemed to cut through him as if he were vapour, getting louder and louder.

He saw the faces of the men and women, wizened, old and wrinkled. He noticed a few looked young, but they all had ancient dress and museum clothes. Something else struck him as bizarre more than their clothes and language; at first they looked familiar, but mystifying, and so foreign somehow. Then after a moment, as they blurred into focus, he realised it was their faces. The men and women – they all looked like him. He saw his grandfather, and somehow he knew him to be his grandfather. Dadda Jan had also risen out of the ground, and stood before him. His confusion gave way to certainty. He identified his grandfather's soul, but he wore Jimmy's face.

'Where do you belong? Where are you going? Where do you belong? Where are you going?' Dadda Jan asked him, over and over, louder and louder.

Then the ground under Jimmy's feet felt soft, and his legs quivered.

He turned to escape the surrounding apparitions and leave the graves, to get back home and be rid of the spasm that spread to his arms, and the nausea that gripped his abdomen. As he turned and flailed, he nearly lost his balance and fell into the deep, dark hole. His own grave seemed to open up wider before him and his feet slipped, almost pulling him in; he could not see the bottom. With a huge effort, he stopped himself toppling in.

He turned again as he heard a shout, then many shouts, from the ancestor-ghosts who looked like Jimmy. Now they all surrounded him and pressed on him again, screamed at him, took his breath away so he felt he would collapse. When he thought he would burst and could not last another second, they released him. His eyes bobbed in a green sea where fire fish twinkled all around, and he felt as if he had lost consciousness. Time seemed to stand still; he had no idea if it was a dark afternoon, or a blue night.

When he could see again, his eyes slowly focused. He felt different, but he could not be sure exactly what had changed. The spirits surrounded him and swam in a circle mixing into each other around him; their faces were now joyous. They became distinctive. They no longer had his mask on them; he could see their own faces. They changed their expressions, and the ghosts started smiling and laughing.

His dead ancestors sang: 'Come home! Come home! Come home to us! *O Shaheed Al Islam, O Saif Al Islam!* Come home again *O Shaheed Al Islam, O Saif Al Islam!*'

He did not understand why they were calling him home – he had never been to Pakistan before – or why they addressed him as a Martyr of Islam and the Sword of Islam. Jimmy blinked the sweat out of his eyes and looked back to the line of graves. Then the ghosts turned from him and they filed away, walking calmly now, disappearing into the haze in orderly rows and columns. His grandfather dawdled and, as Jimmy turned, he saw his Dadda Jan smile and motion with his head.

Jimmy saw another apparition: a spectre shimmered into being. He saw himself as a ghost dressed in Arab armour, a knight from Saladin's victorious army with a scimitar: a *saif*. He held the *saif* in his right hand by his side, as if it was a natural part of his anatomy. He had his left arm around his grandfather, who had to reach up to hook his arm around Jimmy's broad shoulders, and both the ghosts walked away from him. His Dadda Jan looked like a tiny old man compared to Jimmy's giant spectre. His ghost turned back to him for a moment and laughed, before walking away following the long line of the graves.

Jimmy wiped the sweat and tears out of his eyes with his palms. When he opened them again, the graves appeared as before. The fresh holes in the ground that had been his father's and his own graves had disappeared. The apparitions had also vanished, leaving no evidence of ever having been there. The dust on the stones had not been disturbed, and he saw the small birds foraging, as ever, in between the dry ancient tombs.

He turned and ran. He did not look back to see if anyone or anything followed him. He ran for an age, running past a group of his cousins who had set out to find him, ignoring their shouts as he passed them and everything else, until he came to the river and plunged himself in, again and again. Finally, he tried to pull himself out, half drowned and bedraggled from beneath the water. His lungs heaved and a pain weighed through his limbs, as if they had been filled with stones from the bottom of the stream.

Jimmy had never felt so mortified, with death so close. He forced his exhausted body out of the water but the earth beneath his feet in the riverbank was soft, and his legs sank deep into the silvery clay. The river eddied and flowed fast, and he thrashed as he crawled through the waist-deep *nulla*. He fell forward and splashed towards shallower water, but as he did so he landed in the slippery mud. The mud felt thick and viscous, it stuck to his body and arms. He tried to pull himself up but fell again, face-forward, splattering into the ooze. Gasping, he crawled on his belly, his face covered with clay. His pulse stuttered a staccato beat on his temples as he levered himself out of the sticky earth.

After rolling over onto his back, he spat mud out of his mouth and greedily drank huge gulps of air. He stayed motionless, baking in the afternoon sun on the riverbank. Time and place merged. His arms felt as if the muscles had been torn at the sinews, his legs like Auntie Yasmin's home-made *gajjar ka muraba*, the sweet carrot preserve he had had for breakfast. His whole body quivered for a long while before becoming still. The mud made him immobile. He looked like an ancient rough tree-trunk.

A migrating flock of Kashmir White butterflies flew overhead. He thought he must look like a clay-covered mound. They landed on Jimmy, and started to suck the precious minerals and salts out of the clay. He stayed still, hardly breathing, not blinking; he could see the white cloud fluttering above his body. He looked like a terracotta warrior from the army of the Emperor of Qin, completely covered in butterflies. A clay angel with thousands upon thousands of independently beating white wings.

He provided unexpected nourishment for the swarm of Kashmir White butterflies migrating back to their breeding grounds on the Russian steppes, back to the land where his maternal grandmother had fled from. Just as abruptly as they had arrived, they flitted off en mass, and began their journey home, back to Samarkand.

That night, Auntie Yasmin guessed that something unusual had happened to him. She said not to worry – that people often saw *Jinns* in the graveyard, and especially during the worst of the heat at the height of summer. Many *Gorah Sahibs* had known in history what he had felt like today; he was not the first *Gorah Sahib* to suffer heatstroke on the plains of the Punjab.

'It has beaten many of your fellow countrymen.' His Auntie had laughed at him; she held onto her stomach and said not many *chiteh offsar*, white officers, could stand the Punjabi heat in June, which was the full flush of summer's youth.

Jimmy refused to tell anyone what had happened. That night he sat with his feet in a bucket of ice, and slept with more ice in plastic bags surrounding his body. He shivered and shook all over but he would not let anyone remove them. He would rather risk dying of ice exposure, an unknown occurrence in the middle of a Pakistani summer, than let the heat get to him again.

That night in his dream he saw a clay angel, flying into the brightest blue sky with thousands upon thousands of beating white wings.

*

Jimmy forced down the memories that he had so rarely allowed to surface since that ghostly, heat-filled day. He looked at his father's gaunt face. 'We'll get the operation privately, yeah. I'm going to get you into Park Hall hospital.'

'You know we can't afford it...that'll cost thousands.'

'I'm going to pay for it, right? You just rest now, and it'll be okay. You'll see.'

Jimmy imagined his father as he had been in his childhood, and still could not get used to this different Ahmad. Every day his father's head left a smaller dimple in the pillow. Jimmy noticed how he looked at him with half-closed eyes and sweat-sheened face, and how he made a small shake of his head in protest.

'I can't take your money. I can't use your money. You know that. It's *haram*!'

'Why not, *Abbo*?'

'I'm sorry, Jimmy.'

'I do it for you. I risk my life every day on the streets so we can afford things we ain't ever dreamed of before, yeah, but you've never taken my money. Why not?' Jimmy had never before alluded to his criminal activities, but had often made a simple offer of money, which his father had always refused. Jimmy's scar burned with a tingling pain.

'You know I can't. I can't risk the fire of *Jahanum*, and my eternal soul, so that my body can have a few more days of earthly life.' He paused and closed his eyes. Jimmy saw him purse his lips as his chest moved faster; he could see the skeletal structure under the sheet.

'Whatever I'm suffering now, I promise you Jimmy, is as nothing to the torments of Hell.' Ahmad's chest heaved, as he looked away.

Jimmy breathed in, and held his breath. Something hung stinky and unsaid. He had expected his father to refuse his money. His father's eyes had a look he had not seen since his early dealing years. The way his father's eyes would express disapproval... no, it was not disapproval. What was it? He remembered suddenly: disappointment.

He sensed his father's disappointment, but he did not know why. Jimmy knew that his father often disagreed with his lifestyle, but after the early teenage arguments Ahmad had chosen to ignore his Anglicised way of life, his girlfriends, alcohol and clubs, just as he had pretended Ahmad's prayer mat, Qur'an and mosque just did not exist – or if they did, he made them irrelevant. Jimmy just never spoke of it. He realised both of them lived divorced and different lives that would never have crossed, except for father and son love, and they became closer for each other's tolerance. Now he knew his father had something to say.

Ahmad opened his eyes and tried to sit up, half succeeding. 'You were drunk in that club you go to, the Blue Flamingo. You started a fight a few days ago and battered a man half to death, spent the night in a cell in Southall Police Station, and you're being charged with assault.'

Jimmy's eyes widened as he puffed his cheeks and shot the air out of a small hole in his lips like a pistol crack. He knew there were plenty of informers in his father's community who lived for such gossip. Now, he did not meet his father's gaze. He never could look into his father's eyes at such times.

'Who told you?' he asked, not because he cared, but he did not know what else to say.

'Do you deny it?' said Ahmad.

'I don't want you to worry about anything. Let's get you better; I want to take you to -'

'I worry for you.'

'Don't. I told you before, innit, don't. I've been looking after me for years.' He scratched his scar.

'That's because you won't let anyone near.'

'You're close to me and I'm gonna get you to Park Hall, then we can talk about it.'

'What do you want?'

'What?' Jimmy kept his hand on the right side of his face and caressed his scar as if his fingers possessed an, as yet, undiscovered healing touch. He knew his father would put up resistance to the private treatment, but he had not expected Ahmad to start questioning his life.

'What do you want? Stop!' Ahmad said, as Jimmy thought about mouthing a meaningless: *I just want you to get better*.

'I don't have much time. What do you want, what are you going to do?' said Ahmad.

Jimmy had not discussed his future with his parents for many years. Even then, he remembered how they told him what they wanted for him, and no one had asked him his desires. *Why does everyone assume I have no dreams?*

'I ... I ...don't want to go through what you did. No way. I don't want to work all week and then be crushed by the gas bill, innit? I don't want to be spat at, yeah, and called a "dirty fuckin' Paki" on my way to the foundry. I don't want to be a stranger in my own country. I don't want my kids to grow up without. Drowning in a lack of everything amongst a sea of nothing. Just like we did. We grew up with fucked up feet – *deformed* was the word Dr Patel used – because you couldn't afford new shoes.'

'You can't live like this, you're not happy. I always did my best for you –'

'I'm fine; I know what I'm doing. I just want you to get better, innit?

People beat cancer all the time.' Jimmy tried a half smile, dropped his right hand away from his face, and stopped pulling at his scar.

'It's time. Time for me. It's written; every breath is written. I can't force one more in or out no matter how hard I want it, or how much you want me to go on breathing when there's no breath left. And the truth is, I don't. Don't want to force.' Ahmad closed his eyes and sank back on the pillow. 'I just want to be in the front row of my mosque again, just one more time...'

'You don't want to get better? You want to die?' Jimmy could not believe his father would just give up and not fight. Ahmad had been fighting his whole life. He had seen the daily struggle to make ends meet, dragging his tired body off to the foundry. Then later, when he was older and unable to manage heavy work, he had seen him leaving for the Royal Mail sorting office at Harrow at dawn, and returning when Jimmy and his siblings were in bed.

'Just one more *Jummah* prayer in the front row...'

'*Abbo*, I'm going to book you into the hospital,' Jimmy said.

'Will you go to the mosque?'

'I haven't been for years, what's the point?'

'Then I won't go to Park Hall.'

'What's my going to the mosque got to do with your treatment? That's sick Paki blackmail.' He had numerous explanations in his own mind why his father should use his money, which he did not voice because he felt there would be nothing to be gained at this moment except an argument.

'I want you to find yourself...to look deeper than your current life.'

'I hate the mosque, and they hate me.'

'Just promise me you'll go before I die.' Ahmad sat upright. 'Even if it is blackmail. I feel I have earned the right to use it this once. For me.' His eyes regained their old intensity.

'I've got everything I want. I've got my life sorted.' Jimmy had not been to the mosque for seven years, since his father had dragged him along to *Jummah*: he could still remember the fight afterwards when he had told his father he would never go to the *Masjid* again. He had ended up swearing at his father and almost attacking him, something he regretted even years later.

Jimmy gave up. 'I'll go to the fuckin' mosque if you'll get the operation privately.'

'How can we afford that? Only if the money isn't *haram*.'

'Leave that to me, *Abbo* –'

'Where are you going to get the money from? I don't want you to do anything illegal. Promise me.'

'I've promised you all that I can, right, more than I wanted. That's now my problem, innit? I'll sort it out.' He squeezed his huge fingers onto Ahmad's clammy hand and kissed his father's cheek. Jimmy felt as if his thick fingers would press through his father's tissue like skin and porcelain bones.

Ahmad's eyes closed as he sank back drenched in sweat. 'Swear it. Swear it on my head, on my life,' he whispered.

'Okay. Okay I swear. It won't be *haram* money.' Jimmy knew he had plenty of that secreted around the house and private dens around Southall. He had sworn on his father's life, and to him that bond was greater than if it had been made on any Holy Book or the Qur'an.

However, he had no idea how he was going to find the twenty thousand pounds he now desperately needed.

CHAPTER 2

Birmingham – Central

Jessica smothered her body in Purify Ambrusca Body tonic that she had bought yesterday from the Molton Brown shop in Solihull, hoping that it would fortify her spirit. She knew she would have to take another shower before dinner, but this was her habitual morning ablution: she would feel ready to tackle the day. *After dinner I'll use the Unwind Crystal Bath Soak – I'll need it desperately by then*, she thought, *but never mind; just having Hamid makes all the coming discomfort worth while*. Now that her marriage was so close, it made her think of her teenage dreams of an ideal man, just as she did when she was a girl in boarding school. The way she would gaze out over the springtime fields and hedges wishing she could take long walks hand in hand with her Prince, while her Classics tutor droned on about Horace and Virgil and Pliny and taught her about the pantheon. She could not have imagined that Hamid was the man she had dreamed of during double Latin. *You can't help whom you fall in love with*, she thought. She smiled as she recalled how she would sit up straight when it came to the love poems of Ovid. Jessica had not shared her dreams with any of the other girls in the dormitory, who would always chatter ceaselessly and share everything. It would be harder than Hercules stealing the golden apples of immortality from the garden of Hesperides to formalise things with Hamid's family, for them to accept her as part of it, she knew.

Jessica gritted her teeth behind stretched lips and rubbed her arms hard so that they became red, although she had already washed most of the scented body tonic off. She scrubbed herself roughly with the loofah. *Too white! Too bloody white, this soap lather!* She felt glad that she would meet them in her house. Hamid's mother had promised Hamid that she would give Jessica a fair chance tonight. What if they ended up hating her, despite her best efforts? Just as they had rejected her so many times before, on every occasion Hamid had ever mentioned her. Then Hamid would simply have to live his life without them. For some reason, she felt certain that Hamid's mother would lose her objections once she had actually met Jessica. She knew Holly had a point – anybody else might have just given up on Hamid. But soon enough, Jessica knew they would get married anyway. She had felt more respect and love for him when, after the last argument with his mother, he had said, 'I'm going to marry you next month. No matter what, Jessica. That's it – next month.'

Despite the pressure of completing the preparations for the meal, she turned up the heat on the shower and closed her eyes. The water from the shower felt like a fountain in the Taj Mahal, tumbling onto her head.

Her thoughts turned to how they had first met since it was the day of their anniversary; she had met Hamid when he had failed his job interview as a research assistant at the BBC. Hamid would rarely talk about himself or his family, so she would usually end up talking mostly about her life. However, despite his lack of extra words, when she spoke about the tiniest thing that mattered to her or the smallest memory she could think of he would remain interested, and ask all the appropriate questions. In time, she had become used to his quiet ways and private religion; she did not ask why the mosque called to him, as if he could hear the muezzin every day. Time thickened and shortened, hurried away from them, and always seemed to run out before their conversations did.

The soap had softened her skin as if it were sea foam. She reapplied the tonic but quickly washed the smallest flecks of lather off her body and dried herself briefly, putting on a new top and pyjamas. She went into the kitchen to see if the curry she had left on low heat had enriched.

Jessica pressed Hamid's number into her phone; there was no answer. She furrowed her brow and wondered why he was not answering his mobile. She wanted to remind him to ask his manager if he could leave at lunchtime today. She desperately wanted Hamid to make it to her house before his family arrived; she did not feel she had enough reserves let in her defensive shield to meet them alone for the first time. Jessica had reminded Hamid, as he had walked out of the flat, she expected him to be at her place by six, and he had better arrive before either of their families, who were due at seven. He had arranged the dinner thinking that they could relax on Friday evening.

'Your lips are so luscious Jessica. I can't tear mine away from them,' Hamid had said as he kissed her before leaving, a while ago.

Jessica redialled, but there was still no answer. She had almost completed cooking a lamb *bhuna* last night, and had started some of the other preparations then. She dipped a finger into the *masala* sauce and sucked her finger, satisfied with its thick texture and rich, complex taste: coriander and cumin followed by the after-burn of chilli on her lips. Her chicken was more yellow than red, unlike the restaurants. She disliked the artificial red dye they used. She ran her fingers under the tap, before switching the small kitchen television on to BBC news.

However, she did not stop to watch, but moved to inspect the various silver pots that gleamed on the hobs. They blurred her reflection back to her but she did not look at her own image, and ignored the kitchen mirror. Her thoughts, more today than ever before, still centred on Hamid. She had fallen completely for him, despite the kernel of worries and doubts, which she assumed all relationships contained. She had created a protective pearl around these things because he was the only man she could talk to about everything from the periodic table to her periods; she had felt relaxed in a way that ensured she could for the first time become the true Jessica.

She stirred the *bhuna* mix and added some more chilli powder and haldi. Jessica ground the gently roasted cumin with the cloves, cinnamon and nutmeg. *Jeera, loung, dal cheeni*. Reciting the mantra had become spontaneous, the words just escaping her mouth as if she had exhaled. She frowned, and the soft skin of her upper lip formed furrows, as she forgot the word for nutmeg. *I'll add the saffron later*, she thought, and smiled because the word was almost the same in both languages. *Zaffraan*, she practised, as Hamid had taught her.

Jessica remembered the accidental touches that had sparked and sensitised their skin; how he had jumped, yesterday, as she reached for his hand when he was not looking in the Bullring shopping centre. She loved to wrap her limbs around him, much to his discomfort. They had shared so many miniscule moments of happiness that those seconds became the sum of their lives, and now they were willing to risk eternity on it.

She padded barefoot back into the bedroom and then took her phone into the kitchen and pressed Holly's number. 'Oh, hi, you *can* help actually. I might not have enough yogurt for the Hyderabadi *Biryani*, and the chicken marinade could do with some more –'

'Yeah, no worries, I'll rush a couple of pots around in a bit, just dropping Sally to nursery. Two enough?' asked Holly.

'Oh thanks, you're such a darling.'

The television sounded louder than usual in the background; Jessica froze as the news entered her conscious mind. Only snatches of the report seemed to register: '...*a bomb...an explosion...a suicide bombing during the morning rush hour. There have been a large number of casualties...*'

'Oh shit, there's been a bomb,' said Jessica.

'Where?'

'Don't know…'

'*It is feared numerous people have been injured and many killed…*'

Jessica turned the volume up and grimaced as she imagined what the final figures might be.

'*We have had a phone call believed to be from Jaish an Noor wass Salaam, the extremist Islamist organisation who are known to have terror cells all over the world…*'

Jessica knew it must have been *Jaish an Noor wass Salaam*, The Army of Light and Peace – they were the only ones powerful enough to do such a thing, anywhere in the world. She had seen the speeches and threats for months on the BBC news channel.

'*There has been an explosion. A suicide bombing in New Street station, Birmingham,*' said the news reporter.

'It's at New Street. The train, oh fuck! Hamid. Oh no, Hamid's there.' Jessica wanted to know which train had been bombed, which platform. She removed the phone from her ear and moved closer to the television, but the reporter gave no further details. She cut Holly off, and redialled Hamid's number. When she did not get through she put her hands over her face and then pulled at her hair with both hands, yanking the long strands down to her cover her face, as she wondered what to do next. Then she dialled the newsroom.

'Yeah, Peter, it's me, Jessica. Where's the bomb?'

'Hi Jess, I think it's Platform Four, the train station.'

'Tell me everything, quickly,' Jessica said, and as soon as she thought she had enough information she cut him off in mid-sentence.

The thoughts of their anniversary meal morphed into a mess, and caused her to become immobile as the implications of the explosion overwhelmed her. She felt the nausea rise and retched, but her mouth was dry. His phone ringing on the other end sounded loud in her ear.

She stood frozen for a moment. Then she put her palms over her face, shutting out the world. She reached out autonomically and turned the heat down on the *biryani*, moved the raw mince balls for the lamb koftas aside, and sat them next to the marinated tandoori chicken. The mounds of raw flesh, more than usual, felt nauseating to her vegetarian moderation. The oils released into the atmosphere from the *garam masala* spices did not allay the feeling; the restorative aroma did not calm her senses today. She put the phone down softly, felt the tears, and wiped her eyes.

The freshly ground *garam masala* mixture now spilled onto the work surface. Her hands moved uncontrollably, jerking the pots around on top of the cooker.

She knew that Hamid had died as soon as she heard the breaking news. She had felt a sense, something instinctive and abysmal inside, like a choke that started from her depths, which became stuck like a stone in her throat. She had heard a muffled bang earlier but had no idea what it meant; she had seen the birds flying off frightened, leaving the branches bereft. The Birmingham BBC was based in the Mailbox, the same building as her flat; she realised that a camera crew must have rushed the short distance to the train station, and had started broadcasting. Jessica stood with her palm over her face, and with the other hand she picked up the phone, pressing it hard to her left ear. She pushed Hamid's number, and then stood, screwing up her eyes so tight that they hurt.

She had lost the only man she had ever loved. She wondered if the kiss that Hamid had given her this morning before he had left would be their last kiss. Would that kiss that he had lingered over for so long now have to last forever? Things like bombings are supposed to only happen on TV, just like the pictures of the starving stick-insect children refugees with their obscenely bloated bellies. She gave to charity regularly. What could she give to make this better? What would she have given to stop this, had she known?

Jessica tried to reach Hamid again. She clutched her stomach, feeling as if she had fallen overboard and was now desperately reaching for a piece of driftwood in the storm-swollen surf.

I have lost my beloved. She pressed redial again, hoping that her feeling would prove false and somehow she would hear Hamid's voice, full of love and smiles, on the other end. Her call did not connect, now there was no ring. Just a recorded message that kept repeating that it was not possible to connect her call, but the words somehow meant something else to Jessica. Her blood thumped in her ears, her face tightened as her eyelids filled with moisture, the muscles in her face contracted into a grimace until they became painful. She remembered how she had cancelled her holiday-of-a-lifetime with a group of her friends last year, to see Ankor Wat in Cambodia, and had nursed Hamid through pneumonia for two weeks instead. She had known fear then, but this fear now made her hands shake. It caused sweat to cover her as if she still stood in the shower, and her heart to beat faster than metal wheels on a railway track. This fear felt like a stranger, come to smother her breath.

Now she felt with an unnatural certainty that she had lost him.

She nearly dropped the phone as it rang with the Bollywood ringtone. She thought about throwing it down, because it might confirm her worst fears, but then pressed the button without looking at the screen, hoping to hear Hamid's voice.

'Jessica? Jess? What the hell's going on? Say something!' said Holly.

'Sorry. I've got to go. Something, Hamid – something terrible has happened.'

'How do you know? Go where? Don't do anything silly, please, let the police sort it.'

Jessica dropped the phone onto the worktop. She could still hear Holly's voice, faint but strong. 'Don't – don't do anything stupid, it'll still be dangerous. Please Jess, promise me…Jessy, are you there?'

Jessica brushed her hair away from her face with both hands, picked up the phone, then let it go; she lifted the knife, but then dropped that too. The chopping blade clattered onto the tiles from her limp hand and she sank to the kitchen floor, onto her haunches. Covering her face with her hands, she howled without tears. Hamid took the same train every day from the city centre. *Is Hamid dead?* She felt that he was but a tiny wish, like a lonely seed in the dirt of despair, hoped he would still be alive.

They don't need to tell me he is dead, she thought. *I know this before anyone has identified the bodies, before the police come around, before I ring the emergency number for worried friends and relatives. Why am I so sure?* she asked herself. She didn't know; perhaps it was premonition. *If he's dead… what will I do? I shouldn't have let him go to work today.*

She could not find answers to the questions that razored through her like Damascus' steel, pulverising the soft grey matter of her brain. Questions besieged her, as she thought about running out of the building to try and find Hamid.

No, he's not dead – no, he can't be. I'll drag him back from the mouth of Hades if I have to.

Why today – a bombing? Who could and would do such a thing? What is this Islam that makes people do this to their fellow man? It must be them; the newsreader had said so. It was always Muslims – who else would bomb New Street? What sort of religion could allow, let alone condone this? The Church of Scotland of her childhood felt safe and loving. She knew well the Presbyterian strictness, but suicide bombing? What mad god and inhumane prophet would permit this? Not Allah and the Prophet of Islam, she felt sure, from what little Hamid had told her about his religion. She had to find Hamid, to know with complete certainty if he had died. *He can't be dead*, she thought. *Surely not*. Her life would not be the same again, and she felt an almost physical emptiness invading her insides. A space she could no longer see herself filling after Hamid's death. She gripped her stomach, and bent forwards.

She opened her eyes and stopped her tearless cries, as she stabbed the red button to cut Holly off, and then jerked her shaking finger to press Hamid's number on her phone. She missed, cursed, and then managed to ring him. The desolate echo of the of the recorded voice telling her she could not be connected to his phone made her cover her eyes and shout out aloud again.

The memories of her empire that she had built with him dissipated. Fear rose in her that she would lose them completely. His memories were crumbling before her eyes that could no longer see his face, and her ears knew not his voice. Memories were already passing fast into history, turning into less than the dust of ancient bones.

Jessica shrieked again, but then just as suddenly as she had started, stopped her mournful lament. She thought that she was being illogical and without reason, like a desert thunderstorm. Hope flooded over her like the sweat, which was dripping down the side of her face. She put on Hamid's blue coat and her old tennis shoes, grabbed the car keys and press badge, and she slammed the front door behind her. Her hair still dishevelled, she ignored the other people in the lift, and got to the underground car park. She flung the car door open and set out to pull answers out of the dust and debris of confusion that enveloped her, taking her deep into its bosom so that all actions slowed and all sounds were muffled. She felt her chest heave, but it was as if she could not escape the sticky dust that coated her lungs or the viscous liquid that surrounded her body; she was thrashing with her arms and legs and her breath was running out, the surface invisible above. She did not know what to do or where to go – she had an urge puppeting her, as if her arms were controlled by another's strings. She knew she had to find Hamid, had to bring him back, no matter what, even if she had to bribe Charon, the boat man, not to take his soul across the river Styx.

Jessica slapped her hands onto the steering wheel, slammed the clutch down, punched the gear into first, and pushed the accelerator until the car sounded like a dog being tortured. She could barely focus clearly enough to drive; she wiped her palm across one eye, and then the other, to clear the mist. Jessica realised that the road to the city centre would be blocked by emergency vehicles and she would get there quicker without her car. She got out, slammed the door without locking the car, and ran out of the Mailbox building.

The loss of happiness and his unfulfilled promises; the piracy of faithful fecundity; the theft of security, of being with a man she could trust gave her a new impetus. Jessica wondered how it would force her life through twists and turns, maybe through ways she had not conjured in her dreams.

She did not know if it was the Fates or Kismet or some other unknown force that propelled her as she ran, already breathless, towards New Street train station.

*

Jessica left the car park of the Mailbox. She ran up Queensway and realised that the police had not yet established a cordon. She approached the train station and saw numerous people at the end of the road. A few of the emergency services that had arrived early crowded around the entrance. She ran across the wide street and approached the station. She saw officers that she knew must be from the transport police; their offices were on the same road.

Chaos, born from the bomb, had escaped from the station and taken command of the immediate vicinity of the city centre. The television teams must have arrived in minutes, Jessica realised. The BBC, where Jessica worked, was also based in and ran operations out of the Mailbox, the old post office building, which had been converted into modern offices, bars and luxury flats.

A couple of railway workers led the walking wounded away, and a community police officer administered first aid, trying instinctively to provide life support. Jessica imagined that within a few minutes the station would be like scenes she had seen on television of previous bombings. Panic already held people in a chokehold and soon many more emergency vehicles would descend, and the police would establish a cordon.

An ambulance crew mechanically busied themselves. Jessica assumed they were attending the seriously injured, but her thoughts fled back to Hamid. She knew she had to find him, and she wondered if he was injured and already in an ambulance. She imagined many would need urgent blood transfusions and emergency surgery. She saw the crew bundle a woman who seemed barely alive into the ambulance, which rushed off to hospital with sirens screeching. *Where the hell is Hamid?* The train station reminded her of their first coffee together, after his job interview. She would have been his boss had he been the successful candidate, as she often reminded him later. However, he had been so awkward then and simply too weird to employ, so he had been rejected by Jessica's manager. Hamid had been shy and reserved but Jessica had thrilled him with her laughter and enchanted him with her smile during the feedback session, as he often told her over the following months. Hamid had told her later that he could not help but accept her invitation on the first day to Starbucks, and he had also realised that she had taken him by storm and disrupted his withdrawn existence. She knew he had never received a proposal from a woman such as Jessica, with her penetrating arctic eyes: Hamid said they were like an ever-moving torrent, and he had become swept up in them. Some things about Hamid had irritated her right from the beginning. Memories of those shared coffees, lunches and dinners would make her grind her teeth, especially in the early days, because of his lack of words.

Jessica had ripped Hamid away from his angular, gangly self, pulled him out of his inner city mode; she hated the fact that he did not easily join in with mainstream society. Jessica turned him from being an outsider into someone who, three years later, could almost (but not quite) fit into the trendiest bar or gourmet restaurant in Birmingham. He often objected but she would drag him by his collar, choke him out from his hole like a lizard afraid of being baked at midday. She distanced him from his protected and well-established habits, far from his parental culture, his Pakistani-Muslim ghetto-womb, introducing him to the shiny world of the other England that she inhabited.

A lone police officer was trying to herd people, without success. As Jessica approached the policewoman, she reached into Hamid's coat pocket and pulled out her press badge. She flashed it at the young woman, who had an amiable face. 'BBC reporter,' she said, looking into her eyes, and ducked past her. She saw people in frenzied disorder; they could not be controlled by the few police officers present. Skirting past the garrulous fire engine, she could make out people clambering over the debris and each other like workers on an anthill.

Jessica saw shapes shifting in front of her. Her mind no longer controlled her limbs, and thoughts of Hamid made her eyes blur. She tried not to focus on the shattered remains of the station building, partly collapsed and misshapen, ugly like a broken nose. There was no access from the main entrance: part of the roof near the drop off point had fallen, and some police officers had blocked the entrance, trying to regain control of the hysteria. A trolley trundled some distance in front of her, and she realised the red shape was a man on a stretcher. Paramedics rushed him into the air ambulance. In the ensuing chaos as the helicopter took off and people sought cover from the whirlwind, she ran into a side street, but before she could get into the station a policeman stopped her and sent her back.

Jessica knew the city centre area intimately; she had changed trains there on her way to King Edward's School for seven years. She thought if she could only get through the inner cordon that was being put in place as a physical barrier, she would find a way onto the platform and help Hamid.

Jessica ran up and down the streets that were being sealed off, still trying to find a way past. She felt as if a giant hand had bunched its fingers around her stomach and squeezed it in a steel fist. She stopped, put her hands on her knees and retched, spitting out bile and phlegm.

She knew she had to get into the train station, onto the concourse, and take the stairs down, in order to get to Platform Four, where Hamid's train left from everyday. From the thousands of isolated and apparently meaningless moments such as the fleeting glances and stolen smiles that could mean nothing even to an astute observer, they had nurtured nonsense words and secret codes. Through this teasing they had created intimate names like Hammie and Gul-e-Shabnam that went on to become abbreviations, invented words that had come about through a natural wandering of the tongue, a private communion in their separate world. Her lungs wheezed out a strained screech of hermetic pain. Thousands of tiny icicles stabbed in her chest with every breath. The blood in her neck thumped like wild hooves, erratic and spooked.

Once more she tried to get past the inner blockade, under the police tape, but they repeatedly challenged and stopped her. Finally, with growing desperation, she tried to push past a huge policewoman. 'I'm press. A BBC reporter. Got to put this on the lunchtime news.'

This time the press pass did not shake the stern woman. 'Emergency workers only!' The policewoman held out both her arms. 'It's still dangerous.'

'I've got to get through. Platform Four...Hamid was on Platform Four. Please –'

'Miss – step back – move back right now. Otherwise you will be arrested,' shouted a more flustered police officer. Jessica realised that he must have seen her earlier, and despite the chaos, she had now come to his attention. Jessica moved away. She could see survivors buttressed by people turned steadfast; most of them transformed into unlikely heroes by the crisis, those who may often have needed supporting on nights out in the city centre.

She had never thought of herself as a spiritual person, but the presentiment of what had happened to Hamid made her mutter something. She was not sure if it was a prayer, and if it was, to whom she had directed it.

Her thighs shook as she half-walked, half-ran. Her calves wailed as if white flames licked them, and refused to respond. There seemed no way around, and no way through. She shook her head and scrunched up her face as she imagined Hamid caught up in the explosion. Jessica brushed her hair away and forced her chomping muscles, that seemed to be eating her legs, to work. She ran the length of the barrier without being able to touch it, like a wildebeest that had met the flush Mara River. She came back to the main entrance.

A man she had seen twice before as she was running brought out another survivor, helping the wounded woman past the inner blockade into an ambulance. *He must have seen something*, she thought.

Blood smeared his hands and face, some patches half-dry and others still sticky. Burgundy stains like an accretion, evidence of his injuries and his attempts to help others, covered his face like rust. Jessica ignored the few firefighters that milled around. She realised that many of the rescuers must be inside on the concourse.

She made for the bloody helper who had come out of the station. The man passed the police tape; the police had still not completely established control. She ran, and as she swerved past a large advertising board, the man changed course and started walking in her direction. She collided with him full force, crumpled, and clattered into the pavement. Although dazed, she thought about trying to crawl under the tape. From her sprawled position, she looked at the barrier again. *I've got to get past the tape somehow, into the station,* she thought. *This man can't possibly know anything.* She tried to get up and run again, but slipped. A firm hand helped lift her, the grip holding her steady.

'Let me go!'

'Where are you going?' asked the man.

'I have to get to Platform Four –'

'There's been a bomb.'

'I know. That's why I'm trying to get there,' she said, panting. 'Get away from me!'

'It's rubble. Stuff is still falling. The roof has caved in,' he said, as she tried to jerk free again. 'Look, there's police everywhere, and the bomb squad will be here soon.' His deep tones would have been reassuring, but Jessica seemed not to hear him.

'What's your name?' he asked her, and when she didn't reply, he jerked her arm. 'There may be more bombs.' His voice became harsh, cutting her like the broken shards of stones that lay scattered around, and for the first time she looked up at him. She froze momentarily, surprised by his grim, but calm, face.

'I don't care. I need to get to the platform.' She struggled, sliding like a salmon, pulling in every direction but it made no difference – she could not move her arm.

'Tell me your name, or I won't let you go.'

'Jessica, Jessica Flowerdew.' Her chest was heaving. 'Which platform were you on?'

'Jessica, why are you wearing pyjamas? The bomb was on my train,' said the man. 'I'm Sebastian.'

She feigned helplessness and tried to squirm free again. 'Stop wriggling. I won't let you go. I can't,' he said, holding her without effort.

Jessica tried pleading. 'Please. Hamid was on that train. I told him not to go to work today. Please let me go.' She let out a mournful cry.

'You'll get yourself killed.'

Jessica looked at the destruction heaped upon the station. 'Hamid! Hamid!' she shrieked.

'What did he look like?'

She did not answer or look at him. Her nose dribbled and mixed with the spittle that ran down her chin, but Jessica made no attempt to wipe her face. She stood with her feet, naked now, on the cold street – she had no idea where her tennis shoes were. Her milky feet paler still against Hamid's dark blue coat.

'Did you see an Asian man with a red stripy shirt?'

'Was he wearing a grey suit with a red tie, clean-shaven?' Sebastian asked.

She folded the loose coat tightly across her chest.

'I don't know for sure, but he got on near the centre of the train. I stood and talked to a chap dressed like that, on the platform before I boarded. But I went to the end of the train, and – and I was knocked unconscious for a while. I don't know how long. I'm sorry.'

'No – no, that's not possible!' She looked at him, searching his eyes, her own eyes flicking randomly, about to lose focus. She fell to the floor again, onto all fours. *Maybe this man is mistaken, but what if it was Hamid that he saw? I need to check the bodies, the wounded, talk to the police... but I can't seem to move.* She could not have conceived that Hamid might be dead within the hour. No nightmare, no precognition, told her that she would never see him again. Before she had heard the news, that thought had been as far away as the most distant black hole. Her imagination at that time did not extend to her love being disembowelled first, and then shredded by the explosion.

'The bomber detonated in the centre...I'm sorry.'

The clamour of sirens mixed with the jabbering of blood in her ears, gushing uncontrolled fluid, like her tears. She feared her whole being would become unbridled emotion and she would liquefy into mush. Some jelly-like substance now seemed to fill her lungs tight; it cemented her irregular beat, and her heart felt like pain pumping against the solidity of loss.

'Let's talk to the police,' said Sebastian.

'I don't want to talk to the police – or anyone.'

'Well we may have no choice; here they come,' he said, looking around. 'Look let's walk out of here. Let's talk about it over coffee. I know I need a cup of tea.' When she hesitated, he continued, 'Was he your husband?'

Jessica looked up and saw his face, covered with grease and blood. His suit trousers were torn, exposing a gory knee below the serrated edge. His tie hung askew, his hair stood like a dark crown at the front of his head, topped by ruby red jewels of blood, encrusting it into an upturned forelock. She could not help noticing his unwrinkled brow, his face square in its symmetry, despite the evidence of debris. She thought she saw concern in his azure eyes, a purple bruise across his left cheek already a swelling aubergine. He winced, let go of her arm, and rubbed his thigh. As she noticed his features her breathing slowed, her nostrils flared. She smelt his sweat, felt his hand warm on hers.

For the first time, she noticed the other smell: of burning flesh, a taste of metal in her mouth. The fires created a rank odour of incinerating humanity and made her retch again, but nothing came out. In spite of this, because of the man's fingers on hers, she felt her chest heave less, and her sweat cooled. He helped straighten her, barely touching her when she stood up, but his strong hands were ready in case she tried to dash past him. She felt like a jumper on a tall building and he had talked her out of it – had empathised her out of potential danger.

Jessica saw a policeman approaching, so she let Sebastian lead her, more by his presence than physical strength. She let him put a gentle hand on her back, and she felt safe because of it, as he guided her away from the entrance for a short distance. Jessica wanted information, treatment, comfort, but she knew the emergency workers had too much to deal with at this time to consider a recovery area for the walking wounded.

The quiescent feeling that had overcome her for the shortest time suddenly vanished, as she heard more sirens and a police loudspeaker announcing that the station and the surrounding area had to be cleared: calmly. Although the voice did not give a reason, Jessica knew the threat of more bombs could be the only explanation.

A throng of police officers walked in a cordon. Jessica watched them approach as she pulled her fingers on one hand and then the other, as if deciding whether to talk to the police now or later.

'These bloody extremist Muslims. That's what they said on the news,' said Jessica, wanting to hate.

'We don't know who it was,' said Sebastian. 'I know these so called "extremists" – it's my work.'

She looked at him, mouth open, eyes wide. Her hands curled into spontaneous fists, as tremors almost made her body shake. *How could he be so calm*, she thought, *how could he defend these violent extremists?* She only seemed to be able to make the connection between Muslim and suicide bomber, forgetting that Hamid also subscribed to that religion. He had never made her feel like this. These were some other sort of Muslims – terrorists, maybe like this Sebastian.

'Are you one of them?' she asked, but without waiting for a reply, she continued. 'There's another bomb, maybe loads more.' She recognised her illogical behaviour, but irrationality bit her mouth and made it twist. Her rational senses seemed to escape with the dirty smoke, as it thinned and coalesced into the blue sky. She turned away, but he walked with her.

'Listen, perhaps we should talk to the police and see if they know anything more?' he said.

'That's what I'm going to do. I have to find Hamid – maybe he's –'

'I'll come with you, if you like.'

'Don't you think you've done enough already? Where are the other bombs?' She looked at him. Her eyes felt like rivets in her iron-masked face; her anger ate her mouth into a grimace. 'Tell me! Tell them!' she spat the words, and pointed to the officers who were closing in on them. 'Tell them where the other bombs are.'

'I'm sorry, you're distraught, but here…' He reached down into the inside breast pocket of his tattered jacket. 'Have my card, come and see me anytime. You don't even have to ring,' he said, and she saw him try to smile, which failed to materialise.

'I'm a journalist. I work over there for the BBC, in the Mailbox.' She waved a hand in the general direction without wondering why she told him her occupation, or even that she was making no sense. She continued, 'And I know your sort.'

'What? You know most people assume they are Islamic extremists, but –'

'I know what you fucking terrorists get up to.' She leaned towards him and then shook her head. She could not believe he was defending bombers. She had to let her anger out, not caring if he had anything to do with the bombing or not. To her anger-misted eyes he was a terrorist sympathiser, although she could not understand why he was trying to justify and defend Muslims – he obviously was not one of them. Her humiliation over the last three years of being treated like pig filth, a *Gandee Goree*, a Dirty White Woman, by Hamid's Muslim family was spilling over like a religious diatribe.

'Listen... you might want to talk. You'll probably have lots of questions,' he said. 'I'll try to help discuss if you want –'

'You can discuss what you like with your bombers in Hell when you discover that this is not what your God wants, to blow up innocents. Which God would want that?' She looked directly into his eyes. 'In Hell!' Jessica shouted at him, as he thrust the card into her hand, despite her instinct to throw it away, to rip it up in front of him. She shoved it into her coat pocket. She had to let her fear and anger run across the field of near-madness.

'Blood thirsty bastards.' She stared at him, daring him to respond. He said nothing, but he infuriated her further as his face seemed stuck, his pursed lips forming a straight line. She started to walk away. 'In Hell!' she shouted, without turning back.

London

Jimmy paced around his private retreat, safe in his harbour from the affliction of expectancy, where the day's fermented dread could be discharged. As the butterflies fluttered around his head he moved deliberately, aware of the vibrations and convections caused by their flight paths. His breathing slowed as a bright maroon Atlas moth fanned his face with its wings. His mind, as always, attuned automatically to the needs of his butterflies. He moved a short ficus tree bearing three small figs to a brighter spot, sprayed water on to the rambutan, and then he misted the small guava and citrus trees that the atlas moths needed to breed. As usual this felt like his harmonious time, in the Butterfly House, where all the discord and nonsense of the outside world washed away as soon as he entered the safety of heat and humidity. Away from the flick-knife uncertainties of life and the foreshadowing of frequent death, far from the talcum *powdari* deals and the shotgun burden of working his boys on the streets.

He hummed as he applied his blubbery hands to the delicate tasks. The sweat drops gathered on his lip, and in the scar on the right side of his face, creating a pearl rivulet. He felt his body soften as the melodious moment overtook him and a glut of tranquillity choked the Jinn of fear in him. In the presence of their gossamer-fragile wings and silken tongues he felt filled with strength, entrenched like a huge hardwood in the rainforest, and the sap of life flowed through him. The insects in his Butterfly House were like a charm, an amulet he needed to protect himself. He remembered Sofia telling him stories of how people would use Qur'anic quotes to protect themselves when they walked through the valley of the *Jinns*; his mother would almost shiver. Jimmy knew he needed a shield from his demons of hate, anger and revenge.

He liked to be alone. He stopped and looked up, immediately identifying in mid-flight the Cairns Birdwing, Eastern Tiger Swallowtail, and the Bright Babel Blue; he whispered their names. He saw a Common Nawab feeding on an orange. He imagined an Englishman naming it in the days of the Raj who did not quite know what Nawab meant, and smiled. Others fed on the rotting fruit from the same group, a Black Rajah and a Leopard Lacewing. He glanced at the feeders he had already topped up, and saw a myriad of butterflies swooping around them in a dazzling array of colours and shapes. Peacocks, Glasswings, Red Pierrots. He especially loved the butterflies from the Indian sub-continent, the Fluffy Tit for its tortuous wings, the Indian Sunbeam for its bright orange shades, and the Purple Sapphire for its iridescence.

The plain ones interested him too and he never ceased to be amazed by their feeding preferences, their reproductive differences, and their unique flight patterns. The infinite colours bewitched him, ever-changing depending on the light and time of year – a lustrous, shimmering, opalescent collection of shades on a unique artist's palette. They seemed to release an unimagined poetry in his thoughts, from depths that he had not known he possessed. Their life cycles enthralled him; he found himself enchanted by the differences between the males and females, the varieties of morphs. He had been mesmerised by them from the time the flock of Kashmir Whites had landed on him, and he had bought his first pupae on returning from Pakistan.

He looked towards the small greenhouse attached to the main butterfly area, which he always kept locked. Not even Sofia had ever entered this secret sanctuary. When his mother's sister came from Pakistan, he had not allowed her into his private area. Most people knew only of the larger greenhouse, which had been especially converted by him, and had its own heater, ventilation system and humidifier. He disliked outsiders entering any part of his Butterfly House, and would only let them into the main area at his mother's request.

Jimmy could hear Sofia proudly showing a group of women around, at the opposite end from where he worked. They could not see him because of the dense foliage. *Loads of her friends are visiting again*, he thought, *just like a bunch of Paki inconsiderates*. Sofia led them around the greenhouse, pointing out the different species, how they fed and what the temperature had to be. She explained a chrysalis to them, and what metamorphosis meant.

Jimmy stopped spraying the plants, glad he had already filled up the feeders, and walked towards the adjoining smaller greenhouse before they could reach him and assail him with numerous, mostly nonsensical questions. The majority of Sofia's visitors of her generation had no idea that caterpillars became butterflies and they would stare in wonder and shout out like small children at the especially colourful ones. He scrunched up his face when he thought of the way they treated it like a zoo, and soon started bringing their friends and family around to view the lurid, kaleidoscopic display. The way they would shriek at all hours as the insects landed on their hands and heads. They usually ending up disturbing the butterflies, and often damaged their wings with their handling and cooing.

Most of all, he wanted to avoid hearing the comments that inevitably followed. These would rise to a faithless fervour when the women went back into the living room, and Sofia would disappear into the kitchen for tea and samosas. Although he could no longer hear them marvelling loudly at Allah's creation in the Butterfly House, he locked himself in the smaller greenhouse for a period of peace. He crouched down behind the foliage, even though the glass walls were opaque. He hid as he tried to escape the gaggle of women. Jimmy reached into the bottom of a deep clay pot and brought out a small bag, full of white powder.

*

The women spread themselves comfortably in the living room, and Sofia excused herself to serve them. Sadia felt guilty for being with the group. She knew that, as Zoya's best friend, she should do her utmost to ameliorate the inevitable gossip. She watched and waited as the women jostled to get to the choicest seats on the sofas.

'Butterflies! Butterflies? *Hunh!* Such rubbish, in the greenhouse plants and all, what a dump. *Areh yeh Sofia ka Betah tithli chor hai.* Where did Sofia's son steal all these butterflies from?' said Bilqis, the eldest of the women. She sniffed, and the others laughed. She naturally assumed the position as leader of the pack. She gestured; a dismissive wave with the back of her hand towards the kitchen to affirm Sofia's failure as a mother.

'Just an excuse to hide the white stuff amongst all that rubbish in the Butterfly House,' said the first of two scarlet aunties who sat so close together on the large sofa, they nearly touched. They looked almost identical.

Then Sadia groaned internally when, as expected, the second auntie asked, 'What white stuff?'

'*Areh areh* didn't you know? *Ooff* Allah! *Everyone knows.*' White powder, *po'darr sho'wdarr.* Heroin, of course,' said Bilqis.

'Bloody drug smugglers. No breeding,' said the second of the twin aunties.

'Did I tell you their real secret – what they think *they* are keeping so secret?' asked Bilqis. Her eyes darted around the five women, conspiratorially.

'Is it the illegitimate thing? Whispers have reached my ears over years – but, of course, I didn't say anything,' said one of the scarlet aunties.

'No wonder their son is drug dealer,' replied the second auntie.

'Illegitimate? *Yeh sab Harami hai*? Are they all descended from a bastard? *Areh chee chee*!' said Sofia's *Brahmin* neighbour, shaking her hands as if trying to dislodge some infective contagion.

'They think it's *such* a secret but I know. Knew Sofia's mother when she escaped from Samarkand. *Hunh*! Samarkand, she says. Her mother probably ran from the next village because she was up to no good. *Badmash aurat,*' said Bilqis, with a smirk. 'How do we know? After all, one of them did it with a *Gorah* after all and got pregnant – not even they know which one.'

'Come on, *Nani* Bilqis, that must have been centuries ago,' said Sadia, trying to curb her gossiping by giving her the honorific of maternal grandmother. As the youngest of the group, she found it hard to censure the women. She had thought Bilqis was the one who had most supported Sofia over the years. 'If it's true, and that's a huge *if*.'

'Really, *nani*? *Kasam se*? Come on... you're just teasing. Do you swear?' asked one of the scarlet aunties, who both looked intensely similar, although they were unrelated. Sadia had difficulty in telling them apart at first glance. They both wore red *salwar kameez*, which clashed with their crimson lipstick, both bickered constantly, and they went everywhere together. They perpetually insisted the other was older and therefore always referred to each other as *Auntieji*.

'May Allah paralyse me with a stroke if I tell a lie! See this milk here, I usually don't make oaths, oof Allah. Ahmad is dying and he thinks the secret is going to die with him. But I know, and I won't let it die with him, the secret must be known. *Hai hai* – what can I do? It is Allah's will.'

'Tell us *Nani*, tell us,' chimed the scarlet aunties together, putting themselves in the same age range as Sadia by addressing Bilqis as '*Nani*'.

'*Areh areh*, look at you gossip mongering women an' all. Shame on you! Sadia, go and help Sofia in the kitchen – we can't all sit here pretend she doesn't need our help,' said Bilqis. The old woman put another *paan* into her already betel-stained mouth and chomped with great enjoyment, her mouth a mixture of hard gums and rotting teeth.

Bilqis shifted her pale green *dupatta*. Sadia knew Bilqis had been told light colours gave elegance and dignity to her aging skin, and since then she only wore delicate shades. The *dupatta* covered her iceberg-white thatch of hair which she had cut fashionably short, exposing the nape of her neck, but she refused to dye it. Orange betel nut-stained spittle escaped from gaps left by the two missing front teeth, and landed on the cream leather sofa. Sadia's own saliva stuck in her mouth. Engrossed with the rest of them in the story, she did not move. None of the women dared breathe; they leaned forward.

The white haired woman settled down to tell the story. 'This is not like me *kasam se*; I swear I never ever talk about other people. May God forgive your wagging tongues and backbiting,' she said with her routine absolution, encompassing them with a remonstrative finger. 'They have a real white man somewhere in the family…'

'Oh please, *Nani*, you can't stop now. Are they really *Gorah*? White blood? Was it forced or did she do it willingly? *Ya Allah*, please let it be a love story,' said Sadia, letting her breath go at once, as her vivid imagination took over.

'You see this milk here, ready for *Chai*?' Bilqis gestured to the milk pot. 'See what you women are making me do?'

'*Nani, Nani*, we will take responsibility,' said one of the scarlet aunties.

'Well, *acha*, if you insist. I swear by this milk, this is *noor*. By this purity, I swear one of them had a baby fathered by a white man.' She chomped her betel nut and talked simultaneously.

'Really? *Sacchheee?*' They screamed together, failing to hide the noise but managing to smother the higher pitch just enough, ensuring that the sound did not carry through the closed doors to Sofia in the kitchen. '*Sacchheee?*'

'No. That's impossible! The shame. How could she…how would she get married? How could she survive? She would be killed,' said Sadia.

'I always knew Zoya was too good looking for a Punjabi, *hunh*! I thought she was a beautiful Kashmiri like us, but now we find she is half *Goree*,' said a scarlet auntie.

'Hardly half, auntie. Maybe a small percent,' said Sadia.

'It's enough. White blood – any corruption – that is more than enough. It makes all the difference and carries the taint along with their disgusting habits down the generations, you know,' added one of the scarlet aunties.

'That's how they got the name Regus. What the hell is Regus? Have you have heard of a Muslim or even a good Punjabi of any religion ever named Regus?' They all shook their heads, even the *Brahmin* neighbour. Sadia realised because of their surprise and shock at the new revelation of the old woman they forget to reprimand themselves for not picking this up obvious fact years earlier.

'What are we doing?' said the *Brahmin* neighbour. 'We are about to eat and drink in an illegitimate person's house. *Eeehhhh! Cheee – Chee – Chee!*'

At that moment Sofia walked in with a tray laden with *mitai*, buffalo milk *barfi* and gaudy *cham cham*, pakoras, samosas, *shami* and *nargisi* kebabs.

'I'm sorry – the kebabs took slightly longer than expected. The tea is brewed, and I'll bring it through in a moment.' Sofia smiled as she carried the tray.

'Oh no, sorry, Auntie, I should have helped you,' said Sadia, remembering her loyalty to Zoya, but still flushed with excitement at the revelations.

'*Kiyon kiya*, all this trouble for us? No need. No need. You should rest. And poor Ahmad, *hunh*?' said Bilqis. Orange saliva with small bits of betel nut had flown out of her mouth and landed over her lower lip and chin. She wiped the mess away with her hand and then adjusted her *dupatta*. Her fingers made brown marks that stained the pastel green head covering and told their own tale.

'No trouble of course, it's nothing, you should all stay for dinner –'

'In fact, we were just on our way out. We didn't want to cause any trouble, did we?' said Bilqis, turning to the other women. 'We know how difficult it is with Ahmad being sick an' all. How is Jimmy by the way? We never see him anymore, *hunh*?' she added, giving Sofia a wide gap-toothed smile. She continued chewing and splattering her *paan*. With that, before Sofia could protest, they twittered out, leaving her wide-eyed, holding the tray.

Sadia excused herself, covering her mouth with her fingers. She realised that Auntie Sofia had no chance to tell them about Ahmad's illness or Jimmy's problems; they all left before she could serve them the nearly-brewed *Chai*.

*

Zoya came into the room as the group of women were leaving, and took the tray from Sofia's sweaty hands. 'Don't worry *Ami*, we'll eat the food. Why are you sweating so much? It's not that warm.'

Sofia wiped her hands on the sides of her salwar. 'Those women, why did they leave like that? Even Sadia left with them.' She paused, lost in her thoughts for a moment. 'Warm, hah! It's never warm. It's summer and it's so cold – rain, rain, every day rain.'

'Oh, you know what these gossip *budi*-women are like. I wish they would leave Jimmy alone. But I do hope one day he will come out of that bloody Butterfly House.'

'And you, too? Forget about these *budyon ki bak bak*, these old women are always talking rubbish. I'll call Jimmy in for dinner. You help your *Abbo* come down.'

Sofia went into the back garden and pulled Jimmy out of the Butterfly House. 'It's cold. Sleet already. Winter has not even come. British summer? Hah! What a country!' she said, as they walked back from the greenhouse.

The British weather was something that Sofia never could get used to. 'When I was little girl in Pakistan, spring started everywhere…' Sofia continued once they got back inside, as she and Jimmy joined Zoya in the living room.

'February – the first of February is the first day of spring in Pakistan,' said Zoya, almost aping her accent. 'We know, mum.'

'There were flowers everywhere, so many colours – and hot, it was hot!' Sofia just could not understand why spring was not warm and the flowers did not come out in February, like in Pakistan. 'This country, why does sometimes summer not come at all?'

'*Ami*, maybe you should just accept the British weather. After all, you have been over here most of your life,' said Zoya.

Sofia smiled as her daughter hugged her around her plumping waist and squeezed her small chubby cheeks; she felt glad that, despite middle age, her skin had remained soft on her almost-moon-face. Her body was lingering for longer than most in the purgatory that existed between youth and sagging skin. Her skin that had once been fair now had nut-coloured blotches, almost almond-sized sprinkled on her face. Like the decorative fruit on the *kheer*, the Asian rice pudding she made on weekends, Sofia sometimes thought, *but not nearly so attractive*.

She expected the winters to be cold, but surely summer was supposed to be hot everywhere. She could not conceive of a place in the world so foreign and alien where the summers would be dark and damp, instead of bright where the sun was white and hurt your eyes and brought out the rainbow flowers like her childhood in Ramnagar.

'You should be more British than Pakistani, you practically lived your whole life here – accept the British weather, just like the British have accepted you,' said Zoya, as she threaded Sofia's blue *dupatta* over her mother's shoulders.

'We ain't British,' said Jimmy.

'You are British. Especially you – you were born here,' said Zoya.

'What you talkin' about, yeah? Don't matter where you were born,' said Jimmy. Sofia looked up at Jimmy and smiled, hoping to allay his anger.

'What are you, then? At least *Ami* has an excuse,' Zoya replied.

'I ain't sure what I am, but I know I'll always be a Paki to these people.'

'Oh come on, Jimmy, you can't tarnish the whole country because of a few BNP idiots. We have them too, you know,' said Zoya.

'Look at Tony. I ain't talking about the fascists. It's all of them... you can see the hatred in their faces, just under their white skin. Tony got an accountancy degree. He should be assistant manager, at least, and he can't even get a bank teller's job. We will always be dirty Pakis, innit?'

'*Areh!* I don't want Tony to be a *mamooli* clerk,' said Sofia. She pronounced clerk like *klah-rakk*, swamping the word with pejorative disdain just by her inflection. 'He will get really good management job in bank, you will see, *Inshallah*.'

'Not with that straggly beard and them stupid trousers hitched up halfway up his legs. They're scared shitless he's a terrorist.'

'Not my Tony, areh, it's bad kismet. Don't talk like that! He's too good, boy.'

'*Ami-jaan*, it don't make a difference to them if you're good or bad, they hate you anyway – they hate all Pakis.' Jimmy scratched his scar. Sofia realised his agitation was making his scar itch. 'Tony's just a walking bomb to them. Today or tomorrow…' he said.

'That's not true. Both Tony and I went to uni, and you just have to work hard. I'm a teacher…'

Sofia knew that Jimmy had never been comfortable in any institution – from primary school, which she forced on him like his Weetabix breakfast, through to secondary school, which he shrugged off like an ugly shirt as soon as he could. And the mosque had felt like a contagious disease to him. She looked at him, unable to smile now as he spoke.

'I don't wanna be tryin' in their system, right? It's not about hard work, or being good… it's about being strong an' getting what you can, innit. Look at Tony – he would kill himself working hard, but he ain't got no chance to prove it. An' so honest, gentle, never hurt his enemy – he ain't got no enemies. Wouldn't steal bread even if he was starving, praying five times a day, head banging the fuckin' floor for his Allah, and where has that ever got him? He couldn't even pay the bills if it wasn't for my –'

'Yeah but what you do…' Zoya said, but Sofia saw that her green eyes did not meet Jimmy's stare, and she dropped them to look at the floor.

Sofia watched Jimmy and Zoya, not sure when and if she should intervene, as usual. She looked at Zoya's long hair, fairer than her own; her body slim, unlike the central weight that Sofia carried. Zoya looked like a Mediterranean beauty with her pale cream skin, slim face, thin lips and pointed jaw. They gave her an elfin air of frailty, which made Sofia more protective of her.

'What I do? What I do pays the fuckin' bills an' puts food on the table.

It put you through uni and will in the end pay for *Abbo*'s operation, even if he doesn't like to admit it,' said Jimmy.

'Don't talk so loudly. He might hear you,' Sofia said, looking around at the doorway. 'You know that would kill him before his time if he thought your money...' She hushed them with her expression. She turned the television on. She bunched the lines in her forehead and her eyebrows knitted together at the long-standing rift between her children. The news channel reported the bombing in Birmingham.

'I just use the system, mum, but I'm outside – not Muslim or Paki, and not British. See – I'm not like these crazies,' said Jimmy, waving at the television. After a pause, he looked back at Zoya. He asked his usual question about how they would live if he did not support them – Zoya had only recently started her teacher training – in a low voice but he held firm, as Sofia knew he would.

'I know, Jimmy *mera Betah*, I know but I hope one day...' said Sofia.

'One day, one day! Well I'll just keep riskin' my life an' make sure we're okay while *Abbo* keeps doing whatever that bastard *Maulvi* Uncle Younis says, an' for all you know Tony might take over from him once he's dead an' make sure we stay slaves of the mosque forever. You keep dreamin' that one day everything will be perfect. Maybe when your precious Tony stops playing the bomber and scaring the *Gorahs*, the Whiteys, has a shave and actually gets a job. Even if he gets one, it'll be shit. How far will that get us?'

'I'm going to bring *Abbo* down. Don't let him hear you, Jimmy,' said Zoya.

'Jimmy, stop! Tony doesn't go to mosque every day. He just prays at home... you know that.' Sofia started crying silently, and went to the kitchen to prepare the evening meal, through her tears.

After a short while Ahmad struggled downstairs wheezing and coughing, helped by Zoya. Whining noises emanated from his chest, like his own independent respirator. Sofia returned to make sure he was comfortable.

'What's going here then? Talking about me? My palms are itching. I thought that meant money,' said Ahmad with a smile. Sofia guided Ahmad into his comfortable chair; she looked at him and forced a smile at his incongruous attempts to keep the mood of his family relaxed.

'I'll go put the heating on for a while. *Ami*, you're always feeling cold,' said Jimmy, as he left the room. Sofia followed him into the kitchen. He switched on the small TV on the worktop turned to the Indian B4U Bollywood channel; he knew his mother loved music. Sofia wiped her eyes with her hand.

Zoya came into the kitchen. 'Oi, that's loud! *Abbo* is trying to relax.'

'Don't worry – he's in the other room. Come on, *Ami*, let's warm you up. You're always too cold.' Jimmy grabbed Sofia and danced with her, forced her despite her resistance. Sofia felt her breath puff too quickly, her muscles too soft to maintain the stamina of a dance. Her son twisted and twirled her around in a bad imitation of Shah Rukh Khan. B4U played: '*Kis ka hai yeh thum ko intezar meh hoon na, dekh loh idhar tho ek bar meh hoon na…*'

Jimmy danced and translated badly, forcing Sofia to his rhythm. '*Who are you waiting for I'm here, look at me I'm here,*' he warbled. Zoya started laughing and he pulled her in with one hand, and forced her to join their skipping circle going around the kitchen. '*Why are you quiet? Say whatever you want to, how much love does your heart desire, ask me for that love…*' Jimmy sang as he tried to imitate Shah Rukh Khan's actions to the song, exaggerating them unsuccessfully. He nearly tripped and fell over, which made Sofia laugh. Then they all laughed Jimmy scooped up Sofia even as she tried to resist and sat her on the kitchen work top, and danced a jig around her.

Ahmad struggled into the kitchen. 'What are you people doing?' They stopped dancing.

'Oh nothing *Abbo*, Jimmy was being silly,' Zoya said waving her hand and turning away, as Jimmy helped Sofia down. Sofia saw Jimmy's face was screwed up as he looked away. Ahmad disapproved of singing and dancing and Indian movies, but he had never stopped his family from watching them. Sofia remembered how he said they were a corrupting influence. Ahmad had always said that, unlike Bollywood, rebellion most often does not succeed against authority and love cannot conquer all. Jimmy, Zoya and Tony had grown up watching the movies with Sofia; she had allowed them that pleasure mostly when Ahmad visited the mosque.

'It's time for *Maghrib namaz*. I've got to pray – help me, Zoya *Beti*.' Ahmad turned to leave the kitchen. 'It's such a shame, shame for the family that none of you pray, only poor Tony, who's upstairs in his room reading Qur'an even now as you are dancing in the kitchen. Everyone knows.' He shuffled towards the bathroom to make his ablutions before prayers. 'You will regret it, long after I'm dead and gone. One day, you will regret it,' said Ahmad without turning around. His voice seemed to echo in the kitchen. 'I just want one more *Jummah* in the mosque, in the front row, and then I can die content.'

Damascus – The Old City

Abu Umar Al Baghdadi sat at a street coffee shop in the ancient part of the city, and surveyed his team. He knew that the other four Chiefs had arrived here at varying times in the day, having journeyed through tortuous side alleys, each taking a random route unknown even to their intimate bodyguards. As their *amir*, leader, he had given them separate directions which he had decided at the last moment; but the planning had not reduced his dread. He felt vulnerable to assassination, and so he had been meticulous in his method. He was the head of the Middle East Chiefs and lived in Damascus most of the time. Abu Umar also had responsibility for Iraq. He coordinated most of his activities from Damascus; Baghdad had been deemed too dangerous to stay in continuously by the *shura*, the council, even for one of the leaders of a revolutionary organisation like *Jaish an Noor wass Salaam*, *The Army of Light and Peace*. The council operated mostly from Dubai and Mumbai. After a consultation with Amit in India, the head of the revolutionary council, he had called the Chiefs to this emergency meeting in Damascus.

Abu Umar used the title Al Baghdadi only when he was in the Middle East, where the very name Al Baghdadi ensured everyone knew his heritage and pedigree. During his recruitment excursions into Europe, he made sure he was known as Abu Umar.

He and Amit commanded the activities of *The Army of Light and Peace*. Abu Umar had responsibility for coordinating *Jaish* in the Arab world, and for recruitment in Europe. In the capitals of the West he often used his stories of battle against the Kuffar, which had become legend, to inspire *Jihadi* cells committed to martyrdom operations.

Abu Umar dug his nails into his thighs and arms again. *What happened – where is my wife?* His wife had simply disappeared during the Kuffar invasion of Baghdad. Since then, her constant silent screams in his ears deafened all other noise. His wife's howls for help smothered his thoughts. He asked himself again. *What happened – where is my wife? Did she shout and beg me to help her?* The questions seemed to eat at his flesh, and made him itch and scratch his body almost continuously since her disappearance. The skin on his arms and legs felt burned, and looked scarred like old rock in places by his incessant excoriation. The perpetual questions had hooked their fangs into Abu Umar, pumping venom into him like a Levantine viper; they sprayed poison directly into his heart and made his flesh crawl, as if his skin was covered in stinging scorpions.

He looked at the men as they sat on rickety chairs in the street. Each Chief had his personal bodyguards, who sat, trying to look like ordinary customers, but formed a protective fan on the outer tables. The coffee shop spilled into the street and occupied most of the narrow alleyway. Abu Umar glanced at the Egyptian but did not speak to any of the Chiefs, as they tried to look relaxed at the small wooden tables. They had all ignored each other as expected and to any casual observer they would have seemed different in looks and age, and especially in dress. But the heads of Egypt and the Levant were identical twins. The area of the Holy Lands, the Levant, was historically known as *Al Bilad ash Sham*. The Egyptian sat disguised as a suited European tourist, in cream linen: the other twin, the Levantine Chief, looked like an old blind beggar with milky blue marbles for eyes.

The Egyptian sucked hard on his *shisha*, and then exhaled the vanilla smoke through his nostrils. The smoke floated over to Abu Umar. He could also smell the coconut flavour tobacco of the other twin as his water pipe bubbled. The brothers gulped sweet mint tea in between each long drag. Neither ate anything while their bodyguards put away large amounts of *mezza* that consisted of chunks of mixed vegetables with herbs.

Abu Umar ordered Arabic coffee. He told the coffee waiter to stew the coffee into an almost thick black paste in the *ibrik*. He saw surprise on the waiter's face when he spoke, because he had forgotten to hide his educated accent. He flicked his eyes, behind his Ray-Ban sunglasses, from the waiter to his men and the bodyguards, but none of them had reacted. He reminded himself to keep his language simple. He had worn a bright red T-shirt and trendy jeans, so that he could pass as someone who would never be associated with any revolution. He scratched his arms again, aggravating the deep marks. Some became bloody and fresh, while others were drying out like wet bark, but he had not bothered to wear a jacket. People would stay away from him if they thought him diseased.

He appreciated the way the bodyguards did not look directly at him. Despite their unfettered appetites, which made his stomach roar like an unsatiated lion, Abu Umar did not order any food: poison was a plot as old as the Euphrates herself. Any of the waiters or casual observer could be a potential spy and assassin, so he kept his eyes on the waiter like a peregrine falcon watching a Houbara Bustard. The waiter brewed the coffee, which he had ordered because he knew it would be prepared within sight, and he made sure he understood all his movements. Abu Umar watched the youth take the ibrik off the charcoal and then wrap it in a thick cloth to stop his fingers from burning. He kept silent as the *ghawaji* brought the coffee over to him in the silver jug.

Abu Umar sipped the black liquid, scratched his thighs, and watched the bodyguards as they relished the sour taste of the herb-covered salad and dived into the lentil soup. The bodyguards had different training and so showed none of the reserve displayed by the Chiefs. They laughed and talked loudly from across the tables, as strangers might in old Damascus, in between chomping on the mouthfuls of food – friendly without knowing each other, in the Levantine way. Their fingers became sticky from the gelatine released by the *makkadem*, a local delicacy. The thick sauce dripped down the chin of one of the bodyguards but he made no attempt to wipe it away.

The sheep's trotters reminded Abu Umar of how he would beg his Lebanese mother to make the dish for him during his childhood. Growing up between Lebanon and Baghdad, his father's home city, meant he would often go via Damascus. Living and travelling between three countries had given Abu Umar a unique and detailed insight into the Arab mind. The bodyguards gorged on minty spicy lamb and on the delicate charcoal-flavoured roast chicken with rice, which they ate with obvious vast enjoyment. Abu Umar remembered his father, as he watched without smiling. His father would often barbecue a very similar dish, *dajaj al riz*, on weekends, during his teenage years in Baghdad.

Abu Umar scratched his scarified arms as he heard the bodyguards laugh and order dessert. He realised they were looking forward to the pastry filled with cream cheese and covered with syrup, but he got up without acknowledging anyone. He instinctively knew it was almost time, so he walked further into the old city, to find the nondescript highrise building where he had arranged their meeting. He did not look back.

The others would follow in an uncoordinated way, to give a random impression to the inevitable but invisible secret police; he hoped they would not be recognised. He knew the spies would be there watching, melting and morphing into the old wooden framework of doorways and creeping past the high shadows of narrow streets. They appeared like dust clouds; *dirt devils*, Abu Umar preferred to think of them, that would suddenly materialise, only to become ghostly again after a puff of wind.

He looked around and almost broke his own disguise and discipline by calling out in shock, as he noticed the Saudi, Abdul Wahid, had rebelled against protocol and was following him. He cursed under his breath. *What in all of* Jahanum *is he doing?* he thought. *Why is he following me without any bodyguards?* He forced himself not to walk faster; he glanced at his bodyguards to make sure they were alert. His breathing rasped in his throat, and the aftertaste of the coffee seemed burnt now.

Abu Umar knew the Saudi, who was the Chief of *Al Jazeerat al Arab*, had had a tough tortuous journey. He had responsibility for the Gulf States, Yemen as well as the Kingdom of Saudi Arabia, although no one in *Jaish an Noor wass Salaam* ever called it that. Abdul Wahid had travelled up through Arabia by a variety of means, including camel train, creeping past the Iraqi border, and finally smuggling himself into the Syrian Desert through the northern part of Jordan.

The Americans and the Israelis had made desperate attempts to assassinate the Saudi Chief of *Al Jazeerat al Arab*; he continued to be one of the most wanted men in Arabia, although Abdul Wahid did not officially exist, not in his own identity, and the Saudi government did not publicly admit to his presence. They had also failed in their attempts to kill him. Numerous near misses later he was lucky – or divinely protected – Abu Umar had heard the Saudi's relieved bodyguards breathe to each other. So many times an almost-victim, a corpse on the front pages like the after pictures of successful assassination attempts he had seen.

Abu Umar slowed down once in the ancient souk and stopped as he passed a shop selling carpets. Could this be an assassination attempt on me? Could they be using one of my inner-circle to get to me? He dismissed the thought as remote a possibility as anything could be in this life, but he knew the enemies of *Jaish an Noor wass Salaam* could get to anyone, and everyone had a price or a breaking point. Would the Saudi not crack if his three year-old daughter was put in a sack with feral animals: rats and wildcats? Abu Umar knew these things were not simply apocryphal myths. They had been witnessed by previous agents of *Jaish*, not only in Saddam's Iraq or Gadaffi's Libya, but in many countries. The ones who had been stupid or unlucky enough to get caught before they had managed to taste the bitter almond of the cyanide pills all operatives had secreted on them, usually sewn into their clothes.

Abu Umar gestured discreetly to his bodyguards. Three continued walking, but one of the four followed him as he ducked behind a rug hanging in the windowless shop front. The bodyguard hid in a side alcove but Abu Umar knew that he had him, and therefore Abdul Wahid, covered with his pistol, through his clothes. As soon as the Saudi got close Abu Umar hissed, '*Aysh*? What?'

'I have no choice. I have information I couldn't tell you before. The cursed Kuffar Americans know about our meeting. We're going to be hit today –'

Abu Umar grimaced as he tried to hide his shock. 'Get back to the plan.' He almost screeched through gritted teeth, despite trying to control his voice. The other man turned and walked away. The Saudi had to take the risk and warn him; he knew not to use the secure phones. Abu Umar felt glad he still had enough discipline not to argue.

Abu Umar had, as always, suspected a traitor. He lived with the ever-present threat of drone strikes with Hellfire missiles – but he had not realised that the Americans had already put plans into motion, if the Saudi's information was correct. It was too late to abort and rearrange now. *Allah will protect us*, he thought; and anyway, Abu Umar had received his orders from The Leader...

CHAPTER 3

Birmingham – Central

Jessica sat leaning over her desk at work in her BBC office. She looked with glassy, damp eyes, at the pictures of Hamid on the other side of the desk, which she had put up over the years. The telephone rang; she answered it and then sat up straight as she heard an unexpected, but vaguely familiar voice on the other end.

'Hello Jessica, this is Sebastian,' he said with deep inflection. 'We met at the station a few days ago.'

'Sebastian Windsor?' she asked. 'How did you get this number?'

'Oh, it wasn't hard once you said you worked for the BBC, it's all a linked web... I have friends.'

Jessica did not reply. She had arrived in the office a short while ago; interrupting her compassionate leave, although it had been a week since the bombing, for a brief meeting with her boss, Penny, who had told her during the phone call that a decision needed to be made on the imminent Baghdad assignment.

Jessica looked at her desk which, as usual, stood like a lonely spreading mess. Her work space occupied a corner in the open plan area and she had spread files and discs on the floor, so that no one could work close to her – she did not want to make inane chatter once she was immersed in a project. Today she wished she had not created such a solitary arrangement. Her desk had files and papers and pens in multicoloured profusion scattered on it, like a display at an exotic orchid show; modern art at work, she sometimes joked.

The photographs of her and Hamid that she had plastered on the back wall caught her eye again. She did not usually bite her nails, but had started chewing her thumb since the bombing. She put the knuckle to her mouth as she saw the photographs of their weeklong holiday in Scotland. She knew she should take the pictures down now that Hamid was dead. The police had confirmed this to her. They had told her they had found his DNA, but she had refused to believe them at the time. She tried looking away and concentrating on the desk, thinking about why this man was phoning her now. *Dr Sebastian Windsor* it had said on the business card that he had thrust into her hand at the station on the day of the bombing. The surprise of him ringing her had brought her out of her private world of grief. Her hand tightened around the phone and she breathed deeply, but her eyes flicked back to the photographs.

Jessica remembered when her mother had had a heart attack last year. Hamid had taken his annual leave to help her as she cared for her mother at home, and Jessica had supported her father through the shock, whilst making him think that he was really looking after her mother. She often wondered why doctors made the worst nurses. Her parents had long ago accepted Hamid, after they had administered the ritual warnings to her. Hamid would help by coming to her parent's house every day with her and cooking for them, usually Asian dishes. Although Jessica's mother did not enjoy spicy food, once she had recuperated she would not hear criticism of Hamid, even from Jessica.

The pictures showed her in various poses: cavorting in the highlands, running on St Andrews Beach, pretending to do the jumps. She told Hamid they had filmed Chariots of Fire there, so she had imitated the runners while he snapped numerous moments of playfulness. They had visited Stirling Castle where they filmed Braveheart, and she had stood there on top of the Wallace Monument, shaking her arm, holding it aloft and crying *Freedom! Freedom!* – not caring that there was no such scene in the film. In most of the pictures Hamid stood with his hands in his pockets. In two of them, where he stood with his arm around Jessica he smiled, but mostly he stood alone, his coat zipped up to his neck.

Jessica had shown him the sights; Hamid had never been to Scotland before. She knew Scotland intimately from her childhood visits, as her father had taken her there on holiday for at least two long weekends in a year. He always said he had been a 'true loyal Scot, lost in England.' He would then turn to Jessica's mother and add: 'Because of my Sassenach wife – beautiful, aye, but Sassenach never the less!' and laugh. He would always make the same joke during those memorable trips. Jessica remembered how her father's face seemed to become rubicund and his small, perfectly set teeth ever-ready on display, as soon as they crossed the border. It was as if the air was suddenly purer and had cleansed the city smog and the water ready-distilled, and only that aqua could wash away one year's worth of pain and grime off his body; a healing that her father, the doctor, needed regularly.

So, during her formative years, Jessica had revelled in the hills. She had marvelled at the clarity of the lochs, and played in the heather and gorse until her skin became 'prickled and scratchy', as she used to call it. As the sun left golden embers filled with silver memories when it reflected in the loch before setting every evening, she would run back home and find her father sitting on the porch of their log cabin in the highlands, near the Falls of Dochart. Daddy would sit her on his knee and sip his Dalmore single malt; she loved the silver twelve-pointed stag embossed on the bottle. Then, on the porch in the warmth of a setting sun, her father would fish for creams and tickle out unguents from his big, black doctors' bag and apply liberal amounts of the weird-smelling potions to her arms and legs and face. He would then whisper, 'Ach, that's nothing lassie, a mere scratch. These are the medallions that all of Scotland's braves carry. When I was your age, do yer ken, I ate three thistles for breakfast!' Jessica would laugh and giggle even more when he tickled her face with his whiskers. She would breathe deeply and savour the aroma of his pipe-smoke as it surrounded her like a protective force field.

Jessica had tried to impart some of her memories and the beauty of Scotland to Hamid, telling him the story of 'three thistles for breakfast'. She felt she had succeeded in convincing Hamid that Scotland was special, because he had pressed and dried three thistles, without her knowing, which he had gathered from the sand dunes of St Andrews beach. He had then set them between two pieces of thick glass and presented the trophy to her on their return. She looked at the thistles as they lay on her desk, but she jerked up as Sebastian's voice broke the mirror of her memories.

'I phoned to see how you were doing,' he said.

Jessica replied, wiping a hand over her eyes. 'Hamid *was* on the train. He's dead.'

'I'm really sorry…' After a hesitation, he continued, 'I think it would be good for you to get out a bit.'

Jessica wondered why he wanted to meet again. She needed some time to think.

'I wanted to ask if you fancied getting some fresh air... to go for a drive this Sunday?' asked Sebastian.

She jerked backwards. *Go for a drive?* she thought. *Who does he think I am? Audrey Hepburn in a fifties glamour movie?* 'What? Where?'

'I need to talk to you. Well, it'll be a surprise.'

'What for?' she said, not caring that she was being short, because he was being so forward. *Does he like me?* she thought. *Doesn't he realise I'm grieving?*

'I just thought going out might make you feel better. I've been asking around, using some of my contacts, and I have some information.'

'About the bombing?' asked Jessica.

'Well, actually, about Hamid.' After a pause, Sebastian continued, 'And I thought you might want to talk about things?'

'What about Hamid? I'm not – I don't think I'll be in the mood for a drive, and I don't know what people are saying about Hamid.' The police had suggested he might have been a suspect – a suicide bomber – but she had rejected the possibility immediately. Then there were the journalist's questions that she had refused to answer. 'I'm not sure I want to know their rumours at the moment...' she said, unsure if she did or not. *After all, it's normal to be in shock,* she thought. *Even if I do need to go out, why should I admit it to this man?*

'I thought I would take you out, even if you don't need it.'

She sat up straight and felt like telling him to leave her alone and stop being pushy and arrogant. She was not sure exactly what was motivating him, and her desire to know more made her hesitate, and chew her lower lip.

'I talked to some people around the city and found his mosque. As it happens, Hamid was known to quite a few of the regulars.'

'You've been spying on Hamid – on me?' she said.

'No, but I use my contacts sometimes. Ali and some other people at the mosque seem to think that Hamid had something to do with *Jaish an Noor wass Salaam*,' said Sebastian.

Jessica slammed the phone down so hard that it clattered onto the floor. Her fists tightened and her jaw locked. She forced her hands open and then leaned forward with her elbows on her table, massaging her temples with both hands. She had refused to accept the suggestions made by the police during their questioning that Hamid had anything to do with *Jaish*. Now this strange man was making the same connections, the journalist implying the same thing. *The Army of Light and Peace* again thought Jessica, as she stared into space and let the silence hang like an unbelievable apparition, one that would not disappear no matter how hard she glared at it.

She took out his card from her bag and rang him back. 'What are you trying to say?'

'How much do you know about them?' he asked.

'No – nothing...I mean yes, of course, everyone's heard of them, but no, I don't know much about them,' she muttered. The shock and disbelief confused her, and her voice sounded alien to her. The usual cadence and confident rhythm was lost in the stop and starts, as if her body did not know how to react to the confusion flooding through her mind and muscles. She could not help her anger, just as she could not when the police had suggested the same thing, and she could not help her shock, or disgust. She had not yet admitted to herself the possibility that she might have been so easily duped for so long. Could she have been taken in? She had known Hamid better than anyone else. It was an impossible thought that made her screw her eyes up tight, but she could not help the silent wetness that spilled over, but brought no relief.

'Well, I've also had this crazy journalist, Blair, chasing me,' Sebastian said.

'Oh yes, I had lots of questions from him too. He just keeps ringing me up, and he's been to see mum and dad, Hamid's family, the mosque.'

'He's using the considerable power and money of his rag to dig this story, like a monkey picking at a scab. I don't think he's going to let Hamid go,' said Sebastian.

'Is he determined to prove that it was an Islamic suicide bomber?'

'More like determined to prove that Hamid *was* the bomber,' said Sebastian, confirming Jessica's fears. 'I'd be very careful what you say to him, Jessica.'

Jessica pulled at her lower lip, and thought she had spilled out too much already to the journalist.

'Well he knows a lot about Hamid, and he's been prowling around Hamid's mosque every day. Anyway, you're on your way to a meeting now, aren't you?' he asked.

'Since Hamid died, nothing feels real. I was supposed to go to

Baghdad to make a documentary, but don't know what to do now...'
Jessica chewed the knuckle of her thumb, and then played with her lips.
'Well the past few days have been a bit of a blur, really.' She felt she could be more open since he had started discussing Hamid.

'*Jaish* have their Arab headquarters there; some say they even mastermind their world operations from there and Damascus,' said Sebastian.

'How is it that you're so well informed?' she asked.

'I know these people, Jessica, studied them, and lived with them for years. I speak and write Arabic better than most of them, and have spent more years in Damascus and Baghdad and Cairo than I have in London. So – see you Sunday?'

'I can't wait till Sunday now. Can we meet any sooner?'

'Well I'm going to London, back to SOAS for a couple of days, then I've got lectures –'

'What about after that?' she asked.

'All right. See you Thursday, at three.'

Jessica felt compelled to give him her mobile number, even more confused than she had been before the conversation. She put the phone down and stared at the photographs again. The questions about Hamid kept staring at her, their reptilian red eyes firing lasers into her soul, no matter how many times she chopped off their heads. They reappeared like some self regenerating serpent, a multi-headed hydra. Every time she cut off one of its heads, two grew back.

On the short walk down the corridor to her manager's office, Jessica felt as if the questions infected her body like a virus, self-replicating until there seemed to be millions of voices in her head. They felt like shards of glass, all shouting, laughing and deriding her.

Was Hamid the suicide bomber? she thought. *How could he have been the bomber? If he was, why didn't I suspect?* The last kiss that he had given her lingered like gentleness; the light touching of lips, their breath mingling, eyes closed. Was that because he knew it would be their last kiss? The question was too horrific to contemplate, and she made sure it was stillborn, but the ugliness of the deformed image of her love would not leave her.

The voices in her mind laughed and said: *Your relationship was a lie: a joke. He used you to hide, to disguise himself as a liberal. Hamid never loved you at all!*

Damascus – The Old City

Abu Umar let his breath out slowly. *So maybe I won't be killed by one of my own,* he thought. *Not today, at least.* He wondered how his own battered and bloated body would look when his time came to be martyred... he knew it would be the lead in every news bulletin. He imagined his face, with its death mask wrapped around his features like a lover's embrace. He recalled all the attempts to kill them, littered through the memory of their lives like seasons. Each one of them had been a wanted man for years.

The Saudi Chief had been the most targeted, and maybe that was why he had become nervous today. Mossad had tried the classic honey trap on him. Abu Umar knew the Israelis loved using women; that was how they got Mordecai Vanunu. Saudi secret services had failed with poison. The Americans missed with their drone aeroplanes and missiles, and none had ever managed to catch him in time. Nowhere could be called home, and, everywhere, the *Jihad* continued. Abu Umar knew Abdul Wahid simply did not stay in one place for long enough. More importantly, he had supporters all through Saudi Arabia's cities and countryside, with sympathisers in every village in Arabia. On hearing the name of the legendary and mythical leader, Zulfiqar bin *Hijaz*, they would provide him with a room and an evening meal. Even the poorest Bedouins would be able to lay down a thick blanket and supply a meal of dates and camel's milk.

Although Abu Umar knew most people were not sure if Zulfiqar bin *Hijaz* was real, and if he was a physical entity where he existed, his name was sufficient to inspire awe and ensure their continued cooperation. On the rare occasions the Saudi Chief needed to invoke the name of Zulfiqar bin *Hijaz*, it ensured instant obedience, because every child in Arabia knew of *Jaish an Noor wass Salaam*. The people knew that the revolution would come soon; for, judging by the malaise and dis-ease in the mind of the *Ummah*, the Muslim Nation, the revolution could surely not be delayed any longer. When it came it was impossible to imagine any group other than *Jaish an Noor wass Salaam* being in control.

Abu Umar slowed down, regained controlled of his breathing, and looked up into the sky as it became rose-tinted with the setting sun, trying to enjoy the city he had always cherished. He loved the way the evening business continued around him unabated, the high-flying pigeons that wheeled and wheezed in, exhausted, unerringly to their lofts.

He adored the smells of hot unleavened bread from the clay wood-fired ovens, mixing with Arabic coffee, that seemed to intensify when the light dimmed, as evening sought permission to enter the enlightened city. The aromas flowed gently through the narrow streets, diluting as they passed the small shops in the souk, and permeating into the red and gold crumbling sandstone. He knew intimately the secret covered walkways that rose suddenly, appearing from latticed windows and balconies as they spindled outwards from troglodyte dwellings, which unevenly packed the narrow streets where the direct rays of the sun rarely penetrated. Yet, scattered date palms and ancient olive trees pillared upwards between St Paul's Church and the Umayyad Mosque with their roots deep in Aramaic clay, spiralling up to meet the flowing calligraphy on the walls of the monuments, their branches shading the tombs of the saints and martyrs. Damascus went about its business as it had done through unnumbered centuries, and Damascenes hurried to catch the short time for *Maghrib* prayers in the Fragrant City of a thousand mosques.

Abu Umar had dressed as a student with HARVARD LAW SCHOOL plastered on his t-shirt, still in his Ray-Bans; he had wanted to hide his distinctive yellow eyes, which had brighter flecks of hazel in them. He stroked his short auburn beard, which was trimmed neatly on a square jaw and pale face. He smiled deliberately to keep up his disguise as a tourist walking through the old streets; his bodyguards now surrounded him again in loose formation. Ostensibly, he strolled through the passageways, his tennis shoes squeaked as he walked. He ensured that no one followed him before he approached the tenement. He grimaced as he thought about what he was about to do.

He entered the building and went straight to the basement, waiting for the others, as they dripped in to join him. The building was a maze of apartments with children running through the narrow corridors haphazardly, with their mothers echoing back from the grey walls, but Abu Umar had ensured that the basement would be empty.

The other four men joined him, as he sat on the floor of the empty room. He sat with his dark blue jeans pulled up to his knees, shins exposed. They automatically formed themselves so he became the head of the circle. As they sat cross-legged in the cellar their limbs seemed to move in an uncoordinated way. The Middle East Chiefs fidgeted and shuffled, despite their usual discipline. The room had one thick door, with no windows. The bodyguards patrolled the corridors and outside, in the narrow approaches to the building.

Abu Umar knew the inhabitants of the city were oblivious to the gathering below, under the tread of their sandals, that would permanently change their lives. He sat still, watching his acolytes. He had thought this meeting, the final meeting, was a risk worth taking; he had no choice but to do this personally, to see and instruct them all at once. To stay in Damascus meeting them individually would take too long and arouse too much suspicion.

Abu Umar observed them carefully, as the pressure of history weighed heavier than the aged bricks above him. He had consulted with Amit, who headed *Jaish's shura*, the council, which moved headquarters depending on need between Mumbai and Dubai, but Abu Umar had received the final order personally from Zulfiqar bin *Hijaz*: *Let it begin...*

Abu Umar stopped his habitual scratching, and gripped his knees so hard that his knuckles turned pale. He controlled his short breaths and rising nausea as he realised that what he was about to enact would change the future map of the Middle East, the history of the world, and the fate of mankind forever. He stared at the cold grey concrete blocks, which formed the basement walls. They seemed to hold a fascination for him; he let his mind wander in meditation. Dripping water stained a patch a darker grey on the wall opposite, which had a brown mould growing over it. The floor looked cement grey and felt hard as granite. The sharp gravel that was spread over it hurt his legs and thighs, but he was oblivious to the discomfort and pain. He forced himself to sit motionless, trying not to show any fear.

It had been eight months since he had given them their last personal instructions but they had never met like this, all together, under one roof. The risk was simply too great.

Abu Umar now looked at the Chiefs. He felt his arms stinging, but stopped himself from scratching them. He remembered how he had, years ago, apportioned sections of the Arab world to his trainees. North and sub-Sahara belonged to the Chief of Africa, who had responsibility for the entire continent, except for Egypt. He had come via the Red Sea through Jordan, past the ocean of tourists in Sharm El Sheikh and the Gulf of Aqaba. The African was the only one of the group dressed as a traditional Arab with a flowing *Jilbab*, and *Keffiyeh*, the Arab headdress.

Abu Umar remembered how he had to argue for the Egyptian and his brother to be made Chiefs; the *shura* thought them to be too young at the time. They had eventually been accepted by The Leader. Since then they had proven their worth and repaid Abu Umar with phenomenal success. Egypt had its own head; it had always been far too important to be under the suzerainty of any other province. The Egyptian Chief had arrived upstate on the Lebanese coast, hidden in the back of a small boat. Once in Lebanon, the rest of the journey had been comfortable, in a GMC Yukon 4x4 to Damascus. The Chief of the Levant was in Beirut when he got the call, and it was a simple matter to come to Damascus. He had removed his lenses that made his eyes look blind and milky, and now they were back to their usual brown.

The men formed a circle around Abu Umar; the twins sat next to each other. The Egyptian in his Italian linen suit and the Chief of the Levant, the blind beggar, looked dissimilar even when sitting together. Abdul Wahid looked convincing as a flash pimp; he continuously opened and closed his fist throughout the meeting. A single gold earring with a drop-pearl glinted in the dim light of the flickering strip light.

He obviously has information from one of his sources – maybe the American drones are secretly based in Saudi Arabia, thought Abu Umar, as he looked at the slim older man, and smiled. The Saudi did not return the smile but sat unnaturally in tight red trousers, his skinny legs gripped by the cotton cloth. He flexed his stiff fingers, unused to the multitude of rings. Abdul Wahid was uncomfortable in disguise and hated not being able to keep his beard.

Abu Umar knew what the four men would be thinking. No one realises that our final plan is so close. *They might suspect, but I know the truth*. There was no way to avoid the risk on this occasion. He had to pass over the secret codes and final instructions – on whom to contact, whom not to trust – and, thereby, successfully implement the final stage. He could read the thoughts of his group. They were all thinking the same thing: the long dreamed-of, but not often dared hoped-for, revolution had arrived. Maybe in the perennially prayed-for final action plan, the ultimate solution had come to pass. Abu Umar had trained them in his own fashion.

He looked at the group, each metamorphosed upon reaching Damascus. Now they allowed some of their real personas to show through. Abu Umar closed his eyes, intoned a short prayer and started the meeting.

'I have been asked to call you all here today because the final phase is in place.' The faces with their wide eyes stared back at him; they had not been told that the planning had reached such a crucial stage. They did not know of the twelve *Qiyama* Machines. He had mentioned the words '*Qiyama*' which meant judgement, several times to them before, but nothing of the specifics. Abu Umar smiled as he dreamed again the ever-dominant dream: that the day of victory for Islam was at hand, and revenge for the atrocities of Baghdad was imminent.

Birmingham – Central

Jessica chewed the knuckle of her thumb and tried to control her breathing, as she stood outside the closed door of her manager's office. She went to the toilet to wash her face and reapply her lipstick, before returning. She knocked and entered the office without waiting for a reply.

'Hi Jessica. Come in, come in,' said Penny, getting up to lightly embrace Jessica. 'Oh, I'm so sorry!'

'Thank you, Penny,' Jessica said, as she sat down.

'It must be awful to be going through what you are, I can't imagine... '

'I appreciate the compassionate leave, I think I will really need that to help sort myself out,' said Jessica, looking around the neat and tidy office. Her boss always wore a dark two-piece business suit and captained a well-organised ship.

'That's no problem, I'm sure you should take it easy when you do get back to work... for a while at least, anyway,' said Penny, shaking her brunette mane in her special style, as if that would show more sympathy with Jessica's predicament. 'I'm sorry to call you in after only a week, but it's just so that we can make a decision, and then you can continue with your leave.'

'Is it the Baghdad story?'

'You remember our contact there; we made a short film about him last year, calls himself the "Iraqi John Wayne"?'

Jessica brushed back her hair; she remembered how she had refused the assignment. Hamid had not been keen for her to go, saying it was too dangerous. Jessica had told Penny that it was too close to her wedding.

'Yahya worked as a translator for the Americans and now he's disappeared – maybe, well, almost definitely, taken by the insurgents. We need to do a follow up film about him and his family, see what we can dig up,' said Penny, thrusting a file filled with papers and pictures into

Jessica's lap. 'We can arrange the dates and exact details later, but I need a yes or no from you Jessica, because I have to submit plans, reports, finances. You know how it is.'

Jessica flicked though the pictures of a short man with a thick moustache, who did not look anything like John Wayne, and pictures she assumed were of his wife and children. The file contained other information – about Baghdad, safety issues, food advice, and information about flak jackets.

'I don't mean to be insensitive, Jess, but now your plans have changed and –'

'You mean there's no wedding?'

'Sorry... but I need to know. Anyway you're the best person for this job, and who knows? It might inspire your documentary making again,' Penny said. Jessica realised she was rushing her words because she felt guilt at applying pressure on Jessica so soon after Hamid's death.

Penny leaned forward, and put a hand on her knee. 'And I really believe you would benefit from a change of scenery. A week at the most. Maybe two. Think of the excitement such a break would bring. Baghdad!'

'Well, it's not the Bahamas, but I know what you mean,' said Jessica, without looking up. She had no more excuses left, no more reasons to say no. Hamid was gone and she had no direction to go in. All roads led to the future, whatever that was; she did not need a compass. *Leave it up to fate*, she thought. It may be just as well to drift, rather than planning and forcing things to happen. After all, where had all the scheming and pushing got her over the past three years?

'Can I let you know by the weekend?'

'Of course, of course you can,' said Penny getting up and moving as if she was almost about to comfort Jessica, but then just patting her on the shoulder with the palm of her hand. 'Now that you have no more excuses, I'll pencil you in, shall I?' she said. Before Jessica could answer she had shown her out, and through a half-closing door added, 'No later than Monday!'

Damascus – The Old City
Baghdad, thought Abu Umar, as he surveyed the men in his customary reflection before speaking. A new well of hatred for the occupying forces overflowed in him. *The Crusaders are here again*, he thought. They were coming in the guise of liberators to democratise the barbarous dark

peoples of the Middle East, just as they had tried when they were the invading and crusading semi-cannibalistic Franks: out of the deepest, darkest forests of Europe, where mostly non-human creatures lurked. The Arabs thought them more bear and wolf than civilised man. After the siege of *Ma'arra* during the first Crusade their troops ate boiled Muslim adults; they impaled their children on spits, and devoured them half grilled. Abu Umar, in turn, fed on these stories, growing up on them. These were are the one and same people, except now they had a veneer of culture and a thin sheen of democracy, with the might and confidence of technology behind them. *They come to eat us up again. This is part of their continuous war against Islam. The ignorant cowboy with his Smith and Wesson no match for the noble Indian; we have been civilised since Babylon, but you barbarous Frank-invaders are in dire need of re-education, your pretence will be wiped out Inshallah, God willing. You will soon be exposed for the true ignoble brutal boors that you are,* he thought.

With these visions in his mind he closed his eyes and intoned another prayer for a few seconds. He took out his rosary beads and subconsciously started counting off the ninety-nine Glorious Names of Allah.

'Let me tell you a story, brothers, which will inspire you and keep you strong should you ever have doubts about our project. It's the oldest story ever written by man. Found on clay tablets in Sumeria, the country that used to be known as Iraq. That land is no longer an entity, no more a country, so I dare not call it Iraq,' said Abu Umar Al Baghdadi.

'What do the ancient Kuffar have to do with our battle against the modern Kuffar?' asked Abdul Wahid, clenching and unclenching both fists.

'The ancient Kuffar were our ancestors. All Kuffar work on the same principles, modern or ancient. It's a story of the journey of a man towards civilisation. Enkidu was civilised by Shamhat, on the advice of Gilgamesh. Shamhat the whore, and the man-beast Enkidu was a man in animals' clothing. He wore their skins and lived like them. Western Civilisation is a beast in the guise of Man. Not a normal animal of Nature, but a foul-fleshed, rotting, half-decaying putrefying creature, more dead than alive.' He looked away as if addressing someone not present, staring at the brown patch on the wall as he spoke.

'Afghanistan, Palestine, Iraq and the war against Islam is your Shamhat, transparent through your lies and deceit. You have whored yourselves once again for material gain. We will take back our lands and revenge will be delicious, for the shame and humiliation of the centuries. Soon we will cut the head of the Beast.'

'Who is the Beast? Is it a man or a nation, *ya amir*?' asked the Egyptian.

Abu Umar turned to face him, noticed his tight-skinned face with bright brown eyes, his thin Gamal Abdel Nasser style moustache, his hair flicked back in the same fashion. 'It is both, my brother, just like the anti-Christ is both.'

'Who is it?' asked the African, straightening his blue *Keffiyeh*.

Abu Umar looked at his large flat nose and wide forehead, his short beard which grew like velvet, and bright teeth which almost always showed, whether he smiled or not. Abu Umar ignored the question, and thought, *Baghdad was once the capital of the world. A city full of fragrant learning and sweet art and dizzying culture. Even the Mongols did not massacre and mutilate as much. They have not only destroyed the physical entity, but desecrated the memory, crippled and laid waste the generations to come, so that Baghdad can never rise again. I am a Baghdadi, and my father and ancestors Baghdadi for over two thousand years.* Although Abu Umar said nothing, through his barely controlled anguish he thought of his family and the atrocities they had experienced.

'How shall we avenge your family and our people?' said Abdul Wahid. The wrinkles on his forehead deepened into trenches, and his eyes narrowed. The others hung their heads, for they all knew how Abu Umar's family had suffered torture. His father and brother had died in Abu Ghurayb prison, and his daughter had been raped. He had been able to bury them eventually, digging the graves with his own hands. His wife had simply disappeared. *What happened – where is my wife?* The questions seemed to eat at his flesh, and made him itch and scratch his body almost continuously since her disappearance. The skin on his arms and legs felt burned as if by acid from his incessant excoriation. His nails formed channels of sorrow into his limbs.

'I swear by Allah, and his Beloved Prophet, by the *Rasul's* relatives and the *Sahaba*, all his companions, by the saints and martyrs buried there – if the least of those martyrs or the most insignificant of Baghdad's saints walked the earth today, not even the best from their Western Civilisation could match them. The greatest their materialistic empire has ever produced, any of them are less than a speck of dust from their sandals. Abu Umar lapsed into speech without conscious effort. 'I swear Baghdad will be the greatest city in the world again despite your attempted annihilation of a nation and race. It will be a greater phoenix than you dreamed possible. We have had many enemies. You are not the first, and you are not the last to try.'

He knew why the other four looked down, to give him face and respect. They could not share in his agony any further lest it provoked their own stories and woke the ogres of their memories, which would make them lose control and so be shamed in front of their *amir*.

'*Inshallah. Inshallah!*' They echoed his wishes.

'Mesopotamia. For so long the capital of the world, the light of its eyes, the reason behind the world's imagination, mother to all the world's subsequent civilisations, all have suckled at her breast. The greatest achievement ever to come out of the labours of humanity. Adam fell out of the sky into the land between the two rivers, and made a new Eden there.' Abu Umar knew his men were motivated, but felt the need for continued inspiration to pour out of him like a Holy River.

'How is Baghdad now? I wish I could be there and take the battle to the enemy,' said Abdul Wahid, as his eyes shone in the dim light.

'Now in Baghdad, where fear stalks the ant-humans like shadows and death spreads his grace like the blue sky over them, the living beg for that small mercy. Death comes disguised as oxygen in each breath, and death transmutates to water in every drink, and in Baghdad, death can masquerade as food at every meal.' Abu Umar knew that Afghanistan and Palestine also occupied their thoughts, but he focused on Iraq. He would never let the recent history be forgotten. *Even if the Crusaders left*, he thought, *they would leave their swine in charge to rule and defile the Muslim lands*.

'I want to take the field against the Americans again – to make what they call Saudi Arabia into *Dar Al Islam*,' said Abdul Wahid, his breath rasping and his pearl earring jangling as he thrust his chin forward, and stiffened his back.

Abu Umar's eyes widened; he sensed their eagerness to begin the real fighting. He had been told in the past that, at moments of emotion, his eyes seemed to blaze a brighter amber. The hazel flecks in them looked like volcanoes erupting in a sea of yellow lava. He used this to good effect now, as he looked at each one of his men in turn. 'I will enact the plan, the long-awaited and ever to be hoped for, never-dreamed-possible plan to destroy, once and for all, the barbarous West at the zenith of its achievements. Their 'civilisation' will be nullified, and the flag of Islam will be raised above the parliaments of Europe, the Jewish-Zionist merchant banks of America. This time there will be no Charles Martel to stop us at Tours-Poitiers. This time we will not knock on the gates of Vienna or the doors of France. This time, we will smash them down.'

'*Ameen! Ameen!*' they said together, as at the conclusion of a prayer.

'Are all aspects of the plans in place?' Abu Umar asked the Chief of Egypt. 'Are you all ready?' Egypt was the most populous Arab country, the *Invincible*, flagship of the Arab fleet. He knew now that Egypt has fallen, it would make revolution in the rest of the Arab world infinitely easier. Although *Jaish* had orchestrated the revolutions in the Arab Spring, the real Islamic takeover would be instigated when the Kuffar West were too preoccupied to intervene.

'Our people have been ready for years, *ya amir*,' replied the Chief of Egypt, taking off his neatly pressed jacket. Sweat showed darker blue patches on his shirt, even though the room was cool.

'Are the Army officers ready?'

'Army, police, newspapers, TV – even the slums and the grave city people of Cairo are waiting for your order my Brother,' said the Egyptian. He stroked his hair back into place, and smiled.

Abu Umar returned his smile. The dream would imminently become reality. The power of Egypt, the might of the pharaohs, would be his to use in serving The Cause, and for the greatness of *Jaish*. He rubbed his upper arms through his T-shirt and then naked forearms, unable to hide the itch.

'Make sure that our take over happens smoothly... no killing. No more than absolutely necessary. The ordinary people must not suffer,' ordered Abu Umar.

'It's all set to happen at four am. The president will think he's dreaming. We will catch Egypt snoring. The first revolution was just a feint, for democracy, hah! *Inshallah*, you just name the day, *ya amir*,' replied the Egyptian.

For a short while Abu Umar fell quiet again as he looked them up and down by habit. His Chiefs were not perturbed by his silence; he often wandered in the sanctuary of his own thoughts. He knew they had become accustomed, through prolonged discipline, to waiting. They shifted less now. One grimaced, and another pulled at his lower lip.

'When the twelve bombs go off simultaneously, destroying the Western capitals of Kuffar, then will their cities be laid waste and millions of their people neutralised...' Abu Umar trailed, off not realising he had spoken, but then he said deliberately, 'If that is the price for the victory of Islam, then it is a small price to pay. Let us render the world into peace out of the furnace of democracy, away from the crushing anvil of capitalism, and back to the tranquillity of the Golden Age of Islam.'

He recovered from his pained thoughts of death and Paradise. The financial crisis had proved the Kuffar system was doomed to failure. The panic that *Jaish*'s plans would cause in their money markets would bring their artificial construct crashing down, leaving them without the big numbers on a screen, so they would have no resources to fund their international terrorism. *Jaish* would use the *Kuffars*' own oppressive, monstrous, god against them. He did not regret speaking his thoughts aloud. He felt he could trust, *should* trust them, after years of training. Each one of the four had proven his mettle.

"Anyway, it is too late now. The bombs are already in place," he said. His men realised immediately the implications of what he had said. Their haphazard movements started again; they picked at their faces, and folded then unfolded their arms and legs. They did not know what to do with their hands. A new ardour entered their eyes, and their fevered mumbling became louder, but more incoherent, as it gripped their mouths.

'Is it the final stage? Is it the end of... ?' said the Egyptian.

'It is, for them,' replied Abu Umar. 'We must be quick. We're taking a huge risk today.' He paused for a moment, as if unsure whether he should tell them, and then continued, 'We are already recruiting a new white woman for London. The other one disappeared...'

'Disappeared?' asked the Chief of the Levant.

'She dissolved. Like salt in the rain. She tried to walk away from us after joining the cell.' He looked at them, making sure they understood him. 'A white woman. We are working with a blonde one – I shall confirm her in London.'

There was an unsure silence. Abu Umar realised he still had surprise and shock in his power, like a dove to release at his whim to send fluttering up into the sky, so that they would all stare at him like school boys.

'The final stage is close –'

'What exactly is the end, final stage? I mean – how will we bring about the Golden Age of Islam?' asked the Head of the Levant, his voice loud.

Abu Umar knew he had never interrupted before. His acolytes had all been hand-picked out of thousands for their aptitude, and each one had had their natural intelligence and ability honed under the personal tutelage of Abu Umar. 'Revolution and take over of the Islamic world. That part you have known and prepared for a long time. Each of you realises what you have to do. Be concerted and synchronised. Let's show them what united Muslims can achieve…'

'Yes, but how will the Kuffar, especially the Americans, be stopped?' asked Abdul Wahid, pulling at his earring. Abu Umar knew he was constantly aware of the American presence in his country; they were hated more than Satan.

'We have a new power over them; our scimitar is poised over their jugular. Are you frightened? *ya akhi*, my brother, Abdul Wahid, do not be.'

'I swear as Allah is my witness I would walk unarmed and bare-footed into the palace of the King, declare him the great tyrant, traitor to Islam, and be done with it.'

'Then you would surely be dead before you completed your sentence.'

'Did you ever know me to be frightened?' The older man showed his teeth; he locked his spine again and sat up straight. '*ya akhi*, my brother. I have been a commander in the field in Bosnia, Kosovo, Afghanist…'

'We all know of your great battles, brother.'

'Did not our beloved Prophet, upon whom I send blessings and peace, say that is the greatest *Jihad*? For surely, then, I would be killed. The most courageous *Jihad* is to name the oppressor as tyrant, to his face.'

'Then you would be very stupid and very dead very quickly. And you would have wasted years of training and sacrifice, and have betrayed the trust of our great Leader Zulfiqar bin *Hijaz*.' They interrupted each other. Abu Umar saw the other three were shocked despite the crisis, by the open display of bad manners.

'He will not abandon you at your moment of need. It's all been taken care of –'

'I believe and trust. And I am not afraid to die.'

Abu Umar looked at all four of them in turn, and smiled. 'I know your personal courage. Each and every one of you. May Allah grant us all the patience of Brotherhood and the highest of Gardens in the hereafter.'

He looked directly into the Saudi's eyes, and bore his will onto him. In response, the older man seemed to soften his mouth. Abu Umar half-smiled but Abdul Wahid did not return his smile. 'What about *Al Jazeerat Al Arab*?' Abu Umar asked the Saudi.

Abu Umar had ordered men and women placed in strategic positions over years, and secret cadres had infiltrated numerous organisations; revolutionaries ready to take control. There were also thousands of agitators and rioters ready to burst out simultaneously onto the streets and bring about a revolution of the masses. The proletariat pictures of the people taking power during the Iranian Revolution had inspired him. He did not need to reiterate that the Saudi royals were slaves of the Americans, who were servants of the real shaitaanic Israelis, and wiping them off the map of the world was one of the ultimate goals; this fact was so obvious it did not need revocalisation.

'We are ready, Brother *Amir*, completely ready. Those royals will soon be kissing my feet for their supper. Where shall we start? Jeddah or the *Har'am*? Does that mean that The Leader will be coming soon?' said the Saudi, his words bursting out of him, despite his years of trenchant discipline. Mecca – the most inviolable place of Islam – was known as the *Har'am*.

'I do not have the honour of knowing what our great Leader plans – but the sooner he appears in Mecca and declares himself *Al Momineen*, The Leader of the Faithful, so everyone knows the truth once and for all, so much the better,' said Abu Umar.

Now they all looked at each other, smiling. Some laughed, and the brothers slapped each other on the back, even though the men were masters at controlling their emotions.

'I'm sure the royals will all want to join the *Jaish an Noor wass Salaam*, then,' said Abdul Wahid, grinning.

The fact that Islam would once again have a Caliph, a *Khalifa* – a true Muslim leader to challenge the West, to hasten again the new Golden Age that would last forever this time and establish The Kingdom of Heaven on earth before The Judgement – filled Abu Umar with the light of peace. He knew this was the culmination of their collective dream. He did not move or scratch. He did not fear the drones. The meeting was taking only minutes, but his mind ranged to eternity.

'Take it over. All of it at once. Together. The rioting should cause insurrections and chaos must lead to revolutions. They must be concerted and simultaneous... not just in different cities of the same country, but in each of your territories across the Muslim world, so the West can't come to the aid of their pet lapdogs. The Leader will decide when and where to declare himself.'

'How will we stop the Americans interfering?'

'Measures are in place –'

Abdul Wahid interrupted Abu Umar and shifted uncomfortably, again pulling at his red trousers. 'But surely we would be able to plan better. You know you can trust –'

'It's not about trust. Even today we are at risk despite the measures we have taken. There's been a breach,' said Abu Umar, and screwed up his face at the Saudi. *How can he be so stupid and insist on asking me these questions when he told me himself that we're targeted?* he thought. *Perhaps that's what has spooked him.* 'The bombs and triggers are in place – I tell you it is so.'

'The sacrifice of our people can't be wasted. Too many good men and women have been killed, true Muslims tortured and killed in Arabia alone, lost. We have waited too long,' replied Abdul Wahid.

'Success is in the hands of Allah... the Americans will have more than enough to keep them distracted.'

Abu Umar thought of the bombs. What devices! Not ordinary explosions like London and Madrid. No poor man's substitute for real mayhem and destruction. Nothing puny and insignificant like the passenger jets used in 9/11 by Mossad. Osama Bin Ladin had been a useful façade for *Jaish*, who had used him so their real power and plans could stay hidden. Abu Umar did not worry that Mossad and the CIA had also played on the spectre of Osama Bin Ladin to enact their own war crimes across the globe – after all they had armed and trained him. Abu Umar knew they would always create a monster of the imagination as soon as they lost control of their pet terrorist. Abu Umar smiled as he thought of how he had given up Osama Bin Ladin, once he had outlived his usefulness. His mind turned to the bombs again.

The practical solution for the Kuffar. Dirty nuclear weapons with chemical warheads: surrounded with biological material so the explosion would spread the agents over a wide area. If any did escape the blast they would be destroyed by the chemical weapons, and the effects of the biological weapons would last for generations. A cocktail so powerful and lethal that even the ones left alive would be disfigured, crippled and unable to breed for decades, generations – destroyed. Their cities would be uninhabitable for centuries. A terrible price, but one worth paying. Madeline Albright's comments had filled him with a cold, glassy-eyed fury, when she had said that the death of a million Iraqi children, 'was a price worth paying.' On that day 'they' became his enemy, and since then he had become robotic. The casual comment of yet another Jew. *How do they wheedle themselves into the most powerful positions?* he thought. No wonder they had the world in their rodent-like jaws. Their long-established global project for world domination had succeeded. The dishonourable deaths of his family and the disappearance of his wife had turned his cold fury into hot lava, set his determination into rock solid reality of action. He had vowed to present back to them in greater measure what they had inflicted on Iraq, Afghanistan, on him and his kin. *I will visit on them a Yaum Al Kiyama* for the *Kuffar*. A true day of Reckoning for the Infidels, and then we can destroy their real masters, the Zionists.

Los Angeles, San Francisco, New York, Washington D.C., London, Paris, Brussels, Madrid, Berlin, Rome, Moscow and Sydney: Abu Umar strung the name of the cities together in his mind like the prayer beads he rolled between his fingertips. *Israfil's Trumpet* – all synchronised, set to go off together, in twelve of the most important cities of the world.

Destruction of the cities was assured, along with a concerted attack by a virus: a worm, a multi-headed hydra released into their defence and financial software systems. Combined with the systematic and simultaneous uprisings all over the world, it would activate the secret cadres of revolutionary men and women so carefully and strategically placed in the crucial departments in the vital countries that mattered to overthrow the corrupt puppet regimes. Thereby *Jaish* would enable a complete a true Islamic revolution and takeover of the Muslim world, at the same time. This would ensure a collapse of the Western order and their civilisation.

'Then *Jaish an Noor wass Salaam* will rewrite the Kuffar lies out of history and I will help remake the world map. A true New World Order.' This was what Abu Umar had come to enact today. He and two other people in the world knew of the exact plans.

He quickly ensured each country and region had the planned uprisings in place.

'We have very little time today. There's no time for questions – you will all be given further directions and given the order with the codes that will start the Final Plan. I have information that we will be targeted today.'

Despite the years of self-restraint, he felt a flutter run through him. *Is this the day I will die, not by assassination,* he thought, *but by my enemies' cowardly remote controlled bombs? All our plans to come to nothing? Like an illusion within a dream? I put myself completely in your hands – O Allah…*

Abu Umar saw fear kiss their eyes, making their lids flutter as if butterflies had brushed the faces of his men. Some cheeks flickered, and other mouths grimaced from involuntary muscle spasms.

'As much as you gasp for martyrdom, we have no need to make Paradise our destiny so soon, do we eh, gentleman?' he said, and grinned, determined to show indomitability. The Chiefs of the Levant and Egypt smiled. No one hurried him or changed position. All hands and feet became motionless. Abu Umar did not scratch. After about a minute of controlled breathing, that seemed to be one long breath, Abu Umar smiled and said, 'You see, my brothers – it will only happen when Allah wills. Not one breath less or more than he has written.'

He detailed the timetable, and handed out small personal digital assistants. 'These PDA devices can only be activated after fingerprints, retinal scans and saliva DNA samples all match.'

This was why he had taken such a huge gamble to gather them together, so Abu Umar could personally ensure the right person got the correct PDA device. Security was too important to risk doing this third-hand. 'They contain your new orders, and the final codes will be sent to you when the time is right. I will inform you how to retrieve them; they will not be given to you the usual way.'

He gave new instructions, deliberately changed old ones, and then set up fresh secret codes and passwords. He ensured all understood the modified PDAs and the message delivery systems. 'Do not take anything up from your old drop-off points. They are compromised. All the old codes are finished, and the new ones are in the PDAs.' There were no problems, and Abu Umar did not expect any.

'Let's take it over. Each of you.' He stared at them, but they needed no second bidding. Their eyes were already wet with anticipation, with visions of how soon they might return to the Golden Age of Islam.

'The final day is not far. Make sure you are all ready to take over your countries immediately, as soon as you arrive back, if necessary. You must have all your forces marshalled, and you must be alert, but silent, with immense power like the atom. Power to be released, once we reach our critical mass.' His eyes crinkled a fraction at the analogy. 'When I receive permission from The Leader you will have four hours to change the world, *Inshallah* – make sure it is so!' Another short prayer completed the meeting. With that they hurried out, and their bodyguards joined them as they started to leave the building.

At that moment, two Hellfire missiles rained down onto the sprawling old brick structure. As rubble fell around him, Abu Umar knew that a MQ-1 Predator drone plane had fired the bombs, controlled by a pilot with a joystick sitting in the back of a truck watching them through a coloured screen hundreds of miles away.

The missiles crumbled the building to the ground and destroyed the church of St Paul, razed a mosque to rubble, and incinerated the ancient olive tree of Abraham.

CHAPTER 4

London

As the family sat in the living room after the evening meal, quietness covered Jimmy like a pall. He had so much to say, so many things to do before Ahmad's death, so many hurts he should put right. A cloaking shadow covered his mouth. Jimmy had always felt the absence of his father from his life because of Ahmad's love for the mosque; Jimmy could not make himself forget how Ahmad prayed there five times a day before his illness, which used to take up most of his day.

Everyone in the family knew how the mosque, the *Masjid*, as Ahmad called it, and his friend Maulana Mohammed Younis Khan *Imam Sahib* would take almost every spare moment, sucking up money and love from Ahmad like a starving miser. No one would mention it, because talking about the mosque inevitably would lead to Ahmad asking Jimmy to accompany him for worship, which had caused arguments in Jimmy's teenage years. He remembered how during the moments when fury swallowed him he had shouted and sworn and threatened to kill his father. He had even grabbed his collar once when he was fifteen, and flung him across the room. The fear of the almost catastrophic fights ensured that none of the family would broach the topic of religion with Jimmy.

He felt that the subject was a catalyst to his anger. The *Imam*-Ahmad-*Masjid* triumvirate was like a demon put away in a box where he usually hid his hostility – a box he would not dare to approach, least of all open, for fear that the Jinn would be let out. The arguments had continued, about many things but especially about the way Jimmy chose to live his life. He could not stop the Jinn from coming out. He felt the pleasure-pain, the desire to release, almost overwhelm him, as he had argued with Sofia and Zoya about being British. He knew that, when let out, his temper would be small at first, almost comical – like a toy figure. He could put it back in the secret box at will, or just leave it out and play with a while. Jimmy felt he could control himself. Then the demon would grow rapidly; it would become a beast. A gobbling beast of fire with a huge mouth, which would consume all the family. The arguments grew and became all-important, the fire fed by familial love and consideration. Love and consideration were demonic monsters unfettered.

Jimmy could hear what his father had said over the years, even now, as clear as a snow-fed mountain stream. 'I want what's best for you. Why you can not see that? You should go to the mosque, pray, be a good Muslim man, you have to know your identity and culture, your history. I just want you to be successful, because you are my son.'

Jimmy thought that Pakistani parents never said they wanted their children to be happy, even at times of emotional blackmail. It was always successful. *We want you to be successful and do well. It's not like you're going to give us anything.* They always said that, but most expected everything at all times. Not just money, but somehow they expected their children to provide them with respect and status, something they had never been able to achieve for themselves. They wanted every heartbeat and every breath. It was never *we love you and we are proud of you, my son*.

'Mum why do Pakistani parents have such a hard time saying *I love you*?' asked Jimmy. In fact, he was certain his father had never told him he was proud of him. Not even once in his life.

Sofia did not reply for a while, and then she repeated what Ahmad said. 'We just want you to be good, to be a good Muslim. Go to the mosque and learn!'

'I already know what I am. I don't need a fat *Maulvi* in the mosque to tell me.' Jimmy had established that as his standard reply to his father's requests to be a good Muslim. The sentence made him think again of the fights that had shaped his life so far.

He remembered how the fire of the argument would be inflamed, and the little demon that seemed so insignificant would grow visibly. The small idol would play with his ego as more family members joined in the conflict, so that Jimmy felt it would consume the space of the room physically, not just emotionally. Soon he could not manoeuvre out of the things already said. There was no way to breathe, as the monster pressed up into his throat. There was no way to take back the hurt and pain caused by the comments.

His mother, brother and sister and father would all shout and compete with each other, but Jimmy knew he could shout the loudest. The Jinn had fire in its lungs that would suck the breath out of them, eventually. It created a vacuum in the room, with nothing more to say. No apology was acceptable, and none was given. Shame walked large and proud, and finally shame alone killed the demon. Demons died, and new relationships were born, but the seeds of rebirth were stored away by love. Jimmy could never quite slay the beast. The fire smouldered, the monster shrunk back into a small thing that could once again fit into the box, and he had to force it into its secret place. Sofia could always make the demon shrink and dissipate.

Jimmy could not be swayed and never gave in, because he simply did not believe in what his father told him, but afterwards he felt regret and shame because he had screamed and sworn at his father. Although he was unmoved by religion and he had digested the British culture he had grown up in, cultural fragments of his parents' beliefs had embedded themselves in him, as if they were raisins deep within a Christmas pudding, like the ones he had enjoyed at primary school. He had wanted to make Sofia happy and so he adopted many rituals of her culture. Tradition became like the much sought-after silver sixpence in the festive dessert. He had never quite removed the stain of guilt and disrespect to his father from his own mind.

They sat in the living room, each holding a mug, no one saying anything. Jimmy's skin prickled at Sofia's fear that the argument about identity might lead to religion, which would draw his father in. He glanced over at him in the armchair. Ahmad sat leaning back, gasping, looking wizened and old – a shrunken version of his former self, his wheezing dominating the room.

'I'll put some more tea on, and get that Victoria sponge that I got from Sainsbury's yesterday after dinner. Jimmy, you come and help in the kitchen, and I'll make some *pakoras*,' said Sofia.

Jimmy always helped his mother when she cooked. She had asked him since the day he became old enough to toddle, although she would rarely ask his brother or sister. He loved to be with his mother in her citadel of the house. His favourite thing had always been peeling the fresh ginger and garlic she would inevitably need, and mashing them into a pulp in the heavy pestle and mortar. The task was reserved for him, a special chore, from the time when he could barely wield the pestle.

He entered the kitchen. Sofia had dispelled the sick feeling in his stomach, for a while at least. He smiled at her, gestured at her turquoise and cream *salwar kameez* miming his admiration, parodied a bowing action and kissed the silver embroidered hem of her *kameez*, which, as always, made her laugh. He then grabbed her fingers, stopped her from crushing the mint and coriander for the chutney. They felt like small fluttering doves in his meaty lumpen hands. He brought them up to his nose and breathed deeply with closed eyes. He kissed both her hands in turn. '*Ami*, will you look after my butterflies?' he asked as he pushed and twisted the pestle down onto the garlic and ginger in the mortar.

'Why, where are you going?' she said still chuckling. 'You should smile more often. All the *kuriya* will realise how handsome you really are, hmm?'

'If I couldn't anymore... if I wasn't able to, I mean?'

'What are you talking about, Jimmy? Nothing will happen to you, *inshallah, inshallah*. You are my hidden pearl, that's your true self. Soon you will leave this – this bad things, I know, I know you hate me say it, but, *Betah*, they are bad things. That's not the real you.'

'Do you promise to look after my butterflies, right? You won't let them just die of starvation, will you?'

'You can look after them yourself. Just don't hide yourself forever, *Betah*.' She stroked his livid scar without applying pressure, which made his features seem as if he was grimacing. He fought the impulse to pull away because of the weird sensation it gave him on his face. In some places he could not feel her touch at all, near his right cheek and jaw. Yet below his right eye any touch felt too sensitive, as if a flame was held to his skin, and his right eye would water heavily at times. He loved his mother's touch – it relaxed him – but he took her hand and made her rub his spiky gelled hair, because his eye had started leaking again. He remembered how he had a fist fight in school when another boy had tried to touch his scar and laugh. He had split the older boy's lip and broken his cheekbone.

Jimmy inhaled deeply again. He loved the smell; strong and overpowering, yet familiar and strangely comforting. The scent of bruised herbs on his mother's skin, of peeled garlic and ginger all ready for him to pulverise, of the freshly released essential oils that filled the cooking area. It was the long familiar fragrance of playing for hours as a child before dinner, the smell of his mother's hands mixed with all the aromatic condiments she used in her sumptuous dishes, aniseed and bay and cardamom.

He would often get fragrant hits of herbs that she had used, mixed over time with her body's smell, even after she had stopped cooking.

'I don't even know what's in the other greenhouse,' said Sofia, as she went back to crushing the green leaves in the mortar.

'I will let you see one day, maybe, *Ami*. It's hard for me to explain.'

Jimmy loved that unique fragrance that he inhaled in hungry gulps when he pressed his lips and nose into her fleshy palms to kiss her hands. Her hands did not smell the same during the day. He looked at her now and smiled, as she moved around the kitchen. She put her *dupatta* on a stool, her long hair raven, with a few wisps of grey that escaped the torrent, like spray on the surface of a black river. Her hair came down to the middle of her back and made a contrast with her traditional *salwar kameez*. He saw she carried slightly too much weight around her middle and over her round face, which had large eyes, her lips, as usual, tipped over into a smile.

'They only smell like that for you, Jimmy,' she repeated. She always said the same thing when he smelled and kissed them before bed every night. 'It's like when the rose is enveloped by *naseem*, the morning breeze. You are my hidden dewdrop within a rose, the special little gem that comes from within the flower itself,' she said.

The same message again, he thought. '*Ami*, I ain't a dewdrop, yeah, or any gem. You look like one of my butterflies in that suit all funny colours an' silver, a bit like my Bright Babul Blues.' He fetched the chutney bowl out from the corner cupboard without looking up. He knew Sofia still had to add the green chillies and cracked peppercorns, and he had not yet added all of his special ingredients to the mix, before finally stirring in the yogurt.

Jimmy kept the mix a mystery. Zoya was forever demanding, 'Tell me what else you put in your *Raita!* Why don't you tell *Ami*, at least?' Jimmy had promised to tell her the secrets of the best ever *Masala Raita* when she got married, so she could make it for her husband, he had teased her. Even Sofia did not know all the ingredients. He smiled as he realised he had been saying the same thing for years. He scraped the mortar clean, while Sofia continued with her preparations. His assured hands now twirled the heavy pestle that crushed the ginger and garlic together, whilst Sofia's fingers were a blur as she chopped the green chillies.

The *tak a tak tak tak* of Sofia's knife on the chopping board sounded the signal for the cooking melee to begin. Out of the seeming chaos and flurry of activity would come a startling array of dishes – mostly exotic, but some a fusion of styles with western touches. Yet all were essentially eastern, each finished with a unique flourish that they had invented over time. If any unannounced guests arrived for dinner Sofia could entertain them on a truly hospitable Asian scale, and Jimmy knew that his mother never worried about friends arriving or surprise visits by his *Chacha* Waqas, his father's cousin from Bradford, who always became *Chacha Baqwas* to Jimmy and Zoya: 'the uncle who talks rubbish'.

Being in the kitchen reminded Jimmy of their cooking sessions, how he and his mother would get faster and faster in their habitual co-operation, as they manoeuvred around the kitchen with ease; anticipating and relishing each other's movements, side-stepping and whirling back to the work top, without needing to look up. Silver pots gleamed on the hobs as onions caramelised with black mustard and fenugreek pods in some, and cumin, cinnamon and coriander seeds roasting in others. Jimmy and Sofia always flowed in the kitchen, intermittently throwing spices into the mixture, adding an ingredient or tasting, roasting and frying, then decorating and garnishing. An artistry that, to any observer of the finished plate of food, belied the coordinated rhythm that had unconsciously given way to dishes, which had become natural, irrespective of who had added the spice or salt. They were neither too hot, nor too salty, nor too sweet.

'I wish I was as pretty as your butterfly.' Sofia paused from making the pakora mix and looked at him, took his face in both of her hands, barely managed to cover a cheek with each palm. 'Secret from all the world, unknown to yourself even, until the rose fully opens and that drop of liquid which comes to release the perfume makes all the other flowers in the garden smell beautiful.'

'No one ever says I smell beautiful. Look at auntie Bilqis. She says I stink.' Jimmy knew Sofia would ignore his negative comments.

'You will provide fragrance to all those who come close, and inspire them.'

'Auntie Bilqis says I smell of the gutter…'

'That's the nectar the butterfly drinks from.'

'I love you, *Ami*, but you ain't real! Only you could see a Paki *pow'-darri show'dari* dealer as nectar.' Jimmy laughed.

'Shh, *chup*! How many times have I told you?' She clasped her hand over his mouth, barely able to reach him, as she had when he was a boy and had said something rude. '*Chup*! Don't ever say that – don't say it! *Kabhi nahin*! Those silly women don't know you like I do.' Sofia turned away from him with a frown, and continued preparing the herbs and spices.

Jimmy remembered how, particularly at night when she put him to bed, after a hard day's labour and sweat in the kitchen, she released her perfume. Like an Indian Jasmine, that gives up its perfume in wafts of sweet concentrated aroma only after the evening dew settles over its flowers. Jimmy always kissed his mother's hands before going to bed every night. He had started doing this when he turned five, and discovered her sitting on a wooden rocking chair by the gas fire, one winter's night, weeping because of the pain in her hands.

'I cart heavy jeans around in the factory all day,' she had answered when he asked her why she sat alone crying. Sofia would sew the metal buttons and zips on them. She earned a pittance fifty pence for every piece she produced, but the daily humiliation by her boss hurt more than her hands. He realised later in his teenage years why she could not tell her five-year-old son that. So he had knelt down and kissed her palms and each of her fingers in turn. Just as she would kiss him better when he fell over and came to her crying with his little scrapes and bruises.

Then he declared, 'There, mummy all better now!' After which he sat back on the floor cross-legged with his face in his tiny hands and smiled up at her, immensely pleased. This had made her sob loudly and hold him tight to her bosom for a long time, but Jimmy could not understand why.

'I remember when I was a little girl in Ramnagar, we used to have so many butterflies come through the village in spring,' said Sofia, as she pulped the garlic and ginger.

'Were they Kashmir Whites?' he asked.

'They were many colours, but I remember lots of white ones always settling on the village *dheer*.'

'The village shit pile?'

'That's where they threw a lot of the rubbish in a big heap, and yes, they did dry the buffalo dung there in those days – *thapis*, cowpats mixed with straw. They stuck them to the village walls to dry so they could burn them later, but of course, no-one uses those anymore. We've had gas and electricity for thirty years. Our house was the first to get a phone, I remember.'

'They probably came for the minerals.'

'Amazing that such beautiful creatures would land on the *dheer*. And so much beauty... thousands and thousands of white wings –'

'See, *Ami*, you're the only one who thinks they're beautiful. Everyone else just takes the piss out of me.'

'I don't think that happens anymore, butterflies on the *dheer*.'

'Beauty out of shit!'

'So many memories,' said Sofia, as she stared longingly into the bowl of the mortar.

The pestle and mortar had been in the family a long time. Jimmy felt it had always been there, like his mother had always been a part of the kitchen. Once, when he had not been strong enough to lift it, he had asked his mother where it had come from.

'What's it made of?' He asked the same question again.

'It's marble, *Betah*. It's very, very old. It's really extremely rare and special, and it's so precious, you know!' Sofia gave the same reply in a heightened voice. She would use hyperbole when describing something precious. Or maybe it was the Urdu language that lent itself to exaggeration, Jimmy could not be sure.

The mortar was golden yellow with a honey glaze, there were small swirls of green intermixed with the sulphur. He often stared long and hard at the outside of the mortar bowl and imagined he saw eastern landscapes there, peaked hills through which silvery rivers snaked out a path, the sun veiled by high slopes, setting behind the mountains, making deep, dark valleys with twilight and a gloaming gathering there.

'It comes from the village. It was my mother's, a part of her marriage dowry. She was a Pathan and brought it with her from Samarkand,' Sofia said, dewy-eyed. She said *The Village* as if there was only one. Jimmy thought she spoke of it as if even now she was running through the narrow uneven dirt streets, and splashing in the *nulla* flush with monsoon water. He would press her, wanting to be fascinated and thrilled with stories and anecdotes, desperate to be fulfilled and nourished by her. Mostly she remained quiet, and eventually said, 'Let's leave those things that we have left behind, memories. This life isn't what you choose to make it, but mostly just flashes of things past. Memories.'

*

Most days Sofia would say that, but not on all days. At some special times, she loved to regale him with stories of how her mother had escaped the unwanted attentions of the Prince of Samarkand. Sofia's mother, with her younger sister, had escaped in the dead of a freezing winter's night on two ponies, and made their treacherous way south to Afghanistan, and then eventually onto the parched plains of India. Once in the Punjab, she had arrived at their ancestral village where Jimmy's grandfather rescued her from the clutches of a 'woman dealer'. Her father then married the elder of the two sisters, and his younger brother married the younger sister. Sofia told him that her mother had brought with her a strange floral perfume, so delicate and exotic, sensual and fragrant, that the house always smelled of it. So much so that the scent resonated and reverberated throughout the house, taking over and changing its character. Sofia's father had renamed the house *'Gulistan'* which meant literally meant 'Rose Garden,' but hinted at Paradise.

A perfume made from the flowers of Samarkand, Sofia's mother would always say. Sofia had grown up with that perfume. The perfume lingered for a while after her mother had died, but eventually faded away.

Sometimes Sofia would sneak into her mother's room when her father forgot to turn the key in the ancient iron lock. Sofia knew he was unable to believe that her mother was gone; he would mostly keep her mother's room jealously barred. There, she could escape the midday sun, and sit in the cool and dark. She remembered how she would sit on her mother's bed, and sometimes a little shiver would pass through her. She would blink her large eyes a few times at the midday darkness, having just left the white light outside, whilst everyone else slept. The room had no windows to the outside world. Sofia would furtively take out her mother's clothes and hold them to her mouth and press her nose into the ancient material, closing her eyes. Then, once again, she could smell the flowers from her mother's stories. The simplicity of a thousand lines and wrinkles on her mother's face came to her, and she could see the honesty within them. When she held the old cloth to her face and closed her eyes, she could always imagine the beauty of Samarkand.

Zoya came into the kitchen and fitted in naturally with the other two. She always tidied and cleaned after them, but never joined in making the main dishes whilst Jimmy shared his mother's space.

'My *Ami*'s face was always without make up.' Sofia turned to Zoya. 'Zoya, you can chop some more onions.'

'Why, *Ami*, why?' said Jimmy and Zoya together, just as they had since childhood, although Sofia knew they both remembered the words off by heart.

'Mum, I hate chopping onions,' said Zoya.

Sofia's mother's face was never artificial even when she was young and beautiful. On her wedding day she had not worn any kohl or rouge. Sofia knew she had refused *Mendhi*, the traditional bridal henna on her hands. So she had married Jimmy's grandfather 'just the way she was'. Sofia's mother said she wanted him to see her reality, so he knew she was not fooling him. She wanted him to know and see her, to smell her, to recognise her unpainted and unadorned, without any contrived construct or customs and dowry. Naked as much a society would allow, she wanted him to understand her as she had been on that night she escaped from Samarkand. 'See, nudity is not always a bad thing,' laughed Sofia, as she interrupted her story.

'In our culture it always is a bad thing. You'd think there wouldn't be any of us left in the world, the way they talk about it,' said Zoya.

'Yeah, maybe your mum was the only honest one out of all of these lot. Your auntie's friends all makin' like they ain't never been naked but they had six kids before twenty five, and the world is overflowing with Pakis. Typical – all pretending, innit?' said Jimmy.

Sofia told the story. One night, her mother and her auntie had to escape with nothing, the thundering horsemen of Samarkand pursuing her, their breath froze in the night air. The moon gazed on full and low in the firmament, open-mouthed. The two teenage girls fled, dragging their virtuous maidenhood behind them, kicking its heels in the dirt. Sofia told them how her mother's family had been wealthy aristocrats, part of the landed gentry in fact, descended from Samarkand's nobility. The family lost all that when the Prince of Samarkand killed the male members, and the two sisters left their worldly wealth behind.

The same story was told in the same way, from the time when her children could hold a memory in their minds; Sofia understood that this was what made the telling so special. They all knew what would come next. The pattern of words gave structure to their youth. She realised that when Jimmy was older he had discovered that his grandmother could not have been a Pathan, and was more likely an Uzbek; that the two teenage girls fled because the male members of their family, their father and brothers, were murdered by the Prince in a long running family feud over a land-grab.

Sofia knew that Jimmy had seen things made of the same material as the lovely honey-coloured pestle and mortar on his trip to her homeland, and that they could be found in any handicraft shop in Pakistan. He had seen one just like it in one of the local ethnic curiosity shops on Southall High Street. She felt sure none of that diminished his love and fascination for the stories. And anyway, Sofia had reassured him, the pestle and mortar in the shop were just tacky copies of the original. This one original, she would always say, is a priceless work of art created by a master craftsman, an *Ustad*, a guru who was ascendant at the zenith of his art. This is a unique piece of carving that showed his virtuosity and spontaneity, because the sculptor had left the mortar bowl rough and unfinished on one side. In fact it looked more of an irregular rectangle shape than a circle, not shiny and lacquered like the cheap imitations in the shops.

Sofia told the stories to them less and less as her children grew older, but she realised that they seemed to become more and more significant with each telling. Tony usually missed out; he would mostly stay in his room, even as a child. She did not mind that Jimmy and Zoya cringed at the embellished and adorned Urdu words. As her voice trilled and rose in timbre she became breathless, wide-eyed and gesticulated as if performing for a primary class. She felt it was vital to tell the tales in highly expressive terms so that the culture would penetrate every pore and drip out into their own children in time, even if it was in diluted form, and thereby keep her civilisation and traditions alive.

After dinner, Jimmy and Zoya helped Sofia clear the table, while Tony took Ahmad back to his room. Sofia saw the effort of eating downstairs had exhausted him.

'I've got to go and see that bastard Uncle *Imam Sahib* now,' said Jimmy, when Ahmad had gone.

'Oh, my poor *Bhai!* Be brave, brother,' said Zoya, smiling. 'It might do you some good to go to the mosque again.'

'If I don't come back tonight, yeah, you'll know I'm in hiding, and Younis is dead.'

'*Oof, Allah!* Don't even make jokes about such things, *Betah*. *Ya Allah*!'

'That's the only way *Abbo* will ever be free, innit,' said Jimmy. He added, 'Okay, okay... I'm only half joking, *Ami*.'

'Please don't do anything stupid, *Betah*, please,' Sofia implored him, as he left the house.

CHAPTER 5

London
Jimmy saw the mosque as he turned the corner of Springfield Road onto Whitechurch Road. He felt a forgotten sense rising deep within him, which brought back memories like a scent, suffused on the air; he felt some old part of him arrive on that long-forgotten wind. The breeze reminded him of the river's breath in Ramnagar village during summer. He remembered how the currents had been sweet, redolent with the fragrance of mustard flowers before they were harvested in the early morning. Jimmy's memories made him smile but then he wrinkled his nose as the sight of the mosque took over; it burnt his senses like acid. He could see the mosque looming ahead. He had not visited the local *Masjid*, his community mosque, for years. His father had been a fervent worshiper there for the last twenty-five years. Jimmy had not been in any mosque, not since his father had taken him physically to *Jummah* prayers a many years ago. He had not entered any church or synagogue or temple. It had just not occurred to him.

The asphalt felt sun-stained, and almost melted as he walked on it. The autumn's last gasp of heat stuck cloyingly to his rubber-soled shoes. Sweat stunned his eyes and made them swim, and he worried his light blue shirt would cling to his back. The sweat made dark moist pools of blue and indigo in irregular and irreverent patterns.

The converted house had a modern extension built over the rough ground they had recently bought, and they were now erecting a huge green dome, which dominated the skyline. Jimmy looked up and it seemed as if it was the mosque that was walking towards him; to be getting closer, transforming itself into a green giant that loomed and stood astride legs apart, challenging him to take another step forward as it blocked the street, making sure there could be no escape. His father's mosque. Or at least, that was how he had always thought of it. His father's possession. Belonging to him, something that his father had a relationship with, a thing that remained an integral part of his life. Just as the *Masjid* possessed his father. It was something they never spoke about, a dirty secret; like a mistress, or HIV. Or like Jimmy's drug dealing.

Jimmy forced himself out of his reverie. His feet slowed, and seemed to sink even more into the road. As if the surface had turned semisolid, he had to drag his feet out of the mire with every step. He willed himself forward and tried to walk at his normal pace, but his legs did not respond in the usual way. He had not thought the heat would affect him so much; he wiped the sweat out of his eyes.

As he walked through the front entrance of the mosque, a sweet, musky miasma filled his nostrils. It brought back memories of his childhood, spent in overcrowded small rooms with forty other boys. The smell of sweaty socks felt familiar, an aroma that instantly reignited the dynamite of childhood memories. Jimmy's senses recognised the sounds and feel of the mosque, like a signature. The *Masjid* enveloped him as soon as he entered. It was simply an old house that had rising damp, which was cold in summer and colder in winter. He almost smiled as he remembered the boys' teeth stained black from secretly eating 'Mojos' and liquorice 'Blackjack' sweets, and the way they stuffed the Arabic books with comics, copies of the *Beano* and *Dandy* hidden in between the larger, religious books. All the boys knew it was far too dangerous to smuggle crisps into the mosque. The *Maulvi Sahib* had headmaster-like hearing, with ears like red cauliflowers. He could slap one boy whilst quizzing a second about his homework, and still hear the rustle of a packet of crisps from thirty feet away, which he would swiftly confiscate, to consume later. Before doing so he would whip his bamboo cane around, or, if the distance was too great, he would throw his mosque slippers. Often the teacher would throw any small hard book he could reach without moving his body. He threw it, as long as it was in English. For even in moments of rage, the *Maulvi Sahib* would never throw a copy of the Qur'an. The boys would have been shocked, and would have reported the incident to their fathers.

The semblance of religiosity had to be preserved even in the heated moments; Jimmy's master had let slip. It was a sentence he did not quite understand at the time. Jimmy looked around him. He could hear the faint hum of boys hard at their rote memorisation of the Qur'an from an adjacent room. Everything was suddenly familiar and nauseous. He thought he had submerged the smells when he had drowned the memories of the *Masjid*, but they bobbed in the sea of his subconscious like a cork boat.

'The old decaying order of centuries of neglect, abuse and regression of the Muslim youth is continuing unabated.' Jimmy remembered the words of Hamza's father. Hamza had been his childhood mosque friend, and his father had only allowed Hamza to attend the mosque to keep up a pretence of peace with his wife.

Hamza's father reminded him of a clever schoolmaster. Jimmy did not remember much from the occasional days he attended school, but he remembered Mr Fox, his English master and his favourite sentence. 'The stultifying of youthful brains is continuing its inexorable slide down its exponential decline,' he would say to a non-comprehending Jimmy, although Jimmy felt the frustration in his voice.

Jimmy had refused to play the part of Shylock in *The Merchant of Venice*, because Shylock was a Jew. He did not really know what a Jew was, but he had heard some of the other boys saying that Jews were the enemies of Muslims. At school, Jimmy thought being a Muslim was wearing long robes to the mosque, eating his mum's kebabs with *biryani* on Saturdays, being brown, and not eating smoky bacon flavoured crisps. The *Maulvi Sahib* had not helped him understand when he later asked him why Jews and Muslims were enemies. He had to learn extra *sabak*, rote memorisation of the Qur'an, for asking stupid questions.

The boys' voices from one of the rooms filled his ears like an ocean of oppression. The sound took him back to the shrill jangle of noise that his class made, and the thousands of multicoloured old pieces of chewing gum stuck under the small benches on which they rested their copies of The Final Book. Some of the boys wore small white hats with gold embroidery on them, some were bare-headed, and some were bald, their hair shaven off at the beginning of every summer holiday.

The teacher would sit at the head of circle of boys; bearded, large, and unable to speak English. He had a slim bamboo cane that seemed to be an integral part of his hand. The bamboo cane would leave a red weal with white raised skin around it, after the teacher had suddenly and unexpectedly whipped it across a boy's back or hands. Worst of all was when

Maulvi Sahib rapped it across a boy's knuckles; the skin would then turn dark blue.

Jimmy remembered how the *Maulvi Sahib* reserved the special punishments for the boys he took into his small office, where he would bend them over and whip their naked buttocks. Jimmy would often get the 'special treatment', and sometimes he felt he actually deserved it; he hated learning his *sabak*. He had learnt most of the final small *Surahs* in chapter thirty of the Qur'an because he had to, and he endured the beatings until he turned twelve.

Many dark thoughts crossed Jimmy's mind as he entered the mosque, put his shoes on the rack and forced himself through the dark, narrow corridor. Jimmy had attacked the *Maulvi Sahib* with his own bamboo cane, and nearly blinded him; the memories gave him a flush of pleasure, and made him strong.

One day after class, the *Maulvi Sahib* had taken Jimmy into his office and beaten him on his bare buttocks. *Maulvi Sahib* had said to him, 'Let's put some cream on that. Let me soothe it for you, you poor boy. Your arse looks so sore, and it's red hot. But I will make it nice and cold, all better.'

He covered Jimmy's buttocks with Tibet Snow cold cream. Jimmy knew he had brought it with him from Mirpur, in a vain attempt to turn his swarthy complexion creamy. The teacher had tried to make his face fair, like the woman on the jar who had rosy cheeks, but even after dogged years of industrial application he remained dark as a mamba. The *Maulvi Sahib* had smiled at him as he stroked Jimmy's buttocks up and down.

Jimmy stopped for a moment and put his hand on the cool wall, wiping away the sweat which always pooled in his scar on the right side of his face. The air of the mosque seemed so alien, unbreathable. He felt choked as he sucked a deep breath in, and then coughed; it tasted as if he had breathed in a half-rotten, dead dog.

He remembered how the teacher had then casually slipped his hand to the front and fondled Jimmy's penis and testicles. 'You're a lovely boy, so lovely and smooth,' he said. Jimmy ripped the bamboo cane out of *Maulvi Sahib*'s hand unexpectedly, with a surprising strength. He smashed it across the left side of his teacher's face, thrashing him harder and harder. The bamboo cane struck almost the same spot every time, just below the *Maulvi Sahib*'s left eye. His teacher became stupefied and fixed, too surprised to react. He looked as if he had a red swollen tomato growing out of the left side of his face. Jimmy pulled his trousers up with a huge dignity and pointed the cane at *Maulvi Sahib*'s good right eye; the left one had started closing up.

'That was for Hamza. You bastard! I'll fuckin' blind you if you ever touch a boy again, you fuckin' cunt,' he said in English. He held the bamboo stick a centimetre from his teacher's right eyeball. Although the *Maulvi Sahib* had been in England for six years, Jimmy knew he still did not speak English. He had been imported from a Kashmiri village just to teach memorisation of the Qur'an. But at that moment, Jimmy felt certain he understood every word.

Hamza had been Jimmy's closest friend in the mosque for years. They had started Qur'an lessons in *Masjid* even before school, at four years old. He had been his best friend since primary school, and continued to be his confidant as Jimmy had developed his patch, dealing heroin at secondary school. Hamza had stood by him, and when Jimmy had been knifed in the face and almost bled to death, Hamza had been there right next to him, two of them fighting a full gang of much older boys. The scar on Jimmy's face was a constant reminder of Hamza. They had walked to mosque and back home everyday since they had been young children. They joked and laughed and played catch, spinning and throwing tennis balls at each other in the manner of Shane Warne, Jimmy's leg spin hero. One day Jimmy had come back into the classroom after lessons, when he tired of waiting outside for him. Jimmy saw Hamza coming out of *Maulvi Sahib*'s office, distraught, with silent tears streaming down his face. His friend would not say what had happened. He just wanted to go home.

Jimmy escorted Hamza to the toilets, where he locked himself in a cubicle for ten minutes. Jimmy saw the blood stains on the back of his white *salwar* before he could cover it up with his long *kameez*. That day, *Hamza* had been wearing the traditional Pakistani dress. The red splashes staining the back of his white salwar were like a disease, an accusatory and threatening contagion. The spreading pollution defiling the purity of the white traditional baggy clothes his friend had worn. Jimmy watched silently, pain growing inside him, as *Hamza* washed his face with cold water and put his small white hat with the gold embroidery back on his head. The two boys did not speak. Jimmy had looked into Hamza's wet eyes, and words became superfluous.

Jimmy put his arm around his Hamza, and walked him home. They both fought to hold their tears back all the way to Hamza's house. Jimmy tried a smile as he left Hamza on his doorstep. 'I'll see ya tomorrow, bro. I'll teach you how to bowl the googly, I promise,' he said, and waved. The smile came out all twisted, and he felt his face was ugly.

Hamza never came to mosque again. Jimmy did not see his best friend for six months, and then things were never the same. After the drug fight where he had saved Jimmy's life, Hamza disappeared. Jimmy had not seen him since that day. The memories of Hamza had become a continual wound, which bled every day; the scar on Jimmy's face may as well have spelt *Hamza*. The *Maulvi Sahib*, after Jimmy had beaten him nearly blind, was never seen again, either.

Mumbai – Gulf Software Security Systems Boardroom

The skyscraper shook slightly with the rising wind, a gathering storm about to spit its venom on Cuffe Parade in the Colaba district. Amit Bahadur looked down from the top offices of the building. The rooms formed a penthouse suite and had luxury living quarters attached, occupying the whole top floor of the high-rise. Amit had had them disguised when the rooms were being built to look like offices, and they were virtually invisible from the street. There was a small corridor that led to stairs, which linked the top floor of the Gulf Software Security Systems building to the normal work offices on the lower levels. Today Amit had not come through main offices of the software company, but as usual used his secret entrance: a hidden door, which led directly into the boardroom, accessed by a tiny service elevator operated by a special key. The elevator started in a little alcove at street level, disguised as a door; it only stopped when it reached the boardroom.

Amit stayed aloof from the rest of the employees who helped to run his successful software company, based in Mumbai and Dubai, which ensured he could commute between these cities. Most of the rest of the world was not sufficiently secure for him to travel freely. The company had been well managed for fifteen years by his Vice-Principal, a south Indian graduate of the Massachusetts Institute of Technology. Amit kept his distance from the everyday microevolution of software design, that occurred at a speed unimagined even by the prescient Darwinian brain. As long as GSSC made huge profits and so gave him virtually unlimited finances, which he was trying to metamorphose into unlimited power, he had no further interest in software design and sales. He was betting on the financial collapse and ruin of the western systems; the plan had started with the crash of the markets. He knew he would run these programmes that would rewrite the future of the world, change the history of mankind in a greater way than even the silicon chip had ever done. Becoming the reclusive mystery man behind a multi-billion dollar company had been a natural thing, although he continued to relay occasional orders concerning overall strategy and direction through his Vice-Principal. Amit's position afforded him the best cover; like a chameleon that needed no effort to blend in, but had found foliage already matching his passive state.

Amit looked out of the floor-to-ceiling windows. The business district of Mumbai looked like any other business capital of any major city in the world, but the curving road along the beachfront and the panorama of the harbour filled him with nostalgia. It was the view that numerous Indian film scenes had embodied from Amit's youth. When the films depicted the rich and powerful they pictured them driving on the beachfront in 1970's Chevrolet Impala convertibles, more gangsters than businessmen, in cream suits and long cigars with oversized sunglasses. Amit remembered the way the movie scenes would cut to the high-rise offices, like the one he looked out of now. Here multi-million rupee deals would get done on an emotional whim, as a miscreant son tried desperately to rectify past misdeeds. Who would have, inevitably, despite his mother's tears at *Durga* goddess's altar, become a deviant from the *Devi's* path. The camera would pan to a view of the Arabian Gulf, the parallel panorama that Amit could see now. Indian movies had made an indelible impression on Amit's mind, like celluloid film being exposed to light, and that had stained his conscience and formed his culture. He had insisted on being called Amit during his childhood, when he had become completely overwhelmed by Amitabh Bachchan. The demi-god of celluloid usually played the ordinary-but-wronged-angry-man of Indian cinema. Amitabh Bachchan fought the corrupt and powerful. Amit would flinch with every blow, and felt every injustice done to Amitabh Bachchan like a whip to his marrow. Amit would laugh and throw his arms up, wipe his sweat, and dance his way home from the cinema when Amitabh Bachchan eventually defeated the baddies, beating nearly insurmountable odds.

Most of all, Amit loved it most when Amitabh Bachchan played the prodigal son, how he always attempted to achieve his mother's oh-so-near-yet-oh-so-far redemption. *I am a prodigal son of India. Ready to return to the embrace of my mother and the comfort of her bosom*, he thought. *I shall soon redeem myself for the pains and humiliation she has showered upon me like the monsoon. My own India, because I am the unacceptable, rejected and reviled Muslim son of a Hindu goddess-mother. I shall revenge on her, and find redemption through her, because I love her! Jai Hind! Long live India!*

Despite the coming storm, he could still see it was the same scene laid out in front of him, like a frame of film frozen from the Indian epics. It now looked grey, as the waves beat the beach. *The uniform monopoly of globalisation grows every day*, he thought, *and spreads its tentacles into the very heart of Mother India. From these tentacles grow skyscrapers and concrete buildings like parasitic organisms of business. The saprophytes of commerce, these investments, will bring unimagined returns. It will not be long now, God willing, before I establish the real New World Order, end the War of Western Terrorism and create the Golden Age of Islam: the final Kingdom of God on earth.*

Amit looked at the gathered *shura*, the council members, each of the eleven men representing different parts of the world, multiple colours and races. The only woman sat near the front of the table, the Sister-in-Charge. Amit had long known her to be a committed worker. He looked at the unembellished female as she sat still in her usual dark brown, her headscarf always matching her *Jilbab* in its austere plainness. Plain Jamila had become an adopted name of her own choosing, and whenever Amit addressed her as such she seemed to glow with ever increasing piety. *Ya Allah*! he thought. *I hope Abu Umar manages to recruit someone a little more pleasing to the senses; this one rankles like grains from the dunes of the desert in my eyes.* Although useful, it would be so much helpful to the cause to have a beauteous blonde who could go anywhere and do anything in London without being questioned, even triggering the final phase. *Israfil's Trumpet*! Amit thought in English, almost saying the words out aloud that went through his mind. He had long been aware of his imperfect English, and so he imagined the words with a studied practice, at times almost moving his lips as he tried to correct his syntax and grammar.

He looked at the *shura*, ensuring that no one had noticed his lips quiver, but none of them gave any indication of having noticed. Amit squinted at them, as if sending out a challenge with his narrowed eyes. All of the men wore suits, except for two. The Indonesian's wispy beard contrasted with his traditional white dress and cap. The incredibly tall American sat cross-legged in beach shorts and sunglasses, his flip-flops loose as his foot moved rhythmically, and his Hawaiian shirt supported birds feeding from exotic red flowers.

Amit paced behind the twelve seated at the table in traditional conference style. It was like the thousands of business meetings taking place in Mumbai at that very moment, but he knew the large antique oval table in front of him was different, not simply because it was old. Its age was indeterminate; although it was certainly ancient, it did not look shiny and lacquered, as in most other boardrooms of modern Mumbai. Amit breathed in deeply as if he could imbibe remnants of history, like cocaine, in his nostrils, from its wooden splinters, holding secrets within the swirls of its grain. He knew the rosewood body had witnessed and withstood the political machinations of the British, their rule and removal. Its sturdy legs had borne the upheavals of partition, and its walnut top may have taken Bahadur Shah Zafar's palm prints as he laid his hands upon the table – before a forlorn parting look from the last Emperor of India at the Red Fort on his way to Rangoon, exile and shame.

Amit turned, and saw his reflection in the large windows of the boardroom. His *churidar* pyjama clung to his legs, his arms hung too low by his sides, and his knees appeared knobbled and stony, set in the middle of *langur* legs. The open top button of his white cotton shirt exposed his chest hair. Although he kept his facial hair neatly trimmed, it was so thick that no skin was visible underneath the moss-like growth. His beard did not stop at his Adam's apple, but instead continued sprouting growth down to his neck, until it became confluent with his chest hair. A cream waistcoat hung flat over his stomach. The white Ghandi cap completed his Nehru attire. He had felt it appropriate today to demonstrate his nationalism, in view of what he had arranged for the *shura*. Amit did not feel uneasy at his Indian Hindu attire. It gave him the confidence of a poly-limbed deity-chimera – an animal, like Amit, that would transform itself and use any culture or history and even any religion to further its own aims and fill its belly. He held his stomach, as a ripple made his muscles contract involuntarily. He almost smiled as he imagined the show he had planned, and he did not allow himself to worry about his hirsute chest, or even the way his arms hung like jungle vine creepers. He stared at his reflection, and forced himself to ignore his gorilla-thick, stumbling legs. He had often felt his life would have been different had he not had such a simian gait, which made his arms swing when he walked; something that had incited most of the other children at school to call him *Lamboo Langur*, Lanky Ape.

Power in *Jaish* had nearly banished the memories of school and almost eradicated the more painful ones of his time at college; his failures with women. Such spectacular rejection would inevitably have ensured the end of his line had he been a new species of half-man half-ape, as one of the girls in his college in Allahabad had suggested, when he asked her to see an Amitabh Bachchan movie with him (*Silsila*, an unrequited love story). *So what if she laughed at me and made fun of me every day for a semester?* The boys in college followed Amit for weeks, aping his weird walk, bursting into fits of laughter every time he turned around to face them, until he managed to catch one of the ringleaders. He pinned him to the ground with his huge bulk and then smashed his fist repetitively through the bridge of his nose, so that the boy had a brain haemorrhage, and struggled into a coma. After battering the boy, Amit had to leave Allahabad. He had never returned to his childhood village, five miles from the city; his family's money and influence had been insufficient to protect him, and so Amit had escaped to the anonymity of Bombay. He never did find out what happened to the boy he had beaten up.

This whole world is less than a mosquito's wing! he thought, as the old memories dried his mouth. What is the most gorgeous girl in the world compared to my *Jihad* in the way of Allah? Nothing! He will reward me with the pleasures of Paradise; the finality of Firdous will be upon me like the joys of *Jannah*. What is a woman's earthly beauty? Nothing at all. Nothing.

Amit set his face firm, and turned to the table. 'We shall expose the frailty of all this, this so-called reality,' he said. He faced away from them again, looked out through the ceiling to floor glass; he waved his arms to encompass the panorama. 'This seemingly rational concrete solidity they think they are having, this hard and firm quicksand they have built on. We will expose their false righteousness, the naked lies; the truth will lay bare their artificial construct.' He stopped, and turned around. He did not look at any of them directly, but noticed them shifting nervously. 'Their premise of the New World Order will be shown for the mirage it really is, artificial, self created and self perpetuating. Nothing in their New World Order is real: all is an illusion,' he said. Holding his arms out in front of him, he encompassed it into his bosom, as if the view in front of him were a poster and he could disrupt the illusion by pulling the picture off the wall.

Amit went closer to the huge one-way glass windows, and saw his broad nose with forever-flared nostrils above his thick, blubbery, lips. He tried to straighten his slightly bent back, but slumped again into the natural posture of a lifetime. He leaned forward, taking his weight on his hands, almost as if trying to escape and fly free from the crystal cage. His palms made giant prints on the glass as he continued speaking.

'This illusion will be coming tumbling down about their ears harder than the seeming concrete of their lies. We will use their own technology, their own licence and democracy. They are calling it "freedom of speech and equal rights" – and now, their own "New World Order" will be used to destroy them. As Allama Muhammed Iqbal said, in the national song of India, "*Saare Jahan Se Accha Hindustan Hamara*", *Our India is better than the whole world*. I sang it in school every morning. As Iqbal said, "*By its own hand will this Western Civilisation destroy itself, by chopping down the axe on its feet*."' He turned to face them, and this time he looked at each one of them directly, until they averted their gaze. Amit resisted the temptation to stroke his neatly trimmed jet beard. He held his rough hands immobile, his head steady and his whole body still. The power flowed from him. He felt them shiver. *No one will be thinking of my agrarian upbringing, now,* he thought. *Or my Uttar Pradesh village background, my dolphin lips, and the way I walk. Or even the fact that I have misquoted Muhammed Iqbal.*

'We will facilitate our great leader, the one and only, the *Shamsuddin*, Sun of Islam. *Al Jabar Al Islam*, The Might of Islam. *Salahuddin*, The Righteousness of Islam. *Al Faris Ad Deen*, The Knight of Islam. The might of the *Tigris* and *Euphrates*, the sweetness of *Kosar*, the fragrance of *Firdous*, the noblest species of modern man. The new *Khalifa*, the *Amir Al Momineen*. His very name is the essence of Islam: Zulfiqar bin *Hijaz*. The great and magnificent true servant of Allah, our Leader of *Jaish an Noor wass Salaam*. The true party of God, *The Army of Light and Peace*.'

Cries of *Allah O Akbar! Allah O Akbar!* broke out amongst the seated delegates; a couple raised their hands above their heads.

'The Leader will be the vengeance, the avenging tool by Allah's hand. Allah says *And when you strike them I will strike them, I will be your hand!*' Amit looked glazed. He felt inspired at this time, just before the final delivery of Allah's judgement and justice onto the Kuffar, and the urge to inspire others flowed through him like the confluence of the Ganga and Jumuna rivers.

'Especially those that call themselves Muslims, these traitorous betraying dogs... dogs have more honour and loyalty. Even swine, like these *khanazeer* who scoff and slurp at the trough of their western paymasters, will be rooted out and treated like the wild pigs that they are. Wild boars cannot help what they are; they are animals of God. These spies, these traitors are not men of Allah, despite their masquerade – no, they are not even animals of The Creator. They are faceless infiltrators deep within us, in our societies and groups planted decades ago; everyone and everything has been infiltrated. Trust no one – not even me. Only the Great Leader is true and inviolable. Even I may be one of these... is it possible?'

He looked at the scant hair of the Scandinavian, noticed his high cheekbones and long face and even thinner body with gangly legs. Amit resisted the temptation to smile at the Dane. The Malay sat with thick rolls of flesh, making him seem even shorter next to the tall European. His meaty cheeks hung and shone as if oiled by the coconut milk from Nasi Lemak, and the fat skin glistened in the artificial light, brown and shiny. The Chinese sat next to him. Amit knew he had a genetic lack of a beard so kept a thin black moustache, one side slightly higher than the other, as if a child had missed with a marker pen.

'No, no!' A chorus of astonishment and disbelief greeted Amit as he paced around the conference table.

'Always question what I do, brothers, always question! With your tongues, and your swords if necessary.' He looked around into their faces: Malay, Chinese, Indian, Slavic, and Scandinavian. Fear made saliva drip down the lips and snail track down the face of the Malay. He made no attempt to wipe it from his opulent suit, and the rolls of flowing fat over his collar were now sweat-covered.

'Before that, gentlemen, I have a treat for you – a special show, you might call it. Even in this land of Hind, of the Hindu, there have been people willing to fight the forces of evil, colonisation and imperialism. This New World Order is just a fresh wave in that ancient eternal struggle... a new phase.' Amit loved history and now wanted to reinforce his favourite lesson: The Clash of Civilisations.

The office door banged open and a man burst through, chased by security guards with drawn guns who were just about to fire their weapons at him. They hesitated for a split-second, fearful of hitting any of the gathered high priests of the Gulf Softsystems Computer Company at the full conference table, long enough for the man to run towards Amit and throw himself at his mercy. The young man landed on his knees in front of him, and with eyes clenched and his face a grimace, he bowed his head. The desperate man looked terrified as he grasped Amit's hands.

'I want to convert. I couldn't wai...' said the man, but before he could complete his sentence, four security guards jumped on him and tied him in a bundle to the ground.

'Let him go,' said Amit.

'But, sir, he could be dangerous! He tore through security, hit three of my men,' the security foreman said.

'I said, let him go! Bring the three who couldn't stop him to me later.'

'Yes sir, of course, yes sir,' said the sergeant of security, glad he might still get away with his job. Amit knew he feared Amit's retribution more than losing his job. He ordered his men away from the man who was grimacing in pain on the floor, rubbing his arms, trying to get the blood circulating again. He rose to his knees and Amit came to stand in front of him.

'Accept me as a Muslim, please! I want to bear witness that there is no God except Allah and I believe in our Leader. I heard you speak in college three days ago and since then my spirit has been on fire. I will give my body and soul to bear witness... please accept me as a sacrifice. I want you to bear witness to my submission and surrender on the day of Judgement,' said the man, his voice lust-filled and greedy for martyrdom. He rubbed his shoulders and arms where the joints had been bent into impossible angles by the security guards.

Amit said the *Shahadah*, the testimony to convert him into a Muslim. The man already knew what to say and repeated it after him, consuming it hungrily. Amit smiled at the fallen man, lifted him gently and sat him down next to him at the head of the table. 'Now you are a Muslim, and must remain one forever. You must fulfil your obligations and responsibilities to *Jaish an Noor wass Salaam*. One day you may be called upon to do your duty, and that day may never be, but if it does become your destiny you must be doing it as you will be trained to do it, unstintingly and unquestioningly, and having been asked to do it only once.'

'I – I will. I will. I swear, protect, and serve Zulfiqar bin *Hijaz* with my life, my family's life, my blood and my soul. I will.' He kissed Amit's hands.

'You are knowing what to do and say without being asked? Except we only kiss the hands of our beloved leader, Zulfiqar bin *Hijaz*.'

'Three of my brothers are already in *Jaish*, and each one is ready to be a *Shaheed*.'

'How lucky and blessed is the woman who gave birth to four such sons. *Umm al arba Shuhada*. The mother of the four Martyrs she will be known as from this day forth.'

'My brother is Raju –'

'Raju? Raju…' Amit held up a hand, as he realised that the teenager's older brother was already one of the Alpha Ansar in California. 'You then, brother of *Raju Ban Gaya Gentleman* from today will be *Om Shanti Om*,' he said stating another of Shah Rukh Khan's films. Amit codenamed all of his agents after the superstar's movies. 'You will be carrying, in future, the banner of Islam and becoming the beacon, the torch of *The Army of Light and Peace*.' All the gathered men smiled with Amit at the convert. He knew none dared groan at the continuing Bollywood *filmi* connection. Even Plain Jamila almost smiled. 'Maybe we should be selling him some of our software systems now that he is becoming one of us,' said Amit. Restrained laughter greeted the comment.

Amit continued, 'Before that, as promised – some entertainment. Since we are in India, we should try to fit in with the local traditions. One of the leaders who stood against the forces of colonialism and imperialism was the great Sultan Fateh Ali Tippu. He used *Jettis*, Hindu holy strongmen, who implemented his special wishes along with his famous tigers.' Amit nodded at one of the guards at the door, who went across to the other side of the conference room to a hidden door, and he slid it open.

Four giant men, hugely muscled and wearing nothing but tiny loincloths, sauntered into the conference room. They wore gold bangles across their biceps, and their oiled bodies glistened and shone in the fluorescent light. They padded, softly jogging to their positions, two to each side of the conference table, behind the seated men and one woman.

The group looked at each other nervously; Amit noted their apprehension at this unexpected development. Nothing like this had happened before. The Dane removed his glasses from his blue eyes and wiped them on an immaculate silk handkerchief, before lighting a large Cuban cigar. Amit stared at the Dane, without moving or blinking. *I wonder if you are being quite so calm on the inside, my Scandinavian friend?*

The fat Malay shifted continuously as he rocked on his leather chair, sweat staining his blue collars. He took his jacket off to reveal mounds of meat covered in a shirt that clung to the folds of flesh, revealing darker blue pools of wetness. The nakedness of the *Jettis* contrasted with the dark pinstripe suits worn by most of the men.

'We must gather our forces for the final showdown. But before then... what to do when something is rotten from the inside? How can we be strong and defeat the enemies of the true faith if we have *dheemak*, termites amongst our midst? Eating away at us and destroying our very structure, devouring our sacrifices and gorging on our souls, making us rotten to the core?' asked Amit. He walked slowly around, and stared at each man in turn at the table. Most were now discomfited, fidgety and nervous. One or two coughed and brought out handkerchiefs of Egyptian cotton, and blew hard. The Chinese and Indonesian looked quietly confident and made eye contact with Amit, smiling.

'We are having a traitor amongst us... '

The *Jettis* now circled, slowly jogging clockwise, around the backs of the seated men. The smell of almonds filled the conference room. The *Jettis* shone, their vast muscles taut like canvas, oiled, shiny nutmeg-brown and liquid chocolate. Their long queues of hair hung out beneath their turbans and straggled down to the small of their backs, signifying their vows to their *Devis* and *Devtas*. No mixed blood, no Arab, no Mongol, and no Aryan; pure, devotionally deadly, Dravidian Hindu. Just as the Tippu Sultan had used the Hindu strongmen to punish his enemies and traitors, now Amit was about to re-enact history. *I wish the girl who didn't go with me to see Silsila was here today.*

All those gathered, even David Gul, the undisputed don of the Mumbai underworld, knew of the folklore that still grew out of the Tippu's stories over two hundred years after his death, in a country where centuries are like hours and history keeps the blood circulating. They knew how the ogres twisted the necks of men like chickens to kill them, or simply crushed the victim's skull between two giant palms until it crunched like an eggshell. The Tippu's *Jettis* had devised numerous ingenious ways with which to kill his enemies and traitors.

'Mir Sadiq betrayed the great Tippu Sultan – and Mir Jaffar, who sold Bengal to the Britisher dog Clive, and so started the disintegration of Muslim India. We have them still.'

Amit looked at David with disgust, hidden behind a sneer. The Underworld Don, the Mumbai Mafia. Short and squat – barely five foot – with greasy, curly hair and a small moustache that dribbled into a disappearing chin, which became a thick, bullfrog neck that expanded every time just before he spoke. Amit knew women swooned and vied with each other for David's ministrations. David had years ago slithered his way into the *shura*, and because of his power and influence in Mumbai and Dubai had become indispensible to *Jaish*.

'This is the true India, despite the façade of the new and modern vibrant India; they *are* India. Dark and pagan. Look at them!' Amit pointed to the *Jettis*. 'They sit down cross-legged on the floor to worship their black *Kali Devi*, in the depths of the night, in the darkest of caves, when they think no one can hear or see.' Amit paused. *Did the girl reject me, even though I had almost impossible-to-get gallery tickets for Silsila, because I was a Muslim? Did she worship the same dark Devi as these Jettis?*

Amit continued, 'They will do what I tell them, inspired by their diabolical sooty goddess, so that they can endow a new temple to her. Her priests wait and wail and lament until the day she returns to sweep the new order away. So you are seeing, gentlemen, that these people and American-terrorist-*Kuffars* are sharing more than commercial interests. They have more in common than you realise... they are sharing the same hope. That is what human beings are crying and dying for. They are so thirsty that they will drink the sand. So what do we need to give them? We will give the Kuffar a real financial crisis; money is their only god of strength. We will take humanity away from these Kuffar lies, and show then the truth of Islam. We will be giving them real hope. Hope! If you show them a mirage in the desert they think it is water, and they will drink the sand. They will literally drink the sand!'

Amit saw the fear flood into them, rising like a rip tide through the dozen. Plain Jamila adjusted her headscarf and looked from Amit to the *Jettis*, and back to Amit again.

'Hope...' Amit looked around at the sweaty faces, their darting eyes and spinning heads to try and keep track of the *Jettis*. 'That is what we are. Hope and Light, the real New World Order, against the darkness of any American President, Jupiter, Kali or any other false God. Against any of the one eyed *Dajjals*, any Antichrist that comes, right from the time of Ra, through Mithra to Clark Gable and Harry Potter. Against the might of the Jewish Conspiracies. Money Lenders. Usurers. Shylocks. Rothschilds to Goldman Sachs.'

Amit knew the conspiracy theories that were forever spreading, through the media and especially the Internet, like vigorous bindweed amongst the Muslim minds. They had intertwined with logic, stealing the light of reason, and so strangling the rose of free thought. The conspiracies had been well manured and watered and given new incarnations by *Jaish* to further the *Jihad*. Amit stood still at the head of the table as the *Jettis* rhythmically danced their slow jog, hypnotically circling around the table, not looking at any of the men, oblivious of all.

'Here then, gentlemen, is the true living India, the real beating heart of darkness, darker than any ebony found in Africa. This is what has gone on for centuries, for millennia. In fact, this is what will go on when America is a memory, and George Bush's or Obama's butchery – doesn't matter which president – is another blot on the record of humanity. What do you thinking happens beyond the bright commercial district, in her dank caves and her brooding forests and beyond her swollen rivers? The Ganges, Jumuna and Sarayu feed and fertilise. They have created myths and monsters for aeons. These incarnations,' he gestured to the *Jettis*, 'of Hindu-humming human barbarity, will still be here just the same when the mountains are crumbling and the Himalayas are no more. I grew up with it and I love her, the true India. Maybe I am not agreeing with all of my Mother India, *Maa Hind*, but I love being Indian. It gives you a feeling of eternity, of invincibility, of fate on your side and destiny in your hands because we have time. See, look ahead of you and you can see your generations following from you, flowing down like a river endless – one after the other – into Eternity.' Amit gazed without seeing and gestured with his hand into the empty space ahead of him. *You, girl who called me an ape, should have gone with me to watch the film. See – now I am using Hindus to do Allah's work.*

Amit often wondered why he loved India despite its blatant paganism, but she had depths of unfathomable beauty; like the girl at college but even more like his favourite actress, Aashriya. *Maybe that dichotomy made me what I am*, he thought. *Muslim – but in love with Hindu women – and I grew up with Hindu legends. I remember reading all night under the flickering oil lamp, being endlessly fascinated by the crazy stories of the Mahabharata. Of course, I know it's all nonsense, but whoever wrote it in the first place must have been a genius. Maybe I love India, despite her idolatry, but she does not love me. No, my mother has spat on me.*

'Excuse me, brother...' said Plain Jamila.

Amit paused and waited with both hands in front of him; she had flown in from London for the meeting. He gestured and tipped his head forward for her to continue.

'I – I thought we were going to arrange –'

'Yes we are, my sister. Don't be frightened by them.' He smiled at her his voice quieter and gentler. 'They're not here for you. No harm will ever come to you, my sister.' He nodded to the security men who escorted Plain Jamila out. 'I will call you back – and *Om Shanti Om*, you go with them too,' he said, turning to the young man. The new recruit was too untried to trust with what was about to happen, and his sense of chivalry did not allow him to let Jamila stay in the boardroom. When they had left, he continued speaking as if he had never been interrupted.

'Because we are having time, gentlemen, Time. We know that a millennium either way does not matter. Are you really thinking that raising a few skyscrapers and scattering some five star hotels like a rash – a disease over the face of India – and that by putting a few bikini clad Germanic women on holiday brochures for Goa that you will change India, hide and destroy the true India in all her historic, barbaric beauty?' Amit covered his mouth as he said the last part of the sentence, as if unable to commit sacrilege and describe his mother as barbaric, but then he quickly moved his hand down again. He looked around at them, and they stared back quizzically. He knew they had expected this to be a planning meeting, to implement what had been long awaited and was often suspected. The final solution: the victory of Islam in the Clash of Civilisations. This was now imminent. *The* Kuffar *gods were Mammon and Kali... death and destruction that could not be tamed by Shiva*, he thought. *We shall enslave all their gods and rule them through the temples of Wall Street and The City of London. Their markets crashing shall be just the beginning, the financial meltdown dissolving their lies like dross in a furnace; we will chain them with gold.*

The Leader had spoken about their victory and ever-lasting reward in the highest of gardens; for they were the new breed, the super-Muslims, who would very soon bring about a revival of the true faith, the *Deen*, and would establish the Kingdom of Allah. All the Messiah would have to do would be to arrive on earth and wear the throne, claim his crown that *Jaish* would have prepared for him. The leader had often said that *Jaish an Noor wass Salaam* would make his job easy and smooth. The leader would often deliver his speeches and speak at the *shura* meetings via video-link, from somewhere in the Rub Al Khali, The Empty Quarter of Saudi Arabia; even Amit did not know his exact location. Amit would always end the meetings with his head bowed as the Leader prayed with them for the final solution. Most days, however, Amit ran *Jaish* and administered the practicalities to bring about the Islamic World Order as if implementing the Leader's wishes, as if he received regular telepathic communication from the higher spirit.

Now Amit saw how they became increasingly frightened. The rictus of fear gripped their faces as the *Jettis* started chanting. They continued the slow jog, becoming slower and slower, but the cadence and timbre of the chanting rose. Amit knew none of the gathered heads could recognise it. His mind wandered. *Is this your language, you Hindu college-woman that I used to love? What about you Aashriya, who I have secretly loved for so long, the undisputed queen of Bollywood, do you understand this? Can you imagine even in your dreams that this is my secret paean to you?*

The room shook and reverberated with the pagan harmony, the heavy padding of feet kept an inverse rhythm, the guttural and throaty noise completely alien to the dozen, and even to Amit, although he knew many of the tongues of India. It was not a language they recognised or had heard before. He looked at David Gul and wondered how the starlets could spend time with this squat, troll-like man. His typically dark Indian face, his head like a cannon ball, and with his small moustache as usual, he struck Amit as ugly.

Without warning, the Indonesian from the other side jumped out of his chair onto the table and ran towards Amit. His long white shirt fluttered like a prayer flag. He screamed as he flew towards Amit.

'You are the true enemies of Islam, the hated *Khawaarij*, the outsiders and traitors to Islam's true message. *Allah O Akbar!* Death to all *Takfiris!*' he shouted, as he leapt at Amit with his silver fountain pen, now a killing weapon, raised above his head. His white hat fell onto the table and his loose shirt flapped as he readied for the downward stab – but as he jumped off the table, one of the *Jettis* made a huge scything movement, an upward-flying scissor kick. A crunching sound split the fetid air as the Jetti's knee caught the man in the middle of his back, and the strong man brought his other heel crashing down into the man's throat, crushing his larynx and trachea. The man's eyes bulged frog-like; he did not make a sound, but flopped like a jellyfish onto the floor. The Jetti who had performed the martial arts manoeuvre rejoined the other *Jettis* and resumed his slow jog and chanting with semi closed trance-like eyes, almost as if he had not moved, nor broken pace with the others. Amit had not flinched. The rest of the seated men looked too terrified and shocked to move. Amit looked around, ever more confident, unblinking, reaping strength from their weakness. Finally, the American stood up, and tried to mouth something as he pointed at his dead colleague.

'Sit down –'

'But – but… That guy – these guys…' The American's mouth moved, but no further sound came out. He pointed from the body to the *Jettis* and back again, fingering his Hawaiian shirt, as he stood agape and incredulous. Then he stared, unblinkingly at the corpse.

'I – said – sit – down!' Amit repeated slower without raising his voice as he stared at him. The American collapsed panting, back into his chair. His limbs that seemed to Amit to be incongruously long started shaking; one red flip flop had come off his foot. Disenfranchising the American of dignity empowered Amit. He loved the sensation, even though the tall man formed a vital strand of his team.

'They want the old world order to be as it always was. They want to cement their dominance, these *Kuffar* over us for ever, and they believe it will be happening when *Kali Devi* is coming again. Not just the Hindus; the Americans, and all of them. If we ignore their plans we will be having a wound in the Muslim body the size of the Grand Canyon, which is bleeding blood like the Amazon. A liberal modern Muslim bandage, a Band-Aid, will not hold back the flow. Their *Kuffar Jihad* against our true *Jihad* is being fought everywhere, even here. India is dark and she is dangerous. There are secret societies and gatherings and customs, rituals unseen to most human eyes, except to the select few.'

Species to be uncovered by anthropologists, he thought, *more than any lost island in the Indonesian archipelago. India is mostly mystery even to the majority of her own people.* 'They work with fear, and castes, mostly low, they are having rat-eating castes, and their currency is dread. They covet the old world order and they are secretly hungering for the return of Kali, who will extinguish the light of Islam and make the day as black as the night.'

Amit walked over to the American even though others were closer, and nodded to him to him as he gave him sheets covered in charts and diagrams. He gestured to the American to pass the papers around to the others. The gangly man pushed his palms onto the table, before getting up and distributing the plastic covered folders.

'One copy for you all – it's a secret report by the Indian Intelligence Bureau, into the work of so-called Islamic terrorists. They have approved extra-judicial assassinations, and killing by any method. Like Israel, they mean to strike first. They are meaning us, gentlemen.' Amit smiled at their amazement. His self-control made his legs feel like steel, as if connected to the metal running through the building. He looked at their unbelieving faces; he could give them handouts charts with statistics on them, while a dead body lay at his feet.

Amit knew it would get even better before the meeting was over. The men reluctantly took the sheets of paper and flicked through the tables and figures, with a graph on the front page showing the rising strength of *Jaish an Noor wass Salaam*, but he noticed none could take their eyes off the dead man on the floor for long, and they flicked their eyeballs asynchronously back and forth. Amit felt like smiling. Despite their power in their own areas the terror of death had come home to them, and they could not concentrate on the figures presented on the papers. The *Jettis* continued their slow jog and harmonious chanting.

'Only Islam can set them free. Like it set you free, George Geoffrey Davis III,' Amit said, looking at the American, who walked behind the delegates. 'They have remained unchanged for centuries and millennia. Time before history they have remained the same, and they will be remaining unchanged until The Day if we let them stay in the darkness. Money and the Americans cannot set them free, just as it cannot set the rest of the world free. The investment banks and gold diggers live on the dregs of human misery and suffering, interest payments and world debt relief loans from the World Bank. They are all Jewish usurers, paying for the cluster bombs in Gaza, grinding the bones of children to dust with starvation and disease to sweeten their cappuccinos. Do not be making any mistake. No one else can set them free, no one can give them Justice except Islam. History is proof and testament to that fact. When I say India, gentlemen, I mean all India, Pakistan, Bangladesh,' said Amit. He knew he did not need to worry about the Middle East; he expected Abu Umar Al Baghdadi to have that under control. 'And any other false schism or artificial construct they have managed to divide themselves into these last few years. All of them are moneyed slaves to fraudulent finance, which we will soon destroy, Hindu, Sikh, Kali worshippers, Zoroastrians, Parsi, Bahais, Jains – and especially the Muslims of India and the world, like this one who you see lying in front of you here.'

Amit motioned to the limp man at his feet and resisted the temptation to kick the body. *What the hell was he thinking? Tried to assassinate me in my own office. Hah! Are you watching, Aashriya? Can you see my power?*

'These so called Muslims we will start with them. The ones that are not like us, the pretend Muslims, the *moderates* sometimes the *Kuffar* call them. They who don't look, walk, talk, dress eat or even smell like us. I had long suspected him,' he said, and stabbed down with his index finger. 'Today we confirmed him as one of them: a moderate, spiritual Muslim, they would have us believe. That is what the *Kuffar* have always wanted from us, gentlemen – just spirituality, and no action. Fundamentalists – *hardline political Islam*, they call us. They want to wipe out anything that challenges them. I promise you, brothers, it will be so-called Muslim blood that flows in the streets when the real New World Order is established, for it is the so-called moderates, the modern Muslims, who are deranged and dangerous. They are fundamentally wrong, and extremely far away from their true religion. See here... today we had a *true* Muslim, just joined our Brotherhood, *Mashallah*,' he said pointing to door the convert had gone through to his right. 'And here's the traitor. All it took were some naked singing and dancing Hindus to bring out the real traitor, to scare him witless and force his hand. They are not like us, these no-guts, these moderates,' he spat the words out. 'Make no mistake, they don't fight like us.' He smiled at the Dane. 'They don't fight at all. That's the trouble.'

The *Jettis* paced around the table. All four of them still chanted but it was a low hum now, like the murmur of machinery singing in the background, so Amit could be heard clearly.

'Now that the traitor has revealed himself, we can talk business.' Amit looked at the lead Jetti and made a small incline of his head toward the Scandinavian, who had remained calm throughout the meeting.

As Amit stood at the head of the table, he watched without breathing. The *Jettis* completed one last circle and made for the door with their pachyderm, black buttocks glistening. Before they got to the door they reached the Dane, who was leaning forward in the process of lighting his Churchill-sized 'Romeo y Julieta' Cuban cigar. His loose blonde hair, thin at the front but long at the back, became wavy and flowed over his dark suit collar.

Two *Jettis* jumped on him and pinioned him to his seat. Amit did not dare blink, and his eyes widened as one of the *Jettis* jerked the Dane's head upwards and backwards by his hair. Then the fourth colossus clapped his massive hands together like some monster from the Mahabharata fulfilling his demonic master's command. As he slapped his hands together he brought out a huge foot-long nail from the waistband of his loin cloth, and in one smooth movement drove the nail through the crown of the man and out through the centre of his forehead. The Dane's jaw muscles went into spasm as his teeth bit through the still-burning cigar; he froze, arrested in animation, eyes open, teeth clenched, sitting statuesque in mid-motion. The *Jettis* that held his arms released him. The first Jetti gave the back of his head another slap and skewered him face down onto the table, the nail of Tippu Sultan deeply embedded in the ancient wood.

The gargantuan that had driven the nail through his skull clasped his hands together and bowed with closed eyes to Amit. Then the *Jettis*, oil and sweat mingling, now soft and silent, filed through the secret door out of the room. Amit sighed and ignored the looks of horror and masks of incredulity, as his seated subordinates stared at the shiny pool of dark blood which spread and seeped out of the dead man's skull, streaking his blonde hair and staining the historic table dark purple.

Amit lips stretched and his eyes glazed, as if in post-coital climax. He slowly returned to reality and stood facing them, with his hands behind his back.

'We will use their own technology against them, I will find you the best software wizards in the world, and the hottest programmer under the sun; Indian, of course,' he said, with a small smile. 'Their satellites will come crashing out of the skies; they will be blind, deaf and dumb. The secret cadres of *Alpha Ansar* we have infiltrated over decades will be enacted.'

'What shall we do, Big Brother? What do you think? What does The Leader order?' said the Malay.

'Who votes for war?' asked Amit.

'I vote for war!' the Chinese near the back, as he stood up and shouted.

'And I,' said another.

'And I vote for war!' The chorus grew.

And I!' said the last of them. They all stood shouting and echoing, 'War! *Allah O Akbar!* War!'

Amit picked up the fallen cigar off the walnut tabletop and stubbed it out, crushing it into the marble ashtray. 'Then if all the *shura* is agreed, I am having no option but to accede to my brothers' wish.' He looked around and motioned them to sit, but they continued standing and gesticulating, arms raised in war salutes.

'*Allah O Akbar!* War! *Allah O Akbar!*'

'Then let us unleash onto them a *thoofaan*, a storm, a taste of their own creation. Destruction is already assured. All our great Leader has to do is press the button.'

'*Amit Bahadur* – Amit the Brave – *Amit Bahadur* – Amit the Brave!' They took up the shout, translating his name, the title that had become more than a motto, a rallying cry for the *shura* over the years.

The remaining ten men could no longer hide their shock and bewilderment at what war with the West would mean and what the final solution might entail – a possible nuclear holocaust. What they had long suspected would soon become a reality, but Amit noticed how they tried to hide the terror from their faces.

Amit the Brave looked out at the giant screen as Aashriya Aarzoo Romano performed his favourite number, and, as always, he hummed along wordlessly. He turned back to face them, smiling. He glanced back to the screen outside. *Are you watching, Aashriya? With one nod of my head I control the destiny of the world, and soon I will possess you. Just as I love you, you too will have to love me.*

Amit smiled his broadest smile, which still looked like a grimace, and said, 'And I too vote for war. Let us blow *Israfil's Trumpet!*'

CHAPTER 6

Birmingham – Jessica's House

Jessica cradled the martini glass like a memory. She had tried desperately to grasp the fleeting remembrances of Hamid every day since the explosion, pull out their ghostly shapes from the ether; but his memories would become opaque, and then transparent, and then they would disappear whenever she tried to reach out for them. She wondered if it was the confusion following his death that was causing the questions to rise from the remotest corners of her mind, to take over her thoughts and make her lose control of her body. *Could my Hammie really ever have been a suicide bomber? Was our wonderful relationship a pretence? Was our love a lie? Is that why it's so hard to hold onto his memories?*

She gripped the stem tighter, as if the fragile glass was Hamid's soul that might just float away, out of her reach forever. She had not made herself a martini in months. Hamid usually insisted on serving her, on twisting the piece of lemon so that the zest from the rind as well as the juice flavoured the cocktail. She washed her hands and wiped her face with a towel, determined not to let Holly see any wetness in her eyes. She had held onto her best friend and wept numerous times over the past week. She felt she had cried enough since Hamid died enough to salt her bones in a bath of tears, her very own Dead Sea.

The police from the Counter Terrorism Unit had been polite enough, but their questions during the interrogation had cut through her, had sawed at her throat as if she was a sacrificial lamb being hacked by a dull blade. *Did Hamid ever talk to you about Iraq or Afghanistan? Did you ever carry things like packages and bundles; put things away in storage for him?* The implied accusations had cut the deepest, as if her heart was being lacerated by the scalpel-sharp insinuations. *When did he last talk about the intifada? Did he mention Shaikh Yassin? Did you ever hear the name Yahya Ayyash? Or 'The Shaikh?'* Jessica knew by that they meant Osama Bin Ladin. She had replied she had heard these names in her distant memory, but could not recall them at the police station, and asked who these people were. When she realised what the Inspector was trying to imply, she felt a pain grip her chest at being associated with people they called terrorists. It was as if her heart lay on the butcher's table, sliced into strips and dry-cured. Jessica felt, now that she had been exposed to the desiccating air of police scrutiny, she would physically shrivel up. She wanted to curl up into a ball and hide under her duvet, as she used to do when frightened of ghosts in her wardrobes as a child. A little princess to her father, who told her as he kissed her at bedtimes that she had cheeks as soft as baby bunny rabbits, and she giggled when his whiskers brushed her face. In those days daddy would kiss her better and he would say: *goodnight my darling baby, sweet dreams, princess of Solihull!* Words that would help her forget her monsters. She had often felt the need for her father's embrace while she had been interrogated.

Jessica did not believe that Hamid had anything to do with terrorists. She told the police the same thing until she mumbled the words in her fitful sleep. Questions raised themselves and spread through her, as if a blue-black dye of death had been pumped into her veins. She watched it flow through her circulation, taking over her nervous system so that her movements became jerky, erratic. A small muscle in the right side of her face started twitching, something that had never happened before. It seemed as if the accusatory blue miasma caused shock waves in her mind, like explosions she felt rocketing into her, and she shuddered.

During the police interviews, the only thoughts that would come to her were *Why are they asking me these weird questions? The police have got it all wrong! Or the wrong guy at least – maybe it was some other Hamid?* The Inspector had been proficient as any cardiac surgeon and had laid open her core by questioning every aspect of her relationship with Hamid, including their most intimate moments: how often they had sex, when they first slept together, whether Hamid showed any reluctance to go to bed with her. *Did he ever cry in the night?* The police had removed all of Hamid's belongings from their flat including his computer and laptop. Even her work MacBook had been taken.

The Inspector had emptied the room of oxygen, Jessica felt, and she panted for breath as if her lungs had been pumped with noxious gases, an alien contagion which had spread through her body and eventually came out in the sweat which covered her palms, as if she had washed her hands. The questions went on, as if dissecting her anatomy. She felt her vital organ turning darker, until the physical pain made her almost clutch her chest and her temples throb. The pain increased and took over her mind. Her head felt sucked into a vacuum of terror, and all she could see in the airless space with her bulging eyes was the life of emptiness that awaited her. Nausea gripped her chest, and eventually made her retch during the middle of a question. The facial muscle had flickered so hard it almost made her right eye blink, when the Inspector suddenly stopped asking about Hamid's mosque and friends to ask her about her planned wedding day. She could not imagine that water-boarding or beatings could be worse. Her solicitor had asked for the filming and recording to be stopped, and the policewoman had helped her to the toilets and brought her a cup of hot, sweet tea. Going on long walks had made her feel better; able to breath normally again, at least. When she spoke to Sebastian on the phone over the following few days she did not felt able to describe her police interrogation to him.

Jessica forced the feelings of nausea down, picked up the tray with the martinis and snacks, and walked towards the lounge. Nausea had become inevitable, rising every time she thought about the past three weeks, from deep within her. As if to remind her she still had emotions. During the aftermath of Hamid's death Jessica realised that her relationship and even her existence would be denied and rejected by his family. This had made her feel she would never recover enough to feel and sense things beyond the physical.

She entered the lounge and put the tray down on the coffee table. 'Sorry I took so long...'

'Have you been upset again?' Holly asked, peering up at Jessica.

'I'm fine,' said Jessica as she sat next to Holly on the sofa, but Holly still reached over and gave her a hug.

'I really think you should call them. I mean, if it's bothering you enough.'

Jessica had been discussing Hamid and his family before she left to get the drinks. That was all they ever seemed to talk about now, but Jessica had still not come to any firm conclusions. *What would Hamid want me to do? I don't know!*

'You've got the right to go to his funeral, don't you?' said Holly.

'It's not so much a funeral, more like a remembrance service.' Jessica did not look at her friend. 'Well I suppose it is a funeral too... whatever they could find of Hamid...'

'I'm sorry,' said Holly putting her arm around Jessica's shoulder and passing her the drink. 'Do you want me to phone them?'

'There is no *them*. I've only ever spoken to his sister, Farah, and that's only a couple of times, I don't know his mum or the other two sisters...' Jessica drank two gulps of her martini, and then another, almost like an afterthought. Not sure if she should finish her drink, she left a slurp in the glass.

'Do you want me to ring her?' asked Holly, sipping her drink. 'I'm not afraid of them lot. Muzlins or not, it doesn't matter.'

'It's not so much that I'm afraid, Holly. It's more that I don't know if it's the right thing, or something that Hamid would have wanted,' said Jessica.

Jessica knew Holly often said something insensitive and even inappropriate, but it was always without malicious intent; she did not know how to be any other way. *Strange – I seem to have so little in common with Holly, but she's been my closest friend for four years,* thought Jessica. *Since the time she turned up on my doorstep, covered in bruises like a juvenile alien, holding a new born baby...*

'You know what, Holly, you're right,' said Jessica getting out her mobile phone. 'I'm going to phone Farah right now. Ali told me that they have a woman's gallery, which is a balcony area overlooking the main prayer hall, in Birmingham Central Mosque. You can see everything that's going on from up there.'

'Ali's an alright sort. At least Hamid had one good mate, then. Is it happening tomorrow?'

Jessica dialled the number. Her hand gripped the phone and pressed it hard to her ear, but she felt oblivious to the discomfort. She had met Farah once briefly. She had joined Jessica and Hamid for a quick cup of tea, and although she had been friendly and apparently amicable, she had left them in ten minutes. Another time she had said 'Merry Christmas and Eid *Mubarak*.' Jessica had replied in the same way, because Eid and Christmas were within a few weeks of each other. Jessica hoped that Farah would have some positive memories of her. As Hamid's youngest sister, the only one in his family he had been fairly close too, Jessica hoped she would be greeted with generosity, or perhaps even some sympathy.

'Hello... er yes, is that Farah? Hello, this is Jessica, I don't know if you remember me but –'

'What? Who?'

Jessica paused, ignoring the interruption, before continuing, 'I understand you must be upset but –' She stopped and glanced at Holly.

'One minute, can't talk here, let me go outside.'

Jessica tried to listen dispassionately to the unfamiliar woman's voice as she cut in, interrupting Jessica, but she gritted her teeth and grimaced as the memories of Hamid, which came in intermittent violent waves, now washed over her.

'I don't think this is a good time...' said Farah.

'I know, I'm sorry, but I think I need to speak with you,' Jessica replied. 'You understood our situation, Farah, when we met.'

'I just said I would help Hamid Bhai in whatever he was trying to do, but I knew it would never work,' said Farah.

'Well, that's not what you said at the time.' Jessica got up and started pacing the room.

'I was trying to support my brother. Anyway, why have you rung me?'

'Look, I'm angry and confused too, about what's happened –'

'Angry and confused? That's very noble of you. We've lost a brother, and my mother's only son!'

'I said I'm sorry.'

'Tell her you're coming tomorrow, no matter what,' whispered Holly, she sat back with her arms and legs crossed on the sofa.

Jessica turned away from her to listen to Farah, who continued, 'Does that make it alright?'

'What?' asked Jessica.

'Is that how it works with you *Gorah* people? When someone dies, you say sorry, have a few drinks and then maybe a few more... get pissed and forget the dead before your head hits the pillow?'

'What do you mean, us *Gorah* people? Is that what Talat – I mean, your mother, said?' Jessica looked at Holly and shrugged a look of surprise at her. She knew that, although *Gorah* literally meant 'white', it was as hard not to use it in a pejorative sense as for a tiger to live like a vegetarian. Jessica sat down on the sofa and finished off her martini. 'I didn't think you were like that, when I met you, Farah.'

'Like what? What did you expect? A reception committee, garlands of marigolds and open arms, like you see in the tourist programmes, the poor darkies receiving the rich white people?'

'No, not exactly...'

'Yeah, well, it may have seemed an exotic and exciting thing to do, for you, being a liberal blonde babe, to set up with a dark ethnic sort, but mum always said Hamid was bewitched, and he was making a mistake having anything to do with you. She always said we would lose him –'

'I lost him too!' Jessica held the phone so tight that her knuckles turned white, as if she could squeeze some of her anger into the phone.

'You lost the idea of someone you fancied for a bit.'

'I lost someone I loved like no one ever before,' shouted Jessica. 'Why can't you people understand that?'

'Tell that stupid cow you loved him and made him happy, which is more than she or her mum, *Talat: The Giant-Toothed Demon* ever could!' said Holly and Jessica waved her to be quiet. She regretted joking in the past about Hamid's mother. Holly had made up the name 'Talat: The Giant-Toothed Demon', after Jessica had told her the particularly hurtful names Talat had called her. Ali, Hamid's friend, had informed Jessica about the comments. Jessica stood up and paced the room, and did not smile as she usually did at the name Holly had invented for Hamid's mother. Neither Holly nor Jessica had actually seen Talat but had relied on secondhand descriptions, in all of which Talat's teeth had figured larger than any werewolf's.

'Oh – it's us *people* is it? Is that what we really are to you, some "weird creatures"?' said Farah.

'I meant your family,' said Jessica, controlling herself.

'Anyway, how can I help you, Jessica? Sorry for calling you a selfish *Goree*,' said Farah in a calmer voice, and Jessica thought she would almost add, *even if you are a bloody selfish white woman*.

'Well, I – I rang you to ask about Hamid's funeral...'

After a short silence Farah continued, 'It's tomorrow.'

'I know, Ali told me,' said Jessica.

'Can't ever keep his bloody mouth shut, that idiot Ali,' said Farah.

'Well, I – I was wondering if I could come?' said Jessica. After a silence which seemed to hang like the blade of a guillotine above her head, she said, 'Hello? Farah?'

'What?' said Farah, in a voice that Jessica could only hear as filled with disdain.

'Well, I want to come to Hamid's funeral,' said Jessica, raising her voice and almost pausing between each word.

'Tell her she'd better try and go through me first, before having a go at you,' hissed Holly.

'Before now I just thought of you as a selfish *Goree*, but now I think you're a stupid, selfish *Goree*,' replied Farah in an ever-darkening tone of voice.

'What? What are you talking about? I don't understand why my coming to Hamid's funeral –'

'No, you don't understand much, do you? What the hell were you thinking? You could just marry a Pakistani Muslim guy without understanding any of his family background or culture, let alone religion?' said Farah. Jessica heard the growing disgust. 'You obviously don't have any idea what you put us through when you took Hamid away from my mum and set up shop with him, and you don't seem to give a shit what we've been going through for three weeks.'

'I've been through a lot, and I would go through hell for Hamid.'

'You bloody liar.'

'Now you listen to me, I've had enough of your shit,' said Jessica, punching out each word as if she was landing a body blow on Farah. 'You obviously aren't able to hold a civilised conversation, so let me tell you something. I'm coming to Hamid's funeral tomorrow.'

'But you're not – not even a Muslim,' said Farah.

'Yeah, well shows how much a Muslim like you knows about your own faith. I know the mosque is open to everyone. You don't have to be a Muslim.'

'Listen, sister, let me tell you something. Don't blame me for the reception you're going to get tomorrow. If you dare to turn up. And how you turning up is going to affect mum. And what she'll do to you, I can't imagine.'

'Hamid told me she suffers from depression and panic attacks –'

'Don't you dare pretend you know anything about our family!' said Farah.

'I was going to be a part of your family, next month you know, Farah…' Jessica said in a soft voice, replete with memories of Hamid, as if he was even now standing behind her, stroking her hair. 'I'm coming to say goodbye to Hamid tomorrow,' finished Jessica, in a whisper.

'You'd bloody well better not dare!' said Farah, just before Jessica hung up. The tone sounded in her ear like the explosion of rejection, the finality of death.

Jessica turned to Holly and said, 'Well that went amazingly well. Stupid me. What did I expect? To be welcomed as the long lost sister?'

'Well, better put me in the lead tomorrow, Jessy. I'll put my shark teeth in for her, but they still won't be anything compared to Talat's teeth!' Holly guffawed.

'Don't know if I should go, not now...'

'What?' Holly put an arm around her. 'Look, I don't wanna force you or nothing, but you said you wanted to say go to the funeral,' said Holly.

'I just want to be able to see Hamid once more. I mean, I just want to wish his soul goodbye on its final journey,' said Jessica wiping her eyes with a tissue.

'Well, there you go then. What do Muzlins wear to a funeral, anyway?'

'White – they wear white, traditionally.'

'I thought you said you didn't know anything about Hamid's religion?' asked Holly, looking at her sideways.

'I don't,' said Jessica, chewing the knuckle of her thumb. She turned to face Holly. 'Holly, do you think there's such a thing as a soul?'

'Don't know, but if there is, no soul or no guardian angel never helped me when I was being beaten to shitty pulp by FC,' said Holly, and put her hand across Jessica's forehead. 'You feelin' alright? Next you'll be askin me if there's a God,' she added.

'Well, do you think there is?'

'I don't know, darling, but if there is he ain't never helped me with my mortgage, not even last Christmas when I pawned my diamond ring to get Sally all those things she had tantrums for. But I'll tell you what I do know. I'll be buggered before I wear anything white to a flippin funeral!'

Birmingham – Central Mosque

Jessica gripped the steering wheel so tightly that her hands felt numb. She jerked the car around the corners, as if she could control her destiny with the direction of her vehicle. Her breath came in pants, and she tried to control it by blowing out of her puffed cheeks. She pulled up in the car park of Birmingham Central Mosque and parked in a space on the far corner.

'Are you really sure you want to do this?' asked Holly. She added, in a soft voice, 'You really don't have to prove anything. Anyone that matters knows you loved Hamid.'

'It's not for anyone. It's for me and Hamid.' Jessica switched off the car and slapped both hands onto the steering wheel, then tried to give Holly a smile that came out as a grimace. She felt sure that Holly would see through her pretence at bravery. 'You're looking lovely.'

Holly made a snorting noise; she had eventually agreed to put on a long white dress and a full-sleeved shirt over it, at Jessica's insistence. 'I really don't think this is a good idea. I mean you know me. I'm not scared but I can feel trouble brewing in my waters, and they've never been pissin' wrong.'

'We'll be fine,' said Jess, giving Holly's hand a squeeze, and a smile she knew would look more like the mouth of a clown. 'You can wait in the car, you know. I really don't mind, honestly.'

'That first night when I came to yours with Sally... she was just a tiny baby then, remember?' asked Holly, and continued without waiting for a reply. 'I knew something was gonna happen that night, when the bastard battered me and put through the mangler.'

'This is just something I've got to do... look, I'm sorry.' Jessica realised she should not have let Holly come, despite her insistence. 'Please wait in the car,' said Jessica, raising her eyebrows and putting a hand on Holly's, although she knew it would be a futile attempt, just as trying to stop her coming along had been.

'No way. Ain't gonna miss these Diwali fireworks for anything.'

'Hindus have Diwali,' said Jessica, and let out a strangled sound that would have been laughter at another time.

Holly joined in with a whinnying noise. 'Well, you know, whatever. Love getting into these fights.'

They got out of the car and walked towards the mosque. Jessica glanced up at the bulbous white dome and saw the matching white-tipped minaret. Earlier she had driven past, not quite able to understand the sign on the side of the mosque: READ AL-QUR'AN, THE LAST TESTAMENT. She looked now, and saw the blue background of the sign glimmer and shimmer in the autumn sun. She had seen the sign on occasions, when driving back home from work or the flat to Solihull, and she remembered the glowing green light in the minaret; shining out like an exotic beacon, a coloured call to the faithful instead of the muezzin's cry. Jessica had never thought of the mosque as anything other than a place of worship for people who were extrinsic to her life – an extraneous building in an ethnic enclave – and even after she had got to know Hamid well, she had not looked closely at the mosque. Although this had not been Hamid's regular mosque it provided a central location, as Ali had said when he told her that Hamid's funeral had been arranged there. Jessica had never been to Hamid's mosque, but she knew it was somewhere in the Asian area.

Jessica had covered her hair with a silken scarf she had found in a drawer. It had printed floral patterns on it and matched her long skirt. As they approached the shadows of the mosque, she pulled the scarf tighter around her. Holly had refused to cover her head.

'Don't worry, I'll lead the way if you want, they won't recognise me,' said Holly, patting her hand.

'They won't recognise me either. They'll probably just think some mad white woman got lost looking around the mosque,' said Jessica.

'Except for his sister.' Holly stared up at the minaret. 'Looks pretty, kind of, in a weird way.'

Am I just being stubborn? thought Jessica. *Forcing myself into a situation where I'm just not wanted? Worse – am I going to embarrass them, his mother, at a time of family grief? I just want to say goodbye to Hamid...*

'Right, we'll be as quiet as mosque mice. All I want to do is sit through the service, which is starting in a bit.' Jessica glanced at her watch. 'We're not going to bother anyone. We'll go up to the women's gallery, and I'll be happy to sit in the corner. Fifteen minutes, then we'll be off.'

'Yeah and you think they'll just ignore you? They're not that English, you know. We can still go home... come on. I'll make you a martini.'

'Too late now,' Jessica said, and zipped up her coat. She resisted the temptation to hold Holly's hand; instead, she bunched her fists in her pockets.

Jessica, determined to lead the way, strode ahead of Holly. She ignored the smoking men in the car park, who seemed swarthy and full of intent as they stared at the women. Jessica glanced at the rapidly increasing throngs that gathered into small groups in the courtyard. She noticed the camera and television crews had already set up their systems. *I wonder if they're going to add to their scandalous rumours and accusations about Hamid?* she thought. *Like that journalist who keeps ringing me up – he's even been to mum and dad's place.*

'Ali told me it's inside, and then up the stairs to the gallery.'

Jessica dug her nails into her palms and hardened her resolve, still wondering why she had insisted on coming to his funeral. After all, it wasn't possible to know someone in death as you had in life, even if you had propriety rights of marriage. Death and birth and culture were blood ties; she had none. No rights, especially in a mosque with her dead Muslim lover, suspected of being a suicide bomber, whose family had regularly rejected her and wanted to hide her from the rest of their community like an illegitimate child. *Harami, Harami Hamid*. He had been called a half-way bastardised fugitive by his community, for being a runaway slave from Islam whom she had harboured. They needed to scour him with the lash of their gossip so that they could scourge the shame: a shame, *sharam*, which threatened to stain not only Hamid's offspring, but the future of the whole *Biradari*, community.

Jessica knew the fears of the *Biradari*: what if their own children decided to follow Hamid's example? What if their girls wanted to have *Gorah* boyfriends and marry them and make half-caste children? The Daughters of Islam and their future generations lost forever. Jessica had heard the gossip; she had insisted he tell her the stories that were being spread in his family and *Biradari*. One of the mosque elders, who had a white beard like Santa Claus, had taken Hamid aside after *Jummah* prayers one Friday, put his arm around him in a corner of the mosque and said to him in tones so conspiratorial it was as if he was about to reveal Israel's nuclear secrets to him: 'Leave the *Goree puttar*, son! Listen, Hamid – zebras only look good in Africa or in Hollywood films, and you're not in either. What do you think it would do to your mother to see zebras as grandchildren? Hmm? *Sharam*! Hmm? *Sharam*!'

Half-white, half-black, Kuffar-*load of* sharam, *more than his mother could contemplate*, obviously, thought Jessica. Although she had laughed with Hamid about the zebras for a long time, as she often did about many of the comments he relayed to her. She had tried to ignore the way he stood wringing his hands, wet with sweat, his fingers knotted as if hiding secrets of his own shame and embarrassment, and he had always said, 'Oh, don't worry about my family, I'll win them around. And you should forget about those mosque idiots. Santa has three daughters, well, had three daughters. He says two of them are dead now. Tells people they died in a car accident because they ran away from home at fourteen with white boys. He disowned them the same evening they didn't come home. He then stopped his youngest one from going to school when she was thirteen. But now that she's married and got kids of her own, he feels safe talking to me like that, as if the two that ran away never existed.'

Although Jessica had laughed at the way he described Santa and aped his walk and accent, and she had shrugged off the comments by hugging him and kissing both cheeks, and then she made him Pakistani tea, just the way he liked it, boiled up in a saucepan, hot and milky and sweet – that night, Jessica had gone back to her house to be alone.

Even if Hamid was dead, the three years that she had spent with him and the effort she had made and the love that she had received were too much to forget, to simply walk away as if he had not existed, without even going to his funeral. She knew she was attending on principle. Jessica gritted her teeth, but her legs did not feel her own. *Let's see what they've got: what's the worst his mother is going to do?* Jessica remembered a saying of Hamid's he had translated from Urdu. *She can't eat me alive, can she?*

Jessica climbed the stairs up to the women's area. Each step felt as if she had her legs caught like a bear trap. Her thighs quivered and her calves burnt as if the fires of *Jahanum*, hell, were licking at her heels. Her breath rasped in sulphurous pants, and she slowed twice but continued climbing, determined not to stop, not to show weakness to Holly or to anyone else who might see them, but mostly to herself. *I'll show them what this selfish* Goree *can do*.

Just as she reached the entrance to the women's gallery, she turned to Holly and gave her a sign to stay silent. Holly gave her a puzzled look. Jessica wondered why the service had started early. She walked into the women's area. The space was wide enough to allow two dozen women to stand side by side, and women stood, filling the first few rows. The rest of the space seemed to yawn at Jessica like a monster from the deep with a cavernous mouth, but she felt drawn onto the balcony despite herself. She took off her shoes, and Holly copied her. Jessica crept like an insect into the corner, near the back row. All the women stood in prayer, with their backs turned to Jessica and Holly.

Jessica wanted to go near the front of the balcony area and look down to see what the men were doing. She assumed they must be in a similar pose, and Ali had told her the coffin would be in the main hall. Jessica heard the Arabic recitation; melodious, haunting, like music played from exotic pipes made from some otherworldly material, for the glorification of an alien god. She wondered what the *Imam* looked like. She saw the women lined up for prayer; a few empty rows between her and them. Jessica crept forward. She did not approach the women, but went to one side of the prayer area. She stood motionless for a moment and then realised she had to breathe out, which she did slowly, her breath loud in her ears like rustling tissue paper. She pulled her pale blue silk scarf tighter over her head. She knew there was no requirement to cover her head, but Jessica wanted to show respect to Hamid.

She watched with a mixture of horror and fascination, barely blinking, as the women lifted their hands above their shoulders and brought them down again. The *Imam* recited some words in a chant, a voice that seemed replete with history and tradition, as alien as the dromedaries of the Rub Al Khali, the Empty Quarter.

Jessica felt surprise that the women did not bow and touch their heads onto the carpet during the prayer. *Why was there no prostration to Allah during the funeral rites?* Jessica signalled for Holly to follow. She sat down on the carpeted floor in a corner of the prayer area, moving as if any sudden movement would cause a tremor that could reverberate through the whole building, bringing it tumbling down. She looked up and saw the main ceiling of the mosque, formed by the inside of the dome section. Glass lined the inside of the concave cupola, which reflected back numerous lights of the crystal chandeliers, so that it seemed as if the roof had uncountable fairy candles flickering in the vaulted ceiling. Jessica felt like a moth, drawn to a dimming light. A faint but distinctive waft of incense made her breathe deeply.

Within a short time the women looked first to the right and then to the left, and then the prayer was over. Some of the women started crying, while others wailed in louder tones. Many of them started gathering around a middle-aged woman with wavy black hair, which Jessica noticed as the woman's *dupatta* slipped back, revealing the front of her head. She had pale skin and a long nose on an oval face and thin lips that quivered as each woman approached, clouded eyes that poured wetness onto her cheeks with each hug, and rivulets of tears ran down her chin. Jessica heard some of the women recite the mantra: *Bara afsoos huha. Bara afsoos huha,* which Jessica assumed must mean *I'm sorry*. Some of the others beat their legs and thighs and rent their clothes and pulled their hair, before hugging the middle-aged woman and sobbing on her chest.

Jessica saw Farah standing next to the woman who was the centre of attention. Jessica had immediately realised this woman to be Hamid's mother, but seeing Farah with an arm around her confirmed her status as the highest amongst all the mourners. *So this is Talat Khan?* she thought. *This is the woman I would have had as a mother-in-law. She doesn't look like a Gorgon or a baby-eater. This is the woman who could have become more influential in my life than my own mother. The woman who I would have called Auntie Talat next month.*

'*Bas Allah ki marzi. Jawani meh bas…*' Jessica heard one of the older women say and sob, as if her own son had died.

Jessica gestured to Holly to stay sitting, and got up and approached the crowd of women, but before Jessica could get close to Hamid's mother, Farah blocked her path.

'What the hell are you doing here?' she hissed.

'I just wanted to say sorry – to Hamid's – I mean, your, mother,' said Jessica.

'I warned you about coming here,' said Farah, glancing around at Talat, who was now surrounded by a throng of women, some wailing, and many weeping without apparent self-analysis or consideration. 'No one wants to see you, and definitely not my mum.'

'I wanted to – to say goodbye to Hamid…' Jessica craned her neck to look past Farah, with her eyes looking down as she stood on her tiptoes to see down past the balconied area to the main prayer hall, where she knew the coffin would be resting at the front of the mosque. 'Did you mention to her that I wanted to come?'

'You're not welcome here.'

Jessica squinted at Farah. 'You didn't tell her, did you?'

'What's the point?' Farah put her face closer to Jessica's. She put her hands on Jessica's arms and pushed her around so she faced Holly, without making it obvious that she was forcing her. 'Do you see any of your kind here?'

'What's that got to do with it?'

'I can't let you upset my family more than you already have.'

Jessica felt the pressure from Farah's hand on her back, like the village buffalo, guided away from the evening watering hole.

'Don't you get it? 'You're not bloody well wanted here. Why are you here?'

'Because I bloody well want to be here!' Jessica said, letting the words hiss out of her teeth like steam out of a Balti cooking on full heat.

'Get out! Get out and don't ever dare to come back.' Farah shoved Jessica towards Holly, who approached them. 'Get out, both of you. I can't let you pair of bloody selfish *Gorees* upset mum any more. You've destroyed our lives as it is.'

'She's got enough rights to be here, okay?' said Holly.

'Let me talk to your mum. I want to see the coffin,' said Jessica.

'Get out!' spat Farah, with a final push.

Holly put her arm around Jessica and led her out. The long stairs down felt like the slippery slope of failure. The courtyard had filled with men, smoking and staring, mostly at the journalists that lined the back wall. The men's eyes flitted, hard as black bats, between the camera crews and the white women, as if to say *How dare these two just lounge about the centre of the courtyard? That's what they're probably thinking,* thought Jessica, because no other woman stood in the courtyard. She noticed two small groups almost hiding to the side of the stairs, like gazelles shielding themselves from the leopard's gaze.

'What are we waiting for, Jessica?' said Holly. 'Let's go home.'

'I didn't get a chance to –'

'To what? Its over, come on!' Holly pulled Jessica's coat.

'You go and wait in the car,' said Jessica. She heard shrieking, and turned to see a group of sobbing women leading Hamid's mother out of the mosque; they formed a protective gang around Talat.

Jessica walked over to Talat and stood in front of her. Jessica noticed the long face, the buck teeth, straightened by an expert dentist but still seeming to belong to a species of ungulates. Her belly hung as if it contained a child, and was the only fat part of her. Two women supported each of her arms and shoulders, as if Talat would collapse under her own weight. Her arms seemed floppy and she bent over, not quite able to stand straight. She squinted at Jessica through half-sealed puffy eyes.

'*Haaii*, who are you, *hai*?' Talat asked in accented but clear English and looked directly at Jessica, who felt as if she were in a massive coliseum. She shrank back a little, as if its huge walls were towering in on all sides, and in the seats was a crowd who hated her.

'My name is Jessica.' She flushed; her fingers pulled her lower lip for a moment.

'Who? Haaii, what is Jessica?' Talat said *Haaii* in a typical Asian accent. Each *Haaii* became prolonged, trailing off at the end, as if she had run out of breath on her deathbed.

Jessica glanced at Farah, who stood to one side of her mother – supporting her weight, Jessica assumed, so she did not rush forward to cut Jessica off this time.

'I – I was... I mean Hamid and I were about to get – you were going to come to my house before the bomb?'

'*Haaii*, what is this? *Yeh kiya keh rahee hai?* What is she saying?' asked Talat to Farah, without turning, as if she needed translation.

Jessica did not know if grief had driven the memory from Talat's mind, or if she just refused to accept any knowledge of her. Jessica fixed her eyes on Talat, and the other women faded out of focus. She sensed some movement behind her but felt as if she heard the screams of the crowd in the coliseum, who now shouted at her, waving their arms, faces stretched with enmity.

'I was going to marry your son, Hamid. Next month he and I were going to get married,' Jessica said in a firm voice.

'What? *Kiya kaha?*' said Talat, this time turning to Farah who shrugged.

'I said, I am Jess –'

'*Thu kiya kar rahee he yahan?* What are you doing here?' said Talat, her eyes suddenly filled with fever, embers glowing behind the darkness.

'I wanted to say sorry and –'

'Sorry? Sorry? What sorry? Too late now. You kill my son.'

'What?' said Jessica. 'No –'

'Yes yes. You kill my boy,' said Talat.

'She didn't kill your son. He –'

Jessica quietened Holly before she could say anything else.

'Jess, she's accusing you of killing Hamid.'

'Shush, please, Holly.' Jessica turned back to Talat. 'Auntie, listen, I know you've been quite depressed and it must have been a shock –'

'You kill my son! You kill my son!' Talat pointed a finger, which then shook in Jessica's face. 'You kill Hamid, my only son,' said Talat, now standing taller, without the support of the helpers, turned to the women, '*Meh kehthe thi Hamid ko yeh chureyl hai. Hain hain chureyl hai.*' Talat turned back to face Jessica. 'You are a witch. I told my boy first day I find out about you. You are a witch,' said Talat, as she accused her. Her right index finger came closer to Jessica's face and shook as if it bore witness to Jessica's witchcraft. 'Chureyl!' Talat shouted, with a vigour that seemed to draw strength from the earth and the ether.

'I didn't kill your son. I loved him.'

Some of the other women in the gang took up the cry: *Chureyl! Chureyl! Chureyl!* Their arms waved towards Jessica in a throwing motion, as if they were casting stones at the devil.

Jessica did not move, but continued to look at Talat. She felt as if the crowd had closed in on her, the walls of the coliseum were about to crush her, and the chanting crowd was almost on top of her. They wanted to drink her blood; revenge for the death of Hamid. Sweat covered Jessica's palms and the hair stood up on her neck, as if she could feel the 'Giant-Toothed Demon's' breath on her back.

She glanced around and realised that two of the television crews had started filming. The journalist who had pursued her stood next to one of the cameras, grinning. The television crews zoomed in and crowded closer to the women.

'Can I ask you some questions about Hamid?' said the journalist. 'Did you have any idea he was the bomber?' He thrust a microphone almost into Jessica's mouth, and the camera showed her face like a horror movie.

'Shut it, you idiot!' said Holly, and Jessica saw the man withdraw a little into the circus of people.

'You *chureyl* – you eat my son,' said Talat, now casting both arms in front of Jessica's face, almost hitting her with every throw.

'What are you on about?' said Holly, and then turned to Jessica. 'This old crone's mad, Jess. Let's get out of here before I lose it.'

Jessica did not look at Holly. She felt fixed to the ground, and her legs did not respond.

'What are you talking about?' she finally managed to stutter to Talat. 'I just wanted to say goodbye to Hamid.'

'*Hai! Hai! Merah Betah Hamid! Hai hai!*' screeched Talat, her arms casting out the devil from their midst as if she was punching the air. She slapped her own face with both hands, and then stared at Jessica with eyes that turned red, as if they were coals fanned by the breath of 'The Giant-Toothed Demon.'

'*Thu chureyl hai. Abshagun! Abshagun!*' screamed Talat.

Some of the women walked away with short marching steps, without looking back. The rest of the women took up the cry. '*Abshagun! Abshagun!*'

'These lot are mad – come on!' Holly pulled at her arm, but Jessica did not respond. 'Come *on*, Jess. They're filming this.'

'What does that mean?' said Jessica, forced by Holly to half-turn away from Talat, but she kept her eyes fixed on her. Despite the cold wind, sweat gathered over Jessica's upper lip, and her nails dug into her palms.

'You kill my son. You eat my son. You *chureyl. Abshagun! Abshagun!*'

Holly interrupted, 'Listen, I know you're upset and everything, but let me tell you something. I don't know what you're talking about, but this woman loved your son and –'

'She witch – kill my son. She eat him!' screamed Talat, pointing a finger in Jessica's face.

'She didn't kill your son. He was a fucking suicide bomber! He's the one who probably killed all them people,' shouted Holly. Jessica turned to Holly, her face drawn lips trembling, but could not make any sound materialise. The television crews crowded in and jostled for space like hyena on a kill.

'Get lost! You happy now? That's enough, get lost!' said Farah, moving forward.

'Yeah you lot just try it,' said Holly, moving to intercept her, but Jessica pulled her back.

'*Abshagun! Abshagun!*' shrieked Talat.

'*Abshagun! Abshagun!*' her gang of women aped her. Jessica assumed this must be Talat's core gang. The nucleus of hatred, the electrons spun off.

'Okay. Okay.' Jessica finally said to Holly and then turned to Farah. 'I'll go. Just tell me... what does that mean?'

Farah sighed. The fight seemed to have gone out of her. 'Listen, you're probably a nice person.'

'What does it mean?'

'I don't want to hurt you anymore. After all, Hamid liked you,' said Farah.

'Just tell me what it means!' shouted Jessica. 'Why is she calling me that?'

Farah shrugged, 'It's like a Jonah – bad luck, or –'

'Bad luck?' said Jessica, her mouth dry as Asian sand. Her mouth rasped air, which seemed devoid of moisture.

'– cursed. My mum thinks you're cursed. That's why Hamid died.'

'Cursed?' Jessica felt the stupidity rise to her crimson face. Her blonde hair hung lank with sweat, but she seemed unable to say anything else. She felt aware of the crowd that had gathered, the camera crews, but no one seemed to interfere directly, and no one mattered to Jessica. She had to try and understand why Talat hated her so much.

'*Abshagun! Manhoos! Abshagun!*' Talat and the women continued to shout, growing louder, intermittently covering their mouths as if keeping the *Jinns* sealed tight, but instead they worked themselves into hysteria. Their tears mingled with sweat and faces screwed up in agony but no one relented, as if the screaming and casting of arms were a badge of honour, and the first to desist would be a coward.

'*Abshagun* means *cursed*. Even if you weren't before, you will be now, and everywhere you go you will be cursed, everything you touch will be cursed…'

'Why is she saying I ate Hamid?'

'Because you had his body and soul. That's what cursed witches do – eat their men so that they can possess them body and soul. My mum believes you used black magic to make him fall so madly in love with you.'

'*Abshagun! Abshagun! Manhoos Chureyl Hamid ko kah gaheh. Miti ho jahe gi, sab kuch miti… mereh Hamid ke tarah…*'

'The cursed witch ate Hamid, *abshagun!* Everything you touch will turn to dust, like Hamid…' Farah's translation reverberated in Jessica's head, as if it was stuck inside a huge ringing bell which smashed at her temples, and her whole body felt numb. She flexed the stiffened fingers of her hands, screwed up her eyes tight, and wiped away the spittle that had escaped in small white flecks at the corners of her mouth.

After an unknown length of time, blinking the sweat out of her eyes, Jessica looked one last time at Talat. She took Holly's arm and crept away, feeling like a praying mantis.

Birmingham – City Centre

Jessica thought that Starbucks in Birmingham city centre would be a good place to meet Sebastian. So she had rung him back the day after receiving his call in her office, and had asked him to meet her in the Bullring shopping centre. She felt that coming to the same place as she and Hamid used to go for coffee would help force her to come to terms with the his death.

She had seen so many people helping the wounded on the day of the bombing, but no one could have helped Hamid. The bomb had brought the average citizens out of their disguise of uncivility. The self and selfless merging because of the accidental; the impermanence of human beauty shifted into focus out of the fog of everyday ugliness. She imagined the increase in the already unimaginable suffering, the families, the children, so many destroyed hopes... Congo, Gaza, Kabul. Yet another salvo, another meaningless number of people killed. A denominator to add to the subtotal of the explosion. The cumulative figures were finally known; it took days before its struggling and gasping statistics brought the final numbers of dead and injured to an end.

Jessica wondered why she had started philosophising. She could not stop her mind – this precious, transient fragility, humanity realising the reduction of all things to the ephemeral, ensuring the disappearance of the ego. It seemed as if a long time had passed since she had worried about Hamid's mother or her work. That felt like some other Jessica.

Jessica scanned the small seating area to see if Sebastian had arrived, although she was early. Memories of the time she and Hamid had spent in here came floating up, like the aromas of freshly ground coffee that took over her nostrils and shook her brain awake, small hits from molecular hammers in her nose. She breathed deeply as she passed the serving counter and sat in one of the leather seats by the large windows. The rain had stopped but deep clouds gathered low, as if the darkness would invade the coffee shop. The lights looked like fireflies in the reflection of the glass. The huge floor-to-ceiling windows made her feel as is she was in a bubble.

Jessica scanned the heavy horizon, as if her eyes were hummingbirds trying to escape the confines of a trapper's mist net into the wider world. She had sat with Hamid in the same chairs, where she had spent hours watching the birds circle over St Martin's church spire; the time had passed like minutes. Jessica and Hamid had discussed all the important things, as well as the smallest of things, and during their meetings they had been oblivious to the other coffee drinkers. She had shaped her life plans with Hamid, and she tried to mould their lives out of what seemed to be disappearing water vapour in the face of Hamid's family's objections.

Everything has evaporated since then, she thought, lacking solidity like the clouds she could see through the windows. The Bullring Shopping Centre had remained undamaged and had soon re-opened for business after the bomb blast at New Street. Jessica thought that by sitting close to the station she might help jog Sebastian's memory; over what, and how that might help her, she could not be sure. She knew that sooner or later she would have to confront this part of the city centre again.

She waited on one of the comfortable seats, with her head back, still staring up into the changing sky across which autumnal clouds scudded, as if chased by the west wind, blown by the wicked witch. Maybe there was a wicked witch who had bewitched her life. Hamid had told her about the *Evil Eye*.

'Hi, Jessica.' Sebastian stood, tall and poised, already holding two mugs of coffee, smiling as if the bomb had been a different lifetime, or had happened to some other avatar of his. This current incarnation seemed unaffected. 'Got you a caramel macchiato, extra hot and sweet.'

How does he know that's just what I wanted? she thought. She loved the thick heavy coffees on wet afternoons. Sebastian sat down opposite her, and his constant half-smile flickered for a moment. Jessica clutched her small handbag closer to her and glanced at the raindrops from the intermittent showers that were forming irregular rivulets, pulled by random gravity into a meaningless dance.

'The chap that I was talking to... was he your fiancé?' said Sebastian.

Hamid was on the train, and she thought it probably was him that Sebastian had spoken to. 'They managed to get – get some DNA... He – he's dead. Hamid is dead,' Jessica said, although she had already told him that during their phone conversation. She felt her eyes almost close and she leaned her head back on the chair. A tightness squeezed her chest as if some unseen force gripped her; she breathed deeply but resisted the temptation to rub her chest, or cry. He leaned forward and put his hand on hers, briefly.

She looked up, making sure her lips did not quiver. 'Why did you give me your card? What made you do that?'

'I don't know. I didn't know what else to say, to do, to stop you running into the station, and bring you back to reality.' This time he kept his hand on hers. 'I'm glad you're a bit more in-control today...' His half-smile flickered again, as if the sun was threatening to return.

'Well thanks, I think,' said Jessica. She did not withdraw her hand; his palm felt muscular, as it encased her soft fingers. The warmth from his palm over her fingers, and the stillness of his hand, slowed her breathing. He did not attempt to make any other comforting movements, nor did he stroke her hand. His humanity gentled the storms. His touch felt so light that the warmth from his body was almost imperceptible, but she shivered as she felt it. 'How did you manage to survive? Make it out, I mean?'

'I don't know. It must have been – don't know what made me go to the end of the train, away from your fiancé.'

Jessica withdrew her hand at the mention of Hamid. 'They're saying it was Muslims, probably a suicide bomber. What the hell is it with these Muslims?' she said, seeming to forget that she had called Sebastian a Muslim extremist sympathiser during their first meeting at the station.

'How's your coffee? I like it strong and black,' he said, as he moved in closer. 'I talked to police afterwards, told them whatever I could, which I'm sure was insignificant.'

'That's how I usually drink it too, but today this is just right.' Jessica wondered if he changed the subject because taking about Muslims made him feel uncomfortable; she looked down and sipped her coffee. 'I don't know your name. It was on the card, I mean... is it Sebastian?' said Jessica. She realised she was making no sense, so she added, 'This is where we came first. He was taking the train back after the interview. We just had a quick coffee at Starbucks,' she said, and wondered why she mentioned it. 'I really have to know what happened to him.' She brushed the wetness off her cheeks. She looked at him and tried to think of something else to say. 'Is your name really Dr Windsor?'

'We will get to the bottom of what happened on that train. I'll give further information to the police, if it helps you.' He smiled at her. 'Yes, my name is Dr Windsor. Sebastian, I mean.'

Jessica took her mind off Hamid with a huge effort, thinking *I suppose I should make an effort to talk to him – he has done his best.* 'Sounds posh, not just your voice. That's just how I would expect a doctor to sound. Although my dad's a doctor, but he isn't posh.'

'Oh, I'm not a medical doctor.'

'What are you, an archaeologist, like Raiders of the Lost Ark? You look a bit like a young version of him.' Jessica felt surprised that she could make an almost-joke. She felt it was a ploy of her mind, otherwise her control would crumble if she dwelt on Hamid, and what had happened to him and to her at his funeral.

'Well, that's my major interest, yeah. I mean, I'm just a teacher.' He brushed his face with his hands and closed his eyes for a moment. Some dried blood flaked off the cut on the right side of his face. 'Nothing as glamorous as Nazi gold, or the Holy Grail.'

Sebastian's cut and bruised face made Jessica's thoughts turn back to Hamid and the kiss that he had given her in the morning before the explosion, the look that had lingered without regard for time. Jessica's fingers skimmed her lips. Her mouth pursed at the leftover sensation of his affection, which now felt as if it might have been the cut of a scimitar stroke. The burn of his kiss left a scar; she wondered if it would last. She swore it would be a constant reminder until she had the truth, and revenge on all his accusers, whoever they may be. Jessica would embrace the pain, let the burning smother her, combust the perpetrators instead on the incendiary of Hamid's funeral pyre.

'I lecture in Islamic studies and Islamic history, I was on my way back to London – I had a conference on Islam-West dialogue,' said Sebastian.

She noticed his calm patrician face, despite the obvious pain from the bruises and injuries. Jessica noticed he tried not to wince.

'I don't even know what I was doing there, at the station.' Sebastian looked away from her, towards the church, and looked around the city centre. 'Well, actually I do, sort of...' He shrugged. 'I'm doing some research here, on sabbatical, a loan from my usual post at the School of Oriental and African Studies. I was due to go back there for a lecture that Friday, when – when...'

'When you nearly got blown up,' she added. Sebastian drank his black coffee. 'You teach Islamic studies. My God, how do you put up with all those Muslims, so self-righteous and perfect? Don't you get sick of the holier-than-thou attitude?' she asked, sipped her coffee, moved her hair away from her face with her left hand. She leaned forward. 'Especially when they want to bomb us like insects, fleas on a camel... that is how they see us, isn't it? When you hear them on their pre-death videos...'

Her hands shook and she put the coffee cup down. 'Except Hamid,' she said, as she stared at her cup, cradling it in both hands. She looked up at him, in silent expectation of a revelation.

'Well, we don't know it was Muslims. I've been hearing a lot about right-wing extremists... ' He looked down as he cradled the mug in both hands, and she felt his voice soft, gentling her like feathery down, as if anticipating her anger.

Jessica seemed to vaguely remember him telling her that when they had first met. The revelation seemed fresh, and she pushed her hair back with both hands and widened her eyes at him. 'You're supporting these criminals?' she shouted then, barely able to stop her voice from breaking. '*Jaish* – like that creature who crawled out of his hole to blow up the train station. That's how they do it, don't they, suicide bombers? How can anyone kill themselves like that? He blew himself up on Hamid's train.' She threw the wooden stirrer down on the table. Although the coffee shop was not busy, a few of the people turned to look at them. 'Except, Hamid wasn't like that,' she added, her voice a whisper.

The pickaxe thoughts of Hamid being blown up chipped at her self-control; the thoughts of his body that she had touched and loved being disintegrated had reduced her logic to shreds. She wrung her hands, pulled at her nails, picked the coffee cup up and then put it down again as nausea rose up to the back of her throat, and she almost retched over Sebastian.

Sebastian spoke after a while, as if giving her time to recover. 'Yes, the ones that did this, they are criminals. And no, I'm not *Jaish*. Just as you are not the Inquisition – '

'Yes, you are. You're defending them. I know all 'brothers' have trainers and special helpers –'

'– or responsible for the Church's purges, you don't have to answer for the massacres of millions...' He trailed off. 'Sorry. I didn't mean to go on.'

Jessica felt amazed she could have an near-conversation with an almost stranger about the bombing, even if it was degenerating into an argument, although it had been about three weeks since the event; the shock and life-changing memories were burnt onto her brain like a laser marks on a disc. *The fact that we're talking like this is not a surprise,* she thought. *To have a normal discussion is going to be almost impossible, even one loaded with bitterness after the bombing. Is this what it takes for people to talk about these things? Is that the real reason why these terrorists feel compelled to do this? Out of desperation? Because no one ever hears them? This is their shout in the darkness...*

Sebastian's calmness impressed Jessica, as did the way he tried to talk to her, ignoring his obvious pain and shock of the past days.

'We don't know who did it the other day. It may not have been a Muslim at all. It may even have been an accident. Look, every religion has its extremists and zealots. There are white supremacists –'

'Oh, come on. It's not Buddhists who are doing this – this...' Jessica gestured back towards the direction of the train station. She picked her cup up and put it down again without drinking, brushed her honey-gold threads of hair away from her face, and stared at Sebastian. She noticed his eyes were deeper blue compared to her pale icy colour. 'I mean how many attacks have been non-Muslim?' she asked, slapping the table with her fingers. 'That's the problem.'

'There are lots of problems, Jessi –'

'You have to stop making excuses for these Muslim extremists. You have to wake up. Stop acting like it's fourteen hundred years ago. We haven't got any flying carpets to whisk away to Aladdin's palace. See, nowadays, we have information.' She knew she was being insulting, but could not hide the pain or the memories of Hamid, which made her mouth twist. 'It's always Muslim terrorists and their bloody sympathisers, like you.' She sloshed some coffee onto the table.

'I don't know, but if it is Muslims, then...' Sebastian paused, looked at her after a moment's silence. His face twisted as he spoke, as if he was reliving the aftermath of the explosion. 'Whoever it is, I'm sorry for your loss, for this, this carnage,' he said, spreading his arms wide, as if gathering the pain of the city outside the windows, without taking his eyes off her.

Jessica felt he was encompassing her emotions as well as the physical damage. She thought his humanity was touching. Although she knew many people sympathised, she was been surprised to find him defending the terrorists, or at least making excuses for them. This doctor looked and sounded different; he could have been a legend of the silver screen, a James Dean from the golden age of cinema.

'I mean, this is what I say when I teach: would the Prophet of Islam – would he do this?'

'How should I know?' she said, not sure if he expected an answer. *Why does he assume I might be an expert, just because I was going to marry one of them?* she thought. *He could never have been one of them, not that kind anyway... I should have stopped Hamid. They didn't even find his body, only bits and pieces: nothing is left. They won't even tell me anything, except for drowning me in a dark well of endless questions.* Jessica twisted her fingers in her lap, and chewed her lip as she looked out of the window.

'Do you really want to talk about this stuff? Right now, I mean?' asked Sebastian.

'Yes, yes. Actually I really want to know, want to understand – it might take my mind off things. Isn't that what these terrorists want, for us to talk about all this? Maybe they're right for once. These are the things we should be talking about, and anyway, Hamid never did discuss these things,' she said. She realised that her words were running into one another like a pile-up of crumpled train carriages, and her thoughts sped like an engine. She waved a hand, and said, 'Do enlighten me, professor.'

'Would Saladin do this? Jerusalem – Cordoba –' He stopped in mid flow; his blue eyes flashed almost cobalt over his coffee cup. Jessica realised he assumed she would understand the references, and she knew he had allowed some emotion to creep in.

'Sorry, that's not what I wanted to say, but...' said Sebastian.

'But you thought you'd get your world view in?'

'It's been a rather emotional time for you.'

'What about you? A train blew up, and a station, all around you.'

Jessica wiped a trail of brown liquid from her lips and chin. People milled around in the coffee shop, some taking late lunch, students off from college early. Normality almost forced its way thorough the tiny gap in her thoughts, squeezing through the doorway now prejudiced and illiberally tight; the slight space left by the narrow minded terrorists, where the real world could intermittently intrude. The extremists had succeeded through terror in creating gaping chasms and canyons in the hearts and minds of people, greater than the last Ice Age. Suspicion filled spaces that simply had not existed before. Many of the people in the square below them stood on the street and seemed to be obviously discussing the bombing, pointing in the direction of the train station. She watched them as they tried to comprehend, without being able to vocalise the unfolding of a city that would never be able to wrap itself up in quite the same way again to hide the pain. No one had been clearly been able to say what had happened, and why.

'Yeah, but I only lost a suit,' Sebastian said pulling at his blue jacket as if he still wore the one that got ripped up during the explosion. Jessica felt surprised that he had answered after a delay. Maybe he was reliving that day, in the same way as she had numerous times. In some ways it seemed like a dim and distant silent movie. The film of memories could not be exposed to the oxygen of reality, but at other times the memories seemed to crash into one another like a garish cartoon, played out on the screens of her eyelids every time she dared to close them. *Perhaps he's giving me time to gather my thoughts, not rushing in, trying to keep cool,* she thought.

Sebastian gave her a small smile. His eyes seemed inviting, and his expression soft. Jessica steeled herself not to cry in front of this strange man. She closed her eyes for a moment and massaged two index fingers on either side of her nose, so that no tears would spill over. When she opened her eyes again, she studied him for a moment.

Perhaps because of his empathy, she said, 'How – why don't we hear more from people who understand Islam, like you? I mean, we just hear vitriol and venom from those bushy-bearded bastards.'

'How do you know I'm not one of those? Just now, you were saying –'

'Are you?' Jessica was annoyed that, regardless of her insults, Sebastian still smiled at her. He seemed in control, except for the small blaze. She went on despite not wanting to, her knowledge and emotions now mixed like a garish Pollock painting. 'Who want to kill Jews and gays and blow up the West.'

'I don't. I mean, I know there are people who –'

'Not just soldiers in Iraq, but here on the streets of Birmingham.'

'No one has asked me to talk.' He sipped his coffee without rushing. 'The news people interview me sometimes, I suppose. You should ask the BBC why they don't interview me more often.' She wondered if he was saying that because he knew she worked for the BBC.

The corners of his mouth turned up and his eyes shone, but his face showed more than physical pain. He touched the bruise over the side of his face on his right cheek, which seemed to throb with its own heart-beat; a livid, scarlet-purple blot. Jessica felt disarmed. Her shoulders uncoiled and she let her chin drop, and she seemed to be going along with him, despite her resistance.

'I don't know. I – it sells papers, I suppose…' She did not know how to answer.

'You haven't had much of your coffee.'

'I'm more of tea person, really,' she said, looking down and playing with her cup. She realised he had changed the subject to avoid her feeling uncomfortable at having to defend the media.

'How do you like it?'

'Er, doesn't matter.' She looked away as if not wanting to reveal an intimate secret, but she thought he would see her as an old fashioned prude. He inclined his head and raised his eyebrows. 'I love it out of a china cup, actually.' She glanced up to see if he smiled at her peccadillo.

'Oh, you're an old-fashioned porcelain princess?'

'Yeah, I'm afraid so,' she said, regretting the revelation already. 'Well, enough about tea.' Hamid's memories flushed her face, as they took control of her again. 'Got to go and see the police again,' she said, unable to stop herself from screwing up her eyes for a moment. She chewed her thumb, as if her hand in front of her face would offer protection.

'Have they interviewed you?'

'Of course – they've taken the flat and house apart, almost. Taken away the computers...'

'I'm sorry. If there's anything I can do...'

What can anyone do at a time like this? Except to surrender to embarrassment and hide somewhere at home, mostly under the duvet, she thought. She wondered why she felt like revealing personal information to Sebastian. His calm manner acted like a sponge to dampen the explosions in her chest, like a balm that had magic powers to draw out the pain – a solitary splinter being removed from her heart.

'Well, it helps just to talk,' he said, his eyes like a searching blue sea, his voice soft.

'Yeah, thanks, but I've got more questions down at the station.'

'How well did you know him?' he asked, raising his eyebrows.

'Known him for three years, lived together for two, we were gonna get married next month; is that well enough for you?'

'Sorry, but sometimes we know least about the people we think we know the most about.'

'Thanks for trying to put doubt in my mind and desecrate the love I feel for him.'

'Well –'

She screwed up her face and held up her hands. 'No, don't bother. Got to go – thanks for the coffee.'

'Which you hardly drank,' he said. When she got up, Sebastian stood and asked, 'Don't you want to know what I found out about Hamid?'

Jessica walked out of the coffee shop without replying, without waving or looking back.

CHAPTER 7

London

Jimmy forced himself to put away the old memories, the things that he had almost succeeded in hiding in the undisturbed darkest recesses of his subconscious. He steeled himself, and knocked on the door of the *Imam*'s office.

'Come!' said the *Imam*, Maulana Mohammed Younis Khan, in an authoritative voice. Jimmy wiped the sweat off his face and dried his hand on the sides of his trousers. He pushed the heavy door, and walked into the large office.

The office was awash with books. It had books pouring out of the walls, books growing out of the floor, and books seemed to be dropping from the ceiling. There were books in Arabic, Urdu, and other languages that Jimmy did not recognise, even some in English. Some had gaudy hardback covers and even brighter printed writing on the spines. Others had gorgeous Arabic calligraphy on them; the flowing script itself made another picture, a lion or a horse or a sword. Some looked so old it seemed as if the paper could be papyrus, and they had no covers at all. Jimmy could not see a pattern. They occupied the bookshelves randomly with no regard for size and shape, type, or even language, let alone subject matter. They had always been strewn all over the office, even during his childhood. The *Imam*'s desk was covered with haphazard books, so it looked like a patchwork quilt with multicoloured and nefariously differing badges and labels. In spite of himself Jimmy craned his neck to catch the title of an especially large ancient volume, which was open on the *Imam*'s desk.

'Ah, Jimmy. Come! Come! Sit! Sit!' said the *Imam*, as he waved him towards the chair. First he hugged Jimmy three times, to the left and then to the right then to the left again, squeezing him with his arms each time. Uncle Younis smelt of *Attar*, a sweet, slightly sickly-smelling, oil-based perfume. Jimmy knew of the perfume's traditional popularity in the villages amongst the working classes. He had seen it being made on his trip to Pakistan, in huge copper vats, made by hand as it had been for centuries. He saw how the perfumer mixed roses and other flowers, distilled the essential oils that overwhelmed the olfactory senses when used in copious amounts. He noticed that the *Imam* employed the traditional method and applied it to a small cotton bud, which he had placed behind the ear. The smell increased every time the *Imam* came close to hug him, and only became tolerable when Uncle Younis sat some distance away. He pushed Jimmy towards the small blue plastic chair in front of the desk, which was spattered with specks of white paint, as he pumped his arm up and down with both hands. His grip felt strong and his handshake prolonged, as his left hand tightened like a noose on Jimmy's right shoulder.

The priest squeezed behind the desk and sank into his own bat-winged black padded leather chair. He flashed Jimmy a dazzling Colgate advert smile that contrasted with his blue-black triploid beard, which was mostly black and orange, speckled with small tufts of grey where he had missed with the henna. Jimmy's chair was smaller and lower than the *Imam*'s. Younis' chair dominated the room. He slouched in his seat and put his right foot on his left knee in a sub-continental manner, rested his elbows on the large leather armrests, and steepled his fingers together. Jimmy stared at his bright orange hair; the *Imam* also dyed it with henna. Maulana Mohammed Younis *Imam Sahib* looked striking. Maybe it was his orang-utan hair and lack of wrinkles, and especially his lustrous mother-of-pearl teeth, that belied his fifty-six years.

'So long since you visit us in *Masjid*. We think you forget Allah.' The *Imam* used 'we' when he wanted to imply that he spoke for the mosque, and Jimmy knew it to be a reproof implied by the whole community. He knew the *Imam* desperately wanted to speak Urdu, but persevered in English. He did not want to be the first to discuss business. Jimmy would have to ask and so lose face, thereby the *Imam* would gain respect and power. The real business would be done in Urdu, for listening to the *Imam*'s English was like wading through a thick fog, heavily laced with a provincial Punjabi accent.

'Allah will be Allah, whether I forget him or not. He doesn't need me if he is the Almighty, innit?' said Jimmy. 'He's gotta have other things to worry about these days.' Jimmy forced himself not to give in to his anger or frustration, and not let his distrust of the mosque and its people turn into hatred. The *Imam* was guilty. Jimmy judged him guilty of a moral crime because he had been his father's closest friend for a lifetime. His father, who had been a mosque stalwart, lay three streets away dying of cancer, and Uncle Younis had not visited him yet.

'I very busy, you know? We have big celebration, the very big Saint's birthday coming next week, you know, Hazrat Shah Hussein of Lahore, you know?'

Jimmy did not care which saint had a birthday; he never had been able to make sense of it all. 'I ain't never heard of him, man, and I wouldn't give my old whore's left manky tit to find out. My dad's dying. And you've been arranging a birthday party for some dead old Paki geezer?' He could not hide the bitterness in his voice, but he regretted it as soon as the words left his mouth.

'No, no, no not party. We Muslim. No, no party,' said the *Imam*. Jimmy had seen the priest's performances since childhood, and now he thought Uncle Younis forced himself to give his intermediate level of artificial smile.

'I know your dad sick.'

Jimmy got the message. *He's prepared to overlook my behaviour because of my dad.*

'So busy, you know? *Imam* job not easy, you know? Many people, many too many jobs, less time,' he said, persisting in English.

Jimmy tightened his stomach. He felt sick of Younis' hypocrisy, and his worry over his father's illness made him give up on English. He knew he would not succeed in getting what he wanted, because there could not be any real negotiations, or any of the hard bargaining that inevitably lay ahead, unless he spoke Urdu. Partly because the *Imam*'s English was becoming barely intelligible. *Let him think that he has won the game,* thought Jimmy.

'You and my father have been friends for many years and grew up together in your village, Ramnagar, in Pakistan,' said Jimmy, then paused, thinking he might cause the *Imam* to feel regret. 'You're childhood friends. You spent your whole lives together, there and here,' Jimmy added in Urdu and looked down at the desk, not making eye contact with the *Imam* and thereby showing *izzat*, respect and status.

'Yes, yes. You're right,' said Younis, with a small smile of satisfaction. 'And I have always held your father in the highest regard. When I dropped out of school to go to the *madrassa*, Ahmad continued with education. I resented him.' He chuckled and stroked his beard and straightened his *karakul* hat. 'Then he went to Lahore University, and that's when I became so proud and happy. It felt as if I was going too. When he graduated, I felt I had achieved something. All of us friends, the boys, we continued to be so proud and happy. Though he wasn't the first one from the village to achieve a first-class degree, even if his was in engineering.'

'Well, now he's dying. Unless we help him.'

'I will do anything. Anything I can, you know that – whatever is in my power, and also I will pray to Allah to cure him. *Ya Allah Ahmad ki madhath kar, Ahmad ko shifa atha farma deh Ya Maula Ya Karim Ya Rab il Aalimeen!* O Allah, help Ahmad, grant him health, O Master of the Universe, O Beneficent One!'

He translated to stress the point, although Jimmy understood. The *Imam* followed this with some very fast Arabic which Jimmy missed altogether, during which he rolled his eyes to heaven so that only the whites could be seen, raising his arms up above his head with hands outstretched and palms raised to the ceiling, as if he expected divine intervention in the form of the Archangel Gabriel to come crashing down through the roof at any moment. Uncle Younis petitioned heaven with such passion that Jimmy glanced up at the ceiling, and felt immediately foolish. It seemed to him that the *Imam* performed this routine to any of his mosque regulars who pleaded for help.

'He needs treatment. An operation, innit. I have found a surgeon willing to operate, but it'll have to be done privately – the NHS ain't willing to take it on.'

'Why? Why not?'

'The NHS surgeon said the operation ain't gonna help. I think it's about costs, man, they think that *Abbo*'s operation won't be worth it yeah, cos the cancer has spread. It's the final stage. Of course, they ain't sayin it like that, but I know it.'

Jimmy realised the *Imam* knew this from members of his congregation, friends of the Regus family. *The mosque spies*, Jimmy called them, and whenever the gossipy men or women came to call on his mother or father he would leave the house. The *Imam* feigned surprise.

'Really? I didn't know that. That's shocking.' He leaned forward and stared into Jimmy's eyes. 'How can we know these things, *Betah*, if you and your family don't tell us?' the *Imam* said, in a mildly indignant voice. Jimmy always felt insulted if anyone other than his parents used the word *Betah*, even if they did not intend it to be patronising. That, he supposed, might be the English part of him.

Jimmy stayed silent. He did not want an argument with the *Imam*. He needed money, and he needed it fast.

*

'*Ah-reh, ah-reh, achha, achha*. Don't worry; just tell me. I'm your uncle, after all.' Younis now used his paternal voice. He would have stroked Jimmy's head if he could have reached across the desk.

'*Achha*' had a multitude of meanings: it could mean 'good' or 'okay' or even 'that's enough', depending on its usage. In this instance, Younis meant all three. He wanted to remain in control, and he knew what Jimmy wanted and that the boy would do anything to get it. Younis was enjoying the experience of having Ahmad's son in his office under his terms, and about to put his head into his trap. A trap he had long thought about and prepared since he had first learnt of his friend's diagnosis. *Hai hai – it's Allah's will.*

Pressure from external forces mounted on Younis. His sponsors, the main financiers of his mosque, had become increasingly restless. Most of the money came from a group of businessmen based in Saudi Arabia, loyal to Zulfiqar bin *Hijaz*. Not even the mosque committee knew of this secret, or where exactly the funding came from. The *Imam* told them wealthy Saudis gave generous donations, not *Jaish an Noor wass Salaam*. They knew nothing of his promise to provide young recruits for 'The Cause'. No one knew the hidden agenda to channel men to training camps in Afghanistan via Pakistan. Younis had no sympathies with Zulfiqar bin *Hijaz* or *Jaish an Noor wass Salaam, The Army of Light and Peace*; he could not be certain the money originated from them. Nor was he interested in the revolutions that had, in hushed insinuations, been attributed to *Jaish*. The Arab Spring could turn to the dust of an Arab Autumn.

In fact, Younis' mosque was nothing like the usual type of mosque funded by the Saudis; his brand of Islam was an anathema to the *Wahabi* doctrine. They needed recruits, and the *Imam* desperately needed funding to expand the buildings and pay for all the resources to run the weekly activities. *We make strange bedfellows, but needs must,* he thought. *Almost as ridiculous as the Pope and the Whore of Babylon being in bed together – or maybe that's not such a ridiculous idea.* He smiled. Under normal circumstances his type of Muslim and the Saudis hated each other, both accusing the other of corrupting the true message and of being 'deviants'. He also heard every day how the extremist revolutionaries terrified most Muslims. Younis regularly felt the fear of joining them and helping them to take over in any country, especially Muslim countries. He knew the extremists would turn on other Muslims as soon as they had power. Most Muslims did not want this type of Islam. Younis saw everyday, even in his mosque, how many young Muslim men were still more petrified of not joining them. *If the* Kuffar *are not stopped, then they will continue to spread their mayhem in the Muslim world.* The youth felt terror at the fact that the disbelievers would continue to rampage and pillage the world, and it would only be a matter of time before Muslims everywhere would be victimised and persecuted, whether in New York or Nairobi. The *Kuffar* might win as a consequence of their inactivity.

More importantly, Younis could not and would not allow the *Masjid* to close – he would not allow Abdullah to win. Younis could see his face even now, with its derisory laughter, insulting and humiliating him from his mosque across the street. It would have been impossible to run the mosque without *Jaish an Noor wass Salaam*'s continuing support. So Younis had agreed, despite the inner voice nagging at him, to provide willing recruits for The Cause.

Of course, it was a just cause, he had finally convinced himself. After all, what were the Americans and British doing in Afghanistan and Iraq anyway? To Younis, the end justified the means. He had no choice – he had to keep the *Masjid* running. *What harm could there be?* He could not force anyone to go to Afghanistan or Iraq. After all, he could not create a suicide bomber, and he would simply ask for volunteers for *Jihad* and leave it at that. Surely that small sacrifice, that would result in his mosque and his community being kept alive, would be worth it. *Anyway, too late now*, he thought. Impossible to go back, no time for second thoughts. He had taken the money and had already spent most of it.

The *Imam* had been the first to sit on the new carpet, as soon as it had been fitted in the prayer hall. It had a yellow swirling pattern on a blood-red background. The new wing of the *Masjid*, admittedly, looked like bombed-out Baghdad at the moment, but it was coming along just fine. It would be grand when finished, the envy of all the other *Masjids* and *Imams* in London.

All his great work would come to a halt if the Saudi money stopped pouring in, and then the mosque would close. Younis would no longer be able to lead his congregation in prayer five times a day, the elders would no longer have a community centre, the teenagers would lose their indoor football facilities, the girls' lessons on a Saturday morning would come to an end. The women's study circles that his wife loved teaching every Tuesday and Sunday and alternate Wednesdays would stop. He would be out of a job, but more importantly he would no longer be an *Imam*; the centre of his universe, the beating heart of the Southall community. It was the only position that allowed him to hold the shivering soul of the people in his ever-tightening grip. Without it, he would be just another Tariq, Dawood, or Haroon. He shuddered at the thought of not having influence, and so losing power over people's lives.

Younis stopped his musings, and realised Jimmy had to ask him the inevitable question. *I need this treacherous idiot.* Younis chuckled softly, and changed the angle of his Jinnah cap. He had not met his quota for the last six months; his agitation had risen because of the increased demands from his sponsors. They continued to demand foot soldiers for The Cause. The pressure had mounted on him and the thoughts of what they might do to him, beyond stopping his funding, gave him a sensation in his chest like a sword entering from his breastbone and skewering him through his keel. Nothing was forbidden and he knew everything justified to them, as long as The Cause of *Jaish an Noor wass Salaam* was kept alive.

The Army of Light and Peace was not a patient army.

*

'I need £20,000, and I need it now!' Jimmy said.

He spoke more loudly than he had intended. His words ricocheted off the walls in the small office, and hung in the heavy air. He disliked speaking Urdu, though he could speak it fluently. The nuances sometimes put him at a disadvantage, and things would spill out not quite as he had intended. A request could sound like a demand – or worse, because of his reputation, it could be seen as a threat. The silence became dangerous, like an axe hovering above their necks.

Why do people change, he thought, *shine with even more fakery, at the mention of money?* In his experience, the people that called themselves 'Uncle and Auntie' and said things like *Of course we will do anything to help, anything at all!* had proven, inevitably, to be as much use as a bucket of sand in the middle of the desert. Jimmy had grown up used to their hypocrisy.

'So much money. It's hard, very hard to come by immediately... ' Uncle Younis spread his hands out with his palms down on his desk, adjusted his *karakul* cap, and forced out a quasi-embarrassed chuckle. He clasped his goat-like bulging belly.

'I'll pay it back, man, you know I will. I just need it for some time – a couple of months at most.'

'You'll pay it back? How will you pay it back?'

'I got the dollars, man. I got enough fuckin' money, enough to buy you and this fuckin' Mosque. I never asked no one for no money ever before. I got cash, man.' Jimmy interspersed Urdu with English.

'It's not as easy as that, you know. You can't pay it back. I don't think the mosque committee would –'

'Would what? Would want my dirty money?' asked Jimmy, leaning forward dominating the space. He noticed the *Imam* move back slightly.

'It's *haram*.'

'*Haram*? You gonna tell me what's *haram*?' *Haram* literally meant 'inviolable' but was often translated as 'forbidden' or 'illegal'.

'You'd rather be arse-fucked by a wild herd of bull elephants, man, than lend me a single fuckin' *paisa*!' Jimmy saw the older man's cheeks flush and his eyes blacken as he pushed his *karakul* cap back, exposing more of his orange hair.

'I know you've got money, you've got plenty of that – so why don't you use it, then?' asked the *Imam*. Jimmy realised the older man knew the answer, but could not help playing politics.

'Because I can't. My dad won't let me. He – he made me promise, innit. Look, he needs to see the money coming from you, otherwise he won't agree to having the operation.' Jimmy tried being conciliatory, to give him time to think. He searched for ways of getting into the mind of the *Imam*. *Come on – think*, he said to himself. *How can I get through this bastard's defences?* His desperation made him fish the depths of memory. *This is my only chance to get the money for* Abbo, he thought, to get the operation. *There is no one else. No friends or family who could lend money and I can't go to the banks because officially I have no income. This is my only chance to save* Abbo's *life.*

What's the secret to unlock the Imam*? What does he desire, what does he want, and what is his worst fear?*

*

The *Imam*'s love of lucre ensured he worshiped in the temple of Mammon. Younis did not know how exactly how he had planned to sacrifice Jimmy at the altar. He knew simply that the boy must be offered up as a pagan blood totem to his voracious, insatiable god.

'You know how the *Masjid* struggles. Money is always needed. There's the new wing being built with four minarets. We have lots of ongoing projects which are only possible because of Allah's grace and the support of ordinary people like you...' Younis allowed his voice to trail off and gave his customary chuckle, put his elbows on the desk and leaned forward, smiling at Jimmy.

'I would be most happy to help the mosque. Of course, I would always pay back more than owed.'

Now he is playing the game on my terms, thought Younis. '*Ah-reh, ah-reh!* Allah forbid that I was suggesting you give me any money.' He made his face angry.

'You're the *Imam*. We don't need to involve the committee, do we, Uncle? I could pay you back in two months – say, £25,000?'

'That's very generous of you, *Betah*, of course it is, but it's going to be very hard to get that money so quickly without the *Masjid* committee...' *Shameless little pig. Thinks he can tempt me with an extra £5,000? How insulting.* The *Imam* pushed his kidskin cap around his head.

'£30,000 in two months. The Furniture in The Elders meeting room is so very old, yeah? Perhaps a new leather suite would help make all the uncles much more comfortable?' Jimmy said, smiling. 'I don't tell no-one nothing, man, but you know what our peoples is like. They love gossip... '

Younis grasped the clear warning sent out by Jimmy, but he would not let him get away that easily. '*Betah. Betah.* People say and do such terrible things. Here, everyone knows each other, and I would hate for devilish whispers to reach to your father's ears, in his condition. The hurt just might finish him off. After all, I know he has a weak heart. I could never forgive myself if anything happened to him. No, I think it might be better if we just forget the whole thing. Ahmad means more to me than any amount of money could.' The *Imam* cuffed his eyes, shifted his books about the table, and made to get up. The Muezzin started the hauntingly beautiful call to prayer. 'It's nearly time for *Maghrib*.' The prayer just before sunset.

Younis knew Jimmy was a gaffed fish. The boy offered more money. '£40,000 after one month.'

Younis' anus twitched and tightened at the thought of so much money. He kept his face inexpressive, stared down at his desk, and continued shuffling his books.

*

Jimmy's desperation grew, and desperation fed his anger. He felt like getting up and smashing Maulana Mohammed Younis Khan *Imam Sahib*'s face in with his great fists, and then putting him in a chokehold so he could not breathe, not letting go until he agreed to lend the money. Or died. It would be so easy to do, so easy to let the bloodlust take over. He fought back that impulse. The tactics that served him so well on the streets were unlikely to work in this situation.

Then he remembered something one of his working girls had told him months ago, which he had dismissed at the time as just the usual gossip mongering, a prostitute keen to get a laugh out of her pimp and the other girls at the end of a hard day. Shazia told him how one of the *Imams* had used her services. This was not unusual and hardly a conversation-stopper, so no one had taken much notice of her. Until she said they had an orgy; the *Imam* had had a three-way session. Jimmy had looked up at her and, distracted from working out his daily accounts and portioning the takings, he screwed up his face.

'He fucked me up me arse while Shams shafted him up his shitter. Yeah, yeah, that's right – then he took Paul in his mouth too, while he made Shams sweat. I swear, I ain't never seen Shams work so hard, the lazy fuckah. 'Make me a seekh kebab, faster, faster, harder! Oh yeah, so fast, make me into a seekh kebab!' the *Imam* kept shouting,' Shazia said with a screech of laughter. She turned to one of her friends, and continued, 'I couldn't give a shit though, and neither could Shams, 'coz he gave us two hundred quid each on top of the usual. I'm gonna get that amazing Valentino handbag today, been saving up for it. I've wanted that one with the red rose on it for friggin' ages. Yes I fuckin' am, Sunita, and don't you or any fuckin' bitch – you hear, Samantha? – try an' stop me gettin it today. I didn't get me arse all sore and fucked-up for nothing.'

'Yeah, you got arse-fucked for a thousand pound Valentino handbag, innit,' said Samantha. The group of girls let out screeching disinhibited peels of laughter and with that they were gone, shopping. Jimmy went back to his accounts and never did ask her about her special customer. It was a huge risk assuming that it was Uncle Younis, but now he decided to gamble. Jimmy had no choice when he thought of his father lying there, bleeding: drip, drip.

*

'I'm sure – no, in fact, I'm certain – you won't want me to tell anyone least of all the mosque committee about your preference for seekh kebab over any other type of food? Or do you prefer spit roast?' said Jimmy. Younis looked as if he had been shot in the face by a tank shell.

'What are you talking about, *Betah*?' Younis knew immediately what Jimmy meant. He had been careful, as he always was, when he felt the need for his 'special relief', but he had no idea that Jimmy ran that stable of men and women too. *That little bastard's cornered the market*.

'*Oh, make me a seekh kebab, make me into a seekh kebab!*' Jimmy said. Younis saw the younger man's nerves, and the fear on Jimmy's face that he might be mistaken. The *Imam* realised Jimmy would not be worried for himself, but he knew what this mosque meant to the community and to his father, and so it would be important to him.

He released a small chuckle and looked down, piling books in between himself and Jimmy. Younis knew that if his tactic backfired, then Jimmy's father would never forgive him.

'*Betah. Betah.* I think the grief over your father's illness has affected your mind. What has food to do with what we are talking about?' Younis did not panic; he needed Jimmy's co-operation, and he wondered how far Jimmy would dare push him.

'It's not usual for most *Imam*s to take one man in the mouth and another man up the arse, spit-roast-style at the same time, is it, Maulana Mohammed Younis Khan *Imam Sahib*?'

'You little *mahchaud*, who the hell do you think you are? You little pig piss *benchaud*!' Younis felt like dynamite in a furnace. He had never sworn in front of any of his flock before.

'If this was a normal day, Majid's pit bulls and *Tosas* down on the farm would be scrunching on your bones by now, innit!' Jimmy shouted. Younis saw how Jimmy forced himself to sit back down, make and remake his hammer fists, despite his position Younis felt a flurry run through him, and he put his hands over his belly.

'I'm not sayin nothin' and I ain't gonna, as long as I get the money –' Jimmy let his breath out and unclenched his Popeye-like fists. 'Please! Uncle, it's good for you too. Think about it – £40,000 after one month. That's a phenomenal return, innit? And no one need know nothing. Not my dad. Not the mosque committee.'

Younis thought about the money and managed to control himself slightly; he already had his black Mercedes S500, the lack of which had made his wife wring her hands to shreds over the past two years. Younis had been in an unspoken, but much gossiped-about contest between his parishioners and Abdullah's flock, as to who would be the first to get a Mercedes S500. A competition that he had won, to his immense satisfaction, but it had meant taking huge risks to achieve success. *So spick and span that no one knows it's second hand*, he thought, *now that I've added my private number plate with my initials – and I love the way it has a small Pakistani flag in the corner.* He had stopped it right in front of Abdullah's mosque and walked across to his own *Masjid*, ignoring his own special parking space. Younis would park it in the same spot before prayers so Abdullah could see the car every time he came in and out from *Fajr* to *Esha*, at least five times a day. Younis had planned to drive at a crawl down Abdullah's street again tomorrow, to roll past his house so he could see and admire the S500, just as he and Fatima had done earlier today. The car was so burnished and lustrous with its satiny black shine, and Younis loved the way Abdullah's furious face and disabling jealousy had been reflected in its alloy wheels. He let out a small chuckle, as he thought how he and his wife would laugh at Abdullah and his wife.

Younis fixed Jimmy with a reptilian stare. 'Because you are your father's son, I will forgive you. But if you dare to ever threaten me again I will see your mother publicly whored, and I will make sure your father knows agony before Hell. I'm not the type to go quietly, I promise you.' Younis' need for money overtook his humiliation. 'See how much God has given me patience and put the true spirit of Islam in my heart? £50,000 in exactly one month's time. And you will also attend a spiritual meeting this Friday night at midnight. It's a *kiyam* night where there will be inspirational talks. It's about time you, too, learnt some Islam.'

'£50,000?' Jimmy asked. Younis saw Jimmy's mouth hang open. *He thinks I'm a bastard, worse than any loan shark,* he thought. *I know the boy hates the thought of having to attend a religious prayer vigil more than the money.* 'Take it or leave it, and get out. No one will believe your ridiculous accusations, anyway,' said Younis. He smiled slightly, secure in the knowledge that the mosque committee would sweep any accusations of impropriety under the carpet as if they had never existed, especially anything to do with sexual misdemeanours. No-one in his community would dare accuse him openly without concrete evidence, and even then they would just pretend nothing had ever happened. He knew thus it had always been and he relied on the community's lack of moral fibre and fear of a scandal, on their continued cowardice, their intransigence and their deliberate blindness to continue to exercise his rule and authority over them. They would consider regicide before thinking of removing the *Imam* – an affront to God himself – and Younis had long encouraged and nourished the idea.

The *Imam* grinned and showed his lustrous teeth, and thought he was safe enough to let fly a medium chuckle at Jimmy. Now he would pay off his S500 in one lump sum and she would be his, such a beauty. He would ensure Jimmy became fodder to the canon that roared – he would make Ahmad's son join *Jaish*. *Du shikar ek thir ke saath. Two birds with one arrow.* Younis translated for himself.

Younis smiled as if he could read Jimmy's mind.

*

I know you love money, you greedy bastard, but this is taking the fuckin' piss, thought Jimmy. He knew as well as Uncle Younis that none of the money would ever make it into the mosque's account, and the committee would never hear of it. He saw the *Imam* spread his hands, palm-down, fingers open, on the table in front of him, and let escape his final victory chuckle, which had a different timbre to it.

Jimmy fidgeted, trapped, and felt like letting loose some of his choicest street lingo – a combination of English, black and Punjabi swear words. He felt like 'poppin' the *Imam* in his ass', as his boy soldiers would say on the streets. They would point at someone, with fingers forming a pretend gun 'Pop! Pop! Pop!' they would say, and sometimes that was followed up with real gun with real bullets. Jimmy thought of his dying father. 'Okay, okay. Whatever the hell...'

Before he could complete his sentence he heard a sudden commotion outside, and a group of men slammed through the door and burst into the room. Jimmy immediately saw the pistol in the hand of the man who led them. Others had machetes and flick knives; they dragged Maulana Mohammed Younis Khan *Imam Sahib* out, kicking and screaming.

Birmingham

Oh God! It's five past three already. Jessica looked out of the front room window and saw that Sebastian's car, a classic convertible, had its hood down and stood idling on the road outside. She liked the way he waited for her patiently without coming onto the drive. She wondered how long he had been there. She checked her lipstick in the mirror, ruffled her hair out of habit, so that it fell in golden, wavy columns onto both shoulders – although it was smooth, she wished it was not so fine and unmanageable. She touched her nose, which was slim and slightly upturned at the end; she had often wondered if she should have something done about it.

'Hi, sorry, have you been here long?' she asked as she walked around to the passenger door of his Jaguar. Before she could get there, Sebastian got out and opened the door on her side.

'It's still warm enough to have the top down,' he said.

Jessica looked at the car. Its dark blue colour and curves seemed smooth enough to be organic, as if they belonged to something from nature. She looked at its sleek lines and glass-covered headlights, which reflected in the late summer sun like opaline tears. She almost jumped as the engine snarled into life. The noise made it sound animate, as if it came from a secret line of evolution; a weird and highly prized creature, tamed by Sebastian.

'This is an unusual car,' she said.

'My father left it to me. I think he loved the E-type more than my mother.' That dazzling James Dean of a smile, again. She looked at him as he got into the car and noticed the athletic slope of his shoulders, his lithe limbs comfortable in the smart-casual clothes. The pale blue sports jacket formed its shape around his physique.

Jessica stood for a moment, looking at him. *Oh, he's waiting for me to get in,* she thought. 'Erm, yes,' she said and moved quickly and gestured to him as he held the door. 'Ah yeah, please. I mean, thanks,' Jessica said. *Why have I started bumbling just as I got near him?* she thought. As he passed her, his woody cologne made her take a few rapid breaths. She sat down and told herself there was no reason for her to become agitated.

Sebastian got in. He reached down under his seat, and pulled out a short-stemmed bouquet of flowers. 'Sorry if I upset you last time with what I said, I mean, about Hamid…'

Jessica stared at the flowers without making any move to take them. Her nostrils flared as she controlled the rising wetness in her eyes, and tried to stop her breath coming in gasps. She seemed to be aware, somewhere, below a misty surface of consciousness, that his cologne had mixed with the floral scents of the bouquet. He was offering himself as part of his apology, as if in future there would only be the real Sebastian; the last two meetings she had felt unable to understand him. Jessica had tried to pin labels on him, but he had been impossible to define. Muslim sympathiser or not – violent extremist, or saviour? *I have to go along with this if I want answers about Hamid,* she thought. That was why she had finally agreed to go for a drive with him.

Jessica could not stop a pink flush appearing that covered both cheeks like butterfly wings, as she realised she had accused him of being a Muslim terrorist sympathiser on their first meeting, and on the second meeting she had walked out without listening to what he had to say in the coffee shop, without even a goodbye. He had still phoned her and asked her to get together and talk about things. So Jessica had agreed, despite the bewilderment since Hamid's death. Sebastian had come into her life and added to the agitation. She had already been asking herself numerous questions about Hamid, which had become intertwined with her being like ivy around the branches of a tree. However, Sebastian's aura of mystery, combined with his looks and easy-mannered, old-world charm and chivalry, had made the confusion swirl like an identity crisis. Jessica thought she had good protection, but he had lanced his way through her armour like a knight on a charger in a medieval joust.

Her first thought after opening her eyes this morning had been *Sebastian is coming today – I'd better get ready.* As she jumped out of bed, she had stood thinking under the shower. Why had she agreed to go for a drive with him? *I can't let myself over-analyse this*, she thought. *He was on Hamid's train, he knows something about Hamid, and I simply have got to know the truth about Hamid. I just won't accept the police's insinuations that Hamid could have been the suicide bomber.* There were not enough body parts for even the forensic team to be certain. Unusually, on Hamid's train the suicide bomber had used Semtex. Her journalistic determination had convinced her that she should use whatever means necessary to get to the truth. Even though Sebastian seemed lovely, not just his looks, his stunning blue eyes. She loved his understated masculine confidence, which was so different from Hamid. More than anything, Sebastian was so unusual and mysterious...

As she leaned forward again, his musky aroma mixed with the floral fragrances. The smells curled and entwined together to become temptation, which gripped her throat.

'Thanks... that's a bit unexpected,' she said, as she glanced at the flowers, but still did not move.

Sebastian smiled at her again, and moved the flowers nearer to her. He had not attempted to kiss her, and he had not tried to greet her in any other way. 'From my garden. I have a greenhouse' he said, as if that explained it all. He sat with his arm outstretched; the simple collection of small-petalled flowers seemed fragile in his fist. She finally took the bouquet. The corners of his mouth seemed to be upturned most of the time. Now, as they flicked up slightly further, she looked harder, but could not detect any guile. His face seemed almost too beautiful; but his angled jaw and sculptured chin, which had a deep dimple in the centre, made the shape of his face masculine, and his full pliant lips compensated for his beauty. He seemed almost too perfect to look at for too long... almost painful to perceive to a flawed mortal, like her. She knew that he liked her, and wondered if she was betraying Hamid's memory by going on the drive – a date, as he must perceive it.

Sebastian nodded to her, smiling as if encouraging a small child to recognise a gift. 'It's okay. I grew them myself, had a good season this year. They're just flowers...' His dark hair stood up at the front. His easy manner and twinkling outlaw eyes that reflected his unexpected charm forced her to nod her head, which made her feel immature. She looked down at the bouquet and gripped it in both hands. She wondered if it was her vulnerability so soon after Hamid's death that made her so intrigued by him, and by what secrets he might hold.

'Flowers always make me feel better – well, a bit more relaxed, anyway,' he said. His face always seemed to have lips ever ready to tip over into a smile, like fine scales. The balance would find the slightest provocation and each smile, almost every comment, seemed like a favourable judgement to Jessica. Sebastian sat comfortably with his limbs relaxed as he drove, caressing the controls of the car through every manoeuvre.

As he drove to the Malvern Hills, Jessica quizzed him about his past, making conversation about his work, lecturing in Islamic studies. She discovered his special interest had become the 'Clash of Civilisations'. He told her how he had lived in Damascus and Cairo and *Sana'a* and even how he had done a tour of Mecca and Medina like Richard Burton, disguised as an Arab Bedouin. She asked him about the language and discovered that he was not only fluent in Arabic, but had also lived with the Anizzah Bedouins. Wandering on camel back, drinking camel milk, like some modern Lawrence of Arabia between the deserts of Syria, Iraq and northern Arabia. Jessica asked him how he disguised his blue eyes, and he shrugged and laughed, saying that if anyone questioned him about them he had answered that one of his ancestors had come down to the deserts of Arabia from the Caucasus Mountains, and he was really half-*Jinni*, half-Bedouin.

When they got past Bewdley she asked, 'Where are we going?'

'I discovered this place recently, a hill in the Wyre Forest. I love to relax on this drive.'

Jessica put her hand on her abdomen, as feelings mixed in her like the colours of early autumn. She thought about her parents, and how she wished she could have saved her father worrying about her potential marriage to Hamid. Her mother's concern had manifested in restrained inquiries over the years as to whether she had met Hamid's mother, and would Jessica ever be accepted?

What is the truth? The question had become repetitive, rattling her brain like rifle fire. It made emotions swirl inside her, like the leaves that fell around her, which had been turned into foreign colours by the darkening days. The leaves had divorced themselves from their maternal branches and twisted in a dance, their final waltz before winter. She felt mixed up, but she knew no matter how lovely Sebastian might be, her main aim was to discover the reality about Hamid. She cursed inwardly at not knowing what to do easily.

The questions tumbled in her mind like the debris of autumn that floated around them. Sebastian drove without speaking. His calm manner, the comfortable leather seats, and the nature that surrounded them made her close her eyes as the sun smothered her face with warmth.

They stopped at a high point; the Malvern Hills were laid out below them like a rumpled rug. Jessica got out and looked over the Wyre Forest, the trees turning shades of sulphur and chestnut, advertising their final sacrifice in a blaze of glory.

Sebastian went to the boot and took out a hamper. 'Brought something to refresh you. I know a spot we can sit, where you can relax if you get tired,' he said.

They walked down one of the nature trails, and as they travelled in silence, Jessica allowed her mind to fill with the sounds of songbirds. Across to one side she saw an orchard with blushed apples, where a woodpecker tapped out a secret code. As the path got deeper into the woods, it became more twisting and started to climb uphill. Jessica began to pant. The miasma of the city cleared; she breathed deeply, and felt the rejuvenating qualities strengthen her legs. The breeze hummed through the branches and whistled through the bulrushes. It gave voice to the growth, and gathered a symbiotic song of harmony.

'Not too far, now. It's a really good place to sit,' said Sebastian. They soon came to a stream that they followed for a while. Trees grew on both sides of the brook, and without warning, a small clearing appeared to one side of the water, as if the stream had decided to provide them with a front seat to its dynamic display.

Sebastian took out a thick woollen rug and laid it over the grass. 'A seat worthy of Gaia herself,' he said with a small laugh, and bowed in mock courtier style to her.

The scene seemed to be unfolding like a wholesome Hollywood fifties movie, as if she were watching it on a silver screen. The clean harmonised lines of his face made her stare slightly longer than she wanted to. He seemed as patrician as she had suspected on the previous meetings. His accent was clipped and cultured, and he used soft tones as naturally as he wore his Saville Row clothes.

Jessica sat and watched the brook. Oaks, silver birch and maples branched on the other side of the river, shedding leaves like giant artists dripping accidental colours from their palettes. She saw two maple leaves fall into the brook. They swirled on the surface of the water as it reflected the afternoon sun that made their colours seem iridescent; a twig fell and danced with them, creating small eddies and ripples. The twig disappeared under the surface, like foreign secrets that could enter and destroy a self-contained universe. Jessica wondered if all things did happen for a reason. The maple leaves floated downstream, no longer connected to their source, breaking the memory of their origins.

'Would you like something to eat? I've got roast chicken, some cold meats, a selection of sandwiches, strawberries, biscuits and a variety of cheeses?' Sebastian asked. She shook her head.

'Good – neither do I.' He took out a thermos flask and an empty teapot and two porcelain cups, unadorned except for a single wild flower on the sides, which looked like a scarlet pimpernel. The saucers had an inter-linking chain of the small red flowers around the edge. 'I know you prefer tea.'

'Er, yes,' she said, looking from him to the cups and saucers.

'Out of porcelain?'

'Well, ideally…' she said, as a small laugh escaped her, but it did not hide her fussiness. 'The flowers look like scarlet pimpernels.'

'I had the cups printed. My mother, bless her, loved wild flowers,' said Sebastian as he served her tea. 'You're something of an expert to spot them.'

'Don't know much about any kind of flowers, really, just that my mum used to let them grow in her runner beans,' she said, almost not telling him in case he thought she was making the story up because he had told her they were his mother's favourite.

He told her he had them made in his mother's memory, and how she had taught him about wild flowers. He said he was the last of the Windsor line, seemingly without feeling sorry for himself. He poured the tea from the thermos into the teapot and stirred it, waited for a while, and then poured it carefully into the cups.

Jessica did not ask him about his family, although she wanted to know about his mother. They sipped the tea in silence, and she felt he had made it just the way she loved it. Jessica took a second cup but refused a third. They sat still enough for her to notice a kingfisher land for a moment, some distance away, on a branch overhanging the river. They sat back, leaning on elbows, looking up into the dappled sky, where clouds scudded like yachts on a blue sea. The scattered cumulus did not stop but drifted by, as if they had not found solace. They looked like a giant's wish bubbles, continuing their search for realisation, to condense and crystallise into a giant's tears somewhere else.

The harvest sun's rays seemed to warm her from the inside in a way that no artificial heat could. It provided her a closeness to not only the physical, with the cool earth that she could touch if she stretched out a hand, but also created a metaphysical connection that caused hormones to pulse through her body, that loosened the tight coils in her shoulders and back. She felt a link with Sebastian, as if the brook took the cadence from their breasts and spoke, as if the birds translated their thoughts into song and nature conspired to make them understand one another. Perhaps it was because of his silent comprehension, because he had been the only one who had provided companionship without demands. He seemed to know what to do, without the need for speaking, a symbiosis she had not ever felt with anyone, not even with Hamid. She wondered why she could relax with a man she hardly knew. Jessica put her arms behind her head, and fell into a dreamless sleep for the first time since the bombing.

When she awoke she found him reading a book on Wild Flowers of England. 'Went for a hunt while you slept, got a small collection of flowers to add to your collection. Don't worry, they're not endangered or anything – in fact, they're mostly Forget-Me-Nots.'

Jessica did not reply, but looked at Sebastian. *Why is this guy so weird?* she thought. *Is everything so cosy in his life that he can pick wild flowers? I know why I'm here, but why has he brought me here?* She saw him look at her and then glance away, and he took a deep breath.

'I've been asking around, and I've been to Hamid's mosque, and...'

'Go on... after all, that's what we came out to discuss,' she said, brushing her hair away and rubbing her eyes.

'I don't know for sure, but...'

Jessica waited for him to continue; maybe he was being hesitant because he did not want to hurt her.

'Well, last time you got upset.' He looked at her and shrugged. 'But it seems as if Hamid might have been involved in some unusual activities.'

'*Unusual activities?*' She raised her eyebrows. '*Might* have been involved?'

'Well, okay, it's circumstantial. *Jaish an Noor wass Salaam* have been recruiting heavily from Britain, but especially from Birmingham, and his mosque is in the front line. Some of his friends seem to be involved, and Hamid had been seen at some of the meetings.'

Jessica laughed.

'Sorry, I'm not laughing,' he said. She saw his smile disappear, and a rare, serious mood covered his features, as if reality had squeezed his smile. 'Perhaps you don't know much about these people, but I know *Jaish*, and –'

'It's a good job you're not a lawyer, because I can tell you that Hamid wasn't anything like a suicide bomber. He had everything to live for – us, our marriage next month,' she said, her voice getting louder as her face turned into a grimace, and she threw up her hands.

'There's his friend, Ali. There were some late-night meetings, videos of insurgents in Iraq, the recent targeting of Gaza. All these things have been used in recruitment campaigns.' His voice became gentle as he continued. 'Often friends and even families have no idea when somebody becomes radicalise. Maybe Hamid –'

'Was a suicide bomber? Is that what you're saying?'

'It's a possibility. It may be something we can't just discount.'

'And Ali!' She let loose a little laugh from the garrison of self-control. 'He's the loveliest man you could imagine. I've known him since I knew Hamid.'

'*Jaish*. These people can be very persuasive. Sometimes I find myself almost agreeing with them, when I listen to their speeches.'

'*You're* the bloody terrorist helper then? Not Hamid,' said Jessica, louder than she had intended.

'Well, I have been accused of being one.'

On each occasion that they had met she had been rude and aggressive. She felt churlish, especially because of the effort he had made today. She did not really want to discuss any more details of what Hamid might have been involved in, so she said, 'Thank you for bringing me here. It's a beautiful place, and I've relaxed for the first time in weeks.'

Jessica leaned forward and poured the remaining tea, half a cup for Sebastian, and half-filled her cup. 'A peace offering... let's call a truce,' she said, and almost smiled. 'I have to know what happened with Hamid. I'm going to ring Ali, and go down to that bloody mosque if needed.'

'I'm sure you'll need lots of help, I know these people –'

'I don't think I could stop you, even if I tried.' She touched his hand. He really was a decent, lovely guy, and he had made her feel better already. 'I don't want to try to stop you,' she said, managing to smile, and she raised her teacup. 'A truce?'

CHAPTER 8

Birmingham – Sebastian's House

Jessica had noticed the old-world splendour of his house as soon as she had walked in. She sat on the comfortable ancient leather chesterfield suite, that had slightly musty cushions. Rugs lay on the floor and looked as if the Pasha had just stepped off them. There were more intricate runners in the corridors, lying on waxed wooden floors, seemingly from the Sultan of Egypt's palace. Jessica sat opposite Dr Sebastian Windsor, her legs crossed as she leaned back into the thick seat.

'I don't think he's worried about insignificant me... ' He inhaled the fumes deeply and savoured the aroma. 'God.' He looked at her across his balloon glass. 'He is rather too busy not-intervening to worry about my drinking,' said Sebastian, as he swirled the nut-brown liquor. He closed his eyes, and inhaled again. He took another sip of his cognac. 'Oh, I know you're wondering about my drink. I'm sure if that's all He has to worry about then He's a sad man with a sad thing, this religion... '

'This religion of yours, you mean?' said Jessica. She leaned back in the comfortable sofa, but could not help glancing up at the multi-faceted chandelier, which refracted and fired colours at her like kaleidoscopic laser beams. The light reflected in his steady blue eyes that seemed to appraise her continuously, as if marking her responses. *Did he steal that chandelier from the Palace of Versailles?* The ostentation somehow suited him, as if a part of his lineage. He did not seem unreachable because of the grandeur, but more at home. She crossed her arms and legs; determined, this time, not to let emotion stop her from succeeding in her mission, to get answers about Hamid. The funeral and Hamid's mother's response made her muscles feel like cotton wool, as if her sweat had soaked into them and weighed her down. She had lost any semblance of warmth that she had felt on the last meeting and now tightened her jaw and stiffened her back, determined to get answers.

'This religion of *ours*, Jessica, in so far as we are all born into a pure state, without the need to expiate original sin. That's what the Muslims believe. It's society that puts the subsequent labels on us.'

Exactly how Sebastian was linked to the bombing, Jessica could not be sure. She had spoken to Ali, and quizzed the men she had seen hanging around with Ali, and some of them had mentioned Sebastian's name. Some of the teenagers had called Sebastian the *Ustad*, the great Teacher. Jessica felt certain that Sebastian had inspired the terrorists. At the very least he seemed to be a supporter, despite his pretences, and he certainly knew more about the bombing than he had led her to believe. *How could I have been so stupid to fall for his platitudes?* she thought. *Is his liberal exterior just an empty shell? Why does he keep trying to see me, keep trying to get close?*

A few days after she returned from Hamid's mosque, she had rang Ali again. Although his responses to her questioning had been evasive, Ali had admitted that Sebastian had visited the mosque after Hamid had died. Sebastian was on the train. Maybe he lured the bomber there somehow, or maybe he triggered it. She wondered... *maybe it wasn't a suicide bomb?* There seemed so much about Sebastian that did not make sense. He intrigued her, despite her doubts about him, and she often found herself thinking of him since the drive to the Malvern Hills.

The journalist, Blair, had continued to bombard her, but his enquiries felt like stones. He had almost asked her more questions than the police. He blatantly blamed Hamid for the suicide bombing and the deaths – what was his source? *He cannot be certain, because he hasn't printed anything yet*, she thought. Had he truly found out something about Hamid that no one else knew? She knew how the media sensationalised stories and jumped to conclusions. *What if they were right? Maybe Sebastian would have answers? If he's telling the truth about Hamid.* She would not permit her doubts to become a parasite, worming into the one-way-alley of memories to destroy the citadel of love.

Jessica had looked at his name on her mobile phone on numerous occasions over the past few days, nearly dialling his number, and then only half-dialling. She had hesitated until the evening today, before finally ringing him. Sebastian had been keen to see her and had invited her over immediately.

Sebastian's voice broke the crystal of her thoughts. 'I would miss Cognac too much.' He looked away for a moment, and added quietly, 'Maybe I did pretend to stop drinking for a while... Who's always honest in this world?'

The corners of his mouth flicked up further, slightly. She could not detect a hint of apology. His face seemed almost too beautiful, but the masculine jaw and sculptured chin with a large dimple set below expressive lips compensated his masculinity. At least two days of dark stubble prickled his cheeks.

Jessica looked around, and saw that layers of thick hardback books in dark wooden bookcases lined a whole wall. They seemed as if they would crumble on touch but looked precious, as if holding the accounts and fragile secrets of an Empire. They gave the lie to his seemingly physical perfection, and the apparent hedonism of the surroundings created a dichotomy of Apollonian-Dionysian measure. A breaking wave of contrast upon which he seemed to ride nonchalantly: light versus dark, civilisation versus primeval barbarity.

'Does drink help you to inspire the terrorists?' Jessica looked around and saw the Menuet Napoleon Grande Champagne Cognac bottle on the antique mahogany drinks cabinet. 'Must have wanted you, the University – didn't spare any expense, did they?'

'That's some stuff from my London home. The older things my grandmother left me...' Sebastian shrugged at what must have seemed familiar, and looked back to her. 'Didn't Hamid ever do anything wrong?' he asked.

Jessica pulled at her fingernails, pawed the corner of her mouth. The doubts about coming to see Sebastian had returned. The pain of Hamid's death refreshed itself on seeing Sebastian, mainly because of the new suspicions she now had about Hamid. Jessica looked around his house and wondered why he sat here in the semi-darkness in a room which looked more like colonial India, with furniture that might have been from Raffles.

'All the time,' she replied. Jessica thought for a moment about not answering him, of hating him, of telling him that he should go to the same Hell he had condemned her to. She had been skirting the edge of sanity since the bombing, which had only been made worse by the media reportage. The time after the funeral had stretched the skin in her face, and her cheeks had become more sculpted. She could not accept peoples' insinuations about Hamid. Jessica knew Hamid's habits; he trimmed his toenails every three weeks, and Chinese takeaways gave him indigestion. *How much closer do you have to be, before you really know a person?*

She had thought, initially, that she wouldn't answer Sebastian – that she would just ignore him, get him to answer her questions and then leave. His easy manner and inviting eyes that reflected his unusual charm, along with her desire to get answers, forced her into the conversation. Jessica felt the need to talk. She had not allowed herself to be drawn out before now, and everyone else had been too close. Since the explosion, and especially the funeral, she had felt like Hamid's flitting shadow. She had barely spoken to her parents and friends, except Holly. Jessica wondered why she was so reluctant to tell Holly everything about Sebastian... maybe it was because she had such mixed feelings for that man of mystery.

Finally she said, 'Hamid drank, smoked, and often went to mosque.'

'Yet you loved him?' said Sebastian, smiling. 'Would you like a drink? How rude of me not to offer one as soon as you came in.'

Jessica knew he had not offered her a drink as a deliberate ploy. His manners and upbringing would not have allowed such behaviour otherwise. 'No, no, thanks. I've been having too much since Hamid...'

Sebastian rose and easily opened a bottle of wine without hurrying.

'It's all the running. The press, that newspaper guy, Blair had been hounding me.'

'I'll pour you one. I'm sure you need one. Especially now you've come to see me.' He gave her a smile, and she felt the muscles on her face slacken. 'I bet I can guess your favourite tipple.' Sebastian passed her a glass of Australian Chardonnay. 'This one is particularly fruity, although I'm no expert, but pears and peaches I think.' He sat down opposite her, crossed his legs, and leaned back.

Is he always so languid? 'Did you offer drinks to your acolytes too?' Jessica quaffed the drink. The wine tasted cool and refreshing but caused some nausea as it went into her stomach. She put a hand over her abdomen; she could not remember when she had last had a hot meal.

Sebastian's eyes flashed lightning blue over his brandy glass, as he took a sip.

'Before they blew themselves up in the train station?' she asked.

Sebastian sat impassively, looking at her with strong, unblinking eyes, which seemed to smile without mocking even when his mouth did not. His eyes encouraged her to be more open with him. Despite that, she tasted something bitter in her throat.

'Or was it when you were indoctrinating them? Brainwashing them into being suicide bombers? Teaching them about the pleasures of paradise that await them when they're martyred?' Jessica's forehead wrinkled again, and her eyes narrowed to slits. She crossed her arms and held the glass to her chest. All the evidence that she had, so far, pointed to the fact that Sebastian had something to do with extremist Muslims. He definitely knew more about Hamid than he had told her.

She felt ungenerous and unforgiving, but she hid her shame under her smothering anger at the memories of her beloved Hamid. *Lost to these people. Lost to their narrow-minded worldview, to their shallow and introverted Islam. Turban-headed, and dribbling venom. Who hate everyone, even their own sort, anyone who does agree with their tight clique.* She had seen them on television, shouting and screaming, gun-toting ranting and raving, wide-eyed, firing automatic weapons when there was no obvious need to, open-mouthed, straggly beards, flowing robes, burning books, flags and effigies. Oppressing women – no school, commanding them to wear a bloody tent in the roasting sun. Shooting and destroying ancient monuments, like the *Buddhas of Bhamiyan*. Ordering twenty cows to be sacrificed as penance because they were not destroyed fast enough. Head-chopping *Jihad* in Jeddah, book-burning in Bradford, suicide bombers – clubbers in Tel Aviv, babies in Baghdad. Everywhere and anywhere. They did not give a damn, as long as they got to their Paradise. Now here, Birmingham: the train station. Hamid dead. 'Did you offer them a nice port reserve with matured Stilton?'

'Is that what you think?'

'Now you're going to tell me you had nothing to do with it?' She tightened her lips into a tiny pink ball, and did not blink.

'No, we didn't have any cheese and wine parties,' he replied. 'It's not what you're led to believe. They have reason, internal logic...'

She hated his cool manner. 'What did you promise them? Dark-eyed beauties in Paradise?'

'Thinking of the Hashassins?' he asked. She stood up. 'Too much TV, Jessica,' said Sebastian as he stood up too, and diffused her aggressive manoeuvre by his body language.

She looked at him, unsure what to do. His athletic build showed no droop of his shoulders, his smooth walk told her he could encompass anything that was physically demanding with fluidity. With confidence, without seeking permission, Sebastian topped up her glass and gestured her to sit again by extending an elegant arm. His limbs bewitched her as she followed his sleek movements, like liquid being poured from an alchemist's flask. She sat down again.

'What did you promise them? What does it take for someone to blow themselves into small pieces of meat? Why do you promise them virgins, anyway? Can't they get any girlfriends in the real world?' She felt hope rising in her as she saw a flicker cross his face. *Was he insulted? How can I upset him?* Jessica wanted to disrupt him; she disliked not being in control of her emotions. She barely realised that she had spoken, and she could not be sure what would come out of her mouth next. Sebastian was too comfortable. It seemed as if he was too used to being in control, too used to being the cool doctor, the professor all the time. 'No girlfriends? Are you all too ugly or too stupid?' she added, and felt foolish, for she knew Sebastian was neither.

'Porn and Paradise,' he said. 'That's what you seem to believe?'

'What?' she said. Sebastian had already shocked Jessica, but he continued to surprise her. His attitude and demeanour, his appearance – in fact, even his language – was nothing she would have expected from a religious man, a lecturer in Islamic Studies. But then he had never taken the title of *Shaikh* or an *Imam*, both of which Hamid had hated.

Sebastian had not made any claims. He had not shown his piety in anyway; he twirled no rosary. He had no blind eyes or hooks, or deformities of any kind. In fact, he was the antithesis of the screaming Muslim assassin. Why did her mind keep straying, making him synonymous with a Muslim terrorist? All Sebastian had said was that he was a lecturer at The School of African and Oriental Studies, and was taking a sabbatical at Birmingham University. He did not quote Qur'an or *Hadith*, sayings of the Prophet. He sipped fine Cognac and spoke in an earthy way. The doctor could have been a legend of the silver screen, from the golden age of cinema. Yet he worked at SOAS in Russell Square, WC1 – *so homely, yet so foreign*, she thought.

Apart from the shock of what Sebastian had said, he seemed as patrician as she had suspected at the earlier meeting. He sat comfortably, with his long legs draped over the chesterfield.

'Porn and Paradise. That's how it's done. Isn't that what the papers tell you? Get them hooked on all the blue-eyed babes, then promise them brown-eyed, innocent dewy virgins in Paradise. That's how it's done.'

'Is that how you do it?' Her hands balled into fists, then she unscrewed them and gripped the chair tightly as she leaned forward.

'Get them hooked onto the pink flesh and honeys with straw-coloured hair, make them desperate for the seventy-two virgins in Paradise. That's what the media would have you believe. If you can believe that then you can believe the stories about 9/11 bombers dancing their last mortal night away in strip bars and clubs.'

'Seventy-two. Oh, why stop at seventy-two?' She kept brushing her golden hair away from her face, tilting her chin forward at every comment.

'Oh that's just an expression – it means numerous, or unlimited.'

'So you do it for the women? Is that what it's all about?'

'That's all they've got – Paradise – so it gets used. Anything is used. All depends on what and who you want to believe, Jessica. Whose truth do you want?'

'So the end justifies the means?' said Jessica.

'Maybe, maybe it does. Depends what the end is.' After a pause he said, 'Someone as striking as you has surely passed through many such crossroads in your life?'

Mystery surrounded Sebastian like an opaque mist. He was still an enigma to her, a contradiction. She leaned back in the chair, looked down, and played with her fingernails again. He was too good-looking to be a doctor or a scholar of any sort, yet he was easy to talk to, human at the same time. Jessica stole a glance and wondered if she could see some vulnerability in his eyes; the eyes that crinkled at the corners so easily and made him so approachable. 'I suppose that's what I'm here to find out?'

'Are you? Are you going to decipher the conundrums and answer all the questions today? Of life, the universe and everything?'

'Oh, you can get philosophical, but all I want to know is why you and your kind blew up Hamid.' Jessica wondered how he could make her feel warm, make her want to talk to him all night, and then in the next sentence he made her feel foolish. Before she could stop, she was jumping about and hissing in her chair like a spitting cobra, shooting venom at him.

'Who blew up Hamid?' he asked.

'Blew him into thousands of small pieces. Just found bits of his body, and scraped some DNA off the train windows. They wouldn't have known he was even on that train, otherwise…'

'I killed Hamid? I was there at the train station, remember? Why would I bomb my own train? Who do you think killed Hamid?'

'You did. You're defending them, so you're responsible. You and your virgin-seeking bloody followers. You dog!' shouted Jessica, as the pain became too much to control; the primitive emotion took over. She simply knew Dr Windsor was a Muslim extremist sympathiser, a scholar, and so he was at fault. Somewhere deep inside her was the fear that she could be falling off the edge of sanity, into the blackness of the abyss, from where there was rare escape: madness.

'How do you know I'm the dog?' he said.

Jessica noticed how he deliberately drawled dog into *dawwg*. His still-relaxed attitude and the easy slippage into street colloquialisms made her pull at her lower lip again. She thought these weird mannerisms ill-suited him, but she realised he was not bound by convention. *Am I pulling him into the chasm with me?*

'You did. And the people you support and condone. You killed him. You Cognac-sipping bloody hypocrite. Hamid may have done many things wrong, but at least he knew what he was, and he was no hypocrite like you. You are the dog. You dog!'

'I'm not the dog, I'm the wolf and I eat dog. Let me tell you I devour dogs for breakfast. To catch the dogs, you've got to be a wolf.'

'What the hell are you talking about? I don't care if you think you're a bitch –'

'Are you a wolf? Are you wolf enough to know The Truth? Can you handle the Truth?' His eyes narrowed into cognac-fired lupine-slits.

'What? It was obviously a mistake to come here tonight.'

'Come on!' Sebastian threw his head back and howled like a wolf. 'Come on Jessica. Owwwwww! Owwwwww!'

'You are crazy, bloody crazy! It's true what Hamid said about all you lot, terrorist sympathisers. Which part of the chain are you? Crazy pigs.'

'Pigs? Pigs? Dogs are okay. Wolves are good, but pigs?' he said. Jessica noticed he gritted his teeth for the first time, but he quickly smiled again.

'One minute all so sophisticated – port and Stilton – next, blowing people to mincemeat. Crazy pig-dogs!' Jessica shouted.

The doctor lost his smile. 'I've tried to help you in the best way that I could. I know you've been upset, more since Hamid's funeral, but let me tell you something. I'm the reason that there is peace and security out there on the streets.'

Jessica had told him that she had been to Hamid's funeral, but not what had happened there. 'Oh you really are the Angel of Mercy, aren't you?'

'I'm the reason why bombs are not going off everyday. I'm the reason why the planes are safe, why you can ride on the buses. You think it's the Prime Minister or the President who keeps you safe? Hell, it's people like me letting the trains run on time.' Now Sebastian leaned forward, as if he was about to spring off his chair.

'By blowing us all up any time?'

'By stopping those who would blow you up *all* the time. You know how soon there would be chaos on the streets if I didn't stop it?' He paused, leaned forward, and said in quieter voice, 'I have to talk to these kids every day.' He resumed his mocking tone. 'You'd have suicide bombers coming out of your ham sandwiches, and veiled assassins in your sherry trifle.'

'What are you talking about? How do you stop them?' Jessica leaned back, crossed her legs, brushed her hair away again, then folded her arms across her chest.

'They listen to me I know about Islam – I studied in Cairo, Damascus and Medina –'

'Do you believe any of it? I think it got you places you couldn't go, to influence people you wouldn't normally meet,' said Jessica.

Sebastian's eyes flashed, and his fingers tightened on the stem of the glass. He put it down on the side table and leaned back in his armchair. *So you do have to collect yourself sometimes? I bet I hit the spot,* she thought.

'You guys don't understand. You just want MTV perfection, perfumed and intense, the women and the men, dewy-eyed. Each one more alluring, more beautiful, with gyrating and lithesome limbs and bodies approaching perfection.' Sebastian leaned forward again. 'Do you know what perfection is? I know they take your breath away. They're almost so beautiful that it hurts, and makes you cry. The unattainable. Just when you think it's not possible to be more entranced, to be more bewitched. Then just as you are about to look away, to get on with something else in your life, they hook their suckers into you and drink your life-blood.'

'What the hell are you talking about? I came here to talk about Hamid.'

'I *am* talking about Hamid. You can't look away, because there suddenly is someone else you fancy, even more heart-stoppingly alluring and beautiful. Another Adonis, yet another Venus. Then a veil is drawn over your eyes, and before you can think you are transported and addicted, mainlining – and they have you.'

The lecturing mood doesn't suit him, she thought. *I liked his cheeky side better. I've got him all riled and serious now.* Jessica sat still now with her arms and legs crossed, but her eyes almost crinkled at his agitation. 'I'm not addicted to anything...' she said, not sure if she was or not.

'You worshiped Hamid.'

'That's the trouble with you and your Islam; you don't know what love is. Isn't that the truth? You can't love?' she said.

'You eat but you don't taste, you look but you don't see, you read but you can't understand. Then your whole life is devoted to living the dream. You think you are not like that, but really, you are. You're looking for something that doesn't exist, deluded, an illusion. You think that when you find 'The One', he'll fill the emptiness. They tell you stories, and you then live the stories.'

'Who the hell is this *they* you keep talking about?' she asked.

'Before you know it, you're old and decrepit and saying *Oh how I wish I had my life again. I would do what was really important*,' said Sebastian, as if she had not asked the question.

'I *was* doing what was important. Living my life, planning the future with Hamid, before your sort murdered him.'

'Even if you find your Brad Pitt, or as you did, Hamid, the reality is always more disappointing than the dream. Flesh can't match fiction. They can't fill the emptiness. Because they are just people, idols. Idols. They are mortal and physical with hunger and pain and suffering and disease and shit and vomiting and bleeding and germs. Ultimately even the flesh idols lose. To the stealer of the veil. The exposer of the truth: death.' He took another deep drag from his cognac.

'You talk about death as if it were life,' said Jessica, as she uncrossed her arms and legs and slurped her drink.

'It's the final truth, the ultimate.'

'Death before life, that's you lot. Bloody hypocrite.'

'Your soul aspires but cannot comprehend yet, and so there is anger, because you want to climb the dizzying heights towards the peak – to leave behind the pain and suffering of this world. But it's scary. Your soul aspires. I can see that now. But your heart dares not comprehend. It's too attached, too welded, to the material world.'

'Is that a spiritual Saville Row suit? And holy sipping cognac? Are you sitting on a blessed leather chesterfield? Dr *I-ain't-material* Sebastian Windsor.'

He ignored her insults. 'Something. Anything to assuage the emptiness. That's what you thought Hamid was, but really now you are feeling empty after the death of your god. Because that's what mortals are – death waiting to happen. Even if you possessed the material universe, it would not fill the hole; not if you're a thinking person.'

'You don't know anything about me,' said Jessica, but felt he had fathomed more, got closer to the truth than Holly.

'You are lonely, sad and meaningless without the Truth. Because only by enslaving yourself to 'The One' can you become free.'

'Can you hear yourself? You don't seem to have listened to your own words. What's the answer? I don't think you have it, but let me ask you, since I'm here.'

'You want the truth?'

'You know I do!'

'You don't have the guts.'

'Try me. I'll shock you. You don't know it all, doctor.' Her face flushed and sweat beaded her lips. She could not unlock her jaw, and lines of bitterness crinkled into her forehead.

'The truth is to find enlightenment. That's serious. You are too far away from knowing yourself to even be a seeker of wisdom – you don't dare to do it. You don't even dare. Reflections will scare you, and meditating will give you palpitations and a panic attack. I know what I am, you see.'

'You think you know. I can't believe I'm listening to such a false man.'

'What I am may be a mystery to me too. Yes, you're right. I may be a hypocrite, but I'm an enlightened hypocrite. I know the Truth – maybe I just can't follow it all the way.'

Despite herself, Jessica felt warmed by his human honesty, but she could not bring herself to say anything positive.

'I'm not a scared little kid. You can't even look in the mirror. You worshipper of Hamid... you don't even know your own idolatry. You imagine you're in love, but how many people are in love?'

'I loved. I loved. Have you? I dare you to love.' Jessica said. The momentary warmth had disappeared like the cognac fumes.

'Once the lust wears off, then it's looking for the new one. How many?'

'It was never lust. I loved Hamid. Can't you understand? I loved him!' She felt like releasing a vicious string of swearwords at him. She felt surprise at the strength of her emotions, but she allowed him to answer.

'I can tell you of a place where real people meet. The true men and women are there. Go there, then. If you dare.' He challenged her. 'I know I probably drink too much and I live in the castles in the air, because I want ideals, and my ethereal castles may come tumbling down. But you, Jessica, are Alice in Wonderland. The real world is hidden by the thick curtain of deceit they call 'modern liberal democracy' and you don't know it, because you think this is the real world.'

'I don't think you know the truth either, but I've come this far...' she said.

'When you really see the Truth, you will be like a candle held against the light of the sun. You will melt and disappear into the Truth. You will want to be the moth that self-immolates in the flame. I know the ultimate Truth, and maybe I can't follow it exactly. But I know it. I don't need stress relief and cognitive therapy and drugs or empty promises or a Ferrari, or Money or 'love'. The nonexistent stitching that is no longer holding society together. Serial killers on Prozac and kids on Ritalin, mass-murder and fear and want and hunger and loathing of fellow man.'

'If it's true, how do I find out? How will I know for sure? Let me decide for myself,' said Jessica, out of breath, her chest heaving erratically. She had never been challenged in this way. Her hands shook; she sloshed her wine and spilled some onto the thick carpet. She did not apologise. 'There's no such thing. You're not Peter Pan. How can such a solution exist?'

'I can arrange a spiritual session for you. What you make of it, if anything, is up to you. I hope you're brave enough.' He shrugged. 'There might be a road through the morass of pain... '

'I want to... I have to. I have no choice, I need to...'

The wine glass fell from her hand. Her whole body started shaking, and she could no longer control the tears. Sebastian stood with Jessica and she leaned on his shoulder, in a spontaneous search for human comfort. She did not notice his silent tears.

Sebastian did nothing. He did not hold her. Nor did Sebastian wipe his wet cheeks.

'Is there really a path to enlightenment?' she asked.

'Not in this cynical world, but you have to enter a different universe.'

London

Jimmy walked into the room and recognised the speaker, Dwayne Williams, immediately. Dwayne had operated in Jimmy's area over the last couple of years, trying to talk to the teenage boys in the neighbourhood. He had never interfered with Jimmy and so Jimmy had never felt the need to speak to him. Jimmy stayed as far away from mosque types as possible. Dwayne stood addressing the roomful of seated men. He wore a long flowing traditional Arabic robe, a white *Jilbab* that stopped three quarters of the way down, exposing the lower part of his shins. A white cap, not much larger than a skullcap, sat on the crown of his head, but this did not tame his thick curly hair, which protruded through the sides in bushy tufts, so that it looked like a jet halo around the cap. Jimmy tried to step over the crowded rows of men. He willed his muscles not to quiver, forced himself to unlock his jaw. He heard the deep thrill in the speaker's voice, which sounded different to how he spoke on the street, the few times that Jimmy had heard him. On those occasions Dwayne had a smattering of Jamaican patois, which he did not use now. Jimmy felt intrigued by the earthy black accent emanating from the speaker and he was surprised to hear Dwayne's voice had taken on a rich, melodic quality, as it was amplified by the microphone.

'Abu Umar. That's the only name you need to know. Brothers, that's the person that I am about to introduce to you now, and he should need no introduction. You should already know him. Many of you have heard of him, of course, but too many of you don't know him. In fact, each and every Muslim out there and in here must love him. He should be one of our heroes, one of the real heroes of the Muslim world today.' The speaker warmed to his task. 'Are there such heroes, I hear you ask? Are there any such people in the world today? Surely that was a long time ago, during The Golden Age of Islam,' said Dwayne, in a plaintiff's voice.

The memories of the old mosque rose in Jimmy like vomit that would not stay down. He wiped the sweat from his scar, and kept repeating to himself *They's just people, men like me. Just people. Don't be scared!*

'The very fact that we have to ask that question, brothers – that very fact shows us the level of our weakness, the shocking state of our *Imaan*, our belief.' Dwayne raised his voice at the end of the sentence to great dramatic effect, and used his hands, sometimes violently. He used the full range of contortions that his facial muscles and eyes would allow, to create expression. Jimmy knew *Imaan* meant faith and level of belief or state of conviction; he had heard his father referring to his low levels of *Imaan* over the years.

He stepped into a non-existent gap and pushed his way past men, who hardly moved, to make room. He realised it was accepted, turning up late and pushing to make space to sit, at a time like this. The men sat on the floor, so that Jimmy could see heads full of black hair forming a moving mass. They made the room feel as claustrophobic as being locked up in the back of a lorry. Jimmy had arrived just in time that for the main attraction, Abu Umar. Jimmy climbed over seven crowded rows of men who formed a semicircle. They all sat facing the front of the room, craning over each other to see the speaker.

Jimmy squeezed into the last row and sat down with his back against the wall. He had to clasp his arms around his knees so that he would occupy less space, but despite this he made heavy physical contact with both men either side of him. To avoid touching the men seemed impossible in the tiny space, but Jimmy scrunched up his legs close to his chest and folded them in his arms, to stay away from his neighbours. Neither of the other two seemed to mind or even notice him. They were concentrating hard on the speaker; he could hear their breath whistling in and out. Jimmy felt disquieted and edgy. He picked at his scar with his right hand, and occasionally ran his left hand through the patterns cut into his short hair on the side of his head. He had paid the barber extra today to make sure his street credentials were visible when he came to the mosque tonight.

Jimmy's hair design, clothes and demeanour marked him as a dealer and gave him respect on the street amongst the boys, but here in the mosque he felt like a creature of the high mountains thrust into a swamp.

He was keeping his promise to the *Imam* by attending this meeting, and now he was jammed up next to people he had never met before. He hated Uncle Younis anew for forcing him here, but almost smiled as he remembered going to see the *Imam* two days after he had been dragged out of his office.

Jimmy had revelled in the visit, and had looked forward to going to the mosque for the first time in years. Younis kept rooms in the mosque next to his office, where he would often lounge and sleep or hold meetings with the mosque cronies to plan his revenge strategies on Abdullah. Jimmy had not entered the *Imam*'s private sanctum for years. He had last been there as a child with Ahmad, and Younis had asked Jimmy to join him on the long thin cushion. Jimmy remembered the sparkly blue material that covered it since his childhood. The cushion still lay in the same position against one of the walls, and was almost as long as the wall, about a span in height. This spongy material formed a dais and served as the throne for the *Imam*. There was no other furniture in the *Imam*'s rooms. Everyone else sat on the floor. Very few people were invited onto the cushion. Younis had greeted him with disingenuous exuberance, and when Jimmy had stared at his battered and bruised face the *Imam* had, without apparent shame, announced in front of his gathered acolytes that he had been in a car accident whilst being driven by the mosque secretary to perform a *nikah*, a wedding ceremony, in Harrow.

Jimmy imagined – without effort, but with perverse pleasure – what had happened to the *Imam* after the men had burst in and dragged him out. They had saved Jimmy a job, probably. Jimmy felt amazed that the *Imam* had survived, somehow. He must have begged and begged. *I wonder what he's promised those guys from Jaish?* thought Jimmy. *One of the payments Uncle Younis must have made is to let Dwayne and Abu Umar speak today. The Jaish boys told me I'd better keep my mouth shut when they dragged him out of his office, as if I didn't realise that. I wonder how Uncle Younis is going to deliver on the rest of his promises?*

At that time Younis had not been able to speak to Jimmy openly, because of the men who had gathered to see him after his supposed car crash. Jimmy went back to see him later before coming to the meeting, and found him alone. He had found Uncle Younis had lost none of his acid attitude. The *Imam* had told him – whilst wearing his huge black sunglasses, which made him face look like a beetle's carapace – that he better go to the meeting tonight, and the fifty thousand had best be delivered to Younis on the arranged date, before ten o'clock in the morning. Although Younis had mumbled his words and grimaced in pain because of his thick, split lips and face that looked like it had potatoes growing out of it, at the end the *Imam* had still managed a smile when talking about the money, not seeming to care that stretching his lips made them bleed even days after the beating. Jimmy had stared open mouthed at Uncle Younis as he stood there, grimacing at him in pain, making no attempt to wipe the blood from his mouth. He had even tried to convince Jimmy, briefly, that the *Jaish* boys who had burst in had done so by mistake, and that once they had realised who they had dragged out, they begged his forgiveness. Younis even repeated the lie about the road traffic accident. Jimmy had laughed and nodded.

Jimmy felt a fleeting smile come over his lips as he remembered the *Imam*'s face. Despite that, on looking around the overcrowded room of the mosque he felt worse than he had imagined he would, as nausea overtook him. He breathed deeply to clear the feeling but the air rushed in and out, hot and smelly. This was just how he had imagined this meeting.

Jimmy found it strange that this meeting started at midnight when the rest of the mosque was deserted and eerily quiet, except for the *Imam*'s offices in which Uncle Younis and a few close friends sat drinking *Chai*, the hot spiced sweet traditional milky tea of the South Asian subcontinent. Ostensibly the *Imam* and some of the Mosque Committee had organised a late night meeting for next week's celebrations for Hazrat Shah Hussein, one of their *Sufi* saints. In fact, Jimmy felt sure they wanted to keep an eye on the proceedings of the group. Jimmy could see the *Imam* had ensured some of his followers were present amongst the crowd, as spies who would later provide an eyewitness account of everything that transpired.

'Brothers, let me tell *you* about this man, *Shaikh* Abu Umar, and you can decide for yourself if he is a hero or not. I will let you decide. I trust your honest judgment. I know he dislikes – in fact, he hates – me to talk about these great things he has achieved, but I know them to be the truth. People have seen the things with their very own eyes. I have seen them with my own eyes.'

Jimmy waited expectantly, confident that whatever miracle the speaker was about to reveal would be unimpressive.

'I testify by Allah and His Messenger, His Book, that this is the truth. Let me tell you, for example, what happened one time in Bosnia. We were in Srebrenica, the massacre of Srebrenica. Do we all remember that? Yes? No?' The speaker looked intently at the faces seated on the floor before him. 'How short our memories are, brothers, how short. That was the single worst atrocity in Europe since World War II, when the Serbs massacred at least eight thousand defenceless and unarmed Muslim men and boys when they overran the UN-protected enclave in 1995.'

Jimmy searched his memory and found nothing, but noticed a few of the men nodded, some faces twisted.

'These facts and figures are not mine. This report was still posted on the BBC website on the fifth of October 2005. So it has to be absolutely true. Right?' This was greeted with generalised chuckling and mirth from the floor.

'On 16th July 1995, General Mladic congratulated his troops on carrying out the massacre by saying *Finally, the time has come to take revenge on the Turks.*' He spoke the quote in a whisper. Silence covered the room, making the atmosphere thick. Jimmy felt as if it was smothering him, and he was breathing through down and feathers. 'And now they've 'caught' him, sixteen years too late. If they could catch him and Saddam Hussain and put them on trial, why kill *The Shaikh*? When he was unarmed?' After a pause, to let the significance of the assassination of Osama Bin Ladin settle, he smiled.

'We were trapped in the city with thousands of women and children, old people, sick people. We had to get them out somehow. We were trying to make a safe channel out of the city to get these people out. The only way out of the city at that time was across the bridge, through the lines of the attacking Serbs. You know all about these people, these *Kuffar*, of course. They would not let the women and children go.' Jimmy knew that the extremists used *Kuffar* when they meant a group of people they despised.

'The Kosovo Liberation Army had been trying for three weeks to create a safe passage without success. Don't think, brothers, that they failed because they were weak or didn't try hard enough. Oh no. They were some of the best and fiercest fighters I've ever seen. But all they had and all we, *Jaish an Noor wass Salaam*, had, was light arms. We were heavily outnumbered, at least seven to one. The Serbs had artillery, armour, and air support, helicopter gun-ships, fighter planes, and all the things any modern army has. We had AK-47s and some RPG's, and we had each other. More importantly, we had with us the man who is shortly about to come and talk to you. And, of course, we had Allah on our side.'

Why is Allah always on your side? Jimmy wondered. *What's so good about your black arse?* Now he remembered Zoya and Tony discussing some war, ages ago. Jimmy heard the murmurs of astonishment rippling through the room; he could not help but be impressed by the story, if it was true.

'We knew that. But it's scary when you see thousands upon thousands, and yet more endless thousands of them facing you, bristling with weapons and bombs. You know what they want to do with you. You can see the lust of revenge written in their eyes. Let me tell you, my *bros*, there were literally tens of thousands of them. I don't care who you are – it makes your knees shake, and your body quake. It's enough to loosen your bowels.'

This was greeted with laughter. One of the youngsters in the back responded, 'Yeah! I'd fuckin' shite mah fuckin' pants bro', and probably piss meself too.'

'Exactly,' said Dwayne.

'Yeah, Shabbir, but you shite in yo' pants every time yo' Momma calls you in for yo' deena,' replied another, to much raucous laughter.

*

A smile flickered across the speaker's face for the briefest moment. He remembered what it was like to be a black kid growing up in the worst part of Tower Hamlets, a hard-bitten and intractable neighbourhood of inner city London. The language did not surprise or shock him. Not much did after three spells in Brixton Prison, which had loomed large in his imagination and his life. He knew many boys who had ended up there from the ghetto he had grown up in.

'Didn't get very far did you, Dwayne?' His mother would say in her heavy Jamaican accent every time he was 'sent down.' He would get a lecture every time she visited, usually on Sundays after church, when she was feeling particularly evangelical. He never knew his father. His mother told him he died when she was in Jamaica and pregnant with him, so she decided to come to 'Hiinglaand on de boat,' to give him a better life. 'You isn't going get far in life, you kno', if you keep t'eavin dem cars, dealin that ganja, yo kno'? You is gonna live in this stink hole prison, you know? In fac' – you mark my words – you is gonna die in

Brixton, if you don't come to the Truth and the Light that is our Lord and Saviour Jesus Christ. Hallelujah!'

Every week was the same, the same loving lecture delivered in the same way. She did not know how to be any different. As an evangelical Christian, she proselytised in Tower Hamlets on most days, standing almost all day outside the library, giving anyone who would listen the true message. She never tired of saving as many souls as she could.

'Me prays for you Dwayne, me son, and forgives you, prays so very hard every day and every night that Jesus Christ finds you and you find Him and bow down before Him. He can help you. He died for our sins, Dwayne. He is the Lord Almighty.'

Some days she would get agitated and raise her voice. 'He loves you so. He loves us all and I pray he cast the devil out of your heart. He is our Lord and Saviour. Hallelujah. Hallelujah. HALLELUJAH!' she shouted, before leaving him.

Dwayne found the light during his third visit to Brixton Prison, the light of Islam. It ended his years of darkness and confusion. He felt as if all these years he had been drowning and slowly suffocating to death, and then suddenly somebody had grabbed him by his shoulders and lifted him clear of the water. He gulped down the fresh sweet air of Islam's teachings in huge and unashamed swallows. He barely dared believe fifteen years had passed, during which he had learnt more and travelled further than he ever thought possible. His mother had then abandoned him to Satan, whom she felt sure now had full possession of his soul.

Dwayne preferred to call himself a revert, not a convert, for he had learned and believed that everyone is born into a state of innocence, of purity. So Dwayne reverted back to Islam and became Dawood. No one ever called him that, and he was still Dwayne.

Dwayne continued, 'This man did it. He created a safe channel so that the women and children could get out. He did it. Do you know how he saved these thousands of lives? He led them over the only bridge standing, brothers. Yes. That's right. The same one held by the Serbs. He cleared a safe passage right through the Serbs, right through their tanks and armoured divisions, right under the nose of General Mladic.'

The small room reverberated with shouts of '*Allah O Akbar! Allah O Akbar!*' The young men that Dwayne had strategically placed in the crowd before the meeting instigated the chants.

'He did it in four hours. In four hours. Can you believe it, brothers?

The Serbs were powerless in front of this man. What the KLA couldn't do in weeks, what NATO did not manage in months, he did in four hours.'

'*Subhan Allah! Subhan Allah!*' shouted Dwayne's boys, followed by the others in the room. They jumped to their feet now, all of them excitedly raising their fists in the air after every *Subhan Allah*. Jimmy remembered *Subhan Allah* meant Allah is perfect, but he kept quiet.

Dwayne waved them down smiling. 'And do you know how he did this? He did it with the help of Allah. With the help of Allah and His Angels.'

*

Angels? What the fuck is he on? Must be shootin the shit, thought Jimmy.

'Yes. It's true. We saw them with our own eyes – great figures dressed all in white, dominating the horizon. The Serbs soldiers we captured swore they saw them. *Subhan Allah!* Even the *Kuffar*, brothers, even the *Kuffar*, even they were witness to Allah's miracle. The bullets did not touch our leader and only seven of our brothers were *Shaheed*, martyred, only seven of our commandos and hundreds of them killed. Hundreds. The Battle of Kosovo Polje 28th June 1389 – one of their heaviest defeats ever by the Muslims – and then July 1995, when our brothers smashed through them.'

Jimmy had not fully realised that Muslims had been around since 1389; he usually associated Islam with the existence of Pakistan, and at most, Saudi Arabia.

'*Fight against them so that Allah will punish them by your hands and disgrace them, and give you victory over them and heal the breasts of a believing people.*' Surah 9, Verse 14.'

Jimmy felt that Dwayne often quoted the pertinent versus and memorised them in Arabic and English, so he could prove the validity of his struggle to his audience.

'Their bullets couldn't touch us. Their artillery misfired when faced with this great man, and their planes bombed miles wide. One of the Serb pilots later insisted that he saw someone, a huge figure dressed all in white flowing robes, tall as the hills, catching the bombs and missiles and throwing them into the mountains and fields away from the Muslims. That is a sworn testimony of a Serb fighter pilot, brothers. Who did he see?

'And Allah drove back those who disbelieved in their rage, they gained no advantage. Allah sufficed to the believers in the fighting. And Allah is Ever All Strong Almighty.' Surah Al Ahzab, Chapter 33 Verse 25.'

Dwayne closed his eyes as he recited the Arabic and then translated into English. Jimmy pulled his fingers down his scar and wondered how seriously they took all this fantasy. The speaker seemed impassioned, as if he believed every word. *How do they find time to do all this?* he thought. *When I'm workin' I don't even get a shit break. How do they make a living?*

'And how did Allah suffice for the believers in the fighting? By sending against the disbelievers a severe wind and troops of Angels. God will send down Angels to fight with the *Momineen*, the 'True Believers'. This is the truth. Angels fought with us. Brothers, do you know how many Muslim guerrilla groups they were?' He held up his right hand with his palm facing the audience fingers outspread. 'Five groups of six men each. That's all – thirty men, led by this great man.' He curled his fingers into a fist and raised his fist towards the ceiling in a salute reminiscent of the Black Panther's, and then closed his eyes with his head bowed.

'*Allah O Akbar!*' the audience shouted.

The speaker paused and looked at them for a while. Jimmy followed his gaze. *He's very scientific in measuring the effect he has on people*, he thought, *and I bet he's rehearsed this until he can whisper it in his sleep*.

'Don't be fooled by anything anyone says. This is not a one-off unique occurrence; this miracle didn't just happen in Bosnia. This miracle from the *Ghayb*, this amazing miraculous help from the unseen, it happened in Kosovo, in Palestine, in Afghanistan, in Kashmir, and in Iraq.'

Jimmy's brow wrinkled and he puckered his lips as he tried to place the countries in the right geographical zones and failed. He only knew that Kashmir was near Pakistan.

'*Allah O Akbar!*' The shouts of 'God is Great!' reached a new level with the mention of Iraq.

'This man, *Shaikh* Abu Umar, this is what it is to be a MAN. *Ar Rijaal*, brothers, means a man, a true man; this is how the great Muslim men before us were, the great heroes we read about as children. Not these soft, puny, boy-girls that you see out there every day. I can't tell what they are any more – boy, or girl. The fact is, they don't know what they are themselves.'

What the fuck am I doing here? He ain't a man until he's tried to take over someone else's patch on the street and not moved from his corner when the enemies come running in gangs, Jimmy thought. *If he don't flinch when the bullets whistle in his ears, then he's a man.*

'I'll tell you a secret. You've all seen The Wizard of Oz? Bros, I loved that movie when I was a kid. Who can tell me how the Wicked Witch of the West died?'

What the hell? I must sell this guy some Maall, *yeah,* thought Jimmy, *but he seems high without drugs.* The Mosque Elders, of which a few had attended the meeting, had no cultural reference point and stared, stony-faced, at Dwayne. Everyone else shouted out the answer.

'That's right. She just shrivelled up melted away, disappeared in a puff of smoke when Dorothy threw water on her. Let me tell you, brothers: that is exactly what these *Kuffar* soldiers are.'

Jimmy looked around, unable to stop his eyes wandering, amazed that the crowd could be transfixed by such talk. He knew the value of propaganda on the street, but the men and boys looked as if their faces had been stapled into puppet-like smiles. They simultaneously raised wooden arms and shouted, '*Allah O Akbar! Allah O Akbar!*' together as Dwayne affirmed their suspicions that the West's soldiers were all pussy-cowards.

'It doesn't matter if they're British, French, Italian, and especially American. They just want to *Get home to my mommy in time for Christmas dinner and open my presents underneath the Christmas tree,*' he said in an American accent, with a high-pitched falsetto. The audience roared, completely entertained. Jimmy smiled at Dwayne's accent and actions.

'That's all they want and that's all they ever think of – how to run away from the fighting as fast as they can.'

Jimmy watched with admiration. He knew the speaker had them.

'And you know why? Because they don't believe. They don't believe in nothing. They fight for nothing, they live for nothing, and they definitely don't want to die for nothing. But a Muslim, when he fights, he knows he fights for Allah. If he lives he has conquered his enemy, but if he is lucky enough to die fighting in the path of Allah – he is a *Shaheed* – a martyr. When a 'True Believer' stares down the barrel of a

Kuffar gun, he sees success. If he lives he has won, and if he dies he has won. He cannot be defeated.'

'*Allah O Akbar! Allah O Akbar!*' reverberated around the small room.

Jimmy could understand fighting to make a living to sell his *Maall*, to expand his patch in the woods; his 'hood' had become the 'woods' between him and his boys. Dying for religion seemed wholly unnecessary.

'*Think not of those who are killed in the way of Allah as dead. Nay, they are alive, with their Lord, and they have provision. They rejoice in what Allah has bestowed upon them of His Bounty, rejoicing for the sake of those who have not yet joined them, but are left behind not yet martyred, that on them no fear shall come, nor shall they grieve. They rejoice in a Grace and a Bounty from Allah and that Allah will not waste the reward of the believers.* Surah 3, Verse 169 to 171.' Dwayne recited the Arabic, and translated into English.

Despite his discomfort, Jimmy could not help but be intrigued by the recitation, although he did not understand the Arabic. Ahmad talked about praying and inner peace. These guys seemed obsessed with dying. *They should spend a few nights in my streets*, he thought; the woods would soon grant their wish.

'This is just what these *Kuffar* soldiers are, terrified little soft puny boy-girls. Don't let their noise and bluster kid you, don't be deluded by their technology and military hardware – that's just so that they can fool themselves and play at being Rambo. I tell you, when they is face-to-face with real men, they just melt away.' He waited for the derisory laughter to die down. 'They are losing 'The War on Terror'. They are losing everywhere. In Iraq, Kashmir, Palestine – and boy, are they losing big time in Afghanistan!'

Jimmy did not really care about these expressions he had picked up whilst passing through the living room, hearing the news. The War on Terror for him was part of an ongoing racist fight to keep the darkies down, to never let them succeed anywhere in the world. The consensus of opinion on the street was unanimous: they hate us. *That's why we've had to make our own way; there can be no right or wrong if you're a Paki.*

"The War on Terror' – that's a joke, for a start. Ask the Iraqi and Afghan orphans about 'Terror'. At least a million people have died since the 2003 invasion of Iraq by the US, a minimum of one million. These are just ordinary people. Civilians, somebody's mothers and sisters and children. Your fathers, brothers, sisters and children. How many Abu Musab Ar Zarqawis are there? How many *Shaikh* Osama Bin Ladins are there? Not a million, I guarantee you.'

Jimmy knew of Osama Bin Ladin, but had never heard of the other one. *What's that got to do with me?* he thought. *He ain't a Paki, but then, neither am I.* He realised that Dwayne had hit the right note. Some of the men turned to their neighbours and nodded, some gesticulated with their hands, waving, as if shooing the *Kuffar* away from the Muslim lands. The face of every man in the crowd, that Jimmy could see, showed disgust and anger. He knew Iraq was an agonising, painful, festering, open-pus-weeping sore in the Muslim mind, for the liberals and the hardcore alike. He knew enough politics to realise nothing was guaranteed to get more reaction, except perhaps Palestine.

'Let me get back to our leader, *Shaikh* Abu Umar. This brother, this hero, took out three machine-gun nests single-handedly in the mountains of Kashmir. The Indian Army had never seen anything like it. A division of Serb tanks utterly destroyed in Kosovo. Whole battalions decimated in Iraq. Need I go on? The *Shaikh* is living proof, is living proof of the true face of what absolute *Imaan* can achieve. This great and true leader of the Muslim world is a hero. No – he's much more than that. He belongs to the real *Mujahideen*. He is a *Ghazi*.'

Despite himself, Jimmy felt fascinated by the idea of fighting a war. A strange shiver ran through him as he remembered his father telling him stories of great Muslim *Ghazis* returning from *Jihad*. He knew a Muslim who lived after a Holy battle was a *Ghazi*. Those who did not return were Martyrs.

'Here he is, brothers, the man you've been desperate to meet in person. *The Saif Al Islam*, The Sword of Islam, the one and only, salute you: *Shaikh* Abu Umar.'

Everyone stood up. They were all desperate to see the man who had achieved such miraculous victories over such a long period of time against the *Kuffar* wherever he had fought, and still lived to tell the tale. Alive and, unbelievably, here in London. They reached a climax of shouting and chanting. The crowd became too excited to stand still now, and most of them raised their arms above their heads with every exclamation.

'*Allah O Akbar! Allah O Akbar!*' Interspersed with 'Abu Umar! Abu

Umar! We want Abu Umar! We want Abu Umar! Abu Umar!'

With that the door opened and a whole group of bodyguards quickly took up positions around the room, placing themselves strategically at specially predetermined points. Four stood facing the crowd; they forced the men back, creating more room at the front. Two stood on each side, leaving an empty central area. Pairs of bodyguards stood in each corner of the room and a couple stood in the centre facing the audience. Two of them were guarding the inside of the door, and yet more protected the outside.

Jimmy noticed they all wore similar navy blue tracksuits bulging and strained by the muscles underneath, had short cropped hair, and wore impenetrable sunglasses. He could see they all looked under thirty and were incredibly fit and well toned. He noticed that their calloused and gnarled hands and feet and expressionless faces bore testimony to their toughness. The bodyguards, like everyone else, did not wear shoes in the mosque. They took up their positions with military precision, and communicated with each other in low whispers through their microphones and earpieces. No one had been allowed to enter the mosque. All entrances and exits were guarded; he had been one of the last to be granted entrance, and everyone who had entered the small room earlier had been professionally searched. They had selected one of the smaller rooms in the mosque despite the availability of three large halls. *Maybe it's much easier to control and monitor the crowd in a more confined space*, he thought.

Jimmy stood with the rest of the crowd and mumbled when they chanted '*Allah O Akbar!*' Although he knew what the words meant, he did not understand what was going on. Some of the other teenage lads seemed as confused as he was, and they looked around at each other with raised eyebrows. Jimmy just shrugged, but by now they were desperate for the arrival of Abu Umar, although Jimmy knew most of them had never met him before and many of them had not even heard of him before tonight. Along with most of the gathered men, Jimmy's eyes flicked from one bodyguard to the other. He felt intimidated by the presence of the guards. Their demeanour and body language sent a clear message: *Do not mess!*

They spoke to him in the base language of the street, a code Jimmy could decipher more quickly than any verbal linguistics. He had learned that language quickly as a boy, growing up as he had done on the tough streets of inner city London. He had to show respect to the seniors and the aristocrats of the gang world or not survive, just as he now demanded respect and obedience from his own teenagers.

Jimmy looked at the man who exhorted the crowd to passionate chanting and, despite his determination to dislike everything about these people; he clenched his great fists and felt admiration for the speaker. Jimmy looked at the black man now, as he held a raised fist with his head bowed, but he could not understand the crowd's urge to copy Dwayne's Black Panther salute.

'We want Abu Umar! We want Abu Umar! Abu Umar!' they all shouted.

CHAPTER 9

London
Three black cars screeched and slowed down outside the back of the mosque. Before they had fully stopped, bodyguards jumped out of the first and last cars. They ran and surrounded the central car and opened the rear doors, shielding the occupants with their bodies.

Abu Umar stepped out slowly; guards hemmed him in, and covered all four sides. The cars sped off, with their blinding bright headlights jumping over the bumps and bathing the courtyard of the mosque. They strafed the tarmac, like searchlights looking for escaped men from a Nazi prisoner of war camp in a World War II movie. Abu Umar strode towards the mosque. He could hear the cheering and chants of 'Abu Umar! Abu Umar!' As he neared the back door, which opened one step before he arrived, he kicked off his shoes without breaking step. His personal bodyguard immediately picked them up and bagged them.

As expected, Abu Umar saw the low lights through the door, with faces blurred in the artificial twilight. He entered the small backroom to wild adulation and shouts of '*Allah O Akbar!* Abu Umar! *Allah O Akbar!*' The Muslim equivalent of Mick Jagger's arrival.

Dwayne's boys came forward and initiated the hugging and kissing of Abu Umar's face and hands. Only the inner circle, the trusted, were allowed close enough to kiss him. The bodyguards firmly kept back all the others who tried to emulate Dwayne's boys. The bodyguards, however, could not quieten the crowd nor make them sit down.

Abu Umar walked calmly through the crowd, which parted and left a clear passage for him, moving out of either deference or fear. He kissed Dwayne on the cheeks, and smiled and spoke to him briefly. Dwayne towered over him – Abu Umar was of average height. Dwayne bowed down to kiss Abu Umar's hands as a sign of respect, as Abu Umar had been his teacher, and then left the central stage area. Abu Umar looked resplendent and radiant in his eastern garb. He had the accoutrements and appearance of a *Shaikh* a thousand years ago from Bukhara. A brilliant white turban made his head look bulbous, and his chestnut coloured *Jilbab*, a long flowing traditional robe, suited his short auburn beard, which was trimmed neatly on a square jaw and pale face.

Abu Umar turned and looked at the crowd of gathered men and boys. A cave-like silence filled the vacuum, sucking the breath from the chests of the crowd.

At Abu Umar's left side hung a curved sword in a plain scabbard: it was a scimitar, a *shamshir*, a *saif*. In his right hand was the Qur'an. He had gathered the props before entering the room. In the central dais area his personal bodyguards brought forward a large clay pit bowl, sitting on a low tripod stand. Abu Umar stood behind the clay bowl and stared implacably at the gathered crowd. He had the ability, rare even amongst experienced generals, to look at the assembled men in such a way that each one felt as if he had looked directly into his eyes, and each felt he was addressing him personally. Despite the dim light, Abu Umar knew his strange amber eyes glowed. Every member of the audience felt he was the only man in the room, even though Abu Umar had not yet spoken.

He flicked his arm out, the only part of his body to move. He gestured towards the tripod as he opened his clenched left hand, and something that seemed like pieces of silver dust fell into the clay pit. Instantly, flames jumped up, and seemed to respond immediately to his command. Within seconds a fierce fire burned in the clay pit. It seemed as if the blue flames that grew tall would consume the whole room and the mosque with it, so that the people in the front two rows jerked back. He now stood behind the fire so that the crowd could see his face, spectral through the flames.

He started speaking in Arabic: he spoke softly, but his voice carried clearly. The silence allowed his words to flow to the back of the room. He stared, but he did not move. He looked at the gathered men and it gave him satisfaction that they seemed to physically wilt from the intent gaze caused by his yellow tiger's eyes, as much as from the fear of the flames. The fire seemed to grow with his voice and the flames danced, now incandescent blue and white. He lifted his empty left hand towards the flames and immediately green and bright red fire shot up and mingled with the blue and white.

Abu Umar only performed staged impersonations when absolutely necessary. He always used momentous moments from Muslim history. The recruitment crisis had become acute, and the work slowed to a virtual standstill. Thousands of fighters had been killed in Afghanistan and Iraq, and because of the Pakistan government's anti-religious drive numerous *madrassas*, religious seminaries, had been closed. Abu Umar knew he had to have volunteers to continue the *Jihad*, and bring about the victory of Islam.

Today, he was enacting the story of Abdur Rahman III, the Andalusian Caliph. This was his favourite story of all the stories he had heard as a boy – of how the Caliph had treated a mission of Spanish Christians, who came from the north to negotiate with him. The Caliph wanted to impress and awe them by showing them the splendour of his kingdom. So he had lined the twelve miles of road, leading from Cordoba to the gate of Madinat Al Zahra, with a double row of soldiers on both sides, who held aloft their naked scimitars with their tips touching to form a roof. The Christian ambassadors were led between these double rows of soldiers as through a covered way.

Abu Umar imagined the terror that this sight must have induced in the visitors. Further, the Caliph had the ground from this gateway to the reception area of his court covered with brocade. At certain intervals along the way, he seated dignitaries who could have been mistaken for kings because of their rich dress; each time the ambassadors caught sight of one of these men, the Christians fell to the ground before them, mistaking each of them for the Caliph. Then they would be told, 'Raise your heads! This is but a servant of his servants'. Abu Umar smiled to himself, enjoying their stupidity, as he recalled the story in detail, told by his teacher. Finally, he remembered, when they reached a sandy courtyard, there was a man with coarse clothes. He sat on the ground, with his head bent forward. Before him was a copy of the Qur'an, a sword and a fire. 'This is the ruler,' the ambassadors were told, who then threw themselves to the ground.

Now Abu Umar addressed the crowd with the same words that Caliph Abdur Rahman III had said to the Christian ambassadors. *Even if they don't know the story, they will be impressed*, thought Abu Umar. He kept his face stern and his eyes constant.

'God has commanded us, O you people, to call upon you to submit to this.' With these words the Caliph had showed them the Qur'an. Now Abu Umar held the Qur'an aloft in his right hand. 'If you refuse, we shall compel you with this.' The Caliph had indicated the sword. Abu Umar did the same. 'And if we kill you, then you will go into that.' The Caliph had pointed at the fire, and Abu Umar pointed to the fire, in his mind's eye copying the echo of the centuries. Then Abu Umar jumped in the air and jerked out the scimitar in one movement. He brandished it, slicing the air, the Qur'an now in his left hand as he repeated history in his own style. The gaudy colours, the sweet green and plum purple of the flames, reflected in the steel of the sword as he waved it above his head.

The crowd now became amazed and awed. Their breathlessness increased the excitement in him; he knew some of them had heard the story of The Qur'an, the Sword and the Fire. Abu Umar felt like weeping as he was reminded of the great days of the Muslims that turned arid Spain into a garden, who took Europe out of the Dark Ages and into its rebirth. Al Andalus was the mother of modern Europe. He thought of the art and architecture, science and amazing achievements, the knowledge in the numerous libraries. The looted libraries of Toledo and other cities had led directly to the Renaissance, brought about the founding of most of the great universities of Europe, including Oxford and the Sorbonne. He hated them more because no one accepted this fact in Western culture anymore. It was not taught in schools or universities, and a whole millennia of Muslim achievement and contribution to the world had been deliberately and maliciously written out of history.

Spain: the stories of the Muslims being wiped out of the Iberian Peninsula, and the massacres of the Inquisition, were like painful personal memories to Abu Umar. *Why don't these boys know and feel this?* he thought. *Their parents have failed. The Spanish still re-enact battles of the Muslim defeats, like the Corpus Christi in Granada. They celebrate their great* Matamoros, *Moor Killers. Well now the Moor has returned, not for his last sigh, but instead to roar in the face of Christendom again. Here I am. Tremble and fear me and quakingly obey, Muslim and non-believers alike: the message of Allah! Soon you will weep at my victory… the victory of* Matakuffaros, *the* Kuffar *Killers.*

The gathered men shifted, some leaned forward and touched their faces. Abu Umar gathered himself to his full height, imperceptibly blew out a few long breaths, closed his eyes and recited:

The Butterfly Hunter

Shame of Al Andalus haunts our dreams
Sweet garden of light and reason, philosophy
What justice became you?
O bitter wine goblet of Ferdinand and Isabella –
Filled your belly with fire

You drank sulphur suffering after the nightingale left your boughs.
Souls of cities, no more quenched by fragrant juice of learning,
No longer oranges cooled in the fountains of Seville
But the pomegranates of the Sierras still stain your skin!

Why quiet, O Great Mosque of Cordoba?
Deafening silent screams sing rape of marble and jasper
Madinat Al Zahra – spreading cedars and sweet myrtle fed huge by your blood
Satiated Rose and Rosemary veil face under silver leafed olive groves.

Why now inarticulate in Al Andalus, the song of Ibn Arabi?
Left now The Versatile Arabian, how pale your reflection of Al Buraq?
La Giralda – in the minaret they imprisoned the slit throated Bilal
The muezzin silenced for all eternity...

Abu Umar recited the poem again. Despite his Arabic lilt, he knew his voice enthralled the silent crowd. He locked their souls with his unblinking eyes. His keen sense of timing and sensitivity to men's emotions had been sharpened over the years. Now, in the smoky gloom he noticed a few of the men were crying. *Some*, he thought, *are feeling the history of Al Andalus*.

'Cry! Cry now like a woman, because you could not defend it like a man!' He waved the sword again over his head, pointed it at the crowd so that each man was highlighted with the tip. 'When Abu Abdullah lost his kingdom of Granada to the Christians in 1492, the last Muslim kingdom in Spain, his mother said these words to him as he looked back for the last time at Granada, and wept.' Abu Umar had hooked his lion's claws into their souls and now controlled them with his tiger's eyes.

*

This display affected Jimmy deeply because of the striking colours in the darkness, the words and hypnotic power of Abu Umar's voice. Although he had not understood the entire poem, it held him in its spell like a spider's web binding around his heart. Jimmy felt nausea welling up inside him. The sword – the *saif* – took him back to his teenage visit to Pakistan, to that fantastic apparition-filled day in Ramnagar. Suddenly, he could hear the voices of his ghostly apparitions clearly again. The first time it had happened since his visit to the village.

His ancestors whispered to him, and he looked around to see if anyone else could hear them. All were oblivious to him. The voices were there again, now asking and insistent, repeating the same questions: *Who are you? What are you?* over and over again. Jimmy could not see anyone.

'And I say now to you – weep! You should cry. Weep like little girls because your children are starved, your fathers and brothers massacred, your mothers humiliated and your sisters defiled.'

'*Takbeer!*' one of Dwayne's boys shouted.

'*Allah O Akbar!*' came the reply from the crowd.

'Are you going to sit by while they massacre you? They have already killed one million Iraqi children.'

'No! No!' Shouts reverberated around the small room, anger and humiliation showing on the faces of the men.

'Children, just kids like you have at home, just like the ones you see playing in the streets, walking to school in the mornings. The same – just kids.'

Who are you? What are you? asked the voices. Jimmy jerked his head from side to side as if to clear his mind, but the voices only became louder and said the same thing over and over again.

'Are you going to let rip them open your pregnant sisters' wombs?' Abu Umar pointed directly at a teenager in the first row. 'Like in Kosovo?' The teenager shook his head. 'Are you going to let them rape all your sisters?' Abu Umar said, pointing to another at the back of the room.

'No! Never! NO!' The group now stood en masse, and their cries rose to fever pitch. Jimmy felt hemmed in and claustrophobic in the crush of men. Across the room, he saw a new bodyguard enter through the door from the outside and approach the dais, to speak with Abu Umar.

'Are you going to let them slit Bilal's throat?' asked Abu Umar.

Jimmy knew Bilal was a freed black slave who had achieved a never-before-imagined high status with the Prophet. Bilal had been the first Muezzin in Islamic history; he had led the first *adhan*, the call to prayer.

Abu Umar continued: 'Is the *adhan* forever silenced in Europe? Who will take revenge for the blood of Bilal? Who?' Abu Umar had to shout now to make his voice carry.

The mob was at frenzy point, with shouts of, 'No, never, no!' interspersed with screams of *'Allah O Akbar!'*

Jimmy saw the bodyguard whisper something in Abu Umar's ear – then Jimmy thought he recognised him. Hamza... his childhood friend from Mosque. Hamza! Jimmy stared at his familiar triangular face, with its long thin nose with flared nostrils at the end, leading to a feminine small mouth and a pointed chin. He had a thin moustache now.

The voices in Jimmy's head grew ever louder, now deafening, and he resisted the temptation to put his hands over his ears. The sight of Hamza again after years overwhelmed Jimmy; he thought he would vomit and collapse. Then the ghosts of his ancestors appeared in front of his eyes, and he could see them as clearly as he had on that long-ago heat-filled day in the graveyard. They floated above and around him, pressed onto him, took his breath away.

Who are you? What are you? they said, still louder and louder. He could see them now. The ghosts floated above the heads of the crowd. They laughed, and seemed to mock him. He brought his hands up to his ears, closed his eyes tight, but it made no difference. He could hear and see them in exactly the same way. He had to escape. Jimmy pushed himself through the tight pack of men, but it was impossible to force his way through the roused throng.

'Let me through. I'm going to be sick.' No one heard him. 'Let me get through!' The sword, the voices and Hamza combined made Jimmy panic, and he lost control. He started pulling the men out of the way. The first few teenagers he moved easily, and initially no one paid any attention to him. When Jimmy met heavier resistance amongst the jostling crowd he pulled at a few, and then smashed a couple of them with his fists. He lunged for the door at the side of the stage, but he had to pass by Abu Umar. An ecstatic member of the audience held onto Jimmy's right arm. Jimmy realised the man had become frenzied, caught up in the spirit of the occasion, and the man laughed and pumped Jimmy's arm up and down with both hands, with a fixed grin on his face.

'Let fuckin' go of me!' Jimmy shouted. 'Hamza! Hamza! It's me, man. It's Jimmy,' he called out. The man let go of his arm and he fell forward, lurching towards the stage, towards Hamza and Abu Umar. The old memories swamped him. His voice became strangled, and his face stretched as he shouted for his old friend. The bodyguards at the front reacted; they pounced on Jimmy.

'Hey, look at that guy – he tried to attack Abu Umar,' said one man at the front, pointing to Jimmy. 'Another assassination attempt on Abu Umar!'

'Don't let him escape. Get him!' said another.

The crowd gathered around Jimmy, and helped the bodyguards attack him. They thundered blows onto him, so that blood poured from his broken nose, his eyes turned black, and plumed bruises appeared like molehills over his body. Jimmy made a huge effort, and with a supreme struggle crawled and lifted his head up slightly. He saw that the swarm around him had attracted Abu Umar's attention, but his personal bodyguards surrounded Abu Umar and were trying to push him towards the exit.

'Stop! Right now,' he said. The guards tried to push him through the door. 'No,' he shouted. He pushed one of the bodyguards out of the way and flung another easily to the side, with a strength that belied his slight build. The surprised men gathered themselves, and followed him. As Abu Umar got to the pack he pulled men off Jimmy with a proficient mastery, taking a man's collar, shirt or belt in each hand and flinging them aside like a man picking apples off a tree.

'Stop! I want to talk to this man.' The confusion and violence stopped. Two of the men who were kneeling on top of Jimmy climbed off. The others stopped punching him and looked up at Abu Umar. Scarlet streaks stained their knuckles and the carpet of the mosque. Jimmy gasped and grunted, bloodied, barely conscious.

*

Imam Younis sat in his offices in the mosque, swallowed some painkillers with *Chai*, and pretended to close his ears to the noise emanating from across the other side of the mosque. He remembered how earlier in the day, despite his battered face, he had taken his wife out to see her arch-rival. At least he ensured she, Fatima his wife's enemy, would see them as they drove through Fatima's street. Younis now owned a Mercedes S500, it would no longer be on monthly payments, and next month he would have the £50,000. Thanks to Jimmy, he would pay for the car in one lump sum. He had been dreaming of one for years. He hated Abdullah, who ran the mosque across the road. Nazli, Younis' wife had made an enemy of Fatima, Abdullah's wife, on the first day she had arrived from Pakistan by announcing that she would take over the local women's circles, and poaching two dozen women from under Fatima's nose.

'*Areh Nazli chal Fatima ko jealous karte hai*. Let's go and make Fatima jealous,' Younis had said. Nazli suited her when she was young and lithe: *Meri nazak Nazli*, my delicate Nazli, Younis would call her. Now the name sat as incongruously on her as the rolls of fat on her abdomen and the slabs of cellulite that hung from her buttocks like some heavy rubber cloth, too weighty for her small bones. However, Younis doted on her, and called her his *dhumba*, a sheep fattened for the slaughter on Eid. Despite his wandering tendencies, Younis admired Nazli's flesh; he enjoyed watching the excess of adiposity that flowed and jiggled, stealing light and gravity. She was a source of never-ending pride for Younis when they had returned triumphant, he the Caesar and she his Cleopatra, to their village in Pakistan for summer holidays.

Nazli drew admiring, if amused, gasps from the tinder-dry native women, whose bones had become kindling from fetching water three miles twice a day and yearly birthings like the village goats, but with less nutrition. A sure sign of success, that he had made it in England, which had caused the women to renew to fever pitch their exhortations to their sons to go to England so they might achieve the same levels of elephantine lard. Most provincial *Imam*s' wives were lucky to get two *rotis* every other day. All were wholly draped, milk-bottle anaemic, and had rarely travelled in a bus. Nazli had been more isolated than most of them. She had never seen a TV before arriving in England, but now she had fifty-two inches of high definition and two huge satellite dishes. She watched all the channels in the languages she could not understand, and especially loved watching Fala Brasil, the Chinese and Korean channels. When her friends came around she sat there, an unmoving Jabba the Hut, shouting orders to the teenage girl she had brought back to serve her from her last visit to Mirpur.

Nazli loved displaying her gargantuan immobility, bedecked in large thick gold chunks of jewellery, for she would always say, *what was the point of gold if not to wear it?* Who would see it in the bank or bedroom? Even her serving girl and the village girls herding their goats could claim to have vast amounts, and no one would know. Younis had always said he would keep her like a princess when she came to England. He had kept his promise.

'*Miki vi Innggerrrlaand karo. Meh vi valayat jasah. Miki vi Innggerrrlaand karo, naah.*' Take me to England. I want to go to the land of the White Man. Take me to England too. Nazli had wailed in *Mirpuri* to anyone who would listen, while she had waited, wringing her hands harder every day, for her visa after they were married. Younis had left her behind for a year, the most difficult of her life, to continue his *Imam* duties.

In her teenage years she had been lithe as the saplings she planted in her father's fields, and slim as the kindling firewood she carried for miles everyday from the forest. Now it had all become too much to click on the cooker because of her headaches and pain all over her body, and the Asian channels played hypnotic movies and music. So she did not cook most days, but ordered home deliveries of three twelve-inch pizzas for ten pounds, for a *tannah*, as she called it and a twelve-piece family bucket of southern fried chicken and chips, with a free portion of coleslaw.

Younis had waited for Nazli to struggle into the car. As he watched her he thought again of how he had very recently bought the Mercedes S500 even though he had to make interest payments on it, but he would soon be free of those. He had kept this fact secret from everyone, for of course 'eating' interest, as they said in Urdu, meant filling your belly with hellfire – something the Jewish usurers had excelled at throughout the centuries, as he regularly reminded his flock.

They had cruised around the Asian areas. Younis stopped and doubleparked in front of the *Sagar Halwai*, the Ocean/Sky Sweet shop on Southall High Street. He knew the stallholder on the street outside, who sublet the pavement for a daily rate. Oblivious to the obstruction Younis had caused with other drivers honking their horns, he casually made the little man with the greasy moustache – in gleaming overalls and matching white hat, looking like Norman Wisdom playing the milk delivery boy in 'The Early Bird' – fry a whole new batch of *jalebis* for Nazli. A little man stood behind the tiny white stall with orange writing on it. *Fresh jalebis cooked in front of you every day!* the sign said in English and Urdu. The small man never smiled, but splashed half the boiling oil from the huge black cauldron onto the pavement.

'*Jaldi kar yaar. Jaldi!* Hurry up. Can't you see all the traffic is blocked up? Quickly!' said Younis, and made him turn the gas cooker to maximum.

'*Ji Imam Sahib, ji-ji ek minit laga gah*. Yes sir. It will be ready in a jiffy, sir,' said the small man, his voice bright. Oily in patches, his face became scrunched up like a discarded brown paper bag after the *jalebis* had been eaten.

Younis stroked his beard and adjusted his *karakul* cap to a more rakish angle, and ordered half a pound of chicken and half a pound of fish pakoras from the serving boy inside the shop without going in, shouting at the boy to bring them out to him. Younis turned to face the sun. He straightened his black woollen *sherwani*, a knee-length doublet with buttons down the front, stretched by his bulging stomach, which he wore over creaseless white *salwar kameez*. Perspiration smeared his forehead as he saw one of Abu Umar's bodyguards pass by on the other side of the road; he turned away and watched the man's reflection as he passed. The *Imam* closed his eyes and massaged his brow. '*Ya Allah, Ya Allah madath*. O Allah, Allah help me,' he said, as he sunned himself on the pavement.

They enjoyed the hot spicy pakoras mixed with the sweet sticky *jalebis* as they slowly drove through Fatima's street. Younis hoped Abdullah would be in as he blared the horn outside his house, ostensibly to attract the attention of Abdullah's neighbour who worked in the mosque for Younis. He kept his hand heavy on the horn even after the neighbour had come out, until Fatima also came out to see who was making all the noise. Younis drummed his fingers on the steering wheel in disappointment that Abdullah was out – *but never mind*, he thought. He would catch Abdullah before *Maghrib* prayers in front of his mosque. Nazli chuckled, her laughter barely discernable, her fat absorbing some of the sound. Younis then talked more loudly and in more animated terms to the neighbour.

'Make sure you're there for the meeting at six tonight! I can't be expected to make tea and sort everything else out, and make sure you pick up two dozen fairy cakes and some cardamoms. We have a planning meeting tonight.' Younis never made tea.

'*Ji Imam Sahib, ji ji*, of course, yes I will, I won't forget,' said the neighbour.

Then Maulana Mohammed Younis Khan *Imam Sahib* dismissed the neighbour with 'And don't forget the cakes.' When the neighbour turned his back Nazli laughed out loud, as she adjusted the *dupatta* on her head to ensure that none of her hair showed in public. Younis saw Fatima's eyebrows become one long dark caterpillar of fury. He frowned to hide his pleasure at the sight of Fatima's face reflected in the shiny black metallic paint, her eyes burning into Nazli. Nazli pressed the buttons to make the windows slide up as smoothly as buffalo double cream. She turned the air conditioning on full, which felt as refreshing as a summer's day. Neither of them acknowledged Fatima; they never had been on speaking terms. Younis glanced at Fatima, unable to look at another man's wife for too long out of propriety – the streets were watching. Nazli stared as her rival stood in the doorway with bare feet, her pursed lips dry and baked, her fists bunched on both hips. Then both Younis and Nazli looked away, as if they had come to see the neighbour all along. Now, job done, Younis set off, turning the car around and driving even more slowly back down Fatima's street.

Younis roared with laughter once he had got past her house, as Fatima was still standing in the doorway, a statue. Both husband and wife slapped each other on the thighs in congratulation. Neither had laughed so much since Nazli had poached the women's circle. '*Dekha. Dekha woh jal ke aur be kali rakh ban gaye thi?* Did you see how she burnt up and became even blacker ash?' asked Younis.

'*Hai hai. Kitna maza aayah na. Aap kitneh acheh hain.* O, it was so pleasurable. How good you are to me,' said Nazli.

'Yes, yes, I am,' replied Younis in English. He imagined Fatima standing on her doorstep immobile for a long while, staring into the street.

*

After they had achieved success at Fatima's, Nazli went to teach the sisters' circle in the women's area of the mosque. Younis could see the women through the wooden *jali* as they fluttered in for their study circle, from his eyrie high up on the balcony. *It's a social event*, thought Younis, *an excuse for the women to talk.*

Their tongues, now loosened from the constraints of household expediency, flew free and exercised their revenge against the torture of silence heaped upon them by their husbands for the whole week. The release, Younis knew, made them smile and giggle like school girls on the first day of their summer holidays. Their propensity and capacity for fatuous chatter like inane parakeets never ceased to amaze him. They would undulate in and out of the women's area, creating a shrill tumult of giggling and laughing, displaying their multi hued and garish clothes. Most wore *salwar kameez*, but the younger ones were more chi-chi, with countless yards of silky material draped over their bodies and trailing long gossamer *dupattas* behind them. Younis knew how necessary a *dupatta* was in the gathering – a long scarf draped over their chests worn by most South Asian women, an enduring symbol of modesty. They exhibited colours that he could not even describe.

The shades seemed to reflect the food; they wore corals, apricots, subtle stains of salmon intermixed with peach and tangerine. Very few outfits had only one colour, instead merging into a kaleidoscope – slight shades of plum, pomegranate, cherry and aubergine interspersed with amber, pink ochre, cinnamon, cardamom, sepia and sienna, topped with bounteous tones of terracotta, intricately woven with gold and silver thread embroidery forming a myriad of patterns. Younis imagined the Moghul palaces of Agra and Fatehpur Sikri where Emperor Akbar had held court, the wives and concubines of the harem gathered together around the inner courtyards to play and splash in the fountains. This evoked in him feelings of pathos and 'Paradise Lost': a golden age of Muslim rule in India.

Younis loved watching them from his secret vantage point high up in the gallery, hidden behind a large wooden *jaali* screen, which was made up of intricate fretwork carving. The *Imam* could not be seen by anyone looking up into the gallery, yet he could see through the *jaali* clearly. Usually the women would spend most of the time eating *chapli* kebabs, samosas and pakoras with that special tamarind sauce Gul Hameed's wife made so well, which Younis regularly hankered after. Nazli would be sure to save Younis some of the food, and especially the tamarind sauce, every Sunday. He salivated unblinkingly as he watched them unpack the food. *They're going to eat before the circle, not even waiting to the end*, he thought, as he ignored the pain form his injuries.

Last Sunday the women had been especially hungry, and Nazli could not give him any food because they had eaten it all. That had put Younis into a wolverine mood, and he stomped round the house and did not speak to Nazli until she made up for it by cooking one of his favourites: spicy roast tandoori chicken. His condition improved significantly after sucking the bones clean on the third portion of chicken. He mopped up the chilli sauce off his plate with the remaining fragments of chicken meat. He hated wasting food – it was sinful. Younis loved the way the sticky, viscous chilli sauce dribbled down his lips and into his beard when he bit deep into the chicken breast. It felt so spicy and sweet, and made his lips tingle.

Seeing Sofia in the women's circle made him think of Ahmad. The *Imam* knew of Jimmy's activities, of course, and how he made his living. The whole mosque congregation pulsated, agog with stories of the Regus family's decline and Jimmy's illicit pursuits. Many times Ahmad had walked in on hushed conversations of the mosque's elders, gathering in the darkened corners of the mosque after prayer times like shoals of small fish that escaped from the light in the centre of the flow, and congregated in the blanket weed and in the pools and eddies near the riverbanks. The *Imam* had seen how The Elder's posse treated Ahmad, yet he had chuckled with them. He did not dare reprimand them, and he did nothing to defend Ahmad.

'And how are you doing with Jimmy?' Younis would ask when they had all settled down, during Jimmy's initial rebellious teenage years. Ahmad would mouth embarrassed mutterings. Younis knew what he really wanted to say was: *Come and stop him selling heroin. Help me.*

The Elders feared the light of exposure, so would change conversations as soon as Ahmad was within earshot. Some would get up and leave, like woodlice scattering when the centre of an old rotten log is exposed to light and air.

Younis felt surprised that Ahmad's shame – he had, of course, heard all the rumours and stories about his son – did not stop him attending the mosque and making all five prayers. Ahmad usually made it to the front row, and if he did not make the front row he made sure he sat in the first three rows. For the Holy Prophet said the front rows are surely better than the last, as the *Imam* often reminded the worshipers, to ensure the mosque would be full on most *Jummah* prayer times, and at least a quarter full at all other prayer times. Younis knew he had targets to meet.

The *Imam* grinned as he thought of how the Elders welcomed Ahmad with toothy smiles, exchanged knowing glances with each other, shuffled on their bottoms without uncrossing their legs and gathered their baggy salwars about them, making room on the floor for Ahmad to sit amongst them. Inevitably, one of them would eventually offer up a cup of cardamom-fragranced Pakistani tea, sweet and steaming, so deeply ingrained was their sense of hospitality and welcome.

Today Younis did not think of tea. He had his car, and Ahmad's son was meeting tonight in the mosque. He had arranged the meeting for *Jaish*, and although he knew he had many quotas still to fill; the memory of his Mercedes S500 made him quiver with pleasure. His bruises would soon heal, and maybe the kebabs that Nazli was sure to save for him would make his cut lips tingle even more. Younis wiped the flecks of saliva away from the corners of his mouth with the back of his hand, as he waited for the leftover food.

Birmingham

Jessica paced the length of her lounge, at home in Solihull. She clutched a phone to her ear whilst biting her thumb with her other hand. 'Hi Ali, it's Jessica.'

'Oh, hi. How are you?' Ali's familiar voice stopped Jessica pacing for a moment. He had been the only one of Hamid's friends and family who had accepted Jessica, and as Hamid's best friend he had often visited them at their Mailbox flat. On most visits he had stood in the centre of the open-plan apartment, and shrugged his disappointment at Auntie Talat and the rest of the family. Jessica had always smiled at his antics, but she knew the *Biradari* system was a xenophobic force field. At times, she felt it had been designed to keep her away from Hamid's inner circle, and Hamid away from her. Although he was on her side, Ali swam with the great whites. She had never wanted to be seen as an albino seal and she had done her best to stop her relationship with Hamid from becoming prey for his mother.

Jessica appreciated Ali's small gestures over the years, like *mitai* from Ambala's, Hamid's favourite Asian sweet shop. She could never eat the rich desserts, but accepted them graciously for Hamid.

'I saw you at the funeral yesterday,' said Ali. 'Although I was too late to do anything about it, sorry. By the time I came out of the prayer hall, after greeting everyone who wanted to pay their respects to Hamid, well, you and Auntie Talat had almost finished your interesting discussion. I did catch the *abshagun*. I could hardly avoid hearing those harridans with Auntie.'

Jessica wanted to say that it was Talat who had started it but instead she paused, walked into the kitchen, and opened a bottle of water. She peered into the mirror and pulled her eyelid down with one finger, and took a sharp intake of breath at the swellings below her eyes, which looked like red warning flags. Her face had lost its pink blush and seemed sallow; the tawny tinge looked like a spreading fever, as if the accusations of Hamid's mother had surged through her skin.

'Are you all right?'

'Yes, yeah. Where are you? I need to see you.' Jessica gulped the water, pushing back her long hair that hung as if devoid of its usual life force, which normally added so much to her personality. The yellow no longer shone like shavings sparked off a goldsmith's crafting wheel.

'It's a bit awkward just now,' said Ali, and she noticed an unusual timbre to his words.

'I just need five minutes.'

'I know you're upset; after Hamid, we all are.'

'Nothing looks real. I can't seem to taste or touch anymore. If I touch I don't feel anything... it's all unreal, after yesterday. I'm abshagun, like I can walk through walls...' Jessica waited for his reply, but when she heard nothing, she continued, 'Look, you were Hammie's best friend. I only need a few minutes of your time. I'll come to you.'

'What's up, Jessica? But I can't get away from here at the moment. You know its not about five minutes, or fifty, just ask me whatever you –'

'I can't do it over the phone.' She knew she had to see his face when she asked him. Jessica wiped her palms on her shirt, and walked over to turn the heating off. *Why is it that people change after someone dies?* she thought. Did Hamid take Ali's compassion? Did it disappear with his soul?

Just when Jessica thought Ali would refuse, he said, 'I'm at the mosque. Do you know our mosque?'

She had tried to ignore the things that Hamid did, those she could not be involved in.

'Hamid loved our mosque – it's just off the Stratford Road. We're having a remembrance for him today, a *khatam*, where we read the Qur'an. I'll be saying some prayers for him, anyway,' said Ali.

Jessica felt surprise that his voice had changed. He sounded like someone else, his usual dome-smooth tone and minaret-high bright wit was now crumbly and gothic. She told him she did not know where the mosque was. She ran her hand over her face and cursed that her throat would not stay moist, no matter how much water she gulped. She jotted some basic directions. She knew the mosque thrived in a medium she could not breathe in easily: the alien planet of the Asian city, somewhere between the Sparkhill and Sparkbrook areas of Birmingham.

As Jessica opened the front door, she met Holly standing outside. 'Oh, hi. That was good timing.'

'I was just on my way out for a bit,' said Jessica, closing the door.

'Where are you off to, then? I wanted to make sure you were okay after yesterday's fiasco.'

Jessica hesitated on the path.

'Where?' asked Holly. 'Doesn't matter. I'll come with you, could do with a bit of cheering up myself.'

Jessica turned away from her friend; she did not want to cause Holly further stress. 'I'm off to see Ali,' said Jessica, opening the door to her car. 'Well, in fact, I'm going to another mosque, Hamid's. I can't ask that of you.'

'Nonsense. I'll love to come, and maybe we can get some samosas on the way back,' said Holly with a smile, getting into the car. 'I'm starving, and we're bound to be going past Stratford Road somewhere – we'll get some from Mushtaq's take away. He makes nice *Katlamas*, too.'

Jessica never ceased to be amazed by Holly's intuition. *Maybe she understands a lot more than I give her credit for*, she thought. 'Only if you're really sure, Holly? It might not be pretty – not that yesterday was a day at the beach.' Jessica felt relief that she would have Holly. The dread of entering another mosque after yesterday made her shiver, and felt like spending a night naked in the Arctic. Jessica had not yet told Holly about her trip to the Malvern Hills with Sebastian. Not because she wanted to hide her meeting, but because she felt unsure about her feelings towards Sebastian. She was not sure whether they should grow or wilt like the bunch of flowers he had given her, which stood in a small crystal vase in her study.

'The food's your treat, anyway. That's the only way I'm coming,' said Holly, with a laugh and got into the car.

'It's always my treat!' grumbled Jessica.

As Jessica drove along Stratford Road her shoulders hunched tighter as she steered through the Asian areas. Was it just because Hamid's family lived close by? As Holly chattered, Jessica looked at the shops with gaudy signs. Many had bright backlighting and looked like illustrated children's comic books in their profusion of candyfloss colours:

pinks, purples and lime greens. Even the clothes in the shop fronts seemed garish beyond everyday wear. Jessica could not imagine anyone wearing such artificial colours, except perhaps at a wedding. *No wonder they're so emotionally violent, if their clothes are anything to go by*, she thought, but then her mind flashed to the *lengha* she had tried on with Hamid. One question had drowned all else since the explosion, and now it came bursting out from under the surface, as if deprived of the oxygen for so long, gasping for the truth. *Was Hamid the suicide bomber?*

Although the shrieks in her mind had quietened as the intensity of the pain had dampened, the question still made her dig her nails into her palms, as she clenched her fists and her breath became shallower. She had made her palms red and sore, especially since Hamid's funeral yesterday and Talat's accusations. Jessica had not slept and her nausea had increased since dawn, like a returning tide. The relentless waves of alienation washed over her, as if she was buried in the sand on the beach and water was beginning to fill her mouth; she gasped.

Jessica looked around the street as she queued in traffic, to scare away the daydream by forcing the real world into her senses. She saw a shop selling bangles, which sparkled and glittered in the bright lights and attracted her eyes like sensually wrapped confectionary.

'They're nice,' said Holly, as if reading her mind. 'But you couldn't wear them with jeans.'

'Why not? I have before now, when Hamid and I went out for dinner in the Balti Belt.'

'Yeah, but you're weird,' said Holly with a smile, staring into the shop window.

Jessica pulled away reluctantly, and followed the directions Ali had given her. She turned through narrow streets, twisting the car through gaps made between parked and oncoming cars that seemed to leave a finger width of space on either side. She entered a street that had narrow doorways facing each other, some of them opened, out of which children escaped like small brown chocolates tumbling out of a relaxing fist. Jessica pressed the button and lowered the window, to ask for directions. She heard a mother scold a babble of small children as they laughed and ran, clutching their books to their chests. The little girls adjusted their long scarves, which trailed behind them like multihued tails. Jessica assumed the books must be Arabic and Qur'an lessons, and the children were on their way to the mosque for a dish of *rasmalai*, having consumed the bread and butter of a school day. Jessica decided against asking the woman, who had shouted in a language she did not recognise, and parked the car with difficulty.

'Come on then – let's do this thing,' said Jessica. She felt glad that Holly had just accepted whatever she was about to do, without argument. *I suppose after yesterday, Holly has given up trying to make me stop my quest,* she thought.

Jessica led the way along the narrow footpath of cracked paving slabs, past a *Halal* meat shop where a denuded sheep's head, with bulging eyes and long teeth plugged into its skull, grinned at her. She saw a tray of ram's testicles staring up at her, a gross of milky white eyes blinking blindly.

'What the hell are they?' asked Holly, as she pointed at the tray and pulled a face.

'Er, I think they're sheep's testicles.'

'What? They eat sheep's bollocks?' said Holly, loud enough for the man in the shop to look out at them. He smiled and gestured at them to enter.

Jessica imagined herself transported from the back streets of Birmingham to the bazaars of Peshawar, which made her remember a few lines from Kipling, from her father's book. *Perhaps it was those romanticised visions of the East that made me fall for Hamid,* she thought. The poetry had stayed with her:

> *When springtime flushes the desert grass,*
> *Our kafilas wind through the Khyber Pass.*
> *As the snowbound trade of the North comes down*
> *To the market-square of Peshawar town.*

Now the trade was terrorism, and the currency suicide bombing.

Jessica saw the converted house which served as a mosque, with its misplaced tiles and peeling paint, the inner city emblems of decay. She saw the green sign with white writing on it; the Arabic and English crashed into each other like the Clash of Civilisations. The swirling Arabic would have seemed incongruous, except it seemed to be in place, because the whole area felt foreign.

As Jessica approached the mosque, she saw Ali talking to a woman in a scarf. Their heads were bent forward as if in deep conversation, as another man stood and watched. Jessica stopped as soon as she recognised the man to be the journalist, and she turned to look into a shop window.

'Give me a minute please, Holly,' she said. *What the hell is he doing here?* she thought. *Who's that other woman talking to Ali? I don't care. I've got to do this now.* Jessica brushed her hair back and started walking towards them, planting her feet firmly with every step. 'Right, come on,' said Jessica, turning away from Holly and leading the way again.

When she got to Ali, she said, 'Hi, Ali. Thanks for seeing me here.' She ignored the other two.

'Er, hi,' Ali said, and glanced at the man and the woman. 'This is Jamila,' he added, gesturing to the woman. Jessica looked at her and saw her normal brown face merge with her darker brown scarf; her everyday beige coat was too big for her slight frame. Jessica accepted Jamila's outstretched hand, which had a surprisingly firm grip.

'You must be Jessica,' said Jamila. 'It's our business to know Hamid's friends, especially around here. We should all have friends.'

Jessica glanced at the journalist. 'Ah, yes – and I think you know Mr Blair already?' said Ali.

'Heard him, more like,' said Holly. 'Asking questions in Central Mosque yesterday like he was the flippin' Pope at confession. What you doin' here, anyway?' Holly asked Blair.

Blair grinned, showing more teeth than Jessica thought could be contained in a human mouth.

'Ali, can I talk to you for a minute?' said Jessica.

'I'm looking into this Hamid thing,' said Blair, in his Liverpool twang. His huge grin did not waver.

Jessica turned to him. 'There was no "Hamid thing". He was my fiancé, and now he's dead, and dirt bags like you can't stop digging dirt.'

'He'd dig his own shit out, if his mum would let him,' said Holly.

'Now, hang on a minute. There's more to this than meets the eye, and it's in the public interest to know what's gone on around here,' Blair said, looking at Ali. 'Ain't it, Ali?'

Ali's bovine eyelashes fluttered as he shifted his gaze from Blair to Jamila and back to Jessica again, like dark-feathered birds stopping at temporary feeders on their migration. 'Yes,' he said to Blair, but then looked at Jessica. 'Sorry, he pulled me out of the mosque. I have to talk to him – to Mr Blair, I mean.'

'Mr Blair? That's rich. Good name for you,' snorted Holly.

'I only need a couple of minutes,' Jessica said to Ali. She pulled his arm, and led him away. 'Don't worry about scumbag; he'll still be here waiting for you,' she said, and turned to Holly. 'You keep them entertained till we get back, Holly.'

Holly crossed her arms and spread her legs slightly wider, as if daring Jamila or Blair to get past.

Jessica kept her hand on Ali's arm as she led him a short distance away from the group. Ali shifted his eyes all over the street. They darted back to the group, before he pulled his arm away from her hand. She saw him glancing back. 'Look at me, Ali.' She waited for him to turn around slowly. 'You've known me for three years. We've almost become good friends.' Ali looked away again, so she put her hands on his elbows and turned him around, making sure he faced away from the others. She could see Holly talking to Jamila and Blair. *Why is Ali behaving so weirdly today?*

'Okay, even if we haven't become close friends, you were Hamid's best mate, weren't you?' she asked, and he nodded, arms crossed. His chin fell onto his chest and stayed there, and he shoved his hands into the pockets of his thick coat. *Why is he being so recalcitrant?* she thought. *It's almost as if he's afraid of something – or is it because of Hamid's funeral yesterday? I think it's the journalist; could it be Jamila? He must be afraid of Blair.* 'I need to ask you something,' she said.

Ali looked down at his shoes, and shuffled. 'What makes you think I know the answer?' he said, without looking up. Jessica pressed both hands onto his arms.

'I need to know if Hamid was involved in any strange activities.'

'Jessica, I don't think this is a good time. You shouldn't be here now, worrying, I mean.'

'I need to know this. I was with him for long enough to imagine I understood everything about him.'

'Everyone wants the same thing. I don't know any more than you,' said Ali, his voice barely escaping the ruffles of his coat. He kept his face down as he kicked some imagined stone with his foot. 'That journalist has been eating my brains with the same question. 'Was Hamid with *Jaish an Noor wass Salaam*? Who did he hang out with?' *Me*, I just keep saying. He was my best friend. The police – they won't stop, either. They –'

'Who's that woman?' asked Jessica, glancing past Ali to look at

Jamila, who was smiling at Holly.

'Just someone I got talking to in the mosque. She knows a lot about Hamid, she kept asking me stuff about him.'

'Why?'

'I don't know. I don't question these Aunties... they always question me,' said Hamid, glancing back at the group. 'I'll tell you something, though – she isn't one of the usual aunties,' said Ali. He frowned and his mouth twisted.

'Is she one of them?' asked Jessica.

Ali ignored her, and looked around. 'He's still there.' Ali's eyes flashed irritation at Jessica. 'I've got to get back. He's asking too many questions.'

'Okay, so was Hamid involved with *Jaish*, as far as you know?'

'Jessica, listen to me. You're just not built for this stuff –'

'Why, is that because I'm a *Goree*?' she asked. 'A *Gandee Goree*? A Dirty White Woman? Don't you think I know what they say?' she asked, nodding towards the mosque. 'I didn't think you were like that,' she added with a shake of her head.

'Why don't you go home, back to safe and sound Solihull, and enjoy a nice Bordeaux?'

'Don't you bloody patronise me, Ali.' She shook his arms, so that his hands almost came out of his pockets. 'I've lost Hamid, and I need to know the truth.'

'Yeah, but whose truth?' said Ali through gritted teeth as he took his hands out of his pockets, as if that barrier had failed against Jessica's storm. *At least I've got him animated,* she thought. Ali waved towards the grimy houses and the people who seemed pedestrian, whether on foot or in cars. '*Their* truth?'

Jessica saw a couple of men leave the mosque, their white beards matching their small white hats. They waved at Ali, who ignored them. 'The truth is, Jessica, that *Jaish an Noor wass Salaam* are everywhere. Was Aitch involved? Of course! Just like we're all involved, whether we like it or not. That's like saying *have you got anything to do with the British Government?* Do they affect your life in any way?' Ali shook his head.

'What? How the hell is that like the British Government?' she asked, compelled by his unexpected response. *I'll never understand these people,* she thought. *Three years I've tried, although I know their culture and learned how to cook their food and have adopted their manners. I just can't seem to get to their core, their animating life force. What the hell is it about this religion that's everything to them, and everything is religion? It doesn't just tell them when they should go to the mosque, or how to pray – that I can understand – but it orders them in everything, not just marriage, in everything. Eating and greeting and sleeping and even fucking and shitting are all controlled by their religion.*

Ali's voice broke into her thoughts. 'Because every time we switch on the TV, it's Muslims dying. Baghdad and Gaza and Kabul are just the head and heart of the Muslims, and the rest of the body is in agony too. Muslim blood spurts out from our veins…' Ali stretched out his arms in front of her, with such passion that she could almost imagine fountains of blood gushing from his cut arteries.

Ali looked up at her, his arms still outstretched. He stood still, seemingly without breathing or blinking, and continued in a whisper, '*Jaish* drinks the blood, from these ever-bleeding wounds, like a demon who grows stronger on the blood of Muslim suffering.' He leaned forward. 'Now the Jinn is out of the bottle and its trying to get ultimate power – and trust me, this Jinn will not be granting anyone three wishes, but will gift you things you haven't seen in your worst nightmare. Your future. That's what they can do, and will do in real life.' Ali drew back, his face contorted.

Jessica let her breath go and shivered. *It's just the cold*, she thought; the autumn sun came through the clouds and ripened the blush on her face.

'Listen, it's easy for them. They're everywhere. They use what happens everyday,' Ali said, as if explaining to a small child. He paused, and looked around. 'They have videos, and films and recruiters talking to kids, whilst others train the teenagers, day in day out.'

'Was Hamid involved?' she asked again, not caring that he would think her stupid or stubborn.

'I told you everyone is involved,' he shouted, but managed to control himself.

'Hammie wasn't like that. He was gentle and kind –'

'And?' Ali leaned forward again. 'You just don't get it. Have you ever known me to be cruel?'

Jessica shook her head. 'Well, exactly. When these kids grow up – not even talking about Hamid and me – at least we had some chance in life.

But look at them...' Ali gestured to a group of boys in their teens. They shoved each other and guffawed, as they all tried to get into the mosque door at once. 'They've got no future. No education, and more importantly, no identity,' said Ali, in a voice pregnant with wonder bred by exasperation, which gave birth to sarcasm, fertile with cynicism.

Jessica looked at another similar group who passed, and some nodded to Ali. A few had short beards and Brummie accents, but most spoke a mixture of languages in an accent uniquely unidentifiable, except attributable to future failure.

'They have as much in common with your part of Solihull as they do with the Klingons. They look more like Klingons.'

Jessica saw how they had short hair, with patterns cut into it, and some had short beards, which showed double tramlines. She had no idea if they shaved like that out of fashion or gang culture. She felt sure now that the tramlines led to a desolate tunnel, down a blind alley of despair.

'They reject their parents so feel alone, and when they get rejected by everyone else they feel not only alienated but under attack. When you have a grievance that would normally just fizzle out, but you put it into the pressure cooker of failure: of family, of society and culture and throw in some *Jaish* spices – keeping the current climate in mind – then you have a uniquely hot curry. After that, then it's "us against them," especially when that's the message they receive from both sides. They take the law of the street, and apply it.'

'So you're a part of these *Jaish* terrorists, then?'

'We all are. That's what I'm telling you. We all are. Not all of us are violent extremists. Frankly, I'm amazed at how few do go on to do anything stupid.'

'What do you mean? You either support them, or you don't?' asked Jessica, crossing her arms. She had almost started to regret coming to see Ali. It seemed he would not give her any answers, but just throw rings of confusion around her already tight chest. He had never said anything like this before – he had always been bright and pleasant and sociable.

'Disillusioned, disenfranchised, demonised. You tell any group of people you're on a crusade to wipe out them and their religion, and how do you expect them to react?' said Ali. She did not move. He continued: 'You don't allow them to take an identity or be a part of this country. That's like pouring red chillies over nerves that are already raw and jangling in the hearts of the misguided youth. It's so easy for them to fall for the charm and acceptance and love and visions of honour. They provide them with the food and water that these kids need to survive, with delusions of dignity. That's what *Jaish an Noor wass Salaam* offer. After all, they are *The Army of Light and Peace*.'

'I don't get you.'

'No. I don't get me either. And you and me are not the only ones. They'll start wondering what we're talking about, but let me tell you. These boys are desperate, in a drought of love but drowning in a river of want. That's their natural state, ready to be plucked by *Jaish*, to reject the world. Who wouldn't find solace in the arms of the *houris* of Paradise? Who wouldn't want escape?' Ali raised his eyebrows.

'You can never justify it, Ali. I don't believe you believe this bullshit. Are you with them? Was Hamid a suicide bomber?'

He continued as if she had not spoken. 'For some people it's alcohol that makes them forget. For others, it's hate. The desire for revenge. *Jaish* is a black hole that sucks in anything good, and spits out hate.'

'Is that what a martyr means?'

'For these people, hate and revenge are the rockets that martyrdom rides on. *Jihad* and Foreign Policy is the jet-fuel mixture.'

Jessica did not know what to say. She looked at Ali and saw a stranger, with wide eyes that glistened in the sun and lips flecked with saliva. She wiped her eyes, and felt her throat close.

'So you're telling me Hamid was the suicide bomber? Not only that, but that he was right to be one?'

'I'm trying to help you understand,' he said, as he looked at her closely. 'I can see you don't get it. You just don't get it, do you?'

She realised that Ali would not answer her question or perhaps could not. She felt the muscles in her arms clench. He was not denyining the possibility of Hamid being involved. Her stomach tightened. 'I'll prove you're wrong. I'll show you that, no matter what shitty excuses you make and despite the shitty lives they have, some people will never become suicide bombers.'

'Look I'm sorry, but I did try to warn you. All this is too much for a gentle English girl like you.'

'Well, there's granite under this soft English soil – and you're the steel that's caused sparks, and a fire!'

'I wouldn't push this, if I were you, Jessica. It won't be good for you.'

Jessica walked away from Ali, reached Holly and grabbed her by the arm. 'Hey, you finished? I've been watching 'em like a dragon.'

'Come on, Holly, we're off.'

'What? Just when I was getting into it? These two are dangerously funny, some of the stuff they've been sayin', you know.' Holly pointed two fingers to her eyes and then pointed them at Jamila and Blair, and then pointed them to her eyes again. 'Yeah that's right, I'm watching you. Watchin' you,' she said, as Jessica led her away. They walked the short distance to the car. Holly got in, and just as Jessica turned to open the door, she noticed that Jamila stood behind her.

Jamila smiled as she had before, in a matter-of-fact way, and said, 'I think I know what you're looking for.'

*

Blair had stood, watching Jamila follow Jessica and Holly down the road. *I wonder what she's after? Stupid bint*, he thought, as Jessica and Holly turned the corner and Jamila followed. He turned to Ali.

'Got to go in for *Asar* prayers,' said Ali.

'What? Arse prayers? Me arse prays,' Blair guffawed. 'I want you out here in five – I ain't chasin' over that bloody house with a hundred rooms and a million kids for you again, Mu-hammed.' Blair chuckled as Ali entered the mosque. He knew Ali could not just stand with him outside whilst the congregration prayed. Blair had enjoyed calling Ali Mu-hammed since he had first met him – *maybe it's because of Mu-hammed Ali*, he thought, *but I don't know for sure*. Blair took out his mobile phone and punched a preset button with his chubby fingers, flicking back the long strands of hair that covered his bald pate.

'Kingsley? Yeah, hi – it's me. That is you, Kingsley, ain't it? Why are you putting that posh voice on? You're not at work, are yer? I know you're not, cos you never take this phone into work.' He did not give the other man a chance to answer. Blair knew he could allow his natural persona to show, since Kingsley was on his payroll. 'Anyway, listen... I expected you to ring by now. Yeah, well, you owe me a few, pal. Don't worry 'cos I'll look after yer, with some smackers. Always pass a few lovely dollars over, don't I? Anyway, what info have you got for us? Do yer ever do any fuckin' work in CTC?' Blair had been a bailiff two decades ago, before becoming a reporter. The years in London had not dulled his Scouse accent, nor had living in Kensington. London ameliorated the effects of growing up in Kensington, Liverpool. He applied pressure as naturally as he breathed to his source in the Counter Terrorist Command.

'I need some answers pretty quick, quick, yeah. Yeah, I'm down at his mosque. Yeah, just give me what you've got.' *I've got to break this story*, he thought, *and get the scoop out in the next two days, or the fuckin'* Sun *and* Mail *will be rolling all over it, like Bedouins in camel shit.*

'I don't give a Mancunian's turd if youse ain't verified it. You're making this harder than me old mum farting when she's all bunged up. I've got to break the story. What did it say?' said Blair, his accent becoming strained. 'Just tell me what it said. What did the intelligence report say?' He gave no chance for a reply before continuing, 'There's a fuckin' laugh in a cop shop if I ever heard one. 'Intelli-fucking-gence ree-port!" guffawed Blair. 'No fuckin' smart remarks about Scousers – and yes, I know you're not a cop.'

Blair paused to wipe his brow with the back of his hand, and shook his head while he listened to Kingsley summarise the report. *Fucks sake, get on with it*, he thought. *Aren't I paying the twat enough?* He took out a pasty from his coat pocket, threw the paper bag on the floor, and munched a huge bite. He tried to catch his breath at the same time as swallowing, and he almost choked. He coughed and retched, his huge abdominal fat jiggling as he spluttered. He pulled out a bottle of Coke from his other pocket, gulped half of it, and the bubbles went up his nose, making him splutter again. 'Yes, o' course I'm fuckin' alright.' He waited until he could breathe again. 'You were watching Hamid Khan and Mohsin Ali? Yeah, yeah I know Ali, he's another slimy one. They was interested in *Jaish*? Well, ain't that fascinatin'? Half of Africa and half Asia is interested in *Jaish*. And the other half who ain't interested are already signed up to *Jaish*. Tell me something I don't know.' This time, he waited for Kingsley to speak.

'Okay. They've been under surveillance before, and as usual you donkeys stopped watchin' them. Then what? *Huh, un-hunh*. Now we're getting somewhere. They went to Pakistan together? Hamid and Ali have been to the Pakistan-Afghanistan border? Ali and Hamid went last year?' said Blair, with rising glee. 'And they definitely met their *Jaish* contacts there? Okay. Thank you. Keep them smiling down at CTC.' Blair ended the call. 'Twat,' he said aloud, and ignored a passing old man as he stared.

Blair smiled. He lit a cigarette and sucked hard. *I can see the headlines tomorrow: HAMID KHAN: SUICIDE BOMBER.*

Ali came and stood beside him. Blair grabbed him and led him around the corner, to a quiet side street.

'You little greasy-mouthed twat,' said Blair, leaning forward into Ali's face, splattering bits of partially masticated pasty onto his face. Ali wiped his face with the back of his hand. Blair lit another cigarette and waited for the consternation to die down on Ali's face.

'What? I didn't say a word to her. Nothing about Hamid.'

'Yeah, yeah.' Blair came in close, puffing smoke into Ali's face with every word, 'You lot are all the fuckin' same. Don't matter where you been growed up, as my grandfather used to say in the old country. God rest his soul in Sligo. *Some things only flower in pig shit son, so they do.*'

'What are you talking about?' asked Ali, looking around the empty street and putting his hands into his pockets.

'What do you think they'd do to you?'

'Who?'

'Oh, who is it now? WHO?' Blair spun his head and eyes around, as he looked all around the street in mock animation as if searching for someone and repeated, 'I wonder WHO would be interested in knowing your secret?' He grabbed Ali by his coat. 'What the fuck do you think I'm paying you for, sonny? Do you think it's easy to get so much money? Greedy twat. And what do you think *Jaish* would do to you, Muhammed?'

'Listen, I've given you everything I could –'

'You fuckin' went to Pakistan last year. With Hamid. That was what slipped your greasy little money-grabbing mind. All these months I been paying you to watch the mosque, and I should have been watching you.'

'It was a family holiday, Mr Blair. My granny was sick.'

'Probably caught it off your granddad, sonny. She should have kept her legs closed. That was the first mistake she made, letting your granddad into her hole. She ended up having your dad, and he ended up making you. And who knows how you'll end up, because this might be the last mistake you're gonna make.'

'My granny died before I got there,' said Ali. Blair saw fear pull Ali's face back into a grimace as if the Grim Reaper stood behind him, straining on his hair and scalp with his bony fingers. 'No, please – they don't need to know anything.'

Blair chortled and puffed smoke, which ended up in Ali's face. 'You went to the Afghan border, wondered all over FATA, didn't you? Into Dir and Waziristan.' Blair pulled a face, speaking in a baby voice.

'That's where my family are from.'

'Yeah, yeah, I don't know if they care in Guantanamo Bay. I doubt it, but I don't give a shit.' He chomped the last of the pasty, and licked his fingers and spoke as he chewed. 'You, sonny, Mr Mu-hammed Ali, are gonna tell me everything, including how many times you swapped spit with Hamid Khan. Anything and everything – you're gonna tell me, before I ask it.' Blair grabbed Ali's collar and almost touched his mouth onto the younger man's nose. Ali grimaced and screwed up his eyes tight, as saliva flecked his face. 'No more pissin me about and playing Mr Tough Guy – you got it?' said Blair.

Ali nodded, his teeth gritted and his face a mask.

'But first Mu-hammed, I've run out of me ciggies, so go and get me a pack of twenty Benson and Hedges Kings.' Blair shoved Ali, and slapped a five-pound note onto Ali's cheek.

Ali grabbed the money and twisted away from him.

'Oi, twat,' shouted Blair. Ali turned, and Blair added, 'And make sure you don't buy the black pack – hate the fuckin' black.' As Ali lurched away, Blair chortled.

CHAPTER 10

Mumbai – Gulf Software Security Systems Boardroom

The drug baron and underworld don of Mumbai-Karachi-Dubai, David Gul, continued to stare at Amit in stone-faced, silent incomprehension. David had been listening to Amit speak since the start of the meeting. Amit had spoken quotations in a tone he had imagined impossible for a human throat to keep up for any length of time, squawking in a language David believed Amit had invented five minutes before entering the boardroom. *What did he call it? Latin. What kind of animal is that?* David looked on, unblinking, hardly breathing. He almost ripped the nails of one hand with the other, but he hid his fidgeting under the table. He did not dare to glance at the other board members, in case he was unable to control himself and ended up in hysterics of laughter.

Amit continued his pacing in the boardroom. 'Our enemies have long announced their intentions by putting their motto on the Great Seal of America: *Annuit Coeptis Novus Ordo Seclorum*. It means: *He has approved our undertakings*. I ask you, who has approved their *New Order of the Ages*? I will tell you,' said Amit, looking at David Gul. '*Dajjal*, The Antichrist.'

David wondered if Amit was deliberately trying to confuse him, but the look of intensity on Amit's face, as if he was even now involved in a life and death struggle with the forces of evil, convinced David of his passion.

'Centuries ago their Priestess of Apollo, the Sibyl, prophesised a final return of "the age of Saturn, a new child sent from the heavens." These *Kuffar*, and their numerous gods,' said Amit, in a mocking voice. David knew that the greatest sin was to declare there could be more than one God.

Amit spoke some more strange words that David assumed must be Latin, and then translated. '*A brand new great order of the ages is born; for now the Virgin and the age of Saturn have returned.*' Amit held his arms aloft as if looking at the back of his hands, but he started into space, and spoke like a prophet predicting the future.

David glanced around and saw the gathered leaders looking at each other, more confused than ever by Amit, who had often confused them in the past. David thought that most like him were unfamiliar with the classics, but they all knew well the theory of the New World Order. *That's just big words for what my gangs do on the streets everyday*, thought David. *Whoever has the biggest gun, gets the most money.* It was the same goddess. Despite the financial crisis, she was just being herself; an old whore with new clothes and a facelift. David was unsure why Amit was repeating the philosophy in what was supposed to be a planning meeting. Amit was always nonsensical in the pursuit of his ideals.

'*Jupiter omnipotens*. All-powerful Jupiter. *Astaghfirullah*, I seek refuge in the One True God Allah. But that's what they called Jupiter, all-powerful,' said Amit. '*Annuit Coeptis* and *Novus Ordo Seclorum* are from the Roman poet Virgil. This has been the Devil's philosophy since before Time began.'

David felt as if Amit could even quote the page number; although he had not heard of Virgil and he was not really sure know if it was Latin that Amit was quoting. David almost convinced himself that it did not really exist.

'This is just part of the eternal battle between *shirk*, false gods, and The One True Allah. This war has been going on since *Shaitan* refused Allah's command to bow to Adam. They still worship the same devils. They have the same golden calf cults, the same gods as Rome, and Jupiter was head of the pantheon of gods.' Amit paused; *to ensure they were following him*, David thought.

He had problems following Amit's speeches most of the time, so he had not even tried to waste his brainpower with this shit that sounded like a parrot screeching. *If this is what Oxford University does for you, then thank Jupiter I didn't go there, wherever the hell that is*, he thought. David knew the university was somewhere in a white country, but he had never been out of Asia. Amit had to pay such high fees for Oxford that he and his family were in debt for five years afterwards. *Not for all the wondrous pussy in Tartary*, he thought – for he had heard the women there were born with a congenital lack pubic hair – *would I go to Oxford University*. He had heard that story from the Ambassador of Italy, at one of the numerous diplomatic parties he regularly attended. 'The Mongol hordes have runways to heaven that are already smooth.' The drunken ambassador had giggled, 'I want to make that my next diplomatic mission, to Tartary.' Wherever the hell that is.

David knew it had always been about money, and so it would always be. He could not let *Jaish* ruin his empire with their stinking plans to destroy the world's money markets. They dared to sniff at his business, when they were going to put the world into the sewer with the collapse of the financial system.

'Jupiter, the supreme god of the Roman pantheon, is called *dies pater*, shining father. He is a god of light and sky, therefore another *Dajjal*, yet another sun god. This name refers not only to his rulership over the universe, but also to his function as the god of the state who distributes laws, controls the realm, and makes his will known through oracles. And this is still what they worship now. This is the ultimate Truth of the world, this is the Clash of Civilisations, and this will be the final battle. The false sun gods, and behind them *Al Dajjal*, the Antichrist. Sitting high above them all, is, of course, *Shaitaan*, The Devil. That is their true God, their Lord.'

What utter fucking *bhenchaud* bullshit. What are these guys on? David wondered. Inside he was ripping with laughter. He had infiltrated the world's most powerful secret organization and forced them to accept him into their planning meetings in return for his help, but he had to take the oath of secrecy and unquestioning loyalty to The Leader. David knew Amit did not trust him; a vow on any Holy Book was the same to David as swearing on toilet paper. David did not care – he had made himself indispensable to *Jaish an Noor wass Salaam, The Army of Light and Peace*. Soon he would have power beyond his wildest dreams. Money... he had huge amounts of that, but it was a lie. Money was not power. Money was Beluga caviar, Krug Grande Cuvée champagne, luxury yachts, a private jet and an endless supply of butter-skinned, ageless Bollywood starlets and nubile, even more desperate to please Lollywood nymphets. He knew he had even more power in the failing film industry of Lahore than in Mumbai. When he had power, *then* David would have his revenge. Retribution on a world that had birthed him into the sewer, that had made his mother a whore. Revenge on the abuse, spit and filth that he had piled upon him, for beatings that he had endured for years before becoming the Godfather, The *Bombay Bhai* that he was. There could only be one, at any one time, who took that mantle: *Bhai of Bombay*.

Not bad, he thought, *for the day-old baby abandoned in the middle of the night*. The bastard child of some unknown teenage *kanjeri* mother left outside Mount Mary's, crying, shivering, and puny and starved. Black as human sin in Mumbai, forty-seven years ago. The miraculous reputation of the Basilica at Bandra had proved true for David Gul.

Power was fear. Fear that he could inspire in others – and if he could inspire fear in whole nations then that was a heady wine, once-sipped never forgotten, and always to be desired. He needed it in incremental dosages – it was infinitely more addictive than any simple-minded chemical formulaic. David had never felt the need for drugs. His confidence came from being a Mumbai gangster, who ran his multinational empire from Dubai, Karachi and Mumbai. David Gul was born into a Mumbai gutter full of human excrement, and he had never quite managed to remove the stench of shit from his nose and the stain from his DNA.

David loved his world: Karachi the clit, Mumbai the arsehole, and Dubai. Dubai was the centre of joy, a bejewelled paradise of some desert nomad *Shaikh*'s imagination. He thought of the glistening city, and smiled. What a pussy, Dubai: *The Golden Gully of Heavenly Bliss*. He lived in the chilli triangle, Dubai-Karachi-Mumbai, the pubis of the globe. David swam in an enclosed, underworld universe of corruption, which discharged its sticky, offensive effluence from the cunt of the world. David's lust continuously grew new teeth of hunger.

Once, at a party which was full of politicians and Mumbai's elite, where David had naturally been one of the first to be invited, he was shown a map of the world. One of the politicians who fawned on him had pointed out the three cities and the Persian Gulf to David, for he was illiterate. He had replied 'That's not the Gulf – just looks like a cunt.' It was his favourite party joke, and he loved to laugh at the pretend shock of his politician friends' wives.

Over the last few years, David had started working with *The Army of Light and Peace*. He had helped them to infiltrate Mumbai, and tried to pimp them starlets, which had been his original occupation. He saw Amit Bahadur looking at him with disdain and disgust. David smiled as he thought of how Amit always refused the beauties that he offered him regularly. They were the same ones that Amit watched daily on the huge screen, which was playing Bollywood songs outside. David knew Amit hated him with a new and virulent temper every time they met.

David drifted into his own thoughts, his eyes glazed, and he made no further effort to try and follow Amit Bahadur's serpentine, meandering speeches. He gazed unblinkingly into Amit's eyes, and smiled.

*

Amit Bahadur sighed, and looked out onto the beachfront of Cuffe Parade. He thought of Aashriya, the Queen of Bollywood again. He seemed to miss her with every movement of his body, his concentration reduced to seconds.

First, he thought, *I have to deal with this gangster, as well as activate the Alpha Ansar. This is what we have come to: how weak we are that we have to use scum like David Gul. What an irony his name means David the Rose, but even such filth can be used as tools for the glory of Islam.*

Amit turned, so he could see a giant plasma screen showing one Bollywood blockbuster after another. A huge hitlist of songs played. The exotic and tantalising dance numbers assailed his senses through the floor–to-ceiling glass of his office, almost as if he had a personal giant television screen placed outside his window especially for him. He abhorred David, but the slimy tentacles of temptation had reached out and wrapped around Amit's heart. *Anyone would waver*, he thought, *thanks to the breathtaking beauties of Bollywood.* Indian films had made a deep and lasting impression on him, because he had grown up in an ordinary middle-class family in Allahabad. The sensuous beauties of Bollywood had allured Amit since his teenage years, with their juicy, inviting eyes. They were magnetic and fixating, so addictive and lithe. He saw them gyrating in front of him now, as he looked up at the screen. They mesmerised him with their entrancing hips.

None compared to Aashriya Aarzoo Romano. Amit saw her on the screen, performing a dance number. He followed her every movement, and knew her every motion before she made it, because he had seen the songs so many time before. Aashriya had Hellenic skin and Nordic eyes, which were sometimes grey and occasionally green, depending on the sun and her mood. Her eyes shone, flawlessly reflecting and enhancing the light that fell on them. She had a creamy face, with gazelle-eyes, emeralds that hypnotised him. Wet like a sponge, they sucked his soul in. She was smooth and creaseless, no fat or excess skin, no cellulite, so satin-soft and frictionless – no less than an Indian Diana or Aphrodite. Any goddess on seeing Aashriya would tear her hair, whilst running from such beauty.

Amit remembered when David had introduced him to Aashriya Aarzoo Romano. David had invited him to the party, ostensibly a charity fundraiser for a Mumbai orphanage. Amit had seen all of her movies, and was spellbound by her before he had seen her in real life, so he had to still his limbs and grasp clasp his hands together before he met her. Eventually Amit had found himself in her presence, in the same room as her, but long before she had looked at him or he had approached her, he melted and had felt himself flow away. When Amit had finally got near enough to her he breathed her in deeply... not just her fragrance, but as if he could breathe in her essence. He tried to infect himself with her beauty, as if by inhaling some of the cells of her body her flesh could be forever incorporated as a part of his corpus, through his lungs. Some tiny part of her residing in him permanently. Amalgamated and integral to his being and essence, so much a soulful and spirit joining at the cellular chemical level, even if it was impossible for them to be joined in life.

Amit looked away from the gathered *shura*, walked over to the huge window, and put both hands on the glass. He was not worried about what the others thought of his behaviour; he always covered his eccentricities by saying he could think freely by moving around the boardroom. His mind often flitted from the past to the present.

Amit felt the physical pain of missing Aashriya welling up inside him, stabbing and mortal, a reminder of his flesh. He always felt that Aashriya spoke with a glistening speech, no matter how senseless the words or bad their enunciation. Her imprisoning laughter felt like handcuffs for his heart, even if it others thought it was braying and discordant. *She is the staring, unblinking, nonpareil epitome of the goddess tradition,* he thought. *A historic guardian of the ancient art. A paragon of capturing men. She has achieved status as the high priestess, and masculinity is bowing in servility. Mistress of time and tradition, from when the first Man was enslaved to that almost forgotten guile*: so Amit justified his slavery. She was captured daily by lasers, in billions of electronic impulses, an ethereal beauty made worldly forever. She was not the historic, ephemeral beauty vanished, but for a poet's lament.

Amit looked at a film scene, as she walked out of the sea wearing a swimsuit. Her hair and lashes were in harmony, like waves of a dark ocean lapping the shores of her cheeks, made damp by her wet hair. She sighed with relief, which seemed to him to be, like some long lost, lone sailor, who after an age wandering the empty sea finds an inhabited shore.

Since he had met 'A Wish from the Land of God' he had found arising in him an aching emptiness that seemed to take over his body. For the first time in his life he wished he could be another Abdullah, literally a servant of Allah, like most Muslims – if only for a moment. From that time, he wished to be just an ordinary man. At least then he could hunger, without shame, for all the material things. *I want to be Abdullah: free to lust because that was the ever-present* nafs, *the ego-desire.* Amit wanted to love – so rare in life, but common in books and on the tongues of men. Hound: how he wished he could, in his innermost heart, dog-hound after Aashriya Aarzoo Romano, to pursue her like all the other powerful political and business leaders. Amit had seen them with their pink uvula, open-throated-laughs at the parties and fundraisers, usually organised by the underground overlord of Mumbai, David. Amit hated all of the politicians afresh, every time he met them. He had seen how Aashriya shrugged off their amateurish, clumsy, grasps. Amit knew she was inured to those gobbling mouths and black clawing talons of India's political and business elite that so desperately wanted to flense her flesh from the bone.

Amit would not allow himself to be so debased. He was not an Abdullah. He was Amit Bahadur, Second in Command of *Jaish an Noor wass Salaam*. Amit stood in line only after The Leader himself. Amit knew that soon the fate of the world would be decided by what happened in his boardroom.

Amit realised these temptations for women and love came from Satan. He willed himself to be strong, to reject the love of this life, of the *nafs*: the incarnate, the corporeal flesh. He was certain it was more love than lust, but it was still earthly-inspired. He thought of an altogether more spiritual life; he would ask for her in Paradise.

Amit's mind flashed back again to when he had first spoken to her. He had muttered and stumbled and lost his balance, no longer the expert orator, no more the leader and decider of men's destinies. Eventually, he had managed to speak.

'Your name…your name…means 'A Wish from the Land of God.'"

'I know,' she replied, simply. 'My father was a poet.'

'Oh – I didn't know that.' But he did, and Amit did not know why he denied it. He knew all about her father and had read his poetry at university before he learned of her existence. Amit would not want or care for his *houris* of heaven, his innumerable virgins. Since he had met Aashriya Aarzoo Romano, he would ask for her alone when his turn came.

When Aashriya made her excuses and left Amit, he had found David Gul. Amit had no choice but to surrender himself to the question, 'Okay, when can I meet her, again?'

After the first brief meeting, Aashriya had left Amit wiping his palms on his trousers; the nausea making him retch, and his chest heaving like an asthmatic. David had smiled, and said he would arrange another meeting for Amit.

London

The bodyguards dragged Jimmy with his legs trailing behind him, as they started to bundle him away.

'Ya *Shaikh*, you continue here,' said Dwayne. Jimmy glanced up and saw Abu Umar protest, but Dwayne nodded with his head and gestured at the expectant crowd. 'People are waiting for you, *Ya* Sayedi.'

Jimmy's knees burst with explosions of pain. The bodyguards held him down again as he struggled, and they crowded around him. This was their big recruitment drive and Jimmy realised that Abu Umar had to continue with the show, not exhibit any weakness. His actions had added to the theatre and the head of the circus, the legendary American-*Kuffar* tamer, the gladiatorial Abu Umar, had to remain calm and in-control – which would add to his status. The crowd was expectant and becoming impatient, and Abu Umar waved them to sit down. They jeered as Jimmy was dragged out.

The bodyguards hogtied him, trussed him like a boar after the hunt, gagged and blindfolded him, driving him erratically until he lost all sense of direction or time. He felt numerous hands pull him out of the car and carry him some distance, then take him indoors and dump him onto a hard wooden chair. His arms were tied behind his back again, with such force that his head and shoulders were thrust forwards. Then someone pushed his head down further, so it was almost between his legs. They had bundled him to what Jimmy guessed must have been a safe house.

He sensed men moving around him. His instincts were sharpened by the danger after the beating, but he could not work out how many.

'Who sent you?' said a voice that rattled like pebbles in a tin. 'Who sent you, your controller? Who is it?'

Jimmy did not answer, but yelped as a slap on the back of his head jerked him forwards and stretched his hamstrings.

'Who's paying you? When did they recruit you?' asked the same voice, which seemed Middle-Eastern, but confident in English.

'This guy is stubborn or too fuckin' stupid. Put the water on him,' said a different voice, younger – *more enthusiastic for the games to begin*, Jimmy thought. Suddenly he felt his legs grabbed and yanked upwards, so his head hit the back of the chair. Someone untied his hands and retied them above his head, and threaded a pole through the plastic tie to hold them up. Jimmy felt pressure increase on his wrists as a result. The pain became agonising when he was dragged by the pole, but he did not scream. They strapped him naked now, his clothes cut from him, as he was forced flat onto his back. He kicked his legs blindly where he imagined his assailants to be. He felt immobilised and helpless, but he would not go without a fight. Then someone shackled his ankles so that he could not bend his legs. A woollen mask covered his head and face. Jimmy felt his head immobilised. The cold tiles of the floor dug into his back as he laid spread out, arms stretched above his head, shoulders screaming in their sockets.

Water flooded over his face, then stopped and started again. Jimmy started drowning, as some water droplets entered his lungs. A leather strap had been tightened across his forehead, so he could not move his head to either side to escape the water. A corner of the tile cut the back of his head. He felt the hard leather make a groove just above his eyebrows.

The water came in torrents, sometimes slower, and then faster, splattering onto his mask, entering into his breath. Then it came slower again, but it kept coming. Jimmy coughed and spluttered as he tried to clear his mouth and throat. The panic rose in him like a rapidly enlarging stone in his throat. It made no difference when he tried to close his mouth and breathe through his nose, he still felt as if he was under miles of ocean.

Seconds stretched into fear of imminent death. He thought he was in the process of choking, and about to stop breathing. His heart felt as if it was pumping against a boulder. Suddenly, someone released his legs and jerked Jimmy upwards. The plastic ties on his wrists, made to support his body weight, felt like the bite of a thousand hypodermic needles. *I'm still alive*, thought Jimmy. *I'm alive!* He could not breathe or speak or scream. He was dumped into the chair again, naked and bleeding from the wrists and back of his head. He felt the woollen mask yanked off his face, and gasped. The cracked cartilage in his nose sang in pain with every breath.

A torturer removed his bonds and blindfold. His eyes swam in the bright rays of a light that hung somewhere close to him. A man sat opposite, and smoked in semi-darkness. The blue-grey curls of smoke rose in a stream from his nose like from a tepee. He sat motionless, while Jimmy coughed and retched furiously for a few minutes.

'That's what you call water-boarding. What you Americans do to us all the time. That was a tiny demonstration, by the way. It can go on for hours, but usually even the strongest of men break within minutes.' The man blew smoke in the direction of Jimmy, who felt the gust of tobacco thick and spicy. *Camels*, thought Jimmy, as another fit of coughing wrenched his chest. *I need a cigarette*. The man blew more smoke upwards through pursed lips like dragon's breath.

'You lasted nineteen seconds...' A pause, and an almost-smile flickered in between puffs of smoke. 'Who sent you?' he asked.

'Younis,' spluttered Jimmy, 'my dad.'

'Where's he?'

'At home, in the mosque,' said Jimmy.

'Who do you work for?'

'Work for? No-one. Myself.'

'You lying bastard.' After a pause he blew more smoke into Jimmy's face. 'No one can do a job like this alone.'

'What job?'

'Last chance. You want to go under the water again?'

'No. No. No water...' Jimmy gasped the panic returned and made him cough. 'What do you want me to say?' The choking sensation started again he leaned forward as much as he could with his hands tied behind his back. Being cut, when he got his scar, did not feel as bad as the water torture.

'Who's your boss? Your handler in MI5? Or don't you work for the British lackeys – are you straight from the Agency?'

Jimmy did not answer and he noticed the smoking man signalled with his head, immediately he sensed two men behind him move forward and grabbed his hands.

'No, no!' Jimmy's fear of water flooding over his face flashed over him.

'How were you going to kill him? We found two knives on you, one flick knife.'

Jimmy sat naked, shivering and wet. The bodyguards dragged him back towards the water with his feet dragging as they lifted him by the arms. Jimmy felt a mask thrust on his head from nowhere, plunging him from darkness into blackness and screamless panic. He knew they had him and he would do anything, eat shit, say anything; disown his mother. His dignity was held by the slightest incline of the smoking man's head. A spider's web of a nod, and he would be utterly humiliated. This time he knew he would shit and piss himself.

He felt the bile rise in his throat. *I'm going to vomit and choke on my own puke*, he thought, *when they lie me flat this time*. He gasped his breath coming as if through the thick cloth. 'I didn't want to kill him. I didn't. Who the hell is he?'

'Don't give me that. How did you know Hamza was going to be here? I heard you shout his name.'

'I didn't. I ain't seen him for years. I was supposed to teach him the googly, I promised, like Shane Warne...'

They laid him flat on his back. Jimmy felt the tiles dig into his flesh, cold and reptilian, unfeeling, inhuman: the sum of his life. So different from his clay. Maybe the clay tiles in Baghdad or Medina would be warm and comforting; maybe if he lay on Muslim tiles he would find peace. For the first time he felt lonely. His hands shook, as his tongue tried automatically to anticipate and block the incipient flood. Although he knew it would only be a trickle, his logic was drowned. He had faced death in every potential deal for *Maall*, but then he had some measure of control. *Is this the result of all my bad?*

'Please, please don't do this,' he said through his constricting breathlessness, barely able to speak through the throat-gripping, drowning sensation, which still held him from the first episode. His arms shook, his back and legs racked into contortions by painful spasms of his muscles. He tried to make it look as if he was shivering from cold, but failed. Jimmy kicked his legs, smashing them against one of the men who tried to tie him down, but he knew it was futile. They overpowered him and punched his legs into submission in seconds, but he refused to go quietly. He would do anything to avoid that feeling again.

'Bastard assassin got through security with two knives, and flew at the *Shaikh*,' said one of the men who he felt came up close, followed by the footsteps of more men. They immobilised him. He felt that he could not twitch a muscle. His breathing became erratic, and even that did not seem to be in his body. Sometimes shallow, sometimes gasping, but always-insufficient breath. His heartbeat became rushing, gushing, thumping. No longer the cool, metronomic controlled heartbeat of youth, but the haphazard rush of known fear, of terror that could never be accommodated, never accepted as a decreasing nightmare. Logic became dysfunctional, and he could not tell his brain not to panic.

He tried struggling and failed again but he persisted, because he could do nothing else. 'I always carry two knives,' he said, as he recovered from a spate of coughing. 'One strapped to my left forearm and the second in my boot, innit?' There was no reply. He had hidden the knives well enough for the mosque search teams to miss them; Jimmy had long experience of hiding weapons about his body. These torturers were thorough, strip-searching him, and exploring any part of his anatomy that could hide the smallest of weapon, even a vial of poison.

Jimmy heard water splashing about, maybe a bucket being raised on a pulley system. He had caught a glimpse of it as they had lifted him up last time. 'Are you there?' he asked. He got no reply, then a few drops of water splashed onto his face. 'Ask Hamza, you fuckin' bastards. Hamza!' He tried to thrash, but moved only a fraction. He still got no reply. The words tumbled out, past the glottal choking sensation, like a release on a steam train whistle. 'I'll drop you if you do this. Not with a bullet, neither. Yeah you, you fuckin' smokin' cunt, I'm talking to you.' More water, barely a trickle, ran down his mask. 'I know you all. I seen you now, and don't worry. I don't forget, innit.' He coughed. 'Don't you fuckers worry, yeah? You better kill me now, 'cos when I find you fuckers you'll –' the choking cut his sentence. He gurgled and spluttered as water ran down his throat; less than before, slower, but it seemed worse, as if he floated in prolonged agony. Jimmy could not move his head. As soon as there was a pause, Jimmy tried speaking, as if he had could breathe comfortably. He had to show no weakness.

'Fuck you, fuck your mommas.' Then Jimmy felt as if a skeletal hand of death had shoved his bony fingers down his throat, and shot fireballs from the tips into his lungs. 'I'll chop your cock off, smoking man, and shove it up your fuckin' arse before I let you bleed to death.'

The water stopped. 'Oh, we know plenty about you, Jimmy...' The voice muffled against the blood that thumped in Jimmy's ears like a crescendo waterfall, crashing and rising, then rising again to a shrill pitch. Jimmy did not know if his uncontrollable screaming was silent or loud. Did his throat manage to make any noise?

'We know your dealing and wheeling and threats and corruption you spread, the *fitna* you cause. The women you pimp,' said the voice of smoking man.

Jimmy could sense the hatred. The man spat words like globules of gob. Phlegm retched out from the back of his throat, as if he could rid the world of the *Kuffar* by spitting the hatred dragon out.

'You macho man. Pimping women and men. But this isn't the street, and to us you're like a kid who's only ever played toy soldiers and thinks he's a field-marshal of war. Well, you're in a war now, my friend. You little kid – baby Jimmy.' Then the water started again. Jimmy swore he would not let the water in to simply drown him. He would not let them win.

The water stopped. When he could eventually speak, he shouted and spluttered, 'Fuck you. Fuck you and all of your kind.' He paused to cough. 'Fuck your momma and seven generations. I piss on you and all your kind, and I piss on your leader.'

'Oh, weak! So weak and helpless, yet so stupid too,' said smoking man. Jimmy felt hot fluid spray onto his face, and then the tangy, acrid, smell covered his mask. He felt the hot steam rising from the lumpen black of his shamed face.

'It is stupid to say you piss on anyone, but especially stupid when you are tied to the floor, and even more stupid when you depend on me for your next breath.' More urine splashed his mask. 'How does True Believer piss taste like? Piss on your American President.' Then he shouted, 'I piss on all the *Kuffar*.'

Jimmy tried to spit the ammonia liquid out, but tasted it instead.

'I will make sure even a waster like you remembers God, tonight,' said the smoking man.

There was no memory of God. He felt helpless, like a fawn tied to a stake awaiting the tiger's claw. Jimmy remembered he had not kissed

Sofia's hands tonight. It was too late. He would die without kissing *Ami*'s hands.

Now he felt a man sit on each of his legs, and another sat on his chest. Jimmy grunted, tried to scream but could not as he felt something cover his mouth. Then punches clattered the bones in his face, in between the water torture.

Punch, water, punch, punch, water, water, punch.

Jimmy felt himself flitting between charcoal greyness and starry blackness.

Then they released him, the weights lifted off his legs. There was no need to hold him; Jimmy knew he could not move. The liberty of air in his lungs felt clean after the leaden incarceration of a man on his chest, like the newborn's first gasp. The water stopped, restarted, stopped again. A few seconds at a time, but he felt as if he had never been anywhere else in his life. He could not measure what had ever gone before; there was only the immediacy of escape.

The sound of the falling water transported him back to the Butterfly House and his fountain in the centre of the Lep, as he called it. He wondered if his swallowtails had pupated yet. Jimmy often sought refuge in his Lep, although he had never imagined himself as a Lepidopterist. As he choked and gasped, the colours that blazed in front of his eyes were an amalgam of summer's warmth, of swirling wings and spots. *Will Ami know when to move them out of the hatching box?* he thought. She had promised to look after them. His mind fluttered downwards on a meandering course. *When will she go into the small tropical house, what will she think – when will she know my secret, how long after I'm dead? I hope she goes in soon, otherwise they will starve…*He dropped, and his muscles slackened. His mind plopped like a pebble under the surface, into unconsciousness.

CHAPTER 11

Mumbai – Rooftop of the Hotel Gulistan
Petite, slim, everything he thought was good about woman crystallised into the figure before him. Amit saw Aashriya Aarzoo Romano sitting opposite him. He exhaled slowly, in case his breath marked her like Murano Venetian glass. He thought himself an Attila, a barbaric Hun, fearful at entering the gates of civilisation for the first time, scared at stepping through her doors of peerless beauty, formless in front of her art.

Aashriya was an elfin imagination from a fantasy, with pebble-jade eyes and ever-succulent lips, slightly parted. They held the pink faithless promise of fertility. Amit could scarcely believe she had agreed to meet him. Now he owed a debt to the don of Mumbai, and he hated that he had allowed himself to be so enveloped. David had arranged the first meeting and Amit suspected he had fallen into David's trap. Amit was unable to contain his desire and had panted her name to David, asking for her every day after the party for weeks, gasping in the spasms and throws of unrequited love. Aashriya was to Amit as a toy to a love-starved child. He tried to resist, but his usual strength had failed.

Amit realised that he had not yet spoken, or even gestured. He had, unashamedly, without self-analysis, arrived about an hour early. A few days ago he had asked David to book the rooftop in his best hotel, *The Gulistan*, The Rose Garden, which David had named after himself. It was a modern achievement of Mumbai, a place that rivalled the Taj in glamour, except the Taj still held the top spot in the historic hotels, even if it had to be refurbished after the Pakistani attacks. Amit had sent a team of men with specific instructions. He did not expect David to have enough class to organise things. His team had been working since yesterday to arrange the display on the hotel rooftop, so that now Amit was surrounded on all four sides by a swathe of semi-tropical plants and flowers. Amit had personally chosen these for their colours and fragrance, and some had been flown in on his private jet from Dubai. The flora now created a dazzling display, colour-coordinated, with different schemes blending one pattern into the other without jarring to the eye. The flowers formed an almost botanical enclosure around them, hiding Marine Drive and excluding the bustle of the business district below, creating a private garden, an enclosed world. Except for a space to Amit's left where a small patch was left open, so that those sitting at the table would have an unhindered view beyond the jungle canopy of the Arabian Sea.

Amit sat on one of the two white hand-carved chairs that had been set at a slight angle to each other, so anyone seated on them would not be forced to stare face-on, but could glance across, and so would be looking at the sea most of the time.

Amit looked again at the chair opposite, and realised it was still empty. He had only imagined Aashriya sitting there, like a movie scene played out on the curtain of his eyes, but she had not yet arrived.

He looked out over the ocean. The water reflected from its surface a thousand *jugnoo*, fireflies. He squinted at the water, and it seemed as if light-emitting fire fish winked back at him from the waves. He wondered if the world would look the same to Aashriya. The waves twinkled at him, and the sun started falling quickly. The light in chasing the globe overshot its mark and seemed to be falling off the edge of the world, into the chasm. He was not worried whether it would rise again and manage to find its way back from the abyss, or whether the solar light of the Earth would escape the black hole where it disappeared to every night. The blackness felt familiar to him, as had lain awake on his bed most nights, wondering about the emptiness of womanly experience in his life so far. There would be light if Aashriya Aarzoo Romano was in his sight, illuminating his eyes. He imagined a world of the deep, away from the struggles of Mumbai and Dubai life, like the overflowing cornucopia of life he had created on the rooftop; he smiled as he looked at the opulence of greenery.

Amit waited, unable to hide his bulk. He was not sure where to place his limbs, and his legs spread under the table, as he was unable to cross them. His gait was too simian, which would not allow for him to stand

and greet her, yet he must. His features were manly and square, and his normal confidence and calm seemed attractive to many women. His usual singularity of purpose and cleanness of vision cut through the smog of post-modern confusion. He adjusted his cufflinks once again, made sure the top button on his shirt was fastened to ensure that his chest hair, which sprouted in tufts up to his neck and made a confluence with his beard, remained hidden.

Aashriya Aarzoo Romano arrived forty minutes late, which was forty minutes earlier than she would be for a film shoot. She floated in on a waft of Neptune's sea breath, skin like ocean foam, sparkling with a luminescence of pink pearl that seemed to give light to the dying day. She imparted her fragrance to the flowers, bestowed a perfume to the rooftop atmosphere that paled the hibiscus. Aashriya took the only other seat without being invited, offered no apology, and gifted him a smile that eclipsed the white lilies. Neither spoke. Amit was unable to return her smile but grimaced after a short while. He sat back down then pulled himself up and touched his top shirt button.

'You did all this?' she said, waving a regal hand at the floral decorations. 'For me?'

Amit managed another grimace.

'There was no need...' She paused and jutted forward as near a perfect chin as he had seen. 'A *Chai* from the *Chai wallah* on Chowpatty Beach would have been enough,' she said.

Amit could not imagine anything more incongruous than the undisputed Queen of Bollywood drinking *Chai* from a street vendor. 'It's nothing – nothing...' He looked down then unable to stop and hating himself, he said, 'Compared to you, it's less than nothing.' He hoped she did not see his beading sweat.

'Oh, but it's beautiful,' she said, looking at the floral display, 'I'm not used anything like this.'

'But you must be, I mean, people...guys must all the time...'

'It's so lovely,' she said ignoring his obvious statement.

Amit watched her staring with narrowed dreamy eyes at the floral collection, breathing deeply, gathering the concentrated dusk fragrance into her nostrils with closed eyes. He wondered if she was truly moved by the experience. 'It's less than you deserve,' he stuttered. 'I wish I could be doing justice to your beauty...' said Amit, looking down and fiddling with his cufflinks. He suddenly felt conscious of his slightly staid, middle-class English speech. In India, his lack of English-medium education was an indelible stain on his tongue, a black blot that even the University of Oxford had not quite removed.

Aashriya smiled again and he stole another glance, feeling large and inadequate every time she looked at him, disenfranchised of power by her face.

'Thank you for inviting me.'

'It is my pleasure, truly.' He waved a dismissive hand. 'As too inadequate as the preparations are...'

She looked up at the bearer who arrived behind Amit after the apportioned period of time, under strict instruction. He was resplendent in his red and gold uniform, with a silver silken turban shimmering in the dying sun, red and purple now.

Amit realised the waiter had arrived; he beckoned him with a small signal of his hand, without turning away from her. 'What will you have?' He gestured expansively, spreading his arms wide, but unable to stop his left hand shooting to the top button of his shirt. 'Anything. Chicken *biryani*, Bombay Duck, Kashmiri *korma* –'

'Is there a menu?' she asked

'Meaning? Everything is the menu. You can be having anything, you name it.'

Aashriya laughed her bewitching laugh. 'A cup of *Chai*, then.'

Amit was not sure if she was laughing at the desperation in his voice, or whether she was enjoying his discomfort. 'Maybe I should just order a selection –'

'*Sirf ek cup Chai*. Just cup of *Chai*, please, Amit *Sahib*,' she said.

He felt himself unmanned by hearing his name spoken aloud in her voice for the first time. He noticed she did not acknowledge the waiter, who was now hovering and smiling. Amit thought she was giving him control by not ordering to the waiter, in case she insulted Amit's masculinity. He growled at the waiter, 'Chai aur choti moti cheezeh lahoo! Tea, and bring the small things!'

'*Ji Sahib. Ekdam layah*.' Now that he had been ordered the waiter dared to show his yellow, nicotine enamel under a black-waxed moustache. Amit knew he was pretending deference and hospitality, but really laughing at his inadequacy of seduction. Laughing at his failure to lure Aashriya onto his hook-feast – she had wriggled past, an expert at noticing the barbed worm. Amit glanced again at the over-dressed waiter, whose moustache immediately drooped as his smile fell to his chin.

'Bring what I ordered before.' This time the waiter did not speak, but nodded with a frozen expression. Amit knew the servant would not dare to look at Aashriya. She had not given the waiter a second glance. The bearer went to a hidden alcove, and got out a parasol.

'I hope the setting sun is not too much dazzling?' Amit said. He gestured towards the golden globe as if it were an irritant.

'Would you drop the sun out of the sky if it were?' she said, inviting the natural riposte. He wondered if she could entrap him unconsciously.

'For you, I would tackle *Ra* himself, and throw him off his chariot,' replied Amit, aware in the recesses of his mind that the silken web had wrapped its strands around his chest, and this was the start of the falling. He felt like abandoning his breathing to it.

The waiter unfolded the parasol. Aashriya looked up and Amit watched her face change, as she moved her lips to read the Urdu, then English, gold lettering on the side of the parasol:

Pyar bur sukhta hai	Affection can grow
Khabo ki shaam meh jaiseh –	In the sunset of my dreams –
Phool buruf se nikleh	Like tulips from snow

'It... How? I mean who –'

'I have never written Haiku before,' Amit interrupted her, wiping the dribbled sweat from his chin, although he felt the cooling sea breeze. He knew there was no tradition of Haiku in Urdu. 'I used to write poetry at school, though.'

'Love poetry?' she teased.

He relapsed into Hindi and then translated into English. 'My *dost* would be making fun – all my friends.'

'Well, I think it's beautiful,' she said, closing her eyes and putting both hands on her chest.

Suddenly Amit felt his sweat had become the sweet sheen of victory, his nervousness the full flush of love. He looked out over the sea to hide his eyes. The waiter bought up tea in an antique engrained silver service, and a team of bearers followed, carrying numerous trays with elaborate snacks. Sweetmeats, *mitai*, of innumerable colours, rich with *ghee* and cream: the pleasures of India. Samosas, plates of *kheer* and *rasmalai*.

'David said he is having Italian and a Chinese chef, but I love the

Indian things. I hope you don't mind that I am not ordering anything exotic and foreign?'

'Oh, how did you know *kheer* was my absolute favourite?'

Amit just tried to smile. He beckoned the head waiter, who brought forward a large bowl from one of the side tables. 'It's the Hyderabadi *Gil-e-Firdous*, The Clay of Paradise. I know you love it. I think it is your *Ami*'s, mother's recipe, or as close to it as I could get.' The waiter brought over the rich Hyderabadi version of the pudding, which had vermicelli as well as rice and mixed dry fruits: almonds, currants, dried apricots and peaches and pistachios in it. He set the large traditional clay dish on the table and removed the earthenware lid.

The writing floated on the surface of the *kheer*, a flowing script in Urdu and English, side by side, written in saffron paste.

Teri ankhon meh	Depths of your eyes, there
Meri chahateh aks hain –	My desires are reflected –
Tu kehkashan hai	You're my universe

Amit looked down hoping she would not see him wipe his palms on his trousers. 'I know you can read Urdu. Your father taught you.'

'This is too much, Amit sahib. How can I destroy such beauty?' she said.

He thought she meant it. The use of his name followed by the diminutive moved him to a new level of intimacy, and he leaned forward. Sahib usually implied a formal relationship, but he felt sure on this occasion she had used it as an affection.

The bearer brought over a bouquet. 'Sorry, Sahib,' he said. 'I forgot to give you these at the beginning.' He handed the flowers to Amit. Amit saw him standing there, quivering. 'They're not for me, idiot. They are for Miss Aashriya.' Amit had also forgotten the flowers. 'Do the other thing now, too,' he said to the waiter.

The man breathed out and rushed over to a part of the floral arrangement, his long red tunic swishing as he passed. He fiddled with some flowers close to Aashriya, and then he moved the flowers and long leaves back from the arrangement. A new Haiku, written in white unopened rose heads and nestled on a bed of marigolds, was now revealed. The flowers were fixed onto an upright plaque, which nestled amongst the larger collection:

Hoonton ke nami	Wetness of your lips –
Se – sarsabz hotha hai bagh	My life's garden becomes green
Is zindagi ka	And ever more verdant

The sea breeze tossed the loose strands of hair that Aashriya allowed to play on her face, like golden fingers of the setting sun god, which reached out and caressed her skin, as if reluctant to leave his priestess for another night. Amit stared at her hair, his lips parted and parched; his eyes following, transfixed, the rare raven strand amongst the brown spun tresses, as they undulated in the breeze.

'Is that why Muslim women have to cover their hair?' she said.

For the first time he felt embarrassed to be addressed as a Muslim, since his teacher had humiliated him for being descended from an 'Afghan conqueror' and for being 'illegitimately Indian' when he was ten. 'I suppose so.'

'You suppose? That's not like the Amit Sahib I have heard of.'

'Your hair is unique, amazing. I have never imagined hair so brown-golden, so radiant…' He felt himself inadequate again. He should have kept his mouth shut and let the poetry speak. Then he had a flash of inspiration, 'Bring me *qalam* and ink with good calligraphy paper.' Amit saw the question arising in the waiter and crushed it with, 'This is Mumbai, and you work for David Gul.'

He bade Aashriya eat from the *kheer* dish, and insisted he serve her tea himself, which he poured without spilling into the delicate china cups; hot sweet and milky, infused with aniseed. Steam rose from the long curving spout of the teapot as he did so. He caressed the carving on the handle, which had jade and onyx inlay. 'This was Bahadur Shah Jahan Zafar's tea service.'

'The last Emperor of India!' she said. 'I didn't know you collected antiques.' She paused. 'Amit Sahib, I only drink tea without milk and with cardamom…'

'Sorry, sorry.' He turned to the waiter. '*Oii bewakufh! Elaichi walli Chai lahoo*. Oi, idiot! Bring cardamom tea.' He turned back to her and whispered, 'Sorry…'

Aashriya looked back at the clay bowl in front of her. The creamy *kheer* contrasted with the earthy reds and browns of the bowl, and the saffron orange writing highlighted the lighter shades of the earthenware pot. 'I cannot, dare not, spoil such beauty. Let's leave it untouched, let the words of your poem echo out over the sea for all eternity. A gift to the ocean. I will savour the words.'

She recited:

> *Depths of your eyes*
> *My desires are reflected –*
> *You're my universe.*

Aashriya recited the words, like *kheer* dripping from her lips. Amit imagined she was not acting. He stared at her, as she looked serenely over the sea and the setting sun. He did not speak, in case he disturbed her meditative state. The waiter returned with the tea.

They both sipped in silence. He could not be sure how much time had passed, but most of the sun dipped below the horizon, and the sea turned midnight-blue. He had not noticed the waiters placing numerous *diya*, small clay lamps with wicks dipped in *ghee* around the hotel rooftop, at strategic points near the flowers and plants. They had also sprinkled the flowers and plants with water, so that the flickering light from the *diya* reflected from the water droplets. The whole rooftop seemed to be dotted with transient fireflies. On the sides stood lanterns on tall shepherd's crooks, with tea-lights in them. The glass of the lanterns had shapes etched into the surface, a moon or stars, which increased the twinkling of the lights.

The bearer returned with a set of traditional calligraphy pens, and paper that seemed as thick as parchment. He carried a small bottle of black ink, and he placed all three on the table in front of Amit.

'*Tazah Chai layoh.*' Amit ordered. The waiter left to fetch fresh tea.

Amit turned and tried to smile at Aashriya. He felt certain that, if he persevered, it would come out right. He looked at her for a while, and she smiled back.

Then Amit removed his jacket, dipped the thick bamboo calligraphy quill into the ink like a scribe of yesteryear, and began to write, his whole being now focused on the movements of his arm and hand.

The words flowed into his arm and gave it strength. He wrote in the *Nasta'liq* script, the long horizontal strokes and the changing thickness of lines exaggerated by the qalam, the proportions of the letters perfectly in keeping with the rules.

Zulfoon ki chahon meh –	In the shade of your
Imaan keh barooseh par	Hair – on the strength of pure belief
Zindagi choopi	Are my life's secrets

Aashriya read the poem. 'It's a haiku in Urdu and English – they all are.' She did not wait for him to answer. She checked the number of syllables were correct in his poems, both in Urdu and English, by reciting them under her breath and tapping her fingers in time on the table. He felt pleased she knew the format for haiku: *that's what makes her so different from all the others*. He saw her astonishment as she realised the poems meant the same thing in both languages, and were flawless.

'How clever of you – did you just think of the last one just now? You must be the first person to write haiku in Urdu.'

Amit was silent, suddenly self-aware again, gangling and awkward, unused to praise. 'It's so beautiful,' she said, and put her hand on his. He saw tears forming in her eyes. 'I am unworthy. Truly unworthy of this much praise and beauty.'

'No one is more worthy than you. And it is insignificant compared to your perfection…' he said, and with a huge effort he managed not to look at her hand as she kept it on his. On the few times he had tried before in his life, he had failed with women; most memorable had been the college beauty who had mocked him. He felt the bile rising, the familiar stench in his throat. He dared not move his hand, as much as he needed to, for fear that she would feel his sweat or worse sense his trembling; he had to overcome the guilt. He felt his shirt becoming damp.

'No. Mr Amit sahib with the beautiful poetry, I am not perfect. These flowers are perfect, the sunset was perfect, and God is perfect.' She looked at him with a skewed expression, he thought, as if to say *you of all people should realise that, Amit Sahib. Have you not just committed the most heinous of crimes that a Muslim can commit? Did you not just say I was perfect when only Allah is perfect? You have made* shirk. *Assigned false gods with your one and only true God.*

For the first time in his life, Amit forgot the struggle. The tea came, and this time she poured with an elegance and mastery of her body movements that he had not witnessed before. She held the teapot in her right hand, and folded her flapping sleeve with her left hand. Then she lifted the teapot to the correct height above the porcelain cup, so that as the tea tumbled into the cup it made a musical tinkling sound. Aashriya poured for him first, then for herself.

I should have known she likes her tea pale golden and without milk, he thought. *So uncommon in India.*

A silence extended over them as they drank, and it enveloped them, cushioning the need for words. Aashriya reached for her china teapot with the cardamom tea to pour another cup, but he insisted by gesture, took the teapot from her hands and served her. Amit barely trusted himself to pour the tea; he felt clumsy and boorish. Neither spoke. He became acutely aware of the thin strand of telepathy between them that might make this moment immortal.

The bustle of Mumbai below became irrelevant, as the city started on its nighttime rituals. The silence became peace without need for speech. As if any words spoken would be ugly and inadequate.

Pleased that he had served her, he now followed her gaze out to sea again. She put up a hand and refused a third cup. Somewhere deep inside he knew he would have to speak, and destroy the period of perfection.

'If I were to be spending every minute for the rest of my life giving thanks to your unnamed teacher for this moment, then it would still be insufficient...' he finally said.

'No, no. Thank you for this eternal sunset. If the moment became perfect, it was because of your artistry.'

'You are perfect. Eternal.' Amit realised he had fallen into *Shaitan*'s trap, but he could not stop himself.

'I shall treasure this even when I'm old and wrinkled and nobody wants me anymore.' Her hand was on his hand again, and this time it felt more familiar, almost as if it belonged. Amit nearly replied that he would still want her when she was old and wrinkled, but he stopped himself in time. He would embarrass himself further, and become even more ape-like in her presence. He had visions of spoiling her exquisite Punjabi suit with the tea or food. The *kameez* was a rare turquoise with silver embroidery, highlighting dancing and displaying cranes in gold filigree. The darker salwar, stolen from the waves of the Arabian Sea, it seemed, reflected the shimmering colours of the ocean. Amit noticed that her eyes filled again. He reached nearby and picked a dark maroon rose and held it out under her face; he gathered a tear, which watered her left cheek. He brought it close to his eyes and studied the single drop.

'This is more beautiful than any flower here, and more precious to me than all the pearls in that ocean.' Aashriya sighed imperceptibly. Amit knew that now she was truly swept up in the moment. 'You have more art and poetry in you than I've ever seen in all my years of cinema,' she said.

Amit forgot all his awkwardness, his looks, even the *Jihad*. He smiled and held the smile: the first time he had held a smile that was more than his usual fleeting momentary grimace, since his schooldays.

'So, what special plans have you got for me, and dare I ask, for the rest of us?'

Amit did not respond for a moment, as he tried to understand what she meant.

Aashriya smiled. 'I mean... I'm trying to understand what *Jaish* is all about?'

Amit felt shocked, but controlled himself. He suspected that David Gul would have sent her with a mission, but he had forgotten himself in the flurry of emotion.

To the outside world, to those who knew he was Amit Bahadur, he was the de facto CEO of *The Army of Light and Peace*, for barely anyone had seen Zulfiqar bin *Hijaz*. Here, on the rooftop, in a different world, he had tried to be just a man in love with a woman. He was no ordinary man, and she no ordinary woman. Amit knew she had never known love unconditional, but had always traded it like commodities on the BSE, the Mumbai stock exchange. He recited a prayer in his heart as he steadied himself, ready to sell his soul.

Birmingham

On seeing Holly's door, relief covered Jessica's face like the sheets of rain soaking her. Her thighs shook, and her legs ached. She had been chased by the TV reporters and newspaper journalists. Everybody who she had ever known had asked her the same question: 'Was Hamid the suicide bomber?'

A feeding frenzy had started in the media, which had felt like sharks thrashing after her in a small pool. Yesterday, Blair's paper had been the first to print the story HAMID KHAN: SUICIDE BOMBER. The newspaper accused Hamid of blowing up the train at New Street Station, quoting confidential sources. Within hours the story had become international headline news, and had taken over the print, radio and television news. The journalists had tracked Jessica down to her parents' before breakfast; she had been on the run all day. She had changed taxis four times to make sure she was not being followed. The thought of Holly's face on the other side of the door almost made Jessica smile as she brushed her wet hair away from her face, which had darkened in the rain.

Jessica rapped once on the front door, and then banged out her special rhythm loudly. She knew that Holly would immediately recognise her knock, even though it was late into the night.

Holly opened the door, her eyes widening and her eyebrows arched. 'Jess! Oh my God! Where have you been? I've been worried sick.' She leaned forward, and grabbed Jessica in a hug.

Jessica did not move. 'Can I come in?' she asked. The question was rendered unnecessary by years of intimate sisterly support they had provided for each other.

Jessica's shoulders slumped as she pushed her hair out of her eyes, which hung, bedraggled, in lank ropes. She entered the hallway past Holly. 'Had to wait until it was dark – bastards might be right behind me.'

'Who? Yeah, come in. Take your coat off, you're completely soaked.' Holly paused as she took her coat and looked at Jessica. 'God, are you alright?'

'I feel worse than I look.' She rubbed her face, forcing blood into her cheeks and her eyes to focus.

Holly followed Jessica into the living room. 'I've been looking all over for you, sweetheart. I must have been to your house ten times, and phoned you more than a million.'

'How did you get past the wolf pack?'

'There's so many of them. Would never have believed there are so many photographers in the whole wide world. Couldn't get to your front door.'

'Have you seen the papers?' Jessica clutched a pile under her right arm. She let her handbag drop to the floor and put the papers on the coffee table. She pulled at the thick wet jumper, which felt cloying on her skin, her wet jeans uncomfortable.

'You're so pale and ghostly. You all right?'

'You know what's happened,' said Jessica, more loudly than she intended, before realising that Holly must have been shocked seeing her like this; she had forgotten to ask about Hamid being labelled a terrorist.

'Sorry, yeah, yeah, the papers are going mad. Of course I heard about

Hamid and I'm sorry, Jessica, but I've been so worried for you... I can't think straight.' She guided Jessica to the sofa. 'Where have you been?'

'I tried to go to mum and dad's, but they followed me, tracked me down to their house –'

'They're like wolves, you're right. They kept shouting a million questions at me when I went round to yours. 'You a friend of Jessica Flowerdew? Was her fiancé a suicide bomber? What do you know about the terrorists? Did you get suspicious?' They just kept on, hemmed me in. I had to run to get away. Oh, here's you feeling terrible, and me prattling on. Sit down. Let me get you a drink. You get out of those wet things, and I'll get you a blanket,' said Holly. 'Let's have vodka martinis the way we used to. I've still got that shaker.'

'Yeah, okay. Anything... my nerves.' Jessica starred at her shaking hands, as if that would help steady them.

'Oh no – I know what you need. Some hot, sweet tea, and a blanket. It must have been horrible.' Holly went to get the blanket, as Jessica pulled off her wet clothes and struggled with her jeans. 'You poor thing.' Holly wrapped the blanket around Jessica and picked up her clothes. Jessica stood and Holly held Jessica's arms, comforting her. Jessica looked back into her friend's eyes for the first time, and saw the concern. Holly hugged her. Jessica closed her eyes for a moment, and let the tears stream down her face.

'I'm sorry, Holly.'

'Don't be silly, Jess. I really feel for you. I'm confused now... what with after the funeral, and the way his mother and sister behaved, I don't know what to think. I know you loved him. It's been weeks since Hamid died, but it just seems to be getting worse for you. I'm so really really sorry, darlin'...' Holly looked into her eyes, holding her at arms length, and then she hugged her again.

Jessica tried to blink the tears away, but failed. 'I still can't believe he's gone...' she said, and wiped her eyes with her fingertips. 'Not now, not like that. What the papers are saying has put me right back to feeling like I was when he died.'

'It's that lying bastard Blair. How was Hamid's family with you? I mean, has Farah been in touch since the funeral?'

'No, she hasn't. How should I know what they're thinking and feeling, except for how much they hate me? You know what they're like. They know what's going on, but they don't know. After what happened at the mosque, I don't expect anything from them. Maybe they're sorry, now their son has been accused.'

'Too bloody late now,' said Holly. Jessica wiped her cheeks, Holly held out more tissues. 'Relax, lie back. You must be shattered.'

Jessica slumped back into the sofa, kicked her boots off. 'Oh, my feet! Hope I wasn't followed.'

'No worries. I'll show them my teeth – you know me,' said Holly. Jessica tried a smile, but ran out of will; it froze, half-formed, on her face. She closed her eyes and wrapped the blanket more tightly around her body, as Holly left to make the drinks. She came back with some lasagne, and held the plate under Jessica's nose. 'Here, eat something. I bet you haven't had anything solid in over two days.'

'No thanks, don't feel like –'

'Eat,' Holly ordered, and put the plate on a lap tray on Jessica's knees. 'It'll warm you up.'

Jessica knew she had always been great in a crisis, able to take control and calm her, soothe the pickaxe pain that ruffled her brow. 'When you've eaten, there's your drink,' Holly added, setting the tea down on the coffee table. 'I put some brandy in it. I think you need it. We'll have martinis one day, when you're feeling better.'

'Thanks Holly, you're so great. What would I do –'

'Oh, shush it now,' Holly said. Jessica looked at her best friend and noticed her narrow mouth, brunette hair hanging in pencil lines covering her cheeks as Holly leaned forward, cut off square in line with her jaw, which gave her mouth a harsh look.

Jessica felt glad that she had escaped the press pack and was able to finally talk to Holly. Her breathing slowed and she lapsed into dreamlessness as she slept, and her muscles unwound for the first time since the funeral.

Just before falling asleep she remembered the day she met Holly. Jessica was interviewing women who were in violent abusive relationships for a BBC documentary, and she had known even then that the icy pain in Holly's eyes marked her out as different. Holly had talked in a manner all of her own, as she told Jessica about her partner. FC, as Holly had always called him (she allowed Jessica to guess what the acronym stood for), had been a violent philanderer, who had created a patch of bruises in livid colours like a world atlas over Holly's face and body. He had gifted her a newborn child and stolen her life savings, which she had worked for until the skin became opaque on her cheekbones, until it looked like greased paper, her fingers like rolls of puff pastry after washing and wringing soiled bed linen from old people's homes. Holly worked for years as a washing assistant in an industrial laundry operation, and supplemented her egregious income with private cleaning jobs. Despite the divorced women's group and FC's continuing attacks, she worked full time.

Jessica mostly remembered the pride that had shone from deep within; the last embers of a respect that refused to be put out by the effluent of the world, no matter how much FC had pissed on her soul, Holly had said. She had just turned up a week later on Jessica's doorstep. Holly had arrived bloody, broken physically, but had looked Jessica in her eyes as she cradled her baby girl, who did not have a name at that time. 'I've left him, at last,' Holly had exhaled in a matter-of-fact way, as if finally washing out the remains of poisonous fumes from her lungs. There was none of the usual accompanying triumphalism and artifice of celebrating the separation.

Jessica had consoled her, and from that moment Holly had become her friend. Jessica comforted her by simply laying on hands, which had more healing than any miraculous preacher, and she had waited quietly until Holly had finished sobbing on her shoulder. Then Jessica had carefully, although inexpertly, dressed her wounds and put her to bed. Holly stayed with her for three months until she became confident enough to move out following a court order, which restrained him and then got him convicted for assault.

'I'm gonna make a new life, for me and her,' Holly had said, and Jessica knew she had. 'I hope FC tastes fire when he's dead, burns in hell like what he kept me in for all those years. And I swear, Jess, if he ever comes trying to see Sally then I'll stick my butcher's knife in his throat and saw his head off. I swear to God, and I don't care what they do to me.' They had both known there was no chance of contact with the baby, because of his uncontrollable violence. Jessica never did use Holly's segment in her programme.

After a while, when Jessica stirred, she said. 'I know it wasn't him. Hamid could never have been a suicide bomber.'

'I'm sorry for what I blurted out to Talat at Hamid's funeral.' Holly looked at her sideways and said, 'I know I shouldn't – but sorry – I got to – how do you know?'

'Holly – for God's sake. You too?'

'But how do you know?'

'Come on. I was with him for three years – shared everything that was important and a million things that weren't – things that were irrelevant to the rest of the world, except to us –'

'I know, I know – but so did the wives of the 7/7 bombers, and they didn't know anything either.' Holly paused; Jessica felt she looked unsure, as if she had gone too far. 'The papers... it's all over the TV, every day, every news channel. They're all saying it. *Hamid Sadiq Khan, the suicide bomber...* '

'Oh fuck the papers and screw the TV.' Jessica threw the blanket off her.

'Okay. Okay,' said Holly, putting the blanket back over her. 'And I'm really sorry for calling him a suicide bomber at the funeral, but Talat was accusing you of being a witch.' Jessica made no reply. Holly made her another cup of tea. 'At least you're looking a more healthy colour, now that you're all flushed,' Holly said, and smiled. 'I think you're near the end of your strength. Even you have a limit.'

She knew what Holly meant; Jessica pursed her full lips. Her face was always made up with understated, professional colours. She never went anywhere without her pale lipstick, at least.

Holly asked in a softer voice, 'What are you gonna do? Have the police been in touch again? Did you tell them anything new?'

'What else could I tell them?' Jessica shrugged and wandered off into a few blank moments, tea held suspended in mid-air in her right hand as she starred at the black TV screen. 'Do you think it's possible? You shared your life with someone who – who was – would...' Jessica shivered and looked back to Holly, taking voluble slurps from her drink followed by more, to lessen the chances of spilling it from her shaking hands. She brushed her drying hair back with her left hand, only to have it immediately fall back across her face again. It was becoming wavy as it dried out.

Jessica leaned back as the tiredness hit her like a vacuum. Her set face felt bloodless. Hamid was gone. She closed her eyes and realised she should not be angered by Holly's suggestion, although she had been outraged with the police. 'You know the questions. How, why, where, when? All the while I've been trying not to ask myself the question: *could he?* Could Hammie even have had the potential to be a suicide bomber?' She looked at Holly, at her plain everyday outfit, her lanky appearance, which made her shoulders stoop forward. Jessica started shivering, which made her hands shake and slosh the tea. Holly leaned across, took her drink, and set it on the table. Jessica said, 'If you'd asked me the same question a few weeks ago, I would have laughed in your face, but now...'

'Are the police still certain?'

'They seemed so sure when they questioned me, although they don't say that in so many words, and of course I told them it was impossible. But now, with the papers all screaming? It's like they're battering my skull with sledgehammers.' Jessica felt as if her certainty was reshaping into doubts; what she most feared and had not allowed herself to think, was slowly forming into a solid reality. Jessica shook her head and covered her eyes with her palms, as if she was not sure if she had even known Hamid or had lived a life with him at all.

Jessica read the unsaid question in Holly's eyes. 'There was nothing!' Jessica almost screamed without meaning to. Her chest throbbed and her feet felt as if lava flowed over them, and she pulled them up onto the sofa. 'How could I have been so stupid?'

'Maybe you weren't. Maybe they just got it wrong?'

'You know I'm not like that. I mean, I knew Hamid well. Before I committed myself. Yes, I loved him. But I don't even give my number to guys until I know their mother's maiden name.'

'I'm sorry for your loss...' Holly gave Jessica a small hug.

'Thank you, Holly.' Jessica sat up, and thought she should tell Holly about Sebastian, about spending time with him. She had not told Holly yet because of the uncertainty in her own mind about her feelings for Sebastian, which had only been made worse by recent events. Jessica forced herself to take a more conversational tone and said, 'Oh, talking of guys. I met this man. Really weird, but fascinating.'

'Oh, and when was this? You were running from the photographers, and you still met a guy? You meet men even in the middle of a crisis?' said Holly, tossing her head. She took a loud slurp from her mug of tea.

'No, I ran into him; literally fell over him at the train station. I mentioned him very briefly to you, on the phone? When I went looking for Hamid, after I heard the bomb had gone off. I tumbled into him and he helped me up.'

'Yeah, bet he did. Not everyday he gets a Baywatch–Scarlett

Johansson look-a-like running into him.'

'He was on Hamid's train.'

'Did he see Hamid?'

'Yeah well, he thinks he did, even talked to him before the explosion. He helped to calm me down. His name is Sebastian.'

'Oh, la di dah – Sebastian,' said Holly.

Jessica knew Holly could never be entirely serious; maybe that was what she called her 'shit-shield', after FC dumped on her. 'I shouted at him, Holly – had a real go at him and called him a fucking terrorist sympathiser.'

'Now, I really am confused. He helps you, stops you running into a death trap... a station that's crumbling, maybe about to blow up even... then you shout and swear at him? Man, he must have thought it was his lucky day.'

'No, silly, it's because he's a lecturer –'

'Is he rich and good-looking?' asked Holly.

'A lecturer at SOAS. That's a university in London.'

'I know. Well, heard of it at least, anyway,' Holly shook her head. 'What the hell's that got to do with the price of peas?' asked Holly, and frowned.

'He gave me his business card, and said I could visit him anytime.' Jessica took a deep breath, trying not to look guilty. 'Actually, I have met him for coffee, to discuss things.'

'He wanted to meet you, I'm sure. Is he fit?'

'Holly, do you think I was wondering or looking at a time like that?' Jessica blushed slightly, and hoped Holly would think it the effect of her second brandy-laced tea.

'He is, isn't he? I can tell by your face.'

'Anyway, he said he could help, that he knew all about this Muslim malarkey business...'

'Thank God someone does, cos they don't seem to know what the bloody hell they're doing. Oh sorry, just got to go and check on Sally.' She came back with another cup of tea.

'How is she?' said Jessica.

'Sleeping like the angel she isn't, a real madam,' said Holly. In the years that followed Holly's escape she told her daughter, Sally, that Daddy could not see her because he had gone to heaven. As a good Daddy, God loved him and wanted Daddy to be close to Jesus. 'Anyway – you gonna see him?'

'I've seen him a couple of times already, but it's not like that.'

'I mean are you gonna ask him for help, see if there's anything he can do? You're hurting –'

'I need to know about Hamid. I need to know. The more I think about it, these last weeks seem like a different universe, and with him it feels like some other lifetime. When he was alive, I mean... '

Jessica felt her well of tears overflowing again, as the regret of not being invited to his funeral filled her, which increased when she thought about the way she had forced herself onto his family in the mosque. It was no longer the thoughts of his body parts that she had imagined lying in the coffin that upset her most. She had accepted his death after the initial denial – but the outright rejection and exclusion, and being made to feel like something inhuman by Hamid's family at his funeral, still felt like a bloody wound. The accusation of cursed witch, *abshagun*, felt like rejection by a thousand cuts. That pain of that – and the realisation that she had never belonged to his world, and never would have been accepted by his family, despite three years of patience – made her sit back and cry. Jessica cried as if she was alone at home.

How wonderful of Holly. Why is it that men always try and shut you up and don't let women cry? she thought, as Holly silently passed over the box of tissues. 'I've got to try – try and...'

'How? What you gonna do?'

'I don't know. I've got to find out. Even if I have to go and keep seeing Sebastian to try and make sense of things.'

'So, what's wrong with that? You should see him again. Maybe he understands stuff we don't, or we can't...'

'Don't know. I don't know...' Jessica sucked her nail and then chewed the knuckle of her thumb as she stared at the blank TV screen in the corner again, 'Don't know anything anymore... but I do know I need answers, and the truth.'

'Good luck trying to get that out of a man,' said Holly and turned away to reach for the brandy bottle with a *hmmph* sound.

'I've got to. You know what this feels like? My life's mission. I can't live with this confusion any more, Holly. I have got to know if Hamid was the suicide bomber. Even if it kills me.'

CHAPTER 12

London
When Jimmy's eyes blurred into focus, his ears caught broken packets of conversion that his mind could not yet process. He found himself dressed in a bathrobe, in an orange room, sitting on a soft sofa. He was opaquely aware of people walking around him, to the back of him, as he sat in the centre of the room. He shivered; the hair on his body stood up. He had no idea how long he had been there. Men he had not seen before seemed to be busy milling around talking to each other, but no one looked at him.

He coughed and spluttered. Icy barbs stabbed into his guts, with crushed chillies at the bottom of his lungs. One of the men came forward and helped him wipe his face and mouth with a tissue, after he had vomited yellowish-green liquid that tasted like rabid dog's piss. He looked up to find another youth holding a cup of tea. He wondered why there had been a sudden change towards him.

As his vision cleared, he saw a small rosewood table with a single chair. Papers rustled on the table, as he recognised the *Shaikh* Abu Umar.

'How are you feeling now?' said Abu Umar, raising his eyebrows, a sheet of printed paper in his hand. When Jimmy gasped in response Abu Umar said, 'Don't worry. It's just a sensation of choking and drowning. Please don't worry, you will not actually stop breathing.'

'Fuckin' well feels like it!'

'So many times I tell, idiots! I tell them a thousand times. You know very well the zeal of youth. They love, how you say? They have a longing lust for rewards, heavenly hankering.'

'Nearly killed me, heavenly bastards, paradise pussies...' Jimmy retched, but his chest slowed, as his breathing started to return to normal.

'I know you weren't trying to kill me,' said Abu Umar. 'Yes, I've seen that look before.'

'What's that?' asked Jimmy.

'Eyes glazed over and confused, didn't knowing where to run, like a hungry Jewish housewife in Mark and Spencer's food department after one month's long fast,' the *Shaikh* said, and chuckled.

Jimmy coughed. His throat burned with the aftertaste of the acid from his stomach that he had vomited up, and his ribs ached. 'Your fuckin' boyfriends seemed to be sure, yeah. They better pray I don't catch 'em nowhere on the street.'

'Maybe that's just as well, then,' Abu Umar looked at the man who still held the tea at Jimmy's side. The man brought forward a side table, and set the mug down. 'It'll warm you up.' Abu Umar smiled at him.

Jimmy knew before the meeting that Abu Umar was from the Middle East. He found his accent lilting, and remembered a lesson at school about some country near Israel. Now he thought this man belonged to that land, his accent rounded like the hills and valleys that stretched and melted to the horizon, sheened into a cobalt sky. The pictures had made an impact on him, and he had had some framed and put on his bedroom wall. Abu Umar's voice reminded him of the soft blue-green hills of Lebanon.

'I hope you are feeling better?' He did not look like Omar Sharif exactly, but seemed as charming. Sofia loved watching Dr Zhivago, every time it came on TV. Abu Umar's short dark brown beard looked evenly groomed on his pale clear skin. He seemed Middle Eastern, yet not clearly definable. Manly, but youthful at the same time. Jimmy stared at him. Abu Umar then half-nodded to the attendant, more with eyes than head, who picked the mug off the table, cradled it in both hands with one palm under the base, offering it formally. Jimmy wondered if the *Shaikh* had trained them or whether they naturally understood his smallest gesture, some secret social Islamic telepathy. Like the signal of the petals to the honeybee, dung to its beetle, the prey's blood to the vampire bat. How many more Muslim mind games were to come?

Jimmy looked into the mug and wondered if the tea was poisoned, then dismissed the thought as irrational. If they wanted him dead, he would have been dead long since.

'Don't worry, it's quite safe,' said Abu Umar, and looked at him.

Jimmy saw his smile. He took a sip from the tea, and almost sighed with relief: hot and sweet. This man was not like the smoking man. Even his mocking tone seemed somehow on his side, filial.

'Are you from Lebanon?' Jimmy asked, surprising himself.

'Ahh, Lebanon. Do you know *Lubnan*? It means *milk*, some say… the real land of milk and honey…' Jimmy did not answer, but sipped his tea, and looked unblinking at Abu Umar. The *Shaikh* continued, 'You have heard of the Lebanese cedar?' Jimmy looked at him, blank-faced. 'The flag, the tree on the flag?' he asked.

Jimmy nodded, remembering his geography lesson, and Abu Umar smiled again. 'It is a national symbol, and you know the largest forest of the Cedars of Lebanon is on all sides of *Jabal Barouk*? Ah, she is a beautiful lady, the mountain.' He said mountain like *moon-thyen*, with softened syllables. 'She wears the cedars like a spreading emerald skirt, and when the sun shines on her…' Abu Umar gestured with his hands as if plucking stars from the air. '…all over her dress you can see dotted lapis lazuli and turquoise.'

Jimmy stared at him unmoving, wondering if he was taking the piss.

'You know, the boy flowers are found at the end of the branch, which is very short. The purple-brown cones, at first, have a little pink –'

'Who the fuck are you – David Attenborough?'

'These cones take three years to be big, to season. The trees cannot produce cones until they are older than you; but you know they may be a hundred years old before producing either male or female flowers…'

'What are you on about? You nearly killed me because of trees?' said Jimmy, and coughed again at the memory of liquid filling his lungs.

'You see, Jimmy, when the time is right – that's when you get the best.'

'Just let me go, yeah? I don't want –'

'What does time mean?' Abu Umar looked away, and seemed to drift off. Jimmy stayed silent. After some time, he seemed to come back.

'You know, my grandfather brought mountain tulips for my grandmother, red and black. The tulips are red and black, like the Burnet moth of Lubnan. Every day he goes into the cedar forest, and he cuts wood.' Abu Umar looked intently at Jimmy, his yellow eyes searching and feline. 'He loved his tobacco pouch made from scrotums of musk deer.' The *Shaikh* paused; Jimmy wandered if he did it for effect. *Why must stupid foreigners become so personal all of a sudden,* he thought, *telling all about their families?*

'He filled the scrotum,' Abu Umar continued – he cupped his right hand as if weighing the stag's bollocks in his palm – with the cedar's flowers. When he smoked it, sitting on the veranda of the old house, the thick smoke, so thick, would billow through the village, and all the young men would come to beg some cedar-flower-scented tobacco from my grandfather, the woodcutter. He know where to find the trees that just opened their flowers, and so made the best fragrances. Some trees do not produce flowers until they are over a hundred years old...'

'Prickly Juniper, the Burnet moth, the Cardinal butterfly?'

'You see, Jimmy, when the time is right – that's when you get the best. Your time is right. Now is right time,' said Abu Umar. He seemed not to have heard Jimmy. 'Then we had the *Yawm Al Nakba*, The Day of the Catastrophe, the creation of Zionist Monster.' Abu Umar looked away and seemed to drift. His face twitched once. Jimmy wondered if he felt anger or futile frustration made him speechless. Then he seemed to flow back, took a deep breath and puffed his cheeks out. 'You have the killer look, but you're not...'

'Not what?' asked Jimmy, intrigued.

'A killer. With lamb's eyes, and your scarred butterfly face.'

Jimmy thought he should be insulted, and on the street he would have been, but the mention of butterflies slowed his breathing. He looked intently at Abu Umar and scratched his scar.

The *Shaikh* looked at his bodyguards, and inclined his head slightly. They all filed out of the room.

'Aren't you afraid I might try and kill you?' asked Jimmy.

Abu Umar let out a gentle laugh. 'How do you propose to do that, lamb eyes?'

'I – I don't know. I could –'

'You were at the meeting tonight – you heard them.' Abu Umar gestured to the door the men had left from. 'I have taken machine gun nests, and massacred armoured battalions.' Abu Umar's mouth turned at the corners. Jimmy thought his pale face looked interested in him, a rare occurrence in Jimmy's life.

'Aren't you afraid?'

'No. I ain't never been afraid of no one,' said Jimmy, sticking his chin out.

'Sitting there in your bathrobe, breathless. Aren't you afraid I'll do something?'

'I didn't know you... they allowed you Muslims to be queer.' Jimmy's bravado in the face of fear had become a natural response.

Abu Umar laughed louder this time. 'But you're not smiling.'

'I ain't found nothing funny yet,' Jimmy replied.

'You don't strike me as a fanatic or a new convert,' said Abu Umar, serious again. He got up, and came and sat on the other side of the sofa. 'Why did you come here tonight?'

Jimmy did not reply.

Abu Umar leaned forward and scrunched up his nose. 'Did your father make you?'

Jimmy was impressed by his relaxed manner, how his slim body seemed firm under his brown *Jilbab*. He controlled his boys without shouting, or even raising his voice. Jimmy knew that such instant obedience and unquestioned following only came from respect. He realised the *Shaikh*'s bodyguards, at least the lieutenants, must have seen him leading from the front, and so the *Shaikh*'s life had become an example. A sugar idol crafted from the syrup of his words, held together by the treacle of his deeds.

They must have seen Abu Umar in action, fighting, because the bought kind of respect is worth nothing, knew Jimmy. This *izzat*, respect, did not emanate from fear. Jimmy had seen the way the bodyguards fell to serve him. They had vied with each other for that honour. The one who succeeded in getting close and serving the *Shaikh* beamed and seemed to grow tall, as if imbibing strength from the presence of Abu Umar. An infatuation fed by proximity. Jimmy had heard the dons of the drug world talking about the sensation in the past. They referred to the legendary figures in London drug history, in tones approaching sainthood. Those who had met them and had been in the presence of the dons had acquired some of their mystique by mere association. Jimmy guessed it would be much the same in the *Jihadi* schema. He understood how Abu Umar's boys desired that closeness with him, so that they could make a name for themselves, become legends when their time came. For now, however, they seemed content to be trainees in the *Guru-Chaylah*, Master-Apprentice, system. Jimmy had sometimes seen the looks of awe in the faces of his new recruits. Especially when they first came to him. He had the status they aspired to, so that when they saw his wealth their eyes were unable to fix or focus. The amazing, technicoloured visions of money and power made their eyes swivel loose in their sockets like gyroscopes.

None of the street kudos was of any help now. Here, Jimmy rated lower than any novice. Abu Umar's respect had reached a zenith unimagined by Jimmy. His bodyguards would freely give their lives for Abu Umar – no one would ever do that for him. That was more heady than any wine-drug, more empowering than fear or force. Jimmy realised why Abu Umar's bodyguards would go forward to meet bullets, or absorb an explosion into their flesh. They fully believed he was a great *Mujahid* of Islam. Jimmy thought they could not have loved Abu Umar more than give their lives to protect his.

'You came because of your dad?' said Abu Umar. When Jimmy did not reply, he continued, 'You're one of those.' Jimmy looked up, and he continued. 'Your father – he is not happy.'

'What do you know of him?'

'I don't know him. But you can't be here for any other reason,' said Abu Umar, as if stating a fact. Jimmy looked at his pale face, his youthful looks, his searching nocturnal eyes, and the dark brown trimmed beard with redder tufts that jutted out. Jimmy felt Abu Umar's intent gaze, which felt as if the *Shaikh* was peering into his brain with his full-moon yellow eyes. Jimmy shivered, and pulled his bathrobe tighter.

'My dad, he's one of you lot, innit...' Jimmy paused, not sure if he should continue. When the *Shaikh* made no reply, he said, 'Well, actually he's not one of you. He didn't fight no-one.'

'We all fight someone.'

'Well, my dad don't, yeah.'

'How did he manage to convince you to come tonight?' Abu Umar asked.

Jimmy felt the disc-like eyes fix him in their glow and reach into his secret heart; he looked down and lost pretence. 'He... *Abbo* said he ain't gonna have the operation, if I don't go mosque. That my... my...' He looked up at Abu Umar, whose face had softened as he sat with his open arms out, and nodded slightly.

'Your money is *haram*?' Abu Umar finished for him. 'They say you're dealing in drugs?'

Jimmy felt that Abu Umar's voice did not carry any condemnation. Or the usual traces of disgust that, with the mention of drugs, most people could not metabolise out of their system fast enough, before the poison of judgement set in. Abu Umar's voice did not suggest that, even in the undertones.

Jimmy had never felt embarrassed by his profession; there was a demand, and he filled it. For the first time he felt ashamed, and stared into his cold tea, as if the mysteries of why he had become a dealer lay in the milky skin that formed on its half-drunk cold surface. He remembered how Ahmad sat with Sofia drinking tea, twice a day without fail, morning and evening: *soonf elachi Chai*, aniseed and cardamom tea, boiled on a stove, made of almost all milk. He wondered if all Muslim people drank sweet, fragranced tea.

Jimmy thought the embarrassment he now felt, *sharam*, came because of Abu Umar's open voice. If only he would rant at him, call him a dirty street dealer, then Jimmy would be able to defend himself. Jimmy said nothing. The clever arguments had disappeared like the steam from the tea.

'You're quite some man on the streets – a main dealer, they say. You have money like a Saudi prince?'

'My dad wouldn't take it. Had to borrow it from Uncle Maulana Younis.'

'Ah, Younis… I'll come to the *Imam Sahib* later,' replied Abu Umar. 'So your dad, he fights. Do you came here fighting? Like you are fighting everyday on the streets – to make more money?' The *Shaikh* rubbed his forefinger and thumb together in typical Arab style, but his upper lip curled up, as if diseased. 'To keep your patch, that is how you got the scar, right?'

The *Shaikh* obviously disapproved of drug dealing, but his voice was open and not condescending. Jimmy found it weird that he seemed more intrigued, and not disgusted, like most people Jimmy had ever met – especially the religious people in his community, who would have been the loudest in their derision. They would automatically repeat their favourite comments – *Tauba Tauba Ya Allah! May Allah forgive!* – while most snorted or smoked or injected in between the exclamations. *Fuckin' hypocrites*, thought Jimmy.

He fingered his scar and put a protective hand over it. 'How did you know?'

Abu Umar smiled. 'See, Yusuf, we all fight. It is Yusuf Mohammed or Mohammed Yusuf, isn't it?' Abu Umar looked at him, smiling without mocking again. No one had ever called Jimmy Mohammed

Yusuf, except the ghosts of his ancestors. Jimmy tried to work it out. The smile was mysterious, but was it that of a brother, a friend, a teacher? He could not be sure.

He knew people – *Muslim people*, he reminded himself – who called each other brother all the time, and would spit swear words as soon as the brother left the room. He had seen it in the mosque, in the *Biradari*, had grown up with it being inside them, instinctive in their nature. It was slow poison like cholera in their villages, all his uncles, related or otherwise.

Yet Abu Umar did not call him brother or *Ya Akhi* or even *Bro*, as he had heard on the streets. The strange man's language flew straight, and his eyes did not flicker. They gave Jimmy belief in his quick smile without laughter. The earthy *Jilbab* that hid a thin but muscled body belied physical strength, and the languid immediacy of power. It seemed as if faith was the engine, craving instant release of energy. Abu Umar's successes had already assured his psychological dominance, and if he failed and died then he would still win: as a *Shaheed*. Jimmy could see why no lines of panic crossed Abu Umar's brow. He believed in live win – die win.

Maybe that is why he is not fidgeting like me, but measured, thought Jimmy. He seemed almost like slow motion in action. Jimmy looked at him as Abu Umar leaned forward and put his cup on the table, as if every movement knew its end point, all the parts concerted towards a unified goal. Jimmy stole another glance and felt guilty for admiring him. He had rarely looked up to anyone in his life. He stopped himself from scratching his scar.

'It's Jimmy, no one ever calls…uses that – that other name.' Jimmy looked up now, and shot his eyes away. He wanted to get up to escape; the hair on his exposed legs stood up.

'Yusuf…'

'No – I'm not.'

'You are Mohammed Yusuf – you – are – Yusuf.'

Jimmy shivered. Abu Umar had seen sunken memories hidden in twisted mangrove-like roots, got past the colourful corals of his teenage years. *How could he know?* Jimmy cursed himself for imagining Abu Umar could have any idea about what had happened years ago in Pakistan, one hot summer's afternoon.

That was only a part of it. It had happened here again, tonight. The ghosts of his ancestors had appeared to him again. Maybe Abu Umar had sensed or seen something. He had often heard his father tell of religious men who, through their piety, had transcended the physical. They had metaphysical knowledge and controlled the *Ifrit*, *Jinns*. *What if Abu Umar had some kind of Jinn?* But that sort of stuff is for old women, Jimmy admonished himself. His brow became creased and his right eye watered as he rubbed his scar. He could not possibly know anything. How could Abu Umar fathom the ghosts called him Mohammed Yusuf Regus?

Jimmy dismissed the idea as ridiculous. He could not help remember Ahmad's stories from when they all sat as a family and watched *Who Wants to be a Millionaire*. His father said it was educational. Or in Jimmy's childhood, they used to watch Bruce Forsyth's *Generation Game*. Ahmad would allow them to stretch to that, and he loved shouting the catchphrases. Sometimes Ahmad would tell tales of mystics who knew everything you knew, could command powers from thousands of miles away instantly, or even enter your heart and control your body by the power of their spirit. Jimmy forced himself to stop his illogical meanderings. Not before he thought of the girl accidentally beaten to death near Ramnagar, on the advice of a holy man who convinced the family she suffered demonic possession, because she kept shaking all over and frothing at the mouth. So fuckin' ignorant, thought Jimmy, but then there are *Jinns*...

'Spirit,' said Abu Umar, making him jump. 'Spirit – *Ruh* – that's what separates us. Fight for the soul.'

'What?' *How could he know what I'm thinking?*

'That's what the Christians thought they were doing when they were crusading and massacring, saving souls. See, it all comes down to fight. You fight for money, your dad fights for you.'

'Yeah, well, ain't doing him no good. He's dying.'

'But his *Ruh* is not, and never will be,' said Abu Umar.

Jimmy's jaw clenched, and tight ropes of muscle twitched on his face at the idea that Ahmad might be dying, but could live in some way. Jimmy had thought once he was gone then there could never be a way to make good all the things he had wanted to promise his father.

'I fight for Allah. For my soul. There's always been a struggle between good and evil. A *Jihad*,' said Abu Umar. A small smile played momentarily on his lips, as he held Jimmy's gaze.

Jimmy had heard this from Ahmad since he had been a child, but his father had never fought anyone. He said to fight the devil within, through spirituality and worship of Allah to conquer the desires, was the most important thing. To Jimmy, this had sounded weak. His father said these things because he was never in a position to get rich. Jimmy thought the road to happiness, or at least feeling better about himself, led past the filling station of desire.

'Since God created *Iblis*, his *Jihad* is continuing. The devil – he has many helpers. Not just *Jinns* but *Inns*, human devils.'

'Devils – *Jihad*? I thought Muslims did *Jihad*,' asked Jimmy. He felt fixed to the sofa by Abu Umar's deep eyes, as if stony devils were reflected in them.

'Do you believe in Allah?'

Jimmy did not answer, but felt another devil sit on his chest.

'Do you believe in life after death? Will you live forever, or will you die?' asked Abu Umar. Jimmy could say nothing; he rasped a long breath in to make up for the previous lack.

'No one – nothing lives forever – not even the mountains. The moon and the sun are dying as we speak.' Abu Umar leaned forwards and touched him on the hand.

Jimmy gasped, but did not recoil. He stared at his hand and then back to Abu Umar.

'We are dying,' the characteristic pause, and then the gentle voice continued. 'No matter how long you live, this life is but a blink of an eye.' The *Shaikh* moved back, and relaxed again. 'Okay, so you don't know if you're a Muslim. What are you then?'

'I'm just...I'm a – just...'

'When you walk down the street, when you went to school, what were you then?'

'A Paki,' said Jimmy without hesitation. The rabid bite of racism had left its jagged canine scars.

'What does it mean, Paki?' he asked.

Jimmy explained the pejorative term to him.

'What are most Pakis?' Abu Umar asked.

Jimmy found the word strange in his slight accent and the way he almost said 'B' instead of 'P', which made it clear to Jimmy that the word was foreign to the *Shaikh*. 'Muslims,' replied Jimmy.

'What are Iraqis, Afghans, Kashmiris, Palestinians?'

'Muslims.'

'Do you know what's happening in these places?'

'Can't miss it – nothing else on telly, anyway. *Abbo* watches it.'

'We are all Muslims, and so we're their enemies. There are no bystanders,' said Abu Umar. 'You heard the Americans say that?'

'Everyone does something in war, yeah. These places – there's war innit?'

'Even the unborn child?'

'What?' asked Jimmy.

'That the Serbian soldiers ripped out of his mother's womb – to settle a bet – to see if it was a boy or a girl. Ripped her belly open with their bayonets, then strung the body up by his legs from a lamppost after they skinned him. One of them used the skin as a flag on a tank, a souvenir. His mother bled to death, but not before she saw his little body swinging, pecked at by the crows. She saw her unborn child skinned and swinging upside down before darkness closed her eyes.'

Jimmy did not move.

'Or the Kashmiri girls. Thousands and thousands of them,' said Abu Umar. Jimmy looked away, as his fingers writhed in his hands. The older man continued, 'Raped. Gang-raped.' A pause, and the yellow eyes flashed lava as his face froze in animation. 'By Indian soldiers, for being suspected collaborators with the Muslim freedom fighters.'

'Them's just stories made up 'cos we hate them,' said Jimmy, still looking at his hands.

'Mass graves in Kashmir, unidentified bodies fertilising the ground.'

Jimmy looked at him, not sure how much he could have seen.

'Nermina. The Bosnian woman. That's her name.' Abu Umar's voice stayed level. 'Let me tell you a story. I knew a Malaika once. Her mother died giving birth to her younger brother. Her father, old, is a woodcutter, like my father. He goes to the hills to get firewood, sells and buys bread everyday. Malaika, she is looking after her brother, who is six years old and works in a kiln as a brick slave. One day, Indian soldiers come through the little mountain village looking for *Mujahideen*, for us. They find Malaika at home, alone. They gang-rape her. A squadron of them. Again and again – and again.' Abu Umar's index finger tapped his right thigh like a piston. 'Again and again, all day. Until they rupture her womb and her anus. Do you know how she died?'

Jimmy did not answer.

The *Shaikh* continued to stare at Jimmy, with his strange eyes that dominated him. 'Very quietly… She died quietly, because she could not scream any more… '

Jimmy saw his eyes glowing now at the memories, filming over with moisture, like amber stones becoming darker after rain.

'Can you imagine the shame, not to mention the pain? The rest of the village can see and hear. She dies in the worst agony imaginable.' Abu Umar pointed to his chest. 'She was my sister.'

'She was your sister?' asked Jimmy, surprised. He thought Abu Umar was an Arab.

'She was your sister,' said Abu Umar; now, the iron finger dug into Jimmy's breastbone. 'Malaika was your sister.'

Jimmy felt the pain as his finger pressed bone.

Then Abu Umar looked away behind Jimmy. 'She is thirteen years old. To cover their crime, the soldiers try to burn her. But the wooden village catches fire and half burns down. Her father found Malaika's twisted and charred body that evening. The villagers saw the squadron leaving her house with their faces red. Painted with her blood, because it was Holi, the Hindu festival of colours,' said the *Shaikh*.

Jimmy twisted his fingers harder, until they turned white. Abu Umar's eyes felt incandescent on his face.

'I saw her body. I buried her the next day, because there was no one else to do it.'

'What about her father?' asked Jimmy.

'You don't know what it's like to live like that. When you have nothing… all you have is your honour. That's what keeps you alive in those places more than bread and water, *sharam, izzat*.'

'What happened?'

'When the old man came back, he found her blackened, naked body. The villagers told him what had happened. He did not say a word to anyone.' Abu Umar put his right index finger up to his lips, as if hushing a child, for what seemed like an age, and then he blinked. 'He simply poured kerosene over himself, his whole body, lay down next to his daughter and he lit a match…'

'He burnt himself alive?' asked Jimmy, with wide eyes and lips parted.

'He died the moment they raped Malaika. He died of shame. All that was left was his mortal corpse. So he burnt it.' Abu Umar wiped the palm of his hands one against the other, as if dislodging flour.

Jimmy's mouth moved, but he could not form sound. 'Why?' he asked finally. 'Why did they do it? Because she helped you?'

'How could she help us? She didn't have enough to eat.' He paused. 'Because she was a Muslim...' Abu Umar said, still looking over Jimmy's shoulder, his voice a whisper. 'The young boy, her brother – we take care of him now. He's safe in our orphanage in the *madrassa*.'

'What's his name?' Jimmy asked.

'Yusuf. His name is Yusuf,' Abu Umar said.

Jimmy could not sense any flicker of irony or tell-tale signs that he had made the name up to emotionally charge Jimmy. The world became a different place, where he felt projected suddenly to some remote mountainous part of Kashmir; not because they were Muslims, but because a boy named Yusuf had survived.

'No matter how much you think you are different, you are no different, no! You are the same. Mohammed Yusuf – whether you like it or not.' He pointed his right index finger to bear testimony to an unseen sky. 'The truth is like the sun. You can shut it out, but it ain't goin' away.' Abu Umar looked at him, and Jimmy felt a filial affection.

'I think Elvis Presley said that,' Abu Umar smiled and quickly raised his eyebrows, immediately informal. 'You like Elvis?' he asked. Jimmy did not know what to say. Abu Umar continued, 'Born a Muslim – die a Muslim.'

Still, Jimmy did not answer. 'The sun does not disappear if the blind man cannot see. But even he can feel, and only the stupid man tries to destroy the mountain with his head.' Abu Umar tapped his forehead.

'So those bastards – Indians – they got away with it? No wonder *Chacha Baqwas* always calls them Indian bastards.'

'Got away with it?' Abu Umar let out a small laugh.

Jimmy looked at him and waited, and sweated; he did not feel cold.

'We wait and we mark them. We wait and then we wait plenty more until they go out, just that squadron on a reconnaissance mission to scout the hills near our post. Then one day, weeks later, when they forget all about Malaika, we trap them. And since then there have been many – too too many – more Malaikas. For them it become, how you say it? Yes, a mundane exercise. Every day they do these terrible things. They carry them out before dinner, on special order of their captain.'

Jimmy could not take his eyes off Abu Umar; they shone with anticipation. He could imagine being with the *Mujahideen*, hiding in the snow clad Himalayas. The excitement of the chase filled him and his jaw throbbed as he clenched it. He knew what he would have done. 'Did you kill the bastards?'

'Oh, died? Oh yes, they died with masks on their faces.'

'What? Masks?'

'They had no marks their faces and bodies – perr-fect.' Abu Umar wiped his hands over each other in Arab style. 'On their bodies and faces there was nothing. When the Indian army finds them – the largest democracy in the world, don't forget –'

'How did they die, then?' asked Jimmy.

'With blood only on their legs.' He gestured to his thighs. 'Their army will not understand why their legs full of blood, their trousers soaked. No blood anywhere else.'

'What did you do?' Jimmy leaned forward. His scar throbbed, and his nostrils flared.

Abu Umar replied in a whisper, as if sharing a secret. 'Nepalese *Ghurkha Kukri*.'

'*Kukri*?'

'Have you ever seen a *Kukri*?' asked Abu Umar. 'It's a special blade. The Hindus bless it during the *Nava Durga* festival, the nine *Durga* goddess festival. They bless the holy blade. *Astaghfirullah!* So we use their holy blade –'

'Fuckin' cool, yeah, slit their throats.' Jimmy forgot what he had been told earlier, as his chest heaved and the fingers of his hands clenched into great fists bunched on his thighs, the knots visible on his forearms, tense like cables of a bridge.

'We made each one pull their trousers down and squat.'

'I bet they shit their pants.'

Abu Umar held up his index finger. 'And we made each one say one word: Malaika…'

Jimmy wanted more; he nodded as if he understood.

'The hills screamed back: *Malaika – Malaika!*'

'So you shoved these *kukris* yeah, up their holes?' Jimmy had to be sure he did not miss the obvious.

'Each one of them knew a little bit, only little bit, of Malaika's agony before they bled to death. Then we pull up their trousers and laid them across the hills in neat rows, for the Indian army to find them. On each jacket we wrote M.R.'

'What does that mean?'

'Do you know what Malaika means?' asked Abu Umar.

Jimmy stared back at him, annoyed at having the spell broken. He had imagined carrying out the torture himself, slowly ripping each sphincter in revenge; he had been transported to Kashmir.

'They had a taste of Angelic justice. Malaika's Revenge – M.R.'

Jimmy laughed. 'Served them fuckin' good.' He laughed but did not question why, and he laughed louder.

'Malaika. It means Angelic.'

'Yeah, I got it, innit.'

'This is the truth on the ground. Not what you hear in the BBC.'

Jimmy felt slammed and dry, desiccated by the heat from the molten core of revelation.

'The fight against evil – that is a purification that makes you feel pure and invincible against the *Kuffar*. Makes them weak and puny. And they believe I am divinely protected and invincible. And so I am.'

Jimmy felt a surge through his body. He desired to be amongst the winners, the invincibles.

'These so-called moderate Islamists who fight for the *nafs*. No, I say. No!'

'You said we all fight?'

'Cleanse the shame of centuries. This is nothing. So much is happening, Yusuf. I could tell you about Palestine, Afghanistan, Iraq – especially Iraq. We can watch film later – Dwayne will show you some of the realities of 'The democratic liberation of Iraq." A pause. Jimmy could not imagine what could be worse than what he had just heard.

'The truth about Iraq, Yusuf... the truth is shame and suffering without end...'

Another gap during which Jimmy drifted off with him, and then he heard the *Shaikh*'s voice closer, almost covering him, although the *Shaikh* did not blink and his mouth did not move. *And where is Yusuf now?*

'Fight the *Kuffar* and purify. Your body becomes an offering a gift, and your soul becomes pure and lives forever. Like Ahmad, you father. He fought for you his whole life, so he will be a *Shaheed*. He is good man. All the *Shaheed* will be together in the Hereafter.'

Jimmy felt his worldview atomised, no longer sure of what he had been his whole life. All his reasoned arguments were now in smithereens.

'Now, it's time for *Fajr*. Make *wudu*.' Abu Umar did not ask Jimmy if he wanted to pray or if he felt well enough. He simply commanded, and in that command Jimmy felt strength and power. The identity of belief and self-certainty, what it meant to be a Muslim. To take the *Kuffar* on and live to tell the tale. To walk tall and free. This slight man had taken on the world. The most powerful enemies of Islam.

Jimmy cleansed his body. He had forgotten how to make the ritual cleansing before prayer, the seed dormant and decaying for so long. Now he aped Abu Umar. Jimmy rinsed his mouth, splashed water on his face, and washed his arms and legs. Afterwards, he got dressed in the simple tracksuit trousers and t-shirt and stood next to Abu Umar in prayer; naked and exposed to the truthful bitter wind of self discovery.

Although Jimmy towered over Abu Umar he felt dwarfed, insignificant. He felt awed; his breath rasped his tongue dry. He wanted to say so much, to gush, but instead he said nothing. He breathed in the pheromones of freedom. *This is reality*, he thought, *this is a man amongst men. If he does it for God, then is Allah not the King of kings?*

Jimmy did not realise the night had passed. He somehow sensed a new dawn threading the east, and a birthing sun pouring a new silver sky onto a new golden earth. He breathed easily, and felt no pain.

He did not remember how to pray; even most of the words escaped him. Abu Umar recited. The sounds were powerful, and they crashed through Jimmy's chest. Abu Umar's voice encompassed and blanketed Jimmy's shaking and quivering. He did not know why he stood trembling; then his mind became white, and he stopped thinking about anything.

'*Wal aadiyathi zaban wal muriyathi qadhan…*' recited Abu Umar.

Jimmy remembered from his dim past, the verse of the thundering horsemen. The mystical meaning was hidden from common sight, although his father had eulogised over it. It was Ahmad's favourite verse from the Qur'an. The horsemen thundered through his brain, churned up the battleground, which Jimmy had now lost to Faith. Jimmy forgot worry and pain and the potential death of Ahmad. His personal suffering dissolved like a pinch of salt in the sea, and he became a crest crashing onto the beach, as if, finally, the wandering wave had found its shore.

Before Abu Umar had finished reciting the verse, Jimmy stood exhausted, drenched in sweat, cold. His head bowed and his body was completely still, but his soul fluttered a new dance. Jimmy shook with knowledge that he had sinned all his life. He started trembling and shaking again, so that he could barely keep his hands on his abdomen as he stood. His fear of Allah's punishment trembled his bones to jelly. For fear: how would he answer his Creator on the Day? His Lord would ask: *What did you do for me? When you knew there were Malaikas every day: what did you do for good?*

He tottered as his body shook uncontrollably, as if a quake arose from its core; now molten, having felt the magnetic pull of the *Shaikh*. As Abu Umar's recitation overtook him, his cheeks glistened and droplets fell from his scar. Tears filled with the chemicals of terror: of righteousness. They burnt sulphurous tracks of repentance down his cheeks.

Jimmy was determined to find Yusuf.

Birmingham

Jessica spoke into the phone. 'Hi, Penny. Sorry I haven't been able to get back to you, but things have been a bit hectic.'

'I was expecting you to get back to me on Monday?'

'That's what I wanted to talk to you about. I had to do some things, about Hamid, but I'm fine now. I'm ready to go to Baghdad,' said Jessica. There was no reply. 'Are you there, Penny?'

'I'm sorry, you didn't get back to me, and so I've confirmed the assignment with someone else.'

'What? It's only Tuesday.'

'I know, but like I said, I've got to make arrangements, otherwise the documentary won't get made.'

'I need that assignment, Penny.'

'Well, I've asked John.'

'I've been waiting for it for months. You know it was only because of the wedding.'

'I know, I know, but I'm sorry.'

'Well, I've got to go to Baghdad,' said Jessica.

'Why the sudden change? You weren't bothered a few days ago.'

'I've got my reasons. And anyway, you know I'm the best person for the job. Has John got his own translator?'

'No, don't think so, but we can hire him one,' said Penny.

'What about contact with the insurgents? Is he going to get an interview with the top wolf in *Jaish an Noor wass Salaam*?'

'Er, we've arranged interviews with the Americans and Abu Yahya's wife.'

'My granny could get an interview with John Wayne's wife. Isn't that what Abu Yahya called himself? As for the Americans, well, they're so desperate they'll talk to the street urchins of Baghdad. In fact, they're asking the boys for advice on the next Iraqi elections, I've heard.'

'Well, you've certainly changed the tunes on your tabla. How did you suddenly manage to get those contacts in Baghdad?'

Jessica did not reply.

'I suppose you could give your contacts to John?'

'No way. I seem to remember you were a journalist once. Would you give your best contacts to the competition?' Jessica knew she was getting to the limits of how far she could push Penny, who was known as an authoritarian in the office. She had to get to Baghdad, to get the truth about Hamid. To do that she had to meet with Plain Jamila's contacts in *Jaish*.

'I could order you to hand them over, as your boss.'

'Penny, at this moment you couldn't you couldn't order me to hand over my train ticket to Heathrow, let alone my contacts. Firstly, they won't talk to anyone except me, and secondly, I'm going to Baghdad anyway. I've got my tickets to Amman, and got my GMC Yukon truck and driver all booked to drive me to Baghdad.'

'What?'

'Yes – told you I had contacts now. And what's more, I'm going to make that documentary as an independent, if you don't phone John right now and tell him this baby's been mine since nearly a year.'

'You're pushing me, Jessica.' Penny chuckled and said, 'Well, something's happened to you since Hamid died. You've got some steel in the blood.'

Jessica did not add that she always had more than enough steel, but before she did not give enough of a shit to argue. 'Right now you're the magnet to my metal, and I'm coming into the office to sort this out with Head of Section. I've known Mike for long enough...'

'You wouldn't dare.'

'Just watch me. I'll be there in, oh, let's say about an hour? I could always catch Mike over lunch.'

'Okay, okay, but let me tell you – you'd better not be bullshitting me about these contacts, and I want to see those terrorists on the documentary.'

In the time Jessica had known Penny, she had never changed a mission once she had confirmed the assignment. Jessica smiled and said nothing.

CHAPTER 13

Birmingham – Asian Area

Jessica could not remember feeling this nervous at having to enter a building; she had not been in this part of the city before. She never had cause to enter into an area with ramshackle pavements and sloping houses, where the roads were medieval in their lack of planning and the roofs crumbling, with rubbish in the streets. Small children scurried into the autumnal gloaming and she imagined them with Dickensian disease, rickets and gruel for supper.

The approach to the mosque was congested with cars. Someone beeped at her, which jolted her out of her thoughts. Jessica eased through the congestion, wary of hitting the scattered children. She squeezed the car into a tight space. The wipers worked noisily, spreading the heavy rain off the windscreen for a few seconds, before it filled up again with wetness. Jessica sat with the headlights turned off in the narrow street. She shrank back into her seat, and let the darkness cover her. The car was idling and she switched the wipers off, hiding behind the veil of rain.

She wished she could remain inconspicuous; the rain dripping down the glass made a barrier. She felt safe with the doors locked. Jessica thought about driving back down the street to the suburbs. She could be home in minutes. She could stop at the Italian on the way home, order her favourite – fettuccine, with goat's cheese and Taggiasche olives. She imagined opening the Chianti Classico... she loved the smell of berries and relaxation that followed. What the hell was she doing in the ghetto, anyway? It pricked at her, felt alien and wounded her peace, took away her harmony.

She had promised Sebastian. Dr Sebastian Windsor. It felt strange how she felt comfortable with Sebastian now, in such a short time. Tears: *is that what it takes?* she wondered, *a woman's tears in front of a man, to create instant familiarity?* To breed intimacy and close association, which made the heart leap and imagine suddenly, without logic, a future together.

Jessica pulled the blue scarf out of her bag on the front seat. She remembered how the woman in the hijab shop had gushed when Jessica had entered. Her tinkling voice started with *Asalamalaikum*. *She probably interpreted my reluctance to reply as the shyness of a new convert, still uncomfortable with English punctuated by Arabic,* thought Jessica. *She mistook me for a Muslim; why else would I be buying a scarf?*

'That one, definitely that one. The steel blue makes your eyes sparkle, it really lights up your face. Oh, he's such a lucky brother. I hope he realises it. If I had eyes as blue as that, what effect I would have on the brothers! Sorry, I just assume everyone else is looking to get married, because I am.' The shop assistant had said this with a smile, assuming that, as usual, there must be a Muslim man who had inspired the transformation.

Jessica had not said anything. Memories of Hamid flooded through her again and she pushed against the swamp, but she did not show the tears, and the woman's bright manner did not cheer her. Jessica had turned away, as the wetness came silently at the thought of Hamid. Despite herself, she could not prevent a tear from rolling onto her flushed cheeks. She turned away from the assistant, and quickly swept her hand across her face. She *was* there because of a man, but not in the way the woman had imagined.

Jessica felt determined to attend the spiritual circle. Sebastian, even though he was not a Muslim, had said he felt it contained sincerity. She put her head down against the rain and entered the mosque through the woman's entrance. The small hallway of the converted terraced house felt constricting. The scarf felt as awkward and unnatural as the rest of the experience. She had not put the scarf on from home in case anyone, especially Hamid's relatives, had seen her. Jessica stacked her shoes amongst the open-toed sandals, and felt foolish. She wondered why hers were the only ankle boots she could see. *Maybe it's something to do with Ramadan*, she thought. Sebastian had advised her that this was going to be a special circle because tonight was *Lailatal Qadr*, the Night of Power – a night better than a thousand months, when the Angels descend – the night when the Qur'an was first revealed to the Prophet Muhammed. Sebastian had said this was the night Muslims believed their lives would be changed, and destinies written.

There were no signs that she could see, as she wandered into the main meeting hall, of any impending wondrous events that were about to unfold: no writing, no pictures, nothing on the walls, no stained glass in the windows. The square room had a curtain down the centre. Jessica walked past the few who had arrived early. There were small groups of men and women, talking and greeting each other. She was surprised that this plain room with no seats, which was cold and grey, could be a place where Sebastian said spiritual enlightenment might be found. She wondered how any of this strangeness could answer her questions.

After a while everyone sat on the floor. No one spoke, no one seemed to look at anyone, yet they all waited.

Jessica sat with her face to the curtain; to one side was a pillar. She could not see the speaker, but she looked up as a mellifluous voice seemed to emanate from the other side and started the recitation: '*Bismillahirahmaniraheem.*'

'In the name of Allah the most Gracious, the most Merciful.' A different voice translated, which was the opposite of the sweet babbling brook of Arabic recitation – the English was a sonorous, ear-shattering roar of words. Jessica felt frightened by the speakers all around her, some placed high above, others on the ground. The translator's voice seemed to leave a booming sonic wave in its wake. 'When the earth quakes with her last mighty quaking…'

It went through Jessica; her organs shook with every crescendo as if a giant breaker were thumping into her, knocking her flat. The clamour of the man's voice seemed to match the words: 'And when the earth yields up her burdens and man cries out '*what has happened to her?*'

Jessica's heart lost its own rhythm as the ocean of noise from the speakers enveloped her. Her breath stopped and restarted erratically, and she waited in the silent gaps, as she held her breath. She looked around in shock, her pulse thudding in her neck. Everyone else ignored her. They seemed to be taken up by the recitation and translation.

Jessica wanted to escape, to flee the dreadful clamour, to still the uncommon barbarous tempo in her chest, as if her heart would jump out of her breast to establish its own independent motion. The cadence of her lungs rasped a different tune, but to get out she would have to climb over the women who blocked the entrance now, disturb them, some of whom were in a trance-like state. Easily slipping into a heightened plane, it seemed to Jessica, disappearing into a parallel universe, when only minutes before they had been chatting and swirling around, like any group, naturally socialising. She did not want to disturb them lest she break the spell-concentration that kept them mesmerised. Courtesy and consideration would not allow it. The women of the group had been polite. They had smiled and welcomed her before sitting down, although she knew no-one at the gathering.

Moreover, Jessica knew she could not escape, she had promised to stay, to sit out one whole session, at least. She was confused and shaken, never having heard anything as sweet and melodious as the Arabic recitation, or as deeply frightening as the timbre of the English translation. Was it the words themselves that frightened her? She was not sure. What was it that Sebastian had said? *Reflections will scare you, and meditating will give you palpitations and a panic attack*: was this what he meant? Was she having a panic attack? Was the translator's voice barbaric, or so out of her own life experience – was she too barbaric to experience the inner beauty? To appreciate the rich poetry she had heard spoken about? Why did the deep meaning, the implication of what was being said, frighten her? Even in English there was mystique. 'On that Day will she recount all her tidings, as thy Sustainer will have inspired her to do! On that Day will all men come forward, cut off from one another, to be shown their past deeds.'

There was a pause – a silence – where no-one moved or rustled. Jessica seemed to be breathing in a vacuum, oxygen-starved, legs shaking. She peeked without moving her head. Her eyes darted like swallows. A woman joined them; the curtain moved, and Jessica could now see quite a few of the men. Some were dressed in jeans, others wore *salwar kameez*, and a few were in *Jilbab* with a variety of head coverings... from lace white skullcaps, to turned-around baseball caps.

The difference in the faces surprised Jessica. She had expected a collection of Asian people, mostly Pakistanis like Hamid. As well as these she saw pale Arabs, probably Berbers, sitting alongside aubergine-dark Africans and pinched-nose Malays. To one side of her was a Mongol woman with oriental eyes, like small bamboo leaf slits in her face. She looked at the men again. Some looked like they were exhausted after sixteen-hour taxi stints, others she imagined could have been road diggers. Most women wore headscarves, although none that Jessica could see had a face veil. One man sat entranced, eyes closed, in an earthy coloured robe, next to a man who wore designer clothes and had his hair slicked and parted down the centre, like some film star of yesteryear.

'And so, he who shall have done an atom's weight of good, shall behold it;

And he who shall have done an atom's weight of evil, shall behold it.'

The people had nothing in common. The whole spectacle was like chancing upon a field of wild flowers in a clearing: all different and haphazard at a glance, with no obvious relation to one another. There seemed to be no scheme – yet each had a place, a niche, which they occupied with reason, in tune with earthly rhythms. Jessica wondered if there was a pattern here too, some commonality indiscernible to her. The men and women swayed as they sat, some moving cryptically, the meaning only understandable to them. Others described large circles of motion, in keeping with the rhythm of the reading. They seemed to be moved by ethereal currents of power, like daffodils on a windswept hilltop. The swaying increased with the recitation, as if they were drawing nutrients from the fertile soil of the speaker's words.

'Something anything only exists because Allah allows it to exist. Allah is infinite. We are a tiny fraction of creation. And any fraction over infinity is zero. We – you – only exist because Allah allows you to exist…' The sweet melodious voice that had recited the Arabic was back. He spoke English with a patrician accent. The heavy voice had gone. Jessica could see the speaker, now.

It was the same man who had recited the beautiful Arabic. She recognised his voice, but was shocked, not only by the strangeness of the words he spoke, but also because of his appearance. He had milky skin and freckles, with a shock of auburn hair that stuck out of his brown cap like an unruly Etonian schoolboy. He looked as he spoke to the men who were sitting nearest to him, his lithe slim body obviously used to long hours on a hard floor, his green robe spread about him.

He spoke softly. His speech was clear, natural, and free from dialect. He used no acquired shibboleths, nothing untried and experimental; he was sure of his path. The ideas he expressed seemed to come from the desert of thoughts not yet travelled by Jessica. Strange paths, still unenvisaged. She felt sure now that there was indeed more between heaven and earth than had ever been dreamed of in her philosophy. When he spoke, she was no longer fearful. She was beguiled by his voice, and wanted to hear more of this strangeness.

From the tone and pace of his speech, Jessica imagined his life was a more reflective sojourn than her own. Like an orchid that lives and sparkles only in the dappled shade, introspective but radiant under the protective canopy of green. His words reverberated through the ground, into her. She felt them as much as heard them, as if she could feel his heartbeat, as if his beat somehow synchronised with her. He seemed to be speaking to her alone.

'We cannot see in pure light at its most intense. We cannot know Allah, and conversely no one has directly seen a black hole. We do not feel the canopy of leaves He provides as shade; it is that very combination of light and shade which allows us to see. We can know Him through His blessings, His mercy, His *Rahma*: In The Name of Allah, *Bismillahiraniraheem*. We say that all the time. That's because His mercy is above His wrath. In depending on His mercy is freedom. Only by enslaving yourself to the One, The Creator of all things, can you ever free yourself from the slavery to created things.'

Jessica thought of Hamid, his breath on her neck, and how her breath had been dependent on his smile, how she had felt nothing would bring joy without him. Yet he was dead and she was still alive, although she missed him. The words of the speaker felt like her unspoken lament; or was it the lament of humanity? The cry of mankind that he seemed to connect to, which reflected in his voice?

'Allah, Lord of the Universe, Master of the Day of Judgement, has Ninety-Nine Beautiful Names. He is The Constrictor, *Al Qabid*, The Expander, *Al Basit*,' said the red-haired man and paused. Not for effect – he did not look at anyone – but he seemed to be reflecting. 'He is the Ever-Living, Self-Sustaining – *Al Hay Al Qayum*. Breathe it. Breathe it. Breathe it in.'

Jessica no longer felt that his words were alien. She could feel the passion in the restrained voice, she was no longer discomfited. She felt close to the quiet voice, as if no one else was in the room, and the room was not in the inner city. Instead she could sense the rain outside, the dampness of the earth giving birth to fruits. Nature was taking its course, and for the first time she felt connected to it. She had lost the usual connection, which held her close to the metal, plastic and money-created artifice.

There was nothing between her and the sky. Jessica imagined rain on her face with her eyes closed, sweet and fresh. She let the words of the speaker, like raindrops, burst the desert of her spirituality. The sand congealed into damp earth. She could see the stars beyond the veil of clouds. A universe was visible, now that the thick cataracts of cumulus were suddenly swept away, by a divinely inspired breath that blew over her and opened her skin. She let the sweet rain of *Deen*, spirituality, impregnate her every pore. She had once heard the word also meant rain. The dross that filled her heart with desire and greed, lust and envy flowed out of her heart; the cup emptied. For the first time, the vessel emptied and made room for peace.

'*Al Hay Al Qayum – Al Hay Al Qayum – Al Hay Al Qayum.*' The words, started by the speaker, were taken up by everyone else. A beat, a rhythm, a cadence built up to a melodious harmony, and covered the room. It was filled it with excitement, and the sound took over repeatedly and reverberated, warmed the room, transformed it from a cold grey stone to a mammalian organism. Some kept count, most recited *Al Hay Al Qayum* loudly, and some moved their lips without much noise. The Babel merged to become a singing stream of sound. Then, as more joined in, it became a gushing torrent, which swept over Jessica like a flash flood, a tsunami praising Allah.

She lost time and space; she gained motion, and took flight with the Arabic which enveloped her. She swayed to the words. Her heart seemed like a small beating bird, a black dove of fear that was imprisoned by her ribs, and as the minutes passed and *Al Hay Al Qayum* continued louder and louder, the bird rattled against her chest, the bars melted by the power that penetrated her, and fear broke free. Fear was afraid. Jessica was filled with love and mercy of The Ever Living Self-Sustaining. Suddenly, love filled Jessica with the mercy of *Al Hay Al Qayum*, The Ever Living Self-Sustaining.

Perhaps this was what Sebastian meant when he said he knew peace and tranquillity were here, but he had not found himself. The emptiness was now space. The negation of the material left her open to the *Al Hay Al Qayum*. The words resonated within her. Jessica became entrained, drawn to the speaker, as all pendulums are inevitably drawn to the largest pendulum in the clock maker's room. She felt harmonised by his peace and strength.

Maybe this was what Sebastian had meant. They make you embarrassed about your spirituality, but spend time with good, true people, and you will know it is not embarrassing; religion and God are above cliché. At that moment she remembered feeling a surge of affection for him, for the truthfulness on his face that he no longer could hide. She saw past the pretence, and adopted stylistic manners. Jessica felt empowered and free. She remembered how Sebastian had got caught up in anger again, and had said, 'No one is free, past the shame of pseudo-intellectual post-modernist freedom they would have you believe is freedom. You can't even get past the shame of saying *I believe!*' Jessica's affection for him had soon ebbed when he spoke like that.

He had added, 'But when you are near real, true, people you will inhale the fragrance of sincerity and that will bring life to your dead inner self, kiss awake the morose, moribund, soul…'

Jessica did not feel any warmth for Sebastian when he spoke like this; she did not like to think of herself as dead, unable to love. She *had* loved. Hamid was gone, but could she ever consider loving another? She would have been repulsed by the thought, before she had met Sebastian. Now, although she had said nothing directly to him, she felt entranced by him… but she wondered if this was the affection that the kidnapped held for their captors.

'Inhale the fragrance of sincerity…' Sebastian had ordered her.

'*Al Hay Al Qayum Al Hay Al Qayum…*' the recitation continued unabated, flying on independent wings, free from the rules of physics. So Jessica breathed deeply, opening her nostrils and filling her lungs. Air rushed in, bold and sweet. It cooled her still closed eyes.

The pure oxygen of realisation, of spirituality, refreshed and ignited her soul, which burned in conflagration and exploded into light that chased the darkness out of her. It was as if she had never breathed before, only existed. Her senses had been vestigial until today. Jessica now felt certain that in her pre-life zombie-existence, she had never touched, seen or smelt before.

Now she wanted to taste life. And hear the harmony of the heavens, praising The Creator of all the worlds, the earth; all of existence exalted the Almighty.

Al Hay Al Qayum – The Ever-Living Self-Sustaining.

CHAPTER 14

Birmingham – Jessica's House

Jessica twirled her hair between the fingers of her right hand, and held the phone in the other. 'He said he would come around today. He's coming today.'

'How do you know? You sure? You know what men are like,' said Holly.

As usual, Jessica felt Holly's bilious vitriol against men rising, which her friend had worn like a green raincoat since becoming a single parent.

'I thought I knew about men, but since Hamid... no I don't.'

'It's been a while since Hamid, but you're right. You just can't trust them,' said Holly.

'I didn't think I would have to go through it all again once I had Hamid. I haven't thought about men.'

'Now your head's all scrambled eggs and your guts are a bundle of writhing snakes over Seb.'

'No, actually it's nothing like that. He's really lovely.'

'Oh Lord! Don't tell me you've done it already? You must have. He's a really hot –'

'Holly, don't be crude.' Jessica sat down on the sofa and stood up again. 'Anyway, I never call him Seb. That just wouldn't be right.' Jessica smiled, knowing Holly was too. She had expected Holly to tease her about men, regardless of the situation.

'Dr Sebastian, how nice. Well, seems like there's a chance there. Truly, I mean it. I was cleaning yesterday and I found a box – guess what was in it? I'd forgotten all about it, what with everything that's been happening.' Holly continued, without waiting for a reply. 'A hat. I went to that hat shop in town you told me about, where those posh women go before Ascot, and the snotty cow that served me had a face on like she'd come third in the sixth race.'

Jessica could not help a small smile at her observation. 'I'm sorry you'll never get to wear it, now.'

'Oh shush, Jessy. You never know. Life is too long to make statements like that.'

'Holly... what am I going to do, now? It feels like the end of my life.'

'You just don't know. You're not even thirty yet. Look at me – mid-thirties, with a child. That's more baggage than British Airways.'

'Don't be silly. You're pretty – really attractive when you bother.' Jessica thought about Holly's autumnal hair and her unsurprising brown eyes. Speaking to her on the phone was almost as good as a face to face conversation, sometimes. 'If only the guys could see you the way I see you, your golden heart.'

'Forget the heart, you know what they want. It's alright, I'm okay with that.'

I don't know how to respond to Sebastian, thought Jessica. *He's really lovely in many ways, and we have a lot in common, but I've got to sort myself out about Hamid first.*

'I think you should go for Sebastian. God how many times you're going to bump into guys like that. I can see the only way you're gonna do that is if I make you. And yeah, just in case he's got mates you make sure you tell him you got a friend who looks like Angelina Jolie on a bad day.' Holly chuckled, and Jessica imagined her irregular teeth. She laughed again.

Jessica asked herself what the spiritual experience at the mosque had meant. She had told Holly about it, only briefly. Jessica now had a peace of a kind; although she still did not subscribe to any religion, it gave her a renewed confidence.

'Oh, sorry, I forgot. You're religious? I hope I'm not offending you, but you know I love to have a laugh,' said Holly.

'It was a special experience. I feel different, more aware of life somehow. Don't apologise, Holly, I think I really need your humour. I don't think I've laughed in over a month.'

'Yeah, Jesus, it's November. It's been over six weeks since Hamid. Anyway, I don't want to go on about that. Okay, let me ask you what I've dying to ask you for ages. You said Sebastian was hot?' asked Holly, in a rising tone.

'I never said that. I said he's got classical features.'

'Is he gorgeous or not?' asked Holly. Jessica paused, chewed her lower lip. 'Is he, or not? Look this is me... Holly! We've chewed the cud over enough shitty men to last five life –'

'Yes, yes, okay, he is. But it's not like that. He's very handsome and sophisticated and really clever.'

'You've got the hots for him.'

'I do like talking to him – more like arguing and shouting at him – but, you know, he helped me – when, you know…'

'Yeah, but that's all long ago. Once upon a time and all that. If you haven't got the hots for him, you bloody well better have, pretty soon, or someone else will.'

'Well, we've been out a few times since then. I didn't tell you about the picnic we went on. Anyway, I thought you and your divorce circle all passed a *fatwa*, you said all men are –'

'Yeah, well, I'm thinking of you.' Holly stopped for a moment. 'I'm just worrying, in case he's like so many of the others.'

'Oh, Holly, not all. Anyway, I need advice. Not for you to be bloody Germaine Greer, just because you've got a daughter and FC dumped you.'

'He didn't dump me. I dumped him.' Holly paused. 'Anyway, he battered me and ran off with my life savings, and –'

'You've got Sally.'

'And I've got Sally.' Holly sighed. 'Sorry. Have you spoken to Sebastian recently?'

'Those 'Female Eunuch'-reading women, that's your problem. None of them have a man and those two that did find someone don't come anymore, do they? I've been speaking to him, yeah.'

'Don't want you to get hurt again,' said Holly, in a quiet voice.

'What shall I do? Oh, there's the doorbell. Too late.'

'Shall I come round? Oh no, that's not great. Just go for it, Jess.'

'Holly – thanks. And don't worry, 'cos he's lovely.'

Jessica looked around her living room. She had made an effort, as much as her confusion would allow her. The cushions were plumped but scattered a little haphazardly, and a slim porcelain vase sat on the dining table with a single spray of cherry blossom that she had managed to grow out of season in her hot house. A candle gave off a sweet scent as it floated in a bowl on the coffee table; lights twinkled off the water's surface. The warm room was filled with the fragrance of almond blossom, which covered her like a second skin. Turkish rose from another candle permeated through from the kitchen, mixed with the almond blossom. Jessica paused, closed her eyes, and breathed in.

She had made the preparations because he had hinted he might visit, although nothing definite had been planned. After the way she had behaved with him previously she felt boorish, ungentle. *I wonder if he remembers everything I said to him*, she thought. *Or shouted at him...*

Jessica felt different since her weird experience at the mosque. She felt unsure exactly what had changed in her life, but she knew now that she needed spirituality in her life to breathe. Just as nothing could grow in a vacuum, she could not live a purely material life. Her senses had been heightened. She could see previously invisible colours in the falling leaves of autumn, and see shades and patterns unimagined in their veins. She had felt the breeze on her face as the breath of the earth. She had watched the clouds gathering force and she could smell the soft rain waiting to be born, before dawn silvered the eastern sky.

Jessica grimaced as the doorbell chimed again. *And I don't even know if it's him*. She walked into the front room and realised that he would see her peering out, so she came out of the room without approaching the window. She caught herself in the long mirror in the hallway. She picked at her bun, wished she had not tied it up in such an elaborate design, with too many pins and small combs to hold it in place. *What am I?* she asked herself. *I don't know, but I feel more spiritual, protected somehow.*

She hurried for the door before it could ring again, or worse, before Sebastian could disappear. She passed the cabinet of curios where she and Hamid put the small things that he had brought back with her from her trips abroad.

Jessica opened the door, puffing her breath out. Sebastian stood there with one hand in the pocket of his grey woollen trousers; the other held a bouquet of flowers.

That cheeky Harrison Ford of a smile again, she thought. She looked at him but she did not move as she noticed the muscular slope of his shoulders, his lithe limbs comfortable in the smart-casual clothes. The dark checked sports jacket formed its shape around his physique.

She tried to straighten her hair, then realised she did not need to push her hair out of her eyes. She wanted to say something clever, to invite him in with something memorable, but she felt like a fish standing in the door. Her mouth pushed air. He smiled at her again and gave her the flowers, but did not attempt to kiss her or greet her in any other way.

'These are also from my garden and greenhouse...' said Sebastian, and stood still with raised eyebrows, looking at her.

Oh, he's waiting for me to invite him in, she thought. 'Erm, yes...' She moved out of the doorway and gestured him in. 'Do, please, yes.' As he passed her, his woody cologne mixed with the floral scents of the bouquet. Her throat felt tight and she held her breath. She closed her eyes for a moment, and then breathed deeply. She turned away and blinked a couple of times.

Jessica led him through the hallway. She put the flowers on a side table, adding them to a vase which already held some lilies. *I'll separate them later*, she thought, not wanting to leave him sitting alone on the first time he had come to hers. She saw him looking at the curtains in the archway. The brocades and silks hung in the arches of the house, composing layers of rich cloth folded over on both sides of the arch, tied with thick silken sashes to create a *shamiana* effect. Her house had become an amalgam of East and West.

Sebastian sat on the cream sofa without being asked, and crossed his legs. She sat opposite him, and tried to control her hands in her lap. Jessica saw him looking at the Arabic calligraphic artwork on the walls. His eyes stopped when he saw the large gold wine flask that stood by the side of the fireplace. 'Oh that – that's something we...I got from Lahore. It's a replica of one the last Emperor of India had, but it's become an antique...' she trailed off, feeling guilty because she did not mention she had been there with Hamid.

'*In Xanadu did Kubla Khan a stately pleasure-dome decree*,' said Sebastian, looking around.

A small laugh escaped her, as she pushed a honey gold strand back. '*Where Alph the sacred river ran, through caverns measureless to man*,' she added to his line, and smiled at him, the mutual recital settling her nerves. 'Hardly...hardly a pleasure dome.'

Sebastian looked at the gold wine flask again. When his eyes settled on her, she added, 'It's called a *Chuski*. The *Mughals* used to serve wine, *araq*, or –'

'Or opium water,' he said. 'How intoxicating...'

Jessica looked away from his eyes to the *Chuski*. She lingered over the bulbous chased body, followed the thin reed-like curving spout, which had a stylised bird sitting, facing another on the handle covered in floral design. A third bird surmounted the large stopper in the centre. *He doesn't miss anything*, she thought.

'I got some of that Menuet Napoleon Grande Champagne Cognac.'

'You noticed when you came around to my place?' He laughed. 'Just coffee,' he looked into her eyes, 'if you please. You have it black, don't you? Although I know you rarely drink coffee.'

'Oh, you remembered from that day at Starbucks? I thought you wouldn't want to remember much of what I said to you.'

'I remember everything. I remember your hurt from the first day, your confusion on the drive and picnic, and especially your anger when you came to see me in my home,' he said, smiling.

'Well, I've changed since then.'

'You've come a long way. You don't even look the same,' he said and did not blink. 'You seem to be fresh-faced.'

'Thanks.' Jessica stared at her fingernails. *Maybe there is something different about me*, she thought. *Even though I'm not wearing any make up... just lipstick.* 'What?' she asked.

'Oh, the first day we met you were somebody else, and then every time we've met since you seem different. I think you've been changing. Today it's like you've been drinking opium water from that *Chuski*.' Sebastian laughed. 'Seeing you now, I could almost forget about all the anger and accusations.'

'Sorry. I know you must think me rather ignorant, and somewhat rude.'

'No, I don't think you're ignorant – just uninformed.' He leaned forward. 'But I think you are very rude.' He smiled.

'I have a lot to thank you for. That spiritual meeting, it changed my life...' she said, and she saw him raise his eyebrows. 'I'll get your coffee.' She pushed up off the sofa.

'Need some help?' He followed her into the kitchen. 'It's been a long time?' he asked and she laughed softly.

'I imagine you hate that instant stuff?'

'I drink it when I have to. If I'm desperate for a caffeine boost,' he said.

He stood away slightly to the side, watching her. She busied herself with the coffee maker. 'Thanks for telling me about the spiritual circle. I did go to the mosque, and...'

'And?' Sebastian put his hands in the pockets of his grey woollen trousers, and seemed almost to be casually looking away from her.

Jessica poured cold filtered water into the reservoir tank. 'I – I don't know. I don't know how to describe it.' She wondered if she really could not describe the sensations that had come over her during the recitation of *Al Hay Al Qayum*, or if she simply did not want to admit to Sebastian that he had been right. *Probably both*, she thought. She looked at him. 'I sort of felt different. Special, spiritual – like there has to be something more than just the material.'

Sebastian nodded, but did not take his hands out of his pockets. 'You're very lucky if you had anything close to that on your first visit to the spiritual circle. Most people go for years and years, and still don't feel anything.'

Jessica shrugged, and fitted the coffee holder to the machine. 'I don't know, but I'm sure that this,' she gestured around with her hands, but felt as if she was encompassing him and herself in the statement, 'has to be something more than an accident...'

'You mean we're not nothing from nothing? I don't want to be an accident from the Big Bang, and all this to have happened by chance.'

'Even if evolution is a fact, it doesn't discount a higher power, does it?'

This time, Sebastian shrugged. 'I don't know much about science, but I'll tell you you're lucky you had that experience.' He turned away from her, went closer to the sink and looked out of the window to the back garden, which led to the hothouse.

'I know this much is true; it's made me feel warm and protected, somehow.' She started the machine and, as always, breathed deeply as the pungent, slightly acrid smell of the Monsoon Java Malabar coffee filled the air. She closed her eyes as the fragrance combined with the Turkish Rose candle she had lit earlier, filling her nostrils. Her breathing slowed and became more regular.

I wonder what it is that makes some combinations so special? she thought. *Two unique smells entwined to make an even more delicious combination of synergy. I always thought that it would be two completely different things coming together to make the ideal combination – like I did with Hamid. Sebastian and I have a lot in common; would that be too overpowering an aroma?*

When Sebastian did not turn around, she switched the machine off and walked up behind him. *Maybe he's drifted off because of what I said about the spiritual experience,* she thought. *Perhaps that's what has made him so reflective.* Since her emotional awakening she had spoken to him intermittently, but until now not mentioned that she felt changed from within. Jessica was loathe to disturb him; this contemplative side seemed more natural. She felt tempted to put a hand on his arm. Instead she stood by him and said, 'I think you've experienced something similar? Haven't you?'

He lifted his arms up in a gesture and his coat moved over his rounded shoulders. His eyes shone and glistened as he held her stare for a moment.

'Come on – *quid pro quo*. If you want me to tell you what happened, then you tell me about yourself.' When he still did not reply, she said, 'I trusted you with Hamid.'

'It all seems a long time ago. I went through a period where I thought I knew the truth, where I felt as if I was flying high.'

'Is that when you almost converted?'

'I sympathised. It was in Damascus.'

'In the Umayyad Mosque?' asked Jessica – because that was the only mosque she had heard of in Damascus – getting excited, thinking that Sebastian might have experienced a mirror of her own and that would give them a shared emotion.

'No, no.' Sebastian smiled. 'It was somewhere weird. I was sitting on the battlements of Krak de Chevalier in Syria.'

'The Crusader castle?'

'The final citadel of Christendom in the Holy Lands, which to the Crusaders felt like the death knell of Christianity itself and the loss of an empire when Sultan Baybars conquered it…sorry, it's the lecturer in me.' He smiled and continued, as if trying to reassure her he hadn't seen things. 'No, nothing weird happened. I mean, there were no angels with white wings, or anything. As I was looking out over the valley below, flush in full spring, the colours were laid out like a meal, spread out below me like a palette of some great artist. It made me think. I thought of the hundreds of years and the armies and the killing and… And, well, I thought – why must there be an inevitable Clash of Civilisations? When both civilisations helped build each other like bricks and mortar.' He shrugged again.

'No, no, please go on. It's fascinating.'

'I suppose what I'm trying to say is that actually there is only one civilisation. Maybe with different beliefs, but Civilisation – if you really think and study it honestly – is one long continuum.'

'One built on the other?'

'Perhaps at times one is higher and achieving more, and then a century later the other is dominant. I think of it as if we're on a ribbon, twisting and turning in space like a roller coaster. Sometimes they might be flying high in space, and at other times we might be above them. It really all depends on where you're sitting.'

'But, actually there is only one rollercoaster?'

'Exactly! And we've got to travel in the same direction – no matter what.'

'Wow, I must say mine was nothing as cerebral as that, even though I felt I had had an epiphany. But yours seems to have solved all the problems.' She laughed, and Sebastian turned away.

'Shall I pour the coffee?' he asked.

'I'm sorry,' she said smiling. 'I'm not making fun, Sebastian. It's just that I've never thought about it in quite those terms. Not even when I was with Hamid.' She poured the coffee into espresso cups, plain white, with swirls of black paint licking the rim of the cups and saucers.

'Well, at least you're in better spirits than when we met last time. I'll give you credit for having the courage to go to the mosque.'

'I'm sorry,' she said again in a serious voice now. 'For some of the things I said and did.'

'I know you were in shock after the bombing, and also grieving takes time.'

'Thanks. I think I was going through fits of anger and confusion. Actually, I think I've sort of come to accept Hamid passing away, even if I can't ever forget him. But I'm learning to face each day and I do need answers.'

'Does that mean that you're ready to move on?'

Jessica saw him stand, holding his cup in the air, one hand frozen on his brow as he waited for her to answer.

'Sebastian, you're a really genuine man,' she said, her voice caressing already the inevitable hurt she felt she would cause. 'Right now, my life has become a quest.'

'I understand.' Then he wrinkled his brow. 'What do you mean?'

'During the drive – which was lovely, by the way – I think I was surprised by you, and then even more confused, although the tea was a pleasure. I felt swinging emotions. Especially after the funeral and the way Hamid's mother reacted, and then I was on edge at your place last time…'

'It's okay. I didn't take any of that personally, and I said some pretty horrible things too.'

Jessica felt she still had to assuage the guilt of her previous behaviour, even though he understood and ostensibly had forgiven her. *I was blocking everything*, she thought, refusing to consider the possibility that Hamid could have been involved with *Jaish* in any way.

'I've been making enquiries. Initially I went along with you because I thought you had the answers, but actually you had only suspicions and some rumours. Not your fault. That's all I have too. Rumours, and some peoples' suspicions.' Jessica smiled at him. 'Sorry to go on, but don't worry – I won't rant and rave at you anymore. I have to know the truth.'

'So what are you going to do?'

'I'm going to go to Baghdad.'

'What?' Sebastian turned to her, his coffee cup halfway to his lips.

'I've made my boss give me the assignment back. I'm going to make a documentary about a translator and his family. He used to work for the Americans, but he's disappeared. Really Sebastian, and I think I can tell you this, I'm going to find out all about *Jaish an Noor wass Salaam, The Army of Light and Peace*.' Jessica saw his motionless jaw, and his breathing had stopped. He put the coffee cup down on the worktop.

'Well, what – what can I say?' He brushed a hand through his hair, which stood up at the front as a result. 'You're a very unusual woman, Jessica. Very unusual, and maybe very brave. I thought that when you told me about Hamid's funeral, but now…'

She wondered if he thought her stupid, but she knew her life before did not make sense, and her future life would also be meaningless – or at least, would not make any sense either – if she did not find some answers. She wanted to ask how much he knew about them. 'Can you give me any advice?'

'If it was Damascus, then I would say you're going to love it. But Baghdad?'

'Come on, Sebastian.' She turned to face him fully. 'I'll open that bottle of Cognac, and even make you some fresh coffee.'

She saw him staring at her; her eyes, her mouth, and her slightly parted lips.

'I don't think you realise who and what these people are. And as much as I love brandy –'

'Sebastian, I've already got the tickets.' She went over to the small side table and waved a sheaf of papers at him. 'I am going, you know.'

He looked at her unmoving, without blinking, and then shook his head, and eventually chuckled. 'Wowwee. You've taken my breath away... even more than before.'

'Baghdad and *Jaish*. I know you know loads about both. Tell me everything you know.'

'If I tell you just to be careful in Baghdad, that's like saying walk through the desert but don't step on any sand dunes. *Jaish*. They're more slippery than slugs in jellyfish. Saying *watch yourself* with *Jaish* is like saying put your hand in a bucketful of snakes, but don't get bitten.'

Jessica chuckled and opened the brandy.

He shook his head. 'Desert and snakes are not funny.' He turned to face her square on. 'There's no Brave New World but a scared, old and twisted world in Baghdad – so don't say I didn't warn you. You'll probably never be the same person again.'

Jessica thought she saw concern shine in his eyes as he leaned forward. His hand landed on hers for a moment, like an errant pollinator, before it flitted back to his forehead. *Is he afraid of losing me?*

Jessica poured him a generous brandy in a balloon glass. She smiled. *There's no point being frightened now*, she thought, *or showing it*. 'Thanks for your flowers. I did love them; I still have the ones you gathered for me at Malvern, during the picnic. They're drying in the study upstairs. I think I will press them.'

Sebastian took the brandy. He wiped his brow, and then his eyes, with a tissue. She felt sure he must have memories of Baghdad.

Jessica patted his hand, and hoped that would calm him down. She smiled at seeing the strong doctor like this. *Is it because of his experiences, or because he fears for me? He does have cornflower blue eyes, and such an even smile...* She took him by the arm and led him to the sofa in the living room.

'I think you need to relax with that brandy, Dr Sebastian Windsor, and then you can tell me all about it. You need cheering up.' She smiled at him, as she sat next to him on the sofa.

'Right – tell me all your Raiders of the Lost Ark secrets of Nazi gold, or *Jaish*'s plots. Are they after the Holy Grail too? You'll see... when I get back, I'll make it up to you. Who knows – I might even take you to the Wyre Forest and serve you tea in a lovely scarlet pimpernel-covered porcelain tea set.'

'Well, that is generous of you.' He laughed.

'Now you're getting into my spirit of revolution.' Jessica joined in his laughter. 'I might rock your flowery world. Hey, I might put you in my documentary, since you're a bit of an expert on *Jaish*. I once thought about doing that to Holly when I first met her, but now I love her too much.'

'Well, lucky Holly.'

CHAPTER 15

Dubai – Gulf Software Security Systems Boardroom
David Gul stared at the only woman in the boardroom: Plain Jamila. *The Sisters-in-Charge… what a joke,* he thought. He did not have any sisters, and did not want sisters. He had never spoken to the woman, never addressed her, and he did not know what to call her. Most men in the room addressed her as 'Sisters-in-Charge', since they usually followed the example of Amit. When really pushed they would say *Sister Plain Jamila*. She served no purpose in David's schema. *Actresses, whores and fuck buddies – all names for the same thing.* He was not sure into which category he should put the Sisters-in-Charge. He continued staring at her: at her face, her lack of make up, of perfume, her clothes. She was too covered-up. *It must be hot outside in those*, he thought. Those flowing robes, and that stupid *patka*-turban-like head covering. She looked away, fidgeting with her scarf, and he half-smiled at his small victory. He spread himself wider in his chair.

David turned his thoughts to Aashriya Aarzoo Romano. *She can't fail. Stupid woman; she wouldn't dare fail. That would be unforgivable. At least Amit Bahadur is obsessed with her. I will have to make sure she goes to him as soon as possible, make sure he feels sorry for her. She will have to be cleverer. I'm depending on her to get the secrets from Amit.* He sighed, but let the air out slowly between his lips. *The information she gets from Amit might be false; he'll suspect Aashriya, because I introduced them. Amit's got love-crazy written all over his eyes for her. Let's hope that's enough. I better warn my M16 handler too, but they just aren't paying me enough. That bastard Amit has all the secrets – who does he think he is?*

David looked at Amit, who stood at the head of the table, but kept his face blank. The hatred welled up in him again, and he untwisted his mouth to unknot the grimace with some effort. *Some Muslim like him,* thought David, *put my mother on the street, and then in the Basilica at Bandra, and I ended up in the anonymous baby-dumping cradle outside.* The nuns had helped deliver him, named him David. *I have to slay the Muslim Goliath.*

Although he grew up squat five foot with greasy curly hair – his black face almost as dark as his small moustache, that dribbled into his mouth and so stayed wet continuously at the straggly ends – he knew why women swooned and vied with each other for his ministrations. Because of power: his only chance at humanity.

Have I risked the amazing Aashriya Aarzoo Romano for false information? She is a pawn, he thought. *A lure, nothing more. As much as Amit might think she is his Malika, his Queen, she's merely a piece, to be played in the Great Game. She would be stupid to fail. Ah, but if she marches into Amit Bahadur's end square, an agent might become a queen as long as she can get him to sing like a* bulbul. *Then she would be a peerless, priceless pawn. Will I let her stay Queen of Bollywood, even when she's forty?*

Yeh hai Bombay meri jaan; the tune of the old song came to him – Bollywood. So fickle, Bollywood. *That's what I have promised her, but a promise is just a premise, the beginning and end of faithlessness. Is that even possible in such a soul-sucking, feckless business with so many other beauties vying for my favours, all desperate to dethrone and dispel the dreamy myth that is Aashriya?* He mentally ticked off Aashriya against his latest acquisition: Nisreen. A dewy-skinned, creamy-bodied, dreamy doe-eyed teenager. *I could make her the latest sensation,* he thought. *What to do? The pressures of business.*

David was not sure if his mother had been a Muslim. She could not have had a good life. The poor only had one belief system: suffering. He felt that Amit, like most Muslims, needed light relief, entertainment in their fundamentalist lives. He would present Nisreen to Amit if Aashriya did not work out. She would be like snowy relief against his grey, jagged, mountainous life. A surge of excitement rippled through him. He clenched his fists under the table and immediately opened them before anyone had noticed the flinch; he loved being in the business of beauty.

I bring fantastical refreshment, and that's what he needs, thought David, as he heard Amit droning on about the latest dream he had, about how a *Yogi* in some arcane philosophy had foretold that a great *Sadhu*, Holy Man, would return to lead India to its final destiny. David wondered why Amit always made such a *kedgeree* and did not feel weird in quoting Hindu philosophy mixed with Virgil, and Tippu Sultan and Muhammed Iqbal.

He's more messed up than I am. At least I know what I want; Amit doesn't seem to know what the hell he's doing. I wonder if he really believes he's the Saviour of India? Maybe he thinks he's a new Akbar, mixing all the religions – some sort of Christ, Messiah. I should take him to the priest at Bandra... he needs a head-doctor, more like. David could not stop the smile from forming. He nodded, as he thought a wise man might, to cover his lapse, as if he understood every word Amit spoke.

Amit continued speaking, without breaking for breath. *If I have to sit here and listen to more of this bhenchaud bullshit...* David thought. *This shit runs out of his mouth like diarrhoea; I can't put up with it for weeks. I hope that bitch Aashriya fucks Amit quickly, and gets what I need. He desperately needs it more than any man I've ever known.*

He almost smiled, but glowered instead at Amit. Maybe Aashriya would take his mind off prophecies and shitty *Sadhus* and he wouldn't have to put up with him for much longer. His droning felt like a mosquito in his skull. *I wish I could just swat the life out of him; maybe I will, one day. Thinks he can call me a black bastard, uncivilised son of an* Achhoth, *untouchable, gutter whore mother,* and *get away with it?*

Aashriya had gone to America to film her latest movie. David wondered if Amit had given her anything to deliver. David had thought about simply letting Aashriya rot in San Francisco, letting her get blown up by the bomb, which could not be that far off now. He wished he had more details. He could not punish her for failing yet, although he had nothing useful out of her yet. He had promised his handler at MI6, and he knew the CIA was waiting for the information; they were the most desperate greedy guzzlers of all the ones he had to feed. They were all thieves, *Jaish* and the West, just like the thuggees of old. He could not let MI6 down. His word was like an arrow, once it left the bow, never to return. He was not *that* kind of thief. David did not do it for just the money. He had realised he had to help the lesser of the thuggees, the West: MI6 and CIA, who would help him to expand his empire to all parts of the world. *I need their support, and the FBI will turn a blind eye* as I expand into the great US of A, he thought. I've no choice but to help the West. *These extremist Muslims are scarier than a half-pissed monk with a hard-on, in a whorehouse for the first time.*

'Thank you, Brother Amit Bahadur, for bringing us up to date,' said Plain Jamila. The voice of the woman broke David's thoughts. 'As far as the sisters are concerned, we are ready. Everything is in place in our homes and offices. And so are the Alpha Ansar...'

'Are you having all funds and finances in place? Is there any need for more? You can always access the central fund.' Amit nodded to the blonde man at the far side of the table. 'Please just be speaking with Brother Clive.'

'No – everyone has had the initial payments, and all advances have been made.'

'Please don't stop anyone who asks for more. We are too close to the end to worry about money now. *Alhamdullilah* – everything is in place. We are on the cusp of victory, and the sisters' role is crucial,' Amit said.

David held his fists clenched under the table; he consciously unlocked his jaw.

'London is even more exciting than before, because now I have managed to recruit a blonde woman with blue eyes,' said Plain Jamila.

'The one we spoke about yesterday? You sent her to meet *Shaikh* Abu Umar in Baghdad?'

'Jessica. She will have an 'enriching experience' in Baghdad, I'm sure. I will arrange for her to meet *Shaikh* Abu Umar.'

'If Baghdad shakes her up, it might be working out well for us, then. I am thinking that Abu Umar will be more frightening.'

David had never met Abu Umar, but knew that he was in charge of the Middle East.

Amit continued, 'I don't think you'll get her, though, sister. From what I hear, she's a crafty woman.'

'Don't worry – I'll get her. She's talking to someone else who we have worked with in the past. I know all about her,' said Plain Jamila. David saw her eyes shine, as she sat up straight.

David wondered how many people *Jaish* had committed to its cause, and how many funders and how many more sympathisers were in Britain, Europe and America. He had always thought those countries were full of white, Christian people.

'*Inshallah*, I will get her,' said Plain Jamila.

'I bet you won't – but if you do manage to get the blonde woman, what was her name? Ah, yes... Jessica. If you get Jessica committing to the martyrdom cell, well, then you can input the final codes, and make the call that will activate the Alpha Ansar,' said Amit, smiling at her.

Plain Jamila clapped her hands in glee. 'I'll make sure we win her to the cause, don't worry. That's my job, after the weekend I go back to London.'

Amit continued, 'For what man can remain functioning well without a good woman to point him in the right direction?' This led to some smiles and a few chuckles amongst the gathered heads. Plain Jamila smiled and looked down.

Such a display of modesty, David thought, as he stared at her plain features, her dark face, her long nose and teeth; hating her anew. He shifted in the comfortable leather chair, and pulled his shirt forward to stop it sticking to his back. The seat had become sweat-stained, despite the air conditioning. *I'll have to call my favourite babe tonight for my special massage and Manhattans.*

'The *Jihad Fisabilillah*, *Jihad* for the sake of Allah, is at hand, and we are ready to give our lives, brother. Everything is as it must be...who lives and who dies is now Allah's will...' Plain Jamila sighed and shuffled some papers in front of her.

It's not Allah's will, he thought. *It's this ugly woman's, and Amit's, and this Zulfiqar bin Hijaz's will, whoever and wherever the hell he is. Look at her, tight-cunted bitch, look at her. She thinks she's so pious... it's probably her mother who sold my mother into slavery, and twenty-rupee whoredom. I will never let these so-stuck-up so-holy mad extremists win.*

'It's all *Fisabilillah*, for the sake of Allah, and if He is happy then we have won – even in our loss is victory,' said Amit.

Cries of *Allah is Perfect* filled the room. '*Subhanallah! Subhanallah!*' came from the gathered heads.

David knew the standard upbeat dogma that accompanied these kinds of meetings. *They might not be so smiley and smug,* he thought, *when the security services shove truncheons up their asses to get them to talk. I will have to have a special word with the head of* Maharashtra *police.* He did not smile this time, as the thoughts of potential nuclear-biological-chemical explosions that he had heard rumoured filled his mind, and the full implications hit him. He could not help pulling his mouth into a grimace and baring his yellowing teeth. *How can they believe all this ridiculous nonsense? Jihad for the sake of Allah? I know, at least, that my jihad is solely for the sake of David Gul. I don't know Allah. I don't care whatever gods, Christ or Buddha, or any others exist. They certainly don't care about me. If they were real, I'm sure they don't want what these crazy bastards want. No God wants them using His name to blow up the known world.*

'Our brothers that we are depending on, the warriors in Alpha Ansar all over the world, would be useless – completely rendered inactive – if not for the never-ending selfless application and sacrifice of the sisters. *Jizakallahkair*, sister, may Allah be rewarding you with the highest of gardens. The sisters have plied their souls thin for our victory – which – smell it...' Amit lifted his bulbous nose up and sniffed the air. 'It's like the smell of freshly baked bread. It is irresistible. *Pan de Dios*, Bread of God, as they say in Seville.' Amit made a triumphant flourish with his hands.

David noted the look of pleasure on his face and the stench of self-satisfaction on the woman's features. *Fresh bread? You smell more like rancid dog shit.*

General Kafeel Khan now spoke for the first time, 'When do you need the rest of the Alpha Ansar activated? The AA thirds have been swimming in the Breath of God for some three days. Web looters and other decoys are in the final fantasy play level.'

David saw that Amit shushed him with his eyes. General Roop Pratap Singh who always sat next to General Kafeel Khan said, 'We have to know, because there is another layer before you get to the Alphas themselves, the activators...'

Amit's eyes snapped to the other General. David almost laughed at the way the soldiers could not help themselves, as indiscreet as ever. Amit's face did not change but his silence blazed them back; they seemed to shrink into their chairs back into a squab-like like toady silence. Why are these Generals all so fucking ugly, thought David? Why can a soldier never be pleasant to the eye? Once clothed in the khaki cloth they become hairy moustachioed frog spawn, thick-set, offensive to the senses – *immoral, necessary, but darker than my cocoa bollocks,* he thought, as he looked from General Kafeel Khan to Roop Pratap Singh. David knew the bombs had been bought, transported and put in place by the Generals and their teams. They had exhibited exemplary teamwork:

the twins of terror.

What have they been fighting over these last sixty years: India and Pakistan? The Generals had planned and plotted together for years. Both had cooperated like brothers to ensure that the bombs and the support network were in place. Although David did not know the exact nature of the weapons, he knew they had helped *Jaish* acquire the weapons. He looked at them. Their perspiration alone made them fail as civilians, despite their slick suits. They looked uncomfortable sitting to his right. He saw both of the soldiers shift in their chairs, Kafeel sat next to him and, as ever, Roop on the other side.

Their sweat smelt like the dye of death, which left an indelible disgrace on the executioners' reddened hands. David wondered at these principled men allowing themselves to be consumed like Bombay Stock Exchange commodities on Amit's table, for a begging-bowl full of rupees. David still could not believe how thoroughly he had managed to infiltrate *Jaish an Noor wass Salaam* over the past few years, and now found himself in the same company as these great men. *I could sell them for a roti full of rupees and buy them back for a* puree *full of annas.*

Amit cut into his thoughts. 'For you, General Sahibs, payment has been delivered in your cases. As you are requesting, it has been made in fulsome amount into your numbered accounts.'

David saw how they shifted forward together, unable to keep their hands still. He remembered how the goblins of greed had demanded full payment before they agreed to activate the final stage. They now sat, smiling sultans, with more money than seven generations could luxuriate in: *even if we choose to drink silver and eat gold.* He remembered their smug laughter at the last meeting.

Amit nodded, and a door opened by security let in a man. David recognised him as the same young man who had burst in on their Mumbai meeting. Amit stretched out his right arm, brought him close to him by a gesture, and then sat him down next to him at the head of the table. Amit had remained standing and pacing throughout the meeting, David realised he never sat at the table; he stood with paternal hands on the shoulders of the college boy.

'Our young Salman Khan look-alike, *Om Shanti Om*, who is having dreams of starring in Bollywood is here,' Amit smiled.

David still felt surprise that once upon a time Amit shared those dreams. *How could this bandhar,* ape, *ever think he was going to make it in films?* he thought. *What stupid code-names. Why do they all have to be Shah Rukh Khan's films? Amit is obsessed with films, even more than the average Indian. Well, maybe his god made him like that for a reason, to deliver him into my hands. At least he's besotted with Aashriya. He'll soon be on his knees, drowning in his own ocean of love. Then I'll have my revenge.*

'Instead, he has settled for ever-lasting Paradise,' said Amit, to some laughter.

Om looked different since the first time that David had seen him. Although only a few weeks had passed, Om strode in with a longer gait, not crouched with rushed steps and earth-bound; instead, he seemed to be floating, almost. His hair was slicked to the side and his muscles bulged under his yellow t-shirt, like his idol. David thought he had a certain similarity to Salman Khan, the actor, at least. David smiled at how he had, via one of the Generals, introduced Om to Amit, in such a way that Amit thought the young man was someone he had discovered. So Amit had thought he had been the one who arranged for Om to burst into the boardroom in Mumbai – but months ago, David had set Om up for Amit, so that he passed all the rigorous examinations and questions of *Jaish*. Om had proven to be a natural actor. *Maybe I will give him a role with Nisreen*, thought David, *if he ever survives this*.

'*Shukran Ya Sayedi*, thank you, my master. What do you order?' said Om. His gaze seemed stuck to the table.

'Oh please, please be dispensing with the formalities *Om Shanti Om*. You are soon to be a *Faris Al Islam*... A Knight of Islam,' Amit said.

David felt sure he did not believe it himself, since Amit loved formality in the boardroom more than anyone he had known.

'Let's start.' Amit led the man to the side of the room where there was a screen, which had stood, shielding a part of the room. The guards now removed the covering to reveal a huge phantasmagorical computer array like some futuristic, horrific space ship with multitudinous lights, columns and rows that formed banks in a blind blinking display. Amit guided the youth to the seat in front of the set up.

'Please sit, *areh yaar* – no formality, don't wait for me, beautiful one. Remember, whatever is happening you are guaranteed straight to *Jannah*, *Om Shanti Om*, where the memories of Bollywood will be banished,' said Amit, with a flourish of his hands. The man smiled shyly. His hands moved in smooth waves over the touch screen in front of him, and on then on the keys, like an expert lover's caress. Amit turned to the table. Along with the rest of the expectant audience, David had not dared flinch since Amit had revealed the computers. The silence felt gravid with the renascent virus of extremism.

'This will cause the birth of the Empire. We will insert the umbilical virus carrying hydras into their heart, body and soul. I do not know if these *Kuffar* are having souls...' said Amit, and David remembered to laugh along with a few of the other board members. 'To bring their defence systems and their whole technological civilisation crashing to its knees. Not before we destroy their money markets, turning their financial crisis into a crashing calamity. Anyway, it will certainly be enough to give CIA, M16, MOSSAD, NSA, RAW and any other members of their alphabet zoo multiple brain attacks. So they will be too busy dealing with the disabling strokes that these viruses cause,' said Amit and slapped Om on the back,'while we will be detonating the bombs giving them mortal heart attacks.' Amit looked around at the boardroom. David had no need to pretend to be shocked and horrified... the emotions filled his face. *Amit expects us to be impressed and awed*, he thought, and so he did not hide his feelings.

'That's before we stop the oil, especially from Arabia flowing. The whole of the peninsula shall be dry for them,' said Amit, as he walked back to where Om sat. David looked around the table and, as usual, could not be sure who was pleased and who tried to hide their feelings. As always, they reacted as he expected. *That's probably what Amit expects too*, David thought. *Fear and obedience.* They all seemed suitably impressed. The Malay and the Chinese and the English. David remembered the dead Dane; no one else would want to go that way, to Paradise or not.

'What are the chances that the best hacker in the business world comes bursting into the boardroom of Gulf Software Systems?' said Amit.

No chance, of course, thought David.

'*Subhanallah*,' Amit chuckled, 'it's *Qadr Allah*. He has destined us to victory, *inshallah*.'

'*Inshallah! Inshallah!*' echoed the gathered leaders. Some pumped their fists while they sat at the table; David joined in with them.

Amit continued, 'There is no victor except the victory of Allah – *La illah Ghalib illah Allah. There is no victor except Allah.* The motto of the Nasrids, who, in their cowardly tolerance and love of Jews and

Christians lost not only Granada, but the whole of Iberia. They left behind their motto on the walls of the Al Hambra, which says: *There is no victor except Allah*. We will prove the truth of that saying, when the flag of Islam will once again flutter proudly over not only reconquered Al Andalus, but over every citadel of Europe.'

David released a smile so that his thin moustache danced; his smile matched all the other faces that shone now. *Why did the best hacker, with a proven international criminal record, come bursting into your boardroom,* he thought, *so that you could use him to destroy the West's defence systems? Probably because you think you staged it all, the set-up and burst in, to make it look like Allah's will. You're a crafty bastard, Amit.*

David looked at the Generals, pleasure spread across their faces, as they realised that the virus could be used to transfer more money, innumerable billions. David realised that Amit wanted the extra money to make his victory complete. The Generals probably wanted to buy a group of small islands somewhere in the Pacific – one of the few parts of the world left untouched. *Assuming they use dirty nuclear devices, and not thermonuclear warheads: that would be unimaginable, and would affect the rest of the world too,* he thought. *I have to make sure these Generals don't escape to enjoy their islands in the sun once* Jaish *blows* Israfil's Trumpet. Israfil's Trumpet – *The End of Time. Why does everything have to be reduced to some form of Islamic symbolism?* thought David. *What are they trying to prove?*

David's hatred of religion had fed his determination to stop the fundamentalists. He despised them all, even the Catholics of the Basilica. These Muslim killjoys, who would crumble his empire before his eyes, without a thought for what his years of struggle and sacrifice had taken him to achieve. *Jaish* would destroy all that. *No-one realises how hard I have had to work, from a valueless life to one. of the most important lives in the world. I would rather have one day as a free-breathing man, than live a hundred years live a slave in Dharavi, the slum where my mother was probably from. The Western powers will do their utmost to protect me until they need me no longer.*

He hated these Amit-type of Muslims the most, violent extremists, who appeared like mushrooms in the wetness of ignorance to be fertilised by the hate of occupation. He equated them all to the vandals that had until recently held sway in Afghanistan. David wiped the sweat from his palms onto his trousers. He knew the back of his light blue shirt would be dark with sweat by now, despite the air-conditioning. This felt like the most important struggle of his life; it was the struggle for life itself.

I don't care about the so-called differences they may pretend to have, he thought. They would destroy my beautiful empire, and Dubai, and empty the Gulf of all life. Just like they destroyed the *Buddhas of Bhamiyan.* Beauty cannot sit with them in the same dimension. David loved Dubai: get rich or die trying, like an American anthem, which David had sworn to defend, and as a result he had succeeded. MI6 would pay well, and he would use the expedient Americans, who thankfully, had no soul except the almighty dollar to sell, anyway. FBI-CIA-NSA: whatever three-letter label, just a cock and two balls, the holy triumvirate of American philosophy. *That's why we love them and everyone wants to live there,* David thought. *Because of success with* Mammon *or* Dajjal, *Antichrist, or whatever Roman god Amit thinks they still worship. If he wants to equate their gods with the Devil that's fine, because success, even from the Devil's anus smells sweeter than the stench from most of their poverty-stricken Holy Muslim countries.*

David would make his *pooja*, worship, to that god, would put his head on the marbled gilt-edged floor of that altar. The realisation that the Western World – and therefore, as a consequence, his world that deeply depended on the markets and economies of America and Europe – would be destroyed had forced his hand, and dispelled any final doubts he had had. After all, who would want drugs and whores and films after so many explosions, probably nuclear, even if they were only dirty bombs, and whatever else the fanatics had planned?

His thoughts turned back to Aashriya, to how she might be, *must* be, successful. His price would be met. He knew of the desperation in MI6, something that they had disguised too badly on this occasion. Their lack of information was astounding, even more than usual. They had numerous agents but knew very little. No-one fed them anything valuable – he knew that.

David smiled again. He had become one of the most powerful men in the world, unknown and unnoticed by the media and the general masses – but what did that matter, when he held the lives of millions in his hands? He felt a surge, and his heart beat a short patter of pleasure. He wiped his palms on his trousers, as he realised that he was the deciding broker between the two most powerful blocs in the world. The West and the violent extremists both needed him, each more than the other. Both were desperate for his support.

The Clash of Civilisations would not be determined by the ghosts of Saladin or Richard, or by some great mystical figure, dressed in white, some Messiah, or *Mahdhi*, or whatever each side wanted to call him. He would not be descending from Heaven to join one side or the other. Instead, the Clash of Civilisations would be decided by a bastard who had been abandoned on the steps of the Basilica at Bandra, forty-seven years ago. David could not stop a wide grin spreading across his face, despite his determination to remain inexpressive. He wanted the others and Amit to think he was rejoicing at the imminent success of *Jaish an Noor wass Salaam*.

Om worked furiously, his fingers flying over keys, barely caressing them.

Yes, you are a clever bastard, Amit – but I will decide who will win The Final Battle.

David stood up and cheered with Amit, shouting, '*Allah O Akbar! Allah O Akbar!*' with the rest of them, as the screens burst into a kaleidoscope of colour. No one seemed to know what was happening.

I know for sure you didn't set up this man, Om Shanti Om, bursting in and kissing your hands in Mumbai. I have tested and retested him since then, thought David. *So I know for a fact you haven't sent him to spy on me, and I control him, and the hydra-virus he is releasing to cripple your enemies. I can make the boy, and therefore the virus, dance to the slightest choreography of my fingers.*

Now, how do I best use Om? he thought. *Shall I use the boy to cripple the West's security systems and financial markets, so that I can get more out of them: put them in my power completely?*

CHAPTER 16

London

The two men sat awkwardly; the silence of days came between a friendship of years. Maulana Mohammed Younis *Imam Sahib* had arrived carrying a small briefcase, and had been shown in to Ahmad's room. Sofia welcomed him and offered him tea and biscuits. Ahmad saw the shock on her face, despite her best efforts, as she showed Younis into his room, although Jimmy had warned her. Neither Ahmad nor Sofia had seen Younis since the attack. Livid patches covered Younis' face. His swollen nose looked like a bullfrog and dark glasses covered his eyes, but they could not hide his split rubber lips. He walked with a limp now; bent forward, he hobbled into the room. Ahmad bade him sit on the chair next to his bed, as he took off his sunglasses.

'I'll send Zoya up with the *Chai*, I've got visitors downstairs,' said Sofia, as she closed the door behind her.

'I… I heard you were ill. I…the Mosque…Hazrat Shah Hussain's –'

'I know… I know…' replied Ahmad, wishing that his breathing was not so noisy and intrusive.

'Jimmy came to the mosque…he went to the meeting.'

'He got beaten up too. In the mosque. Unbelievable that the *Masjid* has come to this.' Ahmad shook his head. 'He's been so different since then.'

'He came to the mosque at least, and you know Abu Umar saved him?' replied Younis.

Ahmad wondered if Younis was simply reassuring him. He felt glad his friend was finally visiting him, but shame covered him like the smell of pre-death faecal incontinence. 'I heard… I heard about him…Who is this Abu Umar? *Jaish*?'

Younis looked away. 'I have to let them use the mosque for meetings. Don't worry; Abu Umar's a good Muslim, very passionate. Jimmy will be okay now, you'll see. *Inshallah, Inshallah!* He spent the whole night talking to Jimmy,' said Younis.

'Maybe... it seems he's more religious since then. I pray for him all the time. I know the cuts and bruises will heal. But his soul?' A pause seemed to lay a hand on each of their shoulders, as if the pausing of time itself allowed Ahmad and Younis to reconnect to a shared past, which unified them into an unknown future.

'Did you see any of the test match, Pakistan and England?'

'No unfortunately, no *areh areh meri kismet*, too busy, not enough luck; no more can watch cricket,' said Younis in English, before reverting back to Punjabi. 'I hear they are doing well?'

'Do you remember that time when I bowled a hat-trick with three googlies in a row?' asked Ahmad.

'When I played against you, I played for *Vasah* village?'

'You were the third wicket, my hat-trick ball. I always wondered – did you let me bowl you out?'

'That was the summer you caught that huge *mahseer*. I remember how you struggled with it for hours, but wouldn't let it go. You fed the whole village that summer, Ahmad. Why did you only catch fish all summer?' Younis paused. 'Remember – that was the year of the drought you went into the hills, and caught trout and *mahseer* and you fed many people in the village. Remember, Ahmad?'

Ahmad's mind went back naturally to the days of their youth, and he remembered when Younis had accused nature of conspiring with Ahmad, as if the fish were only attracted to Ahmad's lure. Younis would beat Ahmad at everything else, especially cricket, and often Ahmad would let him, to keep his friend happy.

Ahmad could see the scene now as if it was being played out in front of him, of how he and Younis played cricket together as boys in Ramnagar when they were growing up together in Pakistan. Sometimes they played right through dusk so they could hardly see the ball, even when they covered it with white tape. The ball would swing and become vicious with its heavy covering of plastic tape, and the fast bowlers would love to make it rear up in the twilight, from just short of a length on the hard packed mud and dirt pitch, making it sting the batsmen on their backs and chests like an angry cobra. When the ball hit the batsmen through the thin shirts it would make a sharp *thrump* noise. The fast bowlers would laugh later, when the batsmen showed them the crimson and purple bruises and blotches left by the ball.

The *thrump thrump* could be heard by people walking past the village cricket ground as darkness descended, which really had been made from an extension of the sugar cane field. The players could hardly be seen ghosted against the clouds, which rolled off the mountains like the dark treasures of the Himalayas as the monsoon dusk took over. Ahmad could still hear the noise made by the ball as it hit his chest, as if he was batting on the pitch, trying to hook a short ball. He loved glancing up into the night sky as a plethora of stars came out to watch, his own crowd of spectators.

Why were the stars always brighter and more plentiful in that part of the world? thought Ahmad. Sometimes they continued playing if the moon was full and low; they hung paraffin lanterns all around the edges of the pitch and played well into the cool of the night. Dew would settle over the ground, and a cool breeze would sometimes bring the fragrance of the stream and its trees wafting over to them, if the wind blew from the right direction.

Ahmad always said that the wind had to come from the north for it to be so sweet-smelling – the breeze of the Himalayas. He said he could smell the sweet alpine flowers that grew below the snow-capped peaks, and could see glaciers melting to join the tumultuous monsoon rains that came tumbling down through the foothills of the mountains. These swelled the countless small streams and rivulets that fed the mighty Indus, that watered most of the Punjab and thereby the majority of Pakistan, that made the wheat grow and therefore made life possible. Younis just laughed and said Ahmad had been reading too many books again. *Too much school just fills your head with wheat chaff and buffalo dung* he would say, to tease Ahmad.

'I can still smell the flowers in the hills if I just close my eyes.' Ahmad winced as another series of pains shot through him, like a train ripping a new tunnel through his bowels. 'I told you it was the fragrance of the Himalayas,' he said. He had made Sofia spray his room full of air freshener before Younis arrived, but he still sweated with shame, conscious of his ruptured bowels leaking, although his friend did not show any signs of having noticed.

Zoya came in with a tray with two more steaming mugs of cardamom fennel seed tea, *saunf elaichi Chai,* biscuits and *mitai*. She said *Salaam* to Younis, and Ahmad saw her staring at his face just before she left the room.

'I used to say your head was filled with buffalo dung.' They both laughed as the memories of childhood flooded back. 'And it still is filled with buffalo dung. You went to university – that makes it worse.' Younis became serious. 'Now it's filled with worry for Jimmy, too.'

'Yes...you're right.'

'Don't worry, nothing will happen to him. The worst that can happen is that he will become a good Muslim boy. That's what you've always wanted, isn't it?'

Ahmad wondered if the *Imam* simply continued to soothe the brow of an ill man, a friend who would soon be dead, and maybe about to lose his youngest son to *Jaish an Noor wass Salaam*. Despite Younis' reassurance Ahmad knew the reputation of *Jaish*, a philosophy that had been an anathema to Ahmad's spiritual life.

Younis took his Jinnah cap off and stroked his hair; he put it on the bed by Ahmad's feet. '*Ya Allah, Ya Allah madath*. O Allah, Allah, help me,' he said.

Ahmad wondered if Younis could ever be master of his own destiny. After all, it must be some powerful people who had him under their control, if they had dared to beat him into a hobbling limp inside his own mosque. The *Imam* always prided himself on standing iron-back straight, a buttress for the community. Ahmad did not say anything; the silence no longer uncomfortable. He felt sure Younis was also lost in their youth.

Ahmad remembered how, during the monsoon rains, they would abandon the cricket match in the midday heat and go and swim in the *nulla*. The boys would try to fish with fishing rods made from branches they had broken off the trees overhanging the stream. The rough homemade hooks were baited with dough surreptitiously secreted in their *kameez* pockets after the breakfast *chapatti* dough had been kneaded, before their mothers could see and scold them. Occasionally they would use sweetcorn and once in a while, when *mahseer* season came, small worms and beetles they dug up from the riverbank.

They tried to catch the carp, usually smaller *mahseer* and brown trout, and most often Ahmad would succeed. Ahmad caught fish without trying, which would infuriate Younis so that he would throw stones into the water, which meant the end of their fishing at that location. They would then take the fish home for the evening meal; none of the fish were thrown back. Although they had pleasure in catching the fish, the real enjoyment came when they shared them, eating with friends and family. Or sometimes, when they felt adventurous, they would stay out late beyond dusk after the cricket match, smother the fish in spicy *tandoori masala* and lemon juice. The lemons were freshly picked from the surrounding orchards in the right season. Younis had his special job – he would broil them over hot coals. Ahmad would let Younis take over, because he was always better at the practical things.

They spent many long, lazy and humid, heat-haze filled summer afternoons lying in the shade of mimosa and willow trees on the riverbank. They spent most of their summers playing cricket until they were caked in sweat and dirt– the dust from the hard yellow earth baked over their sweat. The perspiration made snail tracks in their dusty faces as it ran off their chins, transforming the boys into unrecognisable *Jinns*. Ahmad remembered the tatty and torn *salwar kameez*, the colours no longer discernable after a whole day's cricket, and then the pure, unparalleled pleasure in cooling off in the *nulla*.

When the boys got to the *nulla* they took off their shirts and hitched their loose baggy trousers up to make shorts, and dived into the glacial clear water. Even Younis would dance in the rain when the monsoon came. The monsoon turned the cricket pitch into semi-solid mire and it changed colour from hard-packed terracotta earth to buffalo-dung brown, churned by the boys' bare feet and open-toed sandals. They stomped and squelched in the chocolatey mud, so that the cool wet clay stuck between their toes in the summer heat. Ahmad and Younis loved it when 'monsoon stopped play', just as much as they loved cricket.

Ahmad looked at Younis, and today, more than usual, the memories assailed his heightened senses. He knew they had never since been so filled with such good food or so fulfilled with each other's company. They never thought that they would one day have another life or that there would be another way to live. The rest of their lives had not turned out the way Ahmad had hoped or imagined. Now, he knew he had to save Jimmy.

'I brought you something,' said Younis and put the briefcase on Ahmad's lap.

'What is this?' asked Ahmad in a whisper, and gripped his abdomen, despite his best efforts to stay impassive.

His friend took out a mobile phone and dialled, ignoring Ahmad. '*Jaldi anah, char aadmi lanah, abhi isi waqt*. Come right now, and bring four men with you,' shouted Younis imperiously, and then he snapped the phone shut.

'Why four men? What's going on, Younis?' He had not opened the bag.

Younis said nothing; instead he stroked his beard, and smiled.

Within a few minutes someone banged the front door. 'Are you ready, Ahmad?' said Younis. 'Ready? What?' Ahmad asked.

'Have you forgotten? It's Friday. Are you ready for *Jummah* prayers?'

'Younis, I can't go to the mosque, I can hardly walk. And Sofia's got visitors downstairs – she can't help me.'

'Do you need help to make your ablutions? I wouldn't worry too much about women's visitors. Come on, it's fine. I've sorted it out. I've even got a special chair for you in the front row.'

Sofia came in, astonished. 'Younis Bhai Sahib – there are four huge men here. They said you called them?'

'Yes, Ahmad's going to be in the front row again. I'm taking him to *Jummah*.' Younis got up, and shouted at the men to come up. He gave specific instructions as they lifted Ahmad onto a stretcher and carried him downstairs, past a group of Sofia's visitors in the living room.

'Oh, stop! Stop!' he said, as they got to the living room. 'Ahmad, you haven't opened your bag.'

'What is it, Younis? I'll look at it after *Jummah* prayers...'

'No, open it now! Sofia, *bhabi*, you do it,' ordered Younis.

The gathered people made room for Ahmad, as the men helped him to half lie, half prop himself over the sofa. The visitors moved but no one left the room. Sofia opened the bag and gasped. 'Younis Bhai, so – much – money. What's this for? What – how?'

'Ahmad's operation, of course. He needs the operation privately. Jimmy told me...'

'Younis, where is this money from? Is it Jimmy's money?' Ahmad said, his face turning red, his voice breaking. His breathing became strained and rasped harder. He knew Younis loved the attention, the fascination on the faces of the gathered guests. The *Imam* hobbled forward, occupying the middle of the room.

'Why would I be bringing it to you if this was Jimmy's money? He just told me, that's all. I've brought you the money...' Younis took off his *karakul* cap, shook his head slightly and wiped a hand across his face.

'Oh Younis Bhai – *Imam Sahib, shukriya, shukriya*. Thank you so much! You are the saviour of our family, you –'

'Wait, Sofia, we can't accept this money like this.'

'How can we ever thank you?' asked Sofia as she wiped the tears off her cheeks with her *dupatta*. Murmurs of astonishment and praise broke out from the onlookers.

'This is nothing. Nothing. Please don't embarrass me in front of all these people, *hunh*?' said Younis.

Ahmad saw Sofia's tears, and stayed silent.

'You are a true *Sufi*,' said Sofia and Ahmad felt sure she would have hugged and kissed Younis if it had been permissible. The *Imam* said nothing; Ahmad noticed pain shooting through his leg as he made to move off. The men lifted Ahmad and started the short journey to the mosque.

'One more *Jummah namaz* in the front row...' said Ahmad.

Maulana Mohammed Younis Khan *Imam Sahib* straightened his black *sherwani* and scuttled out, crab-like. He smiled at Ahmad as he left, but Ahmad saw Younis set his *karakul* cap at a more rakish angle as he walked out. He straightened his *sherwani* coat tails, which wagged behind him.

Baghdad – Al Jassim District

Mariam's husband had disappeared weeks before Jessica had arrived in Baghdad. The insurgents had kept their promise to invest a *mard makhoof* – a terminal illness – on anyone who worked with the occupiers.

Jessica's translator said she knew her husband and Mariam would make a good story for Jessica to report on. So they arrived at her house, without announcing themselves.

The woman cowered on a small footstool in the darkened room; there was no electricity other than an intermittent two hours. Her five children gathered around her, the older ones doing their best to succour the young at the appearance of a strange blonde creature, and two men – Peter, the cameraman, and James, the soundman – in their home. The younger children gathered themselves in the folds of Mariam's skirt.

Mariam was about the same age as Jessica. Mariam looked like the oldest woman of thirty Jessica had ever seen. Most of Mariam's teeth had fallen out, broken and crooked ones were left behind, small stumps. She covered her mouth with a hand when she spoke. Grey hair, dry and brittle, peeped out from under her soiled black scarf, and her skin had an almost green, oily sheen to it. She stirred the soot-covered pot on the charcoal fire; the children blinked their streaming eyes in the smoke.

So Jessica started the interview, she later realised, like most western journalists who did not have to live in post-Saddam Iraq, by asking Mariam how glad she felt that he was gone. The woman translator had a hard time keeping up.

'The devil has gone, but the devil gave us food, free schools and hospitals. Now we don't have any water to drink. This is from the puddle outside – it's dirty – smell it.' She pointed to a bucket in the corner of the room. 'My children don't have water to drink. The youngest one,' she said and stroked the tiny baby's head, 'Musa, he has stomach problems, diarrhoea – but there are no doctors.'

'Why are there no doctors? Did you take him to the hospital?'

'I have no money. This food, this vegetable, is charity.' She lifted the lid off the pot and Jessica saw a gooey brown paste with an overpowering stench.

'So you were happier under Saddam, under the devil? Not now you're free?' Jessica asked, with some surprise.

'How can anyone be happy with devils? As *Shaitan Al kabir bala'a Shaitan as saghir*, the big devil swallowed the small devil, and now it's stuck in his throat.' She paused and stirred the pot with an ancient wooden spoon. 'But it's not the food or water, or that none of my children go to school. Yahya, the eldest sells cigarettes, anything, in the market, and I quake my bones for him. Every time he leaves home my womb twists in agony because of the bombs every day. I would give up *Wallahi Wallahi*, I swear by Allah, I would happily give it all up – food, water, everything. I would even live the rest of my life under Saddam, if only I could have Abu Yahya back.'

'Your husband?' asked Jessica. Mariam nodded. 'Do you have any idea where he is?' said Jessica, as Mariam stroked the hair on the baby's parchment-like head. The baby arched his back and mewled.

'I don't know. *Allah u alim*... only God knows...'

'Why did he work for the Americans?'

'We are poor – what can we do?' answered Mariam.

Is asking for pity the first refuge of the poor? thought Jessica. She peered at the woman through the gravid smoke, looked for signs in the fetid darkness that the woman was crying. She bounced the baby on her knee and stirred the pot. Jessica felt that tears that must have seemed infinite once had crushed Mariam's hopes, but the salty sea had now dried up. Jessica thought most people she knew would have broken down.

'Have they asked for anything, for your husband?'

'How can they ask for anything? They know very well what can they take from me.' She gestured around the almost-bare, squalid room. Despite herself, Jessica felt unclean; she pulled her shirt away from her body. She looked around and saw two beds pushed together, a small table in the corner, soot blurring the features on her husband's picture pinned on a blackened wall, the flaking blue paint barely visible. She put a hand on the head of the eldest boy. 'Yahya, even if they take Yahya, they know I don't have ten *Dinars* to ransom him.'

'Have you had any help from the Americans?' Jessica turned to the translator.

'The only time we see Americans is on the TV.' Mariam pointed to an eighties Hitachi set with dials and wooden panels on the side. Jessica looked at it, amazed that it could still be functional. 'Are the Americans really like in the films?' Mariam asked the translator.

The translator smiled.

Jessica said, 'Well, it really depends which films.'

'John Wayne, Abu Yahya loved John Wayne. My husband started learning English by watching John Wayne, that's why he named my son Yahya – he told me that's the same as John,' she said, in a brighter voice. Then after a pause, 'Why don't the Americans – they are the biggest, strongest – have their own language?' she asked Jessica, who looked at her and smiled, but did not add that they almost do. Her smile dropped as she noticed a small girl of about three appear from behind her skirts, almost naked and say something to her mother, who hushed her and pointed to the pot. 'Don't worry, Allah will provide…' said Mariam, more to her than her daughter, Jessica thought.

'We have to leave – Jess – just had a security alert on the satellite phone. There's trouble, maybe a raid. Jessica, come on!' said Peter, still filming. James nodded his vigorous agreement, already packing up his sound equipment.

As Jessica left she tried to hand over a bunch of dollars to the woman.

Mariam shook her head. '*Alhamdulilah*,' she said, 'we have enough to eat, brothers give us, thanks be to God. We will not start living again, my children and I, until we know where Abu Yahya is.'

Jessica put the greenbacks on the side-table.

'People say these bombs, they have something, something called *dept amnim*?' Mariam said.

Jessica turned around. 'Depleted uranium?'

'*Aiwa aiwa*, they say they make it in your country?' she asked Jessica. Mariam looked directly at her through a pool of moisture, which gathered in her eyes now. Jessica did not need to hear the translation to understand. She looked at the floor.

'They tell us that this, this – what you call it, is in the food, in the water?'

'So I've heard,' Jessica mumbled.

'Can you tell them to stop when you go back, to please stop? Don't put this devil's breath in the bombs. Just make normal bombs.'

'I'm sorry, but I don't think I –'

'Musa, he's sick – he's –'

'Use the money,' said Jessica, as she took out more notes out and added them to the pile. 'Take him to a good doctor, a hospital.'

The baby let out a strangulated gasp, an inhuman sound. Mariam looked down at the child in her lap and finally started crying. 'Our children are dying. They are dying – why?' she asked. Jessica could say nothing. 'We are sacrificing our children, but for what? Not for Iraq, so many dead, but for the American President.' Mariam cried without tears, and then she had composed herself with a dignity unimagined by Jessica. 'I took Musa to the hospital when – when Abu Yahya was with us.'

'Look I'm sorry. Here – here's more money.' Jessica told the translator, without looking at the woman, as she took more green pieces of paper out of her purse. 'It's payment for the interview.'

'It's not the money. No money can help. There are no medicines that can help him, not in Iraq. He has cancer in his blood, the doctor told me. There is nothing – nothing…'

Jessica choked as she walked out of the stifling room, into the heat of a fissile Iraqi sun beneath a burning blue Baghdadi sky and left Mariam cradling her baby in her lap, waiting for him to die.

CHAPTER 17

London
The four strongmen lifted and carried Ahmad on their shoulders. Being held above their heads reminded Ahmad of his childhood again, because the only other time he had been held aloft was after a successful cricket match, when he had bowled a hat trick. He remembered how Younis had walked behind the crowd and separate from it, clapping intermittently, as the rest of the boys cheered. Younis later had used the excuse that he was on the opposing team. Younis had been Ahmad's third wicket, and that isolated success on the cricket field against Younis now seemed trivial compared to the honour being done to Ahmad today, as if he had been victorious in some great battle – but he had done nothing.

Today the *Imam* strode ahead of Ahmad with purposeful steps, at the front of the procession. He adjusted his cap regularly. As he speeded up and slowed down, he shouted at people to get out of the way, although they stepped off the narrow pavement as soon as they saw the weird cortege. He sent a runner ahead, ostensibly to clear the path, but so they could be announced, and would ensure a greater than usual crowd at the mosque. Ahmad did not care that people stared incredulously at the sight of a frail older man being carried on the shoulders of four men, forming a quintet of comedy. Even the mosque regulars tittered and the small boys pointed as the men passed by, but only when Younis could not see who was laughing.

Ahmad watched how the *Imam* strode despite his injuries. His paunch belly led the way, and shiny black shoes clickety-clacked on the pavement. He occasionally stroked his beard, or pulled his black waistcoat down by the lapels with both hands. Ahmad thought he looked like some Mandarin autocrat, but Ahmad did not mind; instead, he smiled. Younis was his friend; Ahmad would not defile the memories of friendship, despite Younis' current antics.

When they were both eleven, they were faced with a separation. Ahmad was due to go to secondary school, and Younis had to go to the *madrassa*. Ahmad remembered how they had sat under a neem tree, and Younis had cried because Ahmad was going to be many miles away living in town, but Younis would continue in the village *madrassa*. He had held Ahmad and made him promise he would visit him every Friday, on the weekend. Ahmad had happily agreed. They had mixed salty tears as bitter as the twigs of the neem with which they brushed their teeth, and then they swore a secret blood oath. Younis said he had seen it in an Indian film with Dilip Kumar, one of the greatest film stars of all time. Younis said he had memorised the words. Ahmad knew no such movie existed – Younis had made up the words – but they affected him nevertheless: *My blood is your blood. I am your brother and you are my brother. My future is your future, your failure my dishonour, my success your pleasure. Your happiness before mine, my brother – your blood is my blood.*

They had held their palms together above their heads. The blood shone scarlet in the dappled shade, and ran down their arms. Younis' grip was firm and unyielding. It took a few weeks for the cut on Ahmad's hand to fully heal; Younis had cut eagerly, with a hunting knife. Ahmad bled profusely but Younis cried more. Ahmad realised that friendships end, and that brotherly emotions remain stuck in the viscous mists of history, or become petrified promises, and fossils of stone that he would carry around his chest even in old age. Granite on his heart, the pain of which he would take to his grave.

Ahmad had a pen, which his father bought for him from *Hajj* on his return from Mecca. He gave Ahmad the gold fountain pen on his sixth birthday. Younis had coveted the gift from the moment he had heard about it, before he had seen it. He did not get to see it for another week, and did not get to touch it for another year.

Ahmad had softly wiped it with a velvety cloth and put it away at the bottom of his drawer at home, hidden under books. He had let Younis see it, finally, after a week of incessant begging. Ahmad remembered how his face was filled with wonder as they both sat under the neem surrounded by keeker trees on a small hillock, their favourite vantage point by the sonorous stream where they fished for trout. Younis had looked open-mouthed as Ahmad slowly slid the cover off. The fountain pen lay in its box still and cold, like a corpse in a coffin, except it seemed to pulsate as the bright afternoon sun shone on it. The light reflected into Younis' eyes, and they turned honey-yellow. Ahmad could see how the pen possessed him at first glance. He wanted to tell Younis that it was made of solid gold, as his father had told him, but he could see by the rictus in Younis' face that he did not need to. His friend had already heard that it was made from real gold. So both boys sat motionless, Younis staring, and Ahmad holding it under his face. Finally, his friend said, 'It's more beautiful than Madhubala in *Tarana!*'

On Ahmad's seventh birthday he took the pen out again, and this time allowed Younis to touch it and hold it until it became warm in his hands. When Ahmad turned eight, Younis wrote with it. Ahmad had insisted he would be the one to fill it. He carefully held the nib in the inkbottle, and gently pressed the rubber bladder. Younis then scrawled his name in large spidery writing in Urdu and, proudly, in English. Ahmad had never written with it.

He remembered the days when wealth was eight brightly coloured dollop sweets for one *anna*. Food was some tandoor-roasted *channa*, the chickpeas burning and scalding their skin through their thin *kameez* pockets, or two corn on the cob munched as they ran back to school after lunch break. How they wrote with qalam, which they made from reeds growing in the muddy side of the *nulla*. They cut the stalks and made pens, carefully crafted nibs that they dipped in home-made ink. Then they would write Urdu and Arabic alphabets on wooden tablets, *takhti*, which had to be washed and evenly covered with new china clay, diligently harvested from the river bank every evening, before school the next day. The wooden slates developed their calligraphy skills, but Ahmad could not match Younis, especially at *Khat-e-Nastaliq*, a beautiful Urdu script, which Younis wrote with a clear and bold hand.

School was a huge spreading *peepal*, under which an ancient teacher taught, with skin more shrivelled and darker than the tree. He wore thick black glasses and taught the only class in the school through their primary years. He would stand with a stick pointing at a wooden board. His bare chocolate legs were exposed, like dry flaky branches, in contrast to his dazzlingly white loincloth *dhoti*. Ahmad remembered how the fig tree provided shade, and he loved the way the morning breeze whistled the leaves and how sometimes the macaques would come and raid the fruit. And how when they were gone Ring Neck parakeets would chatter in flocks, or rarely the brightly-coloured Plum Head parakeets would flutter down from the foothills of the Himalayas, especially when the loquats were in season.

Once he and Younis had caught a small bird, which was unlike any bird they had ever seen before. It arrived after a monsoon storm one night, and Ahmad had found it shivering in the dawn, on their hillock by the *nulla*. They were amazed at its curved beak and the way the feathers became a kaleidoscope of iridescent patterns, changing colours as he warmed it in his hands. The two friends often hunted different birds with air rifles in the wooded hills, and relished the doves of their forest. Ahmad wondered how the small bird had got there, where it lived and what it ate. Younis favoured making it *Halal* and roasting it on the fire he had going for the corn and sweet potatoes. Ahmad fed it a honey and sugar solution, and warmed it next to his belly until it was strong enough to fly. He watched with immense pleasure as its wings flapped so fast they became a blur, and it whirled into the sky like a large dragonfly. Ahmad knew Younis shared the same memories, but he wondered why the light seemed to have gone out of Younis' eyes during his teenage years, soon after he joined the *madrassa*. Then the distance had grown when Ahmad had gone to university. *Had education come between them*, thought Ahmad, *or was it the force of knowledge like tectonic plates that had widened the gap between them, and Younis' lack of formal schooling that pulled him into the chasm?* Ahmad pulled himself out of his reverie as they neared the mosque.

Younis led the way into the mosque and made a spectacular entrance through the main gate. He greeted people effusively; today he seemed even louder than his usual ebullient self. He parted the massed throngs with an imperious lifting of his hands, and Ahmad saw the sea of black hair and white caps, like froth on the waves, part in front of Maulana Mohammed Younis *Imam Sahib*'s stride. Ahmad knew him well enough to realise that Younis regretted not having a Messianic staff to wave the crowd away or to turn into a serpent.

Preparations for *Jummah* were well underway. Younis gave hasty instructions to some of his minions, and they seated Ahmad on a comfortable chair in the front row, an elevated position only allowed to the sick or infirm. Most of the front row regulars knew of his illness and he watched as they looked at him in shock, open-mouthed at his condition. There were many audible gasps as they passed the news down the line, a chain reaction which led to a general, '*Areh Ahmad Sahib, kiya howa?* What's happened to you, Mr Ahmad? How did you allow yourself to get into this state?'

In the centre of the row at both sides of him sat Younis' aides, who were always in the mosque although they had no official title and no work to do. The one to his right followed this up with disingenuous but culturally appropriate, '*Areh*, don't you worry. Now that *Imam Sahib* has given you the money, you can get the operation and start walking to the mosque five times again – just like old times.' The old man with a white beard to the other side of him added, 'Isn't it amazing that Maulana Mohammed Younis *Imam Sahib* managed to get twenty thousand pounds at such short notice?'

Ahmad knew his community intimately, but was still amazed at how fast news spread, like some extra-sensory Punjabi perception. Ahmad tried to smile. Instead he ended up wheezing and coughing, which caused the pain in his bowels to shoot through his mouth and rectum at the same time. He grimaced and hoped he would not shame himself by vomiting, or worse, having uncontrolled diarrhoea.

More men crowded around and formed a chattering melee. Ahmad sat like an old king, whilst the others waited to hear the last words of his will. What instructions would he leave for Zoya's marriage? Would the rift between him and his childhood friend Younis become open? Would he denounce Jimmy? Ahmad sat on his chair barely able to reply, occasionally coughing, but mostly holding his chest and wheezing.

Ahmad looked down and noticed how his white *kameez* was impeccable, his salwar crisply ironed. How clean he looked, despite the internal decay. He wondered if his insides matched the colour of his dark brown waistcoat and the woollen cap that Sofia had knitted for him years before, the same one he wore to every *Jummah*. Ahmad blessed Sofia, as he always did before *Jummah* prayers started, realising her sacrifice over the years.

The crowd of men insisted on asking about Jimmy in particular; they knew Abu Umar's bodyguards had attacked him. Ahmad kept his gaunt face expressionless. He knew most of the mosque elders, who gathered around. There were many old and young men he did not know, but they crowded around nevertheless. Some wore jeans, others *salwar kameez*. Most were perfumed, as usual on *Jummah*. Ahmad could smell the overpowering *attar* as the elders came close to him and hugged him. They sat down around him as best as they could, in whatever space became available.

'Has Jimmy recovered after what happened that day with Abu Umar?' said one with raised eyebrows, when really underneath he was asking the question they all wanted the answer to: *Is Jimmy going to stop dealing and pimping and fly straight, now that he's got what he deserved? Should have happened years ago – maybe then he wouldn't have misled our sons, and maybe they would be with us in the mosque today.* Ahmad knew what they really meant. Jimmy, and therefore Ahmad, had long shouldered the blame for their sons' misdemeanours. A few smiled and some of the younger ones, even the ones who knew Jimmy, sniggered at this.

'Are you feeling okay, *Abbo*? You should be resting,' said Jimmy. He had arrived unnoticed and stood behind Ahmad, a part of the crowd. Ahmad saw that Jimmy ignored the rest. The group of men were stricken, quiet and motionless as if a king cobra had materialised amongst them. A few of the teenagers at the edges pretended they were not part of the crowd and pulled at each other, hoping Jimmy had not noticed them; they turned and fled.

'Oh Jimmy, thank Allah you are here! It's been so long since we've seen you. I was just asking your father about you,' said one who had spoken earlier, stroking his white wizard-like beard, secure in his status as an elder.

Ahmad saw Jimmy's face redden as he rubbed his scar. 'I'm fine, *Betah*, fine,' he said, before Jimmy could answer the man. 'Come and sit down, sit next to me.'

'Oh yes, *haanh haanh chalo chalo, yeh kiya tamasha hai*? What a circus, it's nearly time for prayer. Why are you all standing around looking – go! Go!' berated the man with the Merlin beard, shooing the crowd with his arms as if he was never part of the group. No-one moved, Jimmy looked at them, and when they had his permission they quickly moved out of their stupor and then suddenly melted away – *as if they had never been there*, thought Ahmad.

The muezzin started the *adhan*. Ahmad felt the pure sound, a hauntingly beautiful harmony, fill him with strength as it reverberated around the mosque. Ahmad closed his eyes and let the sound cover him, revelling in its cadence, in its never-tiring simplicity. His face filled with tears that trickled down his face. He was not self-conscious; he often cried in *Jummah* as he prayed after the *adhan*, repenting his sins and asking God for forgiveness.

*

Maulana Mohammed Younis *Imam Sahib* was in his office; he locked the door and changed into his garb and vestments for *Jummah*. He donned a huge multilayered green turban, a flowing white dress, *thawb*, with an outer terracotta robe, which had no buttons and hung loose. The wide lapels were richly covered in embroidery. The stitching created overlapping floral patterns in red and green, radiant in the light.

He combed his orange beard and flashed a shiny white smile at his fully accoutred reflection in the long mirror. He was a striking sight even to himself, despite the healing cuts and bruises on his face, but having accounted for them by saying he had been in an accident, the pain no longer bothered Younis. Today his smile disappeared as he applied copious amounts of his usual rose *attar* into his beard, and put a cotton soaked bud behind his ear. He stood motionless, then looked into his reflection for a long time. The lack of motion in his eyes was strange, and no matter how long he stared into them, his flinty eyes looked back at him, opaque. The sensation discomfited him, and he sighed and moved a bookcase to reveal a cast iron safe. He slid the key from around his neck, which was on a tattered thread. Younis pushed the turban firmly onto his head as he opened the safe; he felt his face moisten. He wiped his palms over his eyes, and was surprised when they came back wet.

In the centre of the otherwise empty safe was a rectangular box, the cardboard dark and ancient. The outer box had blue writing, the brand name in swirling copperplate: *Eagle*. The box was frayed at the edges and the writing on it was no longer visible, eaten by time's teeth.

The *Imam* reverentially took out the small box. He held it for a while, and then slid the inner case out of the box. Slowly, he removed the lid to reveal an old pen lying in its ancient, frangible coffin. He turned to glance at the locked door, saw the mirror, and once again his eyes turned yellow-gold. It was the fountain pen that Ahmad had given him on the day of their Oath of Brotherhood. It sang to him, called to him.

There was a knock on the door and a voice on the other side said, '*Imam Sahib*! It's getting late for *Jummah*.'

'*Hanh hanh yaar ahh raha hon*. Yes, yes, I'm coming. You people can't cope even five minutes without me.' Younis put the pen in the inside pocket of his waistcoat. 'Oof, Allah!'

He remembered how he had told Ahmad that he had thrown the pen away when he came to England, and then another time he had said he had lost it in the mosque move. Younis took it out and moved his hands up and down the barrel. The gold was chipped and rust-brown patches peeked through. Time had rubbed away the glitzy veneer, and exposed the true base metal. For all of that, the pen had lost none of its alchemy for him. He clipped it onto the pocket inside his waistcoat, and left to go upstairs to lead *Jummah* prayers.

The main hall of the mosque was packed with a swell of mostly multi-shaded brown patches, with occasional white or black dots. He could see the faces, many with moustaches, and the occasional babbling beard in front of mouths that created a cacophony of chatter. A veritable Babel of languages, surmounting ziggurats of misunderstanding; the usual scene Younis encountered before starting *Jummah* prayer. These were the tongues that had chiselled the cultural citadel of Islam in Britain out of the sands of miscommunication.

Mirpuri, a parochial Punjabi variant, was the normal language for many of Younis' flock. Standard Punjabi for some, Urdu for a few, English for a handful, French, Somali and Kurdish for a smattering. The *Khutbah*, the main speech, was delivered in Arabic. The *Jummah* address was in Urdu. Most of the English sounding noises came from the far side from the youngsters, with designer jeans and fluorescent T-shirts and inverted baseball caps; they shoaled together and gelled to the back walls. Some of the men were in suits and ties, on their lunch break.

Younis started the speech, and spoke for twenty minutes on the Duties of Brotherhood. Then he recited the standard Arabic commentary, and as usual, because it was *Sunnah*, doing what the Prophet had done; he sat down on the *Mimbar*, the pulpit, which had a few stairs leading up to a platform. It was shaped like a small tower, with ornate and intricate wooden fretwork carving on the sides. The *Mimbar* stood to the right of the *Mihrab*, the niche in the front wall that indicated the direction of prayer, to Mecca.

Younis saw Ahmad make *dua*, a special prayer, as Younis saw Ahmad do every week. Younis remembered the *Hadith* in which the beloved Prophet of Islam had said that Allah descends to listen to the prayers at this time, and the prayers are granted. The *Imam* knew what Ahmad prayed for. He made the same *dua* every *Jummah* – for Jimmy, his family, and for Younis.

*

As the *Imam* stood up, he leaned forward to continue his *Khutbah*. As he did so, his waistcoat swung forward for a moment. Ahmad saw the pen hanging from the inside pocket of Younis' waistcoat. Ahmad sat at his feet now. He had insisted on struggling to the floor for the prayer, despite his physical difficulties, especially the pain that tormented him from his rotten bowels. His whole body ached as if being battered by lump hammers. Ahmad recognised the pen immediately. He looked at his friend, and realised that both of them now knew this.

Ahmad remembered how Younis had wept when he had made a present of it to him, on that distant day of oaths. How he had sworn more oaths by Allah to cherish it, write beautiful poetry with it, to exalt Allah The Most High. And above all, how Younis had promised he would write Farsi poetry, which a liberal-minded *mullah* from Herat had taught him, in the *madrassa*. Ahmad knew only a little Farsi from school and would listen, entranced, as Younis even then had recited in an orator's voice, always the stage performer. Younis knew how to enthral.

Younis would recite Rumi and Jami in Farsi, and Ghalib and Mir Taqi Mir in Urdu. He would let the mellifluous sounds stand in the air after each word, a special pause and every syllable especially formed, like nectar pouring into Ahmad's ears before the meaning had reached his heart: for Farsi and Urdu poetry was to be felt and experienced not heard, Younis had always said. He had sworn he would write poetry in honour of Ahmad, and girls would swoon as sherbet dripped from their lips – who would not want to kiss them? Younis had promised to create a new world.

But he had done none of it. Ahmad knew this. He knew in his heart that Younis had never written with the pen again. Now, Ahmad looked at Younis and saw he was staring directly at Ahmad. He looked at the *Imam* and mouthed: *I forgive you, Younis. Look after Jimmy. I forgive you, Younis Khan.*

Ahmad grimaced in pain; he put a hand on Jimmy's shoulder.

'What is it, *Abbo*, is it hurting?'

'Life is pain, my son. Be a man, my *Betah*. A man's life is hard work and suffering pain with a smile. Be a man!' Ahmad said, in a soft but strong voice. Ahmad knew he could continue to talk quietly during the

Khutbah, not something he usually did. Talking during the actual prayer was impossible.

'Abu Umar – how did it go?' asked Ahmad.

'He stopped me being beaten up. I was half-conscious after their bodyguards attacked me. I was more awake after he spoke to me than ever before in my life. We spent the whole night talking.'

'What about?'

'Everything. Life, Iraq, Afghanistan – even *Jihad*.'

'What did you think of him?' asked Ahmad, wary of the word *Jihad* and the new strange light in his son's eyes.

'He's a great man, *Abbo*, he's – he's unique.'

'You seem to think he's a great Muslim?'

'I want to be just like him. He inspired me,' said Jimmy. Ahmad saw that Jimmy instinctively realised he had made a mistake, and now tried to cover for it. 'I mean, he showed me true power can only come from worshipping Allah, not on the street,' Jimmy added.

Ahmad looked at him with concern. '*Betah*, many people use the words like *Jihad*. But you know that true *Jihad* – our beloved Messenger, may Allah shower him with blessings, said – is the struggle against the ego, the ever present *nafs*, the vile demons within us.'

'See, *Abbo*, I'm here in *Jummah* with you. That's what you wanted, isn't it? Isn't that the first step?'

Ahmad knew he was avoiding the question. '*Shahbash*, well done, I always believed it when your mother said you were a good boy.' Ahmad had no choice except to hope for the best, so he knew he would pray for Jimmy to find the right path, straight and true, the *sirat-al-mustaqeem*, when he went into *sujood*, in prostration with his head on the floor for a few minutes. That was when Ahmad loved to ask God for his innermost desires.

'I believe Allah and His pleasure is the way,' said Jimmy. 'That's why I came to the mosque today – not just because Uncle *Imam* had brought you here. I want to worship the Most Powerful; I'll never miss a prayer again. I want to bear witness with my heart, body and soul,' said Jimmy, breathless.

'The best thing one man can do for another is to show him the right way to live. The greatest gift a father can give to his son before his time is up is to make him into a man. To be a man, Jimmy, is to sacrifice. Sacrifice for others, *merah Betah*.' Ahmad put an arm around Jimmy shoulders and saw the shining light of sincerity, and the pallor of truth stricken across his son's youthful expression. His red scar became like a red swollen rope holding his face together.

'I love you Jimmy and – and I'm proud of you,' said Ahmad, looking into his son's eyes. 'I'm proud of you, Mohammed Yusuf Regus,' he said, calling Jimmy by his full name for the first time in his life. 'Now you are a man.' It was also the first time in his life he told Jimmy that he was proud of him. And the last time; those were his last words.

Before Maulana Mohammed Younis Khan *Imam Sahib* had finished leading the prayer, Ahmad was dead. All went into *sujood*, prostration, put their foreheads flat on the carpet, but when the congregation rose as one, after Ahmad had also bowed down and prayed for Jimmy, Ahmad did not get up. He had died in *sujood*, with his forehead and nose on the carpet, calm in his open eyes, and an almost-smile on his lips. Ahmad died in prostration; he subjugated his cerebral conscious brain by bowing his head to the floor, worshipping his Lord in death as he had in life.

As life slipped out of him, Ahmad said the words three times: *How perfect is my Lord, the Most High.*

Baghdad – Al Jassim District

Jessica insisted to her team that they go back the next day. She said they needed to more material for the documentary programme, which was incomplete. She felt an irresistible urge, despite her discomfort, to return and find out more. They set off in the afternoon, but by the time they reached the area, after an unexpected roadblock, the day had turned to grey evening.

Mariam greeted her like a long-lost relative, kissing her on both cheeks. '*Ahlan wa sahlan*,' she said.

Jessica knew this meant literally *You are walking on the easiest ground, and now you are with your family*. She thought it must be because of the money. As she entered the room, she saw the notes had not moved from the side table.

'Why didn't you take the money?'

'We don't take charity from strangers, from foreigners. You just left it there.'

'You said *ahlan wa sahlan* – now I am not a stranger,' Jessica picked up the money and gently placed it in Mariam's hands. 'And anyway, think of it as payment for the interview.'

'*Shukran*,' said Mariam in a whisper.

The night banged and thudded. The noise and clamour grew outside, more than usual for the poor parts of Baghdad, even Al Jassim. Mariam sat in the same place, making the same vegetable paste as the day before. Jessica noticed there was no bread again today. Mariam invited her and the crew to eat. They politely refused. Mariam insisted on making tea, but she had no milk. So she made it with mint leaves.

'Don't worry. It's made with water from a bottle like you foreigners drink. I made Yahya get one bottle from the market yesterday, because the sister translator said you might come back.' She served tea to each of them in turn, offering it in small glasses which had three gold circles embossed on the outside, near the top. Each glass stood in a small white saucer.

Jessica turned away and wiped her eyes so Mariam would not see. The tea and the way Mariam had served it, with such obvious affection, moved her more than anything she could remember, except for baby Musa and the thought of him dying without treatment. Jessica had locked the hotel room door last night and cried until she wet the towel. She had fallen asleep too exhausted to move the towel off her face.

The sounds grew louder outside. The baby cried, and Mariam shook her knee to console him. He seemed so thin, like skeletal aluminium. Jessica thought he would make a clanging sound as his mother tapped him against her knee, like the wooden spoon clattering against the sides of the pot, which she stirred in the other hand. James fiddled with the sound controls.

Shouting now emanated from outside, followed by gunfire. The children became paler, and the skin of their faces stretched. More shouts and a small explosion somewhere not far off; the children crowded together held on to one another. One disappeared behind his mother's skirts.

'Happens many nights, explosions and bullets.' Mariam said, and shrugged almost apologetically that the noise should disturb their visit. 'The children get frightened,' she added.

Jessica felt surprise that the children had not adapted and become familiar with the shooting they must have lived under all their lives.

'If I live to be one thousand, I will still hate the sound of bullets as much as the first time,' said Mariam.

'When was that?' asked Jessica.

'I was a little girl when,' Mariam replied. 'Saddam.' She gestured as if her body could damn him and his line for eternity; she spat the four syllables of his name like a quatrain of curses. 'Sad-dam Hus-sain came through our village. Some men tried to attack him – no-one knew who they were – but Saddam survived, and came back the next day. He dragged all the men and all the boys over thirteen out of the village. He tortured and interrogated them there. They admitted their crimes.'

'Why?'

'Everyone, everyone *Ya ukhti*. It's better, my sister, if you admit your crimes sooner than later. Everyone admits. My father was working in the orchard on his date palms; they dragged him out, and lined him against the earthen wall.' Mariam paused and wiped her face. Jessica could not be sure if she would continue. Finally, Mariam spoke again.

'Uday, Saddam's son, ordered them shot – in cold blood – like wild pigs. In between smiles he chewed his cigar, and he held a glass of whisky in one hand. He had a gun in the other. He shot as many as he could before the rifles of the firing squad barked his pistol into silence…'

The reality of the experience, once the translator had managed to divulge the story in a croaking voice, and its cloaking immediacy became apparent to Jessica, but she felt the need to ask, 'How do you know all this?'

'I remember I hid in the grove of my father's palm trees. I had gone to help him gather the dates. I hid and I watched… but it got worse.'

'Worse?' Jessica could not imagine what could be worse.

'Uday told my father that if he shot my brother, he would live. He tried to make him kill his own son.'

'What?' Jessica found it difficult to believe. She wondered if Mariam's trials of life over the years and grief had turned her misery into the melodrama of legend. Jessica looked into the woman's eyes. They were wet, but steady as Mariam nodded. She did not look at the translator but directly at Jessica; all doubt disappeared.

'What seems unbelievable, unthinkable to you, happens in Iraq every day.'

'What did your father do?' Jessica asked

'He stood to his full height and faced Uday. He asked him *Do you really expect me to shoot my son?*'

'Then?'

'Then Uday said *Your son is a traitor to the Rais Al Iraq – shoot him and you will be spared by my father's generosity.*'

Jessica leaned in closer, 'What an amazing man your father must have been, Mariam.'

'No, *ya ukhti*, my sister, he was not an amazing man, not a fighter. He was just a farmer.' She wiped her palms against her dress, the baby balanced on her knees. She made a soft sound that Jessica did not recognise, which had a strange, foreign, but soothing quality.

'What did he say to Uday?'

'He simply replied: *Would your father shoot you, Ya Ibn Rais Al Iraq? Oh son of the ruler of Iraq? You will shoot him. You will beg me to shoot him!* Uday then turned to one of the soldiers grinning, and then he said to my father, '*What about your wife and small daughter?*' Mariam looked beyond Jessica at the blackened walls, the memories controlling her.

Jessica covered her mouth with her hand.

'My father held his hand in front of Uday's face and then said: *You can kill me and my son, but if you mention my wife or my daughter, I swear by Allah and his messenger, I will find you beyond death and I will slowly squeeze the life out of you.* My father held his hand before Uday's face and closed his fist as if he held Uday's neck. He spoke without shouting, and looked Uday directly in his eyes. *You are not an Arab. You are not a man.* Those were my father's last words.' Mariam paused, and wiped her eyes with her scarf.

'What happened? I'm sorry... take some water.' Jessica handed over a bottle.

'The soldier standing next to him clubbed him with the butt of his rifle, and as my father fell to his knees Uday shot him point-blank in between his eyes. I still remember the puff of blood that burst out from the back of my father's head. Then they shot my brother. I'll never forget his eyes just before he died.'

'How old was he?' Jessica asked.

'My brother was fourteen and I was eleven. I ran screaming all the way back home and carried on screaming at my mother, until I thought my lungs would explode out of my mouth. My heart had burst. I felt my body liquefy into a bloody mess like the dead I had just seen. We left my father's house in the clothes we stood in. Eventually, somehow, we came here to Al Jassim.'

'So you've been here nearly twenty years?'

'It's our destiny to be here. So it was written...'

Jessica contrasted Mariam with the chemical engineer she had met, and with the woman who had stood for parliament who was a journalist. She continued to work for *Al Hurriyah, The Freedom* newspaper despite the numerous threats on her life; she maintained a standard of journalistic professionalism. *How do they do it, these women?* she thought. So different. One educated and urbane, the other poor and hungry, yet so much suffering in common. The women of Iraq like her two rivers, the Tigris and the Euphrates. They now had the job of birthing a new nation out of the sands of Mesopotamia. Both were emptying their hopes and dreams into the same sea of the future.

Without warning, the door smashed open and US Marines burst in.

'Arms in the air!'

Mariam's shawl fell from around her shoulders onto Musa who lay in her lap, as she instinctively raised her arms. The other children screamed.

'Don't move, stay still! Arms in the air!' ordered a marine. An accompanying translator repeated in Arabic. 'Arms in the air! Do – not – move!'

The baby let out a stifling sound under her shawl. Jessica saw a dark shape shift in the dullness of the lamplight, as Mariam moved her arms to lift the cover off the baby.

The marine who shot her could not have seen much either, Jessica thought later. Three bullets went through Musa and into Mariam, seven rifle rounds entered her body altogether, and then buried themselves into the wall behind her.

Baghdad – Green Zone

Jessica investigated the killing with the Americans a few days later. She met the colonel who was head of PR in Baghdad. He offered her coffee, which she refused, and launched into an explanation without waiting for her to ask any questions. *He must have been briefed about what I wanted to ask him,* she thought.

'We – the marines – had chased insurgents into Al Jassim, and thought they were taking refuge in the houses, which they often do.'

'There were no terrorists there,' said Jessica.

'No marine would willingly shoot unarmed women and children. These deaths are unfortunate and regrettable – collateral damage,' he said, in a flat voice.

Jessica remembered the video of the man shot by the marines, wounded and helpless on the floor of the mosque at Fallujah. Shot dead, although he could not move. Murdered. She did not allow herself to think of the other stories she had heard, so she turned them into make-believe, like fairy tales, and the people of Iraq into fairy creatures and beasts – otherwise the testimony of their reality would grip her throat, and tear her breath.

Jessica had returned to Mariam's house the following afternoon. Peter had tried to warn her as they had left the Green Zone that it was too dangerous, but Jessica had to see what had happened to the other children.

When they got to the house, Jessica had found it an empty shell; the smoke-stained walls were the only remaining evidence of human habitation. The only things left were the spent cartridges that had littered the floor. There were blotches of brown on the wall. The mesmerising evidence that Mariam had sat there only yesterday. Blood had soaked into the fabric of the bricks.

Jessica had noticed a rag doll; one of the children must have dropped it. It lay in a dusty corner with its head twisted. She picked it up, straightened its neck, and put it into her bag.

Jessica now advised the Colonel, 'It's your duty now, an American duty, to find and take care of the remaining four children.'

The Colonel laughed, chewed his gum harder, and said, 'La-dy you can always put a re-quest in.' Then she felt he scrutinised her through the reflective blackness of his Ray Bans, he added, 'Off the record: do you have a-ny i-dea how many orphans there are in I-raq? In Bagh-dad alone?'

Jessica did not remind him that their father Abu Yahya had worked for the Americans, or that Saddam had killed their family, and now the Marines had shot dead the baby and their mother. They had run out of relatives. There was no need to remind him. He knew all of this already.

*

Jessica went back to Al Jassim. Most people would not talk openly. After long hours of random questioning with no results, a woman neighbour signalled to her surreptitiously. Peter was with James, filming in Mariam's house. She knew if she entered the neighbour's house it could be a trap. She had to know what had happened. She had brought the woman translator with her again. So they both entered the small house opposite to Mariam's, and inside she met Aisha, who spoke some English.

'Come in – quickly – come in!' Aisha said as she gesticulated them in, and closed and bolted the wooden door behind her. Jessica soon discovered that Aisha's husband had been killed a month ago in a suicide attack, while he waited in a queue to join the Baghdadi police. Aisha told her she had been Mariam's friend since she had arrived in Al Jassim, and she knew of her kindness to Mariam. She felt scared that something would happen to Jessica. When Mariam's husband died, no-one from the government came to help. After a while, a strange woman turned up and gave her some money.

'Who was she?' Jessica asked.

'They – they are looking after *yateem*.'

'Orphans?' Jessica knew almost no Arabic, but that word was ubiquitous in Baghdad. 'Who are they? Where can I talk to them?' she asked, but Aisha did not answer. Jessica pulled out some crisp dollars.

'No, I can't. They're looking,' Aisha said. Sweat covered her brow, her eyes flitting around as if she expected ghosts to walk through the walls. She pushed Jessica's hands away from her. 'Everywhere – looking.'

'But there's no-one here,' Jessica said, as she looked around. The room was empty, except for the inevitable scrawny children.

Aisha spoke rapidly to the translator. Then the woman almost pushed them out of her house, her eyes growing wider and her mouth running. The translator handed the woman a card, before almost tumbling out of the door into the bright sunlight.

They got outside, and found Peter and James almost in a panic. 'When two women disappear in Baghdad, even for ten minutes, that's an eternity,' said Peter.

'Bloody hell!' grunted James, still recording with his sound equipment.

'Sorry, Pete, we had to take a chance,' Jessica said, and looked at the translator as she they all got into the jeep. 'What did she – Aisha – say to you?'

'*They will be in touch*, they said.'

'Who?' when Jessica got no reply, 'Aisha?'

'*They have been watching you since you first came to Al Jassim.*' The translator shrugged. 'This is Baghdad, and our land. Do you think anything happens here and we don't know about it?'

'Is that what 'they' said, or are *you* saying it?'

'Those are the words Aisha had been told to say, and she said they will meet with you, since you seem to be so interested in telling the story of the poor of Al Jassim. But on one condition.'

'What?' asked Jessica.

'That you have to promise to tell the truth.'

'What the hell is that supposed to mean? Whose truth?'

'Well, that's what they said. No-one tells their truth.'

'I hope you said yes. We can't let an opportunity like this go, eh, guys?' Jessica turned around to Peter and James, who both sat in the back and scowled.

'I gave her your card with your phone number on it.'

'Good girl! This is a story we have to tell. But who are *they*? What do they call themselves?' Jessica suspected 'they' could be not be anything other than *Jaish*. She looked at the translator, who wiped her palms on her jeans and swallowed, before speaking.

'They are *Jaish an Noor wass Salaam – The Army of Light and Peace.*'

At home in England, the words that had been unreal and seemed to belong to some place far away now became as real and hot as the steel of the jeep that seemed to surround her like a speeding metal coffin. Jessica opened her window fully, and although air rushed in, her breath still came in gasps.

CHAPTER 18

Baghdad – Hotel Palestine, Green Zone

Jessica and her team waited for her phone to ring. Days had passed, with no contact. She paced her room in the Palestine Hotel, and watched as suicide bombers raged impotently. She saw many of the attacks on the Green Zone only managed to scratch the cemented surface of fixed American structures, protective barriers put up to keep the Green Zone safe. In the suburban city the bombers found their mark, as the nuts and bolts of undiscriminating shrapnel wriggled into the battered, surrendering flesh of the civilians of Baghdad, yielding like velvet kid bellies under the butcher's blade. Jessica watched as rockets and mortar rounds landed regularly. The ancient battle for defining masculinity raged in the era of The New World Order. The explosions sent up intermittent plumes, rising phallic smoke signals creating a mephitic mask, which smothered all in Baghdad. She wondered if suicide bombings felt the same in other parts of the world. Would they feel any different in Afghanistan?

Jessica started to think that Aisha, the woman who had called them into her house, must be deranged. No one would contact her. She jumped as the phone rang.

'You want to make movie?' said a man's hoarse voice.

'Yes, a documentary. Who's this?'

'You make film – yes – no?'

'Yes. Film – make film, yes!' said Jessica.

'You friend Mariam?'

'I knew Mariam,' Jessica said.

'How many people you?' the man croaked.

'There's cameraman, soundman, interpreter and me,' said Jessica.

'No! No, only you, English lady, come and make movie.'

'I can't make a film on my own,' Jessica said. Fear swamped her, with the rising reality that she would have to put her head at their mercy. She could not imagine going alone. She knew that even with a crew and American guards they could be kidnapped; people had gone missing in the Green Zone. Outside, they could be killed at will.

'Who – interpreter – Iraqi?'

'She's a woman.'

'We don't want traitor. What her name?'

'She's a brave woman.' Jessica willed her voice not to quake as she said, 'She's a friend. She lost her family.'

'Okay. Okay. No woman. Just two mens!'

'Yes, okay,' said Jessica. She realised that the numbers did not matter if she went to meet the insurgents and they wanted to kidnap her; a whole BBC studio could not stop them. The quest and chase for answers, which had overtaken her life since Hamid's death, was drowning her judgement.

The Foreign Office and the Americans had been clear enough. 'Outside the Green Zone you are on your own, off the record: we have no idea where they might take you or what they might do,' the American Colonel had said. His cigar had drooped at the mention of insurgents. Jessica had seen her worried face reflected back in the glossy-blue beetle-eyes of his Ray Bans. His Virginia accent had been slewed into a slurring of words by his cigar.

Now they were on their way. The 4X4 bumped the potholes like a rhino, jumping over fresh grazing. Their driver spoke to them incessantly, as if his mouth had no brake. The jeep's horn seemed to feed him nicotine-addiction like his ever-present cigarette, which hung from the corner of his mouth. So the driver gunned the engine, and used the horn like a siren as they swerved and dodged through Baghdad. He slammed the brake as if he were stamping out poisonous snakes with his foot. He had virtually no English and they had no Arabic, except ten words between the three of them.

They headed out into Baghdad. Fear seemed to prick their throats like thorns, as if they had entered the Great Iraqi Desert without water. Jessica looked at the driver and saw his face bitten into a dog-like rictus; he pulled his lips back as he made canine snarls at pedestrians. He growled continuously. She knew as an Iraqi working with foreigners he would already be targeted. Jessica had no idea where they were.

She had given the driver the same instructions that she had received from the caller. She told him to go to Al Hakim market, which was in a bustling area of Baghdad. The car caused dusty whirlwinds to rise from its wheels as it braked hard. They got out, ignoring the driver who gesticulated and machine-gunned Arabic at Jessica. They crossed into the vegetable stalls thronged with people, as instructed. She felt unsteady on her feet, and felt sure that she would fall in a heap.

'I really hope you know what you're doing, Jess,' said Peter, and she noticed that sweat was already running down his back and sticking his shirt sleeves to his arms. James nodded, habitually agreeing with Peter. They stood out – not only because no westerners ever came to this part of town, but also because their flak jackets with 'TV' marked in white made them conspicuous. Jessica felt surrounded by the market, full of locals; they seemed to stop and stare. All the eyes followed her, as if they belonged to some multi-eyed organism. They had landed in a city full of feral brown eyes.

Her phone rang. She jumped onto her toes and reached for it, as if it would explode if she did not answer in five seconds.

'Cross over the market and go into the side street opposite, past the old bookseller. When you get to the orange seller's stall, take a right,' said the voice on the other end. The people in the market place returned to their shopping, as if the phone call had broken the spell.

Jessica realised no car could follow. They could not be tracked from the air because of the semi-covered walkways and narrow streets, which led to burrowing basements and a spaghetti of alleys, where the sun's rays could not penetrate.

Shoppers thronged and pushed past. Some smiled, and children crowded and begged for sweets. A small boy tugged at her shirt; she rubbed a hand over his bristly head, and smiled at him. His friends rubbed his head in imitation. She gave him a bar of chocolate. His friends gulled around him, cawing for a piece, and when they had swallowed it in lumps, they turned to Jessica for more. 'Sorry, no more.'

Jessica looked up, and realised they had been boxed in by men. A musclebound man stood in front of Jessica, with his arms crossed, like a Genie from *One Thousand and One Nights*.

'Fol-loow – bleese!' He gestured with his outstretched hand, and turned. They followed him, surrounded by four other men. The genie led them into a shop in one of the side streets, which had shutters down on the window.

Three chairs stood in the middle of the empty shop. 'Sit!' said the huge man, and added with a smile, 'Bleese!'

Jessica saw Peter and James look around at the men, and fidget with their equipment bags. She shrugged and sat down; they did the same, and secreted their filming equipment between their legs.

The musclebound genie and his helpers passed some sort of scanner over them and their bags, which emitted lights and beeping noises. Then they blindfolded all three of them.

Jessica said, 'Don't worry guys. This is all quite normal, I'm sure.'

'Never happened to me in fucking Finchley,' mumbled Peter through his tight lips.

'Yeah, yeah,' muttered James.

The men bundled them out through a back door, led them by their hands into a waiting car.

Jessica felt dizzy and nauseous almost immediately. After an indeterminate length of time, when she felt that she had been on a rollercoaster for a week, she felt the vomit rising in her throat. 'Stop. I'm going to be sick.'

The genie said something in Arabic, and the car lurched to a stop. 'We here now. Bleese – you come,' he said.

Jessica jerked off her blindfold, flung her car door open, and sprayed watery vomit in a wide arc.

'You okay, Jess?' Peter asked.

The musclebound Genie smiled, and raised an eyebrow at Peter. 'She okay. You no okay?' The other four men, who had followed in another car and now stood beside them, laughed. 'Come – come!' The genie beckoned them with both hands.

We could be anywhere. No one knows where this place is, Jessica thought. They had arrived. For a moment she squinted, while her eyes adjusted after the regurgitation; she thought they had landed in some Columbian drug lord's hacienda. A grand house with red-tiled roof and white walls faced them, and four walls formed a compound around them. Numerous men, guards, shouldered their semi-automatic rifles and stood to attention, as the genie led Jessica and her team. They saluted crisply, sucking in their paunches as the group passed them. They bristled with facial hair and as much masculinity as they could muster, trying to send the Genie clear signals about the die-hard levels of personal protection they would provide. She wondered if she and her crew would ever make it out of the compound alive, and what an incredible risk were taking as they entered the den of *Jaish an Noor wass Salaam*. She had put her crew's life at risk for a story, and she would never forgive herself if anything happened – *but then, that is how great stories get told and amazing documentaries get made by investigative journalists, she told herself.*

Be honest, did you not take this risk for your own pleasure? Did you not put lives at risk for personal answers? Yes... but I have to know the truth about Hamid. She wanted to run, to escape; she hated her naivety for thinking she could just turn up in Iraq and film in Baghdad, like a stroll in Hyde Park. *Stop it. Remember, they respect courage. You cannot show any fear.*

Jessica stopped herself from making eye contact with any of the men. She fixed her eyes on the door in the middle distance and willed her vision not to blur, or her knees to collapse, or to vomit again. She noticed, in her peripheral vision, their youthfulness reflected in their wispy facial hair. They wore straps of bullets around their chests and necks that hung like garlands, or chains of office.

These boys are fuelled by testosterone, she thought. *They just need sombreros and then they'll look like Mexican baddies, as if from a Clint Eastwood Spaghetti Western.* She would have smiled, except that the bulging muscles of the Genie and the deadly, glistening gunmetal of the guards reminded her that this was an altogether different game.

Jessica noticed eyes again. She became acutely aware of being the only woman, as their eyes seemed to search every angle and turn of her femininity. Their dark eyes were like wells of oil that followed her every move. She shivered, as if snakes had slithered and coiled around her. Some of the guards sucked their cigarettes harder, and blew smoke out of their nostrils, building up steam. Cultural difference – would English insurgents would be polite, and not stare. She forced her mind to ponder this as she walked, determined not to be weak, not to stumble on the rocky ground. She said a prayer. *They stare all over the world – why do we think it aggressive to stare? It's natural to stare at anything weird and foreign*, she thought. Her and her crew fitted both categories.

The genie led them through the ancient timbered doorway. Rusting iron studs held the door together. The gnarled wood reminded her of the janitor in the Hotel Palestine; the old man's skin was dry and brown. His weathered face was a set of wrinkled walnuts interspersed with black moles, like raisins. She had got his story on film. He had eventually told her, through her interpreter, that he had come to Baghdad as a young man when his family lost their lands in Jaffa during the Zionist occupation of Palestine, and no matter how bad things got in Baghdad he had no intention of becoming a refugee twice in his life. He had spoken with quiet dignity, and had never smiled. Jessica had thought self-respect shone in his eyes.

Jessica blinked as they entered a room, which had many doors leading off to the sides. An ornate chair faced her. The genie asked her to sit on the small wooden one nearest to her. She shivered, despite the warm Baghdadi air, and wished she had put on layers – but then she would probably sweat.

'You'll be all right, Jess. At least they're giving us an interview,' said Peter, and the genie hushed him immediately.

An interminable age passed, which she realised could only have been a few minutes, during which Peter blew his nose five times and James tested his sound equipment seven times – *probably hoping he gets a chance to use it tonight*, she thought. The genie crossed his arms and became statuesque; she could hear his nasal snorting as he stood to the right of her. She wondered if he had fallen asleep, but did not turn around.

A man walked in through the door immediately opposite her. He had a short auburn beard on a square jaw, and wore an earthy-coloured brown *Jilbab*. His cat-yellow eyes glowed like sparks, fixed on Jessica, and his pale unsmiling face seemed translucent. He walked without hurrying, as if the ground would shrink to meet him in case he stopped. Normal rules of physics did not apply.

'This great man – Ghazi, Jihad *Fisabhillilah*, *Shaikh* Abu Umar!' said the Genie, muscling forward to hold the chair with a huge amount of deference, before Abu Umar sat.

Jessica looked at the slim man, as he strode into the room with an easy gait that seemed to spread confidence around the gathered guards, who stiffened to attention. The guards almost smiled with pride.

What kind of man is this? she wondered. She had heard of the 'invaders atrocities', as the insurgents called them, which had become hearsay. The rumours fell like rain over Baghdad and Iraq. Standing up with courage to 'the occupiers, the invaders,' – was this what had won Abu Umar so much respect? Because he was the leader of those who had dared to make a stand?

Her gaze flickered from the chair, which had no table in front of it, to the men who surrounded them. She barely dared to look at Abu Umar. He sat in the chair. Everything she had been told about the *Jihadi* crystallised into this man. Jessica folded her hands in her lap, crossed her legs and then uncrossed them, unsure how to sit or address him. She did not know how long she could look at him. Or should she even make eye contact with him? She had long imagined this moment. Now that her long-held desire to meet the insurgent leader, to interview him, to get to the truth and see his motivations past the clouds of propaganda had actually materialised, she did not know how to begin. She glanced up at him, adjusted the folder in her lap.

His unwavering gaze was upon her. She felt that his unblinking stare burnt a laser hole in her forehead. She rubbed between her eyebrows, as if to remove the sulphurous stain of his stare. As if his yellow eyes left the mark of brimstone.

Abu Umar said nothing. She offered the traditional Muslim greeting, and felt immediately foolish, her voice not her own. He did not reply.

'Thank you for agreeing to do the interview,' she said. Still he said nothing. 'Do you mind if Peter sets up the camera and James will do sound?' She did not wait for a reply this time. 'Thank you.' She nodded to the Peter and James. 'We can set up now,' she said, her voice gentle. She turned back to Abu Umar, but he had made no movement.

I bet he expected me to quake and beg she thought, but I can't show him how terrified I am, that's the only thing these people respect – strength. Poor Pete... he thought he would never get a chance to make the film today. She felt relief like a sea breeze, and became aware of the sweat-soaked white cotton shirt sticking to her back. She felt glad she had removed the heavy flak jacket earlier.

The two men elbowed each other for the duty of approaching the insurgent leader. They both stood up at last, and stumbled over their equipment. Both cowered, bent over, using the cameras and equipment as a blockade. Neither wanted to set up Abu Umar. Finally Peter approached him, as if he were a cobra sitting on a landmine. Jessica saw how Peter just managed to stop his hands shaking sufficiently to attach the microphone to the *Jilbab* without touching or looking at Abu Umar.

'It should be me who is thanking you. I thank you.' His voice made her whip her head around, tossing her hair. He made a small nod of his head. 'You people are busy, very busy,' he said.

Jessica could not be sure if he mocked her. 'No, no. For you, we always have time.' She regretted the interruption, but relief at hearing him speak made her words flighty.

'Always telling stories.'

Be careful, she thought, as she brushed her flowing yellow strands out of her face and eyes. She noticed him watching her intently. His eyes never moved from hers but she felt sure he noticed every tiny detail about her. She became conscious of her mouth, her teeth. She did not know if she should smile. She wondered if she should have worn a scarf; she had felt more protected, somehow, after her spiritual experience in the mosque, and had thought about experimenting with it. Did he glance at her hair? At her golden locks, thin as filaments, so rare in the Middle East, that often caused women to comment and men to stare.

Abu Umar sat unmoving, unblinking. She noted his high cheekbones, his weird goshawk eyes. He had a curved Arab nose, his limbs were controlled, unflinching, still: a staring, stony samurai of symmetry.

His gaze penetrated her shields.

'We – I – am very interested in stories.' She stopped, reminding herself not to squander this opportunity in sycophantic comments or Sophism... or was it fear that made her acquiesce? He almost changed expression. Did he want to smile at her nervousness?

'That is the problem, our story – nobody wants to tell it – the truth,' said Abu Umar.

'Well that's why I'm here.'

'Your *Kuffar* TV – CNN – ABC – always telling lies.'

'BBC, and we try not to –'

'BBC – XYZ – PQR – you are all the same.'

'Try me,' Jessica said, her professional integrity insulted; it gave her voice strength. She wished she could let him speak uninterrupted, to tell his unique tale. She wanted to get the story above everything, and she hoped that within that story would lie the answers to the questions that had turned her life inside out. *That's why I risked my life and those of my colleagues*, she thought. She turned to Peter and James saw both almost tremble, as Abu Umar looked at them with his unblinking gaze.

'Well,' Jessica cleared her throat, glanced at the pad in her lap, and back to Abu Umar. 'Where would you like to begin?' She paused. 'I have a list of questions, but –'

'At the beginning,' he said and now she felt sure he almost smiled. 'Let us begin at the beginning.'

She pushed her hair back and pursed her lips, scratched with a fingernail between her eyes where she felt the burn of his stare. 'At the beginning of what?' she asked without looking up, sure this was another test.

'At the beginning of Time...'

I wonder what he wants me to say? What happened at the start of Time? she thought.

The militant leader interrupted her thoughts. 'Before space, before the universe, the Big Bang, there is nothing. Only space is there, and so, no Time. So before space and Time start, there is only the One, Al Wahid, Allah. I am only slave of the One. I am *Abd Al Wahid*. He asks us to bear *Shahahda*, how you say, ah yes, testimony. I will bear witness by giving my life for Allah. Then we will be free from oppression, *Al Zulm*. That is why I do what I do.' He paused with an almost imperceptibly raised his eyebrows. 'Isn't that your first question?'

Jessica made no reply, stared at her notepad. *How simply he reduces suicide bombing to a part of the Great Master-Plan, all related to the Great Architect,* she thought. *I wonder if think she is an architect, creating a Janat Al Arif? The Generalife Gardens* she had seen in the Alhambra had been a sultan's spacious imaginings of heaven. *Does he quite clearly put himself on the side of God?*

He had guessed the main question. She had asked herself the same question so often it hurt her head and made her scowl, which made wrinkles in her forehead. She shivered, as if she felt like a sudden arctic wind sweep down into the Babylonian desert. *Did he make Hamid kill himself? Why does he make suicide bombers?* She felt amazed she had stopped herself from blurting out about Hamid. *Maybe I should just assume all these extremists to be crazy*, she thought. There was nothing mad about Abu Umar. She looked at his burning eyes that could brand through skin, and realised that he did it from utter conviction. He truly believed every word he said.

Jessica had failed to ask what she had planned, and he had blasted clear her battlements with his opening sally. She looked up, determined not to be undermined by the power of his presence, or perverse philosophy.

'Is that – I mean is it – Time and space that causes – sets off suicide bombs?'

'If you ask in your sarcastic way, is it God's will? Then you have understood, Jessica.' The way he said her name in his unusual accent, prolonging the syllables, made her look down and withdraw into the chair. She had not expected him to use her name.

'Then you have understood more in a shorter time than I imagined possible,' he said.

She looked at him and saw the hint of a smile. *Is he mocking, or pleased that he has managed to rile me?* she thought. Or is this just how he always is, and is it my distrust of these people that's making me imagine their everyday expressions as malevolent? Evil where no evil exists? Are they simply misguided but with justifiable grievances? Especially after what had happened to Mariam and the children in Al Jassim?

'It's Allah's will. So it's Allah's will?'

Abu Umar did not answer but looked at her with an almost-smile, an unchanging mask. The silence hung between them like a cup of hemlock; dare she reach out? She knew she had allowed emotion to fog her reporting already, like shadows of clouds' across a plain. The death of Hamid had thrown her journalistic professionalism. It felt as if she would have to the drink poison from the cup of hate, held out by some invisible Satanic hand hovering between them, and she reached for it without conscious effort. She knew she had allowed herself to be cornered on his terms, she had no choice but to empower him – *he already has the power anyway*, she thought. No point pretending otherwise. This wasn't the BBC studio... one gesture from him would reduce them to orange jumpsuits in video films, begging for release, shown all over the world's media. The thought led her to ask an unprepared question.

'Why do you kidnap people? Innocent people, and dress them up in orange suits, and behead them?' The horror they would experience surfaced in her voice, a frog noise, which would not remain submerged nor could be drowned.

'Like Guantanamo Bay, you mean?' He paused. 'Men prisoners into cages like animals, nobody guilty, but like wild animals! This is against human rights, international law, Geneva Convention. They have not been charged. They have no court case against them. There is no evidence. Nobody proves anything.'

'They haven't been beheaded,' Jessica could not stop her fists from clenching, and she tried to stop herself from interrupting him. 'You don't care about human rights and the Geneva Convention.'

'What's worse, Jessica?' he asked, and she felt surprise again on hearing her name spoken by him. She felt his voice, gentle not patronising, as if trying to explain the Machiavellian machinations, the realities of the world, to a wide eyed child. 'Being kidnapped in front of your family, children screaming for fear...' His pronunciation was slow and accented with stress like the tight lid of a hissing pot.

Jessica felt his eyes burning into her, almost causing her eyes to water.

'Terror – those babies know the real meaning of terror – Jessica. You use it hundred times on TV without thinking don't you? Like Mariam's children felt terror when your marines burst in?'

'They're not my marines.' Jessica wiped her brow. She could not help it, or otherwise the sweat would have stung her eyes. She panted; her throat felt full of bits of sandstone. She stopped to take a bottle of water out of her bag.

Jessica felt churlish. Hamid's death – the quest she seemed to be giving up her life for, now – seemed to be worth less than a generation that had grown up knowing nothing other than the fear-whistle of bullets that expired the breath. She knew people were just random interceptions in the terrible trajectory of bombs and missiles, innumerable lives changed for those who found themselves in their arc. People in Iraq were now living a life of subsistence without many friends and family, and wherever they went they were followed by the boom of bombs. This nation had lived through aerial bombardment and invasions, then the insurgents and suicide bombings. Two sides of the un-swallowable depleted uranium like truth. She had learned a lot about depleted uranium since she had arrived. She had been told it found its way through the soil into the vegetables and even, she had been told, into the prickly radioactive bread they chewed on. Fathers disappearing, children maimed, women abused. The infinite stories that had become the web of history for a nation, which, like a generous spider, had woven the silken fabric of civilisation to cover the naked shame of the world in a time before knowledge. She imagined this was how the militants felt, here and in Afghanistan.

Abu Umar mentioning Mariam had dredged up her feelings, which her professionalism could not submerge. *Did Musa feel any terror when the bullets ripped through his baby flesh?* she thought. *Maybe that's what he means when he talks about Allah's mercy; at least the marines saved him the agony of leukaemia. What is the curse on this land? The food, the water, the very air poison, now.*

'Surely suicide bombing hurts only the innocent?' She forced the question out. Her hand wandered to her mouth, and she chewed the knuckle of her thumb.

'When someone has nothing left to fight them with, they use their bodies as weapons.'

'That's *haram* isn't it? Suicide is...' She trailed off as she felt certain she saw the faintest glimmer of a smile, before his feline yellow eyes seemed to flash momentarily an angrier amber orange. The lion within raged: *when will he release the animalistic part of him?* 'You're killing Muslims – innocents.'

'Let God decide...' He pointed his right index finger upwards.

'Aren't these the very people you claim to be fighting for? Your own people?'

'Some sacrifices are necessary to free the land. She is the mother that must be wet with blood to make the land fertile and grow good crops for future generations. She feeds on flesh sacrifice of the invaders. Only then will Allah reward us and free from American slavery.' He looked at her, and she felt determined not to show any more emotion than she already had. He shrugged slightly and continued, 'If they are innocent, they will go to Paradise.' His voice rose at the end, became almost nasal, as if stating a simple fact. '*Jannah* awaits them, see? That is what you people don't understand.'

'Paradise? Is that what you have turned Iraq into for the living?' She felt her disgust rising rapidly, like a torpedo from the depths coming to her face, which tightened itself into a grimace. She felt no fear; more rage like a tornado, which twisted her face at the memories of Mariam, that he could be so comfortable with his justification. Her questions felt like a storm throwing out debris. Her short staccato filled the room. 'Is that why you used the Down's Syndrome women, the disabled, like poor beasts of burden, to carry your bombs?

'Is that what you think of us?'

Jessica saw his eyes flicker almost orange again.

'Those things – they are not done by humans, but by creatures of

Shaitan.' He spat an invective of Arabic; cursing whom, she could not be sure. 'Much worse than animals, like Abu Ghraib, like bodies. They appear in morgues, they have vital organs missing – they are organ-farming from living people. They force, take away pieces of their bodies to be sold on the replacement organ black market every day all over Iraq.' His voice was deeper now disguising a great depth of disgust and anger, she imagined.

'Not to mention the dead bodies lying in the streets. People do not collect them. No one can bury them. The stench of fear stronger than the rotting corpses, fear of Sunni and Shia. Women raped in their own homes, small girls now mutilated, living corpses.'

'So you're saying the Americans do all this?'

'You think Abu Ghraib is the worst thing in Iraq?' he asked. Jessica felt incredulous. She had believed Abu Ghraib Prison to be the worst thing, but these new revelations, even if empowered with the voice of a fanatic, rocketed into her. She did not allow herself physically to imagine these things happening or empathise with the people who had suffered the unspeakable; she did not want to break down in the interview because of her memories of Mariam, so she limited her thoughts to the clinical questioning. He added: 'If only Abu Ghraib is the worst, the baddest, then I will support the Americans today. If only they stole our oil, if that was that the baddest, then no problem. I and we would support the Americans, let them have it, if it brought peace.'

'What is it, then?'

'Let me first expose their lies. If they just want to stop Iraq having weapons of mass destruction, then I would even help the Americans. We have no water any more, let alone aeroplanes. Where are the WMDS? No weapons for us – so Israel can feel safe, okay.'

'What are you fighting for?' Jessica felt confusion and naivety rise from within her and explode like depth charges; she gripped her abdomen.

'They have destroyed a nation, massacred a people, killed the concept of Iraq. Crippled our future generations to come, humiliated us beyond endurance. Shamed us, deprived us of our honour, taken away our humanity. They made us worse than dogs – turned us into devils and demons! These devils and demons appeared out of the vacuum left by their atrocities. The same demons now stalk them in their nightmares. Iraq and Afghanistan have become your Frankenstein's monster.' He clenched his fists on his thighs and gritted his teeth. *I'm sure he doesn't want to get emotional either*, she thought, *but his passion has lent him an eloquence and given his words wings.*

'You!' He pointed at her with his right index finger, as if bearing witness. 'Make this monster by bombing indiscriminately.' The finger froze unwavering. 'You! Use us as Mengele used the Jews for experiments with your Daisy Cutters, and depleted uranium and White Phosphorous. Falluja is dripping in White Phosphorous after the American assault. It covers everything and melts human beings. Now human fat drips off every wall in the city.' Abu Umar raised his arms and looked around him, as if he could see the evidence on the walls of the room they sat in. 'Chemical weapons banned by the Chemical Weapons Convention, which the USA refuses to sign, WP burns human flesh to ash and skin hangs off hands like gloves. They calling them *shake and bake missions*. One of your friends – Seymour Hersh, a journalist – said *they have turned Iraq into a free fire zone – hit everything, kill everything!*'

'No doubt the Iraqi people have suffered, but do you think doubling the pain by –'

'It is nothing compared to what we will visit upon you in return, *inshallah*. You will not sleep safe; no one can walk easy on your golden paved streets. I will not allow you to buy your wholly unnecessary goods in Oxford Street or Rodeo Drive or Les Galeries Lafayette – until we have freedom from you invaders.' His tapped a message with his forefinger into the air in front of his face repeatedly, as if he was tapping a *Quit Iraq* message in Morse.

'You're saying... really accusing the Americans of organ-farming?' Jessica looked up wide-eyed.

'I have seen it with my own eyes. Of all the atrocities of Fallujah, women and children who died not from the bombing and White Phosphorous, those dead from missing organs – this is worst. Although they paint the whole city with White Phosphorous.' His hands made a globular shape as if encompassing his known world. He glared at her. 'These, they are not 'collateral damage'. Thousands died because they were cut open and their kidneys, livers, lungs hearts surgically removed. Our doctors see atrocities but no one reports them. I told you, no-one ever wants to tell our story. Even the Western media that did report Fallujah called it the *hidden massacre*.'

'There must be rogue elements –'

'No! Not rogue elements. Systematic organ-farming. They check them, the unaffected young ones, no chemicals, no radiation. They keep those.' His voice became loud, uncharacteristic, no attempt to hide the white fury that burnt his face into an incandescent red. His emotions mixed, the patchy colour of anger ran into his auburn beard, his face a tropical palette. He scratched his arms through his *Jilbab*. 'That's the problem with you people; even when you are finally told the truth you claim to be so desperate to know, you do not believe it.' He paused and uncurled his fist off his thigh, visibly slowed his breathing down.

Jessica copied his example and wished she could escape or close her eyes, if only for a moment. She tried to breathe regularly, avoiding the shallow draughts that made her dizzy.

'Who blow up the mosque of Samarra?'

'I heard on the news it was your insurgents. Why?' she asked.

'I know it was a controlled explosion that collapsed that huge dome. With the level of protection it had by American soldiers, it is impossible to be one of the brothers. It should be a whole demolition team to set up explosives.'

'That even sounds ridiculous. Sorry, but why would the Americans even want to blow up mosques? Doesn't make any sense.'

'That's right – even to us, no sense. Yet they will do anything to get what they want,' said Abu Umar. He pulled his *Jilbab* to stop it sticking to his sweat stained body. 'That is for you to work out, Miss Jessica, if you can. If you dare.' He looked at her, his eyes now flickering anger and staring in challenge, no longer a mystery. 'You say you're a journalist. Good. Then something you can do for me.' He pointed to her, then himself. 'Before I grant you more interviews, or allow you to follow Mariam's story.'

Jessica almost retched as if she was about to spray vomit all over Abu Umar, and she kept one hand on her stomach. 'I don't – what I – if I can.'

'I will provide help. I can have proofs, and I must have Western verification, to get evidence. Then, I will give you the rest of Mariam's story.'

Despite all the awful things he had told her, which had awakened a deeper morbid fear from the primeval swamp of terror, she did not allow herself to imagine the plight of his so-called victims and so refused to empathise with them. They would have to make do with her sympathy, out of necessity of self-preservation.

Whether all the stories are perfectly true or not is irrelevant, she realised. *He believes them, these people and the masses of Iraq believe them, and Muslims all over the world believe them. He says he's witnessed them, so they are more real than the chair he's sitting on.* Despite her resolve, the thought of Mariam and her children made her cuff the corner of her eye with the back of her hand. Quickly, she blinked hard, and then looked down at her notepad. She had not written anything throughout the interview.

It was much more than an interview. She felt that he had X-rayed her soul, and as a result, her presumptions stood bare. He had somehow knifed though her soft belly and laid open her spine, naked to light and air. These feeling had triggered a nervous reflex in her primitive brain: *he's telling the truth. His truth; it is his reality*, she thought. *He really has seen all these terrible things, but that's why he does what he does. All of that still does not justify the suicide bombers…*

Jessica wanted to ask about the bombing in Birmingham, about Hamid's train. She almost made the words come out of her mouth, but she wanted to maintain some level of professionalism in the interview.

She thought Abu Umar seemed to sense her indecision. 'There was a whole world out there, a civilised society, before the Americans invaded.' He said the word, and recoiled as if he could taste the apple pie contained therein. 'There was no Sunni–Shia conflict, no civil war; we would have laughed if you said Iraq is going to be in civil war. No one even knows or care who was Sunni or Shia.'

He threw his hands up, and then seemed to refocus. 'I will tell you… allow me to tell you something, Miss Jessica. When you think about Iraq, imagine your worst life possible, the worst ever. Then multiply it by the bottom number of Hell. Then you might begin to understand Baghdad and Iraq.'

Jessica did not reply, unsure what to say. The interview had not gone at all as expected. She had expected to hit him with a barrage of unanswerable questions that would make him defensive and shifty and uncomfortable, that would make great TV. She had wanted to make him squirm. Instead, now she felt embarrassed to be British. Sweat stuck her hair to her head in limp strands… not the sweat of fear any longer, but replaced by the sweat of shame. Her neck felt stiff, but she hardly dared flex it. She shifted in her chair and moved her back, which felt as if someone was shoving red-hot pokers into her spine.

'Did you want to ask anything else?' He brought out a white handkerchief from an invisible pocket in his cloak and wiped his brow. 'Hot today, even for Baghdad.'

She looked down at her notepad, no longer daring to meet his yellow-flecked marbles in case he saw acquiescence in her eyes or contrition in her face, or evidence from her posture that he had succeeded in moving her. She no longer felt the thrill of bravado journalism; just the despair of Iraq.

'I can see there is still something bothering you?' he said, leaning forward slightly, almost intimately, despite the space between them.

The memories of Hamid hit her like a rancid stink, like sweat from centuries of unwashed bodies. A smell that lingered and would not leave her body, it had become part of every cell. So she had no choice but to ask. 'There was a bombing in Birmingham – a train…'

'Ah yes. Did it affect you?' He leaned forward again, as if eager to gain insight from every pore on her face, which would reveal her true self through her suffering to him.

'You might say it did,' she said.

Suddenly his face turned, as a crumb of recognition came over it. 'Ah, you are the one. Your man – they say he was the bomber, no?' He pointed at her.

'No!' Anger overcame to her easily now, readily taken from the ether, and it pulled at her lungs harder with every breath. She stared and did not blink. She could have said: *Hamid wasn't a suicide bomber. He was a good man. We were about to be married.* Instead she said nothing.

'Ah, I am sorry – sorry for you…'

'Well, you killed him.' She had not expected to hear an apology or sympathy from Abu Umar. She had imagined before meeting him he would be of the barbarous untamed hordes, with human child-flesh fresh in his jaws, still dripping blood onto his face and hands as he tore into another limb. The humanity – could it be empathy? – made him seem vulnerable, almost like any other man, for the briefest moment.

'How do you know it wasn't him?' he asked.

Jessica hesitated for what seemed like the silence in the aftermath of an explosion, the longest fraction of time. Finally, she said simply: 'I don't know. Not for sure…'

Abu Umar stayed quiet for a moment, as if reflecting or giving her respect – she could not be sure. 'Maybe we can help you? The truth is very rare. Maybe the rarest commodity in the world at the moment. Do not believe it is oil.' He looked into her eyes again, 'That is what you want, most want, why you are here?'

She did not answer.

'That is why you risked your life and the lives of your friends.' He glanced at Peter, who had not peeped out of the camera lens the whole time, and James seemed a sculpture holding the boom mike.

She said nothing; there was no need to. The quest consumed her life. *That's why she had risked everything to interview him*, she thought, that's why she sat there feeling sick, in pain physically, sweating, with her heart banging against her chest and her breathing irregular, as if there simply was not enough sustenance for her lungs in the air of Baghdad. Iraq did not feel like a life-supporting place.

'You investigate the mosque at Samarra. Tell the story of organ-farming. Come with us on a journey. Then I will allow you Mariam's story, and then I will tell you everything you need to know about Hamid Khan…' His voice was quiet as he mentioned her dead fiancés name.

She nodded her agreement.

'As long as you understand you are never going back. You cannot. Once you take the magic pill and swallow, your eyes will open to a scary new world. Your eyes will not feel your own, your ears you will feel sure are deceiving you, and your chest will burst with burning pain of the truth, as if huge searing boulders had been placed on it.' He paused and she felt his power through his glowing, eyes. 'But you will be free – free to choose the truth.' He looked at her again, and for the first time she saw he allowed the faintest smile. Not of victory; it seemed more a smile of welcome.

Maybe he needs someone to record his activities and Jihad, for posterity, for his legacy in history? she thought. Her quest overwhelmed her, greater than her journalistic curiosity. *What is the truth about these people?* Her questioning nature had been her driving force until Hamid's death. Now, that combined with her personal quest ensured that she would go with him wherever he asked, and do whatever he demanded. So she stiffly nodded her head, once.

'Now – would you like to meet Aisha and Mariam's children again?' he asked.

She looked up, surprised. 'Well, come on!' he said, getting up, inviting her with an outstretched arm. 'It's nearly lunchtime, her kids love the melon sherbet drinks,' and then paused, smiling. 'Uncle Aladdin, he make sherbet drinks all the time for them.' He gestured to the giant genie, who had reappeared without Jessica noticing.

She saw the face of non-comprehension on the genie's face as he crossed his arms.

'He spoil them, Uncle Aladdin.'

Jessica imagined him with his bristling biceps and moustache as well as a turban with baggy trousers and upturned shoes, a real genie from the Arabian Nights. Despite her increasing knowledge of Iraq and her people, the reluctance of childhood tales to loosen their hold on her imagination gripped her mind tight, even in moments of intensity.

Abu Umar motioned again until they all followed. He led them out into the courtyard at the centre of the house, shaded by a tall cypress and draped with jasmine and orange trees. There on the rough-hewn table were, with a spread of food like a Mesopotamian Christmas feast, Aisha and Mariam's children. They smiled at Jessica as she entered the inner sanctum of the mansion. Jessica fingered the rag doll in her bag and wondered which girl it belonged to. She took it out and smiled at the children. 'Have you ever tried tahini from Lubnan?' Abu Umar smiled at her.

Is he being friendly or mocking or insulting? she thought. She did not know how to respond, and looked back to the table and children. 'Now, let us have lunch. You must be hungry, working so hard.' He smiled again; this time she knew he was smiling at the surprise she showed on her face. 'I have some of my mother's homemade tahini and hummous. The best in all of Chouf District,' Abu Umar almost chuckled.

CHAPTER 19

London

'Police! This is the police!'

The door splintered and smashed open at five thirty in the morning. The battering ram ate through the wood like a giant invasive termite.

They stormed through the house shouting instructions as they went: *Nobody move! This is a police raid!*

It all happened so fast that Sofia did not have time to react to the first bang. Forty police officers, some armed, covered the front and back of the house. Police helicopters patrolled with thermal-infra red vision and kept up an insectivorous beat with their wings.

Sofia jumped out of bed, responding to the ever-alert instinct, honed to any sound of danger by the rigors of motherhood. She did not realise they had invaded her home and now swarmed all over the house. As soon as she stepped outside her bedroom door, they bundled her downstairs.

'What's going on? Who are you?' she shouted her voice shaking. Two policemen carried her down the stairs like a baggy weight; she could not resist.

'Stay silent!' ordered a voice, when Sofia managed a small mewl through her panic.

'Shut it!' said a second man.

The Anti Terror squad contained the house, ensured no one was armed and dangerous, no hidden bombs, no evidence tampered with. The detective in charge sauntered into the living room. Sofia sat pale with fright, dishevelled. She brushed her hair back with her hand, not used to being in front of strangers bare–headed, dressed in her sleeping yellow *salwar kameez*. She gaped and squinted, disorientated, as the bright lights shone in her face, behind which hid a semblance of the dark, cold metal of the muzzled guns.

'Sorry to wake you like this – I know it seems dramatic – but we have to ensure no one is armed and there are no explosives. We have a search warrant, and I would like to ask you some questions, now that we're here.' A small smile played momentarily at the corners of the man's mouth.

Sofia's lips moved, but no noise came out. 'Where's my family – my son – Zoya, my daughter?'

'I'm Dave Smith, Detective Constable. I should have introduced myself.' He looked down at a file, seemingly into the routine, uninterested in the answers she might give to his everyday questions. 'Where's Jimmy?' he asked, and stared at her.

So finally it had come, thought Sofia. The day she had dreaded; the thought she had kept hidden in the womblike darkness of her innermost heart. Things she may have to face now, questions she had not vocalised, for fear that in verbalising them they might materialise into hard reality. These fears she had not mentioned to anyone, even Zoya.

Since Jimmy's disappearance, her mind had jumped from one thought to another like an ecstasy-crazed jack rabbit. None of Jimmy's friends knew what had happened to him. She had sent Tony to speak to his gang members, but they seemed to know nothing. Jimmy's mobile phones had gone dead.

When Jimmy did not turn up on the third day, Sofia knew something was seriously wrong. She had to break the lock of the small greenhouse, and she fed the butterflies in the main greenhouse. Jimmy had sometimes not come home for the night, but he had never gone three days, not without telling her. Sofia had wrung her hands and not eaten for two days. Then she received a phone call, which made her fear for more than Jimmy's physical safety. A man told her he was Jimmy's childhood friend and that she should not worry – Jimmy was safe, and with good people. She recognised Hamza. She begged him to tell her more, but Hamza simply said that Jimmy was going to fulfil his father's wishes and become a great Muslim. Sofia asked why he needed to disappear to do that, but Hamza had not replied.

Sofia had seen how Jimmy's hatred of the mosque had changed after he had been attacked after the late-night meeting. He wore the bruises like medals. Since Ahmad had died in prayer in the mosque, Sofia had noticed Jimmy had not missed any of the five daily prayers. He stopped going out at nights, and she assumed he was not meeting his gang members. Sofia had smiled and embraced him in the few days before Ahmad's death, loving the kind of strange peace that had come over him, but he had not smiled. He often stared into the distance. He did not hug her back as strongly as he used to do, as if his arms had become limp. For Sofia, the mosque had always been a source of community and strength. After Ahmad's funeral, when the extended family grieved together, Jimmy did not cry with them. When visitors arrived with waves of sympathy carried before them like offerings, Jimmy would leave them with Sofia and Tony, and go into the greenhouse. Afterwards, he would put an arm around Sofia and hug her and tell her not to worry, because Ahmad was now free.

Thoughts flashed through Sofia's mind as she looked up at the police officer, as he towered over her. She felt like a small wet bird, cold and shivering, no longer able to fly, about to be devoured by the feline hungry mouth of fear. Her mind kept returning to the same dominant thought about Jimmy that drowned out the others.

To try and keep from losing herself to the idea that Jimmy had become a terrorist, she had tried multiple escape routes over the past two and a half months. She seemed to have more chores than ever before; her work found her even in the middle of the night, when sleep would not. Her hands automatically sought refuge in physical labour. The calluses and pumice skin of her hands felt harsh when she rubbed them against her face, and she pulled her lips raw. Her palms had become harder in these weeks than in all her years of motherhood labours. She made work smother her suspicions, to carry out an abortion of her thoughts before they could implant seeds and fertilise shoots in her mind that might grow and feed off her like that misguided child she now feared she had lost.

Since Jimmy's disappearance Sofia folded sheets, unfolded them and folded back again. Took dishes out that had been washed and dried and washed them again, until her fingertips splintered. She would start cooking a chicken *bhuna* having just finished a *saag gosht*. She fell into bed when her eyes could no longer carry the burden of her days, and she did not welcome the nights. A lonely bed without her husband did not bring any relief. Ahmad in his grave, and her cold in their bed. *Was Jimmy a terrorist?* That was her last thought every night, as she drugged her mind finally into a soporific stupor.

Soon, the same thought woke her and kept smashing at her temples.

A pain that none of the tablets, none of the gaudy medication, could diminish. The pain encrusted her being until she tried to crack through its icy inhuman grip by banging her skull with her fists. She did not cry. Sofia had not cried when Ahmad had died.

In her darkest hours, before the light of false dawn, she would sit on her green geometric patterned prayer mat and give herself up to the *Fajr Namaz*. A predawn prayer ritual for Jimmy, which ran through her mind. Even now, she mouthed the same prayer to squeeze the driest drops of comfort from the arid stone of her life. Every day she greeted the dawn with the same verse:

> *Surah 94 Inshirah – The Expansion*
> *Have we not opened up thy heart,*
> *And lifted from thee the burden*
> *That had weighed so heavily on thy back?*

How easily *Imam* Younis had said after Jimmy's disappearance, 'Oh and to think this is how he repays you, Sofia *bhabi*, after nine months of carriage and nearly two days labour.' Sofia knew what he meant to say was: *An aborted son is better. Or found you less shame than you are drowning in now.*

If only nine months of confinement and one day and two nights of labour were the sum of Jimmy, then she would be able to forget something that had happened so long ago, even if the prolonged labour pains had been beyond pethidine comfort.

> *And, behold, with every hardship comes ease:*
> *Verily, with every hardship comes ease!*

Did the *Imam* mean it would have been better if she had never had Jimmy? If he had ended up as an aborted red mess on the floor? Like her eldest, twenty-five years ago in the stone floor bathroom of Ramnagar? Sofia remembered how she had screamed at the spurting blood; she had barely noticed the loss of the jelly-like substance. Her abiding memory was one of Ahmad screaming at her state and screaming more, unmanned. The bleary-eyed doctor woke in the middle of the night in the local clinic, said that Sofia could not be saved; he had no blood products, because there was no fridge in the clinic and the nearest blood was in

Islamabad. He had yawned and crawled back to bed.

Sofia had nearly bled to death. Her bridal henna that girls in her village applied for a year after marriage seemed brighter than usual, orange against her pale-yellow hand. Ahmad had squeezed and squeezed her hand, as she lay abandoned by the world on the rough bench. She remembered how he tightened his grip and hurt her hands as if he could squeeze the blood back into it, praying with closed eyes. Tears without end or shame wet his beard, as he had waited for his four-month-bride to die. Ahmad had had his miracle, she always said afterwards, his proof of God, and she had teased him for years. He had never missed a prayer since that day.

And raised thee high in dignity?
Hence, when thou art freed, remain steadfast,
And unto thy Sustainer turn with love.

After two decades of nurture, forgiving love without expectation without significant hope of return, she could have said: '*Imam Sahib* Jimmy is more than my life's labour, more than my memories of Ahmad.' Instead she had said nothing, but looked at her husband's old friend with stony, unblinking eyes and a masked face for a moment, before looking away.

Jimmy is a terrorist! Jimmy is a terrorist! Jimmy is a terrorist!

The thought screamed and swamped her mind; it was a silent scream in her selfless, other universe, into which she would not allow Jimmy and Zoya. Sofia had not cried; she did not make a sound, even when Dan had brought Zoya home, battered and bruised and torn, ripped to shreds. Zoya had looked like a tiny splintered shard – a remnant of the daughter that had left to teach primary school that same morning. Jimmy had beaten Dan, assuming he had assaulted Zoya, not understanding in his anger that Dan had saved her. Sofia had not cried. Why and how she had managed not to break down, she could not think. There was no reason. Just as there was no reason to so many things.

Jimmy had vanished without any noise or fanfare, or even a note. After his disappearance she searched repetitively for something he had said, or something he had touched in a different way, so she could touch the same thing and maybe find a reason there for his disappearance. Maybe that would help her make a connection with him, to help her understand what had happened. Except there was nothing. Sofia had his last memory fixed firmly in her head. Of him turning the handle of the

Butterfly House. She had replayed it in her head incessantly.

Sofia blamed herself for not picking up the signs, not being an astute enough mother to pick up the clues of Jimmy's radicalisation. Except for the 'Will you look after my butterflies, if I can't?' there was nothing. Praying and wanting to become a good Muslim should have made him do the opposite of wanting to kill others. So she held onto the memory of him at the greenhouse with the fingertips of her mind as if she was hanging on to a cliff edge, but her nails were bloody and coming away from the nailbeds. She was not about to fall from fear or lack of will, but if she fell it would be because the strength in her body had failed; she had reached the end. Her anatomy was no longer able to take the strain or to support her body weight. Sofia now felt as if she was being forced and ripped asunder.

The detective's voice tore her back to reality. 'We have to search the house.'

'Yes, yes, of course...'

The officer in charge motioned with his fingers to begin the search downstairs. Within a short time, police teams meticulously started to rip and tear apart the house: carpets, false walls, floorboards. Sofia watched as they destroyed the material fabric of her world. The detective nodded to the team, who were heading out to the back garden. 'Yeah and the greenhouse,' he said.

'Not the small one!' Sofia said.

'We have a search warrant.'

'Jimmy never let anyone in there.'

He turned away to his officers, and nodded again. 'We have to, Mrs Regus – sorry.'

'Look, there's nothing there, I promise you. You can check his bedroom, the living room, anywhere. Even the large greenhouse, the Butterfly House –'

'We have to do a complete check, Mrs Regus. This is extremely important I'm sure you understand.' Then after a pause, he half smiled and said, 'I know this is very distressing for you. We'll be as quick as we can.' Another pause. 'Look, you can accompany the search team to make sure they don't damage anything, and that we log anything we take as evidence.'

Sofia looked at his face that seemed to be reassuring her and keeping her calm; she wondered if she could negotiate with this polite police officer. 'It's private. Jimmy's private place…'

'We have to. But you can go with them.'

Sofia got up put on her blue *chappal* slippers, grabbed a *dupatta*. The detective gentled her towards the search team. 'Take her with you, guys, let's keep everything nice and calm.'

Sofia walked in between the three men and a woman who accompanied her, and followed the search team into the back garden.

They methodically searched the Butterfly House. Sofia added admonishing comments and rushed around after them, fixing and repairing any apparent damage. 'Be careful please. The butterflies are asleep.'

'Stop fussing,' said a short squat officer with rheumy eyes and thick stubble, glowering at her. He headed for the smaller greenhouse.

'No. Please not there.'

'Get out of the way,' he said.

'That's Jimmy's special place – he doesn't let anyone in there. Even me, before he left.'

'Maybe he should have thought about that before he disappeared into his *Jihad* and Muslimness.' He pronounced *Jihad* as *Jee-hard*. She could almost imagine a red neck American saying it. 'I said, get out of the way,' repeated the squat officer.

'No. Please, I beg you! Take anything from the house. Anything you want!'

Sofia feared the desecration of Jimmy's inner sanctum, the violation of his essential memories. She could see him even now, coming out of the smaller greenhouse, closing the door gently behind him; keeping his hand habitually on the handle, as if loath to finally let go. Like a father making sure his sleeping child is not awoken as he leaves his room.

Sofia moved in front of the small door and physically blocked the policeman from entering.

'Okay, that's enough. I'm arresting you for obstruction, perverting the cause of justice.' He moved forwards, but Sofia blocked his path her back against the door with arms spread protectively.

'No!' said Sofia.

'Mandy, arrest this stupid woman. She's obstructing a police investigation, and perhaps she's aiding and abetting the cause of terrorism, eh?' he said, as he turned back to Sofia. 'She's been a pain all morning. Don't know why the boss is pandering to these – these…' He looked away to Mandy and signalled her to come forwards, while at the same time he casually grabbed Sofia by her arm to swing her over to the policewoman, who stood just behind him.

'No. I can't let you,' shouted Sofia and freed her arm with a strength that surprised her. She wriggled, as he tried to grab her again.

He pulled her roughly out of the way; she freed her right arm again. Her slipper came off her right foot and her *dupatta* was dragged off her head onto one shoulder.

Sofia slapped the squat officer. She lashed her palm hard against his face; her open hand made a crack like a rotten tree falling. The noise scared the sleeping butterflies, and scattered them into the air. The policeman's rubicund face turned ruddier on the left side. His sweat-stained shirt stuck to him like embarrassment, highlighting his fatty chest in the heat and humidity of the tropical house. His left eye watered, as if through the haze of humiliation at being hit by a small, middle-aged, Asian woman.

The policeman slapped her back. A slap into which he put his significant proportions, that sent her spinning to the floor. Sofia's *dupatta* fell to the ground; her other blue sequined *chappal* flew off her foot.

The other police officers stared in silence at the dishevelled woman on the floor. Dirt marked Sofia's forehead like some defiled bridal *bindiya*. The bright fluorescent lights glinted off the sequins as one of the slippers landed in a small pool, matching the iridescence of some of the Royal Blues' wings as they flew, having been disturbed by the raucous fight.

Finally, the policewoman came to life. 'Paul, there was no need for that.'

'I told you to arrest the fucking old Paki bitch – not to tell me what to do.'

'Yes, sergeant!' said the young woman, and picked Sofia up from the floor. She helped lift Sofia's stunned face out of the gravel. 'Come on, Mrs Regus, you're shivering. I'll get you a blanket and a cup of tea,' she said, and helped Sofia back into her slippers and put her *dupatta* back on her head, carefully making sure it covered her dignity in the same way as before.

In the moment of the slap, Sofia felt the pain of not belonging. She suddenly felt torn and ripped, like Zoya returning from her assault. She now felt emaciated and weak, like Ahmad just before his death in the mosque. She felt alone and afraid, like Jimmy must have done, just before his disappearance. She felt her fingernails tear and rip from their nail beds. She felt herself falling, free falling now, and tumbling over the edge. Her anxiety out of her body, ghostly.

So Sofia shrivelled up into a small ball and cried. Cried for the first time since Zoya's assault, Ahmad's death and Jimmy's disappearance.

Sofia did not cry because of the slap. The policewoman's kindness, the sensation of her lifting Sofia and gentling her in her arms, placing her slippers back on her feet and the care she took with her head-covering. That had made her finally crumble. Perhaps it was feminine compassion? Sofia wondered if the policewoman was a mother. Empathy washed over her like human rain in the isolated desert of alienation. *Someone out there in the world knew,* she thought, *or wanted to know, how she felt.*

Sofia cried and cried and cried. She wept for the seven days and seven nights she was held without charge in the police station, under anti-terrorism laws. She drowned her *kameez*, and then used countless boxes of tissues, and then she soaked the towel. She wept through all five interviews, forty-five minutes at a time, while the police were deciding whether to charge her as an accomplice to terrorism. Sofia's voice got quieter and huskier until it became barely discernable on the tape recordings; her solicitor had to repeat everything she said for the record.

The police had searched the house and found nothing. In the small Butterfly House, they found a stash of Jimmy's drugs. They took away the flowerpot that he had brought back from his grandfather's grave, in Pakistan. Although Sofia had not seen it for years, she recognised it. She knew the clay pot used to have fragrant white *Nargis*, narcissi, growing in them, placed at the head of the tombstone. In the bottom of the deep flowerpot, hidden under bits of broken clay, they found Jimmy's store of heroin. Sofia realised that Jimmy had never grown anything in it.

Sofia came out of the police station, shivering and feeling skeletal and subtracted, a different version of herself, a blurred reflection of Sofia. She had been torn apart by a week, when she had held herself together for a generation.

Sofia was not charged with anything. There was no recompense. No apology for her arrest. A cold, biting wind, desiccating and dry, which felt to her so foreign and un-British, blew over the Law Courts, down through Sofia as she left Paddington Green police station. It hit her face with the full bitterness of an approaching Christmas, as she stepped out, blinking, into a myopic world which was already dark. She walked out shivering, into the cold dusk of a British winter.

London – Westminster Bridge

As Jessica walked over Westminster Bridge, her eyes flitted over the people who passed her by. She looked at every face, trying to decipher the expressions; she stared intently at the brown faces, and then the black and white ones. It seemed as if every face would betray her, regardless of its colour. She gave up trying to find meaning. How could she find a potential terrorist in London? That was like trying to separate a grain of sand from all the others on a beach. She pulled her scarf lower, put her head down, and reached Café Nero next to Westminster tube station, but before she could enter, she half-turned to see a man had approached up close to her, without her realising.

'You must be Jessica.'

She nodded as if his expected arrival had been unexpected. Abu Umar had told her, during the phone conversation that she had with him yesterday, that someone would approach her, at some point close to Westminster Bridge. She stared at the tall man who stood next to her, noticing his oval face and pointed jaw. He had dark hair that flopped over both sides of his head. Jessica looked up at him and saw that his iris and pupil merged into each other. Both looked black despite the sun; he had liquid eyes, as if they were molten night.

'I'm Hamza.' He held the door open for her. '*Shaikh* Abu Umar told me you impressed him in Baghdad.'

'Really?'

Hamza walked over to order. 'I can see how you would have made a mark.'

'I was petrified.'

'Nah, don't believe a bit of it. You went to his place. That would make many strong men weep.'

'Abu Umar said you'd find me – how were you so sure, in the middle of London?'

'Ve hav vays,' he said, and laughed. 'Ve vill alvays find you!' His thin black moustache wiggled as he spoke. Jessica smiled. 'What would you like?' he asked.

'Just water, thanks.'

Hamza's easy manner and lightness of expression seemed incongruous with his mission. He waved her over to a couple of empty seats, and he had put her at ease before she had sat down.

Jessica's throat felt tight and constricted as she remembered how she had agonised about contacting *Jaish an Noor wass Salaam* on her return to London from Baghdad. She had tossed on her bed, got up and wandered the house in her pyjamas despite the cold, chewing her knuckles. She had turned inquisitor, asking questions, talking aloud, but the night had stayed dark in its silence. She had gone into the bathroom and looked into the mirror. Her blue eyes shone and stared back. No matter how brightly the mirror reflected, behind every mirror there was black.

The days had appeared friendlier on dawning, but by midday they had also proved to be complicit in her misery, making her sit for hours fidgeting on her sofa, unable to keep still. The numerous cups of coffee had made her jump and shred her fingers, as she wrung her hands. Her breathing had slowed and her hands had found a temporary rest with Holly and her parents, but as soon as her thoughts turned to Hamid and *Jaish* and Abu Umar, her muscles became steel cables wound tightly enough to snap. She had made her excuses and left, to return home. She found her house receiving her with the open-armed, empty greetings of a stranger.

What happened with Hamid? Time had not diminished the intensity of the question, which rose from within like her bile and tasted just as bitter, as it burnt her throat. *I have to know the truth,* she thought. *How was Hamid involved; did* Jaish *control him?* Abu Umar had intimated that he knew what had happened to Hamid, but he had not told her anything more. *I have to have to infiltrate* Jaish, *she told herself again. Get deep undercover, so deep that they trust me with all their secrets – then I will know the truth about Hamid.*

Her journalistic instincts and stubborn nature made her go back to the question, even when other thoughts of Sebastian and her developing feeling for him came to her. She told herself she needed closure on Hamid, first. Jessica felt pulled towards a shared destiny with *Jaish*, as if Abu Umar's yellow eyes were beacons that drew her to an irresistible shore; or were they enticing her to smash the ship of her life on the rocks of terrorism? She could not be sure. *I don't know*, she thought, *but even if his eyes were the Volcanoes of Vulcan, I would still do it, to gain justice in the court of Hamid.*

Hamza came and sat with her. Jessica noticed his dapper clothes, his aquiline nose, tanned brown skin. His appearance seemed almost effeminate. He had a silk handkerchief jutting out of his top jacket pocket, which matched his pink striped shirt. In his grey woollen trousers and dark blazer, he looked like a city banker on a lunch break. She had worn casual and comfortable clothes, not sure how she should meet a Muslim man, especially one sent by Abu Umar.

'Got you a latte too, just in case. And water,' said Hamza, as he sat down.

Jessica looked at him, with her head to one side. 'Why do so many men think that women only drink lattes or cappuccinos?'

'Why do so many women think that any act of kindness is misogyny?' he said with a smile, and she smiled back, liking him even more. 'How's your documentary?'

'Oh, you know about that?'

'The *Shaikh* told me you interviewed him in Baghdad? That must have been an unusual experience.'

'I never felt so glad to see a hotel in my life. The car journey back was pretty smelly. Peter, the cameraman, was sick with relief, and James who does the sound, couldn't get out of bed for the next two days.' She laughed and felt amazed that she could feel at ease with someone who worked for Abu Umar. Maybe this was part of their training... how to put new recruits at ease? She told herself to be careful. Meeting Hamza made her feel as if she had bumped into an old acquaintance.

She looked at him. He had human eyes, and they did not look like they had mass murder inscribed in them in some unintelligible, flowing, script. His hands attracted her attention; his fingers drummed the table casually, long and delicate. They could not be the fingers of a terrorist. His nails looked like flakes of almond, with no splinters or frayed edges. The cuticles were smooth and perfect, shining like the skin on his face – she felt certain he used moisturising lotions on his face and hands. She kept her hands under the table. She had always taken care not to bite her nails, but since Hamid's death she had given in to chewing the knuckles on her fingers, and had caused a red, raised disc to harden over her left thumb knuckle.

'It was Abu Umar who agreed to meet me.'

'He doesn't stroll around the streets of London, you know.'

'He did mention he was sending 'my very special boy, Hamza."

'Although it's safer for him here than in Baghdad,' said Hamza, as he played with his espresso cup.

'The scarf seems to belong on you,' he said, smiling.

Jessica fiddled with the back of her scarf, making sure she had fully tucked her bun under it. She felt more comfortable wearing it since her spiritual experience in the mosque; she almost felt it was a part of her. *Is he pretending he likes it, to see my reaction?* she wondered. *Isn't that what you're doing now, pretending to be a Muslim? Isn't that hypocrisy? Doesn't that make you worse than* Jaish? *I would swim the oceans of Islam and cross the deserts of Muslimness if I have to.*

'So... are you here to test me out?' she asked, sipping her water

'Do you believe all this?' he asked, spreading his arms wide.

Jessica immediately understood what he meant. *Did she believe in Abu Umar's dogma and his version of Islamic extremism?* The way he asked made her think he was questioning himself.

'Course I do,' she said, and regretted it immediately, realising it was too flippant a remark for someone who wanted to infiltrate *Jaish*. She knew he could slip a little pill into her coffee as easily as he smiled at her. I have to be subtler. She felt a hot tightness in her throat. The pain between her shoulder-blades that had accompanied her on the train journey from Birmingham had returned, and now its twin joined in as it clung to her neck, like a gremlin that sank its fangs into her flesh. The dull sawing of fear hacked over her spine. The impish venom made her shiver, and she zipped up her coat. She stopped herself from grinding her teeth. *I'd better stick to the truth*, she told herself.

Hamza still smiled as if he understood her discomfort – expected it, even. She wondered if he was laughing at her. If he was thinking, *why is she so keen to die?* Why do you *really* want to be a suicide bomber?'

What if he doesn't believe me for a moment? She could not stop the questions dominating her thoughts. *What if he sees through me with those inky eyes of his, as if he could see through to my bones?* This man did not act or look like Abu Umar; her intuition told her he was different. Abu Umar had grabbed her soul and twisted it, making her question everything about herself. Her previous life had seemed built upon things she had been deceived about, or the false elation of self congratulation: why should she feel pleased at being a Westerner, at being white, being born in a liberal democracy? None of those things were things she could personally be proud of.

Meeting Abu Umar and had made her realise these things, but he held worldviews so drastically different from hers. The way he justified his violence, it seemed as if he had not followed the same line in evolution of Homo sapiens. *According to him, he hasn't evolved at all,* she thought. Instead, he had arrived perfectly formed, when Adam, his direct ancestor landed on Earth: in his own personal purgatory. *He thinks all life is suffering for the Muslim, until he achieves Allah's pleasure through martyrdom.*

That Abu Umar could hold such radical opinions and then justify them with sparkling verve, making them *Halal* by force of his champagne personality amazed her. Abu Umar had enforced upon her a grudging admiration, as she would to Machiavelli; but despite being mesmerised by him during the meeting in Baghdad, Jessica realised that, unlike Machiavelli, Abu Umar's politics had the deadly delusion of self-righteousness.

The way Hamza looked at her did not make her soul twist, but did make her glance away and brush her hair and pull her lower lip. His eyes made her feel like the MRI machine that had scanned her brain last year, which her doctor had ordered for the pain in her neck, and the unexplained headaches she had been getting. *Can he see my brain fizzle under the lies?* She felt she should stick to real events.

'Hamza means lion, doesn't it?' said Jessica, and she saw how he raised two thick eyebrows in surprise. 'Our driver in Baghdad, his name was Hamza. He told us that.'

'You might be thinking of *Asadallah*, Lion of Allah. The Prophet's uncle's name was Hamza, but because of his bravery he was called *Asadallah*.'

'Is that you? Lion of Allah?'

'I wish I was. Maybe one day, *inshallah*,' he said without blinking. 'What about you?'

Is he lying? she thought. *What makes me think that?* The uncertainty of her predicament made her feel everyone wore masks, masks on top of masks. As if even the skin on their faces did not belong to them. Everything felt unreal, as if the laws of physics did not apply in her dimension. The water tasted alien. She sipped again, and licked her lips, as if its molecules contained chemicals that would embolden her to carry out her secret mission. Despite drinking her throat felt cracked with dryness, and it seemed to be tightening as she cleared it.

'So what makes you ready to die? So keen?'

Shit, the time for my test has come! 'I'm not ready to do anything. Well, I'm not sure exactly what I can do.' She looked at him, but he showed no reaction. 'I'll tell you something Hamza, I haven't spoken about this to anyone since it happened, but when I was in the mosque, I felt something. I felt as if I had never breathed before, as if my senses had never been used before that day. I heard the beauty of *Al Hay Al Qayum* – The Ever-living Self-sustaining.'

'You found Allah?'

'God finds people, or at least those who he guides none can misguide, and those he allows to go astray will never find guidance.'

Hamza became serious. *Maybe I've surprised him by quoting the Hadith; he probably didn't imagine I knew any sayings of the Prophet,* she thought. *I'm not a Muslim, but I can still see some things of beauty and wisdom that reassure my trembling heart.*

Jessica sipped her water; she ignored the latte. She leaned forward and looked at Hamza, without blinking. 'I believe that the only way is Allah's love, and love is the only answer, and if I can bear witness by giving my body to His cause the world can realise that. I want to be a *Shaheed*, a true martyr.' She hoped that he would be affected by her argument, that her voice resonated with the timbre of truthfulness. 'I'm so glad Sebastian sent me to that spiritual session.'

'Ah, yes Sebastian. Is he a friend?'

Jessica felt Hamza knew so much about her that he must know the answer already.

'I met him at the train station on the day of the bombing,' she said, looking away.

'I'm sorry about Hamid,' he said without hesitation, in a flat voice, but she felt it contained sincere sympathy. *How do I know he's sincere?* she thought. I don't, but I do feel a rapport with him, as if I should give him a job in my office. I have to trust my instincts if I'm going to go through with this.

She made herself imagine that this man was dangerous, that she was like the gazelle stalked by Hamza, the Lion of *Jaish* , so that she knew she had to open her senses to the slightest rustling of danger. *How do I turn this around*, she wondered, *make them ask me to join* Jaish? If I seem too desperate they will get suspicious. The only way is to rely on the truth, and then to twist it.

'Yeah, in the mosque. I was washed by a spiritual wave, of such purity, as if the water came from the kiss of angels, powered by God's breath.' She held his eyes and hoped that her passionate language would convey some of her feelings.

'When did you convert?'

'We are all born Muslim, aren't we?' she said, realising that the lies were inevitable. 'The door was always open, but I was looking for the key.'

'The *Shaikh* will want to know,' said Hamza, and she wondered if he always became serious when talking about Abu Umar.

'I said the *Shahahda* in Birmingham.' She said the words too quickly, and shifted in her seat.

Jessica realised that her non-verbal clues would be more important than anything else in this conversation; her smallest movement would be a message to Hamza, as loud as fireworks screeching into the sky. *When will my lies unravel? Not before I get answers*, she told herself, the truth about Hamid. *Is it too obvious that I'm not a Muslim?* Jessica felt the Eternal Presence of a Merciful God. She just did not know by what name, if any, to call him. Should she think of Him by one name, or none, or the Ninety-Nine Beautiful Names of Allah?

'You know what, Hamza – although I want to be a martyr, I'm not sure killing others is the way.' Jessica knew she was on the precipice. If she showed too much doubt, then they would reject her. She wanted them to think they could indoctrinate her.

'Oh tut tut, you naughty girl. You know that the *Shaikh* says that revolution is the only way. That's the *Jaish modus operandi*. I'll have to send you to meet the Sisters-in-Charge.' Hamza smiled and said, 'Have you heard of Plain Jamila? She's the Sisters-in-Charge... no harm in you knowing that.'

'I met her in Birmingham, and went to Baghdad because of her – well, partly because of her.'

'And now that you're here means you're ready to join *Jaish*'s jungle of *Jihadis*?'

Jessica wondered if Hamza was being flippant to put her at ease, or whether he really meant what he said.

Hamza glanced over her shoulder out into the street, as numerous people thronged around Westminster and the bridge. 'Are you looking for someone?' asked Jessica.

'I'm always looking for someone.' He looked at her. 'You better get used to never being alone if you join *Jaish* – not even when you're asleep.'

The coffee shop filled with people who entered and left, having ordered mostly takeaway coffees, as if vital organs were being filled and emptied; the respiration of London, which created its atmosphere and life, where people rushed in and out of places like air being sucked into choking lungs.

As the doors opened, gusts of wind swept around and felt crisp, as the air cooled her blushing face. Hamza got up and said, 'I'll get you a double espresso, just like mine, to prove that there's no misogyny on my part.' Jessica smiled, but did not object this time. He returned with the black coffee. She saw some surprise on his face when she sipped it without milk, unsweetened. She almost smiled herself at the unwritten macho rules that applied not only to alcohol but also to coffee; *how surprised would he be if he knew I used to drink whisky neat with Dad?* she thought. Maybe he thinks I'm too delicate for all this potential violence.

'So what's the situation?' asked Hamza, shrugging, as if he wanted to get back to business.

'I believe that the wars against us Muslims are wrong, we have suffered too much for too long, this is just another in a long line of crusades against Islam...'

At that moment a black man entered the shop. 'Just who we don't need right now,' muttered Hamza, and looked away.

The man approached them and said, '*Asalamalaikum.*'

'*Walaikumasalaam*,' replied Hamza and Jessica. Jessica had learned a few words of Arabic from Hamid which she knew were necessary to all Muslims, and now tried to insert them like oil into her machinery of pretence.

'This is Dwayne,' said Hamza. Dwayne had barely looked at Jessica; he glanced and nodded to her, and then turned his attention back to Hamza.

'Wha'appen? What you doing?' Dwayne asked Hamza.

Hamza smiled and said, 'Well, we're having coffee and passing a very nice afternoon in discussion.' He raised his eyebrows at Dwayne and added solicitously, 'Can I get you a drink?'

'I ain't here to drink no *Kuffar* coffee,' growled Dwayne. 'The *Shaikh* said to just get the basics.'

'The basics take time. It isn't that simple. Got to take it easy, no harm in chit-chatting a little first...' Hamza gestured to Jessica and nodded, as if to imply to Dwayne that he should not be ignoring her.

'No time for shit-shatting,' said Dwayne to Hamza, before turning to Jessica. 'Alright?' he demanded.

'Er, yeah,' said Jessica, as she shuffled in her chair and put her hands under the table.

'Right, we'll get some takeaway coffees now that he's here. We'll walk across the bridge. Can't really talk in here, because Dwayne can't keep his voice down.'

Dwayne sucked his teeth in disapproval but sat at the table, leaning back in his chair, staring at Jessica squint-eyed, while Hamza went to get the drinks.

Jessica looked at his curls of hair that peeked out of the sides of his white baseball cap, like black lamb's wool. He had a small hard moustache and beard with tight curls like razor wire. *I'd better watch myself*, she thought. *This guy's completely different to Hamza.*

Dwayne stared at her, unblinking; his mouth pursed into a pinky-orange drawbridge. As he grimaced, she saw his wide-gapped teeth; a white portcullis, shut tight against any *Kuffar* invaders.

Hamza returned, and they started walking across Westminster Bridge. Hamza kept looking ahead and behind. 'Not so easy for anyone to listen in when we're on the move,' he said.

'You wanna be a martyr?' asked Dwayne, not seeming to care who heard.

'I – I don't really know what that means.'

Dwayne laughed, and Hamza smiled. 'You need some serious Islamic education,' Dwayne chuckled as he leaned back. 'I was like you once, sistah, yeah. I was like you once, drowning in a sea of *Kuffar*.'

'She's a Muslim, Dwayne,' said Hamza.

'Yeah, yeah, you know what I mean. Now look at me. I'm flying high on Islam – no drugs, no nuffink. *Alhamdullilah*!'

Jessica could not discern any difference between him and many of the other men of his age walking the streets of London. Dwayne wore a reversed baseball cap that complimented his Nike basketball shoes; as he stopped to tie an undone shoelace, Jessica saw his black boots had straggly laces and *Zoom* written on one side. He wore a Henri Lloyd designer jacket that matched the colour of his boots. Dwayne spoke in an accent through which his patois poked through intermittently, like a smattering of islands on a map – the Isles of the West Indies in an English Sea.

'Me carn't believe it. Never knew no white girl who wanted to be *Shaheed*.'

'I'm really not sure what would be involved. What do I, I mean, what does it entail?' She looked at Hamza, hoping to hide behind a semblance of politeness.

'Well, it's not that easy. What Dwayne means is that first you have to go through a programme.'

'Programme?' asked Jessica, feeling as if Dwayne would insert silicon chips into her. She slowed down and sipped her espresso. Hamza looked down and played with his cup.

'Yeah, what he means is we gotta make sure you gonna tune up and ain't gonna sing like a canary, like a traitor. 'Cos if you do, you're gonna find yourself in the cat's mouth pretty quick.' Dwayne cackled and flicked his fingers, then suddenly became serious. 'But if you wanna learn then we's the people to teach you, sistah.'

'Dwayne, she's fine,' said Hamza.

'Don't worry mate, I've heard about her – she's famous in *Jaish* already,' Dwayne said, without taking his eyes off Jessica. 'We'll teach you everything... from how to pray, to how to make they *Kuffar* wish they had prayed.' He chuckled again at his own joke.

'I know little bits already,' said Jessica, deciding that the serious approach would be safest.

'Well, if you're serious then we have to make sure you don't leave any suspicious clues,' said Hamza. 'Arrange a new job for you – or, at least, that's what you tell the people back home. Get your cover story straight.'

'First, sistah...' Dwayne came closer and jabbed her coffee cup with his forefinger, so that she sloshed some of the coffee. 'Is you up for it?'

'What exactly is involved?' she asked.

'Does it matter?' asked Dwayne, 'Okay, let me put it another way. What did you feel when them *Kuffar* American dogs gunned down Mariam?'

Jessica looked from face to face. *Are they really suggesting that anything is justifiable because Mariam died? I'd better give them something to go on, can't be too negative.* So she relied on the truth again to carry her answer across the chasm of pretence. One slip and she could fall into the rivers of lava that would engulf her and leave no trace, and maybe her parents and Holly too. Having met Abu Umar, she realised what he could do, and *Jaish*'s punishment would be complete. They could dissolve her bones, and even her soul might not be able to escape the black hole of their revenge.

Jessica looked at Dwayne. 'I felt worse than ever before. I felt more responsible for Mariam and Musa than when Hamid died.' The truth gave her power to face Dwayne without allowing her lips to quiver, or her hands to shake; the power seemed to connect her to the basic life force of the earth. Her breath calmed and felt as if it came from a free wind, her blood the sanguine river that could replenish a desiccated land.

She walked between the two men and she looked from Dwayne to Hamza, wondering if either of them would support her. Her mouth tasted bitter, and the gremlin sank its teeth into her neck still deeper. She moved to ease the pain, but did not dare to massage her neck.

Hamza said, 'Well, feeling bad is lovely, but it isn't enough I'm afraid.' He looked at Dwayne. 'This is serious.'

'Give the sistah a chance, man!' said Dwayne. 'Yeah, sistah, it's okay to be confused, it's very early for you.' He almost smiled at her. 'Me knows it's hard to give up you're old life, you know. *Khanzeer*, and lust, and alcohol – they is like an infection in your guts and heart and liver. They won't leave you.' Hamza nodded Dwayne. 'Him don't know this, these born Muslims. They got no idea how hard it is for us sometimes.'

'No, it's none of those things, really,' said Jessica. Although she did not know what *Khanzeer* meant, she assumed it must be bad. She felt surprise that Dwayne sympathised with her. 'It's more my mum and dad, and Holly. She's my best friend.'

'Not anymore – now its Sebastian isn't it?' said Hamza.

'Don't worry, we'll keep your secrets, sis. That's what were good at. And we'll make sure your mum and dad is okay,' said Dwayne.

Jessica shivered and pulled her coat closer around her, but it did not stop the goose bumps, or make her feel warm. They got to the other side; she excused herself, and went to the toilet of the café.

They've done their homework. How casually they mentioned my parents, Holly and Sebastian, without leering or any menace, without raising their voices, as if they could be friends of theirs. She realised there was no need for them to make all the threats. *Jaish* were not cardboard cut-out baddies from Rambo or Arnie movies. *These are ordinary people who have transformed themselves into sharks and they don't need to show their jagged teeth,* she thought. *I wonder what made them into committed terrorists? They seem as if they would have no more remorse at carrying out a suicide mission in London then they would have in destroying an anthill – that's it!*

The way that Abu Umar had spoken about 'the *Kuffar*' had reduced all Muslims who disagreed with him to the status of non-Muslims, and the non-Muslims to non-humans, without feelings and emotions. Incredibly, Abu Umar had argued for Muslims not to be demonised, and had spoken about the slaughters of Gaza, and Iraq. The pain and suffering had been twisted under the pressure of a perverse vice of logic, and Jessica had found herself swept up in his emotions initially. Now she knew that his justification was wrong, and she was right to try and infiltrate them, especially now as they seemed to planning a new atrocity in London. Abu Umar had squeezed the truth so hard that it ceased to be the logic of religion but transformed into a slitheringly fast animal, with rabid jaws, canine teeth and poisonous breath; a unique life-sucking cult.

Jessica could imagine Hamza hesitating before gassing a wasp's nest or pouring salt over a slug if they ever attacked his lettuces or brassicas. Dwayne probably arranged games of basketball for the kids of his area.

When she got back, they both looked at her as if inspecting her. Dwayne came closer and peered into her face. 'I remember when I was like you, don't worry. It takes time for Allah to fill your heart, so that you can give your life for him.' He smiled at her, and this time his nostrils did not flare as he spoke, and the hard line of lips had softened to reveal a smile with teeth that looked like castle battlements. 'I know what you're going through.'

The empathy of the convert. Is that what I want? I need someone on my side to infiltrate Jaish *and to get them to trust me.*

Hamza said, 'Abu Umar has doubts too; he doesn't know if you're strong enough for it. We need to see what your commitment is like over the next couple of weeks. There's a flat set up for you. You need to go there –'

'She can't just disappear, man,' said Dwayne, his eyes widening as he looked at Hamza. 'She got her mum and dad to think about; her mum's got a heart condition, you know.' Dwayne banged the centre of his chest with his fist as if he had a piece of meat stuck there: DUFF THUMP DUFF.

'That's what the *Shaikh* ordered,' said Hamza.

'The *Shaikh* said it all depends on how she is, and I think she isn't ready.' Dwayne leaned into Hamza. 'Yeah, but you gotta give them reasons, otherwise they'll look for her, and then that's gonna make too many questions if she just disappears.' He turned to Jessica. 'Tell them about your new job with the BBC in London.'

Hamza shrugged, and looked out over the window.

'Thank you, Dwayne,' said Jessica.

Dwayne smiled at her. 'Don't worry, sistah, I know you is going to come through. I got a feeling you is special.'

'I don't know if I can be a martyr, but I do know what the *Shaikh* said in Baghdad came like an earthquake and shook my world.'

'He's amazing isn't he? What a man,' said Hamza.

'Me carn't believe he's gonna make me a martyr,' said Dwayne, flicking his fingers. 'You go on home and make sure your mum's okay. I'll ring you in three days.'

Jessica left, the two men smiling at her. On the train home she wondered what made them so happy. Could it be the acquisition of a blue-eyed woman who could go anywhere without suspicion, and help their mission succeed? Or were they smiling because they were imagining Paradise? They had seemed preoccupied with thoughts of impending martyrdom; their own, and hers.

Birmingham

Three days later, Dwayne rang Jessica on her mobile phone. She had already told her parents about her new job. She had consoled Holly, who had cried when Jessica told her that she had to leave for London.

'So, sistah Jess, how you been doing?' said Dwayne. His attempt at friendliness made her think of Holly, who was one of the few people to call her Jess.

'Hi, Dwayne, how's things?' *What the hell am I asking him how things are for*, she thought, *as if he's an old friend inviting me to take afternoon tea at the Dorchester? Instead he's a potential terrorist who's trying to invite me to be a suicide bomber.*

'You all set to be one of the True Believers?'

Oh God, help me! There's no going back after this; once I say yes, they control my life. She did not speak for a moment, breathed deeply a few times and tried to still her heaving stomach, which felt as if every moment new acid whirlpools were being born.

'Yes, yes I think so; well I've made the preparations, anyway.'

Jessica had promised her parents and Holly that she would stay in touch, but she knew she had burned her ships. There could be no way back, because behind her patrolling the seas that she had crossed were *Jaish*'s galleys, ready to tie her to the oars. In front of her stood the dark continent of her mission. She had to infiltrate and find out the truth about Hamid, but all she could see ahead of her were unknown lands with a morass of trees, standing thick and tall. There she could be captured, and also enslaved to the ideals of terrorism. Her determination had grown stronger over the past few days, as if powered by nature, a Gaia, who had enlisted Jessica in trying to redress the imbalance in the firmament created by *Jaish*'s philosophy.

I need to infiltrate Jaish, *to find out what their plans are and subvert them,* she planned in her mind. *I need to stop the atrocities before they occur, but how? Should I spy for MI5?* Jaish *are watching me now, probably listening to my phone calls too – and anyway, I don't think I could do that. I have to be an investigative journalist, and a bloody good actress. Maybe I should have paid more attention to Kate Winslett's films.*

Her fervour flooded her with strength like the rising tide, which she allowed to cut her connections with her family; it drowned the narrow isthmus of her past and, made her feel like an isolated island.

Dwayne's voice broke her thoughts. 'Sweet! I knew you was good for it. I could tell you got the heart of a *Shaheed*, sistah.'

'What about Abu Umar?'

'It's cool, I talked to the *Shaikh*, yeah and he's given me permission – well, me and Plain Jamila is gonna take care of you.'

So Abu Umar, she thought, *the werewolf of* Jaish *has left his Rottweilers in charge. What the hell am I doing getting involved with these people? What about Hamid? I need closure...at least the Americans have useful words for these feelings,* she thought. She felt like some silicon-filled queen in a tight top on an American daytime chat show.

'You is gonna be a great martyr, you have felt Allah calling your soul to its destiny, like a swan. That's what you are, Jess – a beautiful blonde swan. Do you feel the pull of the earth? Everyone has to migrate to their origins, back to where they belong, and our first and last home is Allah. Your heart senses the changing moon, as if you could feel gravity, as if you are at one with the seasons. Autumn is already here, the time that leads to the rebirth. You must have a winter before spring can come. So you see, the end of autumn is the real season of birth, just like our martyrdom is the womb that contains the seeds for our eternal life: we will be reborn and have eternal life in *Jannah*.'

Jessica replied in the way expected of her, '*Inshallah!*', but she thought it doesn't sound like Dwayne – more like something he was quoting, an emotional and poetic speech.

'Happy forever!'

'*Inshallah*, God willing, that's what I want to be – content.' She sat down on the sofa and put a hand over her throat, which felt constricted, as if one of the exotic climbers from her hot house had entwined its coils around her neck. Her face burned as if its toxic sap had seeped into her skin.

'You're a beautiful blonde swan and Allah – The Creator of the Worlds, Lord of the Day of Judgement – is calling you home to Paradise. Fly East! Fly to Mecca! Fly home!'

'Okay, okay. When do we start?'

'That's the way, sistah.' said Dwayne in a voice which sounded full of satisfaction, as if his flight of oratory had achieved success in guiding the migrating swan home. 'Take a morning train, on Saturday down to London, like any normal person starting a new job on Monday would. I'll meet you at Euston station and take you to your new flat.'

So Jessica made preparations to fly home to her new Mecca.

London – Central

As the train pulled into Euston, Jessica saw Dwayne standing on the platform. The whiteness of his smile under normal circumstances would have looked appealing, like fresh snow to an ardent skier, but the feelings of dread made her clutch her stomach. She took some antacids, Gaviscon tablets, out of her pocket and chewed them for the burning sensation, before greeting him.

Dwayne insisted on carrying her bag through the underground, and made general conversation with her until they got out at Victoria tube station. He led her to a nearby flat. Jessica noticed the small spray of carnations on the side table in the hallway before she entered. Dwayne put the bag down. 'Plain Jamila will be here soon, er, I shouldn't stay here too long.' He gestured her into the sitting room but stayed in the hallway. 'There's plenty of food in the fridge, and tea and coffee, of course.'

Jessica looked around, feeling like she was close to wearing an orange jumpsuit in a cage, her eyes trying to take in the comfortable furnishing. The scented air was gravid with incense. She craned to look out of the window to try and get her bearings, but she did not know the street or that part of London. She went over to the large window and looked out, put her hands over her face and wiped her eyes. She turned back to Dwayne.

'Yeah, thanks, that's fine.' *I'm trapped, but I'll feel better when he's gone... got to give myself time to think.* 'What happens now?'

'Well, like Hamza said to you last time, there's a training programme, and Plain Jamila will teach you what you need to know. I'll be around. And hey, don't worry,' he said, taking a step towards her, his tone brightening. '*Shaikh* Abu Umar will soon take you under his wing. He likes to do some of the training himself, and when you're part of the cell then its great, because he does all the *halaqas*, study circles – himself.'

'Yeah, cool, thanks.' She walked away towards the kitchen, without looking at him. 'Going to make a cup of tea.' She spoke loudly from the kitchen, 'Do you want some?' she asked out of politeness, force of habit. To her relief, he refused and left.

Jessica made the tea and put it down on the coffee table, but did not drink it. She paced the flat. It had one bedroom, with the bed made up, and a small but modern bathroom to the side. She went and stood by the large window of the main room, when she heard someone opening the front door. She ran to the door in a panic, to find Plain Jamila standing in the hallway, smiling. 'I see that sending you to Baghdad was the right thing to do.'

Jessica covered her face with her hands and slowed her breathing for a moment, before speaking. 'Well, it seems that Victoria is the new *Ka'ba*,' she said with a shrug, and looked away.

Plain Jamila looked at her with a frown that created dark brown creases over her forehead. 'Okay, we have a lot to cover. The *Shaikh* could call us any time, and he might come and join us too.'

'Do you want some tea?' Jessica did not know what else to say.

The older woman led the way to the sofa and sat down. Jessica copied her. 'Right, first things first. You need to learn how to behave as a Muslim.' Plain Jamila spoke with the trace of an accent; her T's and D's escaped like tigers from the old country.

'What do I have to do?'

'We want you to be able to blend in, whether you're talking to Muslims or non-Muslims, because even I don't know what exactly you will have to do. First, we make you inconspicuous again.' She leaned over and took off Jessica's scarf.

'What? What are you doing?' Jessica felt exposed; her own spirituality had made her wear the scarf intermittently from time to time since her experience in the mosque, and it had become a refuge from world, a secret Shangri La amongst a sea of noise. She also wanted to convince *Jaish* she had fully converted.

'Without your scarf, little sister, you can go anywhere, do anything,' said Plain Jamila. Her face became abruptly stern. 'And learn never to question your trainers. Everything I'm doing is to make your martyrdom easier for you.' She leaned forward as if sharing a secret, and her voice became quieter.

'Don't ever show dissent with the *Shaikh*.' Then voice took on the tone of a maternal aunt again. 'God made me plain, and so I insist everyone call me Plain Jamila, but if you're beautiful Allah made you so for a reason; we have to use that as a weapon against the *Kuffar*.' She folded the scarf neatly, and put it on the table. 'Once you're fully psychologically ready, then the real training will begin. First, let's get you settled in.'

Plain Jamila fussed around the flat like a Muslim version of Mary Poppins. Jessica had no chance to object. She tidied and cleared things that already seemed to be where they should. She took Jessica's bag and emptied it onto the bed, then put her clothes away, passing occasional comments along with instructions. Jessica controlled her temper; *this is worse than being in any army*, she thought. She had not imagined that even her clothes would have to pass the scrutiny of Sergeant Major Plain Jamila.

Then Jamila sat on the sofa again. She looked at Jessica. 'Yes, much better, without the scarf. Now you can be a pretty normal girl walking around London.'

Jessica was surprised at how her attachment had grown to the scarf, mostly to convince *Jaish* about her conversion, but she put that aside and watched Plain Jamila with a mixture of fascination and wonder. How did this woman get like this?

'I know, I know, it's terrible for you. You just started wearing it, and your emotions are high, but trust me, Jessica – you're really working for Allah's pleasure now.'

At least she believes my conversion is genuine.

Plain Jamila smiled, and patted her hand. 'Turquoise or cobalt would bring out the colour out in your eyes, too. This black is too sombre for you. You should wear a blue blouse, maybe?'

Jessica looked at the woman who tugged her brown scarf over her head; she wore the same beige top that Jessica had seen before, with a thick dark-chocolate skirt that seemed too big for her.

'Have you told all your friends and family that you've become a Muslim?'

How can I tell anyone, when I haven't converted! she thought but said, 'Yes – no –'

'Well, this is where it gets tricky, because you'll have to get your story straight. If you've told them, then you'll have to remember to wear the scarf around them. If you get a chance to meet them again, that is…'

Jessica nodded, not trusting herself to say anything. She had not considered the minutiae of her time in London.

'Only if unrelated men are present – you know that, don't you?'

Jessica nodded again, and ran a hand through her hair, which fell onto her shoulders in waves of gold. As the light shone on them, they looked like thousands of optical fibres.

'You shouldn't go out without need. You can give this number to your parents, but don't answer the phone in the flat during the day. You're supposed to be at work, remember?'

'Yeah, sure,' said Jessica, wondering how oppressive the real training would be, if the first day was like this. In some ways she was surprised that her handler had given permission for her to contact her friends and family, but she realised that it made sense for her to pretend that things were normal until the final day, when she assumed she and the rest of the terror cell would just disappear.

'If anyone asks or wonders why you're not in touch as usual, you just tell them that you're working day and night on the Baghdad documentary.' She smiled at Jessica, who grimaced back. 'See, it's not that difficult – you just have to think ahead,' she said, and patted Jessica's hand again. 'Don't worry; we'll be here to hold your hand. We're your family now.' Plain Jamila leaned forward, and gave Jessica a hug.

Jessica had to steel her arms to receive her, and had to harden the muscles in her neck and back not to recoil. She looked up at the woman, at her crooked teeth and face covered in acne. Jessica thought the woman's attempts at friendliness slipped off the mask on her face like grease. Her oily skin shone in the bright light. Jessica forced a smile to flicker across her lips, but she could not make her eyes smile.

'You can call me *Baji*. It means 'older sister," said Plain Jamila.

'Oh, okay, thank you – but wouldn't that compromise my conversion to some people, who might get suspicious?' Jessica knew she had to train in London as an ordinary woman.

Plain Jamila looked crestfallen. 'Okay, okay. I hadn't thought of that.'

'I can call you Jamila, if that's alright?'

The older woman looked at her sternly. 'Plain Jamila! If you use my name, say Plain Jamila! Are you trying to take away my piety and closeness to Allah and ruin my chances for ever-lasting *Jannah*?'

'No. No, of course not,' said Jessica, holding her hands up leaning back on the sofa.

'Good, because nothing, I mean *nothing*, and no one will ever stop me getting to the highest of Paradise,' said Jamila, in a voice Jessica had not heard before.

'No, no…'

'Good. I wear my simple piety like a shield against the non-stop attacks of the *Kuffar*.'

'Yes, yes, Plain Jamila,' said Jessica, shrinking back into the leather of the sofa.

Plain Jamila seemed to recover some control. 'Rest, now. Tomorrow I will try and pass on some of my goodness to you. We start at *Fajr*, the Morning Prayer. Be up and washed for five.'

With that Jamila wrapped her scarf around her head tightly, gripping it with her hand like a lifeline to a heaven, as she made her way towards the front door. As she walked out of the flat, each step chopped into Jessica like a reminder of piety.

Over the next few weeks, Plain Jamila trained Jessica. She taught her how to pray, left books for her that she had to read and discuss every day, so that the texts became like meals and the prayers like water during the days. Jessica went through a tutorial programme, during which she sat and answered questions and discussed philosophy. Plain Jamila did not move onto the next section until she looked deeply into Jessica's eyes, and saw, Jessica imagined, her heart filling with emotions and overflowing. So Jessica obliged, acting out her expected emotions, most of which coincided with her own sensations of sorrow and loss and regret so that tears came easily to her. Tears for Hamid, for lying to her parents and Holly, for a future she had started to think about with Sebastian but would not allow herself to fully imagine, because she felt it was impossible. So she gave evidence to Plain Jamila that all the things that she had been taught had affected the psychological changes that her trainer desired.

Is this what it takes to indoctrinate someone? Why do I find myself agreeing with some of the things that she tells me? she thought. *Why is it horrific to watch the videos of Gaza, Baghdad and Afghanistan and so easy to build hate, so that now I hate some of the American and British soldiers, and loathe the security services in my heart, even though my mind tells me it's not that simple? No matter how sorry I feel for the children of Gaza or Kabul and how confused my feelings, I know for sure I will never trigger the bombs. I would rather die trying to stop them.*

CHAPTER 20

London – Victoria

Jimmy tried to ignore the others, especially Jessica; she was always getting in the way, asking stupid questions. He was enjoying his spiritual session with Abu Umar, one of many since his attendance had started at the special closed circle. It had been over two months since he had left from home. Each lesson seemed to make him grow in confidence and belief. This *'halaqa'*, study circle, was moving him more than many of the previous ones. The *halaqa* had been mostly about the Jews. Abu Umar and Dwayne often displayed their huge knowledge of this topic and quoted the appropriate verses.

'*O ye who believe! Take not the Jews and the Christians for your friends and protectors: They are but friends and protectors to each other. And he amongst you that turns to them for friendship is of them. Verily Allah guideth not a people unjust.* Surah 5, Verse 51.'

Abu Umar paused and then repeated, '*They are but friends and protectors to each other.*'

'Because ultimately the *Kuffar* will betray you,' added Abu Umar. Dwayne nodded his head sagaciously as the *Shaikh* expounded his theory of the *Kuffar* and why the Muslims needed to be self-sufficient, independent and proud, as they had been in history, since the beginning of Counting, since the time of the Prophet.

'That's why we must need a Muslim state a true *Khilafa*.' Abu Umar's words made increasing sense to Jimmy now. Almost as if, suddenly, he had stepped out of the darkness of the cave into the light. Like the parable of the cave dwellers in *Surah Al Kahf*, which Abu Umar had explained in another *halaqa*. Jimmy now remembered the verse which had affected him the most: '*When ye turn away from them and the things they worship other than Allah, betake yourselves to the Cave: Your Lord will shower His mercies on you and dispose of your affairs towards comfort and ease.* Surah 18, Verse 16.'

He also remembered the way the magicians of pharaoh had been defeated by Allah-inspired magic of Moses, which proved stronger when the Moses threw down his staff. It became a huge snake, which swallowed the magician's serpents.

Abu Umar repeated the story, and said to Jimmy, 'These are lessons for us, *ya akhi*, my brother. These are signs, metaphors, how Allah wants us to use the *Kuffar*'s magic and power to destroy themselves. That's why we will use their own weapons of death and destruction that they create every day to destroy them, *inshallah*.'

'Allah won't allow the forces of evil to win, will he?' said Jessica.

'That's right, sistah, yeah. We is the reason why Allah won't allow the *Kuffar* to win,' said Dwayne.

Jimmy looked at Jessica with his lips pulled back into a grimace. *Stupid bloody* Goree*! All this time, and she still don't get it.*

Every time Jimmy heard these stories, he felt his palms covered in sweat, his fingers coiled into fists. Sometimes he was moved to tears, especially if Abu Umar and Dwayne started crying. They always cried after watching the videos of atrocities committed by the *Kuffar* in Iraq and Afghanistan, but Palestine affected them the most. Jimmy realised he had been in a stupor all his life, misguided and misled: by the media, films, TV, newspapers and politicians – especially the politicians. Hollywood was controlled by the Jews, who owned and operated all the conglomerates.

'*Because of the wrongdoing of the Jews, We forbade them good things which were made lawful unto them, and because of their much hindering from Allah's way.* 4:16,' recited Abu Umar.

Dwayne backed him up with further by repeating: '*O ye who believe! Take not the Jews and the Christians for friends. They are friends one to another. He among you who takes them for friends is one of them. Lo! Allah guides not wrongdoing folk.* 5:51.'

'Finally, only one conclusion is possible: the world is controlled, operated, owned by Jew-Zionists-Freemason-Neoconservatives. Call them what you like, *ya ahkhi*, my brother, they have *qullo*...' – the *Shaikh* encompassed the globe in his hands – 'everything!'

Abu Umar added some fast-flowing Arabic, which Jimmy assumed were especially directed choice curses. Abu Umar continued, 'The original Satanists, *Dajjal*, the Antichrist worshipers of the New World Order – they attack us with one mission, and one mission only.' He held up his right index finger and waited for such a length time that Jimmy gasped, and felt like shaking him to know the answer. 'To destroy Islam and the word of Allah. They are trying to establish Dajjalic Antichrist on the throne of this *duniya*, world, to give *Shaitan* the final victory.' Abu Umar held up a copy of the Qur'an in his right hand. Jimmy could still hear the way he rolled his R's and called throne a 'zrone'.

'If these evil Jews have managed to take over the world, can't we fight them in the same way?' said Jessica. Jimmy watched the way she looked at the group, as if she really expected them to understand her drivel. She continued, 'I mean if they've taken over the world, then surely we could play them at their game?' Jimmy groaned audibly. He just about stopped himself from slapping his forehead.

Abu Umar smiled at Jessica. 'They do not understand any language of decency. We have to fight them – it is written.'

Why is the Shaikh *so patient with this woman?* Jimmy thought. *We don't need her, anyway.*

'But,' said Abu Umar, as he kissed The Book reverentially, then held it to his forehead and closed his eyes, 'we have Allah's promise that, no matter how hard they is trying, they will never ever destroy this book and this deen, our religion.'

'*Inshallah! Inshallah!*' Jimmy echoed along with Dwayne. The Afghan copied them, even moving in the same way.

'*Da'iman wa abadan! Da'iman wa abadan! Da'iman was abadan!*' said Abu Umar through closed eyes, clenched teeth. He translated, 'Forever to the end of time!'

The Qur'an was still clasped to his forehead, and when he removed it there was a small red mark where the golden inscription had pressed hard onto his forehead. 'In fact, they cannot – it is impossible to change even a single *haraf*, syllable, in it from the time of Revelation. Much as they tried to prove that it was the work of a madman, or old texts amalgamated. Even they said the Qur'an is inspired by Satan, *astagh – firullah!* God Forbid! They have failed, failed completely to change anything. Don't be fool by them – these *Kuffar* have been trying for centuries. *The Satanic Verses* is nothing new. This is not the final chapter in a long line, a catalogue of historical attacks against The Book.'

Abu Umar held up the Qur'an again; aloft in front of Jimmy's face, pointing it towards him. 'This is the final message. The unchanged actual exact words of Allah, to his final unlettered prophet.' He looked at Jimmy intently. 'Do you know poetry?' When Jimmy shook his head, Abu Umar continued, 'He, our beloved Prophet was an illiterate man, *alehis salatus salaam*, peace be upon him. Yet Allah chose to reveal the Qur'an in unbelievable poetry. It was impossible for him to write this. The Glorious Qur'an is the direct word of Allah! This book contains poetry unmatched till today. Better than the Jahliya poetry, and the pre-Islamic Arabs knew poetry – they were masters of it.'

Jimmy wondered how poetry, even if it was with a slight 'B' sound at the beginning as his teacher pronounced it, could relate to his mission, but he felt tears pricking his eyes because of the emotional rhetoric of Abu Umar.

Then Abu Umar flitted back to the subject of the Jews and quoted a *Hadith*, a saying of the Messenger of Allah, 'Among the signs of the approach of Day of Judgment: *The hour of judgment shall not happen until the Muslims fight the Jews. The Muslims shall kill the Jews, to the point that the Jew shall hide behind a big rock or a tree and the rock or tree shall call on the Muslim saying: O Muslim there is a Jew behind me, come and kill him! Except the Gharqad tree, which will not say, for it is the tree of Jews.*'

Allah's own book had singled the Jews out for special punishment. It was their destiny to be killed by the Muslims before the end of time – *which could not be very far away now*, he thought, *maybe even before I complete my project*. From the way Abu Umar had spoken recently with increasing passion, tears and lectures about the *Signs of the Day of Judgement*, most, if not all, were surely now present in the world. To Jimmy they were as glaringly obvious as the sun that rose from the east for all to see, even for the blind man and only those who had devils sitting in his eyes would not see the truth.

'Their own scholars, the orientalists, agree none have come close and no one will ever produce anything like this Book. That's why the Qur'an is greatest miracle of all, of our beloved Prophet upon him being peace,' said the *Shaikh*. 'And The Book tells us that *Jihad* in the way of Allah is the highest achievement for a Muslim.'

Jimmy wondered why his parents had never taught him any of this, despite asserting their Muslimness.

Abu Umar continued, 'That is why each line is called an *ayah*, proof of His Magnificent perfection. *Subhanallah!*'

Jimmy had been awake since before dawn. He had prayed *Fajr* as usual, with Abu Umar leading the group. Since then, Jimmy had felt swept up in the fervour. He felt the zeal and passion flowing into him through his chest like an underground river. He needed to take action to diminish the dammed-up pressure that would otherwise burst. He had to act to let the water flood out and make the desert of Islam green again, flush the Muslim people, the *Ummah*, out of its apathy and delusion. By his death he would achieve success, if he could bring the Golden Age of Islam to flower again.

Freedom! Before his blood hit the ground! Jimmy thought of the finality of that promise.

He felt like Majnoon, who had gone mad searching the desert for his lost beloved, Laila. Abu Umar had told him the ancient Arab love story, but the *Shaikh* told him that Jimmy needed to love Allah with more passion than Majnoon loved Laila. Majnoon had lost his mind and everything in the world in trying to find Laila.

Jimmy felt the heavy, white cataracts of Western appeasement had been cleared from his eyes. The milk of materialism had been precisely removed by the surgical strike of Abu Umar. He felt determined that Majnoon's love would no longer unrequited; the lover would achieve success, *Shahahda*, martyrdom. Allah loved those who sacrificed their lives in His way. Gladness filled him – at least he understood the meaning of his life, and relief now covered him like freedom. He knew now what it meant for the moth to self-immolate in the flame, as he would combust into the Light of Allah. He felt himself burn for Allah's sake so he could achieve *Jannah*, and defeat *Iblis*, Satan. He wanted to see Allah's face and join the martyrs in *Firdous*, the best of all the Heavens. The highest station a mortal could ever hope to achieve: an eternity of bliss. So Jimmy had worshipped his Lord with all his might and fervour late into the night, had sat up on his prayer mat crying, begging for forgiveness.

Finally, he knew what it meant to be a Lotus Eater. Abu Umar had confused him by accusing him of being one in the first study circle. Jimmy had no idea what a Lotus Eater was then, and even now he still was not sure, except he knew it was an old story about a nation that drugged themselves – a story that white people had told each other, a very long time ago. Dwayne had clarified things with him and explained the *Shaikh*'s intention was not to embarrass him. *This white woman with her stupidly blonde hair is still a Lotus Eater. She can't see the truth for shit.*

Since the first training session, Jimmy's mind had been channelled away from anger, frustration, and worthlessness. His emotions had been built up and channelled into a different direction. He felt as if he had managed to bridge the torrents of incapacity and disabling hatred to reach the hard, firm bank on the other side, which gave way to a clear vision. Especially when they showed him the videos of the rape and torture and the brutalisation of the Muslims in Iraq, Afghanistan and Palestine. Then the curtain of capitalistic confusion, the butter of blindness, and his self-serving selfishness had been challenged and destroyed. Dwayne's words still echoed in his thoughts. He did not realise it at that time, but he had started on the long road but fast-track to self-discovery and truth. He felt he was a well-travelled wayfarer on that road.

Now that he understood that he was no longer drugged by the *Kuffar*, he forced every molecule to believe, so that every autonomic chain reaction in his body sang the praises of Allah. He became fully acquainted with worship and what the expression *Islam is a way of life* meant. He had often heard Muslims use the phrase. In the nights he craved for *Fajr*, the Morning Prayer, and yearned after lunch for *Dhur*, the Midday Prayer, and lusted long before bed for *Maghrib*, the Sunset Prayer, and sighed during the tedious and prolonged training sessions to be alone for *Esha*, the Night Prayer. The nights praying alone were the moments that his mind imagined the time when he would be in Heaven.

For the first time in his life, Jimmy knew what it meant to be a Muslim. For the first time he had an identity, and felt he belonged. The world did not want him. Now he wanted nothing more from the world. It was a society that had robbed and cheated him of fair chances, and so made him live, swim and drown in Southall. His father worked in a foundry when he should have been a design engineer. His mother's hands had become rough and raw from years of sewing metallic buttons on jeans for fifty pence a pair during his childhood. It was a world that kept rejecting Tony for jobs, caused the brutal assault of Zoya, and the whole *Biradari* avoided her because of the taint.

They had put corrupt and greedy *Imam*s like Uncle Younis in charge of the Muslims: a Zionist plot that was succeeding all over the world.

His community, as a result, had been crippled and subjugated by the Jews into a form of indentured servitude, words he had recently learnt from Abu Umar. He would have his revenge on the *Kuffar* of this world. Especially those lowest *Kuffar* of all disbelievers: The Jews! *Al Yahud!* The Jews! The words rang in his ears as if they were the root cause of all evil. Jimmy did not know how, but he hoped that Israel would be destroyed somehow by his actions and he would avenge the decades of torture of the Palestinians and centuries of suffering of the Muslims, since the time that Cursed Race had created the Golden Calf.

Jimmy could now see what the *Shaikh* had meant when he told him that a poor Arab Bedouin called Rabia Ibn Amar, had stood bare feet on the carpet at the court of Chosroes, one of the greatest Emperors of all time, starving, having been lost in the desert. The poor Arab had told the Emperor of the known world: *Come away from the worship of created things, to the worship of the Creator of all things!*

Dwayne had explained to him that was like a semi-naked starving African teaching the President of the World a lesson. Or a Paki kid, from inner city London, defining his place in the world, his true purpose; awakening to that niche, and then achieving it.

'That's what frightens them so much. They are terrified of you!' Dwayne had said.

When Jimmy had asked why, Abu Umar had answered, 'They are petrified you will go to the court of the Emperor of today – Pharaoh – Nimrod – Herod – The President, and say 'Come away from the worship of *Shaitan* to the worship of Allah, or I will destroy you and your civilisation.' Because this is a Clash of Civilisations and there can only be one winner – Allah – and one loser – *Shaitan* and the Antichrist.'

Jimmy was made to understand why Tariq bin Zaid had burnt his ships when he landed on Jibr Al Tariq, now bastardised to Gibraltar. Why a Muslim general, whose name he had forgotten, rode his horse into the water of the Atlantic. He had held the Qur'an aloft in one hand and a sword in the other, asking the sea and sky to bear witness that the land had ended. He proclaimed that had there been more land he would never have stopped, until he took the true message of Islam to the end of the earth.

Jimmy felt acutely the pain of the Caliph of Baghdad when he had cried at the capture and abuse of a Muslim trading-caravan by the Hindu king. The Caliph had sent Mohammed Bin Qasim to free them, after the

King refused to release the Muslim women. The Muslim armies conquered Sind.

The Caliph had drunk and ate almost nothing, slept on the floor until the captives were released, and the honour of the Muslim women satisfied, such was the sense of responsibility and accountability to the Almighty on the Day of Judgement. Abu Umar had told Jimmy that a true Muslim leader felt the pain and suffering of each person under his care. Not like the politicians of today who stuff their faces with exquisite food from silver dishes and use gold taps in their toilets, like the Saudis, while other Muslims starve and suffer and are tortured and live pathetic lives of misery.

So Jimmy's life had metamorphosed beyond his own recognition. Time passed, as if stars had been born and died in the past ten weeks. Jimmy felt that Allah's will had finally been revealed to him. His years of wandering in the wilderness, like Majnoon for Laila, of pain and lonely rejection and humiliation and confusion, had ended. Majnoon had kissed the earth in confusion, hoping Laila would appear, and he had talked to her amongst the graves. Jimmy kissed the suicide belt before every training mission. The old stories swirled and mixed in his head like a whirlpool, full of the essential humours of life. Jimmy felt he had suffered like Majnoon, in the Muslim ghettos of London. There he had seen hopelessness pour out of the bricks he had huddled under, had grown up breathing that dust of despair. Those were narrow streets, where shame loomed darker than the shadows of the houses. For even though Jimmy had more money than he could legally spend, he had no official income. He had to keep up the pretence, and so he signed on for unemployment benefit, like everyone else he knew. The streets where he had grown up were always alien, because fear lived in every turn of the key on returning home. Jimmy remembered that fear, that even now made his chest pump, and made the muscles in his neck stand out like leather straps. What state would his family would be in? Would they discover his secrets? Would the police be waiting, crossed legs on the sofa, his mother feeding them chocolate McVities and *Chai*, crying into her *dupatta*?

In Jimmy's hood, *the woods*, hopelessness and the loss of youth reflected in the cold pallid eyes of his friends. They had teenage faces that laughed, but eyes that did not smile, even on warm summer days. Other children played cricket in the park, or ate a barbecue with their families, or enjoyed treats from the ice-cream van.

Jimmy thought of the *woods* as a place where despair and frustration were drunk directly from the water mains, and the promise of failure and rejection blew in like the wind from the salubrious suburbs. Mental illness followed physical, where the need in psychiatry grew in proportion to the delirium and conspiracy. It was as if illness was pulled out of the febrile fabric of brownness and otherness and alienation. Jimmy thought differently now had learned a language he had never imagined before since his time with Abu Umar. How his life had been weird, living in an alien city in the Paki curry colony. Except for the neon lights and pizza takeaways, it could have been fourteenth century Herat.

Just like the Balti Belt of Birmingham, where his cousins lived, the Muslim areas felt the same all over. They all had the ghetto stink. Those areas had the Alien-Rejected-Never-Part-of-British-Society smell that emanated like the sweat of the ghetto rudeboys of the inner city. That smell was familiar in Jimmy's nostrils: *Destined for Failure*. It had long ago swamped the smell of fresh coriander of his parents, and had never been replaced by the salt and vinegar of British society. At school, for the short time he had attended, it felt as if his teachers had shoved his nose into that same flower of failure every day, until his nose lost the power to smell the real world.

All through their teens, Jimmy and his friends had marked themselves as different. They realised they were failures, but they also knew they were not failing conventionally into rejection. They would be weird even in their old age, because they were a lost generation – lost compared to the success of their parents, who had emigrated and worked hard.

Their parents' uneducated eyes stared at the boys in his gang, uncomprehendingly. The drug-skinned eyes of their sons: his friends and little soldiers stared back without seeing the suffering of their parents, into some oblivion where they found no answers. Jimmy realised that his boys never looked up, except before striking at an opponent or before running for survival. Rare conversations with their parents ran out of topics, because they had nothing in common with their parents.

Jimmy knew the boys rarely spoke in more than monosyllabic grunts, even when pulling *Gorees,* white girls. He wondered why white women held such an attraction. It was more than a badge of honour or rank, or rebellion. There was something else, a self-worth, a verification that came with having a white girlfriend – even if mostly they referred to the girls as *My Bitch*, a status once achieved to be deprecated, an irony which he could now see. It made them feel special, even if it was a one-night stand in a hotel room, or back to her place. They had to call themselves Steve, Dave or John, but he knew it gave them a realisation that they must be worth something, for a white girl to be bothering with them.

We are lost from the British government's point of view too, he thought. *Never to be integrated, unable to speak English in a recognisable form.* Their language amalgamated and bastardised into English-*Mirpuri*-Black American-West Indian slang. *Bastards of Alum Rock*, thought Jimmy, as his cousins from inner city Birmingham proudly called their gang. *That's what most of my crew are.* Jimmy had named his patch 'The Rock; in their honour, since they had inspired him in his early teens.

He had seen the *cuzees* – as all his youngsters called one another, changed from cousin – grow into the drug empire of Birmingham. The very few that made it to university came back and opened a post office, or, at best, an opticians but still could not remove the speech impediment that gave away their Rock roots away as clearly as if they had been branded onto their foreheads.

Not me, thought Jimmy. *I have a date with Destiny, as Abu Umar said. She will be my lover. She will lift me should my legs buckle, and carry me undeterred to my goal: the* houris *of Paradise. Time is my witness, as I give myself body and soul to Allah for His pleasure and glory. I will give myself as a sacrifice and be a martyr.* He now understood what the ghosts of his ancestors had said to him all those years ago in the heat and dust of a Pakistani graveyard, and again recently during Abu Umar's sermon at the mosque. *Come home, O Shaheed of Islam!*

He would trigger the bombs: become a suicide bomber. He would not only fulfil his Destiny, but would turn the course of history of the whole Muslim *Ummah*, and the world forever. Jimmy's name would live until the end of Time. More importantly, for the first time in his life, before his blood hit the ground, Jimmy would be free.

Before my blood hits the ground. Free from pain.

CHAPTER 21

Marin County, San Francisco
The car caressed the tarmac as the road hugged the bends in the hills, braking hard before each tight turn. Raju did not glance at the spectacular views of the Freemont hills across San Francisco Bay. Discipline entrenched by years of practice did not help control his hands or feet much today, as he thrashed at the wheel and pedals. The Mustang Coupe 66 had been a *special year*, he had been told by the 'All-American Classic Cars' dealer. He had been assured it had an industry first, a torque box, which meant better handling. The crimson paint seemed more important to him, however, although he would usually not have bothered about such trivialities. Today it became all-important, because he had heard it was her favourite colour in cars. Despite his years of longing for a Mustang since he had been a schoolboy in Lahore, he had, up until yesterday, only allowed himself a Toyota Corolla.

Raju had to be inconspicuous, and although most programmers drove flashier models in Silicon Valley, being deep undercover and an operative of Generals Kafeel Khan and Roop Pratap Singh, answerable to Amit Bahadur, meant he could not take any chances. Raju thought of his brother, the computer hacker who had burst into Amit's boardroom in Mumbai, and had also joined *Jaish*. He smiled as he thought of the codename Amit had given him: *Om Shanti Om – May the Almighty keep the world in peace*. Raju – his codename was pagan in origin. He would never have uttered such uniquely Hindu words normally. *What an irony, what a mixture Amit is*, he thought. *Just like life... mixed up. That's the paradox of life.*

Amit had not sent Aashriya to California for Raju to fulfil his fantasy; she carried the codes that would activate the Alpha Ansar. He knew the codes would give him instructions on how to awaken the sleepers. Most had been hidden in key strategic positions deep undercover, and others had been bought in the army and defence forces, but he did not know who they were or where they worked. Or, more importantly, how the bombs would be triggered. He knew for sure that he would be involved, and for him there could be no escape. He expected none.

Raju's thoughts soared like the road that he raced up as he climbed into the verdant hills. He had achieved his treasured ambition – to drive a Mustang. He had dreamed of tearing, with the roof down, through the green of the richest place on earth, the capital state of the world. So now he blurred the coupe through the Californian hills. These had been things he had dreamed of, but had not allowed himself the luxury of imagining that one day they would come true, while he was in Aitchison College, Lahore.

Perhaps he could make an impression on Aashriya herself. He had had visions of her, and had whispered sweet little *Gulab Jamans* to her pictures in his dormitory every evening, long before she had become The Queen. He remembered how his sleep-chastened, fitful nights had often become spastic with tumescence, hot and sticky more than usual, because of her presence in his dreams.

Raju's hands slipped on the wheel as he pulled up to her drive. Security, ever-present as always, challenged him. Indian movie fans and paparazzi stood grouped outside like gundogs to the prey; they could track the faintest whiff of a star, and Aashriya left a trail like no other. Nothing about Aashriya Aarzoo Romano could stay secret for long.

The gates whispered open, each half sliding along its well-honed path; the security kept the gathered crowd at bay, as Raju cruised through. He drove at a mild speed and reached the house in a couple of minutes.

Aashriya came out, like a gossamer breeze. She walked in front of the glass-fronted house, as the clouds gathered in the late afternoon. The lights inside twinkled like a fairy castle. He got out and sidled past her guard, and before the other security men could catch up, Raju made sure he opened the car door. She smiled and floated onto the seat. He saw the look of surprise on the faces of the guards.

'Hi – Raju, isn't it?'

'Yes, yes. How – did Amit?'

Aashriya laughed and nodded. 'Of course Amit!'

Raju rushed around to the driver's side; driving on the other side now seemed as natural as the muffins and pancakes he had had for breakfast, at his company in Silicon Valley. He smiled as Aashriya waved her personal guards away. She waved an imperious hand, an empress sending her praetorians back to the barrack room.

Despite the wave, Raju saw a man who seemed to be the head of security say something – a thickset man with multiple rolls of flesh tumbling over the collar of his blue blazer, his red tie made too short by his buffalo neck, his bald head glistening. He mouthed saliva into his hand held transceiver, and a black sedan materialised from behind the house spraying grit as it turned the corner. It followed Raju; he looked in the mirror and saw the sunglasses of the occupants reflecting the setting sun. They wore the same emotionless expression, moustaches blending with black shades. Their hulking frames diminished the space inside the sedan.

'Come on! Otherwise we'll have them snapping at our heels all night,' said Aashriya. 'They'll get us, and then there will be nothing to do.'

Raju grinned, and gunned his foot on the gas pedal of the Mustang. He screeched the turn in the long twisting driveway, and cursed as the pebbles sprayed up onto the paint of the car.

'Shit, the gates,' he said, as he noticed the huge white gates with their intricate mock baroque design were closed against them. *Mock, like so many things in this country*, he thought, and thrust the car faster as he approached the long straight drive towards the gates.

Aashriya giggled, and looked at him. 'Go on then – I dare you!'

'Oh you should never do that, Malika.' He pushed the pedal to the limit. He smiled at how he addressed her as The Queen. He had not seen any flicker of response – *an all too common an occurrence to her*, he thought. *I've got to be careful not to become one of the usual fawning men she must get so sick of.* He jerked the car on the clutch so it made more noise than speed, accelerating intermittently, ensuring that the security guards at the entrance would see and hear them coming.

'They won't open. Not without Kaloo's say so.'

'They will. I bet you.' He immediately realised that Kaloo must be the head of security, and he had seen why the man was nicknamed 'Blackie'.

'I know them. They won't. It's more than their jobs are worth.'

'I bet you they will. Accept my challenge?'

'Okay – one wish. If you get them to open,' said Aashriya. She threw her head back and laughed, just like she did in the movies. *So it is not all acting*, he thought.

'Stand up!'

'What?'

'Stand up and wave your scarf,' he said, and jolted the Mustang so it sprayed more pebbles onto the paintwork. *As long as I impress her it will be worth it. Oh God, please let this work!*

'Wave my scarf?' she asked, standing now in the car.

'Yeah, wave it as hard as you can above your head, wave both your arms! They have no choice but to let us through. They don't know that I'm not crazy.'

'They won't do it. I know I've ordered them before.'

'That time they didn't think you were about to die.'

'What?'

Raju raced along the straight drive, praying desperately they understood his threat. If they did not open the gates, he would smash into them. He mouthed, 'Open! *Open!*' through gritted teeth and cursed the bravado and his showboating. Within seconds it would be too late, and he would not be able to brake in time even if he wanted to.

He wondered what mad evolutionary pressure of selection had allowed through this unrequited need to impress women, even in the face of almost assured self-destruction. He knew if he did crash into the barrier he had better not survive. Dying instantly would be far better than quaking before Amit, answering questions of what he had done to Amit's beloved Aashriya. He recalled Amit's words on the secure line. 'If you bend one hair on her head even backwards, then I will chop your legs and feed them to the dogs.' Amit never felt averse to using corny Bollywood threats. 'David Gul can have the rest of you!'

Raju shuddered but he had to impress Aashriya on his own terms, even if it meant David's dogs scrunched his balls. His brother, *Om Shanti Om*, would also not survive, if Raju messed up this meeting and contradicted orders from Amit. He had been told to get the PDA from Aashriya. The old Mughal philosophy that the whole family should pay for the crimes of one of its members was not lost on the dons of the underworld, but Raju was determined David Gul would never get the chance to turn inquisitor on him. He had the pill, the last-throw emergency vial secreted on him at all times, if he became desperate; but that would be a hideous sin. He had been told the suicide pill would have the sweet scent of almonds, but he knew it would be bitter with regret. He wondered if the taste of cyanide would be anything like Battenberg cake. Whatever it tasted like, it would be better than meeting David Gul again in this lifetime.

Raju pushed the pedal down again, and the Mustang roared and skidded pebbles into the immaculately manicured borders. He saw Aashriya grin, and he felt the thrill of his heart bang against his ribs. His usual secret life felt humdrum, because this was the excitement he had long craved.

Raju glanced at Aashriya; her hair became a dark river flowing behind her. She looked like a wraith, writhing as the wind rushed through her hair and fluttered her black silk shirt. Unfixable to a continent, an eternal and universal desire, a testosterone-inspired instinctual beauty. She held her scarf aloft, candyfloss pink, one hand at each end, waving it like a personal banner. Her naked arms glowed in the setting sun.

Raju drove erratically, braking and speeding up again. He attracted the attention of the guards at the gate, so there could be no doubt who stood waving in the car, fluttering like a bird of Paradise. The black sedan followed, braking hard intermittently and keeping a wary distance, but always within touch. The guards at the gates scrambled, with their walkie-talkies gripped tight. Their eyes flitted to each other; none wanting to take responsibility for stopping the Mustang. Now Raju could see their faces, their eyes rabbited onto the car. The guards pushed each other, getting out of the way. His grip tightened, his knuckles pale on the steering wheel. 'Sit down, now.' Aashriya seemed not to hear him, but continued waving, as if filming a song and dance number. She started singing and swinging her hips:

Woh Yaar Hai Jo Khusbhu Ki Tarah
Jiski Zubaan Urdu Ki Tarah
Meri Shamo-raat Meri Kaynaat Woh Yaar Mera Saiyyan Saiyyan
Chal Chaiya Chaiya Chaiya Chaiya

'Sit down!' He pulled her arm, recognising the hit Shah Rukh Khan hit song. He glanced at the road, and then back to her.

She shot him a glare. 'Ow, why?' she said.

'Bloody God damn! Bloody God damn!' He regretted taking this crazy risk, but it was too late now. He let the clutch out, made the car roar so that the noise reached a crescendo, gulped a huge lump of air and raced straight for the middle of the gates. He saw a security guard, the shock of disbelief on his face, turn and race for the release button, and the gates started to slide open. *I still won't make it!* thought Raju. He saw the black sedan following, afraid of his erratic driving. Obviously trying to avoid inflicting damage on the peerless and priceless Aashriya.

The gates slid open smoothly as they reversed on their automatic path, hushed electrical motors lifting them over a familiar movement in the gravel. *I can't get through the gap!* He glanced over to Aashriya. She still had a smile on her face – *must be caught up in the excitement* he thought. He pushed his foot down hard. *No choice now, or I'll look like a failure, and she'll think I didn't have it in me...*

The guards looked at him wide-eyed, and scattered as they realised he meant to gun them with his car. He bore down ever faster onto the gates. He could see fans and paparazzi scatter on the other side, like a covey of wives in a harem on the entrance of an unannounced man. He smashed through the centre of the partially-opened gates, and the metal screeched in protest, chewed crimson paint and spat sparks. The car howled through the gates and left one hanging at an angle. Aashriya screamed, and covered her head with her hands. *I bet she thought I wouldn't do it!* he thought, and almost smiled. He controlled the car before reaching the steep drop of the Marin hills, stole a glance in the mirror, saw flashes of the photographers. No other car had yet rounded the corner, but he knew a series of black security sedans and the paparazzi would follow.

'Are you hurt?' he asked, not caring that she might hear real concern in his voice. Sweat beaded his face, made his hands slippery as he tried to slow his heaving chest, and calm the nausea that burnt his throat.

Aashriya threw her head back and laughed, moved some silken strands out of her face, while the other hand at her neck held her scarf in check.

'I know a place on the hills overlooking the Bay –'

She laughed again before he finished, and nodded. She looked at him, this time into his eyes, and his heart felt as if it had never contracted-expanded before today. Raju felt he would take his heart out of his chest and place it on a silver platter in front of her.

*

The Mustang received long looks on the small Californian roads, in a land where strange was commonplace and the normal became garish. Although he had been accepted by them and infiltrated them, Raju had never seen such weird people in Asia. They reached the restaurant perched high in the hills. He had often sat outside on the raised terraced area, and dreamed of Aashriya. Of how he would sit with her there, say clever things to impress her, charm her until she had no choice but love him.

Raju helped Aashriya climb over the crunched door on the passenger's side of the Mustang. He wished he did not have to let go of her hand as she stepped down, but pulled his hand away, for fear that she would feel the throbbing pulse that surged through his body.

They approached the balcony area; a terrace on stilts that was raised high on the hillside. Raju pointed her to the corner table near the wooden fencing. A few people milled about inside, but only one other couple sat on the balcony. They spoke loudly. She wore grey cashmere and supported Jessica Alba sunglasses – *her daughter's probably*, thought Raju. The man had a blue shirt with a horseman on it, and a red sweater hung over his shoulders.

Raju loved days like this, misty and close with the evening sun breaking through intermittently. The mist hung like a pall over the Bay, and shrouded most of the Golden Gate Bridge. The foggy air cleared in patches and the Bridge showed her face for a moment, as if she was lifting a veil for her intimate-beloved. A lady of grace, lissom and coy, she almost called and cooed her charms to him since he had first seen her in the flesh. On his arrival to San Francisco he had insisted on turning the picture-postcard images that had lain fomenting into dreams of Californian success, into a reality. So he had made his friend take him straight from the airport to see the 'Golden Lady', as he called her.

The manager came over, 'Ah Raju. How are you sir? The usual?'

Raju nodded. 'Two,' he said. They sat in silence, the mist thicker, surrounding them like a poncho. It made him feel intimate, so he became self-conscious now. He tried not to think about how he looked. He did not bother to hide his sweat, but let his breath out slowly, silently. He stared at the mists around the Bridge. 'These great monuments belong to us all. Not just America.'

'Like the *Buddhas of Bhamiyan?*' she asked.

He looked at her surprised. 'I was thinking more of the Taj Mahal, but yeah, the Buddhas if you will…'

He turned away again as a smile played at the corners of her mouth. The manager brought the crockery pre-warmed. The pale golden liquid without milk filled the cups, its colour virginal in the undecorated white porcelain. Pure, unadorned except for cardamom pods, which floated on the surface; three in each cup, like green oases in an amber desert.

'I love it when she's covered in mist. The Lady wears her veils well, don't you think?' he said, still looking over the Bay with narrowed eyes. He had her now where he had endlessly dreamed of sitting with her. Where he had so often sat alone and caressed his gaze over every curve of the bridge and wondered about Aashriya, for so many morns and noons. He could picture the Bridge without looking and he knew well the waters that churned around her skirts, but The Golden Lady surprised him still with the variety of her shades. He imagined the sea changing colours depending on The Golden Lady's tempers – some days bright and fresh, choppy when the breeze ruffled her hair and she sang to him, on others murky and dark. He loved it when her waters turned unfathomable. Turquoise in some areas, green and blue in others and white and grey on the spume. He felt she turned brooding and moody on those days, awaiting her beloved's return with gifts of adoration. Raju clenched his teeth at the loss of such a work of art from the world. His muscular jaw tightened, as he thought about what he would have to do.

Some Alpha Ansar, he realised, would be activated in virtual worlds where codes and secrets became multilayered, through the essential whiteness of the Internet blizzard into the depths of permafrost, hibernating until the resurgent Islamic spring. Others would be mere messengers or decoys. Devious methods had been employed, loops of deceit built within tissue structures flown on crystal wings, so that the controllers could see immediately if any turned traitor. Or, if their operatives were tailed, the fibre-optic cables of the world web would lose alphanumeric configuration, before the real implementers did what was necessary. Cells operated in isolation, and each man or woman knew only their immediate cell family. Divorced from the extended family structure. Raju did not know the location of the back-up cells, or who was an Ansar. He knew Amit would be furious at what had happened today, that he had dared to take Aashriya away without guards, that he had risked their whole project on a whim. Raju knew he would soon be dead with countless others, and he had pined for her for too long to give up this once in a lifetime opportunity.

Raju tore his eyes away from the bridge. Unlike Aashriya, he could stare at the Lady as long as he liked. He felt regret that the Bridge would be destroyed, a work of genius. He wished they had not targeted San

Francisco. People could be replaced, but never the Golden Lady of the Bay.

'Just how I love it,' Aashriya said, pulling him out of his reverie. He looked at her. 'How long have you known?' she asked

'I've been drinking it like that since College, since I read you did...' He looked down into the cup.

'Did you know that crimson was my favourite colour in cars?' she asked.

'Not much of it left on the car,' he said and she laughed. He joined in, his thoughts of what he must do now internalised.

'It's still a great car, even though it's mangled.' She took a sip of tea delicately, with more grace than he thought possible.

'I couldn't arrange a whole forest canopy, even if I had wanted to,' he said.

'No – don't – this tea – this view, this wildness that surrounds us... it's immortal.' She closed her eyes, and breathed deeply. The honeysuckle climbed the wooden edges of the balcony, and wild rhododendrons and bougainvillea grew on the hillside and assailed the senses. She peered over the rail of the balcony.

'I love that it's so isolated.' She sipped more tea. 'I could never do this in India, or even here mostly. Thank you – the memories will be everlasting.' The dying sun came out, dropped gold pearls and maroon and purple corals into the Pacific Ocean, where its rays met the water.

Raju leaned back in his chair and played with his cup.

'You're not like that at all. So natural,' she said, 'not like Amit. You know all about his rooftop gardens, then?'

'Although I don't smash Mustangs through metal gates everyday.'

She laughed; the echo reverberated within him, full of feminine melody. 'Do you trust me?' she asked.

He did not answer, and she stretched out her arms in feline slow motion.

'I like your simplicity. No food, nothing – just *Chai*,' she said.

He shrugged, implying he could be nothing else. 'Well, babe, I ain't much of a poet,' he said, allowing some of his Americanism to slip in.

'You know how it all it seems, everything that happened?' she asked, and after a small pause and she looked at her cup, played with the handle as he did with his. 'Amit tried that. And his poetry is even more lovely than his calligraphy. He's so talented.'

'Yeah, well – he trusts you, and he's the boss.'

'No one does –'

'Except The Boss.' He stopped playing with the cup, suddenly serious. 'Do you have it?'

'What?'

'The codes,' he said.

'They're in the PDA, in my bag. Do you want them now?' She glanced down at her Valentino handbag.

'No. Later.'

'Aren't you worried about kidnapping the boss's girl?'

'Are you? He loves you.'

'Does he? Do you?' Her grey eyes were made brighter by the dying sun's last rays.

The bridge sparkled with innumerable fairy lights. Raju laughed; *it must be so obvious* he thought. He looked back to the Golden Lady. 'Since I was fifteen,' he muttered.

'I don't mean it, you know.'

'What?'

'The pain I seem to cause.'

'At least you know that,' he said, suddenly bitter and jealous of all the others that dared to suffer his sweet love-hurt.

'I didn't ask for it.'

'Even when you won Miss World?'

'Every blessing has its curse, you know.'

'Bless me with your curse, then,' he said.

She took out the PDA device; he leaned forward pulled it out of her hands. 'I can't work it, or even switch it on,' she said. He noticed her watching him.

'I know, but there are eyes everywhere.' He looked around. The American couple seemed to be busy kissing, and did not pay any attention to them.

'What's going to happen, Raju?'

'When?'

'You know when! What's the rest of your codename? Raju is code, isn't it?' she asked.

He half laughed. 'If I knew all the answers...' *No harm in her knowing a little, what could she do if she knew a few details?* he thought, and said, 'All of us, the operatives, are named after Shah Rukh

Khan's films.'

Aashriya clapped her hands with delight, and grinned.

'Really? So your full code name is *Raju Ban Gaya Gentleman*?' she asked, immediately understanding.

'There's *Don, Mein Hoon Na*, and my brother is *Om Shanti Om*!' He brushed his hand in front of his face, pushed his hair back and waited for her laughter to quieten.

'What – which poor bugger is called *Dil wale Dulaneya Leh Gayenge*?' She held her belly and let her laughter peal out.

'We just call her Dil, actually,' Raju smirked. 'I feel sorry for *One Two ka Four*!'

'Amit's idea, of course?'

'Of course.' Now he could not help laughing with her.

'What's going to happen?' She leaned over to him, moved her chair close.

He felt dizzy as he breathed in, her perfume rare. He inhaled again; his nostrils flared and eyes closed. He felt as if he never wanted to smell anything else again. He kept his eyes closed as she put her head on his shoulder, and a shiver ran through him. He felt her reciprocate as she curled closer, her chin nuzzling his chest.

'I'm scared, Raju…' She moved her head up to his neck. Her hair brushed his face as jasmine overwhelmed him.

Her hair fell in wisps over her face – *like the mists that covered the Golden Lady*, he thought. *But although the Golden Lady is hidden, I know she's there. Where is Aashriya?* he wondered. *Who does she really work for?*

He tried to pull back from the brink. 'Your tea's getting cold,' he said. She ignored him. 'I'm sure some people must recognise you. We're getting looks from inside.' He nodded towards the large glass doors, which led to the inside of the restaurant.

'I don't care,' she murmured, closing her eyes.

'What if they take pictures?'

'What's – where is it going to happen, Raju?'

'Why are you worried? You leave in a few days.'

'So San Francisco is one of the cities?' she said. He did not answer. 'Wouldn't you care if I was upset?' She looked up at him. 'Wouldn't you protect me, Raj?'

'I can't protect myself,' he said, almost laughing at his situation, but unable to do anything except give in to her presence.

'Whereabout? Is it in the centre? How many cities?' She looked up at him again, her face drawing in the day's dying light, giving light out to his face.

Raju's head moved down to her face of his own volition. Her face came close, and her eyes pulled him into grey-green depths of mystique hiding mysteries of passion, her breath soft and full of violets. He started to say something but it came out strangled, an almost-squawk. His eyes caressed her blemishless skin, rested on her slightly parted lips. He drew in closer, pulled by the faithless promise. The hope of nectar in her kiss.

'Where in San Fran?'

'I don't know...' He barely managed to speak.

She snaked a lazy hand followed by a languid arm under his jacket, stroked his chest. He almost jerked away from her touch, and his panting became audible. Breath escaped his mouth in gasps. He felt like the decades-dry Mojave Desert, she the longed-for rain. He burned for her in verdant conflagration. She was the greenness of his desire, the culmination of his fantasy that would turn him into fulfilment. Her large eyes were grey-green, now. He felt his longing soar, as if she had become every woman he had ever wanted. He could hear the rain over the distant hills, more waiting to be born; his senses heightened to a new level, the physical melting. He became desperate to taste her.

'Do you trust me?'

He felt as if he had fallen off the balcony, floated into space off the edge of the world, drifted now into the timeless abyss for love-lost souls. He closed his eyes and wished he never had to open them; her breath enveloped him like a warm sea-blanket.

With a huge effort, he tried to let logic control him. He forced his arm to pull her hand away which had found its way under his shirt. She stretched up; her breath hit his face and smothered his will. Her nymph-like body felt supple as it curved over his. She brushed his lips with hers; she closed her eyes. He melted, kissed her back. She responded, and he drew her to him. He floated, a cosmonaut of passion, jet-propelled by desire.

At that moment the manager came onto the terrace. 'Cars – Raju – down the hill, cars – black sedans,' he said, gasping.

Raju sparked into action, pushed her away. 'Come on – we have to go.' He jumped to his feet, pulling her up with him, caught her by surprise. He leaned over the balcony edge and grabbed a ripe fig off a tree that grew wild on the hillside. 'Let's go,' he said. She laughed, straightened her hair.

Was it real pleasure in her face? he thought. *She's never had this kind of excitement.* She held the fig in both hands as if it were spun glass, her porcelain fingers curving around its pendulous body. They raced for the car, and he pushed her over the crushed door.

'*Areh*, where are we going?' she asked.

'Where do you want to go?'

'Away from here, anywhere.' She looked down the valley. 'Away from them.'

He could see three sedans rapidly climbing up the mountain road, but they had to slow down at every hairpin bend. He got into the car.

'Hey Raju! Hey –'

'Don't worry,' he said to the manager. He screeched the car into reverse, looked in his rearview mirror, and noticed motorbikes following the cars. *Must be paparazzi*, he thought. They rode in two man teams; one would be armed with long lens cameras.

'Bloody God damn! Bloody God damn!' he said, as he realised they had been seen. The motorbikes overtook the cars.

Raju raced the Mustang down the other side of the hill, away from the hunters.

'I've never felt so excited in all my life,' she said.

Glad you're having fun, babe, he thought. Did she think this was one of her movies and she would never come to any harm? She tinkled laughter, which flew at him like crystal daggers in his heart. He ignored her as he tried to keep to the unpredictable curves in the road. The motorbikes gained on them rapidly.

The rain started and within moments became a tropical storm, thunder crashing and echoing off the hills. The Bay was shrouded in a mantle of grey cloud. He swerved round the bends, barely able to change gears in time. She screeched in joy, throwing her arms in the air, and waved her scarf again. Raju thought for a moment he had lost his pursuers, as he threw the Mustang around another tight bend, but they roared around the corner, magnetised by his rear bumper. 'Aashriya, you'll get wet.'

'I don't care! Faster – faster!' She exhorted him to more manoeuvres as she kept turning and slapping the dash and clapping her hands, wide-eyed. He could barely control the car. It seemed to be reborn with the new rain and now it screamed and screeched under his thrashing feet and hands. He had not driven like this – even in his days of training, when they taught him how to drive in emergency situations, during his bodyguard duties for Amit Bahadur.

'I love it! I love it!' She laughed, and he too became caught up in her dancing-with-the-devil zeal. She held the fig in her hand with its patchy green and brown-covered skin, cradled its ugliness in her creamy palm, plump against her icicle-thin fingers.

Then she thrust it into her mouth, tried to shovel the whole of it in. The ripe fig splattered over her lips and face, the soft red insides dribbled down off her chin, and she laughed.

Raju looked at her; he could not help himself. His skin tingled all over. He tried to reach over to wipe the fruit from the pink petals of her lips. Then he noticed the bikes almost within physical touching distance, the pillion riders snapping photos, little packets of white light cutting through the darkness of the storm. He was almost beyond caring. He reached over to wipe the pulp from her chin and lips with his right hand. She giggled and licked his fingers.

Raju looked at her and missed the next turn. The car skidded out of control. He tried to compensate for the skid, but failed. He braked hard.

The motorbikes swerved and veered behind him. One went tumbling over, cartwheeling the riders. The car engine whined as he thumped the brake repetitively. He almost brought the sliding car under control, compensating for the skid, but instead the car slewed across the road into the bend and hit a glancing blow off an on coming car, which sent the Mustang into a spin. It slid over the edge of the cliff, down the precipice. Into the chasm.

CHAPTER 22

London – Sebastian's House

Jessica waited for Sebastian at the small table in his kitchen. He had invited her over to his house, and said he would cook for her. *How egalitarian, non-misogynistic of him*, thought Jessica. She wished she could have offered to let him cook in her house.

'Your place because it's beautiful, and my cooking, because it's excellent. Except that you'll have to come to my house because we're not going back to Birmingham just to cook,' he had said, and she had laughed in relief with him. 'Anyway, it's been ages since I've known you, but you've never been to my place in London.'

'How do you know my food isn't excellent?' she had asked him.

'I don't. It's really just an excuse to get you to come over.'

They had both laughed at this. Over the last few weeks, since her return from Baghdad, things had progressed at a rapid pace. Their relationship developed as if life were concertinaed into weeks, which would have made her anxious, except for the fear that she now suffered regularly since she had infiltrated *Jaish* and had become so aware of her impending doom.

Despite the fear, she was ever more determined to stay in *Jaish*, to keep up the pretence of being a Muslim. In some ways the acting had not been as difficult as she had initially imagined. She had easily become serious in the terror cell, her emotions regularly mixed into each other, blurring like a film speeded up. She had also managed to celebrate with them, but with more difficulty. Laughing at their successes during training was bearable, but rejoicing at their visions of the darkened dawn, which they predicted was imminent, had been almost impossible. *Shaikh* Abu Umar had told the others to treat her with more tolerance, since she had recently lost Hamid – although Jessica felt he wanted to add *she's just an emotional woman*.

'Sebastian... how much do you know about *Jaish*?'

He looked at her, stopped chopping herbs. 'I told you some things about them, before you went to Baghdad, but I probably understand their thinking more than I know about their exact activities. Why?'

'What did you do in the Damascus and Baghdad? I mean, are these people everywhere?'

'Damascus was beautiful. It's a magical city, so much peace in some places. It's a city of dreaming minarets.' Then his eyebrows knotted. 'Baghdad, well... *Jaish* are everywhere, like the virus they are. But some people believe they're really important to make the moderate Muslims build up immunity to extremism. Why?'

'You sound like you think they're necessary?'

'I'm saying that they have spread, they're taken some grievances, twisted them and now they grow, fed by the lack of understanding in the Muslim world and by the foreign policies of the West. The best we can hope for is that most people see the monster and fight against it, but it isn't that easy. Once people become infected by their bite, even seemingly sensible rational people who are emotionally vulnerable become like the minions of Dracula, unseeing, under the curse; and *Jaish* know how to cast many a spell.'

Have they cast a spell over me? she thought. Initially Abu Umar was intriguing, and his weird philosophy fascinating, but now even her pain and need to know about Hamid was rapidly drowning in the increasing breathlessness of *Jaish*'s audacity. Jessica fiddled with her hair under the scarf. *It's not as if he is going to see my hair, anyway*, she thought. *Why did I spend so much time tying it into an elaborate bun?* She had put on her light blue scarf, maybe because she remembered what the shop assistant had said about it highlighting her eyes. She wondered if it would ever become less fiddly, even second nature. *I have managed to convince* Jaish, *and although they were suspicious initially, they have accepted me, mainly because of Abu Umar. Why do I feel more nervous coming to see Sebastian?* She had continued to wear the scarf all the time when she was not in her flat and had told Sebastian the truth: it had made her feel protected in a way she could not explain, more spiritually aware.

Plain Jamila had told her what a great asset she was to *Jaish*, when Jessica had gone through the shortened training programme. Dwayne had let slip that *Jaish* were making exceptions in her case, and taking short cuts, on Abu Umar's insistence. *Maybe they have an imminent attack planned, and they need me*, she thought.

Despite the rare moments of comedy with the Afghan in the terror cell, Jessica felt her spirituality hijacked. She felt betrayed, caged in her worship. At the beginning, when she had tried discussing her spiritual experience that she had had in the circle, or tried reading the great Islamic thinkers, she had been told by Abu Umar that such things were dangerous. He had promptly banned her from reading anything other than what *Jaish* had provided for her.

Once Dwayne caught her reading a reviled text; he immediately pulled it from her. As Dwayne had snatched the book from her hands, she had felt the flower of enquiry wilt, and disillusionment flourished in full bloom, as she stared up at Dwayne's face in nursery-school wonderment. Abu Umar had stopped her attending any spiritual *halaqas* except for his circles, where he would expound his interpretations of Qur'an and *Hadith*. There was only ever one conclusion: destruction of the *Kuffar*, especially the Jews, and the end of their world domination – of banks, of media, of politics and power. Jessica felt certain that Abu Umar's end did not justify the means he had adopted to achieve it. When she had made a hint of dissension by expressing regret for the children that would die, she had been sent for special lessons the same day.

She was sent for remedial treatment to the Sisters-in-Charge. She had to live with her for a week, after Dwayne discovered another banned philosophical Islamic text. It made no difference when Jessica told him it was from the enlightened Golden Age of Islam. She had protested to Abu Umar, and nearly got herself thrown out of the group. She felt she had survived because Abu Umar needed a blue-eyed blonde distraction, who could blend into the crowd and go anywhere. Perhaps she was too deeply involved now, and the plans too close to the end for *Jaish* to risk disrupting the group.

Jessica felt glad she had come through the re-education programme. She remembered how she had to agree politely with the dull and increasingly boring Sisters-in-Charge, Plain Jamila. *No crime to be plain*, Jessica thought – *but to be so rigid… surely that wasn't part of the prerequisite to be Sisters-in-Charge for an international terrorist organisation?* When Jessica had first gone to Plain Jamila's house, her corrective teacher had sat on a dark sofa in a brown scarf, with her beige clothes covered in *chapatti* flour dust. She had apparently just finished cooking the evening meal for her four children. When Jessica had finished her first remedial lesson, both sat sipping tea made from one-cup tea bags with skimmed milk. Sisters-in-Charge informed her that her life was difficult as a mother and a *Jihadi*, and that she had serious worries about her second daughter's school next year. Jessica should be grateful at this unique chance of martyrdom, which was an once-in-a-lifetime blessing. Jamila had married late, she said, because of the Islamic studies she had undertaken in the university to become a scholar. Jessica remembered her face, the deep crow's feet, the buckteeth and greasy skin with spots, which obviously had not resolved despite four pregnancies. The Sisters-in-Charge's commitment had never wavered; Jessica admired her resolve, but thought about her children. She must know that by living in London suburbs, they would all be affected when the bombs went off. Jessica wondered if it was a price worth paying for her as a mother – just another sacrifice.

How could this softly spoken Plain Jamila with lines on her upper lip weigh up and balance her life, menopausal fluctuations, and the *Jihad*? On Plain Jamila, the full flush of menopause was cruel in its verdant virility. Maybe because of the lack of similarity, Jessica felt unsure if she could ever take the Sisters-in-Charge into her confidence and try to get her to help stop the bombing. Plain Jamila had an innocence of belief and a misguided simplicity in her sincerity of action. In the end, Jessica decided against saying anything. She thought it unlikely Plain Jamila would agree, and, anyway, it was perhaps even more unlikely she knew enough details about the plans of *Jaish an Noor wass Salaam*.

Instead, Jessica had nodded sagaciously and complied with Sisters-in-Charge's reductionist commandments and redirection. At the end of her week of reprogramming, Jessica gave her a big hug and kissed her spotty cheeks, before Plain Jamila sanctioned her release into the community of *Jaish* and returned to the safe house of the cell. After a week confined with Plain Jamila, seeing Abu Umar, Dwayne, Jimmy and even the Afghan again felt like fresh flowers. Jamila – the beautiful one, she had told Jessica – had been a gorgeous baby, at least so her mother had informed her. Jessica knew she would make an excellent subject for a documentary. *If only I can get past her gargoyle-ugly madness, maybe one day I will tell her story.*

She glanced at Sebastian to see if he noticed her distance, but he was busy with the preparations. *What am I doing here?* she thought. *Should I be risking Abu Umar's anger by not asking his permission to come and see Sebastian? They told me to act as if everything's normal, so here I am, seeing my friend.* She pulled at the scarf again, and thought she could see how it might make some women feel more spiritual, more private. She had also worn the scarf on the weekend trip home, but had taken it off before seeing her parents.

'Do they always leave suicide videos?' she asked.

'You're a bit grim... why all this death and destruction, all of a sudden? I mean, I could understand it in the beginning, after Hamid, but now...I thought we had something, Jessica.' He turned away from her, and started kneading the dough.

'It's not you, Sebastian, honestly. You said I could ask you anything, and you know things I don't.' She wished she could show him more open affection.

He shrugged. 'They usually do leave suicide videos, but recently something has changed... ' Jessica saw his muscular arms become taut, as he pushed the dough hard,

'There are some rumours that *Jaish* are thinking of new tactics and now they want to spread terror, faceless fear, so some of their operatives haven't recorded anything. If you don't know who's attacking, from where and why, then that's even more frightening. No one is a terrorist. Every man is a terrorist.'

'I don't understand so much of what's happened recently, and it's till not making much sense. I thought they would want their names to live on in Ever Lasting Glory as the saviours of Islam?'

'It's on both sides. When you demonise a people you can do anything you like to them, their families, even their children, because they're no longer human. One side calls the other terrorists and uncivilised, undemocratic barbarians, and the other calls them *Kuffar* back – which more or less translates as the same thing.'

'So it's a fight to the end, then? No way out?'

'I don't believe that, thank God, and neither do most Muslims. I think *Jaish* is planning something really big; there's a buzz on the streets, and in the mosques. The trouble is, the world has never imagined an extremist, violent organisation of this size, sophistication and power. They are unlike anything that's gone before in history.'

Jessica shivered and crossed her arms and legs. *How do I tell him I'm part of that plan?* 'Do you need a hand with anything?' she asked, because she did not know what else to say.

He splashed a measure of Orvieto into a glass. 'Sure you won't have some?'

She fiddled with her scarf and crossed her arms. As usual, her thoughts turned to the terror cell. She wondered if they were watching and listening now, even in Sebastian's house.

I still don't know the truth about Hamid. So many times Abu Umar had teased and tantalised her with shards of information, which convinced her he did know about her fiancé, but now in last few days she had started thinking that *Jaish* knew nothing more, or would not tell her the truth. Abu Umar had promised to tell her yesterday. As usual, when she had raised the issue last night, he had answered with another question: 'What do you think, Jessica? What does your heart tell you?' She had sighed and repeated her parrot declaration that she did not believe Hamid could have committed such a heinous crime, and that he could only have been an innocent victim. Abu Umar had sat her down in her room, and brought in a cup of tea made by Dwayne, looked her in the eyes and said, 'Yes, Jessica, you're right…'

'Right – what?' she had asked, her frustration growing.

'Because you have been faithful and a true servant of the *Deen*, the faith, and *Jaish*, I will tell you this only once.' She felt he would have reached out to her put his hand on hers if he could. 'Hamid was not the suicide bomber.' He paused, and looked out of her open bedroom door into the living room where the others waited for him to lead the *Esha*, evening prayer. She did not reply, but stared at him a long while, during which he fidgeted.

'It's time to pray. You can pray on your own, tonight,' he said. He looked at her for a moment, and almost smiled. Finally she had thanked him, not knowing what else she could do. She did not feel comfortable. She had cried for much of last night, as much for her predicament as for Hamid's loss. Did Abu Umar lie to hide his guilt and Hamid's complicity, or to assuage her feelings? She could not be sure.

Jessica felt as if she had condemned Sebastian as well. They had managed to meet fairly regularly since she had moved to London, and each time she wanted to tell him something, share some of the guilt so that maybe he would help her feel less trapped, but each time she felt unable to draw him into her complicity of terror. She feared he would not be able to help, but he might end up being disgusted and hating her, and she would lose him.

Sebastian put some olive oil and tomatoes into a pan, and turned to her. 'It's great you've got this new job down in London,' said Sebastian. 'I've finished most of my work in Birmingham, so I'll be back home too.' He looked at her carefully. 'You look different, somehow.'

'How? Apart form the scarf? You're still getting used to me wearing it.'

'Perhaps.' He walked over to the cooker and put some pans on the stove.

'Oh – I've been meaning to give you this since I got back from Baghdad, but what with the move to London and everything I keep forgetting.'

'What is it?' he asked, as she leaned into her bag and carefully took out the tile covered in paper and bubble-wrap. 'I know you're interested in these things.'

Sebastian unwrapped it carefully. 'Thanks. It's lovely.' He picked up the tile, and turned it over.

Jessica took out a wrought-iron plate holder. 'Here. I bought this for you to place it on.' She took the tile off him and carefully placed in on the kitchen worktop, so it rested at an angle on the holder. It had been smashed into a few large pieces, and had been wired together. It had fine delicate decoration, which became abstract patterns, a circle formed around a central sulphurous flower. The blue glaze had thinned in some areas, baked into a turquoise in other places, exposing in patches a pale copper green. Dust of centuries had pockmarked the face and scoured it in spots. Two cracks ran down the face of the tile. They almost converged in the centre, before they rivered and flowed away, divergent again. Small blotches of the authentic red showed through, exposing the original earth. Dots formed on it.

She saw him staring at the tile; she wondered if he could see what she saw every time. The terracotta spots, for her, marked Mosul, Baghdad and Basra. The red clay, the primordial earth of humanity, the first map of society revealed itself to her. The two cracks seemed like the Tigris and Euphrates, the lifeblood of the civilisation. The tile revealed an ancient history.

'I was filming all over, so didn't have much chance for mementoes.'

'Is this from Ur?' he asked.

'It's from Samarra, from the mosque,' she replied, hoping that he might say something because of the well-known controversy and rumours that had surrounded the destruction of the mosque. Maybe he would reveal some secrets of *Jaish*.

'I should have known. But I've seen the like in Ur.'

'It's easy to confuse, they have some very similar in the ruins of Ur. They still make them in the same way, paint them by hand.'

'It's amazing that it survived the journey. For a moment, I thought you had been smuggling Iraqi antiquities.'

'Most of those have been looted already. This is just an old tile from the famous mosque, infamous now.' She tightened her grip on the coffee cup.

'I'll make some more,' he said. He put the holder in the espresso machine and pressed the button. The machine forced out a sound through gritted teeth, releasing the essential oils of the coffee, which filled the room. The rose scent of the floating candle on the worktop took on a deeper fragrance, as it mixed with the aroma of coffee. She sat down again and leaned forward with both hands on the table. Her head felt heavy, as the memories of her visit flooded back.

'I seem to remember something weird about that mosque in Samarra?'

'Because of the way it blew up? The Iraqis believe it could only have been a controlled explosion.'

'You mean someone blew it up deliberately?' he asked.

He picked the tile up and quickly put it down again, and stared at it with wide eyes as if it had been contaminated, as if the contagion of betrayal would jump out and bury itself under his skin.

'We were in a Baghdad, a nondescript area. Al Jassim – used to be a mixed area before the invasion began...' She looked away from him. 'I was interviewing people, making a programme about how life had changed for the ordinary Iraqi after Saddam. I was interviewing Mariam. Her husband had worked as a translator.'

Sebastian sat at the table. 'Is the same Mariam and her baby who were shot?'

'Yes.' She had told him Mariam's story, but not that she had tried to investigate how the ancient mosque at Samarra had been devastated. Most of the locals insisted that the Americans who had been guarding it could have been the only ones to set the explosives. The destruction of the mosque had led to huge internecine Shia-Sunni killings.

Sebastian served her coffee. Jessica was lost in her thoughts. He waited patiently, and she told him more details about Mariam's story. She did not tell him about meeting Abu Umar and how he had given her a number to contact in London, and that she had already infiltrated *Jaish an Noor wass Salaam*, undergone the training and joined the terror cell. Maybe she would have to become a suicide bomber.

Jessica continued sitting as he cooked. She became momentarily distracted as she watched his muscular arms stirring the pot in his plain white T-shirt. 'Why did you change into that?

'I always cook in a T-shirt,' he said.

'Why – because it shows your flat stomach and broad chest?' she asked, looking at the firmness of his pectorals, which contoured the soft cotton. 'You're showing off, aren't you?'

'No – because, actually, I can take it off, and I don't take the smell of cooking around with me for the rest of the day. Especially when I cook a Rogan Josh.'

When they both laughed it seemed spontaneous, not excessive, open-mouthed or braying. It was complimentary and without the artifice of flattery.

'Even the Rogan Josh is another Moghul legacy,' she said, remembering their conversation about the golden wine flask, *Chuski*, when he had visited her in her house. She stole another glance and saw him grimace as he saw something in the sauce, which he fished out. She stood to one side of him and saw the sinuous, masculine tendons in his neck stretch; she felt stirred by them, as if they were grappling hooks embedded within her vital organs.

How difficult would it be for her to leave, even today? She moved her scarf back slightly and wiped the sweat that had gathered under the front of its edge. What if she could never see him again? How much of her would she leave behind? What if he left... how much of her would he take with him? *Even though I have my reasons for infiltrating them,* she thought, *would he be disgusted by me joining the* Jaish *terror cell?*

Thoughts of her potential suicide and the annihilation that she would cause had now transformed into an unstoppable gargantuan force. Her fate seemed inevitable; the finality that she had pursued with such passion had gained a momentum of its own. She could see no way out of the terror cell, not without risking the lives of her family and friends.

Either that or the deaths of innumerable innocents, who surely could not share the collective guilt for the atrocities against Muslims, despite what Abu Umar had said. Whether she lived or died at the end sometimes seemed almost irrelevant. She could not be so arrogant, so selfish; it was her fault. She still did not have satisfactory answers to what had happened to Hamid.

Jessica knew she had to do something. She had to find a way to stop the bombing, or bombings, but she did not have enough information. It would be unforgivable if she acted without enough information, and precipitated the attack. *Where and when and how many?* she asked herself again. To be able to affect the course of the bomb, the direction of world history, she needed to be there on the day. Maybe she would be the trigger. Perhaps that would give her the chance to stop the bombing on the day. When she knew more she could act with some confidence, and keep the people she loved safe too. She could not be sure Abu Umar trusted her enough. *They have trained me,* she thought, *and they need me – otherwise why would they have tolerated me for so long?*

There was no way out of the suicide terror cell. She had to pretend, to shout the loudest at times, but also show some dissent at times, so they would not suspect. So that Holly, and Jessica's parents, would be safe. She especially wanted Sebastian unharmed.

What if I can't do anything on the day? she thought. What if *Jaish* had failsafe mechanisms and double triggers, or what if she was simply a feint to draw off the security services? What if Abu Umar had special powers to see into her most secret heart? She did not know what she could do when the time came. Would she even have the courage to stand? To go and meet death? To walk towards it with unfailing conviction, as if she could see in front of her not death and nothingness, but instead ever-lasting pleasures of Paradise? Like Jimmy? *Surely the path to heaven could not be built on the bodies of ordinary people?* she wondered. *How could Allah be pleased if thousands of innocents died?* Jessica had no answers, and there seemed no escape.

There can be no future with Sebastian, so don't get too close to him, she warned herself. She turned away from him so he would not see her gritted teeth and the bunched-up lines of her face, or the sweat that gathered on her upper lip.

Too late, Jessica. How can I not think of a future with him, when I care as I do for him? Too late. How can I not think of him when his thoughts become my slave-master, relentless in dominating my day, as if he's there sharing everything with me? I miss his smile before he leaves me, and his aroma threatens my nights and chases away my spirituality. He, like a considerate angel, comes as my darkness dawns anew, and whips the offended, loving Adam back into me. Too late. Far too late; I love him already.

Sebastian, still busy with the preparations, glanced at her and put on a caricature of an Italian accent, 'I – will – a cook – a – uh – the red Bolog – nese sauce.' He stirred the red mixture in the pan. 'Not – like – a – you ever taste-a before,' he said, bringing his fingers into a bunch in front of her in a classic Mediterranean way. 'We're going to have both, Italian *and* Indian.'

She laughed.

'No – no – no packet spaghetti, *hunh*? Real Modena people don't eat that stuff,' he said, waving a finger at her. 'Instead I teach – a – you how to make fresh pasta in – under – ten minutes.'

Jessica knew the story of his fresh pasta. She watched him roll the dough made from the particular wheat, which in turn grew in only a special part of Italy. He had told her the story, one of the numerous tales scattered like constellations amongst the conversations that seemed to contract the hours of the night. They had talked in a way that seemed to shrink time. Or sometimes time seemed to expand into the realms of the stars, when she was enwrapped in his stories and nothing else existed; when time lost track of itself and the nights often rolled into dawn. Jessica and Sebastian had swept each other up and mixed like deep currents into each other's lives.

Sebastian had been on a holiday-cum-sabbatical at Modena University and had formed a real friendship with one of the lecturers there, as well as with the local village baker. The baker had eventually trusted him his family's secret pasta recipe. He remained friends with lecturer and baker even now, years later. *He has such effusive charm,* she thought.

Jessica moved the bottle of Orvieto Abboccato to the side. He had opened it and taken a drink earlier, as a light aperitif.

'Oh, sorry. Do you mind me drinking?'

'No, no, yes. Well I don't know...' she said, unsure how she was supposed to respond, now that she had to keep up the pretence of being a Muslim to the external world.

'I suppose you do mind now that you're a good Muslim. A proper

Jihadi girl?' He laughed.

'So you think. But I'm more like you than you realise,' she said. She thought of the irony. *I called you a terrorist, but that's what I am. I have had to become a potential terrorist to get into* Jaish. *Is it worth it? It will be, if I can stop the bombs.* She funnelled her brow and puckered her lips. She could not stop herself from chewing the knuckle of her thumb.

If only he knew the truth of what I have become, what I am about to do, she thought. *Would he hate me? My stupidity? The impulsiveness? The rush to answers, as if all questions in the world have a logical, easily identifiable answer? Would he laugh at my naivety of being lulled into the dark, never-ending chasm of putrid, puerile promises of Abu Umar? He still hasn't told me what I really want to know about Hamid. Despite all that, I was right to infiltrate them. For Hamid and for myself. One day I'll make a documentary about this: if I ever live long enough.*

Jessica felt strength flow from her like a sailing ship, slipping out to sea in the dead of night, whispering away on the outgoing tide. She got up and held onto the worktop, leaned her head forward, and brushed her hair, which she imagined had escaped her scarf, back under her head covering.

What if Sebastian finds out? Should she admit her part in *Jaish*, just claim she had started doing errands, keen to find out what had happened to Hamid? She walked towards Sebastian but it seemed to her as if every joint clunked, stiff and painful. Sebastian had said she had 'grace of movement', which he had described so well on one of their previous meetings, but now that grace seemed to never have been a part of her. Jessica now felt like some deep-sea diver all geared up and about to get in the water.

'Are you okay?' he asked.

She felt as if someone had switched the air supply off. Ungainly, she walked to the fridge, poured some orange juice, and wiped her palms on her long skirt. *Bloody hell, he doesn't miss much, she thought.* 'Yes. Yes,' she said, 'just the heat of the kitchen.'

'And no basil – no oregano – no – a – nothing – just a little bit of garlic – I will allow you,' he said throwing his arms in the air.

She tried a smile but felt sure it came out as a grimace, canines bared. 'Anyway, I knew you drank when I first met you. No, not first – the second time I met you, and I used to drink then too, but I knew... '

'You weren't Muslim before.'

'Am I now? I don't know, Sebastian.'

'Neither do I know what I am. I've done a lot to get into places. Mecca, Damascus...' He looked at her and shrugged, which seemed full of pragmatism. 'Isn't that the same question everybody asks themselves about their religion? How much do I believe... am I a hypocrite?'

'Not everyone, but anyway...yes, but I agreed to come here and for you to cook for me today, and I know you drink.' She knew his drinking was irrelevant but she was not sure how to express her mixed feelings of guilt at deceiving him, or how to wrap up her desire about wanting a future with Sebastian. She felt certain that Sebastian could help her. Stop her walking into a catastrophe somehow. She opened her mouth, but her fingers shot up to her lips, and she pulled the lower one. She could not bring herself to tell him about the plot and the terror cell. 'We've come some way since we met,' she said instead.

'Some way, madam?' he said with a mock bow, eyebrows raised. He bowed like an Elizabethan courtier.

This time Jessica could not stop a smile, which became a grin, escaping her face and seeming to dance a jig in the charged space between them. She realised that his affection for her had simply continued to grow, despite her stupidies. In that innocuous comment and boyish gesture lay more emotion and evidence of affection than a thousand starry words. She felt he wanted her to say it.

'Some considerable way, actually, Mr S!' She smiled. 'Or sorry, I mean Dr S, sir.'

He smiled back. 'Really, Ms J? You do surprise me sometimes, you know.' Then he faced her and added in a soft voice, 'To you it could be Dr, Prof, or simply *Oi, You!* And I'll still be here for you.'

'The question is, how far are we going to go?' *This is it. I've said it now. Destroyed the moment, what if the magic disappears? Oh God why am I so stupid?* she cursed inwardly.

''Ow far? 'Ow should I know?' He laughed at his own accent. 'You gonna – wanna go out on another date with – a – me, Signorina?'

Well, at least that's something – he's shit at accents, she thought. 'I'd hardly call the aftermath of the train bombing a date,' she said. 'Even though we've been out lots of times since then, but we've never called them dates – that's all.'

Since the first meetings, they had managed mostly coffees and drinks snatched in between stretched lives. Jessica remembered each one with a grasping desperation. A rapidly growing affection, an almost-normal life jammed in between passing all of Abu Umar and Dwayne's crazy tests. During which they somehow managed to weave veiled and sometimes open threats to her family and to Sebastian.

Sebastian added tomato pulp from a bottle into the pan. 'Hey, that's cheating,' she said, 'I thought you were doing the real deal?'

'Yes it is. It certainly is, *ma cherie*.' He paused and looked up at her, '*Parce que* you should always cheat in life. Wherever possible *n'est ce pas ma petite poisson, ma belle cherie?* But not really cheating, because the tomatoes are from Napoli.'

'Now who are you supposed to be? Which chef?'

Does he really mean the sweet endearments, or is it the wine? One glass slurped dramatically, in an impression of Keith Floyd, showed his humorous, charismatic side. A side she had suspected he had right from the start, which he had gradually revealed to her over the past few weeks with a growing confidence.

Jessica remembered the last time she had spoken to Holly. She had asked many questions about Sebastian that Jessica had been unable to answer. Holly had asked her, why, after the first meeting, Sebastian had howled like a wolf. Jessica said she did not know.

Holly had asked her, 'Have you kissed him yet? How fit is he on a scale of one to ten?'

Jessica had replied, trying to be colloquial, 'He's whacked my Gorgeous-Geiger counter reading up to lethal, and man, it's juiced up and crackling like never before. George Clooney ain't got nothin' on him.'

'You need your volcano unlidding. It's been far too long. And don't use Hamid as an excuse. It's been months, and that's too bloody long,' said Holly.

'Look where that's got you then, eh?'

'Sorry, I forgot you're all religious now – but you've got yourself a sexy man and he fancies the French frilly panties off you.'

'We don't know that,' said Jessica.

'Oh, don't we? Why does he call you Angel Eyes and Caramel Lips for then, *huh?*'

'Well –'

'So sweet,' teased Holly.

'Yeah, actually, it's very sweet.'

'He ain't sweet, he's bloody sexy.' Holly let our peals of filthy laughter. 'Well, you got me thinking I need a hot man too.' Then she added in a calmer voice, 'Would you still be admiring him – I mean, no touching – if you hadn't gone all spiritual?'

'Maybe, maybe not.'

'You'd be all over him like cold cream applied to an arse on fire.'

'Look – I don't know.'

'Okay, okay!' Then Holly asked in a more serious tone, 'Do you love him, Jess?'

'Yes.' Jessica surprised herself by immediately answering.

'Yes – yes what do you mean yes?'

'You know what? I think I really do.'

'You sure? Can't be.'

'Guess what? We went for a drive and then walked in the Malverns and had a picnic that I never told you about, after I first met him. I think I must have been unsure what I felt for him then. Anyway, Sebastian knows I love afternoon tea, so he bought a little flask with him that he had hidden, and when we got to the clearing he poured me some tea in a porcelain cup. He brought the thermos out of the picnic basket and served me tea on the hill next to a stream.' Holly did not reply. 'What other man would be so thoughtful, so considerate?'

'Well, that's lovely.'

'It is, Holly,' Jessica said, stuttering the words. 'Please don't be –'

'I'm not, Jess. I mean it. But what you gonna do now that you've 'connected'? I mean, it should be easy, because you're so similar?'

How do I tell Holly that I haven't converted, she thought, *and that I'm involved in a terror cell? I couldn't tell her even if it was safe to do so – she'd call a psychiatrist.*

'Well, all I'm saying to you, in my own stupid way, is we all need someone special. And of course you can't forget Hamid, but it's time to move on, which I'm happy to say you are starting to do. All I'm saying is get on with it.'

'Everything might have been easier and different if Hamid hadn't taken that train.'

'Look, I'm sorry, but you need a good man like Sebastian. No one wins the lottery twice; you better get serious with this one.'

Jessica returned from her reverie by the hissing of the pot, as Sebastian added the mince. The wooden spoon clanged as he stirred. *We shouldn't even be here. I know, I know,* she told herself. *We shouldn't be alone together; that's what Abu Umar and Plain Jamila would say,* thought Jessica, as she fiddled with her scarf and pulled it forwards. *But I really need someone to discuss and talk with. I can't talk to Holly about suicide cells. She's right. I need Sebastian.*

What if Abu Umar and Jaish an Noor wass Salaam *succeed?* she thought. *What if they start doubting me? They already probably do.*

Abu Umar and Dwayne, who implemented most of his instructions, had tested Jessica over weeks since her induction. They had no reason to doubt her – yet. She felt certain that *Jaish* did not trust her implicitly – not because she was white but more probably because of her journalistic background. She had often, since joining the group, asked herself the same question: why had she really joined *Jaish*? Although she had had a spiritual experience, which had forced her along a meditative path that was not the reason for her infiltration, she had joined *Jaish* because of her quest to find out what had happened to Hamid; if he was the bomber. Once she had joined the cell, her natural journalistic inquisitiveness to find out more about *Jaish* had made her want to infiltrate them to their core. She had succeeded in that beyond her own imaginings.

Jessica's thoughts wondered back to the questions about Hamid which fevered her mind, the questions screaming themselves into a boiling screech in her skull. She went to the small downstairs toilet. She had to douse her face in cold water, but still her cheeks stayed as if scattered with strawberries. *How could I have been so trusting?* she thought. *Was Hamid really the suicide bomber?* I don't believe it. *Yet here I am, forced into potentially doing the same thing. Who would imagine it, to look at me?*

She came back into the kitchen, but had to turn away from Sebastian. She did not want him to suspect her rising nausea. How would she tell him she felt too ill to eat? She felt sweat gather in her hair, under her scarf. *What the hell do I do?* she thought. *Do they really mean to set off the bomb? What sort of bomb will it be?* She had heard whispers about chemical-biological-nuclear devices: cocktail bombs. *Could it devastate the whole of London? What about the millions of people? How many and where were they?*

'Excuse me, I need the loo,' she said, and left him cooking furiously. She went to the bathroom and washed her face again, took off her scarf and poured cold water onto her head, washed her hands and arms and then sat on the chair. She wished she knew an appropriate prayer.

I need help from somewhere, she thought. *Oh God, how can I escape the terror cell? What can I do to stop them? I can't just go to the police or the authorities, my parents, Holly, or even Sebastian.*

It had been made clear to her right at the beginning that there could be no turning back and at the first whiff of treachery her life and anyone she loved would be forfeit. *If I don't do something, then millions across London and the world will die.* The thoughts repeatedly squeezed her brain.

Now, Sebastian… what do I really feel for him? I have to face the truth and stop pretending I don't love him. They know all about him – Hamza had said Sebastian was also marked. Maybe Sebastian will know what to do? He seems so calm and in control. I can't just announce it after dinner, over coffee!

Jessica did not know how long she sat on the chair, her fingers fiddling with her lips, whispering to herself, but it did not resolve anything. As she left the bathroom, she stared at the poster of Mumbai on the wall in the hallway. It showed a view of a curvilinear beach and seafront. The skyscrapers and buildings formed an arching skeletal citysaurus. The gaudy neon lights of Chowpatty Beach and Cuff Parade exploded off the glossy paper. She wondered, without really caring, why Sebastian had a poster of Mumbai in his hallway.

Jessica liked the way he had given her space – he had not followed her up, or called for her. She loved the way he never pressurised her, had never forced himself on her. She kept thinking she had to find a way to get Sebastian's help, because he knew so much about these people. As he said, he had spent most of his life with them. *He even knew the people in Hamid's mosque,* she thought. *He will be able to help.* She was not sure how.

Regardless of what plan Jessica decided to follow, she knew she had to do everything she could to stop *Jaish an Noor wass Salaam*. The only way to do that was to go through with it, to pretend to remain committed to The Cause and the suicide bombing, to the terror cell. To stay deep inside them until the final day become the trigger, and then somehow find and stop the bomb. She had no idea how she would achieve any of these things, but she gritted her teeth and felt her fingers curl into fists. She would stop them, even at the risk of her possible future with Sebastian; even if it meant her life.

CHAPTER 23

London – Victoria Flat

'We interrupt this programme for some breaking news...'

Jimmy vaguely heard Al Jazeera in the background. Jessica had turned away from him. His face was still flushed after the argument; he had barely managed to control himself. Good Muslim men were not, he knew, supposed to shout and swear, especially at women. When Abu Umar had gathered them in the cell for the first time, he had introduced the other members of the cell into the large flat and told them they had to live and work together until the final day. Jimmy had accepted the others grudgingly, but as soon as he saw Jessica he said, 'What the hell is this *Goree* doing here? Ain't no job for no white woman.'

Earlier in the day, Jimmy had nearly attacked Dwayne, as he had tried to intervene when he had been arguing with Jessica about her role and commitment. He had accused her of being a white traitor. Jimmy felt pleased that he still had enough of the hard street in him so that Dwayne had been unable to control him. Secretly, Jimmy had been impressed with Jessica's resolve. Despite his intimidation, she had not backed down nor gone to her room, even when he had towered over her. Dwayne had called Abu Umar. His argument with Jessica had been about who would do what and when, especially on the day of the planned attack itself, the main reason for the dispute. Jimmy had been unwilling to accept Jessica's lead on anything, but soon had to forget the argument on Abu Umar's insistence. Dwayne had earlier tried to explain to Jimmy how a white English woman would be far less suspicious moving around central London, especially if the security forces were on alert that day.

Now four operatives of the cell, Jimmy, Jessica, Dwayne and the Afghan were present; he had arrived flanking Abu Umar. The *Shaikh*'s arrival had been sufficient to take the fight out of Jimmy, and he had seen how the redness had disappeared from Jessica's face. Abu Umar had quietened Jimmy and Jessica simply by arriving in the flat; he had ignored them. Jimmy knew it was unnecessary for him to say anything.

Jimmy looked at the Afghan and felt pride that a Muslim man had passed through such hardships and still wanted to sacrifice his life for Allah. Jimmy had heard the Afghan's story before. No matter how many times he heard the stories, they still made him incredulous. He asked for more details, and became increasingly impressed each time. He had listened, wide-eyed, as Hamza had translated the parts Jimmy could not understand, when the Afghan told of his days in the Bulgarian mountains without food, eating the leaves in the forest and drinking stream water. Over the past few weeks Jimmy had begun to understand more of his broken Urdu. He had walked to Britain from Afghanistan. He had been smuggled some of the way hidden in trucks and boats, but mostly he had walked.

The final member of the cell joined them, and quietly closed the door behind him. He made the flat seem smaller, dominating the space with his long limbs. Jimmy watched Hamza. He still had the same smile, which seemed a vestigial part of his personality, and with his smile he immediately changed the atmosphere.

Jimmy smiled back. Hamza still seemed to have plenty of charm and affection left over from his childhood; Jimmy wondered how he had ever managed to preserve it. His skin was like pale wheat, but not as blanched as Jimmy's. Hamza's colour contrasted with his dark liquid eyes, and highlighted his thin Errol Flynn moustache.

Hamza's arrival completed the cell: Jimmy, Jessica, Dwayne and the Afghan. *Jaish an Noor wass Salaam* always worked in cells of five. They were due to run through their final preparation plans, coordinated by Dwayne, who tried to carry out the duties entrusted onto him by Abu Umar. Hamza had told Jimmy that Dwayne had trained him, but Jimmy had resented Dwayne from the beginning, and had only accepted instructions from him when he had heard Abu Umar order the same thing. As a result, Abu Umar had taken responsibility for Jimmy's training.

Jimmy saw how Hamza, sensitive as ever, felt the tension in the room.

'What's going on, *Ya Sayedi*?' Hamza asked Abu Umar. He addressed the *Shaikh* as *my master*.

Abu Umar waved at Hamza without turning around; he increased the volume of the television, absorbed in the news report. The reporter's words now dominated the room. Jimmy saw Abu Umar's interest in the report, and forgot his argument.

'Breaking news: Israeli fighter jets have attacked the holy cities of Mecca and Medina as well as Saudi strategic defence installations around Jeddah and Riyadh...'

The Afghan broke in with some chatter in Pashto; he did not understand English, but recognised the pictures of the *Ka'ba*. Dwayne glared at him, caught up in the shocking news. Abu Umar turned the volume up again, and Jimmy became as transfixed as the rest of them by the words and pictures.

'Oh my God, what's happened?' said Jessica.

No one answered. Jimmy could hardly breathe. The air rasped in his throat and his chest hurt. 'Fuckin' bastard Jews! Fuckin' bastard Jews!' Jimmy said the words as if they were torn from the pit of hatred, made baritone by disbelief. He did not know what else to say, did not even dare to look around at the others or glance at the *Shaikh*, in case the Israeli attack somehow prevented or might defile his attempt at martyrdom. Dirty Untouchables, *Achhoth*, Jewish bastards, spoke within him the *Brahmin* of certain superiority. The silence of anger gaped open.

Dwayne now stood up, and shouted a furious stream of Arabic invective. The Afghan aped his actions, watching him intently, and Jimmy turned to look at him. Flecks of spittle landed on Jimmy, accompanied by the alien Pashto profanities.

Abu Umar sat on the sofa; the others had all gathered around. Everyone stared at the screen and tried to talk all at once, but Abu Umar hushed them with a wave. Jimmy looked back to the television. All disagreements about how the operation would unfold seemed petty, in front of what seemed to be unfolding on the screen. The anchor woman on Al Jazeera continued.

'This was in response to the news a short while earlier today that a revolution has taken place in Saudi Arabia. Zulfiqar bin Hijaz appeared in Mecca after Jummah prayers...'

All six of them stared at the pictures now being played on the television. *'Al Jazeera has exclusive pictures from Mecca. This film was provided to Al Jazeera from* Jaish an Noor wass Salaam, *by their media relations representative...'*

The scene played on the screen. A man in flowing white robes stood under the black cube of the *Ka'ba* on a raised platform, *Mimbar*. The *Imam* of the mosque had been sidelined, and stopped in mid flow from delivering his *Jummah* speech, *Khutbah*. None of the usual people of the *Ka'ba* could be seen on screen. A member of *Jaish*, Jimmy assumed, in a long *thawb* and red-checked *Keffiyeh* held by a double circle of thick black cord around his head, spoke in Arabic. Jimmy read the subtitles:

'*We welcome you. We, who have waited for years, we salute you! O Shamsuddin wa Salahuddin!* O Sun of the Faith and Righteousness of the Faith! *We acclaim you, the true Khalifa or Islam! We give you Bai'ah!* Our Pledge of Allegiance *Ya Amir Al Momineen!* Leader of the Faithful!'

The crowd surged forwards before he could he could finish, to give their *Bai'ah*. pledge of allegiance. The man who spoke smiled and waved at the security to control the crowd; they were obviously failing to suppress the rising excitement and the exultation at the Leader's arrival. The man who had spoken leaned forward, put his hands on the hands of Zulfiqar bin *Hijaz*, and kissed the hands of the new Commander of the True Believers. He wore a relaxed expression, *despite being responsible for the Leader's security*, thought Jimmy. The *Amir* had been acclaimed in a manner that would have been expected. As if his arrival had been long overdue, most of the crowd were hungry for the new Golden Age of Islam to begin. As many of the crowd as could reach him followed the example of the man who had kissed the Leader's hands; then they lifted Zulfiqar bin *Hijaz* onto their shoulders. Men surged around, arms raised aloft shouting: *Amir Al Momineen – Khalifa – Amir Al Momineen – Khalifa!* The pictures cut out and the newsreader in the studio came on again:

'*It seems as if there is a new Khalifa of the Muslim world. A new Leader of the Faithful. The majority of the Arab world has already declared him to be The Leader, the Amir Al Momineen. Many Muslim leaders have been rushing since the revolution in Saudi Arabia to offer their congratulations and also their Bai'ah. The longstanding differences and enmities in the Islamic world seem to have melted away, since the revolution and arrival of Zulfiqar bin Hijaz in Mecca today...*'

'*Subhanallah!* Allah is perfect! *Subhanallah!*' said Dwayne. He stood up and punched the air and grabbed Jimmy, who saw the whiteness of his smile obliterate the snow-white canine grimace that he had held moments earlier. He pulled Jimmy up, raised his arms above his head. Jimmy understood that the Israelis had attacked the Holy Lands, but that was because they feared a true Muslim being in charge. The revolution of *Jaish an Noor wass Salaam* had come. Jimmy shouted in joy, hugged Dwayne, forgetting his earlier anger. The Afghan joined in and hugged them both. Jimmy saw that even the *Goree* woman smiled. Jessica pulled her scarf down lower over her brow.

Abu Umar turned around, and quietened them. 'Wait – wait! The Israelis have attacked *Al Jazeerat Al Arab* and the *Haramain*.'

Jimmy knew *Jaish* called Saudi Arabia Jazeerat Al Arab, and the two holiest places of Islam, Mecca and Medina were known as the 'inviolable ones', Haramain. Ahmad had pictures of the *Ka'ba* in golden frames at home in the front room. Jimmy remembered growing up looking at the photographs of the Black Cube, with thousands of people swirling around it at the time of *Hajj*, the Pilgrimage, and had often wondered what it all meant. He remembered his father's face when years later Ahmad had realised that Jimmy still did not know why Muslim's performed the *Hajj*. *Maybe with my martyrdom I can make Abbo proud*, he thought. We will meet in *Jannah, inshallah*!

Dwayne said, 'But they didn't hit anything, Ya *Shaikh*. There's our *Amir Al Momineen* in the *Ka'ba* –'

'That was earlier, before the air strikes. What's happened now? I have to find out. We have to plan and regroup. Who's been hit?' said Abu Umar, and Jimmy saw the concern on his face; he supposed it was for the Leader. The television took over again:

'Thousands upon thousands of people have poured into the streets of Mecca and Medina, in fact, all over Saudi Arabia. Reports are coming in of people flooding out onto the streets of Muslim cities all over the world: Cairo, Damascus, Baghdad, Tehran, Islamabad, Jakarta… There seems to be a spontaneous outpouring of people chanting the name of Zulfiqar bin Hijaz, *Khalifa,* Amir Al Momine*en. This started in the streets of Mecca and spread like an epidemic. A tidal wave through the Muslim world. Now we have some more footage: pictures released by the PR officer of* Jaish an Noor wass Salaam.'

The pictures showed the crowd in the *Ka'ba* surging forward, kissing his hands, lifting Zulfiqar bin *Hijaz* on their shoulders. The film cut again as they carried him around the Black Cube, the *Ka'ba*.

'What does that mean?' asked Jimmy, still not sure how this affected their plans and his impending martyrdom.

'It means the final day is near. Our glorious Leader has been declared *Amir Al Momineen*. Allah's will and mankind's destiny is about to be revealed. But this is happening too early! I have to call an emergency meeting.'

Maybe this will bring the day closer, thought Jimmy. He could not stop his arms pumping with joy, until they became covered in a film of sweat. He ground his teeth and clenched his fists in victory; he kept repeating, 'Yes, yes, yes!', trying to keep his voice down, but the words hissed out of his mouth. He felt a surge run through his body, making him feel light-headed. *I can smell* Jannah *now.*

'What about our plans?' said Jessica.

'Typical British *Goree*, selfish to the end. *Shaikh* Abu Umar has just said we have a new Khalifa. Just selfish to the end.'

Jessica said, 'Not all of us are idiots. We have a *Jihad* still to –'

'Shush, that's enough,' said Dwayne, and Jimmy who was about to reply melted as Abu Umar turned to face him. The woman on television interrupted them again.

'*As we go to our correspondent in Saudi Arabia, or Dar Al Islam as it has been renamed since this morning, to Mecca, which I think is still called the same. We can go to Tariq Ayoub, our reporter in Mecca. Tariq – what is the situation there?*'

'Well, Stephanie,' said the reporter, and then paused, as if unsure where to start when reporting the momentous events. 'There has been chaos in Mecca. It seems as if the whole city is out on the streets. People are emerging from everywhere – we no longer have a view of the *Ka'ba*. In fact, we just lost our lights, as the power has gone off. We are broadcasting to you off our emergency generator.'

'*Where is Zulfiqar bin* Hijaz?'

'No one knows where he is. We have had no further communication from his media people. The declared *Amir Al Momineen* has not resurfaced since being swallowed by a sea of supporters who carried him off at lunchtime after *Jummah* prayers. We have no idea what's going on now. People are running in the streets with flashlights. Others have made old-fashioned flares made from oil-soaked cloth. There are just thousands of fireflies visible on your screen as you can see behind me, below in the city of Mecca. It's a medieval scene here. We are on a hill overlooking the city.'

'Tariq, what are the authorities doing, if anything?'

'Stephanie, no one knows. As I said there has been no further communication from anyone in *Jaish*. The police and security forces have disappeared, melted into the crowd. They have become a part of the crowd, it seems, and the army has not materialised.'

'Okay well, that is the current situation in Mecca. What can you tell us about the Israeli planes? I know it's noisy there – can you hear me? We can hear gunfire behind you.'

'Yes, there is small arms fire, mainly Kalashnikov, all over Mecca. We don't know who is firing or why. It may well be simply celebratory gunfire.'

'That last burst sounded a lot closer. Perhaps you should get inside?'

'It seems that the Israeli jets missed with their bombs. The Israelis are saying they have incontrovertible proof that *Jaish* had effected a total coup, deposing the Saudi royals, and that a new regime headed by Zulfiqar bin *Hijaz* is in charge of what used to be known as the Kingdom of Saudi Arabia.'

'That obviously must have felt like a direct threat to Israel? Since The Army of Light and Peace *have categorically stated their enmity to Israel.'*

'The fear in the international community, Stephanie, is for the huge arsenal of weapons – American weapons – amassed by the Saudis. Not to mention the numerous bases and secret assets distributed across the country, which are now presumably in the hands of *Jaish*.'

'Does this justify the strikes, Tariq? The air strikes in the Muslim world's eyes? How will the Islamic countries and Muslim people react now?'

'I can tell you there are reports, as you must be hearing over the wires, that thousands upon thousands of people are pouring into Mecca and Medina from all over *Jazeerat Al Arab*, as *Jaish* call it, to personally come to the defence of the *Haramain*, the holiest of sites in Islam – to be shields. In fact, I have been told that *Jaish* have made an announcement throughout the country after the airstrikes this morning, that any volunteers to the cities will be welcomed and accommodated at *Jaish*'s expense. So there have been reports of thousands of men and women flocking to the two Holiest of places. There are flights being chartered as we speak to bring the new *Mujahideen* here from Muslim capitals all over the world. The young men who I spoke to earlier here have categorically stated their willingness to be used as human shields, and to defend Mecca and Medina with their bodies if nothing else. It may not come to that, since *Jaish* now have sophisticated anti-aircraft and Patriot anti-missile systems available courtesy of the Americans...'

'Why did those systems not work this morning?'

'I don't know the answer to that. But it seems as if there may have been some confusion and panic during the coup and all eyes were looking inwards, and it is likely that there was uncertainty over whose planes they were, if they were detected. One thing is certain now, Stephanie, *Jaish* certainly do not have a recruitment problem. Hundreds of thousands – maybe millions – of people, especially outraged young Muslim men, will move into Arabia over the next few days and weeks.'

'What was the actual damage? We have some pictures that we are running now, Tariq, from earlier in the day. What you are seeing on your screens are from outside the city boundaries. There are huge craters formed outside the city, where the Israeli bombs landed. The bombs seemed to have missed in both Mecca and Medina. Although we do have some footage of damage to Al Kharj and At Taif air force bases, which were severely damaged.'

'*Lanatullah kullu Yahud!*' said Abu Umar, followed closely by Dwayne, who repeated in the same accent, '*Lanatullah kullu Yahud!*'

'Allah curse all Jews!' Jimmy knew the line in Arabic and English. He clenched his fists tighter and pummelled the back of the sofa, as he saw the pictures of the destroyed air force bases.

'*Jaish an Noor wass Salaam* are claiming victory and divine protection, Stephanie, since both the Holy Cities were undamaged. For some reason, the bombs missed in Medina too. No bombs landed within either city limits. Their numbers will be especially bolstered now, since *Jaish* are proclaiming a miracle. I have heard their PR man quote *Hadiths*. Allah's promise is that the cities of Mecca and Medina are protected and no harm will ever come to them, that they are protected by Angels. Zulfiqar bin *Hijaz* will probably want to address the nation – in fact, the whole Muslim world, the *Ummah*. I'm sure he will use the *Hadith* and Qur'anic quotes to explain why the Israeli planes could not attack the *Haramain*, and bombed the desert instead.'

'So it is being seen as miraculous?'

'Yes, definitely. It is being hailed as a miracle. Allah is keeping his promise to the Muslims. The twin cities cannot be destroyed...'

'It doesn't seem a very safe place to be tonight, Tariq?'

'Actually, ironically, Stephanie, I feel quite safe, despite the gunfire overhead. I'm sure it's celebratory. Like much of this country, it's a paradox. There have been no reports of anyone being killed. In fact, as far as we have been able to tell, there has been no fighting at all.'

'What are the people there behind you saying, Tariq? I can hear chanting in the background. There seems to be a mob surrounding you now?'

The crowd shouted: '*Hadi hi Dar Al Islam* – Zulfiqar bin *Hijaz* – *Amir Al Momineen*! *Amir Al Momineen*!'

'I'll just translate that, Stephanie, but I think you can hear that they are proclaiming this as the Land of Islam and the Zulfiqar bin *Hijaz* as the Leader of the True Believers... Some people have been taking up the chant against Israel since the attacks today. They have been shouting the old slogans of *Khaybar Khaybar Ya Yahud! Jaish u Muhammed sofah yaood! Remember the historic defeat of the Jews at Khaybar when they broke their promise by the Prophet Muhammed.* They are reminding the Jews of their defeat, which swept them finally from the Arabian Peninsula. They are saying: *The Army of Muhammed is about to return!*'

'The crowd seem happy – they're smiling, surrounding and milling around you, Tariq. They don't seem afraid that Israel will attack again and not miss this time?'

'I have already asked them this, Stephanie, and they are absolutely convinced they are divinely protected. These young men around me... ' he turned and pointed to the crowd who chanted and cheered. 'What do you think – can the Israelis attack?' he asked, in Arabic. The reporter did not need to translate the answer of a teenager, who spoke English with a Californian accent. He had a small beard, the size of two thumbprints on his chin, and he was dressed in a lime-green Ralph Lauren Polo T-shirt and jeans.

'We are divinely protected – by Allah *Subhanatallah* – The Almighty, The perfect. His promise is final; he has protected us, like when Abrahah tried to attack Mecca. It say in Qur'an, Surah Al Fil –'

Another interrupted, 'Or when a Divine Wind came and destroyed the *Kuffar* during the Battle of Khandak –'

'We will never ever be defeated. *Abadan! Abadan!*' He smiled and the raised two thumbs to the camera. Jimmy smiled broadly, and wished he could hug them.

'Are you sure you will be safe in Mecca tonight?' asked the reporter.
'Every Muslim believes it.'
'We are safer than the Zionist who think they sleep safely in their beds in Tel Aviv. We will wipe the genocidal Zionist regime off the map before we resolve the final battle between good and evil. Zionists are Dajjalic agents of the Antichrist.' The young man broke in to the camera, giving the sign for victory with both hands, smiling as the others laughed.

'Although that is not the official Jaish position – Zulfiqar bin Hijaz has never said anything like this – but I think it is safe to assume that, because the Israeli strikes have succeeded in destroying what used to be known as the Saudi Armed Forces, Israel probably will not risk another attack on the Holy Cities. That could easily widen the conflict, and draw in the neighbouring Muslim countries.' The newsreader in the studio paused for the reporter to reply.

'No, Zulfiqar bin *Hijaz* has never said as much. But the danger of the Israeli conflict spilling over and past the borders of Palestine is already a reality. With Israel's pre emptive attack at the very heart of Islam, I believe the Israeli's actions will have mobilised every Muslim. Afghanistan and Iraq pale into insignificance with the enormity of what has happened here today.'

The young man from the crowd spoke into the camera again, 'I promise, in the name of all of the Muslims of the world and in the name of the Khalifa, I will never rest. We will never rest until Islam's insult is revenged, and no Israeli will ever sleep soundly again. Not this generation. Nor their children. Nor their children's children. *Walallahi! Wallahi!* I swear by Allah!'

'Tariq, let me just ask you a question. Is that a real danger? Do you think that the forces of Dar Al Islam are strong enough to challenge the Israeli Defence Force that has been historically so overwhelming?'

'The real question, Stephanie, is not a match of defence forces... but is there a real appetite in the new rulers of the Arabian Peninsula to take on this issue? To solve the Arab-Israeli conflict once and for all this way? Despite what this young man thinks, if Israeli strikes continue, *Jaish* may feel their hand is forced.'

Jimmy felt pride like a needle that pricked his heart at the young Saudi's statement of defiance. He felt the clarity of kinship, the brotherhood that so tightly bound the Muslim *Ummah*. The centuries of shame were about to be expunged. He understood the love for the black cube, the *Ka'ba*, and why all Muslims would protect it more than their own children. Tears flowed freely down his cheeks. Those inbred, disgusting people were a disgraced race: the Zionists. A word that he had learned from Abu Umar, who used it interchangeably with Jews. Jimmy understood that it might mean something different, after Jessica had tried to explain to him there were good Jews too; he had not accepted her reasoning. Yet another argument had ensued, and he had felt like hitting her. Instead he had reported her heresy to Abu Umar. He had chuckled and said that was the English part of her, and that Jimmy should not hold it against her.

'*So do you think that further strikes are likely? And is there a real danger of all-out war?*'

'It is an open secret that American small tactical nuclear weapons are stationed deep underground at strategic sites throughout the country, for use as a last resort if any country in the 'Axis of Evil' threatened American and Saudi Royal interests – such as Iraq, Iran, Syria, Hezbollah. But these have always been under American control.'

'*Israel also has nuclear weapons?*'

'Yes. Who knows what is being planned in Jerusalem, whether the Israelis would consider a first use of tactical nuclear weapons for self preservation – especially if they felt that the weapons of mass destruction were about to fall into the wrong hands? Although the Israelis lost the war in Lebanon, they felt that humiliation extremely acutely, and faced huge criticism for Gaza. The balance of power is not quite so certain now. I believe if Israel is convinced they are about to be attacked by *Jaish*, they will certainly launch further first pre-emptive strikes – perhaps nuclear.'

'*The only Islamic country with nuclear weapons is Pakistan, so will other countries be drawn into the conflict?*'

'This is the true danger that this could turn into a truly global conflict with numerous countries pulled in by force of their people's emotions, adding petrol to the conflagration. A war between Islam and the rest of the world – the final Clash of Civilisations…'

Jimmy felt his hopes soar. 'Yes!' he shouted. 'Yes!' He pumped the air with his huge fist repeatedly. 'Yes!'

Finally those lazy Paki bastards will get off their arses and wipe Israel off the face of the earth, he thought. Breivik, the facist massacrer in

Norway, wanted to bring about the final Clash of Civilisations with Muslims – *well, it's here now,* he thought. The Muslim world will join together to destroy the West's decadent, *Kuffar* devil-worshiping ways, and the Golden Age of Islam will return, *inshallah*! But I will already be in *Jannah*. And I will have helped make it all possible: the victory of Allah.

'Yes!' He grinned and thumped the Afghan on his shoulders, his meaty hands pumped like pistons of joy, powered by engine of faith. Jimmy felt light-headed, as if his soul had already detached from his body. He felt as if even his body he could float; the feeling caused him to retch slightly, but he kept the smile on his face.

'*Allah O Akbar!*' said Dwayne. '*Allah O Akbar!*'

Jimmy, the Afghan, and Hamza shouted, '*Allah O Akbar! Allah O Akbar!*' Jimmy noticed that even the white woman raised an arm above her head, and joined in. The clamour seemed to pull Abu Umar out of his trance.

'I have to call emergency meetings and contact all the others – heads and operatives...' He trailed off, and turned to them. 'I did not anticipate this is happening so soon. Subhanallah! Only His plans are perfect. Allah is perfect, and He knows best.'

Jimmy heard him rolling his R's in more Arabic style, and his P's changed to B's again in his excitement. He could not stop smiling and laughing – everything seemed to be pointing him towards Heaven.

'We will have to bring our plans forward. I will rush through the changes.' Abu Umar looked at each of them in turn. 'I hope you are all ready, and that everything is ready.' The *Shaikh* raised his hands to the heavens. 'I pray you really are ready to do what you must do,' he added in a voice barely audible, before he walked out of the flat.

CHAPTER 24

London – Victoria Flat

'I should be the one to trigger the bomb,' Jimmy said.

'We don't know who the trigger is. They said that –'

'Yeah, but it should be me, innit. Ain't no job for a woman.'

'I'm as much Muslim as you,' said Jessica. Rising to the taunts had sometimes become unavoidable, despite the pretence she had to maintain in the cell. She could not let Jimmy get away with his continuing misogyny, and the rest of the group almost expected them to argue. She thought she would try some history with Jimmy, 'And Muslim women have fought many times in history.'

'Just tell Abu Umar you can't do it. Tell him you ain't up to it, yeah, 'cos you know it, babe. I ain't gonna lose my nerve last minute, like some soft white pastry girl.'

'Look, are you so stupid?' She paused, surprised that he did not start shouting as usual. 'They won't tell us which one of us carries the real trigger. Maybe all of us, maybe none of us do. What if one of us is a mole, or carries a tail, or simply has a change of heart and gets scared –'

'I ain't scared of jack shit, sis,' said Jimmy jumping to his feet.

Jessica regretted the word as soon as she said it. She should know by now that would set him off; it always did.

Jimmy continued talking, as he walked away from her to the kitchen area. 'I just wanna be martyred. In *Jannah*, with my everlasting pleasures. Away from all this.' He gestured around him, out of the window overlooking of central London. 'Away from all of this shit.'

Jessica looked around, ignoring the Afghan, whom she knew understood nothing of the argument, but he beamed back at her, regardless of the situation. The newly furnished large flat with all its facilities had been one of the few pleasures since her training began. All the days had become training days, but she liked to laze in the Jacuzzi for half an hour at the end of a hard day's training. *No expense spared*, she thought, as she felt the thick rugs beneath her feet. At least the Martyrs' last days on earth would be comfortable. The routines to do with bombs and suicide vests and triggers had made her hands shake as if everything she touched might explode; she would be covered in sweat within minutes, dripping wet, despite the cold of December. If the flat was not home, then it had a temporary hotel-like feeling, at least. The Victoria flat that they came to for their practical, and especially spiritual, training could not become an adopted home for her, despite the physical comforts.

Abu Umar usually led the spiritual circles; Dwayne taught them the practical logistics. Sometimes they were called in pairs and in the past they had also been tutored singly, but as the teaching intensified over the past few weeks they had all trained together and eaten together and prayed together as a unit. Jessica had noted the Afghan's shock, with a smile, as she had lined up behind the men to pray. *It's amazing how ignorant some of these Muslims are about their religion*, she had thought. She had felt no surprise when she saw the Afghan staring at her at the end of every prayer; she had almost expected him to turn around during the recitation, as the rest of the men concentrated, heads bowed in obeisance.

'Look – there's a whole team. That's why there's a cell. We need each other.' Jessica now tried to reason with Jimmy. She found it hard to comprehend that he really meant a lot of what he said, and how much of his diatribe was habitual. Jimmy often looked away, and did not answer her questions directly.

During Jessica's time with Hamid she had learned a little about the average Asian man; a definition which he had insisted on using, but a description into which he had not fitted easily. Some of them tried too hard to be the alpha male, macho, misogynistic and ungenerous. Jimmy occupied a niche of his own.

'You don't know what I can do; you don't know what I had to get through in my life just to get here. 'Cos you ain't never met a real brown man, innit, sis. We, us lot – we ain't like them white, softie *Gorah* boys you is used to. I ain't gonna let you mess this up for me.'

'Don't! Don't you ever presume to tell me about my life.' She turned away, and entered the kitchen. The open-plan flat made it possible to see through to the living area.

'You talk funny. Sometimes you is so funny...'

The Afghan stared on in silent non-comprehension. She looked over to him, his eyes closing and widening with Jessica's every move, and his thin moustache rising and falling with every change of intonation. It did not matter that he and Jimmy were supposed to be her 'Muslim Brothers'; she could not see either of them as brothers of hers, no matter how hard she prayed or no matter how far she let her imagination roam. She could not even see them as friends. There was nothing to hang on to, an absence of commonality, which made her lose sympathy with them.

Jessica looked at the Afghan, fascinated despite herself; usually, she tried to look at him as little as possible. His wiry body and rubicund Caucasian face with reddish-brown hair felt even more unusual to her than Dwayne's blackness, and Abu Umar's pale Levantine looks. Having the whole racial mix along with her own blondeness was a great advantage to the group, Abu Umar had told her more than once. He would look at her with ever-increasing whites in his eyes like fried eggs, mouth half open like a Himalayan trout.

Jimmy and the Afghan communicated in a manner of their own making. The Afghan's Urdu grunts, she had noticed, seemed intelligible to Jimmy, once he had asked him to repeat them in three different ways. Jimmy had eventually got used to his way of talking, and they spoke in short sentences. She noticed how he was patient and eventually understood the foreigner when no one else could, like the mother understands her mute child's garbled linguistics. As a result, the Afghan was overdemonstrative, often hugging Jimmy and sometimes Hamza, forcing Hamza to join in their conversations at times.

She hated the way the Afghan stared and stared some more, and when she felt sure he could not possibly stare any longer he managed to stare some more. His eyes followed her around the room like a ghostly marionette, but with bulging frog's eyes. When she walked into the kitchen, he would come and stand and stare.

The Afghan came up so close to her she thought he might try and kiss her, but then he smiled broadly for no apparent reason. His moustache drooped into his mouth like half-balding rat's tail; it sat on the edge of his mouth as if the rodent had fallen into the dark well of his gap-toothed smile, leaving behind its tail. He had a tongue, which darted out on most social occasions, out of his mouth like a pink mouse. Most of the time,

Jessica saw that it had turned green, into a skink-like reptilian colour. His tongue became lizard-green from chewing his *naswar*, the green tobacco-infused snuff, which he kept in his mouth like a secret but stuffed periodically into the side of his cheek with his fingers, irrespective of who observed him.

Jimmy said he had walked – *walked* – from Quetta, where he had been a refugee from Kandahar, to England. Jessica had laughed out aloud: *walked*. No one else laughed. The Afghan had lived in the mountains of Turkey, where three of his company had died of exposure on the snow-covered slopes. On the mountains he had seen two skeletons, and a fifteen-year-old boy had disappeared in the night, fell off the precipice; the guide had shrugged and trudged on. She understood his desperation to escape Afghanistan, but the fact that Jimmy could be so in awe of the creature she found hard to understand. Then Jimmy had told her, even though she had heard enough, that he had been smuggled into Greece hidden under a tarpaulin sheet on a boat. He had been stopped and deported three times, and had spent a week without food in the Romanian mountains, eating buds off the trees and drinking from streams.

The Afghan was oblivious to all; he had eyes for Jessica only, except when Abu Umar spoke. He listened with a dedication of a sheep to his shepherd, even though she knew they spoke no common language. He seemed to imbibe power and strength from the *Shaikh*'s teachings, and then he went back to smiling at Jessica, when the *Shaikh* had finished.

Abu Umar had explained to her that he came from a culture where people stared, and had an insatiable curiosity. Jessica wondered what exactly men like him thought about when they stared. *Better I don't know*, she thought. Was he one of those seekers of virgins in Paradise? Was this the staring that leads to the desire for martyrdom and innumerable virgins, that even Sebastian had said was used as a lure? The Afghan's attention made her scrunch up her face, and the hard red disc that she bit regularly now had grown larger on her thumb, since her time with the cell. She knew she had fully infiltrated them, and she would soon get answers to her questions, and then stop *Jaish* and their crazy plans. Somehow.

Jessica had never come across such a culture as she found in the cell. She often felt a lack of synchronicity, and did not laugh when they did or shout at the same things as them. Jimmy would just call her 'a weird, stuck-up *Goree*.' Dwayne would often tell him to shut up, and many times Hamza had had to intervene. Jimmy would almost always accept Hamza's intervention; she knew they were childhood friends.

Hamza had agreed with Abu Umar when he said that young Afghan men stared and followed younger men, because there were no women visible in the streets. Old men stared longer and harder – they had less to do – and the *gulley* dogs in the narrow side streets of Kabul stared too, but hunger drove them to *yap yap* too soon. The women did not stare, because the streets were like lava flows to a woman alone, during the time of extremist power. The alleys of infection were dodged and skirted by hiding under eaves and praying the dogs would not bark. Because it would result in more violence than a volcano if a young zealot had caught them, without a *mahram*, a male relative they could justify being with. They could never travel alone. Jessica knew, with a stone-like certainty, she would rather fail at stopping the bomb and lose everything than live under the yoke of extremist Islamist servitude.

'Anyway,' Abu Umar had added with a smile, 'who knows if women stare at anyone under the *burkha*, or if they think at all. Only Allah can understand what they think!'

Only yesterday, Jessica had to shoo the Afghan out of her room, after he followed her. She slept with the door locked since the group had been ordered together. She dreaded mealtimes as Jimmy, Hamza, Dwayne and the Afghan gathered. He sat shovelling food into his mouth with either hand, sometimes spitting out white pieces of half-masticated chicken, which he pushed side to side by his green *naswar* skink tongue. He wiped his greasy mouth on the back of his hands, then his hands on his moustache. They awaited the arrival of the *Shaikh* but Dwayne usually took up prayer duties before food in place of Abu Umar, at times when he was not present.

Jessica looked up from the dining table as they all sat eating; she rarely looked up from her plate lately. The Afghan's moustache became involved and entangled with the grease from the pizza. He managed to eat without shifting his gaze off her. 'How – how does he manage to eat without looking at – how does he taste his food?' she asked Hamza, who shrugged.

Jessica saw realisation like a smirk spread across the Afghan's face. He understood she had mentioned him, because she could not help staring back at him with her lip curled, as her hands hovered in space, her knife and fork suspended mid motion.

'Piss – a! Piss – a! *Accha* Piss – a!' said the Afghan. He slobbered and licked his fingers, picking up a triangle off his plate and waving it in front of her nose – offering her a slice of pizza. 'Piss – a!' he said again, triumphant.

She screwed up her face. It did not matter that he did not know where his family had disappeared to after the American bombing of Kandahar. That he had volunteered for morgue duty without recompense in the refugee camps, despite offers of paid work, did not endear him to her.

'Piss – a?' He sniffed the cheesy covering, so that his nasal hair touched the meat toppings.

'No! No – no, thank you…' Jessica looked down.

Dwayne burst in, followed by Abu Umar at a stately pace.

'Turn on the TV! Put on Al Jazeera!' Dwayne shouted.

Hamza switched the television on.

'What's happened?' asked Jessica.

'Its happening – it – the revolution is happening.'

'What?'

'Yeah, look! Revolutions all over the world! Zulfiqar bin *Hijaz* has ordered it,' said Hamza, as he pushed the remote towards Jessica.

'Yes!' Jimmy lifted his fist into the air. 'Islam is coming. Islam is coming home.'

'*Allah O Akbar!*' Dwayne sank to the sofa, '*Allah O Akbar!*' he repeated, in an exhausted voice.

Jimmy jumped to his feet, grabbed the remote off Jessica, and turned up the volume on Al Jazeera. The woman in the studio said:

'*Revolutions and insurgencies are underway in the Muslim world. I have had confirmation from the PR man of Jaish an Noor wass Salaam that the new* Amir Al Momineen *has declared an end to 'Israeli bullying' in the area, and an end to Americans and the dominance of their 'agents' – by which, we assume, he means the leaders of the Middle East.*'

Jessica looked around at the others, her lower lip hanging limp at the news. Sweat gathered and ran down the nape of her neck, and she chewed her thumb. The rest of them had their eyes fixed onto the TV screen. *Not just Saudi Arabia… now there are other revolutions,* she thought. *Shit! How many? What does this mean, for our mission, for me? Will it make it easier or harder to get out? I wish I could talk to Sebastian.*

The news broke into her thoughts. '*There is chaos all over Saudi Arabia, and here on the streets of Jeddah. You can see from our coverage of Jeddah harbour, where ships from numerous countries are moored. There are uncountable numbers of ships filled with young men and women. They are offering their services for the newly established Dar Al Islam, from all over the world.'*

Jessica pulled at her nails, looked around to see the smiles on the faces of the rest of the cell members. *How can they be so pleased with revolution?* she thought. *How can they turn defeat into victory – like the Israeli bombings? Although they missed Mecca and Medina they effectively destroyed the Saudi Armed Forces, but it made them so happy, as if it was a victory for them!*

A male reporter with a microphone in front of him appeared on the screen, and a caption informed Jessica that he was talking live from Mecca. 'I can tell you that all commercial and civilian flights in and out of Saudi or Dar Al Islam, The Land of Islam, have been cancelled, but the flood of people had started well before then.'

'What do we know of the Saudi royals, Tariq?' asked Stephanie, the anchorwoman who had quizzed the reporter during the earlier scenes of celebration from Mecca.

'Well, Stephanie, it seems the king and his entourage have made a getaway.'

'How did they do that? And, I suppose, what everyone must be wondering – did they have American help?'

'They have their private jets, of course, and the Saudi Royal Air Force – assuming some are still loyal to the ruling family.'

'The Americans must have had some knowledge about the impending coup, Tariq? Perhaps the Americans helped. We know they have often rescued loyal supporters, going right back to the Shah of Iran through to the Kuwaiti royals, after their country was invaded by Saddam?'

'Well, yes, it's highly likely that the Americans are involved, and perhaps the Saudi royals would have known something about the Israeli bombings before they happened, too.'

'Do we have any idea of their whereabouts?'

Jessica felt no concern for the safety of the royal family; she knew the Americans or British would have whisked them out. As much as she hated the philosophy of *Jaish*, she felt disgust at the Americans and her own government for their hypocritical backing of such a regime for decades. For making the family of Saud kings in the first place, and as a result dragging the Wahabi doctrine from the cellar and placing it squarely on the mantelpiece in the House of Islam.

'No, Stephanie, not for certain. Maybe Dubai, maybe Cairo. As I said, the place is in meltdown. Palaces are being burned and looted, and here in Jeddah, on the other side of the city from us, there are mobs rampaging through the streets shouting for royal Saudi blood. Literally.'

'*Have any of the princes been attacked?*'

'Well, there are so many it's hard to know if any of the minors have been attacked. News has not been reliable, but I am very concerned for their safety. The police and senior army officers, many of them, have backed the insurgents and the revolutionaries. This is not just an uprising of the poor masses.'

How can anyone still remain poor in a country so rich, populated by so few? thought Jessica. The level of incompetence and mismanagement needed to achieve this astounded her.

'*Have many officers have been replaced?*'

'Yes, generals, as well as high ranking police officers. We have reports that the highly wanted Saudi dissident, Abdul Wahid, who was long suspected as being the Chief of Saudi for *Jaish*, has been declared Vizier, second in command in *Jazeerat Al Arab* to Zulfiqar bin *Hijaz* himself.'

'*We are getting unconfirmed reports. There has been another assassination attempt by army members loyal to the Saudis, but yet again Abdul Wahid has survived,*' said the anchorwoman.

'Fear of reprisals is spreading through the lesser members of the house of Saud. In fact, one of the princes told me yesterday he feared a massacre.'

'*Thank you, Tariq. A revolution in Saudi Arabia, now called Dar Al Islam – but not confined to that country, because we have reports that the revolutions are spreading…*'

Numerous cries of '*Allah O Akbar! Allah O Akbar!*' broke out amongst the gathered cell members, along with spontaneous hugging and kissing, interspersed with jumping around the living room.

'This time, it's gonna go worldwide. Across the whole world, innit? *Khilafa*! *Khillaafaa*!' Jimmy shouted.

'It's unbelievably real. Truly? Real…' Dwayne replied, through tears running like rivers of Paradise down his face. Hamza switched channels to BBC, CNN, and then back to Al Jazeera. They all carried the same story. She forced herself to join the celebrations, but in her normal, more muted way; she smiled and held up her palms open for prayer, as a committed but reserved Muslim female member of the cell would do.

'Okay, Tariq, we have to leave it there. We have more breaking news of insurgencies and coups occurring all over the Muslim world. This is dramatic and incredible. It seems that a revolution of the masses is occurring as we speak, and in Cairo, we go now to Katya in Tahrir Square. What's the situation in Cairo, Katya?'

'Cairo is ablaze tonight, Stephanie.'

'We can see some disturbing pictures of fires?'

'Yes, people are rioting. They started ostensibly over food, the price of food, especially since the government aided-bread programme stopped. Bread has been unavailable in Cairo to most of the city's poor for over a week. The people are hungry, and they are angry.'

'The government has said today that it is bringing in truckloads of flour, but that doesn't seem to have stopped the riots?'

'No – indeed, the government claims that the Islamic insurgents have stockpiled flour to exacerbate the situation, and are facilitating these riots. It's evening here now, and you can see behind me that some police have joined the mobs.'

Jessica felt surprise that there could be food shortages in a country like Egypt, which she knew was fully supported and backed in every way by the Americans.

'Why has the army not been ordered out onto the streets, Katya?'

'Well, we don't know the answer to that for sure. We have tried to contact the Ministry of Defence, but they're insisting that the police can cope with the situation. In fact, there are unconfirmed reports that the army has been ordered out, but they are not responding to the civilian government. It seems that the overthrow of the old *Mubarak* regime was simply a preparation for *Jaish's* 'real revolution."

'Does that mean there is a coup likely in Egypt?'

'The army seem to be acting on *Jaish's* orders now. The streets are dangerous. *Jaish* are saying the earlier rebellions for democracy were simply a front before their real revolutions, which are now about to take over. We are reporting from our hotel rooftop in Tahrir Square. Mobs are looting and rioting and yes – although it's dangerous to talk about these things, we have been warned by the government – but, yes, rumours of a coup are rife.'

'Egypt, so often the standard bearer of the Arab world, seems to be going the same way as so many of the other countries. The whole of the

Middle East is in complete turmoil… I can see something happening behind you? What's going on now?'

'I think some security forces are making their way up to the roof as we speak, and the crowds are converging towards the centre of Cairo, towards our position here –' The reporter broke off.

The picture shook and went blank of a moment, before returning to the studio.

'We seem to have lost our link from Cairo. There seems to be chaos in Cairo tonight – stay safe, Katya. But I am just being told that we can go to our correspondent in Islamabad. Mohammed Ilyas, what's the situation in Islamabad? Mohammed?'

'Stephanie, I can tell you that the situation is the exact opposite of what you have been hearing from Cairo,' said the reporter with his slight drumming accent. 'In fact, it is deathly silent. We are secretly reporting from the Marriot in Islamabad. You might remember this was the almost destroyed by that huge terrorist bomb, but has since then the hotel has been rebuilt. But despite a curfew and a ban on journalists, we have been reporting from here. The curfew is supposed to last until eight local time tomorrow, when the General Commander in Chief of the armed forces will give a press conference.'

'Do you have any reasons why?' asked the anchor woman.

Jessica hid her shock, but could not prevent her hands from covering her face momentarily before she forced them down into her lap again. She realised that coordinated, concerted revolutions were taking place all over the Muslim world, and this must be part of the greater plan. *Jaish an Noor wass Salaam*, The Army and Light and Peace, were succeeding in spreading their halcyon harmony. Tears wet her cheeks and she wiped them away, smiling with difficulty; she hoped the others would think them tears of joy.

'We have an official paper which we were handed by Brigadier Maqsood earlier today from MI, military intelligence, telling us to observe the curfew; there is a shoot on sight policy.'

'Is that why the streets seem so quiet?'

'It's evening here now, and below us normally you would see the whole of the Pakistani capital alive with late-night shoppers, people eating out in this vibrant city.'

'What has actually happened?'

'Something unprecedented in the history of Pakistan has occurred here. No one knows for sure. There's a news blackout, but I have been told by one of my sources in MI that there has been a military coup and the army has toppled its own. The General has been deposed.'

'Well, we are hearing over the airways that a general by the name of Kafeel Khan has taken over. Until recently, he was out of favour with the Chief of Army Staff.'

'What's happened to the Chief?' asked the reporter from Islamabad, turning the tables.

'I have been informed by another source that he has been killed. General Kafeel Khan long had a reputation as a maverick. He was posted to Kashmir. Thank you, for the moment.'

'Killed by Kafeel Khan?' The reporter seemed unable to stop the question, in his astonishment.

'That's what some of the wilder reports are saying, but we will go back to Islamabad shortly. I have in the studio an expert on Pakistani and subcontinent affairs, Professor Mike Burrows – an expert in that strategic area.

Professor, we have dismissed them as fanciful rumours up until now. He simply walked into the office. They were friends, the Chief and Kafeel Khan, so he knew him well. He stabbed him through the eye with his own letter opener, as the Chief of Army Staff looked over the latest reports with the maverick General from Kashmir. Is that remotely possible?' asked the incredulous anchorwoman.

'Well, we are talking about Pakistan and so yes, anything no matter how outlandish it may seem to us, is possible. But I must say that up till now in the history of Pakistan, the army has been wholly reliable. It is the most professional and strongest Muslim army in the world by far. And yes, the Chief would have trusted General Kafeel Khan out of necessity.' The professor pushed his thick gold-rimmed glasses back to the top of his nose. His bald head shone in the studio lights; he had a thin rim of white hair encircling the back of his head.

Fear rose in Jessica, but she dared not show it. Nausea filled her stomach, but she forced the bile down. She sat covered in sweat, shaking. She hoped the others would interpret her closed eyes and the tremors that ran through her body as the fervour of a potential martyr, who knew her time of self-sacrifice, was imminent.

Jessica knew that somehow these events, the London bomb and her own destiny, were inextricably linked. If she was to survive, if Sebastian was to live, and if she was going to keep her parents safe, then she would have to find a solution.

She forced her eyes open, wiped the wetness out of them that kept appearing, no matter how hard she tried. She ignored the others, not caring that their joy seemed limitless; she chewed her thumb and tried to concentrate on the screen, to try to understand what was going on, to find her own way out of an impossible maze. Her legs seemed to be sinking into the tar of inevitability. She would become a fossilized failure in the history of the world, and no-one would know or care if she failed. The flat seemed to close in around her like an airless coffin. She coughed and choked, coughed and cleared her throat.

The woman in the studio spoke again. '*How is it possible? The security around the Chief of Staff must have been phenomenal?*'

The professor replied, 'Well, there is most certainly more to this story than we know at the moment, but they were at PMA Kakul Pakistan Military Academy together in Abbotabad, the same town where Osama Bin Ladin was killed. They graduated together, but then Kafeel Khan fell out of favour with the politicians. They saw active service together and were both eventually appointed General, but the Chief got the most coveted job in Pakistan and became his boss, and posted General Kafeel Khan to three consecutive tours of duty of duty to Kashmir, where it seems General Kafeel Khan ran a private campaign.'

'*He must have had supporters in Islamabad, though?*' asked the woman interviewer.

'Yes, most certainly – there would have been backers, some in government and ISI. But we also know that *Jaish* have been using Pakistani and Indian generals.'

'*The Inter-Services Intelligence – the agency that some say runs Pakistan?*'

'Well…yes.' The professor seemed incapable of beginning any sentence without saying 'well,' and pausing.

Jessica squeezed her thighs in frustration, not fully understanding the implications of all these developments. The expert had not made anything clearer, that she could relate to the London plot, at least.

'It is the most powerful agency in Pakistan, but this is totally new, because the Pakistan Army has never been divided. They have inevitably been loyal to the Chief of Staff,' added the professor.

'*Why do we not have any protestors on the streets, professor?*'

'The army is in total control, Stephanie. That's how it is in Pakistan and I have heard from friends out there that people have been shot in Lahore and Karachi, so there is fear on the streets.'

'We have further reports from the embassy that General Kafeel Khan has been killed – stabbed in turn by his batman. A Kashmiri man from the border is now under arrest. Incredible events in Islamabad. The old order is back in charge,' said Stephanie. *'I think the White House is about to make a statement. We have to leave it there…'*

No-one seems to know what's going on, thought Jessica. *Oh my God! It's started; now I have got to stop this. How can I? I can't do anything about the coups – but the bombs – London. I have to get people on my side, people I trust, but who? There is no-one except Sebastian, but what can he do? Maybe he can do something; he has had insider information, right from the beginning. I have to trust Sebastian.*

Dwayne and Jimmy broke into her thoughts, as they and the Afghan cheered and shouted and hugged each other. Jessica wiped her face, and looked at them. Abu Umar stayed sitting, and put his hands up in front of his face to pray. He made dua: a long, fast stream of Arabic, broken by sharp shuffles of breath. The others calmed down and copied him, muttering Ameen after every invocation. Abu Umar prayed for the revolutions to succeed, and for the date of the event to be brought forward, so they could all reach Paradise without delay.

Then a spokesman from the White House made a statement saying the *Jihadi* revolutionaries, the lovers of violence and the creators of insurgencies, would not be allowed to succeed. This was merely the latest phase in the battle against terror and freedom and democracy, and America and the allies would win.

Then the television cut to pictures of Zulfiqar bin *Hijaz* – who, as Jessica expected, gave a speech stating that the Muslim world must be left to decide its own affairs after decades of unwarranted colonialism and interference. Finally, Dar Al Islam was established. The others sat, with glory apparent on their radiant faces, in popstar adoration. She saw Zulfiqar bin *Hijaz*'s face appear on the screen. For all the mystery and legend and mystique surrounding the man, he seemed an ordinary Arab that could have come from any of the streets in the Arabian Peninsula. He had an average face, with an average body. His voice rang slow and clear, incongruously deep, like the unexpected baritone sound from an average bell. A man's voice translated into English.

'The forces of *Kuffar*, and their agents who had infiltrated and changed the course of history in the Islamic institutions, will be thrown out of Al Jazeera – not only the Holy Lands. We will never let them stop the Islamic revolution in establishing the *Khilafa*, *inshallah*. And they will be humiliated, their faces black with guilt, to be thrown out of all Muslim lands. The torturers of Baghdad, the invaders of Iraq, and the destroyers of Afghanistan will pay dearly for their crimes against humanity. The crusaders will meet only defeat, huge and unchanging. Just as they had tasted it centuries ago, so they shall taste it from this day forth. Eternal defeat is their destiny, in the *duniya*, in this world, and everlasting hellfire their reward in the hereafter. It is only a matter of time, and it is now that time before the end of time. The time for the Angel Israfil to blow his trumpet, which will signal the end of the world. The Kingdom of Allah will be our final victory…Now is that time. I call upon all *Kuffar* to repent and accept the truth of Islam. I call upon all Muslims to do everything they can to support the Islamic Revolution, not only in *Dar Al Islam*, but all over the world. Once our *Khilafa* is re-established, by the will of Allah, then *Dar Al Islam* will again encompass the lands of all the Muslims, as well as the oceans of the *Kuffar*. *Dar Al Islam* shall stretch from the beginning of the Atlantic Ocean, across the Indian, to the ends of the Pacific…'

CHAPTER 25

London

Jimmy remembered holding Zoya's hand and crossing the main road to school, how he always reached naturally for her hand. He knew that Muslim brothers protected their sisters, from the time he had been five and Zoya a year older. He could hear his father's voice – shame, *sharam karo, taking your sister's sweets, for spoiling her game of dolls, breaking their legs and arms* – when Zoya went crying to Ahmad.

Jimmy did not do it to hurt her; he did it so that he would be seen as a rebel. Chastised by his mother, who in turn would tell her friends how cheeky and naughty he was. Later he would make up with Zoya by letting her read his Dandy comics, as she would always get the Beano. Then he would secretly smuggle sweets into school and mosque for her once every fortnight. He would have saved enough pocket money or stolen enough money from other children to buy her one whole Mars bar.

Jimmy had to return home. He had heard the shocking news that Zoya was due to get married to Dan, the *Kuffar* police officer. Jimmy had attacked Dan when he had brought Zoya home. Ahmad had died in the mosque, and Jimmy's grief gave way to rage, so when he had seen Zoya bloody and bruised with her clothes ripped, sitting in the car with the policeman, he had instinctively pulled Dan out of the car and kicked and punched him.

Since Jimmy had heard about Zoya's planned wedding with Dan, he had seen Zoya becoming a *Kuffar* in his dreams. He knew a Muslim woman could not marry a non-Muslim man and still remain a believer. In his nightmares, Ahmad had appeared to him, crying and imploring him to save Zoya. Jimmy had felt he had let his father and his family down his whole life, and now his sister needed him. His father was not there to put things right, and since Jimmy had not managed to save Ahmad, the responsibility to save Zoya was his.

Jimmy had tossed and turned with the nights, that had seemed to transform into a spirit, which maybe took the form of Ahmad – he could not be sure. The night twisted his body and pulled his sinews apart, and caused pain to take over his body, which sometimes made him vomit. The risk he was taking did not assuage the pangs of guilt that washed over him. Guilt and the sense of failure weighed against the importance of his mission: they merged into confusion.

Jimmy had remained in disguise. He had to come, regardless of the risk. He knew the police wanted him, and MI5 were hunting him. Now, he had made potential enemies of the very people who had protected him; his brothers in Islam. When he thought about them, he felt as if he would collapse. Not at the thoughts of death – he had accepted his imminent demise – but the memories of water choking his throat, the droplets filling his lungs, made his hands shake, and he coughed involuntarily. *I will explain things to Abu Umar*, he thought, *and surely the* Shaikh *would understand my predicament? Somehow I will make sure he accepts me again.*

Jimmy had disappeared two days ago from his cell, without informing Dwayne, his enforcer, or getting blessing from his spiritual leader Abu Umar. Now he knew he was being hunted. The *Jaish* would never let him simply walk away; these things did not work in that way. He knew too much already, although he felt he knew very little. It would be safer, and *Jaish an Noor wass Salaam* would have more chance of success in their project to bomb London if he died, now that he had exposed them to risk by leaving the suicide cell without permission.

Jimmy had left his cell and disguised himself as a middle-aged man. He had stayed in Bed and Breakfasts, where he could pay with cash, and not leave a trace by using credit cards. He had a black wig peppered with white and a false beard, bought from different shops. Jimmy knew that many men grew their beards after becoming religiously observant, just as women wore the scarf. During his training Dwayne had advised him to keep shaving and not grow his own beard, for fear of raising suspicion.

He wore a locust-green salwar, a chameleon *kameez* with a wheat-brown waistcoat. A grey *karakul* cap covered his head, soft but uncomfortable, which he kept readjusting because it was too small to fit snugly on his large head. He had learnt well the early lessons taught by Dwayne; he found the practical crash course delivered to new recruits of *Jaish* helpful. So he now spoke only broken English. He had laughed when he caught a glimpse of himself in the mirror before leaving his room in the morning.

'Thank you, Maulana Mohammed Younis Khan, *Imam Sahib*,' he had said out aloud. *For so much more than the disguise*, he had thought. He had adopted a studied style of walking, legs bandy and splayed out to the side, as if rickets had hurt him in childhood; an affected, almost gravid style.

After two days of taking a circuitous route, mostly by public transport, earlier in the day he had arrived back in Southall. He had walked through the childhood-familiar streets. The bricks of the houses were browned like cinnamon bark, and roofs nutmeg-dark. People from the semi-tropical spice lands had invaded in the sixties, but he felt more of a foreigner than the settlers in his hometown. The streets where he grew up now felt strange to him. No longer home; but Jimmy wondered if he had ever belonged. He had asked more questions of himself in the last few weeks, since being attacked in the mosque and meeting Abu Umar, than he had ever allowed to surface before.

Jimmy looked around and saw the habitual imprisoning walls, the concrete slabs like grey gruel. The cultivated and forced hyacinths in a window felt unnatural against the moss, in the gaps left by the paving stones. The moss grew wildly, pushing past the tree roots like an English dhaniya, coriander; soft under his feet. It brought back the stench of fear, the bile rising again at the memory of having to sell heroin on someone else's patch when he was fourteen.

Jimmy remembered how he had started dealing, by pushing himself onto another dealer's territory. Even with the backing of his seniors, the memory of terror made his scar itch. He scratched it with his right hand, and his left shook. He held it firm against his side. Then, later, as he had grown in confidence, when he had taken over a small patch, he had expanded his empire; in turn, inciting fear in others.

He turned the corner of Springfield road, avoided looking at Uncle Younis' mosque. The image of his father toppled forward, forehead flush with the carpet, frozen in prostration, was fixed like a film still in his head. Jimmy muttered, '*Rahimullah*,' as he passed the mosque, still not looking up. *May Allah forgive him, grant him Paradise*.

Soon I will join him. Despite the anger of Dwayne, Abu Umar and The Army of Light and Peace, I know I will still carry out the mission, he thought. *I will convince them.*

Jimmy knew he had no choice but to return to Zoya. *I'm doing it for them too, for* Ami *and Zoya, so we can all be in Heaven together.* He felt cornered by fraternal compulsion and he knew it was as a result of her sisterly kindness, which had forced together the few joined-up memories of his childhood, the stitching which now held his material self together in an otherwise pulled-apart jigsaw life. His relationship with her and his mother seemed to him like a dot-to-dot puzzle, which enabled him to see the greater picture. Recently, because of Abu Umar, for the first time in his disjointed experience of the world the jigsaw puzzle had started to fit together. It was no longer a sea of irregular black monochrome pieces that seemed to have no beginning or end. Except for those few soft moments of responsibility towards his sister, and warmth from his mother, the rest of his life felt like a concrete knife at his throat. He did not often allow himself to remember much of his youth, which had been harsh and uniform, unchanging and without hope or expectation, like the terraced buildings that surrounded and huddled in on him now in the narrow streets. Bricks that he or his little soldiers so rarely called home, a solidity of structure he had not known.

Jimmy looked down from his wandering chimney-bound gaze and noticed Hanif, a local, who was a mosque regular. He had known Ahmad well; Hanif had been in his class at primary school. Jimmy remembered how many times he had battered him for many reasons, mostly none. *Freak, goody mosque* maulvi's *pet boy*, Jimmy and his friends had called him. Hanif had been a mosque regular, even back then, and he used to bump into Ahmad on his way to at least one of the day's five prayers. Jimmy hated his whining tone and the way he would ask Ahmad solicitously: *How is your health* Chacha Jan? He most often beat Hanif for looking at Zoya askance. He had heard how brothers were protective of their sister's honour and virtue in Pakistan, and it was a direct insult to the brother if the sister was maligned. Then he had put his furtive imagination into practice. Now the sight of the diminutive, mongoose-faced, bespectacled young man made his hands sweat. His feet caught in the paving slabs, and Jimmy almost stumbled.

He had no chance to smile at the irony. His fear of being recognised was real. Hanif knew the scar on his face, his steely grey eyes, which he now hid behind brown contact lenses. Hanif knew his old acne marks on his nose; he had been close enough to Jimmy numerous times to taste the spittle from his mouth during the venomous assaults. *What the hell is he doing out walking the streets at this time? Probably been praying in the mosque*, thought Jimmy, *and now he's going home after a late night* Qiyam al Lail, *the night vigil*.

Jimmy looked down, exaggerated his funny walk, and hoped that Hanif would not notice the padding for potbelly. He instinctively scratched his scar, despite it being mostly hidden by the false beard, and bumbled past Hanif, barely breathing.

Hanif did not notice. He did not even glance up from his habitual street gaze. He shuffled past him without seeing the fat fair-skinned middle-aged Asian man, in clothes that would have been weird anywhere else, but were usual in the ghetto. The *woods*, as Jimmy and his friends had called the Asian areas, the word derived from 'hood'. In their wondering teenage rhyme their tongues often misfired and were as delinquent as their attitudes.

Jimmy turned into his home street. He suspected they would be watching the house where he grew up. Where his mother had shed a blindness of tears. Where his sister's wedding preparations would be in full swing. Zoya must have changed after being assaulted by a group of men, and although Dan had helped her, Jimmy still could not understand why she had decided to marry him. Was three months enough time for her to go through such a transition, for a *Kuffar* man? *Then my world has changed, too,* he thought. *Like a volcano, suddenly erupting and creating a new island for me to live on, where there had only been the sea of rejection before.* Remorse washed over him like the sweat that caked his body, and ran into the false beard on his face.

MI5 and MI6: enemies of Islam had spies everywhere, even in *Jaish*. Despite the danger, he felt the pull of his nest like a homing pigeon that had been lost on his homeward flight. Like Ibn Battuta: Son of the Eagle; wandering the known world, but still missing his home, Tangier.

Jimmy walked past his house. He knew somehow, in some way, he had to stop, or arrange and pay for and then give Zoya away at her wedding. He had to do either one of those things. He could not decide between hatred at the thought of his sister becoming a *Kuffar* and losing her religion, and the potential contentment he would feel at her marriage. He felt the desire to see her happy rise from within him, and his heart pumped hard. Sweat poured out of him. He had to arrange everything for Zoya, make sure she married a good Muslim man. *That's what Ahmad would have wanted,* he thought.

Jimmy doubled back down his street, and when he was sure as he could be that he had not been followed, he ducked around into the rear alley, via the small side street that led to the back gardens. He quickly jumped over the fence, only mildly hindered by his unnatural belly, into the small overgrown garden. He crouched down behind a large laurel bush. He waited, his breath rasping in his throat, prickling sharper than the berberis bush in his back. He waited ten minutes, which seemed longer and harder than all his years of running and more running after *maall*, as his boys called the white stuff. He felt ethnic expectation closing ever faster, tumbling him into the timeless abyss of his heritage. Now, he seemed to have time beyond reason, time to think about the things that he had not had time to do before. His mind raced to all the things he had said, and to those things instead, which he *should* have said.

How he should have told his mother he would give up dealing drugs. How he should have helped Tony find a job. How he should have made his father proud, so he could have walked into the mosque with his head held up high. Not to say, like a typical Paki parent, *Oh my son is a doctor-lawyer-accountant, you know.* Just to say *Jimmy is a good boy. He takes care of his family. He respects his father, cares for his sister and loves his mother.*

Jimmy started to cry silently. He should have told Zoya he felt proud of her, happy she had found love, instead of saying she was a dirty slag: *a white man fuckin' whore*, as he had said when he first confronted her about Dan, when the accusations had spiralled down into slippery shame.

He remembered the lectures from Abu Umar's *halaqas*, the reason for his leaving home in the first place, and the memories caused him to draw strength, as if from the damp earth on which he crouched. Bosnia, Kosovo, Palestine, Kashmir, Iraq and Afghanistan: this degradation and humiliation would never happen if the Muslims were united and cared about their territories. Instead, their land and country was pillaged at will.

The Prophet said about the earth: *Hadi hi ummuhum. This is your mother.* Abu Umar had added after the translation that the *Kuffar* are raping, pillaging and degrading your mother, your *mother!* And you, you sit by and take charity from their coffers. Money in begging bowls, which they originally stole from you anyway. *That money rightfully belongs to us. They give you your unemployment cheque and welfare, and you are grateful to them. And because of that you sit quietly and idly by while they rape you every day. Your sisters and mothers, and even your brothers. Look at Abu Ghrayb! Guantanamo Bay!*

Jimmy could hear Abu Umar's voice, 'Let's not even talk about that.'

Why did I leave the Shaikh? he thought. *I should never have gone away without permission. Maybe they would have let me come, even for a few days.* But Jimmy knew they would never have let him go.

Jimmy had cried and wept with Abu Umar and Dwayne, and the other four members of the private *halaqa*, especially when Abu Umar had added: 'Oh, and Mohammed Bin Qasim was seventeen years old when he conquered Sind and changed the world forever. How old are you, Jimmy? How will you change the world?'

Jimmy wept even more when he personally and physically felt the pain at the loss of Granada and he had cried, just as the Caliph Abu Abdullah had, at the loss of the great city to the Christians. Jimmy now knew off by heart in Arabic what Boabdil, as the Christian world called him, had said, as he took one last forlorn look at Granada. The words of the Sultan's mother who had chastised and humiliated him at the loss of Granada: *Cry now like a woman because you could not defend it like a man!* She had shamed her weeping son further with this eternal rejoinder. That was one of the many historical references that *Shaikh* Abu Umar liked to make. Jimmy would beg Abu Umar to recite *Shame of Al Andalus*; he would finally acquiesce to the request, and recite in a voice filled with pain, loss and pathos and yearning. The poem had started Jimmy's conversion. The reversion: a revolution that now seemed to belong to a different lifetime, in some parallel universe.

Jimmy had to be there for Zoya, or delay the wedding enough so that he could prove the *Biradari* wrong and put to rest his father's shame, by making sure Zoya married a Muslim man. He would put his hand on her head and bless her to protect her instead of Ahmad, now that she was fatherless. Jimmy knew he was the only one in the world who could provide her with that strength that she needed in the face of disgust and weird stares of the extended family and community. A *Gorah*, another *Gorah*: *well, they do say that history comes home eventually.* He could hear the women's comments already, and only Jimmy could stare them down and make a small degree of embarrassment enter their eyes, to take some of the glare off Zoya and shield her. Now, all thoughts of turning back – of running away, hiding and begging Dwayne's forgiveness for going away without leave, and the visions of being forgiven then re-embraced and protected by *Al Jaish* – turned to mist, like the fog from his panting breath.

Jimmy's thoughts shamed him into action. He would be there to wipe Zoya's tears, to let his own salt wet her hair, to place his hands on her head, to apply his huge palms to her scalp: tradition realised into emotion. He wanted to cover her head with his meaty paws, make her feel safe before she set sail on her voyage into an uncharted space, and wish her a happy life as she drove away in her bridal car with the right husband, whoever that might be.

Before that, he would finally kiss Zoya's forehead. In that small gesture lay the tradition of centuries, the strength of propriety Islam. The fraternal pressure and responsibilities had been laid out in civilisations established over generations – *for good reason*, thought Jimmy. *In that kiss hides the promise that no matter what happens you will always be my sister, and I will always be there for you, to help you if you need it, to protect you should you desire it; to love you, my sister, until my last breath.*

Although the self-doubt had been overcome by responsibility and love, he wiped the sweat off his brow and tried to slow his breathing. The fear, once again, became all pervasive.

Jimmy no longer feared death after his conversion to the true path. He had learned to live with the thought of imminent demise since he had been old enough to weigh in grams, and tie up the little bundles that looked so innocuous, like talcum powder. Since his days of certainty had started, he knew death was a lover to be embraced wherever she was to be found.

Jimmy did fear being captured alive. Terror spread through him as he thought of the ignominy and humiliation his family would have to suffer. Mortified, his body froze and refused to respond when he imagined the endless circle of years, the repetitive visits they would have to make to his prison. The ostracisation from the little society his mother had left, after Ahmad's death and Zoya's marriage to a *Gorah*. Being captured alive by the enemy, left alive and not martyred, was stigma – *sharam*, shame – which caused a pain beyond endurance. He wrung his hands and tried to release the cramp, which had gripped his clenched fists.

The Butterfly Hunter

Jimmy vomited at the base of the laurel bush and piled up the dirt and earth over the vomit with his hands, shovelling it into a pile. *I will not be captured*, he swore. He gritted his teeth and wiped his muddy hands on his loose salwar. He was glad that he had stolen the small black vest from his storage locker, from the compartment where he hid the vest after practice exercises, in the training flat. Although, at that time he had no idea why he was taking the vest. It seemed to be yet another thing that made no sense.

Over the past two days on the run, he had finalised the hardest decision. If it came to a choice, Jimmy would rather take all those he loved with him, because he loved them; rather than allowing them to endure the derision-defeat of capture.

He remembered what Abu Umar said to him early on in his spiritual training; 'You don't have to endure the unendurable.' When Jimmy had looked at him blankly, his *Shaikh* answered, 'End it.' His teacher's voice had been calm and gentle. 'But make sure you do something above and beyond yourself. For the greater glory of Islam.'

Despite Jimmy's confusion, Abu Umar went on. 'In your death is their defeat. And your eternal victory. So when a momin, *Mujahid* of Islam fights, whether he is living or dying is no matter. It's the same thing. There is only eternal victory.'

Jimmy knew he would take them with him; they would all be together forever. He had prepared to take Tony, Zoya and Sofia with him, rather than face capture. He imagined Zoya sitting there in the small back room, wearing the scarlet marriage wedding *lengha* suit, henna on her hands and feet, like roses blushed with the morning dew. *Yes, better to take them all with me to eternal success and live in His peace, than to suffer lifelong humiliation and defeat*. Moreover, it would be the defeat of Islam if Jimmy allowed himself to be captured. Yet he knew he would have to walk across a spider's web, spread across the valley. On one side stood the security services, and on the other the ravine that plunged him straight back into the heart of *Jaish an Noor wass Salaam*.

He took a few deep breaths and shinned up the drainpipe with the trellis on the side, which had an old iceberg-white rose climbing up it, and quietly forced Zoya's bedroom window.

Jimmy saw Zoya rouse as he climbed in; he smiled at her. 'Zoya'.
Zoya screamed.

CHAPTER 26

London

Jessica wondered why she had been sent on a practice run on her own today; she had never been on a practice mission alone before. *Maybe this is just another one of their tests*, she thought.

As usual, she had been given a route with timings, and how long it should take her to walk from St Thomas's Hospital to the South Bank and then back again. How many minutes it should take her to cross Westminster Bridge, and how long each tube journey would take. She felt most of these exercises were probably simple feints. One of them could be a rehearsal for the actual journey on the final day. Today, as on her many previous practice runs, her doubts rose. What if any one of these numerous practice runs was not a practice? What if the final day had been brought forward, and she was the trigger? *Will I die today? Will London be destroyed by me?* she thought. She had regularly worn her suicide vest, which carried one of the triggers, under her thick coat. She sweated, despite the December cold.

The vests had the triggers, as well as their own explosives. Abu Umar had explained that they were not only essential, but also a diversion if the police stopped any of them, so that the real plot could stay undiscovered. The operation would have been far more conspicuous in the summer; the explosives belt could not be hidden so easily under summer clothes.

Jessica had almost walked across Westminster Bridge, when she heard someone come up close behind her. She almost jumped as she heard a voice whispering in her left ear.

'Don't turn around Jessica, keep walking. It's Hamza. Walk across the bridge, and I'll meet you in Café Nero.'

She remembered how Hamza had tried to give her obscure hints initially, but she felt she could not trust him, especially since he was so close to Jimmy. They had been best mates in childhood and had rekindled their comradeship. She realised what a huge risk he had taken every time, when he had approached her to talk for a short while. They could not speak openly in the planning flat, but he had often ended up speaking with Jessica after meetings and spiritual study circles. Although he had said nothing specific, she felt he had more to say. She thought maybe he was looking for the right opportunity. This feeling had increased over the last few meetings, but with all of the cell members and Abu Umar frequently present, Hamza had mostly enthused about their project. Every time she had seen a growing need reflected in Hamza's eyes as he sent her his terrible telepathy with his dark pools, a secret message to her. Hamza overtook her and walked straight on, without turning around to look at her.

A thousand thoughts churned through Jessica. Her fear swirled like the waters of the river below her feet, and she stopped to regulate her breathing. Her chest heaved, and sweat ran down her temples. She looked over the side and did not dare glance up, as Hamza walked away from her. She looked at the water as the river eddied and flowed, uncertain currents leading to an unknown future. This dry run, unlike many which were arranged seemingly on the whim of Abu Umar, had been planned the week before. Jessica supposed he could not betray a pattern to their training. She had continued as a committed member, because she felt she had no choice. She had to remain inside the cell if she was ever going to influence the outcome of the bombing. Now this. Shockingly, Hamza had appeared out of nowhere; she had not imagined he would approach her during today's practice run.

Maybe he knew she would not be watched today. The Afghan was always watching: was he watching for them, or himself? He had always accompanied her on previous missions. Jessica missed his looming figure behind her, like a habit.

The Afghan had changed in many ways. Now he might have been any ordinary British man in his twenties, except for his yellowing teeth. The top two front incisors had been knocked out during his walk from Afghanistan to London. His ever-stained, dirt-marked fingernails, were tangible proof of his labouring background. The gap between his teeth a chasm, conspicuous evidence of his third world origins. She thought that was a space, a distance, that could not be bridged by orthodontics alone.

He had told her through Jimmy weeks ago: *I have never seen more golden hair and bluer eyes. You look like a jeweller's shop.* Jimmy had translated. He had grinned with his gap-toothed smile and said: *I lub jou! I lub jou!* in English.

Jimmy had given up trying to teach him how to say it properly, and Hamza had laughed and shaken his head. Jimmy had tried giving him the pronunciation of the three simple words, which the Afghan had supplicated disconcertingly to Jessica, and then attempted on women in the streets of London. She had watched, amazed, as Hamza made vague and none too serious attempts to restrain him.

'Unusual men saying weird things in funny accents are nothing new on the streets of London,' Hamza had said, and they had laughed harder when most women ignored the Afghan and just walked by, faster than before.

Unlike the other times on her practice runs, today she could not sense anyone behind her, dogging her steps. There was no way to be sure as the shoal of faces passed her seemingly randomly. Anyone might be there watching her, to make sure she did not falter and of course, they must be able to remotely detonate the vest she wore. Perhaps Hamza knew that she would not be followed on her dry run, for if she did want to talk to someone to betray *Jaish* she would be unlikely to do it while practising how to be a trigger.

Hamza was supposed to be in a planning meeting. Why had he followed her today? What is he: an avenging angel, or the devil's temptation? How far dare she trust him? Even to meet him like this could be life-threatening. This could be another test devised by Abu Umar. She had come through all the previous tests and examinations, shown her loyalty, and had easily passed through the designed contrivances – one of which had been an offer of money to sell her story to a newspaper. She had been approached by a supposed journalist.

There had been other offers to escape from the cell, to disappear, attempts to convince her she was on a path to terrorism by acquaintances, and then by people she had did not know. Each time she had laughed and refused automatically, without wondering for a moment if the temptations were genuine or not, because she knew they were tests, and she was completely committed to staying in *Jaish* and stopping their plans from coming into fruition.

Jessica reached Café Nero. Hamza stood outside with two takeaway drinks. 'Come on. Let's go for a walk on this side of the river.'

'What's going on?'

He led her to a bench overlooking the river, waved for her to sit, but remained standing, looking behind her. 'So... did you meet your timed targets today?'

'Yes, I think so,' said Jessica, looking at her watch. 'Are you supposed to be here? *Shaikh* Abu Umar didn't say anything about you meeting me here.'

'We have to train in different ways; there are many ways to do the right thing.'

'Did Dwayne send you, to keep an eye on me?' She looked into his dark eyes as he sat next to her, and gulped some coffee, but it was too hot. There was nowhere to spit it out, so she held it in her mouth for a moment.

'I wouldn't worry about Dwayne, and someone always has eyes on you. Although you've got the most freedom. They know there's nowhere you can go or run.'

She swallowed. 'What's going on, Hamza?'

Hamza glanced up at the bridge and looked back towards the South Bank, across the other side of the river. 'Come on, keep walking. Let's go along the river.' He led the way, without waiting for her to catch up.

'Hamza, I've got to get back to the training flat, and then Holly's due to come to visit from Birmingham. I've got to get to my own flat after that.' *Jaish* had allowed a small separate flat so that her parents and friends could visit; Jessica was grateful for the privacy. None of others were granted such a privilege, because they had disappeared.

Hamza turned without warning, climbed the steps, and led her back across Westminster Bridge, to Café Manga. Jessica caught up, out of breath. He queued up to order.

'I need some water,' she said, pushing he long hair out of her eyes. Today, as usual, she did not wear her scarf on the training missions, but had to remember to wear it around people who knew she had converted. She knew she would not wear it on the final day.

Hamza grimaced. His light, joking tone was gone, and his eyes seemed to swirl darker than the waters of the river. Hamza took two bottles of water, and sat at a table outside.

'Listen Jessica, I thought there was something different about you when we first met.'

'So did Dwayne,' said Jessica, gulping some water, which cooled her tongue. She peered at Hamza, catching her breath, but she could not be sure what Hamza meant.

'It's not funny, Jessica.' Hamza brushed his flopping hair away from his forehead, his thin features taut, and she was surprised to see him fiddle with his fingers.

Does he really want to take me into his confidence, or has he been trained to be a good actor?

'You're not supposed to be here today, are you?'

'This thing that we're involved in, Jessica, is big.' He looked at her, hands on the table, immobile.

'Well, that's great, isn't it? The victory of Islam will be complete, *inshallah*,' she said, in keeping with her persona in the cell.

'I'm not sure. These bombs – there are more of them. You've heard the Abu Umar mention nuclear and biological and chemical…' He raised his eyebrows.

'Yes, but surely in war – and we are at war, aren't we?' *This must be another test*, thought Jessica; *they want to see my commitment, to see if I will waver.*

'But so many people…' he said, gesturing to the crowds. 'Let's carry on walking. We can't sit in one place for too long. We'll walk slowly this time.'

'As the *Shaikh* said, the people are not innocent, are they?' she said, following him.

What does he want; is he for real? she thought. It would be so easy to trust Hamza, without applying any logical part of her brain. But that would be abdicating her responsibility; to herself, and the people she loved.

'What about the children? If Mariam's children were innocent, aren't these children the same? All children are the same.'

He's testing my emotions. He knows how I felt about Mariam and the children. 'So you're having serious doubts?' she said, going along with him. 'What are you going to do?'

'Will you tell Abu Umar or Dwayne?' Without waiting for a response, he looked at her; his eyes seemed to be pleading. 'I need your help. To stop the hell. And believe me, it will be hell for everyone, *Kuffar* or Muslim.'

Jessica had been tested like this before. Each time she had seen the predictable approach, and had smiled and shrugged off suggestions made by Dwayne and Plain Jamila that she should betray the *Jihad* of *Jaish*. This time there seemed to be something different about Hamza, in the way he bit his lip before he spoke, and the way he twisted the bottle of water between his fingers so that the label had come off as he walked. They stopped on the bridge again, like tourists, and watched a Chinese-looking man twist lengths of metal and marbles to form names and pictures.

'I know you can't trust me, no one would in this situation, but when the time comes, I will need you to help me.' He leaned forward; his eyes seemed like deep pools peering into her face.

Jessica smiled at him. 'I'm sorry, Hamza. I can't help you. This is the *Jihad*, the final solution, *inshallah*, and this will lead to the victory of Islam and hasten the return of the Golden Age. That's the only way we'll ever get peace in this world.'

He nodded; his lips formed a twisted grimace.

'You're very good at this, really good. Did Abu Umar train you to act out your emotions?'

Hamza shrugged.

'I do like you, Hamza and so I think I'll let you tell *Shaikh* about our meeting and your doubts. I shalln't say anything,' she said, smiling at him, leaving the door of remote possibility that he meant what he said, ajar. 'Maybe you'll be sent for remedial training – maybe not – but I'll leave it up to you.'

Jessica walked away from him. She was due to return to the training flat, but she glanced at her watch and realised she might miss Holly's arrival at her flat. She quickened her pace, and thought she could quickly receive Holly and settle her in to the flat. She was the only one of the cell who was ostensibly living a normal life.

Afterwards, she would go back to the training flat; today's debriefing would not take too long. As she walked, she wondered if Hamza was back and had already told the others all about their meeting, and if Jimmy had laughed at her. She wondered when she would get a chance to see Sebastian, and whether she ever manage to introduce him to Holly. She still had to convince Abu Umar and Dwayne to letting Holly visit more regularly. At least Dwayne would be on her side.

Jessica's thoughts, as usual, turned to Sebastian. Since he had become special to her, she had become even more resolute in her secret opposition to *Jaish*. He had become so precious to her that she could not imagine a life worth living without him. What of his life without her, if she didn't succeed? What if he suffered because of her? If he happened to be in The School of Oriental and African Studies – on the final day?

The pain in the centre of her chest arose in her again, as she panted quickly and covered the short distance to her flat, which was only two streets away from the central training flat. She swallowed hard. Her relationship with Sebastian, if it was allowed to flourish, would be unique. She often thought about the possibilities that might develop... the promise of potential moments of breathless happiness. Her mind wandered to the coming spring, which would bring daffodils and tulips to life again in her garden. She remembered the picnic she had taken with him, after the walk through the woods near Malvern; where birds had sang a lazy melody in the last of the late summer heat, whilst fishermen dozed by the river and dragonflies chased each other, leaving iridescent colours across the stream. Where he served her tea in a porcelain cup.

Jaish took over her thoughts. Abu Umar often misquoted Qur'anic phrases and maligned Islam in the vilest terms possible. That was a fact she knew, even at the start of her journey. She had read many books secretly, things which *Jaish* would never have tolerated, and then talked to Sebastian. She could ask him any question without embarrassment or fear of censure.

She had joined *Jaish* mainly to find answers about Hamid, and at some stage in the future she had a remote hope that she could report on their activities, make a documentary to expose the truth, satisfy her journalistic curiosity. Despite her successful infiltration, she realised now that this would never happen.

She had managed to hide her disgust and anger that had rapidly festered into hatred, a flesh-eating pox that she had to keep below her skin until she could stop the bombings. She became more convinced of her beliefs after the regular conversations she had had with Sebastian. Despite Abu Umar's disapproving comments about the *modern, moderate wishy-washy Islam*, she knew most Muslims saw Allah to be loving and forgiving. *His mercy is far above his wrath*. Her own spirituality, despite not taking the form of an organised religion, had given her a new strength.

She had realised with even greater certainty that *Jaish* had twisted the fabric of truth until it fell apart into shreds, and then they blinded their followers with the poisonous anthrax-like dust.

Jessica's visions of a future with Sebastian increased the potential joys of the temporal, magnified the ephemeral nature of life. It would be a sin to throw it away before time. She breathed deeply, and even the air of central London tasted sweet. The river carried the promise of salt, sea and life. Death was inevitable, but at the right time, not before. Going deliberately would mean losing the battle – just giving up, no bravery involved.

Jessica had come to the only conclusion she could. The inevitable realisation that, despite what Abu Umar said and the justifications he used, and in spite of the atrocities that had occurred in the videos that Dwayne showed them, the end did not justify the means. The slaughter of innocents was not an acceptable Islamic philosophy, no matter what the cause, and her reading of the great scholars and the history of Islam had only reaffirmed this in her mind.

She had not let her emotions control her, but had put her trust in a higher power, just as she now decided to tell Sebastian the truth. *Does it matter if I lied to him about converting, and hid the truth from him?* she wondered. *Can I make it up by loving him? I don't know. I don't know if I deserve his love; does he love me?*

Jessica reached her small flat, threw off her coat and hid the suicide vest in a wardrobe, which she locked, and then breathed heavily. She had told Sebastian she rented the flat from a friend. She often used her flat, where she had initially been installed by Plain Jamila, away from the spacious training apartment the cell trained in, when she needed to be alone. To stay here for any length of time, she had had to make excuses to Dwayne and Abu Umar that family would be visiting, or that Sebastian was coming. She knew *Jaish* had to keep the pretence that Jessica had a normal life because she had not disappeared from home, so they had no choice but to allow her to come. She felt glad to be away from the Afghan's continued staring for a short while, although she felt someone might be watching her here too, and she was not supposed to come to her own flat without getting permission from Dwayne. She was never supposed to come here with the suicide vest, but she had been expecting Holly to arrive from Birmingham any minute – and anyway, Holly would not look inside a locked wardrobe. Jessica thought she would return it to the central training flat later, and put it back without anyone noticing. She had much more freedom than the other members of the terror cell. She supposed they just thought she was a woman who was prone to emotional outbursts, and *Jaish* needed her.

The doorbell rang, and Jessica ran to open the front door, expecting Holly. She had convinced Abu Umar that if Holly did not visit her at all, then it would be suspicious. Although she had no idea how Holly could help, and in fact, it might be dangerous for her. She knew none of the cell members were allowed visitors or to make any contact with anyone since their induction and training in *Jaish* had begun. Abu Umar had allowed her exceptions, indulged her, but she knew almost certainly that *Jaish* watched them continuously. Jessica felt she needed support, and smiled as she thought of Holly on the other side of the door.

'Hi, Jessica. How are you?' Sebastian's mouth turned downwards at the corners, his eyebrows arched high.

'Sebastian! What are you doing here?' she said. He had never come to her flat without ringing first. Jessica realised why he had surprise and concern on his face at seeing her open the door, with her flowing blonde hair trailing behind her.

'Oh, you've taken your scarf off?'

'No, oh shit! Yes, sorry – one minute. I must have forgotten it.' She rushed back into the house, leaving him standing on the step.

Oh God! How stupid! she thought. He's seen me without my scarf, now. This is what I've been dreading. Why didn't I check from the window, as usual? She had run to the door barefooted, hoping she could just show Holly in and then leave because she was late as usual for the debriefing meeting, which had become routine after the practice runs, with Abu Umar at the training flat. Today the members of the cell had to go through the practical points with Dwayne, of timings and which landmarks they should have hit, and at what exact times during the exercises.

She padded back to the front door holding a scarf beneath her chin with both hands, fiddling to tie it. 'Sorry – come in, come in.'

'No, I just – just wanted to drop off some cauliflower I had grown. I have an allotment here in London.' He held out a basket with a variety of winter vegetables. He did not look at her. 'And I wanted to make sure you're okay.'

She forced a laugh; he still lived in a world that grew winter vegetables. She cursed inwardly that she was still not proficient at tying her scarf. 'Why, Sebastian, you surprised me. I mean... what on earth would be wrong with me?' She let her scarf hang limp, untied. She felt sure he would notice the timbre of her laugh, more nasal than she could control.

'Actually, I think I will come in.'

'Sorry, Sebastian, I didn't expect you. I was just on my way to –'

'To a very important meeting?' he asked, as he stepped past her into the living room.

'How could you know that?' She bit her lower lip, the dread rising and spreading through her like a torrent of paralysis.

'I had a very strange phone call today.'

'Phone call? Who phoned you? From whom, Sebastian?' she said, tumbling the questions out.

'Well, this is what I asked the man on the other end, Jessica darling, and do you know – I don't think he ever did give a name. Or perhaps he did... I don't remember. But he seemed convinced that you are in some kind of trouble.'

Jessica did not know what to say; she felt torn. Surely he knew something, now. The sensation of relief that she knew she would feel when he made her spill the whole story almost overcame her. But the fear that he would be disgusted, angry, and would walk out never wanting to see her again clamped her mouth.

Finally she asked, 'What – what was his name?' She pulled her lower lip harder and felt sure he would notice how pale she had become. The blood drained from her face, and she held onto the back of a chair. *What if Abu Umar or Dwayne had got to Sebastian was this another threat? Could they get to anyone at anytime?* 'Where was he phoning from? On behalf of whom?' She came closer to him, as they both stood in the room. 'It's vital. Really important that you remember, Sebastian – please. Did he mention *Jaish an Noor wass Salaam*? Or – or...' She did not know how to continue.

'Jessica, darling, one day you're mine and we have a future together, and then the next you're someone else. Suddenly I don't know you, as if I have no right to ask. Why don't you just stop –'

'Stop what?' she said, and noticed his concern turning to anger. She turned away from him, her thumbnail in her mouth as she paced the room. Then she turned to face him, and the disaster she knew was inevitable. She looked up at his face.

'He mentioned the name Hamza – yes, Hamza,' said Sebastian.

Jessica hoped he did not see the relief on her face; but how far dare she trust Hamza? She felt she had rightly rejected his approach today.

'Are you going to continue pretending?' he said, and she saw his face redden. She felt torn. How much had Hamza said? Sebastian certainly suspected or knew something, but how could she tell him?

'I saw you earlier today, as I walked across the river, with some guy in a Café – drinking coffee with him. Without your scarf on, in public…' he said and flopped down on the sofa.

He's controlling himself pretty well, she thought, as she turned away from him. *I've got to tell him now.*

Making the decision did not dissipate the fear that threatened to choke her breath, and she felt as if she was drowning in her own sweat. She sat down on the sofa, and Sebastian sat next to her.

'I think we've got to talk to Hamza,' she said, feeling the regret, but she knew it was not as simple as that. Hamza was a trap. If she went through with Abu Umar's plans and stayed in the terror cell she would be dead soon, but if she did not then London would be destroyed, and *Jaish* would ensure she would be dead even sooner. She pushed the hair which had escaped from the top of her scarf back, away from her eyes, and blurted the rest of the words that had been eating at her brain like an invasive fungus, the confession that had been chewing her body like an alien growing within.

'And I'm a suicide bomber!' she said, and let out a small gasp at her own audacity, the deadly game of risk. She had thought about it for so long, what she would say if the time came to explain things to him; the elaborate explanations and excuses she had rehearsed now burnt away like mist under the searing sun of Sebastian's suspicion.

'What?'

'I'm sorry, Sebastian. I've been meaning, trying to think of a way to tell you for so long, but I joined *Jaish*, and I'm in a terror cell. Hamza is one of us in the cell.' Jessica covered her face with her hands. A stabbing pain exploded in her chest with every intake of breath.

'What did you say?' Sebastian exploded off the sofa. 'Do you even know what the hell that means? You've been playing me for a bloody fool all this time?' His words ricocheted off the walls, and hurt her ears like rejection. He came up to Jessica, saliva flying, flecking his lips in white, and his face turned red. He fists bunched up at his sides.

She got up but shrank away from him, took a couple of steps

backwards, put up her hands. 'No, Sebastian, please. You don't understand.'

He followed her, bore down on her. 'What the hell don't I understand? I knew you were up to something weird, but for Christ's sake!' He brought his fists up in between them.

Jessica turned away. 'Maybe this isn't a good time. You shouldn't have come, and I'm late for my meeting.' She walked away from him, towards the hallway.

'How dare you? How dare you lie, cheat and then walk away from me? Kick me out as if I'm nothing to you?' He followed her into the hallway. 'How dare you?' he shouted.

'No, Sebastian – it's not like that.' Jessica took off her scarf; *no point in keeping up the pretence any longer*, she thought. 'But this isn't the time to talk about it.'

'There is no other time; it's right now, or nothing. If it's not right now, then I don't matter to you, and you'll never see me again. Sit down. I said – sit – down – right – now!' He pointed her to the sofa.

Jessica sat on the sofa and covered her face with her hands. Sebastian went into the kitchen. She heard the tap run, and when he returned he still seemed barely able to control his face.

Sebastian did not approach her, did not put an arm around her. 'Well, it seems you're not only going to die yourself, but kill numerous others too?' Jessica saw the anger and feared his hatred. Tears came, and made her gulp for air. 'When you've quite finished, phone them, whoever the hell it is controlling you. Tell them you've had an emergency, blame it on me if you want, and tell them you're going to be late for the meeting.' He handed Jessica her mobile phone.

Jessica did not move. She had her face in her palms, and she hid her face with her hands. 'I'm sorry, Sebastian. I'm so sorry.'

'Once, you asked me about being a wolf. Well you better be ready to kill those dogs if need be. Otherwise, if they suspect you've told me, no one will ever find a chunk of your meat.'

Jessica could do nothing except cry more, with her eyes screwed up tight and her fists in front of her face.

'Pull yourself together, and make the phone call. After that we're going to sort this out once and for all.'

'Please, Sebastian please get out – go to Birmingham. Anywhere – get away from the centre as far away as you can. You've no time.'

'I'm sorry. I can't,' Sebastian said. She heard the concern in his voice despite his anger, and her pulse surged. He continued, 'I can't leave you alone in this mess.' He breathed deeply, sat down on the sofa, and leaned back, closing his eyes.

'I got myself into this mess…' she said, and regret enveloped her and drenched her body.

His voice seemed barely-controlled; his eyes twitched for a moment. 'It's not just you, now. That's what I wanted to tell you.' Jessica looked up at him again. He held his hand in hers, but it did not stop her shaking. He breathed deeply, his nostrils flared.

'I know this is the worst time, darling, but I love you. I love you, Jessica.'

CHAPTER 27

London
Jimmy smothered Zoya's mouth and choked her scream before it could wake the house. 'Yo-Yo. It's me, Yo-Yo. Don't scream!' he said, and then he remembered what he looked like. 'It's Jimmy.' He saw the look of terror in her eyes, with no light of recognition there. 'It's Jimmy. It's your brother. Who else would know Yo-Yo?' said Jimmy, calling her by her baby name that he had invented when he could not pronounce Zoya. He had started by saying Zo-Zo, which later became an affectionate Yo-Yo. He gently let her waist go, but kept one hand firmly on her mouth. He pointed to the scar on the right side of his face and tried to tug off his beard, but he had glued it on too firmly. In the dim light he saw recognition replace repugnance over Zoya's sleep-doused face. He let her go.

'What are you doing here?'

'I came back.'

'Where the hell have you been?' Zoya asked, her voice barely contained as she switched on her bedside lamp. Her anger made him mumble something, as if she did not know where to begin. 'Mum's worried herself into a spin of sadness. In fact, she's sick. She's become a nutter over worry for you,' Zoya said, brushing her hair out of her eyes.

Jimmy had expected Zoya's worry and stress to spill over into anger.

'Just what we needed, after dad died,' said Zoya.

'I had to go. *Abbo* said to find myself: to become a true Muslim man.'

'I don't think he meant disappear without a word and turn your *pista* mum into a fruitcake,' said Zoya, easily slipping back into private code, where *pista* shortened from pistachio came from *nut* and meant 'mad' between them. Zoya rubbed her bloodshot eyes. Jimmy saw the cold fury smeared over her face.

'If it wasn't for Sadia's support... she's been here night and day, poor thing. You've no idea what you've done.'

'What's wrong with *Ami*? What's happened to her?' Suddenly he realised for the first time since his departure that there had been such a negative impact on his mother. 'I didn't mean anything, right...'

'Well it has. Where have you been? What have you been doing?'

'I didn't think –'

'Yeah, well you never think. That's your problem.' Zoya paused for a moment, when Jimmy did not answer. 'The police have been here...' She looked down at the bed. 'Well, what did you expect? You idiot. We're your family. We had no idea where you were.'

'You know I can look after myself.'

'How tough do you think you are? A bullet can find you, no matter how hard you are. You're meat! You disappear into thin air, none of your friends knew where you were, your phone was dead.'

Abruptly he looked up at her. 'How are my butterflies? Has *Ami* been feeding them? Has anyone been into the small greenhouse? I gotta go see them, feed them now.' Jimmy stood up; Zoya pulled his arm.

'Sit down! It's three in the morning, you idiot. Butterflies? That's the only thing you ever gave a shit about. You stupid bloody idiot.'

Jimmy pulled his arm away.

'*Ami*'s been looking after them.'

He sat down when he heard that Sofia had been caring for them. 'So you called the fuckin' *suwar*?' said Jimmy, unconsciously translating pigs into Urdu.

'Of course I did. *Ami* thought your body was gonna turn up, if we were lucky, deformed and burnt, handed to us in bits in a plastic bag,' she said. Jimmy saw her anger turn to relief, at seeing her brother alive.

'Sadia even gave up her exams. There was no one else.' Tears pricked her eyes, and Jimmy felt regret and remorse at the tears.

'I'm sorry. I didn't mean to hurt anyone.' Then he realised that was not true, and he had been complicit in a plot to blow up innumerable people. 'I didn't mean to hurt you and Ami, anyway,' he added.

'Come here, you *kotha*. You always were such an ass, dumb as a donkey.' Zoya pulled him close. 'I've been so worried. Tony's been praying even more than normal, even got me doing it,' she said. She turned the bedspread back, and sat down.

Jimmy saw her examining his face closely.

'Are you in danger? Were you followed?' she asked.

He did not reply, but instead looked away from her. She pulled him to sit down on the bed. 'Of course you're in trouble. Jimmy ,what have you been up to, and why are you in that ridiculous get-up?'

'Well, I didn't realise that Uncle Younis would inspire me.' When he saw Zoya did not smile, he said, 'Don't worry about that. I'm here now ain't I?' Jimmy saw the look of exasperated outrage on her face and he tried to lighten his tone again. '*Ya Rabi*, it hasn't even been three months yet. Jesus! I thought you lot could cope.'

She shook her head and got up to make sure her bedroom door was locked. 'Keep your voice down.'

Jimmy heard Sofia go to the bathroom. 'Where's *Ami*?'

'In bed – where do you think? Jimmy, what's happened to you? It's three in the morning, everyone's in bed.' Zoya huffed and sighed as she sat back down, pulling her legs up to her chest. Her dark-brown ringlets fell to her shoulders and partly covered her face, and her wheaten skin shone even in the semi-darkness.

Jimmy squinted at his sister as she stared at him, and some light came in through the window and flickered on his face. She brushed some ropes of hair out of her face, which brought back memories of childhood for Jimmy. He felt filled with fraternal affection. With it came regret, black and malignant like oil polluting and defiling the purity of brotherly love, an oilslick over a snow-covered beach, because he had disappeared. He quickly justified it in his mind. It was for the greater good.

Jimmy felt guilty for having beaten up Dan, assaulted and battered him. The day when Dan had rescued her from the yobs saved her from a possible gang rape and a possible polluted death: a disgrace for eternity. He felt the spume of shame and embarrassment wash over him like a tidal wave, carried deep from the ocean of his soul. On seeing Zoya like this, scared and vulnerable, the dread-hatred of the white *Kuffar* washed out of him. Jimmy knew that Dan had asked for Zoya's hand and, shockingly to Jimmy, Sofia had quickly agreed. Within a short few weeks everything had been arranged, despite Jimmy's absence.

Why had Sofia agreed so readily? he wondered. *Why did she want everything arranged in weeks?* Although Dan was pig, *suwar*, police – and therefore enemy of Islam – Jimmy assumed he loved Zoya, and Jimmy suspected she loved him. That was not enough. He could not allow the marriage to go ahead, unless Zoya married the right man.

'How was it done so quickly?' he asked. 'The arrangements for your marriage?'

'Why, are you suspicious?' She looked at him, her anger rising quickly again. He feared it would become a torrent. 'Are you being a typical bloody Paki hypocrite brother?'

Jimmy saw her cheeks flush. 'It's not that –'

Zoya cut him short. 'Well don't you bloody worry, Mr Muslim hypocrite. I am not pregnant.'

He felt the accusations of the community had scorched her skin, and made her sensitive to any hint of accusation.

'Even an ignorant Paki rude-woods boy like you must realise that I can't be pregnant in three months and not know it,' she said.

He looked down and stubbed his big toe repetitively on the carpet. 'I didn't mean that, innit, sis.'

'What did you mean?'

'I meant with what happened to you, and me just disappearing, yeah, and then *Abbo* recently. I mean... it's been only three months. You know how mum would want a respectable time to pass, at least a few months after the traditional *chaliswaah* prayer rites on the fortieth day. Him dying like that in the mosque and everything.'

'Oh yeah, with *Abbo* gone, that's affected *Ami* really badly too, and thinking about what happened to you on top of everything.'

'You know what our *budi* women are like. There's already enough talk about our family – me the druggie, and *Gorah* ancestors, and *Abbo* dead with his head in *sujood*, which I now realise was the best way for him to go. That's what he would have wanted, yeah, to be in *Jummah* in the front row... But this, your marriage – I mean, hasn't it caused a scandal?'

'Is that what happened to you? You became like *Abbo*?'

Jimmy shrank back. He had never thought of himself to be like his father. He avoided answering Zoya.

After a pause, he said, 'Was it to stop the rellys talking and the old women's gossiping, *ki bak bak*, then?' He scratched at his scar. Jimmy saw Zoya's face turn into a funny twisted smile, just as it always did when he was guilty of jumping to conclusions. She still looked pretty. Somehow he felt this was not the same sister he had left. She had changed from the culturally weighed-down woman who trundled the wheel of life like the blinkered beast of burden at the water wheel he had seen in Ramnagar. Jimmy could never be as he had been in the previous life either, in his life of *Jahiliya*, of ignorance, before he had found Islam.

Instead, Jimmy now felt like a thoroughbred who romped through Allah's green and pleasant pasture unfettered to run the Martyrs' field of dreams; shed blood for His pleasure to be counted amongst the *Mujahideen* and *Shaheed*. A pure Arabian stallion. All the respect and admiration and envy on the streets, the success, the idolisation of his foot soldiers and boys had not brought as much satisfaction as his sherbet-sweet conviction.

'Those old bitches been talking shit about you?' he said.

'Well you know how people talk and yes, everyone was talking saying it was my fault, especially the women, mum's friends...' She almost sank into the duvet, 'For being attacked...'

'How ridiculous,' said Jimmy. He thought it was outrageous, and he bunched his fists.

'Well they said I was in town, in Ealing. What was I doing there at that time?'

'What time? You was coming from work.'

'Yeah, and then they said 'Well, that's why girls shouldn't work. We told you, Sofia, don't send your daughter out to work. It's not Islamic."

'Islam's got nothing to do with it.'

'They said it does, and so it's the truth. *Ami*'s feeling so guilty since that day.'

'These old bitches don't know what Islam is.'

'Then there's Dan, thank God for him – but he brought me home, and they saw me with him.'

'That's pure chance, innit? Allah's will.' Jimmy paused, unsure if he should go on. 'But he helped you; saved you. You – you could have been killed, yeah?'

He looked at his sister, hating the thought. He forgot his disguise and beard, now immersed in childhood memories and swamped by mixed emotions. Dan – a *Gorah* man, a white policeman – helped and saved Zoya when he could not. Nor any Muslim. Not Abu Umar or Dwayne, but Dan, one of the *Kuffar* enemy instruments of the state, which was oppressing Muslims everywhere. *What really happened to Zoya?* he thought, the endless thought. *Did those* Gorah-*bastard-guys rape her? Why wouldn't she tell me exactly what happened? Because she knows I'll hunt them down. Even if it takes me to the last day, I'll find them.*

'Then everyone saw you beat him up,' said Zoya.

Jimmy felt his face flush; he rubbed his beard where it itched. 'But that was – was mistaken, a misunderstanding. You know it.'

'Yeah, but Jimmy, everyone immediately thought – in fact, they were certain – I was sleeping with Dan. And you beat him up because you found out, and when they saw what state I was in, clothes all ripped and everything...' Zoya stopped. Jimmy remained quiet, and did not look at her.

'I'm sorry, Yo-Yo. It was after *Abbo*, innit.' He looked at her with softness in his face, and her green eyes, which usually matched his, except for his contact lenses today, glistened in the small light. 'Truly sorry...' He looked down again and his body felt awkward and too large. He continued stubbing his toe on the carpet, as he perched on the end of her bed.

She pulled the duvet over to her side and he saw her shiver.

'Please forgive me, Yo-Yo.'

Zoya wrapped her arms around her knees, and drew them up to her chest.

Jimmy stole glances at her which brought back memories of how they would sit like this for hours as children, Zoya tucked up at the head of the bed, and Jimmy perched on the end, with the small gas fire that would give out a paltry orange light more than heat. Jimmy remembered the long winter nights and the names she would invent for him in her teasing: Jo-Jo, Jim-bo, Johnny-boo and Boo-jo, which meant monkey in Punjabi. She would tease him, 'You are my little Boo-jo!'

The nights were full of mysterious tales that Zoya would read, or Sofia retell from her mother's stories: Samarkandis, she called them. Sometimes Tony would stand and read aloud, formally, and they would all laugh at him. Each one of them snuggled into a corner of the huge Pakistani *razai*.

Laughter like hot caramel drizzled over popcorn, conversation interlaced with more snacks, tall tales, and riddles. A tradition Sofia started with pappadoms and pakoras in bed, which would have chilli sauce like blood dribbled all over them; the red chutney building the firm bonds of sanguinity. A multitude of snacks accompanied the plethora of stories in between the love-fights-arguments. The samosas bonded kinship. They sprinkled chilli on everything, even over the popcorn. Brit-Pak chips with *mirch* and *chaat masala* powdered over them, accompanied by pink tea made with star anise – *like you get in Liberty market Lahore*, Zoya would say, remembering their trip to Pakistan, but Jimmy knew Sofia's pink tea was better than any *bazaari Chai*.

Jimmy now hoped that Zoya would also feel the past encroach and take them over, narrow the ravine of distance that had grown after his disappearance. The rocks were jagged and sharp, and one slip meant disaster. His memories were like seeds sown long ago. The tree of sibling affection was now watered by her tears, which he hoped would produce more fruit to harvest.

Zoya leaned forward and wrapped her arms around him; the space between them disappeared.

'Yo-Yo... you know why I'm here.'

'No, I don't, Jimmy, and I don't know why you went in the first place.'

'How's Dan?'

'After you battered him, you mean?'

'I'm sorry, so sorry. I've already apologised.'

'Doesn't make it okay. The bruises and cuts might have gone –'

'He's a good guy, but I'm worried. Are you happy? Are you sure, I mean?' Jimmy did not want to say anything that she might consider an attack on Dan and so distance her from him.

'Everyone knows the rumours, Jimmy – everyone knows,' said Zoya, more ashamed, more subtracted now that she seemed to be over her anger.

She seemed less than she had ever been before to Jimmy. *Not a light gone out*, he thought; *more of a cinder incandescent for a moment, as if jet fuel had been poured over her and set alight. She has self-conflagrated, taking the shame of the assault and* Ami's *illness with its full force on herself.* She was burnt-out after the molecules of her being had shone for a moment in the flames of the Zoya she might have been: the loving sister, the accomplished teacher, and the caring daughter. Jimmy thought the only light left in Zoya's heart was like a black stone on a moonless night.

Yet, somehow, he had hope. Hopeful despite his predicament, that in spite of what he saw in Zoya he could achieve something, and discharge the responsibility he felt after Ahmad's death. Beyond the entrapment of light, which had burnt her dreams, he saw hope like a small, single luminosity, faint but constant. It never glimmered or dimmed. He half-smiled; it was his faith that gave him hope, even if he could see death surrounding him. *Imaan*, faith, was the only giving star, which shone with the purity of true belief in an otherwise life-sucking dark sky. Zoya's marriage was a responsibility he had to fulfil – to dissipate the disappointment of his father, to ease the pain in his mother's breast, but above all because Jimmy thought his religion demanded it. He thought of his mother as he heard her shuffle back to her room from the bathroom. Sofia was the only other star that gave light instead of requiring it from Jimmy to stay alive.

The community, the *Biradari*, the patrilineal brotherhood that would, Jimmy knew, if Zoya had been in Ramnagar, have insisted she be shot dead. For bringing shame on the family. Her uncles and male cousins would have been determined to kill her. He wondered why he had never heard of a female member of the family shooting the raped woman, if Zoya had been raped. Did they not feel shame?

Much less would anyone consider ever marrying her or anyone of her line for generations, so the men reckoned she would be better dead anyway, for if she were left alive her life would be so much more miserable. Jimmy had seen one woman left alive when he had been to Pakistan. Her brother could not find the courage to kill her. He had been despised and dishonoured by the *Biradari* for not being man enough to do the right thing. The brother had left the village in shame, disgraced in front of the community. His sister had become an old and wizened hag by the time Jimmy saw her. She lived in a one-room mud hut on the outskirts of the village, near the fields that were infertile and rocky and had never produced anything. Two *rotis*, unleavened bread from the tandoor clay oven, were left for her every day by the women of the village who had established a rota. Jimmy remembered following and watching his auntie one day as she left the roti and *lassi*, a watered salty yogurt drink, for the old woman outside her wooden gate before she had awoken, because she would often rant and attack anyone who came to her door. So his auntie had banged the gate with a stick and hurried away, before the old woman could come out.

That was the best that Zoya could have hoped for, had she been in a village in Pakistan. Jimmy could not imagine such a life for her. Maybe being shot dead was better for bringing malignant *behizthee*, the odium of bad name, upon the family, by being assaulted and maybe raped. Jimmy's uncle had told him he would rather marry the one-eyed leprous daughter of the village beggar than consider a consummation with a woman who had been raped. Jimmy knew of the feelings in his extended family; he had even heard the rumours through Hamza, who passed all the community gossip to Jimmy. They planned to trick Zoya back to Pakistan, to reverse the shame now piled high on them. Jimmy had phoned his uncle in Bradford, refused to answer any questions about his own disappearance, and demanded to know if Zoya were his uncle's sister or daughter, would he still shoot her? His uncle had replied, without drawing breath: 'Yes. I would shoot her, and wash the shame from me that has infected my body and blocked my lungs. I would kill Zoya so the breath could pass my throat!' Thus his uncle had proudly proved his impartiality and sense of justice.

His uncle then gave Jimmy the example of Bano, a village girl seen alone with a strange man in the cornfield. Shotguns had made *keema*, mincemeat, of her body; her face was unrecognisable. They had buried her in the same field. She had been shot by her brother, an example of someone who did have enough courage, enough gharat, shame-honour, to do the right thing. The brother then turned up at the village police station almost literally with a smoking gun, and proudly told the Inspector that he had done it, and would do it again a hundred times if needed. He had been rushed out of the police station by the sergeant, his cousin twice removed, who had told him to shut up and disappear into the city for six months while the stink faded away. He was finally arrested and hanged, after turning himself in at Rawalpindi Central Police Station, and demanding the death penalty for killing his sister. He wanted this to be a lesson to all brothers with *gharat* not to let their sisters wonder. Such was the engrained sense of honour, *izzat*. He was dutifully hanged and embraced the gallows with a smile on his face.

The feudal lord of his *zilla*, district, commissioned travelling minstrels, who wrote ballads and poems about him and his manly *gharat*, in lyrical Punjabi. She would be waiting to receive him with open arms: Honour–Shame that pure maiden would be his heavenly bride, sang the musicians. The teenage virgin brother hanged and died before tasting carnal flesh, they said, but so much better for him to wear his family pride as a death-shroud so the *Houris* of Paradise, wide-eyed and honey-lipped, could embrace him, a hero of Islam. Future generations of troubadours would sing his praises – of how he saved his face, his clan's honour. The Choudhary name would be eulogised as a Punjabi folk hero for all time, and what more could a man hope for than to become an ancestor, a legend?

Jimmy realised he knew enough to understand how Islam had been corrupted by his *Biradari*, and he knew his kinship was forever broken by hatred for the people who ritually defiled his pure *Deen*, faith. Jimmy felt disgusted that the world's media gave it the name honour-killing, in the name of Islam. Those who had raped the woman were free, rich and unpunished. The feudal landlord, *zamindar*, who had commissioned the minstrels to sing songs about the *izzat daar brother*, felt secret pride that his son had succeeded in establishing feudal supremacy by taking his pleasure of the woman. *The brother would enjoy Heavenly Pleasures whilst his son had enjoyed worldly pleasure*, he had boasted to other landlords. Even now, Jimmy knew, the rapist walked tall and at liberty in the village, an open secret. Jimmy thought everyone knew everything, but no one would say anything, because they could not or dare not point the finger out of fear or self-interest. In Pakistan no one threw stones, because everyone lived in *Sheesh Mahal*, houses made of crystal. The whole country was a dirty open sewer. No-one wanted to inhale.

'Who would marry me, Jimbo, who?' Zoya asked, and brought him back from his wondering.

'In Pakistan?' he asked.

Zoya's quiet laughter rattled in reply. 'In Pakistan? Needless to ask, in Pakistan. Even here, Jimmy – who?'

'There is guys... don't think like that.'

'No one has even talked to *Ami*. We have been completely ostracised since then.'

'But this is not Punjab.' Jimmy felt outraged at this news. His huge thighs tightened as he pushed himself to sit upright on the bed, and his scar throbbed.

'Open your eyes... have you lost your mind under that stupid disguise? Our community is tighter than even Ramnagar. You're the one who said 'We ain't British!' What are you, all *Gorah* now, Boo-jo? Don't you know what it's like?' she said.

He became quiet, embarrassed by his own society. Jimmy knew that Zoya was right. He wished that all these things had not happened to his family, but it was Allah's will, and there could be only one way to right all the wrongs he thought, as he gritted his teeth and felt his fists clench.

'People have been telling Tony the same. The aunties have been sending their sons to tell him that, as the eldest brother, it's his responsibility to shoulder the blame, the shame. That he has to cleanse the defilement by sending me to Pakistan to face justice.'

'What?' said Jimmy, shocked that people in his family could consider such a thing.

'Do you know what that means? To satisfy the community, the *Biradari* honour, I have to be a blood sacrifice. They will be less thirsty when they have washed their hands in a deluge of my blood; to purify themselves of my attack.'

'I can't believe *Chacha Baqwas,* Auntie Shamim, and all the others would. That ain't Islam.'

'Islam, Jimbo? What the hell does Islam have to do with any of this? They want to kill me, let alone anyone ever dream of blessing my marriage,' Zoya almost screamed.

'I tried asking you before, Yo-Yo, but what happened when they attacked you?'

'They assaulted me, all right? You know that.'

'Did anything else happen? I mean, did they do –'

'Jimmy, the whole *Biradari* knows I was assaulted, and they believe I was raped. So that's the truth, and therefore it doesn't matter what actually happened. That's totally irrelevant.'

'The truth should matter. That's why we, us Muslims, have to sort all this shit out. This is fuckin' outrageous, an insult for you and a blemish on our women. An insult to the honour of Islam.'

'Jimmy, listen to yourself. Is this the same Jimbo who a few months ago battered Dan for doing the right thing? For having the guts to save me and bring me home? Protected and cared for me, wiped my blood and seeped his shirt in my tears? I don't care if other women say it makes me weak. And now he's going to marry me, not out of pity or charity. Because he loves me. The only one in the world who does. I can tell you, Jimmy, when he holds me in his arms and just says 'Zoya' in the way he does, quiet and unrushed – the only one who ever can say it with so much patience and tenderness – he doesn't even have to look at me. The world, and everything in it, melts into oblivion. I am safe. For the first time ever, I am safe.'

He paused, and waited for her to stop panting. 'If that's why you're marrying him, yeah, out of duty, or 'cos he saved you –'

'I love him, Jimmy. He's more man than all these uncles and cousins braying for my blood despite their machismo, and do you know what,

Boo-jo? He doesn't need to be a gorilla to prove it. I've never heard him raise his voice – not to me, not to anyone. Isn't that what a Muslim is? A true Muslim man?'

'So is he a Muslim, then?'

'Well actually – what does it matter?' said Zoya. 'You know, he's even heard the rumours about you becoming an extremist, he knows the police have been here. But he trusts me. That's what love is. He knows I'm not involved, because I told him that I would never follow those nutters who believe in killing innocent people. That's enough for Dan.'

Jimmy realised she had seen the look on his face. *She has sold herself to* Iblis, *Satan, if she marries a* Kuffar, he thought. He feared that the look of horror that only a convert-zealot's imagination could manage became apparent on his face. As if he could already feel the living tortures of Hell, the *Jahanum* that lay in wait for her. The fire that burned with a flame a thousand times hotter than earthly fire. Where there would be no food, except the bitter Dari, and only boiling hot water that never quenched the thirst. *If she marries a* Kuffar.

'We are already outsiders. No one talks to us, anyway.'

'It's not just about what people say. *Biradari* ain't never done anything for us – not when *Abbo* was alive, and not now he's dead. No one can even say a true kind word to you, so fuck 'em.' He paused and grimaced, and plucked at his scar. 'I can feel the fire of hell, I can feel it so close. I can feel it burning my face,' said Jimmy, as wetness filmed over his eyes. The fluid of fear.

'If I marry a *Gorah* on top of that? How much worse will it be? A *Kuffar*.'

'Is he?' asked Jimmy, looking at her face intently.

'Would you stop me and the wedding next week, if he hasn't converted?'

'Yes. I have a duty, to *Abbo* and Allah. But...no. I have my fate, and you have yours. It's my duty to tell you that your relationship won't be legal and you will be living in sin in Allah's eyes. At least I won't stop you because of false *sharam* and *izzat*, like Uncle Baqwas. I want us all to be together and happy forever in *Jannah*, innit. I want to see you there, Yo-Yo.'

'Would you rather that he converted just to shut my family up and people like you, and then after the wedding celebrated with some Budweiser Beer, like my friend's husband? Who's the real convert?'

'No, but –'

'See – these things aren't as black and white as these crazy *mullahs* teach you.'

'I ain't never met a *mullah* in my life. I'm your bro, your Boo-jo, asking you if you are going to be marrying a Muslim man next week?'

'He converted, or reverted, in your language. Said the *Shahadah* two weeks ago.'

'What?' Jimmy stared at her, his hand frozen over his scar, his lips parted. He saw Zoya look away, and shake her head as she looked back to him. 'Are you sure?'

'What do you mean, *am I sure?*' Zoya brushed her hair back and took a drink of water from the glass on the bedside table. 'I'm telling you, he's a Muslim.' Tears rolled down her cheeks.

'*Subhanallah!* Only Allah is perfect! I'm so happy for you, Yo-Yo!' Jimmy raised his arms in the air and pumped them, as if celebrating a goal. He wrapped his huge arms around her. '*Subhanallah!*' He did not want her think that was the only reason he had come, but he could not stop the soft laughter or the smile from spreading. Zoya said nothing, but sobbed on his shoulder.

Jimmy realised that his acceptance of Dan, now that he was a Muslim, had covered her with relief; she had had her fill of rejection and hate. Zoya must have realised that now he would be fully on her side, no matter what. He did not ask what made Dan convert.

'That's why I'm going to do what I have to do.' He hoped now she understood his philosophy, the reason he had left. He could not be happy living as an outsider, hated by the rest of society: neither white nor brown, having no identity. Then, after he had found himself with Abu Umar, his empathy with the suffering of the Muslims would not allow him to stay inactive.

'Make everyone a Muslim, yeah, like Dan – then no problems, innit. Let's create peace and love and make the world realise the truth of Islam and put and end to the torture of Muslims all over the world,' said Jimmy. 'Before that, I have to see you married off and happy in your own home.' He wiped his hand over his eyes and was surprised to see it came back wet; he had thought nothing could distract him from his goal. He held her tightly to him. 'I gotta do it – gotta get us all to Paradise,' he said, and squeezed her torso still harder in between his arms like a python tightening its grip.

He noticed Zoya did not ask him what he intended to do. She continued to sob and gasp on his chest.

London – Wembley, Zoya's Wedding

Jimmy instructed his teams of boys and professional waiters, pointing and gesticulating. He had arranged and paid for as many things as he could for Zoya's wedding; he wanted to make it an event she would remember with fondness and pride.

After the first night spent remembering their childhood with Zoya, he had arranged a safe house, and then over the next few days regularly went home again, after making circuitous routes around Southall to make sure he was not followed. Sofia and Zoya had tried to resist his plans for her wedding, but he had argued most of Zoya's complaints away. He was grateful that she at least had not used the word *haram*. Neither had Sofia. He reassured them that the money was Maulana Mohammed Younis Khan *Imam Sahib*'s, for Ahmad's operation.

On the first night, as soon as he had been able to, when Zoya had let him go, he had gone to the Butterfly House. He had checked everything was in order, glad that Sofia had managed to do most things the butterflies needed. He had cooed as he opened the hatching box and the smiled as he released them into the main butterfly area. He topped up all the feeders, even the ones that did not need replenishing. The police had broken the lock on the small greenhouse, and they had taken his stash of drugs. Jimmy had put a new lock on the door. He had shut himself in the small Butterfly House, and only opened the door when Sofia banged on it in the morning. She had come looking for him.

Sofia had said nothing, except she kept repeating his name and stroking his face, touching his scar. Jimmy was tormented by the way Sofia had held him for much of the day. He worried that he might have to disappear again any moment, so he hugged her back without embarrassment. She had not asked where he had been after Ahmad's death, what he had been doing, or even why he had left and now decided to come back. Sofia had initially stared at him in a way he did not recognise, as if she had been stupefied into an unblinking zombie form of inaction. Then she melted and said 'Jimmy! Jimmy – *mera Betah*! Where are you?'

Sofia seemed less than he remembered her, somehow subdued, but glad to have her son back. He knew that, despite the addition of Dan into the family, and even though relief flooded through her because Zoya was being accepted by someone who was willingly marrying her, nothing would leach out the black stain of Zoya's assault. No more to carry the responsibility of a besmirched daughter, the burden heavier than a yoke, the weight of which seemed to bend Sofia as she walked and pulled the corners of her mouth down into a droop. Jimmy saw stress scour her face, and sit on her brow, that now looked like brown sand-dunes. He could not imagine that, until only recently, women had commented on his mother's youthful face, now turned witch-like by worry. Sofia's face now seemed lost amongst the wrinkles that stood out like ripples on a beach washed by a sea. He knew Sofia hardly dared hope that Dan would love Zoya. Jimmy felt sure that Sofia did not care whether he loved Zoya or not. It was enough for her to see her *behizthee* – her shame-filled daughter – married.

However, the shame would never wash away. It was like black pigment on brown, now buried deep under their collective family skin, to be passed on from one generation to the next. As if the ink had been tattooed permanently on every Regus forehead, defiling them body and soul for eternity. Jimmy knew Sofia hoped that time and marriage would diminish the shame, but he realised it would be fixed ever firmer by the community at every mention of Zoya, because of the *Gorah* she had married. He had asked Zoya if the police had come around again, and he could see the anguish written in his mother's wondering eyes. She seemed to be saying: *You are lost. A pebble at the bottom of the sea. Find yourself, Jimmy. Find the dewdrop! An unopened bud in a dense forest.*

The natural noise of his gang pulled him out of his thoughts. They carried the *mitai*, traditional wedding sweets, above their heads on large silver trays, brought out by his crew of boy volunteers.

Why didn't Ami *ask me where I went, what I did?* Jimmy wondered. No questions. She cried easily now, once the release had come after her arrest. Zoya had told him about Sofia's ordeal during the night. His determination to exact revenge reaffirmed itself, opened its wings and soared on the thermals of hate. Humiliation crawled out of him and felt like termite eggs filling his skull, all hatching together, alien thoughts that had became integral to the curves in his grey matter. His belief in the words of Abu Umar became exemplified by his mother's arrest, Zoya's assault, and Ahmad's death. *Abbo* should have been saved: living the *straight life* for what? Now Jimmy would show everyone what the True

Path, the *Sirat Al Mustaqeem*, really meant. He fingered his suicide vest; it felt thick under his shirt, but blended in well with his fat belly disguise.

The videos of torture and rape that Dwayne had shown Jimmy day after day caused a new bitterness to rise from deep within him, which was not allayed by the Eastern sweetness of pure belief in his religion. Instead, the anger had increased daily. It was all to keep Israel safe. The world was controlled by a Jewish conspiracy, and money was the key. The truth was becoming ever clearer, his purity of desire reflected in the whiteness of the *barfi* now arrayed on precious trays in front of him. He loved the thick buffalo milk barfi, one of the few remaining concessions to his Pakistani roots. As he watched the boys lay out the sweet chunks, saliva wet his mouth.

How much better, then, would be the pleasures of Paradise? he thought, and remembered how the cell had watched 'Truth' videos, which were always followed by 'Allah O Akbar' ones. Hamza had named them so because that was inevitably how the whole group would end up – standing, florid with emotion, fists raised, shouting *Allah O Akbar Allah O Akbar* until they became hoarse, as they imbibed the films of *Jihadi* victories. These were always accompanied by rousing songs of martyrdom in the name of the Prophet, for the cause of Allah, to glorify Islam and return it to the Golden Age. He understood what Dwayne had meant when he said that the *Kuffar* must die, and Islam must win. The arrest of his mother, whom he had imagined to be a loving woman lost in a sea of Englishness, made the injustice greater. All her life, Sofia had made sacrifices for her family, like the dying salmon that feeds the eggs of the next generation with her own body. Sofia had done her utmost through her glow of love. Her spirit, Jimmy felt, had gone out with the death of Ahmad. Now, as he glanced at his mother, he forced his eyes not to fill up. He feared that even a *diya*, a small lamp's worth of light, would never return to flicker in his mother's eyes. Zoya's wedding was far from the happy ideal Sofia had chattered about at length, when the slightest excuse would present itself over the years. He saw Sofia clear her eyes with the corner of her *dupatta*.

Abu Umar had said 'We Muslims must take power to ensure fairness, defeat the Zionist-Freemason devils, destroy their financial idols, to mete out justice.' Jimmy knew exactly what Abu Umar would say if he were here now. *Are you British? Do they treat you like one of them? Would your mother be so humiliated? Your sister so debased, not to mention your brother jobless, your father dying with only Allah's mercy and no operation or treatment? Look around you, Jimmy. What do you see?* He heard his *Shaikh*'s voice reverberating in his head, as he let his eyes wander across the marriage hall. People mingled, men sat in small huddles, and children ran haphazardly, stained in their *shadi*, their wedding best.

Mitai, buffalo milk *barfi* covered in razor-thin gold and silver leaf, served by his boys and waiters, paid for by Jimmy. He had insisted that he did not want the usual volunteers that could not serve efficiently. No one ate the *mitai*. It was a tradition that the sweet things would be eaten afterwards, when everyone would congratulate the father of the bride first and say: '*Mubarak ho! Mubarak ho! Ahmad Sahib Mubarak ho!*'

Jimmy imagined if Ahmad had been alive, and if Zoya were marrying a Paki, not shamed like today, then everyone would be vigorous in their congratulation. Almost immediately after the ceremony the men would shove *mitai* into other men's mouths, women into women's mouths. They would, out of tradition, force the sweetmeats past the almost-resisting lips. The recipients would protest at the large chunks and the mouths would usually close too early, so much of it would crumble and fall to the floor. He was accustomed to the Paki playtimes. The vile politics of extended family divisions and bickering would be forgotten in the momentary rejoining of happiness.

It was an unusual coming together of family and *Biradari* followed by far too much tactile Asian hugging, he thought, and then the embarrassing middle-aged spread that danced its own independent rhythms and the voices that could not sing, but blared anyway. He had seen it at numerous Asian weddings. He wondered at the irony of his life; the typical parochial Pakiness he had tried so hard to distance himself from all his life was something he now wished for. He prayed that somehow, someone would forget all that had happened, that someone would turn the music on and start dancing on Zoya's wedding day.

The women had avoided Sofia and Zoya after the gossip about the white ancestor, and particularly after Zoya's assault and Jimmy's disappearance, but they could not fully exclude them because of *Chacha* Waqas, from Bradford. He had not yet sanctioned their complete ostracisation. He was the eldest living male relative and so the head of the informal *Biradari*, which held more influence over the lives of the family than any Palace of Justice; there was no court of appeal. *Chacha* Waqas had hushed the gossip, probably because he was a part of the same family. But the gossip had whizzed around his mother's friends more than the relatives. The family had for years resolutely refused to accept the white ancestor but, the stories were now in their genes and they would not die. They were passed on from one generation to the next, like hair and eye colour. *Imam* Younis had forced some people together today. Jimmy felt anything would be better than Sofia's isolated and lonely existence, and today, after Zoya left, she would feel more alone. Tony never did do much for family communication.

The *Bhangra* music started too early, the volume near painful. Jimmy had forgotten he had insisted on music, and reminded one of his little soldiers to play music after the *nikah*, despite Sofia's reservations that it would be seen as shameful so close to Ahmad's death. He wanted the wedding to be as normal as possible, even if she had to marry a *Gorah*, until recently one of the legions of enemy *Kuffar*. He felt glad that Dan had converted to the true *Deen*, faith, for his own salvation.

Jimmy's anger rose as he realised how alone Sofia had been after his father's death and his disappearance. He stroked his artificial beard to stop his hands from becoming fists, meaty lumps of anger. He reminded himself not to pull too hard on his beard. All the numerous aunties and uncles who had sworn fealty stronger than blood ties had not been heard of, since Ahmad's death prayers had whispered and echoed into stony silence. The two aunties, who had come to Ahmad's funeral to proclaim loudly their sorrow at his demise, had also vanished like raindrops in the desert after Zoya's assault.

Jimmy smiled as he remembered – but immediately had to stiffen his face – how Hamza had helped him unquestioningly and how, as if at the return of the old King. All his old crew and little soldiers had grinningly obeyed, and rushed to his bidding. His mystique was somehow amplified by the rumours that he had metamorphosed into a *Jihadi*. So it had been no problem for Jimmy to disappear for a few days, the time he needed to organise Zoya's wedding. Sadia had also proved to be indispensible once he had taken her into his confidence. He knew that she was completely trustworthy. He bought gold jewellery for Zoya's dowry, gave it to Sadia for safekeeping, and then organised a different reception hall. He ordered food and crockery through his contacts; things that had taken Tony weeks, Zoya told him, Jimmy achieved in hours. He knew the previous preparations paled by comparison to Jimmy's celebratory message. He wanted to let the community know that Zoya was not indigent or alone. From the magnitude of expenditure they would realise that Ahmad's family had succeeded, and they had enough class to give Zoya away properly. As well as the preparations, he needed a place to hide from the police and *Jaish an Noor wass Salaam*. So on the morning after surprising Zoya, he had phoned Hamza.

Although Hamza now guarded Abu Umar, Jimmy felt he could trust him, since he knew he had Hamza's loyalty since childhood, which he had desperately prayed was worth more than his allegiance to *Jaish*. He knew Hamza usually had the night shift and did not have to be on bodyguard duty until late in the evening, and then only if Abu Umar was away from the flat. At those times, Hamza always accompanied Abu Umar.

Jimmy had been surprised by how easily they had slipped back to the format of their childhood days, rekindled their friendship from the mosque. Like embers on dry brushwood, the fiery passion had consumed them both. Their shared memories of boyhood and cricketing reminiscences burnt the jungle of time that had grown between them, their doubts blazed to cinder.

Hamza received him with hugs and kisses on both cheeks, after Jimmy had nervously contacted him after returning home. He thanked Allah once more that Hamza had helped him. Despite both being committed to the cause, Jimmy had had doubts whether Hamza would risk the wrath of *Jaish*. His friend had reassured Jimmy that they both worked as *Mujahids Fisabilillah*, God's warriors fighting in the way of Allah and so Hamza had helped hide him in a safe house. They talked cricket almost as soon as they walked through the door of the safe house and once Hamza had recovered from the shock of Jimmy's disappearance, he told Jimmy, 'I thought you was dead, mate.'

Jimmy felt relief that there had been no friction of painful memories... of a blood-spoiled white salwar on a summer's evening, all those years ago. Neither had mentioned that heat-filled summer's day in the mosque – that spreading red – that nauseous stain of Satan. That would, Jimmy knew, brand their souls with a wound that would never heal, but would burn and smoulder for the rest of their lives.

So they talked about the different mesmerising leg spinners that had played in the time of their separation, comparing them to the great Shane Warne, and decided that none compared to him. Both had agreed that nothing could match their own memories of fluorescent green tennis balls, the rubber balls that had been so treasured. He reminded Hamza how they would send them spinning to one another, trying to eke out as much turn as the concrete pitch would allow. If any of the boys hit the ball into the small stream that ran at the back of the pitch where they played, then they would chase each other down to the rickety bridge and wait and pray that the ball would float past, and then fish it out with forked wooden sticks. To lose a ball would stop play. At least, until they had enough money to invest in a new one, preferably a bright orange one. Jimmy smiled as he remembered how the balls would change character once they had the covering fur knocked off them, and then the naked bald balls would have a different value. They could bowl them faster and they would grip and spin more, but rocket off the bat if you hit the shot just right.

Maybe because of those memories, or out of a sense of duty, Jimmy could not be certain why Hamza had arranged a safe house so quickly, without trying to convince him to return to the cell and ask Abu Umar's forgiveness. Jimmy found it strange that Hamza did not offer to intercede on his behalf. He did not question Hamza. He was glad for his support, and so did his best in turn to ensure Hamza's help remained secret from *Jaish*. If they found out the truth, not even Abu Umar's bodyguard would be spared. Hamza had told him it was his cousin's house, which once renovated would be sold, the profits already promised to *Jaish*. Jimmy knew everyone was expected by Abu Umar to make their contribution so that he would keep the cause strong in their hearts, and to ensure that they had the spirit of sacrifice. Although *Jaish* did not need money from their cells, they had enough support from their regular financiers.

Abu Umar said that it helped training, and especially that the small sacrifice would help them to lose attachment to the material world, would get them into the spirit of the greater sacrifice they would soon have to make.

Jimmy had stayed in the house over the past few days and Hamza had also helped him organise Zoya's wedding. So Jimmy had grown to respect and love Hamza even more than before, for his loyalty. He made sure he served Hamza whenever he could – food, tea – and changed TV channels to watch whatever Hamza wanted at the end of a hectic evening, which was inevitably cricket. Jimmy felt a rush of emotion, which even he could only identify as love, although he knew he would never give voice to such a thought. He had a new respect for Hamza because never once did he show disgust, or even question why Zoya was marrying a *Gorah*. Jimmy felt closer to Hamza now than he had ever had to Tony, or even Ahmad. Jimmy ignored the raucous laughter of his boys. He felt shocked by his thoughts; he grasped a nearby chair, and slumped down.

CHAPTER 28

Mumbai, Malabar Hill – Amit's Mansion
Amit watched the drive and fingered the top button of his golden *kurtha*, as the chauffeur-driven limousine turned the corner into his private road. As the car drove past the entrance, the gates closed, reforming their unity. They slowly swung together again, whispering her entrance into his domain. A Diana returning, to give tension once more to the hunter's unstrung bow. He gazed at the top of the drive as the twin guards saluted. He knew they could not see her through the darkened windows; they hailed her mythos.

Amit backed away from the bedroom window, although the car still had to cover the long drive to the front of the white Greco-Roman mansion, with its multi-column supports and curving arches. He knew it did not fail to impress, especially in India. He felt he had to increase the prowess of property, power and wealth needed to impress the sublime Aashriya Aarzoo Romano, by an unknown factorial. Surely she was beyond the earthly magnetism of materialism; he would not allow himself to ascribe base qualities to his *mehbooba*, his beloved. Amit had bought the mansion in the name of subsidiaries. Nothing belonged to him, officially.

Amit shifted his standing position, hiding most of his body behind the brocade curtains, although he knew she could not see him yet and it would be unlikely for her to be peering up from the back window of the limousine. The car neared the house and he imagined her sitting, reclining regally in the back. He smiled, which turned into a grimace, and sent splashes through his stomach like landslide rocks from a cliff, churning the sea below to foam.

He watched the driver get out and the doorman leave his post from the balcony-covered porch, rushing to open the rear door of the car. Half a minute passed before she stepped out. He wondered what she could possibly be doing sitting there, as the two men vied to hold the door open for her. His doorman stood already frozen in stiff salute, a masked face. His thick moustache did not move as he stopped breathing, his right hand stuck to his forehead, with fingertips touching the gold braid on the peak of his burgundy cap. Amit knew this was the biggest day of his life, opening the car door and being the first to greet the impeccable Aashriya.

She finally let a silver-sandaled foot show. Its tapered stiletto heel slipped out of the door; he glimpsed her ankle, and had to look away. He turned back almost instantly, instinctively, to see if either of the two men stared at her, but neither had flinched. They stared, like stony gargoyles, into the clear sky beyond the roof of the car. She put a leg out, swung the other to its side, and lifted her body without touching the car, so that the ubiquitous dust of India could not mark her. *She has more grace standing than most women dancing,* he thought. *How does she stay so clean, so dust free?* He watched as she did not need to adjust her clothes, or acknowledge either man. The doorman's head dropped as she passed him, with relief more than regret, Amit realised. He saw the man take deep gulps of air, the reception duties now passed onto the houseboy once she had climbed the steps and passed the front porch.

Before she stepped up, Amit saw her turn her head and look at the mature trees, the smooth turf, and the swards of grass in the central area. So hard to maintain to such a soft standard, because of the sea salt from Back Bay. A huge circle of sand surrounded the central area. This formed a ring, in which date palms *salaamed* their branches in the moist sea breeze. In the middle of the lawned area, a huge fountain sprayed arcs of shimmering quick-silvered water high into the air. Birds darted in between the sprays, leaving a momentary memory of iridescence. He wondered if she realised the outer area of sand and date palms represented the desert, leading to a central oasis.

The birdsong, the nectar-feeding sunbirds twittering, their radiance, the tinkling of water – did it feel the same for her? The shrill primordial, procreating cry of the deep honeydew flowers, vaginal amphorae built for the pollinators curving bills. Their florid cries felt loud in his ears. The mating game of millennia played out amongst the created artifice of a human fantasy. He hoped she did not see his front garden as incongruous or discordant. Or could it be that she was enthralled by the melody like he was, as he took his breakfast on the balcony – was that why she stopped and stared?

Every morning his houseboy flung the huge through-windows of his room open so he could walk out onto the large balcony, but sometimes he would take breakfast next to the fountain. Or on some wistful starry nights, when he wanted to imbibe the melancholy of a lonely Arab about to set out to conquer the known world, he would spend a sleepless night in the Bedouin tent pitched under the grove of palms in the desert area.

Today they would eat on the lawn at the rear of the mansion, where a completely different vista awaited her. He had invited her for breakfast, on the first day back. She had arrived back from California yesterday evening; he could not stop himself. He hoped she would spend the whole day, but had not dared to suggest this to her. He lost sight of her as the elderly houseboy took her into the reception area, but he knew exactly where she would be sitting, waiting, and for how long. He had given specific instructions. After a short while he moved across the landing to the other side of the house, from where he had a panoramic view from one of the bedrooms. He watched as the servant guided her down the steps onto the lawn. The small silver scarf around her neck shimmered in the early sunlight, as the houseboy seated her in a central area, which was covered with an awning in the style of a pagoda. So glamorous, even in the morning, as if she had just walked off a film set, he thought – but she looked more alluring in her black *salwar kameez* than in her usual period on-screen elaborately sequined attire.

He noticed she wore a silk suit; plain black, except for the silver filigree along the edge of the *kameez* hem and the matching lightly worked embroidery around the inverted Moghul arch, which formed her neckline. The needlework sparkled and the shirt ruffled in the sea breeze as she wafted, graced the chair held by the houseboy.

Amit felt doubts raise medusa-like heads. He thought, *What if she doesn't like waiting? What if the breakfast isn't to her taste? I really messed up with the* Chai *on our last meeting… I hope the cooks can get it right today. They know they have to. One warning is enough.* He usually employed a head cook and two assistants, but had drafted in another two specialist chefs borrowed from David Gul's hotels for today. He steeled himself: *be a man! Wait, wait for it. Let her wait. Keep her waiting this time.*

The five minutes he had promised himself weighed on him like oppression. He went to the toilet twice. Unable to manage the first time, he cursed, 'Bloody rascal piss! Can't even bring rascal piss out.' He splashed cold water on his face, then managed on the second attempt. He resolved not to fiddle with his *kurtha* collar, not to think about his thick lips. He tried to stop himself from worrying about the way his beard merged with his hirsute chest, his arms like jungle vine creepers that hung too low, and his simian gait, which made his arms swing. He ignored his gorilla-thick, stumbling legs.

As he approached down the marble steps, willing his feet not to miss, he was glad she looked towards the other side of the garden, through large sunglasses. She did not turn to him until he almost reached the table where she sat. He wondered if Aashriya would stand to greet him. She pushed her sunglasses up into her hair, and instead she leaned back in her chair.

'*Asalamalaikum*, Amit *Sahib*!' She raised her hand with the palm inwards to touch her forehead and curved her neck forwards a fraction in mock Moghul Delhi Darbar style, holding the pose for a moment too long.

'Hi.' His voice was barely audible as he flopped into the chair opposite her.

'My, my – you really are something of a trendsetting cultivator. Almost a Taj Mahal garden in the front, and these amazing Hanging Gardens of Mumbai in the back.'

He was unsure how much of her tone taunted him... or did his senses abandon him whenever he neared his goal? 'I'm so glad, thank God...' He looked up, momentarily raising his huge hands as a supplicant, '... that you are uninjured.'

'Oh, you know, some bruises and grazes, but –'

'Thank God, *Alhamdullilah*!' He interrupted her uncharacteristically, his hands rose up again. Although he minimised his Muslimness around her, he could not help the *Praise be to Allah* slipping out. She had never made an issue of it; he wondered how much of her Hinduism she held dear. 'Rascal! That bloody idiot Raju.'

'Well, he's dead now,' she said. He thought he saw her eyes blaze for a second and her face change, before she quickly composed herself and her usual half-smile returned to her face.

Amit knew the PDA he had given her to carry to Raju contained some small pieces of information that were true, but it did not contain the codes to activate the bombs. He knew that, even now, the FBI who had investigated the accident would be acting on limited information, and as a result the CIA could not stop *Jaish*'s plans being implemented. Only he and Abu Umar knew the codes to deactivate the bombs. The Great Leader did not need to know. There were enough failsafe mechanisms in place, and Abu Umar and Amit had made sure they had not been in the same place since the final part of *Israfil's Trumpet* was about to be activated. Amit made sure they would never be in the same country until the final victory.

Her aroma wafted over to him; his fleeting thoughts of the *Jihad* were instantly subdued, and then subjugated by her perfume. His nostrils flared, happy to be enslaved to her scent, which in turn easily enslaved Amit. He thanked Allah in his thoughts that Aashriya was unharmed. He had had Aashriya flown home in a chartered plane, with a private doctor to minister to her on the flight, even though she had told him she was well enough to travel.

'Yes, yes, of course, you're right…' He let her look across to the rest of the garden, through to the views of Back Bay. The curve in Nepean Sea Road seemed voluptuous to him. As always, he lingered over views of Nariman Point, and sighed when he saw Chowpatty Beach in the distance, because she had said she would be happy with a *Chai* from a *Chai wallah* on Chowpatty Beach. Since then he had often walked the beach, on the pretext of taking a constitutional.

'Thank you for flying me home, and for the doctor,' she said, and smiled. 'The poor man just kept fumbling with pictures he asked me to autograph, most of the way to Mumbai.' She giggled, and covered her mouth with her slender fingers momentarily.

Amit looked at her. Now her eyes were hidden again as she lowered her sunglasses; parasols for her grey lamps, hiding mysteries of his life's goal.

Amit beckoned, without looking away from her, to one of the waiters who stood on the veranda area near the house. The man rushed down the six marbled steps, which had small fountains to both sides; raised platforms with water flowing in channels down the sides of the steps, and curving aqueducts that took the liquid down the hill to water the bottom of the garden. The waiter arrived and waited with both hands tied in front of him, slightly bowed in the usual respectful sub-continental manner.

'Will you do me the honour of letting me order breakfast for you?' Amit asked.

Aashriya turned back to face him. 'Amit *Sahib*, I'm not –'

'Please, it would be an honour. You would put me in your debt,' he said. As he leaned forward, he inclined his head and put his right hand on his chest, close to his heart. The fear rose in him, like bitter bile, that she would refuse breakfast, and he would have no excuse to detain her further, and she would disappear, swoop away from his influence like a hummingbird searching for something else, lost in the firmament...

So Amit ordered. He gave the bearers special instructions, with spoonfuls of remonstrations (mostly in Hindi) interspersed with a cinnamon spray of English, topped with the grunts and noises he had trained them to recognise over the years. A beeline of insectivorous waiters left the honeycomb of his kitchen carrying silver gilt-edged trays. They filled up the Art Deco table with a confetti of dishes.

'I know you are loving everything American: Mustangs, and American food. So I have arranged an all-American breakfast for you, Aashriya-*ji!*' he added the respectful Hindi addendum, unable to address her by her name only. He felt like an obedient historic Indian wife too worshiping of her *pati-dev*, husband–god, to take his name in isolation. As if the mere enunciation would lead to an imbalance of the godly-demonic firmament.

He watched her intently, as she looked around with widening gaze. Her eyes became shiny like the glaze over the myriad of doughnuts; was she thinking of Raju? He could not stop himself wandering what had happened between them.

Of course I am knowing what happened! he thought. *How naïve of Raju to think I would just let Aashriya into his clutches without watching him. All the time I must be watching. Even spies had to have spies.* Now he commanded Raju's brother, the college boy who had burst into the boardroom and fallen at his feet, begging him to join *Jaish an Noor wass Salaam.* Amit smiled; he felt pleased at how fully inducted Om had become. He had made sure the youth was totally melded and malleable into the ways of *Jaish*, so that he could use him. Or perhaps he could have used him to punish Raju. It was a shame Raju had died the way he did. *Amazing luck is there that boy is a hacker, Om Shanti Om, already internationally wanted for breaking numerous systems...* He smiled. *Maybe the god of the Christians is unfathomable to them, but*

Allah works in none too mysterious ways.

Differing breakfasts signifying varying parts of North America now plastered the table, leaving no empty space. There were a variety of pancakes, some with blueberries, others with delicate unrecognisable Hawaiian fruits artistically spread over them, still others with maple syrup dripping off them, glistening in the newborn sun. Southern hospitality breakfasts, 'Louisiana Seafood Louie', which he had discovered on a visit to Baton Rouge. He had the eggs remade in the original style, or as close as David Gul's chef could manage: an omelette filled with shrimp, crabmeat, and crawfish, topped with courgettes, peppers and onions, with a cream sauce ladled on top. The Texan breakfast had sausages in the form of patties, tacos, and a variety of meats, still oozing bloody pink. Steaming beef from prize winning Texan steers, cereals from Carolina, dairy products from Wisconsin, cream and frozen yogurt.

Amit glowered at the waiters until they disappeared. Aashriya threw her hands in the air, pushed her sunglasses up and pinned her hair with them.

'For you, *meri Malika,* my queen, you choose from all of America,' he said, as he gestured expansively.

'I'm not hungry.'

'Please, please, in honour of your escape and amazing survival.'

'Yes, that was lucky,' she said looking around. The over-application of gustatory delights pleased Amit. She seemed impressed, almost bewildered by the dishes, which could have formed a map of America, each dish a state. 'We have to celebrate.'

'Celebrate what? I just got back yesterday,' she said.

'Your amazing lucky escape. We must be giving thanks to –'

'Thanks to?' she interrupted, smiling, with her wrists splayed out, palms turned to the heavens. Her interjections seemed natural and did not make him flush, unlike the usual boardroom sallies. Although they were rare enough, for his reputation was a thing understood.

'Thanks to Allah or to *Durga Maa*. You know *Durga Pooja* is coming up soon?' She paused, eyebrows raised.

Amit knew well the Hindu ceremonies and festivals, which had held a fascination for him since childhood, like movies that he felt compelled to watch. He knew she was teasing him. 'Thanks to Allah, to whomever…' and added, 'Yes, to Allah!'

Why am I pretending? he thought. She knows my Muslimness can't be hidden. He fiddled with his hands, checked his collar, and just managed to resist the temptation to stroke his beard, in case it drew her attention to their differences.

He cajoled her until she showed signs she was convinced. He watched her as she picked at the pancakes, fiddled with the fork, turning it in the syrup at the side of the plate. Despite her previous protestations, he asked her if she needed anything more. She let a laugh escape, that felt to him like a cherry dropped on the table between them. Amit did not know how to pick the cherries of relationships. He realised the fruits of opportunities had littered his life. He felt determined he would not let this one rot too.

The memories of failure with women were too rancid to resurrect. The thought of a future, of happiness with Aashriya made him unsure whether to laugh with her, or feel even more embarrassed. He felt glad that *Jaish* had no idea of his obsession with Aashriya – how could they? Amit was *Jaish*.

He said nothing, retreated into his usual shell of seriousness, like the withdrawn neck of a tortoise, the lumbering giants of Galapagos he had seen on TV. He loved the BBC documentaries, raising memories of his time at Oxford University. He cursed his inability to say something funny or glamorous, or even appropriate. He offered the maple syrup and, hoped to cover ineptitude with servility. Would she want a man who was an uxorious, servile husband? With her, he could not imagine being different. He glanced at the waiter, who instantly stood to attention. An imperceptible shake of Amit's head, and he looked away again; nothing required.

Amit offered the maple syrup in the silver gravy boat once more, but she refused it. He dusted lightly an untouched pile of pancakes, stopped in mid action, and looked up at her. She just stared back as he applied some more vanilla-flavoured sugar, before finally setting down the shaker. He grimaced and tried to cover a frown. His fingers found their way to his collar as he tried to tuck his chest hair in again, and he closed the top button of his *kurtha* that had become undone.

He had dressed in a manner which he imagined might reciprocate her clothes, so he wore a golden *kurtha*, a collarless Indian shirt, that had thick, brighter golden threads woven about the lapels either side of the buttons. The shiny cloth dazzled in the brightness, blared back the light off its surface, as if even the sun rejected such ostentation. His attempt at elegant understatement stopped at his plain white cotton Nehru pyjamas, tight trousers that almost hugged his legs. He realised she looked relaxed, her shirt not quite a traditional *kameez*, her trousers not quite a salwar. She managed to combine both cultural hemispheres effortlessly, without the need to address trends. He felt his small village Uttar Pradesh background oppressing him, and his Allahbadi parochial provincialism swamped him again. The tendrils of his ancestry reached out and grasped his soul.

A soliloquy of silence played loud in Amit's mind, creating doubt and fantasy: twins raised by the voracious she-wolf of love. She had founded his city – a new Rome of expectation, a civilisation upon which he crashed his worldly goals and risked his eternal Paradise. Could he ever have a life with her?

Now that she no longer toyed with the food and had finished pushing it around, he said, 'Shall we take a walk?' He thought he saw her eyes brighten. *I have got to get her involved and animated somehow. I know I moved her with my poetry last time, but how to impress?* He searched his mind for answers on his desperate, yet impossible, quest to possess her. As he stole another small, always-insufficient glance, his longing and pain soared, weightless.

'I have a lovely secret walkway which follows down by the aqueduct...' He went around and pulled her chair away, so she stood easily. The bearer on the steps rushed to help, but Amit had already completed the manoeuvre. He waited for her to gather herself, unsure as usual where to position himself, then gestured towards the rose garden at the bottom of the hill.

Amit was even more conscious now of her lissom grace in movement and her easily controlled, equal limbs. She seemed to affect him more when walking. He looked away over the bay to the Arabian Sea and controlled his irregular breathing, wiping the beads off his eyebrows, although the day had not yet burned away the cooling morning breeze. He glanced at her legs, accentuated by stilettos; her silky, tight black trouser-salwar contrasting with the pearly fairness of her painted toenails. He had to look away as she took off her high heels and her toes sank into the short grass. He thought she gained power from reconnecting with the earth.

As they walked together, she seemed to cover the ground effortlessly. He shuffled, almost stumbled, led with his left arm then switched back to his right, played with his *kurtha* collar.

This is my last chance to convince her I am the man she should accept, he thought. He needed her to reciprocate the passion that had possessed his soul. *I know she hides behind icy smiles and crystal teeth, but I have glimpsed the melting; the almost-tears. I could swear that she really cried as she read my Haiku poetry on the hotel rooftop.*

As they walked through the rose garden, Aashriya noticed an iceberg climbing the side of a large tree. She stopped to smell it. He reached up to pull the white rose down nearer to her and pricked his thumb on a thorn, but he smiled and led the way through a gulley of rhododendrons and bougainvillea. The blood dripped from his left thumb, slow drops, which did not stop when he put his index finger against his thumb; instead, his fingers ended up being covered in blood too. He had nothing with which to staunch the flow, so he pressed it to the side of his golden *kurtha*, which blotted the fluid hungrily. Amit hoped she had not noticed, but knew that she had. Her sunglasses were down again, and he could not make out her eyes.

The trees and plants formed an alley now, which led down to a secret grove. It would have been difficult to find by chance. He showed her into the clearing. It seemed like a random glade in a thick forest; as he entered, the pungent lilacs and jasmines comforted him. Their perfume felt like warm soft hands, which stilled his chest. He gestured to the bench but she preferred the velvety grass, well kept by his gardeners, made to look accidental. She sat on the sward, her arms around her knees, and she pushed her sunglasses up.

Amit looked at her and imagined an Aphrodite from lofty Olympus at rest, and the breeze, which tussled her hair, as a zephyr of Zeus's breath. Her form was softer than the dappled shade, and her strands of dark hair changed colour, as a ray caught a waving tress in front of her grey eyes. She moved the wisp away, and then she looked up at him. He felt the dryness spread through his mouth, and he thought his breathing would become a solid, cemented structure.

She waved a hand around, 'So beautiful. The accidents of nature are lovelier than manmade attempts, don't you think, Amit *Sahib*?'

He sat opposite her. Her long fingers with perfect nails played a tattoo on her left knee. Perhaps she hummed her latest hit; he could not be sure. His senses felt heightened but confused; was that the jasmine, or her perfume? The sea breeze, or the tang from her skin?

'Amit *Sahib*, you know, how we search... ' She did not look at him, but her eyes flitted around. *So unlike her,* he thought, *not to know what to say.* 'It's so beautiful.' She closed her eyes and breathed rhythmically. 'I can really breathe freely here, as if no one is watching. Don't you find that, Amit *Sahib*?'

Maybe she has entered her real phase, like she did on the hotel rooftop, he thought. *Maybe she is meaning it; after all, it must be so rare for her to be unwatched.* He almost said, *the only time I have ever had problems breathing is around you,* but stopped himself in time.

He turned back to her, having glanced up into the canopy and at the surrounding fragrant flowers and plants, which had been strategically placed in the undergrowth to provide differing aromas, depending upon the time of the day and on which way the wind blew. It was Amit's favourite contemplative place, where he would not allow himself any thoughts except how to surmount the peaks of Aashriya. He felt sure this was not what the great poet Allama Muhammed Iqbal had meant when he had written *Become an eagle soaring above the heights of the Himalayas, not a sparrow on the rooftops*. Poetry had grasped his imagination. His father recited it endlessly throughout his boyhood, with a voice full of pain and suffering and pathos.

All worldly, revolutionary problems had to be considered elsewhere, or at the front, in his Bedouin tent. He looked back to her. She had leaned closer to him; her eyes, now hazel and moistened, stared at him like a doll.

'Please don't mind me saying this, but you have such a style. It's a pity I wasn't hungry, but whenever we have met you have overwhelmed me,' she said.

He looked at her, leaned back a little and adjusted his collar. He felt sure breakfast had been a disaster, like his attempt at dinner. *What has made her change?* he wondered. Maybe it's the setting; maybe it was a good move to bring her down here.

'What I mean is, we are all looking. No matter who we are, no matter rich and famous or powerful like you. We are all human. We all want the One,' she said.

His dreams soared through the clouds of confusion, hunted hope in the blue sky. His eyes searched for the truth, flitted like swallows finding flies in an effortless, instinctive dance. She moved closer; her perfume obliterated the lilac. He thought he would faint. Her breath violets in his face. Her eyes impossible, kitten-glazed, now looking up just below his nose. *Did she say something else?* He could not be sure. The sun, birds and the rustling of the leaves disappeared, and his throat constricted. Desire dived to new depths, plummeted into fathomless dark wells.

'Such a strong man, controlling so many such powerful men,' she murmured. Her intonation matched the *sar a par – sar a sar – sar a par* of the breeze in the leaves. She nestled close to him, touching him, her head almost on his chest, his heart faster, flowing like the rushing-murmuration of water in the aqueduct close by. Time stopped and physical reality lost all meaning, as she put her lips close to his ear, her hand now on his chest, like a branding iron through the silk.

'That is what we all want, isn't it, Amit *Sahib*?' When he did not know how to answer, she continued, 'Happiness and love have to go together – and you know, for a woman, security to know she's wanted, and always will be wanted. Especially by such a mighty man... it means more than show boys racing in the mountains of California.' She stroked his chest, nuzzled his ear with her lips.

He felt his glacial past melt, become verdant jungle fed by the thundering of his heart. 'Raju... I thought Raju...' he finally managed to croak.

'There was nothing. I have been looking for someone who can take care of me, keep me safe.' She wrapped her arms around him, and he froze.

'But surely he – his looks? I mean, you seemed to be happy when you had tea in that restaurant.' Amit did not remember to pretend he did not know exactly what had happened between them, but he did worry that she would realise he had spies on them.

'Why would I want the slave when I can have the master?' She looked now into his eyes, her hands on his shoulders, massaging in ever-smaller circles. He felt as if her hands had tightened on his throat. His windpipe had become smaller. The energy locked up in iceberg-fundamentals of faith became history in his veins, and flowed into his tumescent desire. The fight, *Jihad*, and future of *Jaish* unconsidered, as his heart crashed like a wild stag into virile pastures, left behind the deserts of dogma.

She brushed his lips with hers. Amit felt dizzy. 'You know I want to stop acting, don't you? One day, I mean?'

'Do you – do you really?' He almost jerked back into reality, surprised by her questions, doubts in his mind again. He wondered if this could all be a trap, if he was being seduced, a Delilah to his Samson. *How could it be? Who would – she could not be pretending?* He tried to pull away from her, but only moved a fraction. His muscles would not contract.

'I can't act on screen if my future husband doesn't allow, can I?'

'I – I don't know... ' He did not know what to think; he closed his eyes.

'You can be so silly sometimes, Amit-*ji*, do you know that?'

'No, no I didn't. Can I?' he asked, through still closed eyes.

'Yes! I can't act forever. Even I have to get old.' She came close again, pulled him to her. He still had not opened his eyes. 'I mean, not many Muslim men would want their wives to dance on stage like I do...'

Amit did not know if she was real or another of his imagined visions, which he so often had in the glade of gardens, his secret clearing of persuasions. He dimly wondered if she really was trying to say what he thought. Marriage to him, even – even conversion for him. Would she? Why would she? So many men all over the world crazy for her, desperate to please her – why him? He had heard of women like her who rejected all the pretty boys, the beautiful Rajus, for men with power and strength and influence to make them feel safe. She had lost her father when she was a teenager, he remembered.

How is it possible? The conscious part of his mind screamed at him. *She is Aashriya Aarzoo Romano, and I? I am what I am. And she knows the truth about me. David Gul must have told her – stop! Stop – this must be a trap,* he thought. *She isn't real, and if she is, she is not meaning it.*

'Well, if my husband doesn't want other men to see me on screen and wear revealing clothes then maybe, for the one, I would sacrifice all that... if –'

'If what?' He did not dare to open his eyes and he did not flinch, but he tried not to hear his blood gushing so loudly in his ears.

'If I thought someone loved me enough.'

'Loved you enough?' *How could anyone love you more than I do?*

'Loved me enough to trust me.' She paused as he opened his eyes to look at her. She said, in a softer voice, 'No man ever trusts me... ' and added in a childlike voice, 'it's so unfair!' She suddenly sat up.

He immediately felt the umbilical disconnect, the abrupt loss of feminine warmth, which he had not felt in living memory, not since being nursed. The spell broken, he looked at her.

'Why don't men trust me?' she asked.

'Men? I – I don't know, Malika, why men don't trust. I'm not most men.'

'No, no, of course you're not. You're so different, you know. Everything you do and say. So different…I hope my husband would trust me. I wouldn't marry anyone who didn't trust me.'

'Trust? How can I – can anyone – prove trust?'

'I would do it, you know. I would. For the right man. All religions are different paths up the same mountain, my father used to say.'

Like a scene played out from a Mughal-e-Azam, where he was Dilip Kumar and Aashriya his Madhubala. He knew she had not starred in that movie, but he could not imagine anyone else in that role, since he had fallen for her years ago. He knew that other actresses had married and settled down with men, businessmen and doctors, so why not him?

She came close again. He breathed deeply, desperate to smell success. He tried to make the past into memory and so remove the taste of failure from his mouth. He allowed her to kiss his lips lightly, to sweeten his soul with hyacinths. He felt his hope soar again on thermals fired by her incandescent eyes, which seemed like embers of some undiscovered volcano. *How could it be done?* he thought. *Convert: become a Muslim, leave Bollywood behind willingly? No, impossible. I must not succumb.*

'You are different, Amit-*ji*, so quiet and strong. I love strong and quiet.'

She leaned forward, and this she time put her lips on his; not lightly, but pressed firmly. Her hand searched under his shirt. Buttons became undone without his knowledge. He did not question her tactile ability or her adroitness of purpose. He leaned backwards, his arms almost unable to support him, and lay back on the grass. He found her body had rolled on top of his. She felt soft and voluptuous and sensual, and more alluring than he thought possible.

'If a big strong man told me he loved me, then asked me to leave it all behind, then I would. Of course, he would have to trust me – prove it, I mean – and then I would even become a Muslim to marry…' She moved more comfortably on top of him, to kiss him again.

He melted. He momentarily weighed the worth of his life's struggle against the conspicuous capital of consumerism he had once thought she represented. Before he had met her, he thought she would be incapable of true love like all actresses, but his insight now dissolved. The *Jihadi* made momentous battle against his love.

He put his arm around her, kissed her back inexpertly. She moved her lips all over his. Her body was cloud-like softness, which cut against the knife-edge of his life. The Cause, the *Jihad* – lost against the once-in-a-lifetime kiss, irrespective of his future chances of happiness with her.

Amit looked into her eyes, a final battle searching for the truth, and to him they seemed open pools of shimmering light without form, guileless and refreshing. So he surrendered, and drank deep. He put his fealty of faith to the sword. The scimitar plunged deep into the mission and the *Jihad* of *Jaish an Noor wass Salaam* bled and thrashed its last, to give sanguine life to his love.

He spent the moment lingering, kissing and supping the pink from her lips, which would stay on his mouth until it dripped away with his last breath. They spent the day in the secret grove, and the night in the Bedouin tent, on thick Arabian carpets and brocaded silk cushions. History repeated itself in his thoughts, as once again, a Muslim warrior lost the war to luxurious pleasure. His dulled mind did not register except vaguely: a price worth paying. So with her movements his logic loosened, and his tongue moistened with the secrets of *Jaish an Noor wass Salaam*. Before the next maternal morning sun was born, to heat him back to life out of the curled foetal position he had adopted, before sleep found him and kissed him into a dreamlessness of oblivion; he told her everything she wanted to know.

Amit had not moved from his regressed foetal position all night. She left before he awoke.

CHAPTER 29

London, Wembley – Zoya's Wedding
The wedding hall was half empty, but plenty of people still milled around. Zoya had told Jimmy that *Imam* Younis had ensured enough participants would attend Zoya's wedding to make it look respectable, because he would be performing the *nikah* ceremony. Jimmy worried how he would give Zoya away, if anyone saw through his disguise. He had visions of being seen, of people calling out *Jimmy! Jimmy!* People would be too busy gossiping to ask too many questions; although many relatives and friends had not attended, Jimmy still feared recognition, and thought his make-up would be seen as clumsy and amateurish. They would all be exposed – his mother complicit in aiding and abetting a suspected terrorist. The horror of Sofia being manhandled and bundled off by the police again filled him with a new determination and dread of the future. He had to remain undiscovered, but more importantly, he could not be caught. The thoughts that constantly filled his head with the final glory of Islam made him even more certain that he was on the right path. The path to success led only through revenge on the *Kuffar*. The best way to do that was to use *Jaish*. Jimmy knew he had to find a way back into the cell.

The hall had enough guests to feel busy, with children running around, as always. An invitation to one person always meant an open invite to the extended family. Dan's parents and family were sitting at a table. Children danced around the table, and a small boy in a red bow tie and black waistcoat ran around the few white people at the wedding, shouting, 'Goreh, Goreh!' oblivious to the orange Fanta stain over half of the sleeve of his white shirt.

Dan's mother sat with her lilac dress and white shoes, a broad-lipped matching hat in her lap. Elegant, but Jimmy thought she looked confused. Loud music played as the smell of cardamom curry *biryani*, meat and spinach, along with the inevitable tandoori roast chicken, arrived haphazardly, with double platters heaped at the white table. There was multicoloured rice, and Naan bread sliced into quarters on expensive crockery. Plastic plates and disposable cups were not used, as in most of the usual Asian weddings Jimmy had been to. He had ensured, at the last moment, that a real dinner service with proper crockery and cutlery was made available. He had managed to get a hotel over the last few days, after he had forced Zoya and Sofia to delay the *nikah* ceremony. He had sent a trustworthy runner he had used in the past, who successfully pressurised a friend who knew someone who managed the hotel. Jimmy had always hated the cheap throwaway plastic items. *Disposable marriages*, he had called them, and he swore that Zoya's would not be like that. He would make up for what he had done to Dan, and their marriage would last, even if he would not be around to see it.

Jimmy did not feel regret, and when it did show its cowardly head he ensured it was quickly swallowed by the mouth of martyrdom. Soon enough, they would all be together in *Jannah*. This life was the blink of an eye; the life to come would be permanent and eternal in Paradise, with its gardens and innumerable *houris*.

He looked at Dan's family again, and wondered if he would ever have anything in common with them – with Goreh? Could he even sit comfortably to eat at the same table? He realised for the first time that referring to someone simply by colour was as racist as *Paki*.

The soft Asian music stopped abruptly, and the crowd took up the murmurs like a wave. They sat up straight. Hands came out of pockets, and seniors stroked their luxuriant white beards.

'Oi – quiet! Jamila, stop picking your nose, Maulvi *Sahib* is coming,' said one of the ushers. '*Imam Sahib* is coming.'

Uncle Younis walked in, flanked by men from the mosque, who fussed like oxpeckers on a rhinoceros. Tony, as the only remaining male member of the Regus family, followed him. *Imam* Maulana Younis Mohammed Khan sauntered in with his chin high, eyes looking down, and his *karakul* cap pushed back on his head, so that it seemed to Jimmy that it might fall off backwards. His hair was dyed to a new fresh orange by henna. His backwards-slanting gait exaggerated his paunch. The sparkling white, almost shiny, *salwar kameez* that Jimmy knew no other

Imam could wear with such impunity, contrasted with his orangutan beard. His patent leather shoes clipped and clopped over the wooden parquet floor. His black *sherwani*, the doublet, outlined two bulging breasts packeted by the cloth; the wool was stretched tight over his bloated stomach, like a goat belly.

Men sparked off their chairs, bowed forwards slightly to greet him with both hands extended, as the *Imam* remained bamboo stiff. They garnered blessings off him, while at the same time offering respect by showing themselves to be lower. Heads inclined, necks stretched down by insincerity, their backs laden with disingenuousness.

Jimmy could hear the whispers of the men as he passed through the huddled small groups. He had to stop his face contorting into a rictus of hate as he saw the ever-present hypocrisy. *That's why Muslims are in the state of abject misery*, he had heard Abu Umar say only a few days ago – because of so-called Muslims like these, who only moments ago gobbled at tales of the *Imam*'s philandering.

Jimmy had heard one long bearded *Chacha* say to another two-wives-uncle: *did you know he takes it in his arse? Gandoo! Gandoo! I swear! No! Yes!* Both tittered, one behind his hand, and the other putting his head down so his black teeth could not be seen. They stiffened as Jimmy passed because as Jamshed, Ahmad's fictional cousin from Bradford, he could wield influence in the family now that Ahmad was gone. His middle-aged appearance, beard and traditional clothes were not dissimilar to Uncle Younis' outfit, except that Jimmy wore a pale chameleon-green *salwar kameez*.

He noticed Uncle Younis, effulgent in his *sherwani*, take a seat at the head table with as much fuss as possible. His cronies filled the other chairs. The *Imam* interlinked his hands across his lap; his belly bulge almost formed a table on which he rested his palms. The group of mosque regulars surrounded him, smiling and leaning in.

The *Imam* spoke with certainty, 'Sins cannot be hidden! Crimes in history will haunt you... that's why our elders say the stain of generations comes back to repeat itself. *Harami* in the past, so illegitimate in the future, and now who knows who this *Gorah* man is? *Harami Gorah ke sath shadi...*'

'Surely, *Imam Sahib*, he's a Muslim now?'

'*Areh areh kohn kahtha hai*? Says who? I didn't do the *Shahahda* no *Kalima* no *Musalmaan*!' replied Maulana Mohammed Younis Khan

Imam Sahib, shaking his head and stroking his beard, as he did when passing a *fatwa*.

Jimmy heard one of his hangers-on say, 'They are so lucky to get even a *Gorah*. This all your doing. They should be thankful to you, your money – and Ahmad dead ...'

The *Imam* gave his victory chuckle. 'We do what we can, Allah sees...'

Jimmy heard Younis get up with a sigh; he had agreed to read the *nikah*, in memory of Ahmad, he had told Sofia, and now he repeated it to the men who were with him. Jimmy saw him shift his *Karakul* cap forwards, reapply his characteristic *attar* perfume behind his ears. He entered the groom's section, stroking his beard, face set firm, followed by the witnesses. Jimmy followed them, and saw Sofia adjust her *dupatta* on her head repeatedly, as the *Imam* approached. She waved Jimmy over.

'This is Zoya's uncle from Bradford, Jamshed,' she said to Younis, offering an erratic jerk towards Jimmy before her hand jumped to her head-covering again.

Uncle Younis, and therefore all the other men, ignored Jimmy. Jimmy pushed forward, making sure he did not miss anything the *Imam* did. Hamza followed Jimmy everywhere in the wedding hall, and now he stood next to him. Jimmy saw the warning in his friend's eyes. Hamza had managed to convince Abu Umar he needed to track down Jimmy, and so had been with Jimmy as much as possible over the past few days, helping him at every stage. Jimmy wondered who would be the three witnesses from the groom's side. The *Imam* would select them and so give the men a greater respect by asking them to sign the marriage contract. In many places and in most weddings things might have been done differently, but here, especially with Ahmad gone, they would only be done the Maulana Mohammed Younis Khan *Imam Sahib*'s way.

The *Imam* hawked and cleared his throat. He towered over Dan, who sat on a throne-like chair, with blue velvet and golden arching arms. Some of his friends sat behind him, and his family and Sofia were gathered around. Younis stood with a large register in his hands unfolded, and seemed to be reading from it as he recited some Arabic. Jimmy knew the register contained the marriage certificates and copies. Younis looked down and continued reciting a fast stream of Arabic, until it became a continuous flowing river to Jimmy's ear. He fidgeted with his disguise, even though he usually loved the way Abu Umar and Dwayne would compliment each other with their enchanting Arabic recitation, but today he wished he could silence the *Imam*. Jimmy shifted and grunted, and moved closer to Younis.

Finally, the *Imam* spoke. 'Do you, Daniel Andrew Matthews,' – he paused and repeated the surname, spitting the THE sound, making his accent more foreign before continuing – 'accept Zoya bint Ahmad Regus?'

Jimmy looked at Dan. The *Gorah* looked nothing like he had remembered him, as he sat in a silver embroidered *kurtha* pyjama suit; he knew Dan had insisted on wearing it so Zoya would feel that he was doing his best to fit in. In the foreign clothes, he looked even more incongruous and out of place than he would have in a suit. Despite his reservations, Jimmy admired Dan's courage. He had sat in the main hall smiling and joking, almost carrying off the pretence of being relaxed, with a group of his friends. They were made up of mixed races, men who had dressed like Dan, but who wore pale blue versions of his *kurtha* pyjama suit instead of silver. All the male relatives who represented both families wore lapel roses; the boy's side white, and the girl's guests wore red, the traditional bridal wedding colour. Jimmy would not have as much tolerance, patience or guts to do what Dan was doing if he were ever in that situation. Especially the lilac turban with a silver shiny iridescent sheen on it – he would never wear that. He had almost put his hand over his mouth to smother the noise when he had first seen Dan.

Younis now asked Dan to recite some Arabic *Kalima* and prayers after him. Dan mumbled, slipping over the words like a duck on a frozen Himalayan lake, surrounded by a silence like a Kashmiri cave, except for the pubescent puttering in the background of the teenage boys. Jimmy hated the way Maulana Mohammed Younis Khan *Imam Sahib* was letting Dan slip and slide on the icy Arabic. He bunched up his fists and moved in closer, staring at the priest. He knew Uncle Younis had not offered to rehearse with Dan, because Sofia had not forced Dan to go and bow before Uncle Younis, so that their new recruit could be bloodied and sworn in by the *Imam*. Jimmy knew that Uncle Younis was exacting revenge, like a Shylock extracting his pleasure. Dan's cheeks turned scarlet with white blotches. Jimmy cleared his throat for the third time, unable to interrupt openly. Finally, Younis stopped the torture, which Jimmy felt shamed the *Imam* more than Dan.

The *Imam* was making it obvious, through glances at his assembled team and smiles that became grimaces, that he disapproved of all he saw before him. Despite making a show of Dan's lack, Younis eventually asked Dan to sign the marriage certificate. Four men from Younis' cronies signed the witness sections. Jimmy felt flushed, and wiped his brow. Younis did not ask anyone from Dan's family to be a witness.

Eventually, with his residual limp, which Jimmy thought had become worse after Dan had signed the wedding papers, and without a smile, the *Imam* sauntered into the women's area. Zoya sat in a clearing, surrounded by groups of women. Jimmy flicked his eyes from Uncle Younis to Zoya, and felt glad that her best friend Sadia stood guard over her – ordering girls and even the older women to keep their distance, not to crowd Zoya, and to give her air. Crisis had taught Sadia a new confidence – *or perhaps it was concern for her friend*, Jimmy thought. Sofia was wearing a plain pale-blue *salwar kameez*, whereas most of the attending *Biradari* women wore a panoply of richly embroidered silks and satins and brocades. The innumerable colours melted into an array of iridescent luminous chaos as the women rushed around like random particles, all talking, occasionally colliding. Jimmy followed the men; only intimate relatives of the bride were, by custom, allowed into the women's gathering. He wondered how Sofia and the women of the *Biradari* had allowed Sadia to get away with wearing a black *salwar kameez*, even if it did have silver embroidery on it. What was she mourning?

As the men entered, some of the women scuttled away and others giggled and covered their heads with their slippery *dupattas*. Sofia gave instructions to Sadia and Tony, who were permanent guardians at Zoya's side, to fetch the most important male members of the family, so they could see the *nikah* ceremony. She gestured for Jimmy to come closer to her and Zoya.

Jimmy felt determined to be a witness signatory from his sister's side. He had to control his fists and body so that they would not physically enact the anger, which now seeped through his skin, pouring uncontrollably from every pore.

He left for a while, to give himself some time to think. He knew there would be a thousand interminable rituals and special actions the *Imam* would complete and enact as he took centre stage, before he got around to reciting any prayers or asking Zoya if she accepted Dan as a husband.

Jimmy wandered deliberately through the crowds, past the small huddles and gossipy groups; he did not make eye contact with anyone, but listened to snatched half-sentences of conversations. These reaffirmed his belief in the fundamental hypocrisy of his community, which caused his legs to seize, and he had to steady himself against a pillar for a moment. He felt the duplicity to be more distasteful since his spiritual conversion. No matter which part of the wedding hall he crept through, he heard the same sentiments, the same old curried conversations.

'*Hain hain – oof Allah – Gorah – hai Kafir – police wallah. Kitna jaldi kar di shadi – Allah jane!* Yes yes, *oof* Allah – a white man – a non-believer *Kafir* copper. How quickly they arranged the wedding – only Allah knows why!'

The women covered their mouths as they snickered forwards, and the men leaned back and guffawed and clasped their hands to their bellies.

Nothing new in the way things were said, except they peppered more *mirch masala*, chilli and spice on the Regus wounds. '*Raped – now* another *Gorah in their family! Hai hai hai! Sharam kitne sharam –* shame, so much shame! Disgusting!'

How much shame could Zoya and Sofia be burdened with? thought Jimmy. At least they could pretend his drugs did not exist, but now Sofia stood alone and excluded by the *Biradari*, like the lost gazelle rejected from the herd, so that the hyenas bit into her soul at will.

Jimmy went back towards the smaller antechamber, where he caught sight of Zoya, as always flanked, but controlled, by Sadia. He saw that his sister was almost obscured in the centre of the huddle as he entered the room to the side of the hall, which held the main stage. There Zoya and Dan would sit once the marriage ceremony had been completed, to be received and hugged and given presents ostentatiously by family members. A myriad of girls giggled and added the final touches to Zoya's traditional crimson vestments and make-up, and they would do the same again before she would be displayed on stage. The long blood-red *dupatta* edged with gold lace was draped over her head, and the *lengha* billowed and gathered in sheets over her legs, smothered in gold thread work with mirrors and sequins. A profusion of patterns created by the intricate needle artistry, a lasting symbol of the workers' heritage distilled through their fingers like blood, had seeped into the fabric of the cloth. Jimmy appreciated the eastern mystique and craft that was embodied in the three-piece-suit. *All her dreams come true*: he whispered a small prayer, and turned away before the wetness could take form in his eyes. He felt glad he had come, despite the risks.

Jimmy forced himself to face Zoya again, and noticed how the weight of the *dupatta* bowed her neck; but he imagined it was the pressure of history, and the mass-force of the shame-culture, that misted her eyes. He saw how Sadia held her head high and stared at the gathered crowd, as if his sister's friend was daring anyone to make the slightest sarcastic remark.

The overdose of emotion made him finger his suicide vest, and once again it felt thick and reassuring, a protection against the biting lash of scandal's tongue. *I will do it if I have to*, he thought, as he checked again that the mobile phone trigger was safe inside his *sherwani* pocket. He wore a thick coat on top.

Although most of the women mingled on the other side of the large hall, in the bridal preparation room plenty of women and girls scurried around Zoya. Jimmy had managed to stay aloof and had not mixed freely with the women, in keeping with his disguise as respectable uncle Jamshed from Bradford. As such, he had certain inalienable rights to enter, without being announced, into his niece's room. Some of the stricter women did not tolerate any contact with men, even being in the same room as one, including Uncle Younis' wife and her posse, who had a separate room. He approached the women's area. These remained enclaves of unwritten caution for the assembled men. He did not have to try hard to make himself feel nervous. As a paternal uncle, he would naturally be at his niece's *nikah* ceremony.

He wrung his hands and called out to a teenage girl who ran past him to slow down, addressed her as *meri beti*, my daughter, as a pious man should, so as not to arouse suspicion. He flowed naturally now as the bearded Bradfordian uncle. A younger, more trendy, man would be challenged, especially with so many sensuously dressed and highly perfumed girls that milled about – ostensibly fussing over Zoya, but he knew they were hoping that the boys had already noticed them.

Jimmy smiled as he remembered how Hamza had helped him unquestioningly; into the safe house, and then to organise Zoya's wedding. The memories of *Jaish* and Younis Khan's betrayal of Ahmad rose up in him. Jimmy felt glad he had taken on one of his father's responsibilities, but it made Jimmy stagger. He gathered himself, and wiped the sweat from his forehead, soaking a tissue. He stood and made his feet move forward a little, so that he would not become stiff.

Jimmy forced himself to focus, and took in the sight of the cozening beauties that looked like birds of paradise, little nectar-sipping parakeets, but he did not feel immediate desire for them. He felt a pleasure at his restraint. As he breathed deeply, their perfumes made small thumps in his lungs. He felt like a buyer-merchant in the spice markets of Cochin. *How much more wondrous and alluring, then, the Houriya-Brides that awaited him in Paradise?* With no desire for any other man than him. They had the certainty of loyalty, which was a disappearing bond on the world's commodities markets, Abu Umar had taught him. Fidelity now had less saleable value in this material world than ever, loyalty: a crashed epitaph on the grave of materialism. He felt glad he had learned his lessons well from Abu Umar.

If this had been a normal wedding, then Jimmy certainly would have made a play, chatting to some or as many of the girls as he could. However, normality was a stranger that Jimmy had so rarely encountered on his life's sojourn. Sadia had grown more attractive with time, and seemed to have found a maturity, which surprised him, but now he could only see her as his sister, like Zoya. He had realised since early on in his teenage years that sex and love were monsters in his life that had yet to dine at the same table. Jimmy had never discussed his own future with anyone, not even Sofia or Zoya; because there had never been any stability, he had never much dwelt on the prospect.

Girls had never been a problem. He had stables of them, and he ran them in a professional way. He knew he was master of the desert, because he owned the wells that fed the oasis. Many a wayworn traveller had replenished himself, including Uncle Younis, in the havens of desire he provided. Sometimes Jimmy partook of the fruits, but only when necessary. He felt pleased that now the gorgeous girls did not tempt him, but nevertheless he still made *Astaghfirullah*, and so repented his sins to Allah. He had often made *tauba*, begged his Lord for forgiveness, in the middle of the night, since his conversion. This was when he felt closest to the Master of the Day of Judgement.

He wondered now, for the first time since his disappearance, what had happened to the lorry load of girls he ran. Probably under the expert tutelage of the rival firm, his competitor pimps: Suki, Harv and Hari. Strange, how he had not thought of the girls or the boys since he had disappeared – unlike his butterflies.

As soon as he had been able to get a break from Zoya, on the first night of his return, he had crept past Sofia's room and down through the empty spaces of the house into the butterfly sanctum. Although it had been the middle of the night he had topped up as many of the feeders as he could, and sprayed the plants. He had whispered his love, strengthened sleeping gossamer wings with his moist breath, exhaled on them affection from his soul. He had felt relieved to see Sofia had done it all correctly. She had cared for his butterflies. In fact the Butterfly House had never looked better. Certainly the bowls, feeders and the floor had never been so meticulously scrubbed. The fruit left out had never been fresher. Jimmy had smiled in the torchlight. Sofia did not realise that some of the butterflies needed rotting fruit.

Jimmy came out of his reverie as the girls who surrounded Zoya let out shrill squeaks of laughter, over some private juvenile joke. Uncle Younis had not yet started the ceremony.

Sofia beckoned to him, and introduced him formally to members of the extended family as Ahmad's closest friend and cousin – like a brother, really. So Jimmy received hugs and kisses, with donkey cartloads of sympathy. To non-family, who needed less explanation, she just introduced him as Uncle Jamshed, who visited them infrequently from Bradford, while he muttered greetings and quickly looked away. Jimmy saw Zoya in the traditional *lengha* with her gold nose clip and chain looping around. The *dupatta* covered her hennaed hair like a shawl of comfort. The head covering was dipped and edged with gold embroidery and lace, all melding together to create a grand cacophony of tradition in brocades, sequins and silks.

Zoya sat with her *Mendhi*-covered hands in her lap, looking down at the intricate orange patterns and swirls, with her head bent demurely. She had remained statuesque since he had entered, and Jimmy felt sure she would have a sore neck by now. Sadia forced Zoya to take small sips from a glass she held in one hand, with tissues poised in the other.

Jimmy felt the rising pride of brotherly love. The expectation of childhood dreams fulfilled; he had never seen her, even in her designer clothes, looking more radiant. He breathed out, and wiped his hands on his waistcoat. The risk had been worth it to see the scene before him: his sister, the bedecked Asian bride. Ahmad would have been proud. *All the gathered friends and family must feel some pride, despite their comments*, he thought.

Uncle Younis hawked, and noisily cleared his throat again to start the second part of the marriage ceremony. The *Imam* read from the large register, 'Zoya bint Mohammed Ahmad Regus...'

Jimmy felt a shiver run through him, as he heard Zoya addressed as the daughter of Ahmad.

'*Kiya aap ko in char gawaho ke samne yeh nikah manzoor hai?*' he asked her three times. 'Do you accept this marriage in front of these four witnesses?' On the third occasion, without looking up, she inclined her head. Sofia sat next to her, drawn and gaunt-faced, grasping Zoya's hand so hard that Jimmy could see his mother's knuckles turn pale.

Jimmy had never imagined himself in his father's place. He felt himself to be anthropologically so far removed from any Bradfordian uncle in the chain of Pak-Brit evolution, that he had never dreamed he would be playing that role now and be standing in front of Zoya as her paternal protector. The possibility of him willingly adopting that Paki persona and becoming her guardian had been an anathema, until the internal revolution.

He moved forward, through the shimmering mass of *dupatta*-flapping and sandal-shaking women. Hamza stayed behind in the main hall as Jimmy had expected, unable to accompany him into the inviolable women's space. Sadia did not move. Uncle Younis and his entourage seemed to take an age settling themselves, as they waited for the *Imam* to recite some prayers. Jimmy's thoughts returned to the ever-present fear.

He had seen men who had seemed suspicious, probably MI5 and maybe undercover police in the main hall, a few white men but mostly unknown generic-type brown-skins. People he had not seen before, maybe – certainly spies would be secreted amongst Zoya's friends, and maybe her work colleagues too. *Jaish an Noor wass Salaam* would be watching – waiting. *Why had they not acted, why had they not killed him?*

He thought it strange how the two avowed enemies mirrored each other in outlook and behaviour. As if they had become serpentine coils, their habits intertwined, resting vipers coiled in winter's sleep, but they might make a deadly strike at any momentary slip. Either party could inject poisonous death with a honeyed proficiency. The operatives of both organisations watched and mirrored each other in the dance of death, forming twisted macabre faces underneath plain masks. How uniform they had become – the schism between Neo-Con-Westernism versus Islamist violent extremism.

He forced himself to ignore the threat as he watched Zoya; eyes lowered modestly to her feet, as resplendent as any queen of the Indian silver screen. He wished Ahmad could have been here to savour the moment of his dreams. Zoya looked up at him, flashing green ice. He thought he almost saw her smile at his appearance. He leant forwards, put his hands on top of her *dupatta*, bent his back and pretended to be uncomfortable as his large belly stretched over his strained *sherwani*. Jimmy felt none of the clichéd melodrama of historical Bollywood precedent. None of the contrived artifice of a brother-father, or uncle adopting the paternal role after the father's death. He knew he would do anything for Ahmad's memory, but mostly for Sofia.

'*Babul ke duwayeh lehteh jah, thuj ko sookhi sansaar mileh...*' warbled Mohammed Rafi's melodious voice over the speaker system. Jimmy automatically translated to himself the long-dead singer's classic hit, *Take a father's prayers with you, may you find happiness wherever you may go...* The same old song that he had recoiled from at clichéd disgust now fomented emotions in his mind because of Ahmad's death, and his sister's marriage to a *Gorah*. *How easy it was to judge,* he thought, *when I wasn't in this position.* Some idiot had played the song too early.

The *Imam* scowled and looked up at the speaker system as if it had personally offended him, and men ran to switch off the music. Uncle Younis made a great show of standing, brushing down his *sherwani*, and clearing his throat numerous times. He then seemed to re-perform the *nikah* ceremony, almost repeating everything that had happened, until Jimmy's muscles tightened and his back stiffened. Finally, after the *Imam* had asked for the third time, Zoya, without looking up, replied quietly: '*Kabool Hai*. I accept him.'

With that, the religious part of the *nikah* was complete, and Zoya and Dan were married in the Islamic tradition.

Jimmy made sure he hugged her first. He clung to her, and then, fearing that he may have crushed her, he smoothed her *dupatta* back into place, made sure the gold embroidery did not scratch the soft skin of her cheeks and forehead. Sadia helped make Zoya's heavy *lengha* more comfortable, and moved to the side to give Jimmy space. He said a silent prayer for Zoya and then he held her close again, pressing her head to his belly as she sat on the chair.

Then Maulana Mohammed Younis Khan *Imam Sahib* reached inside his *sherwani* to the top pocket of his waistcoat and took out a gold pen with a flourish, which he held under Zoya's nose so she could sniff it. Jimmy saw the old chipped gold covering and recognised it immediately as Ahmad's pen that he had given Younis when they were boys. Ahmad had told Jimmy the story, and about how the *Imam* had claimed to have lost it. During Jimmy's childhood Uncle Younis would sometimes fish it out of the safe in his office, when Jimmy and Ahmad visited Younis for tea in the mosque.

Sofia reached up for it.

'No – no!' said Jimmy, and stopped himself calling Sofia *Ami* just in time, 'Here, use this,' he said and produced a new pen.

'No good, that pen,' said the *Imam* grabbing the pen that Jimmy had given to Sofia. He put Jimmy's pen away. Then he took the cover off Ahmad's gold pen for Zoya, and handed it to her. 'This special pen, very *Mubarak*, blessed. You use this one!'

Jimmy stared at his father's best friend, his teeth clenched, his fists pumping against his thighs –unable to stop himself, his rage building into an impotent climax. Zoya scratched her name on the paper, which had Dan's name on it; soon to be stained by Younis' signature, as well as the three witnesses. With her signature, the contract was officially sealed. The boys lifted the *mitai*, which had sat on large silver trays dotted about the rooms; they now carried them above the heads of the milling children.

'*Mubarak ho!* Congratulations! *Mubarak ho!*' rang out, as Jimmy had expected and clattered like pebbles in a tin can to his ears. They went back to the groom's section and pulled him out into the main stage to sit him on one of the red velvet throne chairs, where Zoya joined him. *At least these congratulations are different to church bells*, he thought of saying to Dan. The men grappled with the groom, surrounded and smothered him, and then each other in turn, with bear hugs and overly intimate gestures of sub-continental disingenuous happiness.

Jimmy knew most were laughing at him and his family's predicament. The same thing happened almost a moment later in the bridal section, because as usual the women received the *mitai* after the men. The wrestling seemed to go on for an inordinate length of time. Some hugged thrice, others just put their arms around each other, before disengaging to grab large chunks of the creamy buffalo *khoya barfi* to be stuffed from one mouth to another by eager hands. Thick chunks of luscious *barfi* fell to the floor, to be trodden on by heavy soles and *kusheh*, the pointed curvy shoes worn with the traditional dress – like the kismet of the Regus family. *We are trodden and shamed*, thought Jimmy. *I will reverse that – if not in this life, then in the Hereafter.* He stopped his hands, and forced himself to stop scratching his scar, in case it gave him away. He did not want anyone to notice the anger and pain. *I want them all with me; Ahmad, Sofia, Zoya, even Tony – and Zoya can have Dan, if it makes her happy.*

The temptation to end the agony and suffering pulled at him like lust. He felt his eyes lose focus as he imagined the detonation, here, in the wedding hall; but not enough *Kuffar* were present to take to everlasting Hellfire. *Wait. Wait,* he told himself, and breathed slowly, in and out. He knew most people would not notice his disjointed breathing as he puffed his cheeks out in the melee. *I've got to go so much bigger and better,* he thought. *I can't let the* Shaikh *down. Our project will change history.*

With a huge effort, he pulled himself back from the brink of the abyss. He moved his index finger away slowly from the mobile trigger in his *sherwani* pocket. *Soon. Soon, inshallah! Peace.*

London – Sebastian's House

Jessica's feeling of fear had diminished over the last few days, as she realised that Sebastian would not simply walk out and abandon her, leave her covered in an overwhelming shower of disgust. The dread at the future explosions that the terror cell had now fully instigated could not be diminished. The day, on which they would detonate the bombs, was surely imminent. They had all trained to a high level of proficiency. Jessica knew she could be asked to take any one of the possible five main routes, which she had memorised, and could walk any of them, so that she arrived at the exact places where she was supposed to be, within a given thirty-second margin of error. She knew the number of steps it took her to walk across Westminster Bridge.

Discussing things over the last few days with Sebastian had not resolved anything. Talking openly by phone was impossible. She had only managed short snatched conversations, due to the pressure of training, and she did not want to create any extra suspicion by leaving the training flat any more than necessary. Nothing had been said to her about Hamza's approach by anyone, *but that's not unusual*, she thought. That's how *Jaish* operate: layers of falsehood, concealed amongst folds of secrecy. During the short times together since her admission, Sebastian and Jessica had talked more about their feelings, which seemed impossible to avoid despite the urgency of her situation – especially now that he had declared his love for her.

Jessica felt glad in a perverse way; she would not be alone in her hour of need. Her concern for him, and the need to keep him safe, had not allowed her to echo the sentiments back to Sebastian. 'I care for you, Sebastian and I want to make sure you're okay.' That was all she had permitted herself. Despite a famine-hungry sensation she now felt every time she saw him, of wanting to take him in her arms and make him wrap her up tightly, she resisted touching him. She wanted to kiss the pink off his lips.

I've got to do something, she thought, *but I don't know what. Let me make sure Sebastian's safe, first.*

She perched on his kitchen table, then got up and paced around the large kitchen, thinking about how she could bargain herself into a position where he would trust her to stay in the cell and operate from within; that was the only possible position, anyway. No matter which way she grappled the problem-monster over the last few days, it seemed to dissipate into a fog, becoming a haze, which she could not physically grip. Finally, she had realised that anything other than maintaining her position within the cell at this stage was simply too risky – for herself, her family, and Holly.

Sebastian entered the kitchen, smiled at her, and gave her a hug. He held her at arms length and looked into her eyes. 'I meant what I said, you know, the other day.'

Jessica hoped he had not told he loved her simply because he had been overwhelmed by her revelation. She pulled away, and moved towards the table.

'I know. Please don't think I don't appreciate it. And thank you for understanding.' She brushed her hair back under the scarf, which she had to keep on around Sebastian so that *Jaish* would not be suspicious. 'I'm sorry for deceiving you, and I know you don't agree, but I do hope you understand.'

'We'll get through this. Don't worry, we'll think of a way through. Then I'll let you make it up to me.' He smiled at her, and then suddenly became serious, and then sat down on the table opposite her. 'No matter what, Jess, we have to stop the bombs – that's the most important thing. You can't go through with this.'

'I know but it's not that straightforward – my parents, and your life.'

'Look, I don't want to die, but in the greater scheme of things it's unimportant. Knowing these people like I do, there can't be just one bomb. Jessica... we're talking about utter devastation.'

'I know. Don't you think it terrifies me too?' She wished she could just escape, run away, and take all the people she cared about with her – but where, and how? She realised, as soon as she had thought it over the past few days, that it was in impractical childish dream. There was no end to the rainbow in real life. 'Like you say, it's not just your life and my life, but so many innocents, and maybe the end of the world order as we know it.'

'Okay. Let's call the police, let's get the security services involved.'

'It's not as simple as that. They're probably watching –'

'I know they're watching for sure, but don't worry. I've had this placed checked out by a professional security team over the last couple of days, swept for bugs and so on. They're not listening to us right now.'

'Are you certain?'

'I know the way they like to operate – they have people followed, and they like eyewitness accounts. They know you're here and that's fine, because you've told them that. So yes, I'm as sure as I can be, as sure as anyone can be of anything. All of life is a balance of risks. So we just have to go with the best option. Let's call the police.'

Jessica felt relieved that he had had his house checked for electronic surveillance, but his desire and emotions were controlling him, as she watched him chew his lower lip and flick the fingernails of one hand with the other. His eyes darted around the kitchen, despite his previous bravery. 'That might be the worst thing of all,' she said.

'Why?'

'We could do that if we actually had some information to give them. What are we going to say? *Oh, there's a bunch of terrorists who have planted bombs and I've been training to trigger the one in London, and we don't know where it is or what it looks like, or on which day the attack is expected, or how to defuse it.* If we find it.' She shook her head, and saw his lips curl down at the corners in misery, so she continued in a soft voice.

'Sebastian... you understand their emotions, their Kamikaze finality, as much as anyone. They will set the bombs off immediately if they suspect we informed the security service, and then we'll have no chance.'

'No, you're right. You have to stay in the cell.'

'They can remote trigger the bombs, but we don't know from how far, we don't know who the real trigger will be, and they probably have reserve cells we don't know about. Unless we have specifics, they will win. We need exact details.'

'What about Hamza?'

'I've thought about that, and that's just another risk. Maybe that's a risk we'll have to take if we've no other choice.'

'I don't know, Jessica, darling. I'm so worried for you.' He held her hand. This time she did not withdraw, but stroked his. She saw his eyes glisten, and then he looked down at the table.

He's always been strong, she thought, *and seemed to know what to do. Maybe this is love; maybe this is what it does to some people. He's still brave, but confused and hurting, and so I'll just have to be firm. I don't know how I've survived so far. I want to collapse into his arms... but not until it's all over.*

'I have to pretend everything's fine, continue in the cell. I'll try to get more information from wherever I can, and I'll especially work on Dwayne. He's always liked me, and maybe I'll even take a chance on Plain Jamila, but I won't say anything else to Hamza unless he says something to me first. Jimmy's disappeared over the past few days – maybe the *Shaikh* sent him on a secret training mission?'

'Let me make you some tea, I'm not much use for anything else. Sorry...'

She looked into his eyes, her face soft. 'I'm here because of you, and I won't collapse in a heap because I know that I have you. We will succeed, no matter what happens, because I want to see you again.' She smiled. *What a consummate liar I am*, she thought. *Promising him success, no matter what. But it's a lie that's wrapped in the death shroud of truth. I do want to see him again, and to have a life with him.* She flexed her stiff fingers; her body felt cold, and her heart growing like an ice-ball earth entering a new frozen age.

Sebastian got up to make tea, and took out the porcelain scarlet pimpernel tea service. 'I can't just watch you go through this on your own.'

'Sebastian, do something for me. Go to Birmingham; carry on with your work.'

'I can't do just do nothing.'

'No, not nothing. Listen, you know these people, you have contacts. Find out what you can.'

'I can't. You're just getting rid of me, making sure I'm away from here,' he said, in a voice about to break.

'You infiltrate them in your way, wherever you can – here and abroad. Use all your contacts and influence. I'll keep going in my way, until we know what we need, and then I promise. We will contact the police immediately, as soon as we know the essentials.'

Jessica got up, and put a hand on his to stop him filling the teapot with hot water. 'No, not that, Sebastian, not now.' She smiled at him. 'When it's over... then we'll drink tea from that service.'

CHAPTER 30

London – Zoya's Wedding

Uncle Jamshed from Bradford got pulled into the celebrations, which continued on the raised stage area where Zoya and Dan now sat. He disentangled himself as soon as he could, brushed off invisible dirt from his clothes, specks of evidence of other men, and wiped his palms on his *sherwani* – hating, as always, the intimate physical contact.

Then the time for the *Rukhsati, The Departing,* arrived. Traditionally, when they had been to other people's weddings, this was the time that Jimmy and Zoya had disliked the most. The time when the bride had to leave the marriage hall for her new home with her new husband to start a fresh life; no longer the virginal princess in her paternal home, but the child-bearing queen of future generations. It was always a time when people cried.

The women, who seemed to cry more than at any funeral Jimmy had been too, even the women who had barely known the bride, would hang their heads on the bride's mother's shoulder and wet her *kameez*, each vying with the other to show the most empathy. There would then be a conglomeration of family to facilitate more tears, which would merge together, and somehow give comfort. A sharing of salt at the impending genetic loss. The girl's side bemoaning the loss of a daughter, but glad to have discharged a 'responsibility' in front of the whole *Biradari*.

Jimmy remembered how he and Zoya, sometimes with Sadia, used to laugh secretly after most weddings, and guffaw after watching the inevitable six-hour-long films. Zoya would say, 'Oh, but her dad's over the moon really – look, look! He's not crying. He's thinking: *thank God! Got rid of number three, never thought anyone would ever marry her. Fat cow!*' They would giggle as if they were back in primary school again.

Now Zoya's henna-stained hand crept into his like a small beige butterfly, fluttering and afraid, seeking a brother's love. The difference in size now seemed greater than it had in their childhood, and it made him feel more fraternal and protective. Sadia held onto Zoya like a conjoined twin and cried more tears, but softly. *She doesn't want to disturb the family by sobbing loudly*, he thought. Jimmy knew the pain he felt was real; it hurt to see his sister going away. They might all soon be dead. He might be responsible. So he cried with the rest of the clan, unashamedly putting his arm around her as she walked to the bridal car.

At the doorstep of the wedding hall, he held her to his chest and sobbed as she wet his *kameez*. He ignored the fear that the wetness flowing into his artificial beard might melt the glue. She clung to him, like a drowning sailor in rigor mortis to a broken oar. This was the time to play the Rafi song, about the daughter taking her father's blessing with her as she left home, but some over-eager Paki had played it too early.

Sofia finally pulled her away from Jimmy, and said, '*Beti*... it's your kismet. Be happy with your Destiny!' On hearing his mother's comment, Jimmy knew Zoya's finality had arrived. Even Sadia could not help, now that the surgical intervention of Sofia had separated Zoya's body from Jimmy's arm. He gave Sadia a small scroll sealed in a black cardboard roll. 'Give it to Zoya once she's in the car, yeah?' he said.

'What? What is this?' asked Sadia, in between her tears.

Jimmy did not reply; he could not explain it was the secret recipe for his Masala Raita. It would have seemed trite or maudlin to all others. No-one could understand... not even Sadia. Nothing could turn Zoya back from her fate, but at least he could give her some good memories of them growing up together. *The recipe will be a reminder,* he thought. *It's too late, whatever happens now. I bet she's thinking just that: it's too late.* Jimmy almost said the words out aloud. *What if she feels that her family had turned their backs on her, just because she had married a white man? What if Zoya never again feels welcome in her parental home?*

He saw her face, looking garish and macabre because of the tears. The beauty parlour make-up made Gothic streaks down her cheeks, smudged panda rings over her eyes and left thick powder marks over her eyebrows. Looking at his sister at that moment Jimmy could only imagine her as a little girl crying and rubbing, then twisting her tiny fists into her face as she cried, just as she used to when he broke her dolls, ripped their arms and legs.

Zoya and Dan sat in the back of the bridal car as Tony drove away, with Sofia in the front. She had insisted on dropping Zoya off at her new home, although Jimmy knew that was against custom. Most of the people started to leave, but his relatives were expected to make their way back to the Regus home for more tea and tears.

Throughout the time at the *nikah*, Jimmy had noticed a youth flitting in and out of the rooms; he thought the boy might be from *Jaish an Noor wass Salaam*. Now he noticed the same youth, who looked like he could have been one of Jimmy's new recruits from the streets. He could imagine the boy asking him for work to push Maal for him. The kid approached close to him. Jimmy tried to ignore him, and half-turned to leave.

'Uncle, uncle, a word – one minute,' said the boy. The youngster seemed out of breath. Jimmy turned back and saw a dark youth with lines, razor cuts designed into the sides of his head where his hair had been shaved short. He had a small wispy moustache, too young to grow full bristle; the boy had a face that would have been ordinary, even in complete isolation. Generic: unidentifiable to caste, creed or city, just like the uncountable others. An unending supply of brownskins that the ghetto houses exuded, zombie-like in unremitting quantities. Jimmy knew they were all desperate to usurp his position at the slightest sign of weakness, like African wild dogs on a long hunt. Jimmy saw the same look now in the boy's face, as his eyes scouted around, but his head did not move.

The teenager gestured with his hands. His speech seemed an impediment to communication. His thick fingers had bitten nails, and supported thicker gold rings. The chains around his neck were a paler imitation of the ubiquitous on-screen LA gangster-rappers. Although Jimmy felt certain the boy had never left the borough, Jimmy walked over to the boy, who then led him away from the others. Jimmy imagined himself to be like the miscreant youth a few years ago, but shuddered in denial. *Surely not: I was never like that!* he thought.

He followed the youth, despite his instinct that the boy was a *Jaish* recruit, and he almost certainly knew who Jimmy was, despite his disguise.

'I need you help innit? Yeah, def need yo' help, definitely,' stammered the boy.

Jimmy looked at him. 'Help for what?' After a pause, and without any need to remind himself to keep the accent going, he said, 'I'm Zoya's

Uncle Jamshed from Bradford.' Another glance at the boy. 'I don't even know anyone around here.'

'Yeah, yeah, Uncle Jamshed. That's right, Uncle Jamshed!'

'Maybe you'd better ask Tony – he's her brother.' Jimmy nodded towards the crowd. 'Look over there.'

'It's okay Uncle J, Mr Jimmy. Enuff respeck – enuff respeck to yo', respeck to yo'!' said the youth, flicking the fingers of his right hand almost up to Jimmy's face with every invocation. He bowed his head down as he did so, out of deference, paying respect to the legendary self-made king of the Southall drugs world. Jimmy's reputation was legend amongst the boys of the woods.

'Look, son, you wrong! *Puttar*, you is wrong,' said Jimmy hoping that Punjabi for son might throw him off his scent; he pulled his beard and scratched his scar.

'The *Shaikh* sent me. The *Shaikh*, innit, yeah.'

Jimmy felt shocked that he had been so easily recognised. *But then Jaish did teach me the disguise,* he reasoned; he hoped MI5 and the police would be less able. *If they had identified him, why was he still alive?* he wondered. *Maybe I should just blow the belt now.* He flicked his hands towards his midriff, near the *sherwani* pocket. The boy reached out and stopped him, firmly, but without violence.

'Sorry, Mr J, yeah, but the *Shaikh* told me you would be dressed like this and wearing that, innit,' said the boy, gesturing with his eyes his hands still on Jimmy's. Jimmy thought of the suicide vest, which lay close to his body like a hibernating reptilian skin, warm now, but forever alien.

'Don't worry, you little shit. I ain't in no hurry.' He put his face closer to the boy's. 'In the woods, yeah…' Jimmy paused and starred into the teenager's eyes. 'Can you touch me?' he asked.

The boy looked down as if to confirm he had touched Jimmy, then jerked his hands away from Jimmy's as if they were poisonous snakes. 'Sor – sorry – sorr –'

'What you want?' Jimmy said in his normal voice, as he pulled the boy into a small side room. *No need to pretend now*, he thought. He saw the youth's lips tremble at having touched him, his hands quivered at being alone with him, despite having the backing of *Jaish*; he knew Jimmy's street rep. He felt an obstinate leftover pride that he still could inspire terror in the boys of Southall.

Jimmy pulled the shorter man up by his coat. 'What do you want? Hurry, you little bastard!'

The teenager's body shook in waves now. 'The *Shaikh*, Abu Umar said...' The boy calmed a little at having mentioned the name of his talismanic keeper and guardian. 'Younis Khan, yeah, Maulana Younis –'

'I know who that shit fucker is.'

'Get him! *Shaikh* said get –'

'What the fuck do you mean 'get him'? What d'you want me to do?'

'Nah, nah boss, no way yeah...we do our own work,' stammered the boy.

Jimmy nearly laughed out loud at the way the kid equated himself with *Jaish an Noor wass Salaam*. Instead, he loosened his grip on the boy's army coat.

'You, Mr J, you is AWOL – yeah, AWOL.'

Jimmy grabbed the youth by the throat. 'Shut up. Stop talking shit. What do you want?'

'Get *Imam* Younis round the back. There's a big bins area, yeah,' said the boy, choking. 'Re – recyclin' area, innit, with big metal bins.'

'So?' Jimmy released his grip slightly. One hand almost encircled the boy's slim throat, but Jimmy could not see any fear in his eyes.

'Then you – *Shaikh* said, yeah – you can come back to *Jaish*, innit?' said the messenger boy.

Jimmy flung him into the wall and he bounced off, seemingly glad to be getting away. He wiped the spittle that had dribbled down his mouth, and cleared the hanging mucous off his nose with the back of his hand.

'Thanks Mr J, yeah,' said the teenager, coughing. 'Thanks!' He gave a mock salute, and grinned.

'If this was the woods –'

'Be there in ten minutes, ten minutes, yeah,' said the boy. The boy gave him his mobile phone number. 'Ring this when you's ready. Just give me a missed call.'

Jimmy saw him growing in confidence now that he had released him. The youth put his hand on the handle and half-opened the door. He made sure he was half out, before he said, 'Be there in ten minutes, yeah or – or – fuck you!' He opened the door fully and bobbed through, but stuck his head around the door and added, 'The *Shaikh* says, innit.'

Jimmy almost laughed at the boy, as he realised this was the chance he thought would never come. Abu Umar was offering him forgiveness and a way to return to the comforting fold of *Jaish*: if he delivered the *Imam*. He kept his voice harsh, with effort. 'Ten minutes exactly, innit. Or I will fuck you,' said Jimmy, with his business look.

The boy grinned, showing some gold-capped teeth, and disappeared.

A way back! he thought. *I can still do it! A way back into the cell. I can still be a martyr. Legit, innit, yeah – be a legit martyr. No need to kill the few* Gorahs *here. Just deliver Younis Khan to* Jaish's *tender mercy. He's my* Abbo's *best friend, but better to have a cobra as a friend. He signed Zoya's* nikah *documents with Abbo's pen. He thinks I don't know,* bhenchaud *bastard.*

Jimmy walked back into the main hall, to find Younis surrounded by cronies, taking money off Tony in thick piles in the most reluctant manner possible. It seemed as if that was the last thing he wanted.

'*Areh, areh, nahee, nahee! Yeh kiya?* Oh no, stop this... what is this?' said the *Imam*, looking surprised as Tony handed him another thick wad of notes. Uncle Younis held out his hands with the notes on the palm of his right hand, while his left gripped Tony's arm so he could not withdraw it.

'No, uncle, take it. Take it,' said Tony.

'*Areh, areh!* What do you think me? *Nahee, nahee!*' said Younis, chuckling.

Jimmy saw how he pretended to pull his hand away from Tony's, and he showed a writhing movement to the gathered men with his upper body, as if Tony held his arm firm.

Jimmy felt his fists clench and blood like murder coursing through his arms, a refreshing feeling of rebirth he had felt many times in his life. He resolved to deliver Uncle Younis to *Jaish*.

Finally, when Tony had pulled out some more twenties and added them to the bundle, Younis chortled and let him go. '*Ohee khoyee!* No need! *Ohee khoyee!*' He tucked the notes into his coat. 'If only Ahmad was alive today to see this... he stop this *behizthee*. Such *sharam*, dishonour and shame,' he sniggered, and shoved the money deeper into his *sherwani* pocket.

Jimmy saw how the money made an obscene bulge below his guts. He knew Uncle Younis pretended he meant the shame of Tony paying him for performing the marriage ceremony for his best friend's daughter, but really he implied the shame of the marriage itself, a raped Zoya marrying an infidel *Gorah*.

'*Ek minute, Imam Sahib*,' said Jimmy, bowing low and shaking him by both hands. He slipped back easily into his middle-aged Bradfordian uncle speak.

'*Lagtha hai ke aap ko kaheen dekha hai*... it seems as if I have seen you somewhere?' asked Younis.

'No – no. We Regus all same-looking.' Jimmy moved forward, still holding both of Younis' hands. 'Need important *baath* with you, talking something important with you,' he said, glancing around at Younis' henchmen furtively. He maintained broken English, not trusting himself to Urdu.

'*Bohoth* sorry, *bohoth* busy, *heh heh*,' said Younis, pulling his hands away and patting the bulging pocket that contained the thick notes. 'Too hot, too hot, *nahh*?' He opened his *sherwani* and Jimmy saw the flash of gold: his father's fountain pen, poking out above the top pocket of the waistcoat. Younis chuckled, and patted the pocket again. Jimmy thought the *Imam* seemed comforted by the manoeuvre, and he ungritted his teeth, with some effort, before Younis could see.

Then Jimmy moved in close to Younis and put his hand over the pocket with the money, before the *Imam* could turn away. Jimmy pretended to hug him. As he pulled him close he looked into the older man's eyes, glad he wore brown contact lenses.

'*Areh areh, Imam Sahib*,' said Jimmy with the same inflection as Younis. '*Aap ko kush karna hai*. I will make you happy.' He whispered and squeezed the pocket with the notes in it as he hugged Younis, so no one else could see or hear what he said. Jimmy released him, then leaned forward and kissed him on both cheeks. 'Outside, behind the bins, five minutes. Alone, and you will be happy and rich,' he muttered in Younis' ear. Jimmy gave Younis' pocket a last squeeze, before smiling broadly and walking away.

He went to the toilet, pissed with difficulty, readjusted his *karakul* hat and splashed water over his eyes; stared at his reflection in the small mirror.

'What about *Abbo*?' Jimmy asked the image.

'What about *Abbo*?' answered the reflection. He stared back at Jimmy with bloodshot eyes. In the thundering silence, his pulse crescendoed in his neck and ears, until he could stand the silence no more. He turned and rushed to the back of the wedding hall, then went out through a small side exit.

Jimmy waited around the back of the building, and lit a cigarette. He doubted that Uncle Younis would come and if he did even more unlikely that he would come alone – *it was rare for his lackeys not to be carrying his bollocks around for him day and night,* thought Jimmy. This part of the building was deserted and hemmed in to create a tight quadrangle, which was open on one side and had huge bins lined up against a wall. It was the sort of place his boys might go to shoot up or smoke. He knew he had used the right bait. Jimmy had called upon the money-god and the lust-god of Uncle Younis; the twin-headed voracious idols that had whipped Younis' life into animation. Their canine-sharp, triangular hooks deeply embedded into the flesh of Younis' soul. Uncle Younis would not be able to release himself from those barbs until the day he died.

Younis came sauntering around the corner, burping and picking his teeth with a wooden toothpick, having eaten a huge wedding meal. The smell of his sweet *attar* perfume preceded him and overwhelmed Jimmy with nausea, the effect only intensified with the physical arrival of the *Imam*. He seemed surprised to see Jimmy's cigarette. Jimmy inhaled smoke deeply, to hide the perfume. Uncle Younis burped louder this time, without making any effort to cover his mouth. The wedding meal had, unusually, been served before the *nikah* ceremony. Jimmy had seen the *Imam* and his numerous cronies stuffing their gaping insatiable holes, lavish food into gourmet-demanding mouths, a buffet of bastards. Younis cleaned his yellow teeth with the toothpick, which he clenched in claw-like nails.

'Heh heh heh,' sniggered Younis, and then after a lingering look at Jimmy, he added, 'You calling me here?' He stared at Jimmy's cigarette, and then closed his eyes. Jimmy thought as if to say *Don't worry, I won't tell dar-ling, if you don't. Kiss me, quick!* The *Imam* giggled in a high-pitched falsetto.

'*Kiya bath hai, aap cigarette waleh bohoth he shareer hai!* Oh, you cigarette smoking peoples are so naughtys!' said Younis, and blinked and shimmied. As he dipped his shoulder a fraction, his eyelids fluttered. He giggled again.

Bastard thinks I fancy him! thought Jimmy. *Must have squeezed his tateh... maybe I got his bollocks when I held onto him. Whatever it was, it worked – he's here.* Younis came close and put an arm around Jimmy's waist, and rubbed his hand up and down his flank.

'Which mosque you *Imam*?' Younis flashed his pearly teeth.

'We want you to come and speak and recruit, *Masjid*, in Bradford.'

'No, *nahee nahee* – I don't do that,' said Younis, and moved closer to Jimmy, almost nuzzling his face. He tried to suppress his rising sickness, not just because of the homosexual overtones, but also because of Younis' oily skin as he slithered his way around Jimmy's body with his face and hands.

'I come, will be coming – if – if you training boys...' The *Imam* grinned and sniffed Jimmy's neck, almost brushing it with his lips. He fluttered his eyes, took a cigarette from Jimmy. Younis caressed the shaft and giggled before putting it deeper in his mouth than necessary; he leaned forward and sucked, as Jimmy offered him a light.

'We will give money before – before you coming.' Jimmy tried to squirm out of his grasp, and crushed his own cigarette under his heel.

'*Nahee, bohoth paisa hai*. No, I've got loads of money,' said Younis.

Jimmy wondered if he had overdone it. No one offered money up-front, especially not to Younis. 'Boys, lots of boys in *madrassas*,' Jimmy said, understanding the *Imam*. 'Now I will send boy to you, right now, and he bring plenty dollars for you.'

He forced a smile as he pushed the *Imam*'s slithering, slimy hands off his face, extricated himself from Younis' attempts at grasping him. Younis puckered his lips at Jimmy and reluctantly slid his hand from Jimmy's shoulder, but grabbed him with the other hand and held on for as long as he could, before Jimmy prised himself away.

'How much?' Younis asked, as Jimmy faced away from. He turned back and saw Uncle Younis' smile broaden.

'Five thousand for weekend,' said Jimmy, walking away slowly and waving, indicating for the *Imam* to stay there. 'I will send my boy. If you like him, I will give money.' Before he turned the corner, he stopped and winked at the *Imam*.

'*Nahee nahee* – no, not for whole weekend,' Younis protested.

'Okay, okay, and boys what you like in *madrassa*.'

'Young, young *bacha*,' said the *Imam* with lascivious intent. Jimmy thought he heard the joy in Younis' voice as he left.

Jimmy felt no regret as he pushed the redial button on his phone. In doing so he alerted the boy from *Jaish*.

It would be over in seconds. He walked around the block and returned in a few minutes via the deserted small side street, back to where the metal bins stood.

As he approached he saw Uncle Younis impaled on a metal bin, his weight supported by the handle that jutted out halfway up the bin. The *Imam* sat astride the handle; there was another metal spike through his chest. His arms were spread out, with nails banged through the palms of his hands: crucified. The black *sherwani* he had worn was cut along with his shirt, both hanging loosely to the sides. In the centre of his midriff, Uncle Younis' bowels hung out in thick loops, blue-veined with yellow fatty streak, like blind snakes intertwined, hibernating in winter's sleep.

His mouth was stuffed full of twenty pound notes, his eyes bulged out of their lids like roulette balls trying to escape the wheel, all white, with small black spots. Inhuman – amphibian – unevolved.

'Better hurry innit, yeah, Mr J? Enuff respeck, yo' did it. Enuff respeck to yo' though, innit.' said the boy. 'The others, they gone. You bettah leg it, them police *Kuffar* fuckers, they's after yo' – they's gonna be here any sec, yeah.'

'What about you?' he asked, despite himself.

'Get going yeah, get goin'!' The boy looked around, and added, 'Don't worry, the *Shaikh* he looks after me, he's waitin' for you, he's waitin', innit.'

The memory of the *Shaikh* Abu Umar re-awoke the zeal for his mission again.

'Yeah, gotta get this back to the *Shaikh*,' Jimmy said, pulling at his suicide vest. 'We're gonna need this for the final mission. But first, one minute…' He leaned forward and took Ahmad's pen out of Uncle Younis' waistcoat pocket. He heard footsteps pounding around the corner. The boy pulled him, and they ran.

'That was for *Abbo*,' said Jimmy, as he turned to look at Maulana Mohammed Younis Khan *Imam Sahib*'s grotesque gargoyle, before running again at full pelt.

That evening, when he reached Westminster Bridge, he leaned over the side of the bridge and held his arm over the dark waters of the river. He threw the pen into the Thames. He watched it fall like a golden teardrop. The pen slipped silently into the water, like a laser-guided magic bullet. It disappeared into the swirling, murky depths: to its target.

Jimmy leaned over the bridge and stared into the black waters of the river for a very long time.

CHAPTER 31

London – Westminster Abbey
Jimmy edged past the crowds near to the Houses of Parliament, but resisted looking up at the clock tower that loomed over him, that seemed to be shadowing him like his future. He entered Westminster Abbey and did not see the overwhelming pillars or the soaring arches, but he sensed them bearing down with the pressure of England's past, which for so many centuries, he now knew, had been the determinant of world history.

Jimmy went into the nave and stopped at Charles Darwin's grave. *How much of what he said is true?* he wondered. *Is it really true that we're apes by another name?* Then his mind turned to the old question: *and is it also a case of you are with us, or against us?* He knew the forces of evil. The Western powers had said all Muslims in the world had to decide whose side they were on in the War on Terror. There was no in-between, no room for grey in their candyfloss, gaudy world. Abu Umar had taught him so many times that you have to stand with the forces of good, for the victory of Islam against the *Kuffar; it is Allah's order*. Both messages sounded the same, but Jimmy knew that the Islamic version was the truth, that it came from the words of Allah himself.

Are we savage beasts with the thin sheen of civilisation? he thought. That sheen which would evaporate, like the sweat that filmed his brow, as soon as the cold wind of self-interest blew? *Will I help to destroy all this?* He felt sorrow slowly take over him, like a chrysalis emerging from its cocoon. It surprised him that he could feel regret over a long dead *Kuffar*. Charles Darwin collected butterflies from all over the world, and Jimmy had knowledge because of people like him. He had his beautiful butterflies, maybe because of the long-dead, weird looking *Kuffar* man. He longed to see all the colours again. He was worried about the pupae box. *Will Mum know when to open the box and how to make the nectar just right every time, and what about my inner green house, the secret one? Of course, since I left home* Ami *knows what's in there, but she's promised not to tell anyone else.*

He looked at Darwin's grave again. *They are the* Kuffar, *out to destroy Islam, as Abu Umar says.* His thoughts flitted from one idea to the other without seeming resolution – sometimes so Western, and yet essentially Eastern. He cursed, and punched one of the stone pillars just hard enough to swear. He rubbed his grazed knuckles, and wiped the sweat from his forehead. He berated his indecision.

What kind of coward are you? he asked himself. *What are you really: Eastern or Western, English or Paki? You can't be both; the Americans have clearly told you so.* Thoughts of identity lead him to one inevitable conclusion. *I'm a Muslim: a Jihadi first and last. So help me, Allah!*

He left Westminster Abbey and made the short trip back to Victoria. When he got back he found Dwayne waiting for him, nostrils flared and arms crossed, his eyes spewing incandescent contempt at Jimmy. He kept his shades on as he entered, but he felt Dwayne's eyes almost lasering holes through them, into his own eyes.

After what seemed to Jimmy an interminable age of staring, and another age of dirty looks and head-shaking, Dwayne spoke. 'Me carn't believe it. You nearly jeopardised the whole mission. You great big fuckin' ape.'

Jimmy did not answer; he turned away from Dwayne, and walked into the open-plan kitchen. He started making some tea.

'Me carn't believe it. Do you have any idea what you've done?' said Dwayne. Jimmy selected the small saucepan. 'You was watched, at your sister's wedding,' continued Dwayne, as he entered the kitchen. Jimmy turned to the sink, and half filled the saucepan with water. He set the saucepan on the hob, took out the cardamom packet, opened some cardamom pods with his fingernails and threw them into the water, followed by some cinnamon bark.

'The kid there at the wedding – he was following you for days,' said Dwayne, coming around to face him. Jimmy turned, to look at him.

'Yeah, we did. You're bloody lucky, fucking lucky, mate,' said Dwayne.

Jimmy took off his coat, draped it over a stool, and watched the bubbles in the water. He added a whole star anise and a pinch of nutmeg powder.

Dwayne came up close, 'If this was, if you was someone else, then –'

'Then what?' Jimmy asked as he turned suddenly, squaring up to Dwayne. He used his street look: unblinking, not breathing, fists almost clenched, feet ready to spring. He was slightly taller than Dwayne, who also had a barrel chest, but Dwayne had sinuous arms and legs, which made him look lighter than Jimmy.

'You what?' said Jimmy, his spittle landed on Dwayne. His face was one nose length away. Jimmy did not breathe, and he saw that Dwayne had not jerked a muscle in his face. Neither looked away.

'You gonna do what, bad ass?' asked Jimmy, using his street lingo. He wanted to free his limbs. *It's been a long time,* he thought. *I gotta thrash him into the ground. I'm getting soft – ain't fought for too long.*

Jimmy felt the automatic response, and his blood almost breached the dam of self-control as it thumped through his tight muscles, each one now coiled like steel serpents. He longed for the lust-pleasure of smashing Dwayne into submission. *No, no – wait, wait for the real test!* he ordered himself.

'You lucky you ain't on the street, innit? I eaten enough like you, yeah, for breakfast – you fuckin' black nigga pudding.' Jimmy came still closer. His eyes lost focus, and breathed out on to Dwayne's face. After a pause, which cut like racism, Jimmy said, 'No... didn't think so. Don't you go pretending you is like the *Shaikh*, yeah, just cos you sit next to him.'

'You's lucky you his bluey boy, but if it wasn't for the *Shaikh* you'd be feeding sharks in the North Sea,' shouted Dwayne, without flinching.

'The pigs would scrunch your bones so fast, bro – if you didn't work with *Shaikh* Abu Umar, you'd be black nigga pig feed. My mate Majid's got Pit Bulls and *Tosas*, and he got a farm full of wild pigs too... and they all love human meat, innit.' He stared into Dwayne's eyes, almost touching nose to nose. 'Especially dumb black nigga pudding.'

'I care about the cause. I ain't letting no little snot rag screw up our project, and my *Shahadah*. I – will – be – a – martyr!' said Dwayne, and turned away from him.

No – gotta get back with Jaish, he told himself. *I know they need me to complete their mission. They're one man short; they can only work in teams of five. Each one is essential, and Abu Umar has told me I'm special so many times. It's too close to the big day. It's gotta to be the way the* Shaikh *wants. Gotta impress the* Shaikh *– and beating this dumb* *puppet won't impress* Shaikh *Abu Umar.*

Jimmy managed to control himself, and then added milk to the boiling water. 'Shit, forgot the *saunf*,' he said aloud. He threw in two pinches of fennel seeds: Sofia's recipe for Pakistani *Chai*. He was glad he had not fought with Dwayne; he felt he had achieved better discipline since meeting Abu Umar.

Before the milky tea boiled again, it released the fragrance from the spices. The promise of Eastern rapture that Jimmy knew awaited him with the first sip, the tea that could subtract problems and add harmony. He had not believed his mother when she tried to get him to drink it for years, then when he had tried it finally, only recently, it had quickly become their ritual, morning and evening. They sat and sipped traditional tea twice a day. All other activities stopped, and he made sure he would always be home for *Chai*. He did not worry that he now loved Paki tea, or that he had embodied some part of the village lifestyle, things that would have bothered him before. He remembered how Sofia and Ahmad also used to sit twice a day and drink the tea made by his mother in the same way. Jimmy had learned how to make it from her, and now timed his day from the diurnal rhythms of *Chai*. Tea, morning and dusk; the cooking of water and milk with spices, until they boiled three times, had become one of life's essential rituals. He knew he would never be able to fill his father's space, but making time with Sofia, trying to reduce her loneliness, had only increased the guilt for the years of filial neglect – and then he had left home.

Jimmy thought of his father. How calm Ahmad had been during his daily rituals. He now wished dearly that he had joined in, or even eavesdropped on his father's smiling, wistful conversations, on his mother's meandering tales of a halcyon age in the village of Ramnagar, where there used to be people who loved and cared for you without expectation of return: Paradise Lost.

He wished he had imbibed the tea, drunk the nectar of wisdom, and picked the rose petals from his father's dying breath as Ahmad sighed out his last days in front of him. And Jimmy had known they were his last days. Yet he had done nothing: just the attempt to get money for the private operation, from Uncle Younis. No open father-son talks, no promises, and no apologies. Not even thank you for being the best father you knew how to be. Not even *I will miss you*, Abbo.

I miss you, Abbo. *I miss you,* Abbo.

He wiped his eyes, glad that Dwayne had disappeared into his bedroom to sulk. Jimmy looked up, made sure the door to Dwayne's room was shut, then whispered a quiet prayer for their togetherness, for him and his father to be reunited in *Jannah*.

Had things been said without being said? Jimmy wondered. What undercurrents had his father passed on to him? Could there have been a sacred strand of telepathy that existed in the moments before Ahmad's death in the mosque? When he had dumped his memories, beliefs and hopes into his son before his death? Jimmy hoped *Abbo* had given him a parting gift before Azra'il, the Angel of Death, grasped Ahmad's soul from his body.

Abu Umar had taught them that death was always painful, even for the good Muslim. The soul would be wrenched out for the bad person, except the martyr. The *Shaheed* would feel no pain, and would embrace death joyfully. He would smell the sweetest breeze. The most wonderful fragrance of Paradise, before his blood hit the ground. Death would be so pleasurable if he died fighting in the way of Islam, that he would beg Allah to be allowed to go back and die in the way of Allah again and again. As would all martyrs.

Jimmy had seen Ahmad die without obvious pain or struggle; he had whispered himself out of life. *How perfect is my Lord!* Three times in *sujood*, prostrate, breathing the words out for the third time. Jimmy felt as if he could hear his father whispering the Arabic next to him. Like a hummingbird sipping its last drop from the flower of life, before cold winter's hand descends and it migrates to feed on some other, ethereal, nectar.

He poured the tea through a small sieve, rolled his shoulders to try and relax his muscles before sitting and taking his first sip. He was roused from his wondering by the sound of Abu Umar's special knock, before the *Shaikh* opened the door with his key.

Jimmy's hands trembled and he put the mug of tea down, but he forced his mouth into a broad smile before turning to face the door. He saw Abu Umar smile in response to his own. *Yes! I'm back in* Jaish. *I will be a Shaheed! Yes!* He punched the air with both fists. 'I made you some *Chai, Ya sayedi*, my master,' Jimmy said.

Abu Umar just smiled back.

CHAPTER 32

London – Westminster Bridge
Jessica walked across Westminster Bridge. She looked up at the tower of Big Ben; dread, like the unyielding stone of its huge structure, weighed on her. The clock chimed half past three, and each chime rang in her ear as if she was inside the bell.

This is the day, she thought. *This is the day. The day of the bombing!* Her brain electrified and jolted nervous random signals to her limbs, which seemed uncontrollable, and jumped with small contractions.

They had left the flat all together, about half an hour ago. Abu Umar had given them a collective blessing; he gathered Jimmy, Jessica, Dwayne and the Afghan around him, as he chanted special prayers and catechisms for the success of their mission today. He raised his hands to heaven, petitioning Allah, his fair skin contrasting with his brown beard. The lines of his features were distinctive and unmoving.

'Oh Allah, Master of all the Worlds, Lord of the Day of Judgement, yours is the power and the glory. Grant us, we are becoming your true servants, success today. We are worshipping you as you have instructed us, with our tongues, bodies and souls. Today we go to make the highest sacrifice: the thing that is most beloved to you, when a servant sacrifices himself. We are offering our bodies as sacrifice, our lives as tribute to bear witness, to be *Shaheed*, to bear witness there is no god except Allah: *Laillah illalah!*' The *Shaikh* lifted his right index finger up, pointing to the heavens, bearing witness in characteristic style.

'Oh Allah, make our hearts steady and firm, chase away any doubts about the justness and righteousness of our cause which is your cause.' He had stopped the prayer for a moment to look at Jessica before closing his eyes again. 'Be the power behind our hands, the strength in our arms when we strike. Let it be the strike of Allah.' A pause as he looked up at the ceiling with arms outstretched.

'Today is a day of reckoning for the *Kuffar*. Grant us victory, defeat our enemies. The *Kuffar*, they are your enemies, *Ya Allah*. As we render onto them a *Yaum Al Nakbah*, The Day of Calamity, as they have made us suffer so many days of calamity, for so long. Today we right the wrongs, we avenge the losses: no more Charles Martel at Tours-Poitier, no more Jan Siebowski at Vienna.'

'*Inshallah! Inshallah!*' the group had intoned at the right time.

'Today Europe, America and the whole world will fall down in terror, and accept the victory of *Jaish an Noor wass Salaam*. They will never dare to challenge us again. Today is the first day of the new Golden Age of Islam, until the Kingdom of Allah comes – until Eternity.' He wiped the tears from his eyes, before drifting off into a semi-stupor, his eyelids closed, flickered. Jessica wondered if he was seeing the historic events being played out in front of him.

'Today we will cleanse the world from the corruption and evil, from all the *Dajjals*, false prophets and anti-Christs. The cities full of vice and inequity will be flensed from the skin of the world, their hearts purified from financial disease. The contagion will be cured. The filthy philosophy of the *Kuffar* will no longer stain the earth, and your final message your *Deen*. The victorious flag of faith will fly and all will be *Dar Al Islam*. All will be beautiful and pure. *Inshallah!*'

'*Inshallah! Inshallah!* If Allah wills,' they all echoed. Jessica remembered how Abu Umar had cried and wet his beard and Jimmy and Dwayne and the Afghan had cried. Even Hamza had managed some wetness in his eyes, though how much any of them meant the emotions, she could not be sure. She felt guilty for being the only one not to weep, although she had cuffed her eyes in pretence. Abu Umar had continued, through his veil of tears:

'Today is our victory. The might of Islam, the roar of the lion, *Asadallah*, The Lions of Allah: you,' he looked at each of them in turn, pointed a finger into their faces. 'You. Each of you is *Asadallah*.' Jessica willed herself not to recoil.

'*Asadallah*, make no mistaking, these *Kuffar* have to know you rule over them, just as the lion rules the lesser beasts of the jungle.' He paused and seemed to smile, but Jessica found his unchanging expression hard to fathom during his emotional phases.

'Those who are making injustice after injustice, genocide and hate against Muslims. They have been try to wipe out Islam for centuries, and today is their defeat by your hands, by the will of Allah. Today, the final Golden Age of Islam under our great *Amir Al Momineen*, may he rule forever, Zulfiqar bin *Hijaz*, starts. These *Kuffar* will never ever again hold sway in our domains. Revolutions all over the Muslims lands will make sure of this.'

Jessica thought of the insurrections, more joining them every day, chaos and mayhem.

'And soon our flag will also flutter proudly over the capitals of *Kuffar*. This time we will not be kicked out after eight hundred years, like Al Andalus. This time will be forever. Until *Yaum Al Qiyama*, The Day of Judgement!' Abu Umar paused as the tears of the men rose to a new crescendo, swallowed up by more cries of '*Inshallah! Inshallah!*'

Jessica noticed how openly Jimmy cried, how deeply affected he was, and how he smiled through the tears. Then he laughed and hugged Dwayne and the Afghan: she imagined Abu Umar's words playing out in Jimmy's mind, like a film predicting the near future. The dreams of victory and success so near, so tangible, like grapes of Paradise they could almost reach out and grasp. All would soon be feeding in gardens with rivers of milk and honey: happy forever with their *houris*.

Her determination to do something, to approach Hamza or Dwayne, to take any risk – she was going to die, anyway – had grown in proportion to her desperation. She had made plans with Sebastian, and now she had no choice but to trust that they together might be able to do something to stop *Jaish*.

Her stomach had become knotted, and she left to vomit twice, as Abu Umar's exhortations flowed viscous and ever–hotter, like molten rock from an erupting core, burning the greenery of her life to a charred stump. In the time she had known him, the *Shaikh* had spewed enough to create new worlds. Except Jessica knew that *Jaish an Noor wass Salaam*'s gospel would only destroy her world: the fire of hate, and the flames of misrepresentation. Abu Umar's breath seemed to form speech that whipped up a burning wind, which scorched everything, leaving behind only the flowers of his vile politics. *Al Jaish an Noor wass Salaam, The Army of Light and Peace* did not create fertile volcanic earth to grow oases, but instead their dogma spread like a disease: it had hunger, like a desiccating desert wind. And the only thing that gave it flight was death. Abu Umar had *Jahanum*-Hell breath, and his lava was about to create malevolent unliving islands of self-interest; unsatiated holes of hatred caused by the wolf-hunger of power.

During Abu Umar's exhortations, she felt estranged. So, to keep in the mood, Jessica had thought of Hamid, of Mariam and her family. Tears welled in her eyes, which she blinked away. She would not cry in front of these people. The Americans and the West had, in so many countries, used the same style of rhetoric as the extremists who had sat in front of her, except much more cleverly. The so-called neo-cons, the Western fundamentalists, used the same Machiavellian machinations, the same expediency, the misrepresentation of fact: plunged deep that dagger into the heart of Truth. They managed to slay facts by creating statistics and suspicion.

Abu Umar often misquoted Qur'anic phrases and maligned Islam in the vilest terms possible. *I knew that at the start of my journey,* she thought. She had read many books secretly, which *Jaish* would never have tolerated, and had continued to discuss them with Sebastian. After her admission and her explanation why she had infiltrated *Jaish*, she felt could ask him any question without embarrassment or fear of censure.

She remembered looking at Abu Umar during his prayers earlier in the day, at his face screwed up tight; *he thinks he's at the end of knowledge, certainty and time,* she thought.

'*Allah O Akbar! Allah O Akbar!*' Abu Umar had exhorted, and they all shouted. Jessica joined in, swept away by their stretched faces and searing breath. Heat that warmed the room physically seemed to flow from their dark eyes, except Abu Umar's yellow-flecked marbles glowing orange – *lion's eyes,* thought Jessica – whenever emotion overtook him.

When she had discovered more about *Jaish*, she had hid the disgust and anger that had rapidly festered into hatred, a heart-blackening virus that she had to keep below her skin. The full horror of what she and the suicide cell were about to enact made her feel as if quicksand was drowning her, and filling her lungs. She took deep slow breaths. Did Abu Umar realise the full implication of destroying a city full of civilians? Innocents massacred on the pretext of an unjust foreign policy, and continuing international terror. The vast majority of Londoners do not know the difference between *Kuffar* and *Momin*. This led her back to the question which would not go away, but only hid behind the ongoing crisis. *What am I?* she thought. *A believer, but in what? God, yes, but*

I don't know. The lines on her forehead tightened.

As she walked across the bridge her thoughts turned back to Abu Umar, and the loud sobbing noises he had made when beseeching Allah, which made her fall into the vortex of confusion. She could not be sure what she really believed, but he always seemed to be so sure of himself. How easily he had hijacked Islam, to say he is doing this in Allah's name. Did the *Shaikh* believe his actions to be for all Muslims and his version of vitriolic, violent Islam to be the true message of God? Does Allah want massacre of humanity? Jessica felt sure she could never believe this. *Even if it costs me my life, I have to stop these crazed* Jaish an Noor wass Salaam *terrorists*. She still had no idea yet how she was going to do that.

She looked back at the Afghan; he was the fixer, the connector between the cell and the *Jaish* trainers in Afghanistan and Pakistan. He proved to be the bridge between East and West, the explosive experts, the logistics and the triggers. He followed her on Westminster Bridge as he had on almost all of her journeys. The Afghan trailed her, puppied her footsteps as usual, panting a pace behind. She felt sure he had no idea what was really going on regarding the final plan, but she had no way of communicating with him except for sign language.

Jessica noted the way he had changed; he now wore a peachy top with cargo pants and chains around his neck, a thick gold necklace around his left wrist, and a luminous Fossil watch on his right wrist from which she knew he could not tell the time. So far away from his tatty *salwar kameez* that she had first seen him in, which was always dirty and creased; he had looked as if he was still wandering the forests of Bulgaria, while he waited for the people-smugglers to come rescue him. She wondered if he ever thought about the skeletons in the mountains of Turkey. He seemed not to have been affected, even though he had left a couple of his own group behind as offerings to the voracious mountain demons, so desperate was he to fulfil his blood sacrifice to his own God.

She glanced at the Afghan again, walked slightly quicker, and he aped her exactly. He was clean-shaven now, no more the straggly beard that grew only on his chin, the rat's tail moustache long gone. His dark-brown hair was cut now so it flopped over both sides, his large hook nose the only immediately recognisable part of him. He grinned back at her.

Jessica bit the knuckle of her thumb, and breathed her own cloudy air in and out faster, panting. *Oh God, where's Sebastian?* she thought. *What's he doing now? Will I ever get to see him again despite our plans?*

That day looked very far off, as she saw Hamza crossing the bridge from the other side and the reality of what they were about to do hit her: destroy London and eleven other cities, commit suicide, and end the modern world. Abu Umar had only now finally confided in them by telling them the true plans of *Jaish* – blasted at her like a shockwave, as if the red London bus that passed her had just hit in her face at full speed. She brushed her hair away from her eyes and felt her explosive vest under the thick winter coat, and wondered what the last-minute Christmas shoppers would do if they realised that a suicide bomber had just passed within inches of them. What would her parents think? Their little Jess, with her wide cornflower-blue eyes and two golden ponytails that she wore to primary school, had turned into a monster? A little princess to her father, who told her every evening as he kissed her goodnight that she had cheeks as soft as little baby bunny rabbits, and who had giggled when his whiskers brushed her face – she was now fully involved in a plot to destroy the Western World. To bring about the Golden Age of Islam, Allah's victory, as imagined by Abu Umar.

Jessica had never believed violence would bring victory for either side, and after joining *Jaish* she was certain that triggering the bomb with her suicide vest would not bring about any kind of Golden Age, or solve the world's problems. She felt more certain with every passing moment that Allah did not want or need this victory. She could not allow herself to imagine the aftermath; the dead and injured the children, with melted and mutilated bodies, for fear that she would run screaming to find retreat into immediate lunacy. Or throw herself into the river in case she was the trigger – anything to prevent the calamity.

Her phone rang and both her feet nearly left the ground in fright. She had been strictly ordered to leave everything personal behind, anything that might identify her. Just before she left the house, she had hidden the phone where she knew none of the men would dare look. She stopped walking to answer.

'Hi Jessica, it's Sebastian.'

'Sebastian, what are you doing calling me?'

'Look, I'm in London –'

'What?' she screamed, her worst fears realised: he would die with the rest. 'I thought you'd be back in Birmingham.' They had agreed that

Sebastian would try to help from Birmingham, where he would use his contacts within the *Jaish* circles to find out their exact plans, and then inform the police – but all without putting himself at risk, or immediately threatening Jessica's covert position. She knew it was a pathetic plan, with little or no chance of success, but that was all they could do.

'I know. I know. But I'm so worried.'

'Sebastian, you promised!'

'Sorry, Jess... that's one promise I couldn't keep.'

'Please, Sebastian, please get out go to Birmingham, anywhere. Get away from the centre as far away as you can. You've no time.'

'I'm sorry. I can't,' Sebastian said. She heard the concern in his voice and her pulse surged. He continued, 'I can't leave you alone in this mess.'

'I got myself into this mess...' she said, and regret flooded over her like her sweat, which drenched her body.

'It's not just you, now. I've managed to talk to some people. And like I said before, I won't leave you, because I love you.'

She froze, eyes fixed on the swirling water in the river below; she did not know what to say. The dreams that she had repressed, the life that she thought she would never have. Now she wanted that life so desperately. Her inevitable future gripped her throat. As if the fingers of Time were pressed hard, deepening their hold on her flesh, digging nails into her jugular. *I want to live!* Her windpipe felt crushed; she coughed and spluttered. *Let me go! I want to live!* She almost screamed out loud.

'I'm so sorry, darling, but I do love you... I can't help it. I have to show you that you must not do this – you – we – all of us must live,' said Sebastian, as he repeated what he had said to her before, when they had planned furtively. She heard the desperation of sincerity, which was leading him to an uncharacteristic loss of control. 'I talked to Hamza –'

'What?' She tried to walk faster but failed, gathered her emotions, which slowed her, but she forced her legs to move. 'He's here. Walking towards me.'

'I know! I know. I have spoken to people who know. Jessica, please listen, darling, we have to get back the hospital flat, to the last safe house, before Abu Umar leaves. Trust me, Jessica – its vital. Get back to St Thomas's Hospital with Hamza as fast as you can. It's okay... you can trust him.'

'I'm not sure, Sebastian. How do we –'

'We have no choice. It's the only chance. It's too late to get out of

London now, anyway. It's Christmas madness.'

'What about Dwayne?' she asked.

'I don't know about him. Hamza didn't say anything.'

'He didn't leave with us – I think he's going to be with Jimmy. He doesn't trust Jimmy.' She did not want to stop talking to him, though she felt time run faster and further, speeding them away taking their lives into another dimension. The insurmountable regret at their imminent deaths would not stay hidden. The wasted lives, but especially at the lost opportunity of happiness with Sebastian. She would not cry, as she had done in her room at nights. She had too much to do, and Hamza had almost reached her. Her conscious mind still fixed itself on Sebastian, as she heard him say he would meet her at the flat; she did not reply.

He had become everything she had ever wanted, despite their unusual start. The weeks felt like years, and she had immersed herself into a life with him. Now she could not imagine anyone else, or a life without him. She realised her situation was full of contradictions. Love and death, hate and life, all in the same breath. She had got herself into an impossible position. Despite the danger to Sebastian, she felt glad, in a weird way, that they would be together at the end, fighting the unwinnable battle. The bitterness that he had not escaped to carry on her memory, when she was gone, stabbed in her breast like selfishness.

Now there would be no life, anyway, she thought. *How could they be stopped? Jaish an Noor wass Salaam* seemed invincible, and they held all the ace triggers. Maybe M15 and the security agencies were involved; perhaps Sebastian *did* know something, and had made contact with the right people. Perhaps those people did not know enough to stop *Jaish*, without Jessica leading them to the bombs? *I can lead them to the bomb!*

As she walked faster, the thoughts of all the small things hurt her more, things that she would now not have. The feeling of holding hands with Sebastian, walking through the swathe of bluebells in spring, of picnics near the river in the glade. She had always loved the woods near her house in the season of rebirth. Maybe even, one day, giving their children enough education and the chance to make a better world, as she had failed spectacularly to do.

In their long hours of discussion she had come to realise that Sebastian was right; how anger and grief, along with her insatiable journalistic curiosity, had led her down a deep, dark tunnel. She did not need much convincing that the terror cell would not remake the Golden Age of Islam, but once it did exist, for periods of time. Sebastian had told her that, in places like Baghdad in the true Golden Age, and Jerusalem, and Cordoba of Al Andalus, the cities had embodied the three Abraham faiths. In Spain, instead of killing the *Kuffar*, the Muslims gave refuge to the Jews who had escaped the Reconquista, and found protection from the Christian purges going on in the northern Catholic kingdoms.

Despite her waning commitment to the cause, her spirituality buoyed her. Since the early days her small pool of belief in *Jaish*'s cause had become very rapidly dry and dusty; insubstantial like wheat stalks, her life's harvest now dedicated to stopping the horror.

She felt certainty and strength in her belief that God wanted her to stop the bombings. She thought that her spiritual power, along with Sebastian's support, were the only things that buttressed her. Stopped her buckling and falling into a heap of despondency, kept her from becoming a formless jellyfish-like lump from fear.

Her motivation had been the desire to know the truth about Hamid, but now she wore her determined stubbornness like a mask of armour to prove *Jaish an Noor wass Salaam* wrong. *Even if I fail today*, she thought, *then the God of all sees all, and he knows my intention was to save the massacre of the innocents*. She remembered reading in one of the banned Islamic texts that *He who takes a life is as if he has killed all of humanity, and he who saves a life is as if he has saved all of humanity.*

'Hamza! Hamza, we have to get back to the hospital flat. I think it's Abu Umar,' she said, her words tumbling out of her mouth like projectile vomit. 'Sebastian hasn't left London. He's on his way there.'

'I know. I phoned Sebastian – we have to get to Abu Umar, before he escapes.'

They turned and hurried back towards the flat.

'He's bound to have a helicopter waiting to get him away from London. I'm sure he doesn't want to die here today, no matter what he says.'

'What about the bombs? What about all the other cities?' she asked, becoming breathless.

'We have to worry about ours for now. That's why we have to get Abu Umar before he leaves,' answered Hamza. He turned to the Afghan and spurted a spiel of fast Urdu, something about Jimmy. The Afghan sped off towards the Houses of Parliament.

Jessica and Hamza raced back over Westminster Bridge, to the doctors' accommodation at St Thomas's Hospital. Abu Umar had a sympathiser in the doctors' accommodation, from whom he had requisitioned the flat for the final few days of the operation. It was the last safe house, minutes from the bomb, which Jessica knew must be somewhere near The Houses of Parliament. At the flat, Jessica saw Sebastian stopping his car outside the block of flats. He got out of his car.

'Come on!' said Hamza to Sebastian. 'I've got the keys.'

All three burst in to surprise Abu Umar, who sat at the table with a small-hand held device.

'What – what the hell is going on? You should be at the Houses of Parliament by now,' Abu Umar said, getting up from his chair. Hamza and Jessica approached him, closely followed by Sebastian; the two men pushed him back into the chair. 'Who the – who's this guy?' He tried to get up again, but Hamza put his hands on his shoulders, keeping him seated, while Sebastian stood to the back, ready to help. 'Hamza – what do you think you're doing? Get him out of here!' Abu Umar ordered.

Jessica saw the shock of disbelief on Abu Umar's face, which had rendered him inactive for a moment. She saw how the realisation that Hamza no longer obeyed him turned his face into red and purple fury. He tried to push Hamza away to get out of his seat, but Hamza jumped on him with his full weight, and Sebastian grabbed his arms from behind the chair.

'Jessica – get something to tie him up with,' said Hamza.

Jessica went to the cupboard where she knew the plastic ties were kept; they had practised how they would be restrained if arrested by the police. Abu Umar had used the plastic strips to tie each of them up in turn during some of the training sessions. The two men had to use their full strength, but still struggled to keep him restrained in the chair. Jessica returned to find Abu Umar's face turning more mottled, as he tried biting Hamza's arms, and spat a spate of Arabic invective at them. He kicked and struggled as she bound his wrists and ankles with the unyielding plastic ties.

'How dare you? You traitors! You God damn traitors!' shouted Abu Umar.

Jessica saw he could barely get the words out in English. Despite being tied, he did not stop trying to free himself. He struggled, and flecks of saliva landed on his face, dribbling down his chin.

Hamza tipped him out of his chair, so he fell backwards. The chair toppled over; he landed awkwardly on his back. Hamza and Sebastian turned him over so that his face was pressed into the carpet. Hamza sat on his back. Sebastian grabbed the PDA off the table, and stood near Abu Umar's head.

'What's the code?' Sebastian asked Abu Umar, who could no longer struggle with Hamza on his back, his arms tied behind him.

'What's the code?' repeated Hamza. 'We'll get it from you, one way or another.'

'So you are the traitor. We wondered for so long who,' Abu Umar grunted in pain, but continued. 'Leaking our secrets.'

Jessica saw he had controlled himself enough to speak, now that he could not struggle.

'You're lucky you last so long. You should be feeding for pigs now. Jimmy –'

'Shut up! Tell me what the code is!' said Hamza, applying more pressure to Abu Umar's back with his knee, and pulling his arms up harder. Abu Umar, winced and Jessica turned away as Hamza smashed his fist into the back of Abu Umar's neck. 'We've no time to mess around, you fucker,' he said.

Jessica turned back to see Abu Umar's reddened face split into a grin and he laughed. 'You expect me to tell you? And you're trying to frighten me by pain?' He laughed again. Jessica felt disconcerted, but of course Hamza should have realised that he would never give up the codes willingly. Even the threat of torture would not be enough for someone who had gone out, actively seeking death for so much of his *Jihadi* life.

'We might try and play our tunes in life, but the music sheet we play from is already written by God. You've lost. So you might as well tell us, because MI5 know all about you and your plans. You've failed!' said Hamza.

Jessica realised he had to try and bluff.

Abu Umar laughed again. 'You jokers! I know they be here instead of you amateurs if they knew. They don't know nothing. They can't move. Because they are scared. They know I can remote trigger, but not from how far away, and where the bomb is. They have no idea. None of you do.' His chuckle became a strangled gasp of pain as Hamza pulled his arms; his face reddened more as Hamza pressed again, harder. Although his head faced to the right, Abu Umar had to struggle to breathe. Blood seeped out along with spit, which covered his chin and stained the carpet.

Hamza punched him again. *Maybe he had bitten his tongue*, Jessica thought. *How does he take the pain? His shoulders must be almost dislocated.*

'It's too late. Far too late. Only the bombs matter – you traitors, the cause of Muslim suffering for centuries. No more, no more!' Abu Umar gasped as Hamza released the pressure. 'You – all in the bottom of *Jahanum*, forever.' Hamza pulled him to a sitting position; the relief did not seem to dampen his fervour, 'May Allah curse you worse than traitorous Jew-dogs for all eternity, to the worst imaginable torture.'

'What are we supposed to do with this?' asked Sebastian, standing over the two men. Hamza still controlled Abu Umar by holding the tie that bound his arms behind his back; Jessica saw that the tie had cut into the *Shaikh*'s flesh, and blood oozed over Abu Umar and Hamza's hands. Abu Umar laughed again. 'You cowboys like Americans – little boys in big boy's games.'

'Here – give it to me, and hold him!' said Hamza. He swapped places with Sebastian. Jessica saw the mocking laughter turn to disgust on Abu Umar's face, as he saw his torturer. Hamza took a small stylus out of the side of the PDA; it had a swab on the end of it.

'Now, open wide like a good boy at the dentist,' he said. He bent down, and brought the swab close to Abu Umar's mouth, who wrenched forward and tried to bite Hamza's hand, but Sebastian held him. Then Abu Umar spat at Hamza, cursing in Arabic, the spit splattering over Hamza's face.

'Thank you!' said Hamza, and wiped some of the saliva up off his cheek with the end of the swab. Then he forced Abu Umar's right index finger into the screen of the PDA. Abu Umar grunted in pain, as Hamza pushed him onto his back. 'Hold his head,' he said to Sebastian. As Sebastian fixed his head in position, Hamza sat on Abu Umar's chest and put the PDA, which had a circular area built into the back to Abu Umar's right eye, forcing his eye open with his fingers. The PDA beeped and flashed into life.

'It won't make no difference, you idiot,' said Abu Umar.

'I know what to do. How to work your secret device – but you're right, I need the code to deactivate the bomb,' said Hamza.

'*Abadan! Abadan!*' said Abu Umar. 'That's something you'll never never get.'

'Tell me, or you will die a worse death than you have ever inflicted on any of your victims.' Hamza pushed Abu Umar so that he lay flat, then put his knee across his throat, until he nearly choked – then, Hamza released the pressure.

'We all going to die soon. None of us can chooses our ends, anyway.' Abu Umar gasped, coughing. '*Lanatallah alehha! Lanatallah alehha!* May the curse of Allah be upon you and your Jew-Zionist masters!'

Hamza jumped off him. 'Come on. We're not going to get anything out of this crazed bastard. We don't know who the trigger is, or even what time the bomb is supposed to go off. Tie him up properly.' He wiped the sweat off his face, cleaned his hands on his trousers. Jessica helped Sebastian secure him to the chair. 'We'll let the police take care of him later. I'm sure MI5 will have a few questions,' said Hamza.

Jessica saw Hamza trying to work the PDA, which shone and flickered with a myriad of lights like the false star of Bethlehem. Hamza prodded the screen a few times, which flashed in response.

'Shit, we need the alphanumeric code to deactivate the bombs, but we can still get some info now that it's active. Let's go!'

Jessica watched as he tried to convince Abu Umar a final time by putting pressure on his throat, and she realised desperation led Hamza to violence, when surely he must realise that Abu Umar would not give up anything. At least, not without systematic prolonged professional torture-interrogation, and time had nearly run out. She felt guilt and ambivalence. She had known this man and sat with him for months, and when Hamza hit him again and she heard the cartilage in his nose crunch, she said, 'We're not like him, Hamza – come on.' She had to pull Hamza away from his final frenzied attack. They left *Shaikh* Abu Umar gagged, bound, and hog-tied to the chair.

Hamza led them back to Westminster Bridge. On the way, he reaffirmed the fact that twelve cities had been targeted and that some information had been gleaned. He knew how to activate the PDA, but the alphanumeric code was not known. Jessica thought the security services must have suspected but they didn't know for sure; how many people in the world knew the codes? Abu Umar was certainly one of them.

As they walked, Hamza confirmed their suspicions and told them of the dozen cities to be bombed: Los Angeles, San Francisco, New York, Washington D.C., London, Paris, Brussels, Madrid, Berlin, Rome, Moscow and Sydney. The names confirmed like the twelve tribes of

Israel; each had its own humanity-nation destroying devices.

Jessica and Sebastian stared in disbelief as he named them. She knew the explosion would be big enough to destroy much of central London, and the dirty nuclear bomb would do the rest. The destruction would spread out, like ever-weakening ripples, followed by the chemical and biological weapons. WMDs: real Weapons of Mass Destruction, in central London. Poised and ready to explode in hours or minutes. Exactly how long, she had no idea.

'Who are you, Hamza?' Jessica said after a moment, as the names of the cities registered. 'Whose side are you on, anyway?'

'I don't think even I know that anymore,' he said, and his dark eyes seemed to swirl with blacker currents. She imagined she saw regret in his triangular face, with its long thin nose with flared nostrils, leading to a small, feminine mouth and a pointed chin.

He surprised her by continuing, after a pause, 'They ain't singing carols or doing Christmas shopping in Baghdad, or Kabul... more like scraping their kids' skins off the walls after –'

'What? Stop!' Jessica covered her face as she remembered Mariam's children.

'I'm just trying to stop people from dying. We'd better get moving, or no one will be shopping on Oxford Street for very long time.' Hamza's phone rang, and he put a small device into his ear. 'We have fifteen minutes left,' said Hamza, and she saw his hands shake as he consulted the PDA.

Fifteen minutes. What can we do in fifteen minutes? Jessica coughed and retched; neither man asked her if she was all right.

Annihilation. The consequences were unthinkable. This was world domination. The final clash: assured destruction of Western civilisation. Not small puffs of dust to be cleared by the prevailing wind like 9/11, or 7/7. Jessica knew *Jaish* thought those attacks to be a poor man's staple, blowing up a few hundred in passenger planes: insignificant amoeba on the evolutionary scale of terrorism, compared to the multi-headed chimera now exhaling, about to breathe fire into the lungs of the *Kuffar*. This would be terror from the King's table: a feast of the most violent acts in the history of mankind. A real bonfire of Western vanities.

Hamza took the PDA out, and tapped the screen.

'Well we've got the location. The map didn't make sense to me, but it looks like the bomb is near the Houses of Parliament somewhere.'

Jessica knew from the practice runs and her training that the Houses of Parliament would be a favourite and obvious target, as she and Sebastian craned to look at the map. Neither said anything.

Hamza's phone rang again, and he repeated the procedure of putting the small device into his ear, which almost completely disappeared inside his ear. 'We need info, fast,' he spoke into the earpiece. 'I know it's just around the corner from the Houses of Parliament –'

'Jimmy is the real trigger.' Jessica could hear a tinny voice coming out of his device. It had the tone of calm authority, which could only be produced by certain knowledge. 'The time is five o'clock. Repeat – five o'clock. Jimmy is the real trigger.'

Hamza looked at his watch. 'We've fourteen minutes left. Where the hell is Jimmy?'

'The device is in a disused old tube station. Follow the map on your screen; there are no road names. But you can follow it once you get to Westminster tube – that's marked with a circle,' said the man's voice.

Hamza led then as they raced crossed the bridge, dodging past shoppers and Christmas tourists.

'Right, you better get all the services involved. Call the local police, anybody – even Bobbies on the beat – although it's too late for all that. Abu Umar can't trigger anything now. We'll do what we can over here to stop Jimmy.' Hamza turned to Jessica as they ran, and said, 'Shit! Jimmy, he's the real trigger!' Then he put a hand over his ear, and spoke into his earpiece again. 'But we need the code. Come back to me in less than ten minutes, or you and me'll be cinders, mate – and there ain't no Prince Charming waiting for us on the other side.'

In her desperate hope that Hamza could get some vital information, despite her suspicions, Jessica did not question how he had got the special earpiece through which he seemed to grow in strength and power, despite the increasing crisis and imminent calamity. She prayed the voice on the other end of the earpiece could extract them from the jaws of *Jahanum*. She felt like a gazelle in the crocodile's mouth, with a futile, forlorn hope of living again. She could feel Abu Umar's teeth grip her windpipe.

They reached the other side of the bridge, ran into the tube station, and down the stairs. Jessica panted harder; her legs felt as if they had been filled with mud, and she had started sinking into the tar pit of history, soon to become a fossilised remnant. *I've condemned the world to destruction,* she thought; *hundreds of thousands, maybe millions, of people will die. Because of my personal desire to infiltrate* Jaish an Noor wass Salaam, *and now* The Army of Light and Peace *would exact a price beyond wealth. And I still don't know the truth about Hamid.*

So many times Abu Umar had teased and tantalised her with shards of information. Then there had been Abu Umar's uncertain declaration that Hamid had not been the suicide bomber. *He knew that's what I wanted to hear.*

Jessica felt as if she had condemned Sebastian as well. She glanced at her watch – ten minutes to five. Ten minutes of life left. What would she do in her last ten minutes? She felt like taking Sebastian aside, sitting down somewhere, quietly looking into his eyes, and telling him she loved him too. How she wished they could have all the small things that mattered: the walks, the smiles at each other's peculiar habits, the way he pursed his lips after dinner as if sucking the flavour of the dessert in. The way he always made her tea, patiently rinsing her mug with hot water first, and the way he added just enough milk and exactly measured the sugar by the grain, it seemed. Her mind raced back to the drive in the Malverns, the smells of the trees that had seemed brighter and more acute, and the yellowness of the primrose; yellower to her than ever before, more real than any previous memory. She wanted it so desperately, but she immediately dismissed the thought. Only one thing mattered now: *don't be so weak!* She forced herself on. *I've got to find a way to stop the bombs.*

She could hear the sirens, and she realised that the operatives Hamza had been speaking to had set the emergency services in motion, the police and bomb squad. *Too late! Too late!* her brain screamed at her, the terror rattling her bones to dust, with a skull full of fear, which took over any logical part of her brain. *It's all too late. The bomb squad won't make it in time, and people can't be evacuated. They'll achieve nothing by cordoning off the area; they can't get through the mass of shoppers on time.*

She remembered the Birmingham bombing. That would be a flyspeck compared to this. No way to run, either. Safety might as well be in a black hole behind *Alpha Centauri*. She followed Hamza and Sebastian, as they ran down the stairs of Westminster tube station.

There is only the here and now, she thought. *Can I live a lifetime in a few minutes, lose myself in the eternal time and space?* She tried to calm her heart, which seemed as if it would punch through her chest wall. Her mind dipped into an almost-subconscious, soft, plane. She thought about her special time with Sebastian in the glade in the woods, sitting with him on the tartan rug amongst the gentle hills, with sweet grass and hay fragrant in the warm autumnal afternoon. The way he made her tea, served her with affection in his eyes; she saw joy in his face at her surprise, and in her laughter. Jessica loved the way Sebastian's own pleasure was vanquished by the only thing that could subjugate the selfish ego – serving the beloved. The memory of the way his eyes filled with love, even now, made her clutch her stomach. She remembered how they would sometimes sit for hours, hand in hand, as they looked out over the fragile surface of the lake near her home. No words would break that mirage-mirror, until the sun had set. *Has it all been a mirage? A lake of love in a desert of hate?*

The reality – a dirty nuclear bomb, with chemical and biological weapons attached – shook her daydream, and fragmented it into detritus. Abu Umar had laughed and said, 'The three dimensional Weapons of Mass Destruction are set for the *Kuffar*, which they had searched for in the ruins of Babylon and in the heart of every date palm of the Mesopotamian desert are right here, sitting right under their bottoms!' *This would lend a new history to the memory of Guy Fawkes if they could not stop it,* thought Jessica.

Hamza's earpiece flashed again. 'Yeah, we're in the tube station, following the PDA, yeah – turn where?'

Jessica and Sebastian followed him, struggling through the throngs of last-minute Christmas shoppers. *They really picked the right day and time*, she thought. They passed a group singing carols, which reminded her of her grandparent's village in Lincolnshire, memories of homemade pies and antediluvian furniture, slightly tired rooms that were gloriously well-lived-in. The thoughts of the inevitable log fires warmed her still.

They pushed their way through the underground station, unable to run, and shouted their way to the end of the platform, trying to avoid the angry throng. Jessica thought they would create panic any moment. Some people shouted back.

'Where now?' she heard Hamza say. 'Come on!' he shouted, as he jumped into the service entrance. Jessica and Sebastian followed him as he ran in the darkness for a short while. Hamza tried a door handle. When it did not open immediately he put his broad shoulder to it, and crashed through the old wood. They ran down a flight of stairs, and entered a disused tube shaft. She could see that this tunnel looked like something out of a World War II movie; the dusty atmosphere and the old platform made her almost imagine air raid sirens overhead and families taking refuge in the station.

'Where are we going?' she asked, but Hamza ignored her, and listened intently on his earpiece.

'The PDA attaches to it. The bomb can only be diffused by attaching it and entering the code. They're saying there's a slot built in. I have to slot it in. The police are coming in through another entrance – shit!'

Jessica had seen a group of armed police officers that were patrolling the area outside. *They must be trying to head us off*, she thought, *but they definitely don't know the exact location of the bomb, otherwise they would have shut down the tube station.*

'Have you got the code yet?' Jessica gasped, barely able to keep up with Hamza.

'Three minutes to go. He's the trigger. Can't even get him out of range in time, now,' said Hamza.

'What's the trigger range?' Sebastian asked Hamza.

'Doesn't matter. It's too late! Where the fuck is Jimmy?' shouted Hamza. They followed again, as he raced around, a corner and crashed into Jimmy.

CHAPTER 33

London – Westminster Underground Station
Hamza and Jimmy smashed into each other; both sprawled on the floor. Jessica helped Jimmy up.

'Come on, Hamza!' said Sebastian pulling his arm.

'What the hell are you lot doin' here?' Jimmy finally asked. He felt confused and dazed. 'None of you's supposed to be here.' After a pause, he continued, 'Who the hell is this guy?' He came closer to Sebastian.

'It's okay *yaar*, come on – we've no time. Abu Umar changed plans, last minute, to throw the *Kuffar* off the scent. Come on, for God's sake!' said Hamza.

Jimmy allowed himself to be pulled by the arm by his old friend. 'What happened to *Shaikh*?'

'He sent us, sent Sebastian with us, to help you.'

'What you talkin about, Zee?' said Jimmy using Hamza's old nickname, 'I don't need no help. I'm the trigger. I'm in range, yeah –'

'No, we need to put the *Shaikh*'s PDA into the device, otherwise it won't go off,' said Hamza. 'MI5 have disabled the remote triggering mechanism in our vests, put a sonic blocker on it.'

Jimmy looked at his old friend, and saw the compassion and desperation in his face. 'Fuckin' bastard MI5!' he said, looking at *Shaikh* Abu Umar's PDA. Jimmy remembered seeing him use it furtively during training sessions in the flat.

'It's okay, *yaar*, don't worry. You will still be a martyr, *inshallah*!' said Hamza, smiling briefly at Jimmy.

How well Hamza knows me. All these years later, after a childhood full of friendship and cricket, he realises my deepest desire to be a martyr, thought Jimmy. '*Inshallah Zee* yeah, we all will be,' said Jimmy, relieved that Hamza shared his vision, his doubts disappearing. For, of course, *Shaikh* Abu Umar would have alternative plans with many layers to throw the *Kuffar* off the scent, in case they tried to foil our glorious plan.

Jimmy had long felt remorse and regret that many Muslims who lived in London, and some of his family, might die; he knew that Zoya and Dan wanted to move nearer to central London. *Thank Allah, Alhamdullilah, they haven't,* he thought. *Harrow is too far away – surely they won't be affected. The bomb blast will be confined to the central area.* Abu Umar had promised him that. As for the Muslims who did die in the bombings – well, they would be *Shaheed*, if they were true Muslims. A price worth paying. For what could any true Muslim want more than to be a martyr and be with Allah forever in Paradise?

Abu Umar had reassured him and flashed him a snowy smile, and had said, 'They are lucky; we are paving the road for their martyrdom! Subhanallah! *Allah O Akbar!*' Abu Umar had reiterated his oft-repeated phrase of *Allah is Perfect! Allah is Great!,* and chuckled. 'You must not think of things like that. That is above us. Judgement is for Allah only. He decides who lives and who dies. If those people are destined to die, then it's *Qadr Allah*, Allah's Destiny. Don't forget, it is He who decides every last breath, and the final heartbeat. To believe anything different is to be like the dirty pig *Kuffar*.'

Jimmy had felt reassured after that, and prayed harder for martyrdom, and also for everyone he cared about to be martyred with him – if it was their destiny – so they could all live in Paradise together, forever.

Jimmy now looked into their faces, which were pulled and taut with emotion, and saw the determination on Jessica's face – a look she had worn during some of the practice sessions. He had doubted her resolve when she had muttered the words and said 'Allah O Akbar' without sufficient vigour, but it must have been because she's a girl, he had thought. *Jaish* had regularly made them recite their final words. Jessica had told him afterwards that he had sounded like Abu Umar in his practice sessions, except with a London accent, and he had smiled back at her, liking her for the first time. He felt he had achieved success to be likened to the greatest *Jihadi* of modern times.

He remembered how Jessica had told him of her journey to Baghdad, of Mariam's story, how she had first lost her husband Abu Yahya, and then how she and the baby were shot by marines. He had always thought of her as a cold white bitch. When she spoke about the numerous deformed children she had seen, especially in Fallujah after the chemical attacks, Jessica had become tearful, and he had found himself surprised. He had felt his face, as if to confirm the wetness on his cheeks, after watching Jessica's Baghdad film, which Abu Umar insisted she should show them. Jimmy had to leave halfway through when the infants with deformed skulls and cancer appeared on screen, with red fleshy alien growths, some bigger than their heads, that seemed to be forever enlarging out of their faces, in contrast to their little twisted and deformed limbs. He had wept openly, loudly, when a mother from Fallujah had said she could not take the suffering of her little daughter. Watching her every day in that state without medicine, without painkillers; just lying on a hard hospital bed, waiting to die. 'I wish I could kill her and kill myself, to end the suffering, and finish the anguish beyond agony', she had said. Jimmy had felt more convinced than ever that the cause of *Jaish* should be victorious.

The words of anger and revenge had formed his mouth for the first time into eloquent sentences of retribution. He would unleash an expectant plague, gravid with millions of biological babies. A mother's chastisement: revenge for the mothers of Fallujah. His tongue had rolled into unnatural syllables. Shibboleths of subculture fell from his lips, like broken prayer beads from the hands of a mountainous-desert *Jihadi*. He remembered how he had stood and delivered an outburst, despite the presence of Abu Umar, to the rest of his cell about the desperate urgency to rediscover Muslim dignity: the need for their mission to succeed, for Mariam, for Musa. For the memory of his tiny shredded body.

'Don't know. I'm not sure,' he had told Jessica afterwards, when she asked him what had moved him in the film so much. He had surprised himself with his polyphonic voice, and eloquent guttural utterances.

The sight of Sebastian standing next to him, gesturing at Jessica, pulled Jimmy back from his thoughts. 'Is he wearing a vest?' Jimmy glanced at Hamza, after pulling the lapel of Sebastian's coat.

'Jimmy, you've got to trust me. I'm your friend,' said Hamza. Jimmy saw him staring into his eyes. 'Let's go!'

When Jimmy did not respond immediately, Hamza said, 'Where's the bomb, Jimmy? Look, any one of us wearing vests could be the trigger.'

'But *Shaikh* Abu Umar said – he told me it was me.' Jimmy had the look of a disappointed child who had not got his expected present on

Christmas morning. 'Anyway, I thought you said MI5 –'

'It might still be you,' shouted Hamza. 'There's no fuckin' time Jimmy. Let's get a move on if we're going to trigger the bomb. The fuckin' *suwar* will be here any second. Do you want to get arrested and spend the rest of your life in a white man *Kuffar* prison, for fuck's sake?'

Jimmy had no choice but to trust Hamza. *After all, this is my childhood friend*, he thought. *The one who I put my arm around and walked home after that bastard Maulvi abused him – raped him – he's Abu Umar's personal bodyguard.* So Jimmy ran, and led them to the central platform area of the disused underground station.

'It's somewhere here. That's all I know... I have to be on this platform. That's all I know, man. Zee fuckin' hell – I ain't lying to you, man,' said Jimmy, as he saw the look on Hamza's face.

Hamza pushed his earpiece, as the voice started again. 'Which storeroom?' He followed the directions to halfway down the platform.

Jimmy panted as he watched Hamza, who had stopped momentarily in front of an antique brown door, which seemed more likely to contain mops and buckets than a nuclear device. Hamza crashed his shoulder and then smashed a foot into the crumbling door, which Jimmy thought might lead directly to Winston Churchill's War Office.

Then Jimmy saw the bomb, as Hamza recovered himself. It stood occupying the whole space of the storeroom, taller than Hamza, and as wide as the four-foot space. Jimmy felt surprise at the large metal tubular structure. It had no flashing lights, no timer counting down, no malevolent blinking display on the front like in the Star Trek movies, which he loved so much. It looked just like an unimposing hulk of metal, a tube crafted for a giant's fissile cigar.

Hamza listened intently for a few seconds to his earpiece, and then reached down to the side of the canister and opened a flap. He retrieved Abu Umar's PDA from his coat pocket, and slid it into the receiving slot. The display on the PDA burst into an array, and showed a timer. Jimmy looked at it, fascinated: ninety seconds to go.

'You got codes? What are the fuckin' codes? The bastard machine is asking me,' shouted Hamza, holding onto the earpiece with his left hand. His right still gripped the PDA, although Jimmy could see that it fitted snugly into its docking station.

A shout echoed in the tunnel. Jimmy turned to see a group of armed men burst in from the other end of the platform. He realised the police must have followed them because of their suspicious actions, and were now arriving in formation.

'Stop! Stop right there!' said the man in the lead. They all had automatic weapons, raised with white lights that flashed onto Jimmy's face. 'There will be no second warning,' shouted the same man. 'If you move, you're dead!'

Where the hell have these fuckin' pig-suwar Kuffar suddenly come from? thought Jimmy. *How were they able to follow us?* He knew that were armed officers always patrolling the area around the Houses of Parliament, and they would have radioed the control room for more information, and been in continuous communication with control; he had learned his lessons well from Abu Umar.

This is not the plan! his mind screamed. *This was not supposed to happen! Hamza – is he supposed to be touching the bomb – why hasn't Hamza set it off already?* Jimmy knew he should have triggered the bomb. He was supposed to make a call, at one minute to five exactly, from this platform. He had done it in secret training with Abu Umar so many times. The same underground security man had let them into the old train station every time. *The* Kuffar *must not be allowed to win*, he had told the world in his suicide video. This would be the final victory of Islam. The return to the new Golden Age. All the aggressors' sins would come back to haunt them, in more spectral forms than they had ever seen in any nightmares.

Jimmy saw the police guns pointed at them: time seemed to slow down. He felt nauseous, and retched bile into his mouth, but he dared not spit it out. The suicide vest now felt heavy and cumbersome, limiting his breathing, when earlier it had felt a part of his skin.

He vaguely heard Hamza say, 'No, it's okay. I'm trying to stop it,' but thought he could not have heard right, or Hamza was buying time, waiting for the relief-bringing explosion. 'Tell them. Call these local coppers. Tell control I'm on your side. I'm trying to stop the fuckin' thing!'

'Stop! Who are you talking to?' screamed the lead policeman, as he came closer. 'What's that in your ear? Don't you dare move!' He approached, with the gun pointing directly at Hamza. His assisting officers fanned out now, and covered the rest of the group, and they paced closer, so now Jimmy could see their features.

'Don't you sneeze or itch – you're dead!' The head policeman walked

– deliberately, it seemed – to Jimmy, as if aware of every breath he made, although the pig was still thirty yards away. Jimmy could see dark muzzles of the automatic weapons snarling at them like canine jaws. The strong lights fixed on top made the guns blink like dog-bright eyes every time the officers moved. *The result of a mongrel nation*, thought Jimmy. And the policeman's voice was like its mongrel-vile breath.

'We're out of time! Check with control. Call in to your control room!' said Hamza. 'Where's the bomb squad? We'll all be dead in less than a minute if I don't stop it.'

Jimmy could not understand what Hamza meant. Was he playing for time? Why did he not set off the explosion? End the agony of waiting, show these *Kuffar* that true Muslims know how to die. Maybe he did not know the codes to trigger the device – but he must do – Hamza said Abu Umar sent him. The thoughts swirled in his mind, and his pulse was murdering his brain, so that it felt as if the top of his skull would blow off his head. His eyes refused to form images momentarily, but then he saw patterns of the Milky Way instead. Jimmy had no time to dwell on his increasingly unreal paroxysm; he saw Hamza turn his head slightly, to look at the time on the PDA display. Jimmy stood beside and slightly behind Hamza, as they all faced the oncoming police and guns. Jimmy registered Hamza's movement out of the corner of his vision, but dared not turn his head; he stood rigid, as if in a trance. His eyes stayed fixed onto the lead policeman. Jimmy saw the man's face change; the man's gloved finger tightened a fraction on the trigger. He saw Hamza still in the motion of turning his head; Hamza had not realised the imminent danger.

'No, Hamza! No!' Jimmy shouted, as he thought Hamza was about to reach for the PDA.

'I've got the code! The code number has come through!' said Hamza.

'What code, Zee?' Jimmy asked

'Israfil's Trumpet!' said Hamza, and Jimmy saw him face the policemen. 'I know the terrorists' code word. And I know the numbers. The numbers to stop the bomb are real, because they used the code word. It's come through, in my earpiece: it's *Israfil's Trumpet*. Check with control.'

'Shut up! Both of you – one more word, and you're both dead! Not a single word!' shouted the police leader. Jimmy heard the hoarseness in his voice; it had a raw edge, and was dark like obsidian.

Jimmy had not flinched or taken his eyes off the lead man. It seemed to him that he would never move again; he stood like sculpted stone. Jimmy knew that his mosque friend, his childhood cricketing mate, was in mortal danger. Hamza would try to enter the code into the PDA screen. He was about to be shot. Hamza had been the only person who had stood by him whenever he had faced danger, despite the fact that death might be in dripping from any gangster's knife, without ever asking a price. The only friend for whom Jimmy would have happily risked Ahmad's eternal displeasure, as he had done by attacking the pederast Maulvi *Sahib* who had raped Hamza. Jimmy would have done it over and over for Hamza, because Hamza had been constant, had helped him save Jimmy's drug-dealing patch, and then had saved his life. Hamza had been the only person who had never sneered, not once – not even at Zoya's wedding. The only one who never judged him.

Without warning or understanding, strength flowed through Jimmy. He felt he could achieve the impossible, like a sick man with no hope of life: cured suddenly, without reason. He heard his mother's voice. Sofia was singing the Punjabi song she so often sang to him in his childhood; it had never made sense to him. Often it had softened his hard muscles to sleep as she stroked his head, made his eyelids flutter like butterfly wings. He had never asked her why she sang him such a strange lullaby. *Apne jaan deh ke auron noh bacha lehyeh... my pride for you knows no bounds, a mother's love. O you who gave your life to save others...*

His friend was in danger and he felt compelled to act, so he lunged forward, tried to pull Hamza back, managed to cover him with his own body, twisted to face the police, and screamed, 'No!'

The bullets thudded into Jimmy's body.

As soon as he had fired, the lead policeman held up his hand to stop the rest of his team firing. No one else had moved. The leader of the group put his hand up to his earpiece.

Hamza screamed at him, 'I'm MI5! I'm MI5, you, stupid bastard – what have you done?'

Jimmy slumped backwards onto Hamza, who tried to hold him up. 'Let me stop this thing. Look at the timer. Less than thirty seconds left. You stupid fucker! Or the whole of London is dead.' said Hamza, struggling with Jimmy's weight.

Jimmy felt no pain. He could not see or hear clearly, light-headed; his eyes swam, blurring colours, as if he were floating. Then he heard strange voices and saw the weird faces again that he had first seen in Ramnagar. The ghosts of his ancestors appeared once more, their faces smiling, some laughing, and swirling around him. For the first time they felt familiar, strangely comforting.

The ghostly apparitions started singing as one with their unique high-pitched voice: *O Shaheed Al Islam – come home – come to success! Come to victory O Shaheed Al Islam! Come home!*

Jimmy saw his father; he stood with outstretched arms. As Jimmy went to him, he saw a baby appear in Ahmad's arms. His father looked down at the infant, and then looked up at Jimmy with an expression he did not know. Then he recognised unbridled pride in his father's glistening eyes.

'Just like the day you were born, *mera Betah*,' said Ahmad. Jimmy looked down at the baby. The ghosts of his ancestors swam around and around. They floated, suspended, singing in happy voices. Jimmy looked up to see the apparition of his grandfather, standing behind Ahmad. He came around and put one arm around his son, the other around Jimmy.

He felt his body opaque. His mind became almost gaseous, not understanding. *How did he get here? Why had his father and the ghosts appeared?* He turned to see his friends, who were now a short distance away. He noticed the police had put their guns down. Hamza pressed some buttons on the PDA attached to the tube, and lights flashed. His friends seemed distant – their voices did not make sense – and they were unreal. Jimmy smiled at them, tried to call out, but stopped as he saw a body at Hamza's feet. A body covered in blood; his face pulped into dark red, unrecognisable for a moment, but then Jimmy saw it was him. He turned to his father. '*Abbo* – what –'

'It's okay. It's okay, *Betah*,' said his father, as the terror rose in Jimmy like the final clarion call. 'Shushh, shush.' His father's voice comforted him. 'Just look at this baby – look – don't you recognise him?'

Jimmy's grandfather smiled, and put his arm around Jimmy, pulling him close again. His ancestors swam, merged into one another, without feet – like shadows in water. Faster, faster, louder and louder, they surrounded him like children holding hands, making a circle around the three of them, playing a game.

The baby gurgled. Suddenly, Jimmy recognised him; he wore Jimmy's face. It *was* Jimmy.

'Who – what?' Jimmy tried to turn, to look around at his friends again, but his grandfather stopped him. His father said again, 'Jimmy - look at the baby. Look at his smile! Isn't he beautiful?' Jimmy looked again. Ahmad looked into Jimmy's eyes, and said, 'This is Mohammed Yusuf Regus.'

Then his ancestors came in close, and then closer. *O Shaheed Al Islam – come home – come to success! Come to victory, O Shaheed Al Islam! Come home!*

Jimmy was floating, weightless. He could not feel his body.

His father said something as everything blacked out... words Jimmy had read on his gravestone. A dim memory that now flooded his being with light. Ahmad recited:

Martyr of Islam
Rest in Paradise with the Martyrs
May you be in Firdous – the Highest of Gardens. Be happy in Jannat Al Firdous
May you be enshrouded with Allah's Love, covered by His Mercy
Live close to His face forever. Live forever.

*

Jessica screamed, 'Jimmy! Jimmy – he's still alive!' Hamza turned away from the screen; he saw Jimmy's eyes flicker.

The timer had stopped. The number three illuminated the screen, radiating a malignant light over Hamza's face. He bent over his childhood friend, tears streaming down his face; he cradled Jimmy's head in his lap.

'The ambulance – where is it?' Jessica shouted at the police, who now milled about on the platform.

The leader stopped talking to his earpiece. 'Ambulances are on the way.'

'It's too late,' said Hamza, in a voice that barely escaped his lips. He straightened Jimmy's head gently, put his arms by his side, and closed Jimmy's eyes. 'Thank you, my friend. May Allah bless you. Thank you.'

CHAPTER 34

London – Paddington Green Police Station

The next day, when she expected another round of endless questioning, Hamza walked into the interrogation room, smiling.

'Hamza – oh, thank God!' Jessica got up, and gave him a brief hug.

'Hi, Jessica! How are you bearing up?' He sat down in the chair opposite her, and put his hands on the desk. 'I've spoken to them, and told them that you and Sebastian were instrumental in stopping the bombing.'

'What's going on? Are you really MI5?'

'I'm afraid so. Sorry.' He shrugged, looked down at the desk, and scratched the surface with his nail.

'What are you sorry for? You're a hero.' Jessica got up and hugged him.

'I'm not a hero – always was too much of a coward for all that,' he said, still looking down.

'What happened to the bombs? All the other bombs?'

'Well, *Jaish* were so keen to totally disable and cripple the West that they centrally linked all twelve devices, because they wanted simultaneous explosions all over the world.'

'That's great news. Thank God!' Jessica wiped her hands over her face, but her eyes still glistened. 'So none of them exploded?'

'No. That was *Jaish*'s trump card, to make them go off together, so that none of the security agencies would have time to intervene or react. But that was also their weakness. They didn't believe it to be much of a weakness, though, because only three people in the world had the code word – *Israfil's Trumpet* – and the alphanumeric key.'

'So how did you, I mean MI5, get it, then?'

Hamza seemed to force a smile. 'Remember when we first met? I told you: *Ve have vays of getting what ve vant! Ve have our ways!*'

Jessica smiled. 'Yes... but how?'

'Like all good, exotic things, such as mangoes and kulfi. We got it from our sources overseas. And, needless to say, there was a beautiful Indian woman involved.' He looked at her and she saw his mouth turn up, but his eyes did not smile. 'Sebastian's a lucky man. I hope you two make each other happy; that's what really counts.'

'Thanks... I believe that too.' Jessica smiled, but it stopped, half-formed, as she suddenly remembered Jimmy. 'Hamza... I'm sorry about Jimmy.'

'More importantly, the twelve cities are safe,' he said. He looked down, and started scratching the desk with his fingernail again.

Jessica put a hand on his, and looked into his eyes that seemed even less penetrable. 'Will you be all right?'

Hamza looked up at her. 'Jimmy was my friend,' he said simply. After a pause, he continued in a more normal voice. 'I'm afraid there will be lots more questioning and interrogation. Of course, you expect that. There's nothing I can do about it, but don't worry. Just remember to stay calm, and tell them your side.'

'I've told them everything.' There was no hiding place anymore during the interrogations. The truth had tumbled out of her and felt like relief, a like a fresh mountain spring which had been dammed for too long, flowing over her face.

'I've already cleared it with my bosses, and you and Sebastian won't be charged with anything. I think the relief that people are feeling will make sure of that, and everyone needs heroes, so you and Sebastian are going to be the people named for stopping the bombs.' Then he almost smiled again. 'You're going to be heroes, Jess!'

'I don't want to be a hero, and especially since I'm not one. What about you? You're the one who stopped the bombs?'

'Spooks and heroes are like secret lovers who can never get married. Anyway, I've been a spy since I was a kid, so I know what to expect. And if I were interested in stardom, I'd go on X-Factor.'

'But that's unfair.'

Hamza smiled at her, and she brushed her hair away to hide her sudden release of emotion. *Still so naïve after all I've been through*, she thought.

'Don't worry – you'll be fully debriefed, and then given guidance on what to say to the TV and press people. Remember, when you do talk to the media, you don't know any Hamza, because officially I wasn't even there.' Then he looked down, and muttered, 'No medal will ever cleanse Jimmy's blood off my hands.'

Jessica did not know what to say; anything she now said would feel a false consolation. Hamza knew he had saved countless people, but he had not been able to do anything for Jimmy.

'Thank you, Hamza.' She put her hand on his.

Hamza patted her hand, looked at her for a brief moment during which time she thought she saw his eyes lighten. As he got up, and turned away from her to walk out, Jessica heard him whisper, 'Jimmy was my friend.'

London – Sebastian's House

Jessica had been unable to contact Sebastian over the past few days. The period in between Christmas and New Year now seemed like a lost time, where her emotions had emptied down the life-sucking whirlpool created by the media storm in the aftermath of the foiled bombings. She knew from Hamza that Sebastian had been released on the same day. They had done the unending media interviews, and then he had disappeared.

Jessica knocked on his door, and her hand shot up to her throat when it half-opened; the other brushed her hair out of her face. 'Sebastian – where have you been? I've been so worried.' She gave him a hug of relief.

Sebastian stood on the doorway, holding the handle. 'I've been away for a few days – just got back.' He frowned, and puckered his lips.

'You haven't been answering your mobile.' Jessica looked up at him, squinting up at his face. 'Can I come in?'

'Yes... sorry.' He held the door open for her.

'You don't look yourself,' she said, as she took her coat off and walked into the living room. Sebastian followed slowly, seemingly stooping. She looked up at him. 'What's going on, Sebastian?'

He did not look at her. 'I needed some time to think, to think things through.'

Jessica pulled her lips and then twisted her fingers in her hands. Sebastian had always responded to her calls and normally implemented her slightest suggestions as if they were commandments. Her eyes flicked over his face. This attitude and demeanour made her question what had happened over the last few days. *Has he changed his opinion of me?* she thought. *He helped me to stop the bombings, but was that because he had no choice? Is this what I feared? Is this the end?*

'What were you thinking about?' she asked. 'Come and sit down, you look all stressed.' She held his hand and led him to the sofa, sat down on the other end, brushed her skirt down, and looked up at him. 'Okay... and so, what did you think?' she asked speaking slowly, attempting a smile.

'What do you really feel about me?'

'What? You're really being silly, Mr S! Come on Sebastian, that's hardly something to wonder about, after everything we've been through.' A small grunt of a laugh escaped her.

'Well, that's exactly it, Jessica. Why did we get close? Was it because of what we were going through, or more exactly what you were going through with Hamid?'

'Hamid? Is this about Hamid? You know I loved him, I grieved for him, but that was a different lifetime ago. So much has happened since then, between us.'

'Was it between us, or was it that you needed someone in the middle of a crisis?'

'Are you saying I used you?' She looked at him, lips parted.

Sebastian stared at her; she had never seen him this serious. Even when he had been angry at her revelation, he had turned it around and made it into a positive. 'I'm asking you. I have to know what you feel.'

'Firstly, let me say what I have wanted to for so long. Thank you for helping me. Thank you for being there. In the final days, my breath came and my legs felt strong because of you. Even when you shouted at me I felt relief. It was like a protection, because I knew you cared. I was prepared to go through with it. Maybe I would have found a way to stop the bombs, and maybe I would have contacted the police, taken a risk. I don't know. Then Hamza contacted you, and that really was the thing I was looking for, an excuse to bring you on board, to let you into my dirty secret life. Because it was such a secret I was ashamed that I had got myself in so deep. And I was terrified that you would hate me.'

'That I would hate you?' he asked, raising his eyebrows.

'That's what I was really afraid of.' Jessica shrugged.

'How could I hate you? I thought you were naïve, stupid even maybe...' He shook his head and his dark hair flopped over the sides of his head. 'But I love you!'

'Do you?'

'You must have known that since the early days?'

'That's what I think about you. That you must have known I had feelings for you from very early on, but I couldn't do anything because of my confusion over what had happened with Hamid, then Baghdad, then Abu Umar and *Jaish*.'

'So what are you saying?'

'Oh, you can be so blind sometimes.' She leaned forward put both hands on his. 'I loved you since you cooked the pasta and the Rogan Josh, and no, it wasn't because of your shitty impersonations.' She leaned in close to him. 'I love you, Mr S!'

Sebastian smiled. 'Well, I have loved you since the picnic.'

'Oh, you will have to take me there again and maybe this time I might really be able to appreciate it. You can be such a gentleman. My perfect doctor. Mr Raiders of the Lost Ark!'

Jessica laughed, and Sebastian joined in. she leaned forward and looked into his azure eyes, in which she saw her own blue reflected with a brighter sheen. She loved how he complemented her. Her breathing faster; she looked at his lips, slightly parted like her own. Jessica leaned forward, closed her eyes, and she kissed him.

She felt him respond but then drew back, for fear of losing the moment to passion. She laughed. 'Well, now that you've kissed such a naïve girl, professor, you will simply have to marry me.'

Sebastian became serious; he looked at her without moving. Jessica did not breathe, or blink. 'Jessica Flowerdew, will you do me the honour of becoming my wife?'

'What?'

'Will you? Make my dreams come true?' He held her hands and she saw the sincerity in his eyes.

Jessica laughed, leaned forward, closed her eyes and kissed him again.

Sebastian got up, took her by the hand and led her to the kitchen, switched the kettle on, and took out the porcelain scarlet pimpernel tea service. Then he rinsed the china out with hot water. He placed the teapot carefully on the worktop, and looked into her eyes. 'I do believe it's time for a cup of tea.'

Chowpatty Beach, Mumbai

The queue curled around haphazardly on the beach, like a snake dissembling itself into its many parts. As usual, every day before sunset

Mumbai started its evening phase, tuning into a different level of wakefulness, like a playful boy changing moods but never dozing. The ritual line formed in front of Gupta's twice a day; and twice a day, like the tide, the *Sadhu* or *Yogi*, an Indian holy man, appeared.

The queues formed more quickly and stood longer today, as the Ganesh Chaturthi festival gathered momentum. Ganesh, the son of Shiva and Parvati, would bestow his blessings on earth for all his followers.

Gupta's *Bhel Puri* shack always had queues twice as long as any other on the beach. Gupta looked at the irregular line, and smiled. A small girl pulled her mother's red dress; another boy bombarded his brother with a toy aeroplane.

Fairground rides blared, blurring colours and noise into one another, swirling centripetally, churning stomach contents; the Ferris wheel screeched with cigarretted-corned beef joy riders. Camel rides, stray dogs, the luxurious unemployed gave way to families de-stressing en masse, Mumbai-style. The city changed moods and clothes, donned eveningwear to enjoy Chowpatty – garish and smelly and noisy. It satisfied Gupta's olfactory senses with the comfort of familiarity.

Gupta knew *Pani Puri* would be consumed in uncounted amounts. Innumerable small round shells piled high on the sides of shacks and carts, or *Gol Gappas*, dough filled with potato and chickpea mixture with yogurt sometimes added, drowned in a thin *Imli* sauce or in *Aam Adrak*, mango with ginger sauce; the tamarind contrasting with the yogurt, giving bite. Gupta saw a family order two dozen small *Gol Gappa* balls from his wife, who served beside him. She threw on a generous pinch of black salt and chopped coriander with a flourish, at the last minute. Stalls also served *Kachoori* and *Pav Bhaji*, but the favourite snack of Mumbai on Juhu and Chowpatty was still *Bhel Puri*, and Gupta's had long ruled Juhu Beach.

So Gupta sold more *Bhel Puri* than anyone else on Chowpatty, his own unique recipe, which had developed over decades. He used fresh mango, fried his *Sev* for seven minutes, timed exactly in his mind's eye, added the puffed rice only at the last minute. He used a secret blend of spices to create the pungent sweet spicy snack, which he served with either a dark brown tamarind-date or green coriander-mint sauce. His fame had spread far and wide, from the impoverished slums of Dharavi to the heart of the rich Juhu gated communities. He knew that the Lotus Café or even the Indigo with its fairy-lit finery could not match his taste bud tingling experience.

'*Bus kya areh Haila Haila roz paka atrangi ban rahela kiya? Ekdum bekar hair roz mangna. Hai hai side marna, dhasu idea yaar Sadhuji!*' What a strange circus you have going on everyday, begging like you do. Why don't you get lost, yeah, move over – great idea, *Sadhuji*,' said Gupta, speaking *Bambaiya*, the street lingo. The *Sadhu* moved awkwardly. His arms and legs seemed too long for him as he shuffled.

'Is that anyway to be talking to customers or Holy Men?' His wife reprimanded him, her hands a blur in making the Sev. She served a couple *Bhel Puri* with puffed rice on fried *puris* that were crispy, but collapsed once in the mouth, along with the ubiquitous sugar cane juice and *shikanji*, Indian lemonade.

Gupta watched as the English couple, with their police escort, walked along Chowpatty Beach, hand in hand. Nothing passed him by on his stretch of sand. The beach often had Westerners sprinkled about, like white yogurt spots amongst Gupta's dark-brown tamarind sauce. The couple now joined the queue for his stand, and he smiled with expectation. Gupta's radio crackled into life as he twisted the knob. A newscaster's voice broke in over tinny music.

The *Sadhu* came and stood by the side of the shack, separately from the queue and, Gupta knew, although the Holy Man never asked, he waited for his daily *Bhel Puri*.

'*We have some breaking news. Just in: a shock story. A bomb has exploded on a yacht off the coast of Goa, a ship on which the screen legend Aashriya Aarzoo Romano was filming. We have eye-witness accounts that a small boat carried out a suicide attack as we speak. The undisputed Queen of Bollywood has died in the explosion whilst filming her latest movie,* The Eve Connection, *about a female suicide bomber...*'

'Did you hear that, *Yogi*?' asked Gupta.

The *Sadhu* started hopping from foot to foot.

The *Bhel Puri wallah* saw a mask of silent incredulity and shock spread across the dreadlocked face, his soul seemingly entangled in the numerous brightly-coloured beads threaded through his hair. The *Sadhu* now flicked them away, first with one hand then with the other, from his face, only to have them fall back again immediately obscuring his features. Then he tossed them away again, whilst hopping all the while from foot to foot, as if by removing the hirsute impediments from his vision, he would more clearly understand what had happened to Aashriya.

The *Sadhu* held his hair up with both hands and opened his eyes as wide as they would go, and stared at Gupta. 'What?' he said, and as suddenly as he had started stopped hopping, and froze, statuesque.

Gupta noticed the English couple had moved forward in the queue, as his wife and son continued to serve the line. Unremarkably, like many honeymoon couples, they held hands, but a police security team accompanied them. Gupta noticed the woman's blue eyes, a fiery aquamarine in the bright early evening light. He turned the radio volume up and the newscaster repeated the story.

'No! Too bad! Impossible! *Yeh nahee ho sakhtah!*' said the *Sadhu-Yogi*. 'Too bad! *Nahee!*'

'*Hanh hanh* too bad, too bad! *Kiya angreji bak rehela?* What English bullshit you are talking?' said Gupta, and looked at the *Sadhu* as he stirred his pot of bubbling oil, frying innumerable *Sev* and puffed rice. Sweat coated Gupta's arms like Vaseline. His hair seemed to have been oiled from his cooking pot, and his huge buck teeth could not stay hidden – even if he had managed to close his mouth, which was perennially open, spitting invective in *Bambaiya*, the Mumbai slang that no self-respecting street survivalist could cope without. Gupta spoke it because he knew no other form of Hindi, let alone English but he knew he must continuously give the impression to the taporis, the roadside footpads and pocket cutters, of strength and aggressive vitality, in a soup-milieu where weakness caused meat to leave the bone faster than great whites could sense a bucket of blood in an shark-infested pond. Either that, or invoke the protective spell-charm of David Gul. Every shark had to be afraid of the biggest cobra-tiger-dragon of them all: the chimera that controlled Mumbai with a nonchalance worthy of the greatest of emperors.

Gupta knew most Indians would laugh at his uncouthness; gangsters or ridiculed clowns used his slang and accent in Bollywood. Gupta did not care at the smiles and sniggers it raised intermittently on the beach. He continued to make money in bundles, which he converted the next day at the bank into piles of multicoloured one thousand rupee notes. He loved the red twenties the best. Each piece meant one *Bhel Puri* snack sold, and he loved to see the inches grow under the counter in the takings box. He glanced over and saw his wife's habitual heavy hand on the lid of the money tin. He looked at the empty space, just next to the takings box, where a small circle made a lighter colour. Here, a small four-inch version of *Lakshmi Devi*, the goddess of wealth, had stood from the day he had opened his stall, for a quarter of a century, until recently, when he had knocked over and smashed the clay figurine. The tiny idol had been witness to the gigantic movements in Mumbai, until she became victim to Gupta's own seismic upheaval. He had not replaced the statue.

He did not care what antics most people got up to on the beach; the extraordinary had become mundane through years of having had a front seat view. He watched the colourful preparations and celebrations for the Ganesh Chaturthi festival, where thousands especially waited for a huge clay idol of the elephant god to be immersed into the sea by the end of the evening. There would be numerous idols drowning by the end of the day, but the largest one was now being carried around the beach by a group of men. It dominated the skyline. The festival meant the beach became a living organism like an ant's nest, and they all needed to eat. Gupta's held the premium place and reputation, which meant more red notes, more money. A deity which sat astride Gupta's visible horizon ruling the Indian pantheon – flattening any other gods, having won the battle for Gupta's soul long ago.

'*Sach hai. Sach hai.* It is true,' repeated Gupta. Then he watched as the Holy Man's mouth moved but no sound came out of his mouth, and his hands froze in horror partly, holding his dreadlocks by the side of his face. '*Mar gahee. Mar gahee.* She is dead,' said Gupta, with more glee than he had intended.

'*Nahee! Nahee!*' said the *Sadhu*, as Gupta saw pain twist his bulbous face into a toad-like expression; he started hopping from one foot to the other again. '*Nahee! Nahee!*' the automaton *Sadhu* spoke. Then he reached one arm out in a begging style to Gupta, then the other, hopping and alternating arms. '*Ek Chai. Ek Chai. Bas ek Chai Aashriya ke liye.* One tea. Just one tea – one tea for Aashriya. *Ek elaichi wali Chai ek Chai meri Aashriya ke liye!* One tea – a cardamom tea for my Aashriya!'

Gupta stirred his black pot of oil faster and looked away from the hopping man, scowling. He wiped the sweat off his small feathery moustache that became more straggly towards the ends, so that it drooped over thin orange betel-stained lips where a small bird-like tongue sometimes darted out, which was otherwise encaged by huge incisors. His white vest was stained by turmeric and *imli*, tamarind sauce in brown patches that matched his cocoa skin. His thick toes made indentations in his cheap flip-flops, like ponds which squelched when filled with sweat from his feet, lonely evidence of his human anatomy. His brown shorts had become legendary, seemingly having organically grown from his scrawny legs, so it became difficult to tell where shorts stopped and legs began. His eldest son, who was identically dressed, stood behind him, similarly stirring another black cauldron, looking like Gupta twenty years ago – except he had a less luxuriant moustache, which had not yet drooped into his mouth. Gupta felt annoyed that his son had felt it necessary to have the familial buck teeth fixed whilst in the States.

Gupta gave the *Sadhu* his attention. The man in flowing robes leaned forward and put both hands on the side of Gupta's stall, which stopped waist-high, and shook the stall; the whole flimsy structure rattled. Gupta looked up from his continuous frying, scowled at the man, and threatened him by raising his metal ladle, which had sieve-like holes in it to drain the hot oil from the frying cauldron.

'*Kaikao roz lafda kar rahela hai? Aashriya aap ko kalti diya?* Why do you create trouble everyday? Has Aashriya given you the slip? *Is Chowpatty peh bada bada pista aur badami item bohoth maal ahtha hai Sadhuji. Areh Aashriya ko hum jaise log kiya karna?* We get a lot of pistachio and almond gorgeous goods, beauties on Chowpatty *Sadhu*ji. What do people like us have to do with Aashriya?' said Gupta, looking up and nodding to a kaleidoscope of colourful clothes which became a group of giggling girls that fluttered by, in the latest provocative Bollywood styles. Gupta knew they were pretending to be self-absorbed in a private joke, but their eyes were darting around the beach, fully aware of the hair-slicked, smoking heroes, who lolled casually in smaller cocksure groups and tighter trousers.

'I just want Aashriya – *siraf Aashriya,*' said the Holy Man, shaking the tin shack harder.

'*Mar gaeh hai*. She's dead.' shouted Gupta, stirring the puffed up *Sev* and removing the golden brown ones. He looked down, trying to ignore the mad man.

'Where is she? Where?' the *Sadhu* asked, looking around frantically, searching faces without seeing, looking back to Gupta. '*Ya Allah, kidhar meri* Aashriya? Oh Allah, where is my Aashriya?'

'You're really weird, so secretive and irritating. You're scamming everyone. You're a Muslim, *Sadhu*!' Gupta almost smiled as he looked back into the face, which seemed not to register the contradiction.

'*Bas* Gupta ek cup *Chai*, dood nahee, no milk, *meri Aashriya ke liya*, for my Aashriya,' the *Sadhu-Yogi*-Holy Man said, and held up one ape like finger, begging in the sub-continental style. '*Meri Aashriya ke liya*. For my Aashriya.'

'*Khatam finito*. If these street rowdies know I give you free *Bhel Puri* every day then I'll be finished,' said Gupta, drawing his thumb across his neck. He continued talking to no one in particular. 'And this *bashtara* – he wants cardamom tea!'

When the *Sadhu* made no movement to signify he had accepted defeat, but maintained his begging stance, he became a petitioner dominating psychologically, forcing Gupta to react.

'Your Aashriya is dead. Look for her in the sea!'

The Holy Man started a loud growling noise from his depths, and started pushing-pulling the shack, causing the hot oil to splash. Gupta jumped back and shouted at him. '*Cut to cut baat karne ka, apun ko faltu bakbak karne ka aadat nahin hai. Bas! Khallas!*' Say what the fuck you want, I don't talk extra rubbish. Enough!'

This only increased the *Yogi*'s fervour, and he shook the stall harder; the tin rattled, and some oil spilled.

'*Mar gahee teri Aashriya. Samundar meh dhoond!* BOOOMB!' said Gupta, and mimed a huge explosion with his hands. 'Your Aashriya is dead. Look for her in the sea! BOOOMB!' he repeated, and mimed again. '*Bas! Oi bashtara!*' Gupta shouted, which was the closest he could get to bastard. '*Sagar meh – teri Aash sagar meh.*' Your Aash is in the sea.

'*Henh? Sagar?*' asked the enraged *Yogi* and looked around, as if he had just noticed the ocean. 'In the sea?'

'That's exactly what I'm saying to you, baby. There's your *Aashriya*,' Gupta said, pointing now with his ubiquitous ladle towards the sun setting on the far side of the Arabian Sea. 'Go – if you dare. Go and fetch Aashriya out of the sea!' Gupta added with his standard asperity. He stirred his pot and suppressed a cackle, which became a goofy grin. He glanced at the queue and saw the rising consternation on the white faces, and the growing impatience on the brownskins in the crowd, some of whom made generic Indian insults and caterwauls, long used to weird ascetics making a fuss. A quotidian experience for the regular Chowpatty-*wallahs*.

Gupta turned to the *Sadhu* again. 'Look for her in the sea! BOOOMB!' Gupta said again, with his hands expanding, as if he could visualise the corpus of the Bollywood queen exploding in front of him. He gave a huge buck tooth smile.

The weird but usually sapient Holy Man stopped shaking the shack, but seemed to become more agitated, in his eyes.

Gupta saw the *Sadhu* scan the crowds frenetically, his eyes oscillating from side to side, and they finally settled on the sea. He froze, as if seemingly recognising something in the distance. He turned and ran towards the incoming tide, waving his hands above his head, saffron robes flowing behind him like an alien peacock's train. He was screaming at something, eyes fixed on the horizon, shouting, '*Aashriya! Mereh pas abhi hai. Ek elaichi wali Chai ek Chai meri Aashriya ke liye. Aashriya!* I've got it now. One tea – a cardamom tea for my Aashriya!'

A couple of men who stood holding hands in the snaking line shouted out to him as he passed them by, and some others waved arms in the air. Most continued the prescribed humdrum of chase and kiss, kiss and tell, tell and retell of Chowpatty Beach.

The *Yogi* did not slow down as he approached the water. The sun was setting low over the western horizon, casting a ghostly shadow of the *Sadhu* back over the beach, which swirled as he moved. Soon the shadow became lost amongst the candyfloss colours of the ever-brightening lights from Gupta's stand and others on the beach. The skyscrapers loomed like giants behind him on the beachfront. The Ganesh party continued unabated; the concrete buildings seemed like ogreish aggressive guards, aliens of Mumbai.

The sun met the water and set it on fire; *sholay* burst from the surface, as if readying a traditional funeral pyre on the Ganges. The Holy Man's saffron robes flowed behind him like prayer flags, and many stared now as he ran, nearing the water. Gupta thought the *Sadhu* enacted the part beautifully. How well he kept up the pretence of being crazy, in such an original way too – that must be the hardest part, thinking of new, weirder things to do. He watched the *Sadhu* and fished out some more newly puffed *sev* from his cauldron, his eyes flicking up and down. He fully expected the *Sadhu-Yogi*-Holy Man to return for his daily *Bhel Puri*, as he had done every day for weeks, which Gupta had today filled up to double portion size for him.

Once the water washes his nether regions and the cold reality of the returning tide bites into his balls, he'll be back, thought Gupta, *and I'll make sure he has his* Bhel garam garam, *very hot, straight off the pot.*

Today I'll offer him some green elaichi wali Chai. *After all, he really has entertained us and pulled in the crowds, even more than usual for Ganesh Chaturthi. I'll even make the crazy* bhenchaud *some green cardamom tea myself!* He felt sure this was the only food the ascetic ever ate. And tea. Bottomless amounts of tea, the *tea wallahs* on Chowpatty plied him endlessly in return for blessings, fearing his curses; *superstitious* chuthiyas, *pussies!* Gupta thought, ignoring his own daily charity. The tea was always milky, never green with cardamom. *That's not in your destiny, my friend.*

He looked up now and squinted into the setting sun, as he automatically set the ripped muscles of his forearm to turning the ladle, like a clockwork pendulum. Surprise turned to concern as he caught glimpses of the *Sadhu* inbetween the passing people. He stopped turning the ladle. The Holy Man lifted a single finger up and shouted something; Gupta felt sure it could be nothing other than '*Ek Chai. Ek Chai. Bas ek Chai Aashriya ke liye!* One tea. Just one tea – one tea for Aashriya!' Gupta saw him shouting and waving his arms above his head. The Holy Man had repeated the same things on the beach. The *Sadhu-Yogi* splashed through the water, faster, ever deeper, with arms raised above his head, waving and shouting as if at something in the distance.

With that the *Sadhu* disappeared into the sea, his arms outstretched, as if reaching for some apparition on the horizon. The waves swept him up, and encompassed him like a lover's embrace. Gupta saw the shock on the faces' of the white couple. They had reached the stall, but all thoughts of food seemed to have vanished as they watched the *Yogi* disappear.

The *Sadhu* went without pause, like a man desperate to lose himself in the arms of his waiting long-lost beloved: melded into her immortal embrace. Surya the sun god had sent his goddess, Aashriya, to receive her most devoted worshiper. She came riding Surya's chariot pulled by seven horses, whipping her steeds ever faster to take the *Sadhu* away, and then pull the sun into the black abyss for the night.

The sea turned orange as the red globe dipped below the horizon, where the Arabian Sea became the Indian Ocean. It turned blood red. The body of water that the Holy Ganges flowed into, where Ram and Sita had met. There, on the Sarayu, Sita had washed and her sweat had mixed with the water of the Sarayu River that then flowed into the Ganges, which had purified the sins of her people for eons. Gupta, like all Hindus, believed in the renaissance-giving power of the mother Ganges, which gave birth to the Indian Ocean. Gupta saw, as he did every evening, the sea turn cardinal carmine red with black patches, as if immorality and wickedness had stained her skin, washed off human flesh from upriver.

Mother Ganga, which flowed from Vishnu's Lotus feet and Shiva's matted hair from heaven and purified India, now met one of her sons, and had cleansed the hurt from his breast. Blood red now, like the history, present and future of his motherland.

At least Amit Bahadur is free now. Unbelievable! he thought. *How clever of David Gul to have created a pre-recorded news report, which he had just played – the* Sadhu, *Amit Bahadur, had no idea.* Salla chuthiya! *Fucking pussy! Pretending to be a* Yogi-Sadhu. '*Salla chuthiya*, Amit Bahadur,' said Gupta out loud.

'Who? Was that Amit Bahadur?' asked the white woman; she had reached the stall, escorted by the police.

'I thought it was a mad *Sadhu*,' answered the man with her. 'Who's Amit whatever, Jessica?'

'You know, Amit Bahadur – in charge of *Jaish*.' Hamza had told her about Amit Bahadur, and the stories and legends of his love for Aashriya, which had resulted in Hamza finally receiving the codes, had turned from speculation to myth in the media.

'No! No – not Amit Bahadur,' Gupta came back with a shock. 'Some rascal idiot Holy Man,' he said in English, with a grating accent. He flashed his goofy-toothed smile again, pretending not to have made the slip. 'Free *bhel puri* for you, lovely, lovely honeymooning peoples,' he said. '*Garam! Garam!* Hot and hot!' He turned and snapped orders at his wife.

How clever of David Gul to have known this is exactly what Amit Bahadur would do, Gupta thought. *I now believe David to be the wisest man in the world, and fully pledge my allegiance to him.* He clicked one of the preset buttons on his phone under the counter, and sent the message to David Gul: *All happened exactly as you said. Amit Bahadur will only ever get to drink* ek cup Chai *with fishes*.

Gupta could not read Hindi, let alone English, but he had had his son – a Harvard-graduate-MBA-from-Wharton-Business-School-returnee – type it up for him earlier. Gupta knew his son stood obediently behind him without turning around, and at that moment he knew Lucky Blade was sweating in a white, stained T-shirt, making dough, standing in blue flip flops, an image of his father two decades ago. So much so that no one would guess that his chocolate sparrow ankles had ever been out of the slums of Dharavi, let alone won a scholarship to the most prestigious business school in the world. He turned and looked at Lucky Blade and felt pleased that his son stopped and looked at him, expecting his father's next order, an obeisance that filled Gupta with joy every time.

Education isn't everything, he thought. *Got to be savvy and have balls like David Gul. What a man! I would serve him for free every time even if I did have a choice, which I don't. He is the master. The mother of Mumbai's poor, who feeds us all. The idol of Chowpatty Beach: we should erect his statue in front of the waves, not Ganesh.* He looked up from his frying as a commotion gathered near the spot where the *Sadhu* had disappeared. A couple of zealous youths dived into the waves. Most people had barely noticed the *Sadhu* disappearing, so great was the commotion, but the two men came back with nothing from the ocean. She was a jealous mistress.

Further along the beach, a huge idol of Ganesh was being floated off into the waves of the Arabian Sea, resplendent in gaudy painted colour. His elephant trunk curled around characteristically; his right hand held in salute, garlanded with marigolds, and his face and eyes animated by the flickering lights, the hundreds of small oil lamps, *diya*, that floated and surrounded him. Light and water, fire and air, as well as clay from the idol, mixed, and celebrated the renewing of death-life-death.

Gupta swore under his breath at Amit Bahadur. *What a gutless bastard Amit was, for succumbing so completely to Aashriya's serpentine charms and losing his head, and then his life. No woman is worth that.* And he swore at David for being the complete unadulterated bastard he was, for doing what he had done and winning such a complete victory. His idolatrous respect for David Gul grew a new head to worship. He chuckled and smiled his sweetest smile at the white people, as his wife served them fresh *Bhel Puri*.

Gupta chanted the old song badly, '*Eh dil hai mushkil jeena yaha. Zara has je zara bach key eh hai Bombay meri jaan!* O my heart, it's an uphill struggle to live here. Laugh a little, watch yourself a lot, be streetwise – this is Bombay, my love!'

Gupta waved and scowled at the white couple, turning down the corners of his mouth as the white woman tried to pay his wife, and then he smiled when Jessica finally put her money back. Because of the bought intimacy, and for no apparent reason, he turned to the white man, but his ladle did not stop its metronomic metre. 'You beautiful peoples honeymoons Bombay?' He grinned without trying to hide his teeth, 'You peoples too good. Too good! USA – A O-K! *Zabardast Ammrika!* USA – A O-K!' he said, and stuck both his thumbs up momentarily, before grabbing the ladle again.

Then, for even less reason he jerked his calloused thumb behind him. 'My son, he come Ammrika. Bhortin bijnis collig. He going!' shouted Gupta, loudly so as many people could hear him over the noise as possible. He hoped they understood *Wharton Business College* despite his accent, and his son, Lucky Blade bobbed his acknowledgement. Gupta gave his full-sized gap-toothed grin, and showed a pink shrew tongue. *And don't think I don't know who you are either, you* Gorah *English fuckers!* he thought. *David Gul sees all.*

'*Areh bashtara Lucky Pyarelal Blade!*' he commanded his son, who leaped forward. His flip flops squelched full of sweat under his flipper-like feet. 'Give them double free *Bhel Puri!*'

'Yes, of course, at once, beloved father,' sang Lucky Pyarelal Blade.

Gupta grinned again. 'USA – A O-K! TIGER WOODS TOM CRUISE – A O-K! *JAISH* – BOOOO!' He gave the double thumbs down sign. *You may look at me like I'm a weirdo,* he thought, *but David's been following you since you got to Bombay. You think you are the heroes of London, but really David Gul controls the world. He's promised me I'll be King of* Bhel Puri *on Chowpatty Beach for the rest of my lifetime.* It was a personal fiefdom granted by his overlord. Gupta had played the part of the dumb *Bhel Puri wallah* perfectly.

He knew of the small hidden cameras that had been surreptitiously placed by David's team. They were dotted around, in the signs, cleverly concealed in the structure of the shack. They had recorded everything from many angles so that David Gul could enjoy the film at his leisure, although Gupta felt sure David Gul was watching live.

Gupta shook hands with the white man. 'Thanking you! Thanking you!' He levered the man's arm rapidly with both hands like a water pump, and beamed his best goofiest smile.

Bhel Puri King of Chowpatty Beach.

CHAPTER 35

Mumbai, Malabar Hill – Amit's Mansion
David Gul sat in Amit Bahadur's bedroom, with the balcony windows open. The sea breeze ruffled his silk shirt. The chittering of exotic birds, some captive, others attracted by Amit's exquisite planting scheme, assailed him with an experience, which had fast become everyday, but it had not lost any of its delicious sensual flavour. He had wandered around the grounds daily, finding something new, something small and undiscovered over the past two weeks, enjoying the detail Amit had created. Now he felt completely comfortable in his new domain, and cared for the terrorist's birds and plants as if the whole thing had been his own idea, and he had dirtied his hands by putting every flower in personally.

He supervised the team of gardeners he had inherited, morning and evening. He played the role of Lord of the Manor naturally, as if born to it. *Change or be eaten up*, he thought. *That's why I'm in Amit Bahadur's house, in his bedroom, waiting for his dream woman. No shame in being a chameleon. The fly that evolves into a spider spins a fine entangled web to catch its enemy. Adaptability.*

David had watched today, as he did habitually, the show that Gupta broadcast every evening on the huge TV screen live from Chowpatty Beach. He looked up at the screen on the wall and smiled, leaning back and sipping his third Manhattan cocktail of the sunset. He watched the golden orb being pulled by the ocean, defeated by earth's gravity, falling off the edge of the world, before dropping pastel shades into the Arabian Sea.

A daily ritual since he had appropriated the mansion from *Jaish an Noor wass Salaam*. Amit Bahadur had disappeared without an apparent trace. David had had him followed, and knew he hid in a tiny hovel in the slums of Dharavi, disguised as a *Sadhu*. David smiled, as he thought of his agent who had helped Amit settle into the slum area. Amit had no idea. He thought he had managed to disappear. Gupta, the man who fed him every day on David's orders, also ran David's agents in Dharavi. What had come first: Amit's madness after Aashriya stole his secrets, or his fear of assassination? Maybe both had led to him dressing up in saffron robes in the guise of an eccentric Holy Man. How much of the madness was real, and how much affected? David could not tell, but he knew Amit was suffering. He felt glad that Aashriya had got the codes from Amit, and so David had helped stop the bombs. His empire was now safe. It had been three months since his success, and the scent of spring was full on the sea breeze. David breathed deeply.

An uneducated, uncivilised, black bastard son of a kanjeri, *whore from the gutter of Dharavi! That's what Amit had called me,* he thought, *had publically dared to call me.*

David had easily asserted control after getting most of the ruling *shura* of *Jaish an Noor wass Salaam* arrested by the senior police officers in his employ. No one knew for sure what had happened to Abu Umar in London. He had somehow disappeared from the flat; David knew he had sympathisers all over the city. David did not care about what had happened in most of the Muslim countries, except Dubai. Zulfiqar bin *Hijaz* was still making speeches and stating the revolution had succeeded in establishing *Dar Al Islam*, but David did not know how long he and *Jaish* could last now. The foetal truth was swallowed up by the black mouth of propaganda, in the aftermath of aborted revolutions.

The other members of *Jaish* who David needed to establish his control had submitted, and kow-towed to him. David smiled at the way they had bowed their heads. *They would have fallen over themselves to stick their tails in air and worship me, if I but suggested it.* Both Generals Kafeel Khan and Roop Pratap Singh had disappeared, once they had been paid. Probably back to Kashmir – David's people were working on tracking them down. It would probably be the best piece of Indian-Pakistani cross border co-operation; by now, both governments had most likely assassinated them. *Most probably they would never find any DNA evidence, let alone their bodies,* David thought. Although he had heard rumours that General Kafeel Khan had been killed when he had tried to take over in Islamabad, by his own Kashmiri batman, but he was not sure if he could believe any news out of Pakistan. Once Kafeel Khan had stabbed the

Commander–in-Chief of the Pakistani Armed Forces, he had gone into hiding and taken his faithful servant, who had proved less than faithful.

Bloody Pakis, never could get anything right, he thought. *Can't ever trust a Cunty Kashmiri, no matter which side of the border they come from. Maybe we should make Karachi an independent city-state like Dubai… then I can carry on my business without hindrance from these incompetent Pakis. Why don't they learn from us Indians? A thief like me could never be President here, yet they put the same* chor–thugee, *thieves, back in power across the border. Unbelievable. How did these fucking Muslims ever manage to rule over a cesspit, let alone the whole of India and most of the known world?*

David felt pleased that the Generals never did get to buy their island in the Pacific. Now he was the most powerful member of the *Jaish an Noor wass Salaam* council. Although they were essentially defunct as a powerful terrorist organisation, David would appropriate the role Amit used to have, to ensure control of any rogue elements – and he felt sure they would be useful in expanding his empire. It had been easy to take over everything that belonged to *Jaish* and to Amit. *The others are no threat,* he thought. They cower before me more than they did with Amit, now especially since the head of security has pledged his allegiance, and I control the agents and the *Jettis*.

He had won. The Sisters-in-Charge, Plain Jamila, had been meek before him. He could always control pussy. *I'm a Rottweiler, and any catty-pussy herding I can do with just a growl,* he thought. *Like the one coming to see me now, Aashriya, the one that idiot Amit lost his mind for! And he dared to call me an uneducated, uncivilised, black bastard son of a* kanjeri, *whore from the gutter of Dharavi!* The insults had burnt his brain since that day, cut into his mind like a laser playing a disc on continuous repeat.

MI6 and CIA will not dare touch me now after I saved their pathetic white gands, rasmalai-*bacon behinds. I'll expand my empire into America – maybe I'll become American, maybe even Governor of California.* He chuckled out loud and sipped his drink, as he thought about the actors turned politicians.

God save America? Fuck them! Amit Bahadur was right about one thing: HINDUSTAN ZINDABAD! *Long love India! And I'm as much a part of India, as much a vital part of her future as Ghandi and Nehru were of her past. That bitch Aashriya should be here now. Talking of pussy... I'm hungry!* he thought.

He rang the bell and Amit's houseboy came within seconds, dressed in his usual shorts and carrying his drooping jowls with difficulty. He knocked and entered without waiting for an answer, made his obeisance.

'*Ji Sahib!*' He bobbed, folded his hands across his front, and looked at the floor, neither happy nor sad. David knew the servants hated him and wanted Amit back. He enjoyed their hatred, revelled in their discomfort at being ordered about all day by him. He smiled broadly every time he made a decree, a pleasure he knew they could not understand, that grew for him on each occasion, because he knew he had the power and they had no choice. A lifetime of indentured servitude meant exactly that. This was India, not Cali-fucking-fornia; Amit was right about that too, no matter what anybody tells you.

A servant cannot become a master in this country, as much as the sea replace the sky. That's what's so beautiful about India, he thought. *Every* bhenchaud *has to know their place. A country full of cow worshipping Dalit-achooth – Muslim, Christian, or Sikh – untouchable bastards, like me! That's why I'm unique. But even I have to stay in the shadows.*

The fact that he did not know his caste but was almost certainly low-born no longer bothered him; it had been so long since anyone had dared ask him his caste. He felt himself above any such system. He smiled at the houseboy, enjoying his discomfort. The man fidgeted, and his dark hands flitted like one of Amit's caged mynah birds.

The elderly man was humiliated, unable to meet David's eye, and as always, bobbed again. '*Ji Sahib!*' He folded his arms in front of his concave abdomen, tight through years of eating servile leftovers, with which he had fed his family. David knew his story without asking; it was the story of the dark of India. The dark people of India had a different destiny.

David Gul knew that the houseboy's eldest son had managed to elevate himself enough to be a checkout clerk at one of the new grocery stores downtown. *That's one that got away. I could make him come and work for me too*, thought David. He dismissed the idea as unimportant, because David had his father's daily humiliation to pleasure himself with, should he find his tension rising and need light relief. He looked at the elderly servant, who stood with eyes downcast with the weight of centuries of subjugation. Ageless: age unknown, but like everyone from the darkness of India old before his time, skin stretched and parched by years of sun, mouth cracked and bleeding at the edges from malnutrition, hands like gnarled old *neem* tree twigs. His life experiences just as bitter as the tree's sap, with fingers like ancient roots poking through the ground, after years of labour: thick simian, insensate.

David had never bothered to use the servant's name. The houseboy would be houseboy till his final day, which would probably happen serving his master's food.

'*Kahna lagao!* Put dinner on!'

'*Ji Sahib!*'

David saw the hesitation.

'Sir…'

'Balcony!' shouted David. 'Miss Aashriya Aarzoo Romano is coming.'

The scrawny man raised his thickened fist to his head and scurried away, back bent as only an Untouchable's can be. David Gul knew the servant felt fortunate. No real high caste, Rajput or *Brahmin* would let him enter his home. David knew not so long ago it was believed bad luck for a high-born to see the face of a low-born, and if an Untouchable's shadow crossed a *Brahmin*'s path he would have to bathe and re-purify himself. *The houseboy thinks it's a secret; he's pretended to be something else, a slightly higher caste his whole life. Secrets within secrets.* David chuckled. *Just like India. In India there is no hiding. The crowds and anthills of people only make the differences more apparent, and everyone knows who you are, by name, by race, and mostly just by looking at your face.*

David had watched the live feed from Gupta's. '*Bara bhenchaud actor hai!* That sister fucker is a real actor!' He had slapped his thigh and chortled and cackled his way through a series of Manhattans. David had had his cocktail waiter specially brought in from his hotel for the day. He had drunk Manhattans since he had found out it was the richest part of New York, although he had never been there.

His delight had increased exponentially at Amit Bahadur's discomfort and dishonour. When Amit shook Gupta's stand, David had stood up and punched the air as if team India had hit a six from the last ball to take the Cricket World Cup. David had stood and toasted Amit with his glass, as a warm blanket of success caused tears of pleasure-revenge to course down his face when the *Sadhu* had walked into the sea.

Amit had refused to meet David before *Jaish an Noor wass Salaam*'s situation had forced him, and then he had had no choice.

'I don't want to see that son of the slums,' Amit had once said publically, years ago before David had started working with *Jaish* – before they needed his influence, his empire, to spread their terrorist tentacles into Mumbai and Dubai. Calling David's mother a whore once was enough. Even if it was the truth.

He wondered if Amit saw visions of Aashriya as some idol, a goddess floating above the waves far in the distance, that he had so desperately tried to reach out with arms raised in worship. David had laughed at his stupidity. Not even a real Kali or *Durga Devi* riding the waves on her chariot, if such things ever existed, would entice him to walk into the ocean. He knew he had caused Amit's goddess to materialise on the sea, who called him to her eternal embrace. The Arabian Sea was Amit's shroud, and the Indian Ocean had become his open coffin.

David had fulfilled an ancient Indian duty: no son may rest or leave this world or ever have hope of rebirth, as long as an insult to his mother or father is left unavenged.

Now he brushed aside the rich brocade curtains and stood on the balcony, watching the beauty queen drive through the gates of the mansion down the serpentine drive. He had given specific instructions to the houseboy and servants. He watched the doorman open her car door and salute, and then had the houseboy take her inside, well-versed in their routine. The houseboy sat her in the hall for two minutes exactly before bringing her up to David in Amit's bedroom.

David spread his arms and legs wide as he sprawled on Amit's emperor-sized bed. He did not bother to get up or move as she entered.

'Hi, David *Bhai!* You look so good on that bed. How are you?' she trilled, brighter than usual.

He did not reply. She worked for him, yet she had been Amit's desire, not David's idol. *Funny,* he thought, *how one man's goddess that he can leave the world for, yet never fully get to caress her skin to his satisfaction, can be just another man's pussy-ass.*

Aashriya smiled; '*Kiya hal hai?* How are you?' she asked, in a voice that drowned the birdsong. He savoured the fact that she was desperate to know if he was pleased with her, and so made her wait. She put her handbag on one of the chairs, walked over to him, seemingly unsure what to do, then leaned over and kissed him on both cheeks. He barely looked at her. The houseboy stood both hands folded, expectant.

Because she had done so well and was the key to his success, he turned his face from the blank screen, which he had stared at as she had arrived. He loved the technology that had brought him knowledge of his victory. He had watched it earlier lying on the bed in the same position, quivering with joy at Amit's demise. David turned to look at her directly for the first time. She stood smiling, her fingers picking at her nails first of one hand then the other, intermittently pursing her lips. He knew she awaited his command.

'Shall I come back later if you're resting, David *Sahib*?' she asked and smiled, and he saw her eyelids flutter a couple of times as she made a kiss with her lips. 'Or shall I help you relax?' Her fingers worked hard at her nails, starting to spoil the perfect nail varnish. 'How about another drink?' She nodded to the empty cocktail glass with the maraschino cherry at the bottom. 'Another Manhattan?' She turned to the houseboy. '*Ek aur* cocktail *Sahib ke liye!*'

'*Ji memsahib!*' The small man rushed off to find the cocktail waiter. She stood and waited, her nails becoming increasingly ragged.

David watched her silently. He did not return her smile. He had not touched her in all the years he had known her since she had been a teenage beauty queen, and he had turned her into the undisputed Malika of Bollywood. Now, she was offering herself. As if he ever needed her to offer. His mouth flickered at the corners as he wondered whether he should take her now. On Amit Bahadur's bed? David had not changed anything; he still used Amit's sheets. *Maybe she recognised them*, he thought.

Aashriya had shown no surprise when he had asked her to come to Amit's mansion. She knew today was the day of Amit's expected demise; she had shown no emotion when he had told her that, either. *That's what makes this Brave New Bollywood so great*, he thought, *as long as everyone gets what they want. There is nothing else. No morals, loyalty or fidelity.*

'I've left the Bedouin tent as it was outside, the lawn – in fact, nothing is touched.' He looked into her eyes for a response.

'I saw it on the way in.' She shrugged almost imperceptibly.

He liked it that she did not ask how he got Amit's house. He knew she just accepted it as the reality, the truth that accompanied the winners in the world. Winners took everything, like strength from food; no one ever asked how the exotic dishes got turned into shit in the process. The houseboy returned with the drink. He did not knock, and he put the drink on the side table by Amit, who dismissed him with a small wave.

'The tent is where you 'loved', where you took his heart and all the secrets of *Jaish*, didn't you?' he asked her. He sat up slightly, sipping the Manhattan, his eyes continuously fixed on hers over the rim of the glass. He saw they did not flicker but remained a steely grey, as she shrugged.

'Well, that's where we should eat tonight,' he said and then allowed himself a grin. 'After we watch the movie.'

'Movie?'

'Yes – your darling Amit Bahadur became a movie star. *Salla chuthiya ko hero baney ka tha!* Made the fucking pussy into a hero, after all!' David played the movie for Aashriya on the large screen, from the radio report to Amit's disappearing under the waves, arms outstretched shouting: *Aashriya! Aashriya!*

David watched her closely through his own pleasure, which he put away to be savoured when he would replay the film later. She simply shrugged, laughed when he laughed, hummed and swung her hips from side to side, like a naughty student made to stand outside class. Then she sang to herself like a schoolgirl on the last day before summer holidays, swinging her hips faster, rising to a climax. David had not invited her to sit, so she stood and he continued to lie on the bed, spread as wide as possible, watching Gupta and Amit's antics on the big screen. David stared at her over his empty cocktail glass.

The houseboy and servants served the food, laying it on the table on the balcony.

'Ready?' David asked. The houseboy stood waiting to the side for his master's next command.

She looked out to the balcony.

'Today we are having only one dish, to celebrate: *Bhel Puri*.' David turned to the houseboy and gave him a flurry of orders; he then went to implement his master's wishes without wincing. '*Bhel Puri* on the lawn, in front of the fountain, by the Bedouin tent.' David waved at the houseboy to change the settings to the lawn.

She laughed. '*Bhel Puri* – my favourite. From Chowpatty Beach?'

'From Gupta's!'

'From Gupta's. Of course!' She jumped up and down, and clapped her hands in delight.

David realised that her emotions were fluctuating wildly, since she was still not sure what he had planned for her, how pleased he was, and whether she get her reward in full. He got up, and turned his face fully to her for the first time.

Maybe I will let her service me in the tent, as a special thank you to Amit Bahadur after all the pleasure he has given me, he thought. His emotions were already heightened by the sensual pre-orgasmic experience of having succeeded in causing his enemy's death. David felt as if his testosterone detected her pheromones through her exquisite perfume; it made him feel like a gun dog with erect nose and tail, when pointing out prey. She had done so well and because she would be thrice as willing, without being asked, to perform for his pleasure he decided to throw her a morsel, like the hawk master he had always been; and as such had only ever allowed her to feed off his fist.

'Oh, and of course, your reward, princess. You'll be Queen of Bollywood until you're forty.'

He stood and looked up at her. Aashriya stood four inches taller than him, and he seemed not only like a different race but a separate species from some undiscovered planet. He looked like a squat, black alien from Tatooine.

She squealed and shrieked her unintelligible response, clapped her hands harder and faster in an ever quicker staccato beat before throwing her arms around him, letting him go, and then squealing again, and hugging him. 'Thank you, David Bhai. Thank you. You're so good to me,' she said brushing away her tears of joy from the corners of her eyes before they could spoil her make up. 'You're so good to me!'

'Yes – yes I am,' he replied, in a flat tone.

'I love you. I love you.' She went on as if he had not spoken.

He felt sure she had never told that to anyone else before, as she wiped the wetness from her face, and he knew she was unaccustomed to shedding tears in sorrow. *Stop your stupid shrieking, you puerile pussy!* he thought, as he led her down the stairs.

She had failed in stemming the flow of liquid that flooded her cheeks and made her eye liner run in garish streaks, making her beauty more like a horror movie extra. The vampire queen of the undead. Her shrieks turned to gasps as she failed to control her tears, and sublime puffs of joy escaped her goddess lips, like mortal but morbid cadaverous kisses.

'Yes, you are beautiful, *bohoth kubsoorath meri Malika,* and you'll be Queen of Bollywood until you're forty,' he repeated. He regretted it almost instantly, as her cacophonic feminine fervour of high-pitched howls rose from her, so that her words became mumbled and strangled in her throat. She sobbed openly, holding onto him. They were halfway down the right side of flight of steps of the grandiose movie set-like staircase.

David extricated himself from her sinuous arms, and felt himself stir when her soft skin of her upper arms grazed his cheek, and her breast nuzzled against his wide chest. 'Got the best champagne in the world, of course, for you in the tent, cooling in an ice bucket,' he said, and she squealed yet again. He hated champagne; the bubbles always went up his nose.

Why did she emasculate and enervate other men? he thought. She seemed to jet-fuel his masculinity, which spontaneously combusted in millions of small explosions throughout his being. Amit had been the catalyst.

David led her with her arm on his, like an old duke and duchess coming down the curving staircase to dine, as if they had dressed for dinner, and were now ready to receive the landed gentry and aristocracy of England. *Now… how long do I really give her?* thought David, as he led her across the immaculate lawn, the birds, flowers, and fountains: a paradise gained by him. Better than any Elysium fields, nirvana, or Jannat. He had his *Houris* of the Highest Garden right here. The present was all that mattered, all that he could taste and feel. After all, who in their right mind had seen any of the millions of gods? And which one, if any, exist, and if they do, which one is the right one? *I'll let them fight it out amongst themselves*, he thought. *Meanwhile, I'm here and now with the most gorgeous woman in the world, who will do anything if I but crook or waggle my cock; she has somehow become all the more alluring by my victory, and Amit's death.* Paradise? *When I'm gone, feed my body to the dogs on the dung heap!*

He wondered how he would solve the new conundrum. *I've already promised the new starlet: Nisreen, that she will be Queen of Cuntistan.* He looked over to Mumbai with all its filth and stench and dignity and beauty. She would reign as mistress over all of this sticky mess.

I'll give Aashriya six months. Yes, she will have six months left before she's on the used actress dung heap. That's the shiest stinkiest heap of them all. No one will even fuck you when you're there.

He turned and smiled at her. 'Queen of Bollywood, undisputed

Empress of all you survey, until forty!' He waved a hand over the sprawling city, the view which encompassed Napean Sea road. He could see Nariman's Point and Chowpatty Beach, where only a short while before a love-stricken *Sadhu-Yogi*-Holy Man had self immolated on the ocean's flames, to reach the burning image of his goddess as she floated far out on the waves. In so doing he had become a human sacrifice to his Devi-goddess: he had set the ocean alight all the way back to the funeral pyres, the fires of the Ganga at Benares, the holiest city of Hinduism.

'The most famous actress in the history of Indian cinema. Aashriya Aarzoo Romano – A Wish From the Land of God. Queen of Cuntistan and Bollywood!' he said, and threw his head back and smiled as he closed his eyes to the sky. He felt the wind on his face, the rain waiting to be born in the firmament.

David laughed for a long time, as he looked into the distance over the Arabian Sea.

CHAPTER 36

London – Southall
The streets of Southall felt alien as *Sana'a*. Rows upon rows of houses stood, as if begging to be pulled into the current century, hiding faces behind crumbling Victorian paintwork facades, greens and creams and pale pinks. She could imagine small children running in between the alleys. Urchins chased by scolding mothers, fighting over food, free games with bicycle tyres and sticks, sick-skinned from lack of essentials. Lives full of grime and Dickensian disease. Except now, most of the people exhibited various shades of brown. Jessica parked one road away from Jimmy's house, and walked the high street of Southall. People everywhere, all sorts of people full of difference.

Multicoloured clothes and hair, peculiar perfumes, weird shoes, and not just multi-coloured clothing, but multi-hued humanity. All races and sizes, all voices and tongues. She heard wet guttural groans and drier clicks, screeching sounds. She thought the human tongue and larynx were incapable of such sounds; it was like a conference of alien worlds. Here she heard languages that she did not recognise, from places she did not know existed on the globe. The noise became a veritable Babel, surmounting minarets of misunderstanding, to reach a British heaven.

Smells and fragrances washed over her. Some, as they brushed close by on the crowded pavements, had obviously decided on no deceitful embellishing perfume at all, just allowing their natural body aromas to shine through.

Jessica saw mostly ex-colonials. She looked into their faces, trying to understand. They seemed long resigned to the consequences of Empire that had despoiled the mysteries of the noble heart of darkness. Now its former inhabitants were exposed, naked and hungry, by the daughter of

Empire: Capitalism. They tried to catch up to her, by buying ever faster the goods she flaunted in all her gaudy glory. Living the First World dream.

Jessica wondered if Sofia felt the price had been worth paying. She had met a woman like her before – a neighbour in Solihull who just sat, isolated, in material splendour all day, unable to go out and with nowhere to go, husband and children at work and school all day. The woman – who, like Sofia, had left her family, her village, her language, as well as her culture and customs, in the prime of her life, to become a reviled and misunderstood foreigner in Britain. Jessica could not image how it might feel, after decades in her adopted land, to be an orphan, a stranger still, in clothes, manners and ethos – despite helping to build a generation in her country of settlement. Jessica felt the power of rejection.

Despite the inner-city squalor, she recognised a familiar presentiment. She had had this feeling before, upon entering the mosque, where she had attended the spiritual circle. She remembered how she had been surprised there to discover space, created by the experience. The emotions cleared a whole dining table in her mind for food and drink of a different kind. When the words had washed over her she had found a unique dimension, a new plane of existence. There, in that other never-before-visited world, that no-map-marks-the-spot land, where no-directions-can-be-given-to-get-there, she had found aliens who had transformed her being. She had seen beauty and found joy in spirituality, and trembled at the truths. Jessica had found her place in the universe, her miniscule niche that had an all-important significance for her; it signalled her role, from the creation to the end. From the Big Bang to the Small Suck. Explosion-Implosion. From nothing to nothing: except for the Almighty and Everlasting. In Truth; from The One, back to The One.

Even if a single religion did not have a hold on her, she felt the positive sensations running through her, although her nervousness at the strangeness of Southall made her movements jerky. Despite the empowering thoughts, however, she could not imagine living such an exiguous existence. She remembered a soft life growing up, in spite of her teenage rebellion, her doctor father providing the middle-class contrast of Solihull that denigrated the lives of those in the ghettos to a third world status.

She stood and looked into a shop window selling gaudy Asian wedding clothes. She looked at a turquoise *lengha* and wondered who would want to get married in *that*. Then she cursed herself for her cowardice, and forced herself to turn towards the right direction. She curled her fists into balls, and did not change her pace, lest her legs slacken, until she got to Jimmy's front door.

What would she say to a mother who had just lost a son, recently a husband, been ostracised by her community for the assault of her daughter?

Hamza had told her Jimmy's story after his death. Hamza had been a saving angel, *her protective lion* she had called him. He had used his connections at MI5 and with the police to provide evidence that Jessica and Sebastian had helped in foiling *Jaish an Noor wass Salaam*. So much so, that they had been seen as fully working and co-operating with Hamza to stop the bombings. Hamza had claimed Jessica was his operative in the *Jaish* cell, and they had not been charged. He had arranged for the special security team in Mumbai, and so Jessica had agreed to honeymoon there, because she knew it had long been Sebastian's wish.

Hamza had been transformed by Jimmy's death. Jessica had tried to console him, after the initial tears. They had shed more tears of relief at having stopped the calamity. Jessica put a hand on her chest and whispered another small prayer, yet again thanking God that the twelve cities that had been linked to the London bomb. When she had spoken to Hamza about it he seemed not to hear her words, but she reassured him that he had done the right thing. He kept saying he had tricked and lied to his childhood friend.

Jessica thought he wore guilt as a mask, and shame seemed to cover him like a second skin. She knew he could never remove the guilt; it was the death knell to his future contentment, even if he did eventually drink the love-philter of having saved countless people. Maybe even that would not bring relief. Guilt had become woven into his strands of muscle, until the end of his physicality. She felt some of his power-shame, having played her own part in Jimmy's decline, the near-death of Sebastian and destruction of the Western World.

Is that the only reason why I'm here, because of my guilt? she thought. To make a token gesture, to see a widowed mother, a white woman bearing gifts of false consoling and condolences? So she had brought nothing. Empty handed; she had refused the emptiness of normal social graces. Hamza knew she was coming to see Sofia today, but had not offered to come with her, nor had she been able to ask him. Jessica and Sebastian had become international heroes in the aftermath, and

Hamza had melted away into the facelessness of a security agent. *Blessed anonymity*, she thought, *after the recent days of relentless interviews*. The media attention had calmed down, in the time following their return from their honeymoon.

Jessica straightened her shirt and brushed her hair out of her face, glad she no longer had the scarf to contend with. She tried not to, but cleared her throat anyway, as if preparing for a speech. She reached Jimmy's front door, trying to lose her thoughts of race and culture and belonging. She tried leaving them behind, in the high-street melee. She knocked on the door, barely allowing her knuckles freedom of movement, hoping no one would answer and she could escape back to Solihull with its easy wide streets and greenery hiding middle-class sprawl.

Her area had always provided comfort, nevertheless – comfort that she felt she urgently needed now – despite the prevalent selfishness hiding behind the mask created by the soft suburbs. The ghettos looked like disease and death, like a face filled with scurvy. She rapped again, and this time, almost immediately the door opened. She drew back slightly at the sight of a bearded man in *salwar kameez* and white lace hat.

'Sorry, I was just reading my prayers. Yes?' He seemed to pause, as if wondering why he was explaining himself to a strange white woman, a *Goree* at the door – a rare enough occurrence in this neighbourhood, she felt. He stared harder as if expecting to find the solution written on her face, to the conundrum why this woman – blue eyed, golden-haired, and pale cream skin – had turned up at his door.

'Er, is this Sofia's... I mean is Mrs Regus in, please?' Jessica managed to stutter. She saw the look of surprise on his face, before recognition spread like a ripple across the lines of his face, which seemed as if it did not know whether to smile or cry or twist in hatred. Instead, she thought he did almost all three.

'You're – you're that woman.'

'Yes, I am that woman.'

'*Ami*'s in the back garden. You'd better just go through.' After a hesitant pause, during which his eyes screwed up as he looked straight at her, he said, 'They say you helped Jimmy –'

'No, no I didn't,' she blurted, looking away from him. She pushed past him.

'Thank you. Thank you for helping Jimmy, innit. I was praying he didn't suffer much. At least, I'm praying he ain't sufferin' much now,' said the man in a rising voice, as she walked away from him. 'Straight through. The corridor leads to the back garden, carry on through the kitchen...'

She walked through the narrow hallway, surprised that she could be near tears already. This had to be Tony, Jimmy's brother, although the similarities were very few. He was shorter and slimmer than Jimmy, except his demeanour and voice gave him away, but he did not have the innate inner-city aggression of the woods that Jimmy had been unable to smother until the last. His brother had a long beard that fizzed out of his face, each hair making its own independent tortuous path as if singly shocked by electrodes, which made him look shorter and slimmer still. She had noticed his hair uncombed, the black pressure mark on his forehead from innumerable prostrations, she realised. More black patches were visible on his ankles; they were bare, like the Islamic literalists. His *salwar* was hitched halfway up his shins, with unmistakable piety. *These are the people everyone assumes to be fanatics,* she thought, *but here he is at home looking after his mother and Jimmy. Where was Jimmy?* She could not be sure, so made no attempt to answer her own question. *Render unto caeser those things that are caeser's – sumnes manu dei – ita amen!* We are all in hands of God – amen! She remembered the Latin liturgy from her school; her private tutor was a Catholic nun whom her mother, despite being a Scottish Presbyterian, had employed because she was the best Classics tutor to be found. The nun had drummed into her lessons in Latin, as well as the inevitable Catholic doctrines.

Jessica forced herself to think of the present. What would she say now, to Jimmy's mother? How would she address Sofia? *Should I continue my pretence of being a Muslim, to better console her? What type: brown, white? Are there harlequin Muslims? Which god? Do all worship the same?*

Her spirituality had increased since the day they had succeeded in foiling the bomb plot, and she had continued to pray in her own way. She realised she did not know many things, but she felt beyond any doubt that God was not vindictive and spiteful, or desperate to throw everyone into everlasting fire and damnation. The God of the Christians did seem sleekly attractive: he who forgave no matter what the crime, implausibly and unquestioningly. Forgiveness achieved too easily was an excessively slippery concept, after what she had been through. Jessica felt certain she would not be coming into this world again and again, in any form, to rectify past misdemeanours. This was it. A singular performance on a complex stage in front of a braying world – and Jessica felt she had better make it a virtuoso performance.

She knew His love was greater than His retribution, that His mercy was far over his wrath. *Your Lord is as you perceive him to be,* she remembered part of the *Hadith,* the saying of the Prophet of Islam, but could not recall the rest, from a book later confiscated by Dwayne. The long tradition of Muslim religious censorship continued unabated. Ironically, she knew it was something that the Church had excelled at for centuries. It was always about control, Jessica had long realised for what had now become an uncomfortable length of time, since her association with *Jaish an Noor wass Salaam* and the terror cell. What an unbridled genius George Orwell was, and how close to the truth he had got with his thought police. How easy it had become to lay all the easy clichés and assumptions, to hang them all on the beards of the terrorists. Her country that had instilled in her values of enlightenment and libertarianism was lurching towards an authoritarian control, a despotic boundary-less walled thinking, a worldwide enslavement of ideas and freedom. The media had covered the story in the typically sensationalist way: hype and gore, and sword-wielding Muslims coming out of the bricks and mortar of our very homes, to chop us down and eat our children while we sleep. Life is shades of grey, she decided – more like Muslims, who can be shades of brown-white-yellow-black, and even an amalgam.

Jessica put her ever-present wonderings to the back of her mind, tried to push them away with her hair. She had spent more time thinking about philosophy, about the future of Britain, the Western World and what the future might hold, now that the Clash of Civilisations had started but aborted: but would the foetus find nourishment, still? Would American Presidents continue to say things like Crusade against Terror? Either you're with us, or against us. How many more Iraqi-Brits, Afghan-American, Palestinian-Canadian deaths?

Tony had followed her, and overtaken her with enthusiasm. He had introduced himself but she had barely heard him. Now he politely held the kitchen door open for her, and then overtook her.

'*Ami*'s inside,' he said, and when she hesitated he added, 'Don't worry, just go in.'

He opened the large greenhouse door and pointed with his head, gesturing with his chin, gently closing the door behind her once she had walked through the metallic insect screen, which had patterns of stylised butterflies on it, and oriental writing down the side.

She stepped over the threshold tentatively, thighs quivering, her breath loud and burning her throat with every puff. At first glance, she saw only myriad butterflies. She let go of the metal strands, which formed the curtain to contain escapees. The heat and humidity increased her sense of agitation. A botanical cacophony of plants and flowers assailed her, perfumes and tinkling of splashing water from the central fountain. She forced her breathing into a more regular pattern, took a few irregular steps towards the water. She saw patchy painted fish in the pond and small exotic birds darted above the surface, like a flurry of sheen and an iridescent memory of colour.

The overwhelming sense was one of an *Aladdin's Cave* of butterflies. As if she had stumbled upon a secret trove, in a forest deep within a lost valley. A chasm which hid multiple species, intermingling colours; but all had the uniformity of wings and a proboscis with which they fed, sucking and swirling, forming a conference of butterflies. Flutterbies – so many fluttered-by – flutterby – butterfly.

Colours, shapes and sizes – she could not keep track of them all, or even follow one for any length of time, as an even brighter one or more interesting one fluttered by.

Flutterbies – this was Jimmy's 'Flutterby Whimsy'.

Suddenly a woman stood up, quite close by, seemingly growing out of the foliage that she had been bent over, and had obviously been tending to. Jessica saw a small watering-can in her hand. *She might have been filling up some of the colourful sugar feeders*, thought Jessica. She had missed the small figure completely amongst the flowers.

'Oh hello, Mrs Regus...'

'*Hanh*, yes – who are you?'

Jessica saw the woman dressed in green *salwar kameez*, which had helped her camouflage in the plants, bend down stiffly and place the small plastic watering can on the floor. Sophia straightened her *kameez*, which had become tangled, and pushed back the few strands of hair that escaped her straight-combed back plait. She shuffled, almost in pain, but before she could move her awkward limbs any further, Jessica covered the short distance between them, without replying to her question, and stood facing her.

'You – you are that woman!'

'Yes!' Jessica said too quickly, in a louder voice than she had intended, and regretted the interruption.

'From TV, newspapers...'

'Yes.'

'My Jimmy...'

'I'm Jessica Flowerdew, Mrs Regus, and I'm sorry about Jimmy,' Jessica blurted out, not sure what she could say. Her own guilt felt accusatory. She wiped her palms along the sides of the trousers, cursed the humid heat, and cursed her cowardice even more. Neither had made a move. 'That was why I could do... I did nothing...' She glanced at the older woman, before looking at the floor. Butterflies swam around their heads; some flew lower, and visited the feeders. Jessica looked at Jimmy's mother, her face stretched with bags under her eyes. The pale of her eyes seemed to shine too brightly. The whites of her eyes had pink blotches in them, like crimson veins on thin-skinned leaves.

'I'm sorry...' said Jessica.

The woman took Jessica's hands; she felt the rough calluses, the thickened fingers – sausages of suffering formed through years of labour.

'There is nothing to be sorry for.' Sofia paused, and looked deep into Jessica's eyes. 'Did he do his best?'

'What?' Jessica asked, and flinched back physically, unsure how she meant the question.

'His father...' The older woman blinked hard, but did not look away. 'Allah have mercy on him.' She wiped her hands on her *dupatta*, which hung over her shoulders and down her back. 'He used to be always saying: "*Betah*, just do your best, and leave the rest to Allah."'

Sofia came closer to Jessica, so that she could feel her breath on her face. She repeated the question in a much slower, more considered way, almost pausing in between the words. 'Did my son – did my son do his best?'

This was the moment Jessica had been waiting for, the question to which she had prepared a stock response. She knew she would be asked how Jimmy died, and that seemed to be Sofia's search now.

'Yes, Mrs Regus. Mohammed Yusuf Regus died saving Hamza, his best friend, who then saved everyone else. Mohammed Yusuf died doing his very best.' Now she had said the ready-made lines, the rest disappeared. She had prepared clever follow-ups and reassurances and false sympathy. She had thought she would say to Sofia that Jimmy had had the hope of life eternal in the hereafter, and the mother of a martyr would be sure to be a martyr too. All the religious condolences vanished, by shame, which was caused by the pain in Sofia's eyes and honesty in her demeanour, the factors which seemed to constitute the very essence of the woman in front of her: her fortitude.

'His grandfather gave him that name.' Sofia wiped her *dupatta* across her eyes. The thin veil turned darker green, but she made no sound. 'But Jimmy to his father, to me, and for you – always – always Jimmy…'

Jessica saw the silent tears, like clear pearls floating across a beige skin river, leaving currents swirling for eternity. Sofia made no further attempt to wipe them away.

'Thank you. Thank you, Jessica, for being a *Baji* to my Jimmy,' said Sofia. Being addressed as the elder sister of Jimmy the *Shaheed* made her feel the full force of her hypocrisy. Jessica felt tears wet her face. She saw that the other was still weeping silently, so she leaned forward and gently took Sofia's *dupatta*, wiping the older woman's tears from her face. Then, without thinking, she hugged Sofia, who seemed to be waiting like a dry riverbed for the affection of a flash flood. Sofia hugged her back, with a surprising strength. Both women cried as one leaned on the other; both wet each other's shirts.

'Now I will be *Baji* to you,' said Sofia. 'Don't call me Mrs Regus. It would be honour to be your older sister…'

'Oh *Baji*! Thank you – I don't know what – thank you.' Jessica wiped her face with both hands, feeling undeserving that Sofia would want her to use such an intimate term. She knew how important that was in Asian culture; she had learned the significance from Hamid. She had failed Jimmy, and yet was being accepted wholeheartedly without questions or anger or resentment. No thoughts seemed to cross Sofia's mind such as, *why did you survive and Jimmy die? Why didn't you do something? Why didn't you guide and help him? He was just a lost boy.* Jessica had here least of all expected to find such love and affection in Jimmy's Butterfly House. The sister word from Sophia broke the final bar in her cage of fear, and her spirit soared free. Having lived in a one-child family caused the sibling epithet to feel as if Sofia had opened the gates to the City of Belonging. Jessica felt as if she had skirted its walls and camped outside for most of her life.

'Oh *Baji*! I can't thank –'

Sofia cut her sentence short and held her, this time in a soft embrace. Both women hugged each other for an unknown length of time. Jessica felt hurt leave her with the salt of her sweat, and pain flowed through her tears. Her breathing slowed, and her heart padded a soft cadence against her chest.

Jessica did not want to withdraw from the embracing stillness, the listless comfort, as the numerous butterflies fanned their faces and brushed their hair so that silken strands, black and blonde, wafted by the wind of the butterflies' wings, floated free, momentarily.

'Come – Jessica! Come!'

'Where, *Baji*, what?'

'Let me show you something. A special thing that no one even knows.' Sofia led her by the hand to the back of the Butterfly House to the hidden door.

Jessica saw the lock and door had been broken, and recently replaced.

'This see – this is what Jimmy – no one ever came here. Not even me, before Jimmy went away…'

Jessica followed Sofia into the small greenhouse, to find thousands upon thousands of white butterflies surrounding her. Everywhere she looked, sideways, down, up at the ceiling there fluttered uncountable white wings – so many that they seemed to be bumping into one another.

'What – what is this?' she asked.

'Kashmir Whites.' Sofia took her hand conspiratorially, and led her the short distance to the other side of the greenhouse. 'Shush – shush – come – come!'

Jessica saw Sofia looking up at the shutters on the roof, and then at a button on the back wall. She felt certain this controlled the shutters.

'They all hatch in Jimmy's pupae box. In the last few days, thousands and thousands. No one knows, so many eggs – all hatched, and born white butterflies,' said Sofia.

Jessica followed Sofia's gaze again, and saw her looking at the two large shutters in the roof which had a mechanism on them. She realised that was the sliding system that would make the shutters swing open like large windows. They had probably been designed for ventilation when the building was meant to be used as a greenhouse, before Jimmy had converted it into a tropical house. Sofia pulled Jessica over, closer to the button. 'No, I can't – no,' said Jessica, looking at Sofia, wide-eyed. 'These are Jimmy's.'

'Yes, yes, these are Jimmy's.' Sofia pulled Jessica's hand over. 'Kashmir White butterflies – Jimmy's.' Sofia took Jessica's hand again, put it over the button, and kept her own over it this time.

Jessica stopped breathing. Unsure what to do for a moment, she looked out through the side of the greenhouse glass, some of the top panes were clear. Jessica could see over the short garden wall. She thought she saw Hamza's car, felt sure she recognised his car, and then she saw Hamza standing to the side of the road, staring at the greenhouse. She gulped in air like someone scared of drowning, faster and faster. She looked at Sofia, who smiled and nodded.

Jessica pushed the button. The windows swung open surprisingly quickly. At first, nothing happed and Jessica exhaled through pursed lips. The butterflies stayed, mostly milling around the feeders.

Then, without any reason – as if frightened by a ghost – suddenly, *en masse*, they became one organism. The Kashmir White butterflies flew up towards the opening.

Thousands upon thousands of independently beating wings, as if they had become an ascending white angelic body. Like uncountable small heartbeats without which there can be no whole. They flew up through the shutters.

The white wings floated up and up: higher and ever higher.

They soared into the clear blue azure sky.

Max Malik is a doctor and he has had a highly successful career in hospital medicine and General Practice as well as complementary medicine. He was working as a doctor in the RAF Stafford Air Force base when the terrorist attacks occurred in the US on September 11 2001.

Max started writing the novel after he was suddenly taken seriously ill a few years ago. He was in intensive care, in a coma, for two weeks with septicaemia. During this coma, and at the brink of death, he had dreams and visions, which became the basis for the novel. On awakening from the coma, Max took a career break from medicine to write the story for *The Butterfly Hunter*.

Max grew up in Britain and, as a result of a mixed ethnic background, he has travelled extensively and so has gained knowledge of many cultures, religions and philosophies. He has worked in the United States and Asia.

Max has researched in the Muslim community for reasons and causes of violent extremism and radicalisation. He is also intimately familiar with Islamist and extremist ways of thinking and has had experience of issues relating to extremism.

Max won the Muslim Writers' Awards, Creative Writer of the Year 2007, for a combination of his earlier writing.

The Butterfly Hunter has been shortlisted for the Muslim Writers' Awards Published Writer 2011 and also for the Brit Writers' Awards Published Writer 2011.

Max has written and produced a radio play. He also writes short stories and is currently writing the screenplay for a film based upon the novel of *The Butterfly Hunter*.

Max is an frequent commentator on Muslim issues in the media. He lives in Birmingham, England.